REFERENCE

MASTERPLOTS II

SHORT STORY
SERIES

MASTERPLOTS II

SHORT STORY
SERIES

6

Tha-Z
Bibliography
Indexes

Edited by

FRANK N. MAGILL

SALEM PRESS

Pasadena, California   Englewood Cliffs, New Jersey

Library of Congress Cataloging-in-Publication Data
Masterplots II: Short story series.
    Bibliography: p.
    Includes index.
    Summary: Examines the theme, characters,
plot, style and technique of more than 700 nine-
teenth- and twentieth-century works by prominent
authors from around the world.
    1. Fiction—19th century—Stories, plots, etc. 2.
Fiction—19th century—History and criticism. 3.
Fiction—20th century—Stories, plots, etc. 4. Fic-
tion—20th century—History and criticism. 5.
Short story. [1. Short stories—Stories, plots, etc. 2.
Short story] I. Magill, Frank Northen, 1907-   .
II. Title: Masterplots 2. III. Title: Masterplots two.
PN3326.M27   1986   809.3   86-22025
ISBN 0-89356-461-3 (set)
ISBN 0-89356-467-2 (volume 6)

LIST OF TITLES IN VOLUME 6

MASTERPLOTS II

MASTERPLOTS II

SHORT STORY
SERIES

THANK YOU, M'AM

Author: Langston Hughes (1902-1967)
Type of plot: Realistic sketch
Time of plot: The 1950's
Locale: An American city
First published: 1958

> *Principal characters:*
> MRS. LUELLA BATES WASHINGTON JONES, a large woman
> ROGER, a fourteen- or fifteen-year-old purse snatcher

The Story

It is eleven o'clock at night; a large woman carrying a large purse slung over her shoulder walks down a deserted city street. Suddenly a boy dashes behind her and with one tug jerks the purse from her. Its weight throws him off balance and he falls, legs flying up. The woman calmly kicks him.

Pulling the boy up by his shirt and shaking him, the large woman demands that he return her pocketbook. When she asks if he is ashamed, the boy finally speaks. He answers yes and also denies that he meant to snatch the purse. Not deceived, the woman tells him that he lies, discovers that he has no one at home, and drags him off. Frightened, the boy begs to be released, but the woman simply announces her name: Mrs. Luella Bates Washington Jones. The now sweating boy struggles desperately but finds the woman's half nelson difficult to resist.

As they enter her furnished room, Mrs. Luella Bates Washington Jones leaves the door open. She asks the boy's name; he replies that it is Roger. Calling him by name, she tells him to wash his face, then turns him loose—at last. Roger looks at the open door and looks at the large woman; he chooses to wash.

When the woman asks if he took her money because of hunger, the boy replies that he wanted blue suede shoes. The woman only says that she has done things that she would tell no one. Then, leaving him alone by her purse and the open door, she steps behind a screen to warm lima beans and ham on her gas plate. The boy does not run; he does not want to be mistrusted.

While they eat, the woman asks no questions but talks of her work on the late shift at a hotel beauty shop. After they share her small cake, she gives the boy ten dollars for some blue suede shoes and asks him to leave because she needs her rest.

Mrs. Luella Bates Washington Jones leads Roger to the barren stoop and says that she hopes he behaves himself. He barely manages to say thank you before the large woman shuts the door. He never sees her again.

Themes and Meanings

Merely alluding to the economic problems that cause widows to work late shifts and parents to leave unemployed teenagers unsupervised, Langston Hughes focuses on the universal power of love and trust in "Thank You, M'am." Hughes portrays the nobility of common people and the vitality of his Afro-American culture in his works. Mrs. Luella Bates Washington Jones, whose name ironically recognizes both the slavery codes of the founders of the United States and the dignity of the common person, gives spiritual and physical gifts to the young boy.

This large woman first recognizes the dignity of the boy's name, Roger. Then she offers him cleanliness and self-esteem. Equality and trust are other spiritual gifts. As a woman who must heat ham and beans on a hot plate, Mrs. Luella Bates Washington Jones knows that food and money are necessary to maintain dignity. Finally, she gives Roger the greatest gift of all: the right to direct his own life. She closes the door; he is left to choose what he will do. As in most of Hughes's poems, satires, and sketches, circumstances and society may be unfair, but the individual has a choice. Roger, like Mrs. Luella Bates Washington Jones, must create his own dignity and freedom.

Style and Technique

Langston Hughes chose to write in the idiom of black America and for more than forty years experimented with its cadences and accents. Most of "Thank You, M'am" is written in an urban dialect. This reliance upon colloquial dialogue to reveal personality is one characteristic of the traditional Afro-American oral style which Hughes often employs. Other characteristics are a deceptively simple sentence structure and a presentational style of narration. Hughes has the woman and the boy speak directly; they seldom demand or declare but simply ask or say. Hughes also has the narrator speak in a colloquial voice. The narrator tells the reader, "The large woman simply turned around and kicked him right square in his blue jeaned sitter."

In addition to capturing speech cadences in his works, Hughes experimented with the sound of the blues in his poetry and prose; the blues, which sing of the common person and of survival, are heard in "Thank You, M'am."

Charlene Roesner

THAT EVENING SUN

Author: William Faulkner (1897-1962)
Type of plot: Psychological realism
Time of plot: c. 1915
Locale: Jefferson, a small town in Mississippi
First published: 1931

> *Principal characters:*
> NANCY, a part-time domestic servant, the protagonist
> JESUS, her husband
> JASON COMPSON, SR., for a time Nancy's employer
> QUENTIN COMPSON, Jason's son, the narrator
> CANDACE "CADDY" COMPSON, Quentin's younger sister
> JASON COMPSON, JR., Quentin's younger brother

The Story

Nancy is a black woman who has been filling in as cook in the Compson household during the illness of their live-in servant Dilsey. She has an unreliable husband, and she has taken to prostitution to supplement her income. She has been knocked down and kicked in the face by a white client from whom she demanded payment, after which she, not he, has been jailed. While in jail she has made an attempt on her own life.

At the time of the story she is visibly pregnant, and Jesus, her husband, has gone off, first vowing vengeance against the father. Afraid that he will return and menace her, Nancy begs Mrs. Compson to let her sleep at the Compsons' house, but Mrs. Compson will not permit it; therefore, except for one evening when she sleeps in the Compson kitchen, Mr. Compson and the three children escort her home in the evening. Between the Compson house and her cabin is a ditch, which she views as the likely place for an ambush.

After Nancy's final day with the Compsons, when Mr. Compson will no longer accompany her, she cajoles the children, all under the age of ten, to accompany her. Upon their arrival at the cabin, she is so terrified that she uses every ploy she knows to delay the children's return, offering to tell them stories and make them popcorn, but her hospitality falls short of pleasing the children.

Finally Mr. Compson comes for the children and offers to take her to a relative's house, but she will not leave. When the Compsons depart Nancy is sitting, petrified, in her house and moaning. The author does not reveal whether her fears are groundless.

Themes and Meanings

Although the story touches on such aspects of early twentieth century Southern life as the imposition of technology on a culture of traditional handicrafts, the awkward and frequently cruel adjustments of the races to social change, and the inequality of the races under the law, "That Evening Sun" is mainly a story about fear—fear rendered all the more terrible by Nancy's total isolation among others who cannot understand, share, or relieve it.

The title of the story derives from a well-known blues song. Nancy's moaning, which Quentin, one of the Compson children, describes as "not singing and not unsinging," occurs when the evening sun goes down and her imagination is most active. Her state exceeds ordinary blues melancholy, with the result that her "unsinging" lies beyond the control of music to give pleasure or consolation. Quentin, the narrator, knows what has happened to Nancy, but neither he nor anyone else in the story understands her despair or the all-consuming nature of her terror.

Although her husband has vowed vengeance against the presumably white father of Nancy's child, she realizes that any such act against a white man would be suicidal and that if Jesus does take action, she can expect to be the target. The Compson family are uncomprehending in their various ways. Mrs. Compson simply resents her husband's leaving her to take a part-time servant home, the children are too young to understand what besides skin color and external subservience distinguishes blacks from themselves, and Mr. Compson's suggestion to Nancy that she "let white men alone" indicates how little he fathoms her vulnerable situation.

On the night that the family allows Nancy to sleep in the kitchen, she awakens them with her moaning but is too frightened even to respond to the question of whether she has actually seen her husband lurking outside. Given a cup of coffee, she cannot hold it and does not notice that the coffee has spilled out. The children's naïve questions concerning what she has done to make Jesus so angry only add to her despair.

Nancy has neither the sense of belonging to a settled familial and social order, such as that to which her slave ancestors could cling, nor any enforceable legal rights such as those a person in her position might begin to enjoy a half century later. Her nominal rights have been ignored, her unfortunate relationship with a contemptible white man has disfigured her face, and her husband's subsequent abandonment of her has destroyed such stability as her life had offered. Unlike the earlier slave generations, she must contend with the threat of unemployment and the caprices of her white employers. While Dilsey has steady work and an obviously secure place within a household, Nancy represents the nominally free black woman at the mercy of a husband who himself suffers, without any possibility of legal redress, bitter insults to his own manhood and may avenge himself by cruelty to her. She is, as she several times observes, "just a nigger," and although she is religious, she feels that God will no more stand by a "hellborn" creature such as herself than will the Compsons.

Ultimately, she is left to the mercy of the Compson children. If they leave her, she must face the uncertainty of the night alone. Her story to the children about a queen winds up with that royal lady pursued by a "bad man" in a ditch. Knowing that queens do not have to cross ditches, the children reject the story. In this and in a remarkable variety of other ways Faulkner conveys her fear. She burns her hand on the hot globe of a lamp and does not notice the damage until Caddy calls her attention to it. She cannot concentrate on as simple a task as popping corn for the children and burns it all. She breaks into a cold sweat and inadvertently recommences her eerie moan. The arrival of Mr. Compson temporarily relieves her tension, but he has come to take the children home, and she is left to her private hell.

It is important to realize that Faulkner not only has given a graphic picture of Southern intolerance, injustice, and violence, which generates lonely terror in a person such as Nancy, but also has enacted fictionally a sensitivity and sympathy for such a victim that is ordinarily beyond the scope of those who have not lived in a town such as Jefferson. Even when, as in this story, there are no characters who share this sympathy—Dilsey is too much a mainstay of the Compson family to share the burdens of her temporary replacement—Faulkner's story implies a moral responsibility unknown to the millions of Americans who have not been compelled to live with, or even notice the existence of, the Nancys and Jesuses of Faulkner's region. "That Evening Sun" communicates not only the sins but also the conscience of the South, and the "I" who hates to see the evening sun go down is not only Nancy but also any reader whose conscience Faulkner's story has constructed or reconstructed.

Style and Technique

Faulkner deploys more narrative resources in developing his themes than any other American writer. The effect of his stories is a function of his way of telling them; therefore, no summary of action or theme can do them justice.

In "That Evening Sun," Faulkner uses a retrospective point of view. Quentin, the oldest of the three children, relates events of fifteen years earlier. Between 1915 and 1930, as he observes at the beginning, much has changed in Jefferson, the seat of Faulkner's mythical Mississippi county. Shade trees have yielded to electric poles and wires, unpaved streets to asphalt, and black women lightly bearing laundry bundles on their heads to black women at the same task in automobiles. Immediately the author establishes the distance between the time of the action and that of the telling. By the absence of any comment on changes in attitudes and by Quentin's matter-of-fact tone, Faulkner implies the lack of any humane compensations for the loss of the old rhythms of small-town life.

The retrospective method also allows Quentin latitude for necessary exposition of facts which as a child he could not have understood, while at the same time the narrator can attempt to achieve immediacy and vividness by reporting recollections of an experience from his tenth year. When he focuses on the scenes that he witnessed with his brother and sister, Quentin's narrative becomes childlike in its language and sentence rhythms, as if he is striving to replicate the perceptions of fifteen years ago. Thus Faulkner achieves an unusual blend of the perspectives of the adult and the child, with the transitions managed so skillfully that they blend smoothly.

Another effective technique is the juxtaposition of the adult conflicts and the children's more circumscribed world. Faulkner creates a counterpoint consisting of Nancy's troubles with men and her remonstrations with the elder Compsons, on the one hand, and, on the other, the naïve questions, petty quarrels, and self-seeking artifices of Quentin's younger siblings, Caddy and Jason, most of which are ignored or shushed by the adults. To a certain extent the children's talk mirrors the preoccupations of the older generation. Young Jason, for example, is particularly interested in determining the status of blacks, while he and Caddy both spend much of the time on the path between their house and Nancy's debating whether Jason is indeed a "scairy cat."

The overall effect of the counterpoint of children and adults, however, is one of stark contrast. The youngest child's attempts to establish who is and who is not a "nigger" represent only an embryonic version of the adult code which condemns Nancy to insecure servitude and Jesus to base humiliation, and the children's utter incomprehension of the nature of adult fear heightens the reader's sense of Nancy's isolation. The world of the children is not precisely innocent, for they have already absorbed many of their parents' attitudes, but they have no intimation of Nancy's inner turmoil. As yet they are cruel and pitiless only in the manner of inexperienced children against whose naïveté Nancy's hopelessness stands out in sharp relief.

One more aspect of the narration deserves comment. Faulkner expected his readers to "see through" his narrators in two different senses. It is only through Quentin that the story is available at all, yet the reader must also see through Quentin in the sense of seeing beyond his field of perception. In his objective account there is no sympathy. In Nancy's hour of need, the Compsons, though in no way legally responsible for her, nevertheless abrogate their moral responsibility not to abandon her. Quentin shows no sign of recognizing this responsibility fifteen years later. He can be trusted to get the facts correct, but the author leaves it to his audience to appreciate their significance.

Robert P. Ellis

THEME OF THE TRAITOR AND THE HERO

Author: Jorge Luis Borges (1899-1986)
Type of plot: Mystery
Time of plot: 1944, 1924, and the early nineteenth century
Locale: Ireland
First published: "Tema del traidor y del héroe," 1944 (English translation, 1962)

> *Principal characters:*
> AN UNNAMED FIRST-PERSON NARRATOR, the writer of the story
> RYAN, a historian and the great-grandson of Fergus Kilpatrick
> FERGUS KILPATRICK, a patriot in the Irish rebellion of 1824
> JAMES ALEXANDER NOLAN, Kilpatrick's oldest companion

The Story

On the eve of the rebellion in Ireland in the year 1824, Fergus Kilpatrick, a patriot, is assassinated. One hundred years later, his great-grandson, Ryan, who is compiling a biography of the hero's life, tries to discover the identity of the assassin. His search entails the examination of historical records which prove to be enigmatic rather than illuminating. The contents of these documents recall episodes and characters from literature. For example, an unopened letter found on the cadaver forewarned of the assassination attempt in the same way that Calpurnia's warning did not reach Caesar in time to save him. Ryan wonders about the possibility of a secret form of time, a drawing of lines that are repeated, like the systems proposed by the Marquis de Condorcet, George William Friedrich Hegel, Oswald Spengler, and Giambattista Vico, and like Hesiod's degeneration of man. Yet Ryan notices that history has copied not only history but also literature, since certain words recorded from a conversation between Kilpatrick and a beggar are originally from William Shakespeare's *Macbeth*. Another discordant element in the investigation is a death sentence, signed by the usually merciful Kilpatrick, from which the name has been erased.

Finally, Ryan is able to piece together the clues. At Kilpatrick's request, Nolan, Kilpatrick's oldest companion, had learned the identity of the traitor to the cause: Kilpatrick himself. Because of the latter's popularity among the Irish people, Nolan conceived a strange project in order not to compromise the rebellion. It was arranged for Kilpatrick to be assassinated under deliberately dramatic circumstances which would endure throughout history. To this end, Nolan, who at one time had translated the principal works of Shakespeare and written about the *Festspiele* (vast theatrical representations with thousands of actors, which reiterate historical episodes in the cities and mountains where they occurred), wrote a script for the assassination. The play was performed, although not without a certain amount of improvisation by Kilpatrick, who, getting carried away with his part, would often speak lines more dramatic than those of Nolan, who had, in turn, plagiarized material from Shakespeare. Ryan suspects that Nolan intended those scenes to be clues for a future investigator.

Themes and Meanings

"Theme of the Traitor and the Hero" narrates the deeds of Fergus Kilpatrick and the events surrounding his assassination, but it is about the nightmarish fatalism that is existence. The story takes the form of an investigation into a century-old unsolved crime, conducted by a biographer who deciphers the enigma through the interpretation of some historical documents. Yet while this evidence furnishes the information that leads to the final solution of the riddle, in the process it has raised disturbing questions about such notions as a secret form of time and reality copying the imaginary. Various passages contained in the documents remind the biographer of certain texts, authors, and protagonists (historical as well as literary), dating from classical and biblical times to the present. Patterns emerge which not only enable the reconstruction of an incident in the past but also partially reveal the essence of being. The explanation of what actually happened—that Kilpatrick was a traitor who agreed to act out a staged assassination in order to save the rebellion—may satisfy Ryan's curiosity, but at the same time, it advances a malevolent hypothesis about how reality occurs. The solving of one mystery leads to another, greater and virtually unresolvable one.

In "Theme of the Traitor and the Hero," there are three story lines: an assassination, an investigation, and an invention. The story is told by a first-person narrator who "perhaps" devises a plot about a contemporary narrator, the latter, in turn, a biographer of his great-grandfather's life as set down by Nolan and others. These characters belong to three distinct time periods: 1944, the present of the anonymous writer; 1924, the year in which Ryan carries out his investigation (retold using the historical present tense); and the early 1800's, the era of Fergus Kilpatrick. Certain texts correspond to the different narrative threads, each having a source in other writings, and all are linked: the first-person narrator acknowledges the influence of Gilbert Keith Chesterton and Gottfried Wilhelm Leibniz in the construction of his plot about Ryan's biography, which is based on historical records, including Nolan's drama, which derives from both the works of Shakespeare and the Swiss tradition of *Festspiele*. Furthermore, the three texts are products of discoveries: The first narrator has had certain partial revelations about history, Ryan figures out Nolan's strange project, and Nolan discovers the identity of the traitor. Common to all three stories, then, is the author-discoverer who rewrites texts from the past that are to be rewritten in the future. The same pattern is repeated again and again, like infinite mirrors creating a labyrinth with no exit.

Such interminable reflections are evocative of the type of existence envisioned by Leibniz: the perceiving and being perceived among all elements in the universe. In "Theme of the Traitor and the Hero," writing is the particular mode of perception: It confers existence upon its subjects and its authors or creators by its practice (they are perceived through the text); conversely, it derives its being from (perceiving) what already is. Inasmuch as writing represents existence, it becomes an act of creation, literally as well as figuratively, demonstrated when, for example, history copies literature, written documents anticipate future readers, and plots justify their inventors.

From Kilpatrick's double identity (not as traitor and hero but as patriot-hero and protagonist-hero), other heroes and traitors may be inferred. For example, Ryan is the protagonist-hero of the invented plot, and, at the same time, he is a traitor in that he sustains the myth of Kilpatrick, that is, through his role as author. Nolan also commits treason through literature in the form of an elaborate, deceptive drama. Yet these specific acts only serve to point to the larger betrayal which is writing itself, the perpetuation of existence as it is known.

Style and Technique

"Theme of the Traitor and the Hero" belongs to the genre of mystery stories, Borges adapting its conventions in order to express his message. The writer after whom he models his story is Chesterton, whose detective fiction is characterized by reasonable explanations of the apparently inexplicable. This is clearly the case in "Theme of the Traitor and the Hero," as Kilpatrick's culpability (leading to Nolan's plan) accounts for various incongruencies and gaps in the original testimony. This, however, is only one aspect of the interest Chesterton holds for Borges. In an essay in the collection, *Otras inquisiciones* (1952; *Other Inquisitions: 1937-1952*, 1964), the Argentine author concludes that Chesterton's work consistently has traces of the demonic, the nightmarish, with such images as jails of mirrors or labyrinths with no center. It is this dimension of the mystery writer that seems to lend meaning and impact to the other borrowing, the structural device, in "Theme of the Traitor and the Hero." Evidence in the story itself may be found, for example, in Ryan's noteworthy absence of reaction to the discovery of Kilpatrick's guilt, in contrast to his utter astonishment before the possibility of a secret form of time. While the former is at the literal center of the text, it is a much less significant moment within the narrative. Furthermore, mention of Leibniz's preestablished harmony introduces a metaphysical concept more akin to an atrocious observation than a reasonable explanation.

Besides supplying background information about the inception of the story, the first-person narrator in the initial paragraph creates an immediate subjectivity, shrouding the remainder of the story with a veil of uncertainty. His use of the Spanish future of probability, *"escribiré tal vez"* ("perhaps I am writing"), coupled with an obscure view of history, places the subsequent fabrication within the realm of the conjectural, precise dates notwithstanding. The epigraph taken from William Butler Yeats's *The Tower* (1928) suggests that what he will be guessing about is that which makes men move.

Krista Ratkowski Carmona

THERE WILL COME SOFT RAINS

Author: Ray Bradbury (1920-   )
Type of plot: Science fiction
Time of plot: August 4, 2026
Locale: Allendale, California
First published: 1950

The Story

This futuristic story has no characters but centers instead on the single house left standing after a nuclear blast has destroyed the remainder of Allendale, California, in the year 2026. It is the story of one day in the life of the house: the day the house finally dies after having lived on for days after its inhabitants were killed in the blast. All that remains of the couple and two children who once lived there are four silhouettes in paint on the otherwise charred west exterior wall of the house. Such is the technology of Bradbury's twenty-first century world, however, that the house continues to go about its daily business, oblivious to the total destruction around it and to the total absence of human life: "The house was an altar with ten thousand attendants, big, small, servicing, attending, in choirs. But the gods had gone away, and the ritual of the religion continued senselessly, uselessly."

Mechanical voice boxes hidden in the house's walls announce the date, the weather, and noteworthy events of the day. A voice clock sings out the passing hours. The mechanical stove makes breakfast for family members who will never return to eat it, and robot cleaning-mice scurry out of their burrows to carry away any chance bit of debris. The family dog, the only remaining living creature, starves to death outside the kitchen door while inside the kitchen the uneaten breakfast is swept down the garbage disposal. The mice, sensing decay, scurry out again to carry off the corpse and toss it into the incinerator.

Time ticks away as the house prepares for a bridge party that never takes place, draws baths for its missing inhabitants, prepares dinner, warms the beds, and even lights a pipe for its absent master. At ten o'clock, the house starts to die. A falling branch breaks a window and sends a bottle of cleaning solvent shattering across the kitchen stove. Fire races through the rooms as the house fights desperately to save itself. All of man's twenty-first century technology is brought to bear as the battle rages. Voice boxes scream out warnings to the inhabitants for whom the warning comes too late, chemical foam gushes from the attic, and mechanical rain showers down from the walls. Finally, however, the reserve water supply that has kept the house functioning for days is used up, and the fire rages out of control.

As the house's wiring, its nervous system, starts to shrivel and burn, pandemonium breaks loose. The stove turns out huge quantities of breakfast as the flames eat up what has already been prepared, the mice rush out to try to carry away the growing mounds of ash, and the walls resound with a crazy chorus of voices, one quietly reading poetry as the study around it burns. When the house finally comes crashing down, dawn is showing in the east, and from the one wall still standing a single, last voice repeats over and over, "Today is August 5, 2026, today is August 5, 2026, today is . . ."

Themes and Meanings

By 1950, Bradbury was well aware of the looming threat of nuclear holocaust and of the irony that the technology that could be used to make life more comfortable for humanity could also be misused to bring about man's ultimate destruction. In creating the house that is the focal point of the story, man has made his scientific knowledge work for him to render daily life orderly and carefree. Before the nuclear explosion, the inhabitants of the house clearly lived a pampered existence, and it was the house itself, man's creation, that pampered them and that indeed even did much of their thinking for them. The house cooked, cleaned, and protected itself without the expending of any human energy. Martinis and sandwiches appeared readymade for the bridge party, and the cards were even mechanically dealt. The children were entertained with fantasy worlds on film projected on the walls of the nursery, and their parents with poetry read at their request by a voice box. The house also reminded the owners to pay their bills, to acknowledge birthdays and anniversaries, and to take along galoshes and umbrellas. Ironically, once the house made possible by man's technological advances started to function, it no longer needed man. So smoothly did the house run itself that it might have lived on much longer had not nature interfered.

In Bradbury's prophetic look at the future of modern society, man by the year 2026 has advanced to the point where he can control his material realm, but he cannot control his own destructive tendencies. The implication is that the nuclear blast is the result of an act of aggression against the west coast of the United States. Whether war or nuclear accident is responsible for the devastation, however, man's power to use science for his own benefit is juxtaposed to his powerlessness to control his scientific developments in their more destructive forms.

The end of the story also illustrates man's powerlessness in the face of natural forces. The manner in which the house dies emphasizes the ability of nature to endure in spite of man's ultimately fatal attempts to control his environment. The wind blowing down a tree branch starts the series of events that end in the total destruction of the house. Dawn breaks in the east as the destruction is complete. The natural cycle goes on regardless of whether there is a single human being left alive to witness it. Man's puny recorded voice calls forth that a new day has begun, but the sun rises to shine only upon a heap of rubble.

Style and Technique

At the heart of the story's irony is a poem by Sara Teasdale that the mechanical house chooses to read when the former lady of the house, Mrs. McClellan, is no longer there to express a preference. The title of the story comes from the first line of the poem: "There will come soft rains and the smell of the ground." Teasdale goes on to create a poetic world in which swallows, robins, and frogs continue their singing, oblivious to man and his wars:

> And not one will know of the war, not one
> Will care at last when it is done.
>
> Not one would mind, neither bird nor tree,
> If mankind perished utterly;
>
> And Spring herself, when she woke at dawn
> Would scarcely know that we were gone.

The irony exists in the way in which Bradbury's fictional world in "There Will Come Soft Rains" parallels the imaginative world of Teasdale's poem. By placing this poem in the middle of the story, just before the house starts to die, Bradbury draws attention to the role that nature plays in its death, but also to nature's lack of concern for man. There is also the additional irony that this poem about nature's lack of concern for human life is picked at random by a house designed to operate at the beck and call of people who are no longer even there. The house, with its mechanical voices, carries on, unconcerned, just as do the birds and frogs of the poem, with their natural voices.

The personification of the house throughout the story serves to make even more obvious, by contrast, the absence of human life. The house is full of voices, but not one of them belongs to a living human being. When danger arises, the voices scream and wail as if the machines behind them were capable of feeling fear. The house fights valiantly to save itself, and the fight becomes a battle as between two human entities. The fire lies in beds, feeds on paintings, stands in windows, feels the clothes in the closets. The fire is clever. It sends flames, as with conscious intent, to destroy the attic brain that controls the water pumps. The house's defeat is described in anatomical terms: "The house shuddered, oak bone on bone, its bared skeleton cringing from the heat, its wire, its nerves revealed as if a surgeon had torn the skin off to let the red veins and capillaries quiver in the scalded air." Its collapse becomes a burial: "The crash. The attic smashing into kitchen and parlor. The parlor into cellar, cellar into sub-cellar. Deep freeze, armchair, film tapes, circuits, beds, and all like skeletons thrown in a cluttered mound deep under."

Humans, in their attempt to be godlike, have succeeded in creating a dwelling that practically takes on a life of its own. In the absence of its human creators, however, the religion for which the house itself serves as an altar is reduced to an empty ritual. The ritual continues for a time, but the "gods" that it is designed to serve have gone away. All that remains is nature, which scarcely knows that they are gone.

Donna B. Haisty

THEY

Author: Rudyard Kipling (1865-1936)
Type of plot: Psychological fantasy
Time of plot: Early twentieth century
Locale: An Elizabethan house in the Sussex Downs, England
First published: 1904

Principal characters:
AN UNNAMED NARRATOR
AN UNNAMED BLIND WOMAN, the owner of the house

The Story

When driving through the Sussex countryside in early summer, the narrator, who appears to be an English gentleman of adequate means and impeccable manners, loses his way. In order to regain his bearings, he stops at an impressive mansion, where he sees two children at an upstairs window and hears a child's laughter coming from somewhere in the garden, two events which are of far greater significance than he can possibly realize. A woman approaches him from the garden, and he realizes that she is blind. In the ensuing discussion it becomes clear that the narrator is fond of children, and the woman (whose relationship to the children in the house is unstated, although it it clear that she is not their mother) asks him to drive around the grounds so that the children may see the motor car—the presence of a car in that area being something of a novelty. The children, however, are extremely elusive, always hiding and leaving only reminders, such as a toy boat in the fountain, of their presence. There is something very mysterious about them. "Lucky you to be able to see them," the blind woman says, but her words contain an irony of which neither narrator nor reader is yet aware.

One month later, the narrator returns to the house. Curious about the children, he tries to attract their attention by making an elaborate show of repairing his car. He hears the faint tread of a child's feet on the leaves, but the children flee when he makes a sudden sound. Then, as he sees the blind woman approaching, he appears to discern a child clinging to her skirt, but the child disappears into the foliage as the woman draws closer. The children are so shy, she explains. They come and stay with her because she loves them. She does not know how many there are. They are not her own, since she never married.

The narrator is puzzled by his conversations with this woman. She has beauty, sweetness of voice, and depth of soul, and yet she is marked by sadness and regret. He discovers that she possesses telepathic powers; other people's thoughts appear in her mind as colors. Some colors hurt her; others make her happy.

Their conversation is suddenly interrupted by the appearance of a distraught woman who is running frantically toward them. It transpires that her grandchild has fallen seriously ill, and the local doctor is unavailable. In the hectic events that follow—the search for a doctor and a nurse, the rush to collect medicine—the story snaps into dramatic action and becomes charged with the sense of the fragility and uncertainty of human life, and the reality of human suffering.

It is not until autumn that the narrator returns to the area. He learns that in spite of all the efforts made, the child had died within two days of becoming ill. On arriving at the house, he hears the blind woman singing:

> In the pleasant orchard-closes,
>   God bless all our gains, say we—
> But may God bless all our losses,
>   Better suits with our degree.

She shows him around the house for the first time. The evidence of children is everywhere: toy guns, rocking horses, dolls. Yet the children themselves are nowhere to be seen; only the rustle of a dress or the occasional patter of feet betrays their presence. An odd kind of chase ensues, from room to room, passage to passage. The children have plenty of places to hide. Finally, as the narrator reaches the hall, he sees them, deep in the shadows, hiding behind a leather screen. He resolves to make them reveal themselves by pretending not to notice them. It was, he thought, a game between them. When the blind woman is distracted by the arrival of one of her tenants, he slides his chair back and taps on the screen. Moments later he feels his hand being clasped and kissed by the soft hands of a child. Instantly he knows the truth and senses that he has known it since the day he first saw the children at the window of the house: They are the happy ghosts of the youthful dead. The woman, realizing that he knows her secret, confesses that she feels undeserving, as if she had no right to hear the children, since she has "neither borne nor lost." They came "because I needed them. I—I must have made them come." The toys were unnecessary, but she disliked having empty rooms.

The narrator listens and ponders the meaning of his realization with increasing emotion. He seems to be grappling with an equal measure of joy and sorrow. He knows that he can never return to the house. He reassures the blind woman that it is right for her to possess spiritual insight, but it would be wrong for him to cultivate it, even though it seems to come naturally to him. He gives no reason for this belief. The story ends as he sits silently by the screen, lost in the intensity of his contemplation.

Themes and Meanings

The origins of "They" can be traced to a tragic event in Kipling's own life.

He and his family had traveled to New York in 1899, and during the trip both Kipling and his seven-year-old daughter became seriously ill. Kipling recovered, but his daughter did not. Kipling's grief was deep and enduring. Back at his home in England, according to his father, he would see his daughter—like the children in "They"—"when a door opened, when a space was vacant at table, coming out of every green dark corner of the garden, radiant—and heart breaking." There is no doubt that "They," underneath the luxuriousness and beauty of the setting and the apparent gaiety of the children's presence, carries a heavy weight of sorrow, which only gradually unfolds itself.

The theme of the story is of the continuity of life and the continuity of grief, in the face of the raw facts of "losin' and bearin'," the human experience of birth and death. The theme has two crosscurrents. In one sense the story is uplifting; the ghost-children, after all, seem happy enough, and they can be perceived by those who possess love and spiritual insight. Love reaches beyond the grave, and the dead are a comfort to the living. Yet they are a torture also. There is no mistaking the sadness and sense of regret in the unnamed blind woman; her voice "would have drawn lost souls from the Pit, for the yearning that underlay its sweetness." It is as if her psychic gifts must somehow be paid for, and in this respect she resembles the character Mrs. Ashcroft in "The Wish House," another of Kipling's short stories set in the Sussex countryside.

In the final pages of the story the full force of the sorrowful aspect of the theme is brought out, as the inner life of the narrator come to the fore. His soul is "torn open," and his realization that he can never return to the house where the presence of the dead is so vivid is "like the very parting of spirit and flesh." Perhaps here the autobiographical strain of the story surfaces once more; Kipling, as the narrator, must put his grievous loss behind him and channel his psychic energies into further creative work.

Style and Technique

Structurally, "They" falls into three sections, corresponding to the three visits the narrator makes to the Sussex Downs. The very first paragraph effectively but unobtrusively leads the reader into the unusual world in which the story takes place. The references to Roman roads, Norman churches, and an old smithy that had once been a hall of the Knights Templars evoke the vast reach of time in English history. The narrator enters a world that is full of the passage of time and the imprint it leaves. Paradoxically, however, it is also a fairy-tale world that is beyond time; retracing his route on a map the narrator can find no name or information about the old house on which he has unwittingly stumbled. He realizes that he is "clean out of [his] known marks," a thought which has more significance than he realizes: He is entering a place which is unknown to him not only geographically, but spiritually as well.

The anonymity of the two central characters—they are never named—contributes to this effect. Not only does it surround them with a slight aura of mystery, but it also suggests that they possess some kind of universal significance, beyond the localized boundaries of time and place and larger than their individual personalities. As a significant contrast, all the characters in the poignant little episode which makes up the second section of the story are named: Arthur the sick child, Jenny the mother, Mrs. Madehurst the grandmother. The subtle and the mysterious gives way to the concrete and the real, and this prepares the reader for the revelation contained in the final section.

The force of the third section comes largely from the unexpected shift in focus from the house, the children, and the blind woman, to the sudden intensity of the narrator's feelings. Up to this point in the story, he has been a model of politeness and courteous detachment, as much the observer of sights and events as their direct participant. The fact that the sudden surfacing of his inner life is so dramatically effective is a tribute to Kipling's skill as a storyteller. Throughout the story he has inveigled the reader into seeing and experiencing with the eyes and the mind of the narrator, in his puzzled innocence. When the carefully cultivated sense of suspense, strangeness, and mystery is resolved in the final, overwhelming flash of realization, in which all the events of the story fall into place, the reader finds that he has been inexorably drawn into the experience, and as the story closes he finds himself, like the narrator, silently contemplating thoughts beyond the reaches of his soul.

Bryan Aubrey

THE THIRD BANK OF THE RIVER

Author: João Guimarães Rosa (1908-1967)
Type of plot: Mystery
Time of plot: Perhaps the twentieth century
Locale: Probably central Brazil
First published: "A terceira margem do rio," 1962 (English translation, 1968)

> *Principal characters:*
> THE UNNAMED NARRATOR
> HIS FATHER
> HIS MOTHER
> HIS SISTER
> HIS SISTER'S HUSBAND
> HIS BROTHER

The Story

One day, quite unexpectedly, the narrator's father orders a canoe made. His wife thinks it absurd for a man his age to think about hunting and fishing, but the man offers no explanation. When the canoe, sturdy and built to last, finally arrives, the man solemnly paddles it into the middle of the river. During the first few days after this strange withdrawal, the narrator worries about his father and regularly leaves some food along the riverbank for his father's sustenance. The days become weeks, months, years, and it finally becomes clear that his father will never return to his family. His father manages somehow to ride out the floodwaters every year, though he barely touches the food left for him by his son and by other members of his family. The daughter marries and has a son, and the family gathers by the river in the hope that the man will come to see his new grandson, but he does not appear.

The daughter moves away, and finally the mother goes away to live with her sister. Finally, only the narrator, out of some profound sense of duty, stays. When he realizes how aged he has become, he knows that his father must be very old, and he goes down to the bank at last and calls out that his father's duty is finished, that he, the narrator, will take his place in the canoe. The father approaches in the canoe, but the son panics and flees. His father is never seen again. Finally, the son longs for a place to die, a canoe.

Themes and Meanings

A story of such open-endedness, in which characters have no names and nothing is explained, is naturally one that invites a great variety of interpretations. The story's lack of specificity is complicated by its title, which calls for the reader to identify a third bank, a process that would require an evaluation of the extant two to determine which is the first and which the second.

The easiest procedure for approaching the third bank phenomenon is to consider the story in the context of the volume in which it was published, which in the original Portuguese was entitled *Primeiras estórias* (first stories), although it was Guimarães Rosa's fourth book. While nothing more than authorial perversity may be the reason, it is true that ordering, numbering, and ranking are rational procedures that depend on a grasp of the external configuration of things, a perception of the real. Yet the author is demanding a perception of essence, not subject to ordering, numbering, or ranking, because it cannot be seen with the eyes alone. The stories in this volume are all about human beings who are disconnected or alienated from the mainstream of social machinery; thus, their perceptions are not received community perceptions, which tend to be linear and symmetrical, but rather eccentric and individualistic, ranging from childhood wonder to second sight and across to the third bank.

When the father leaves in his canoe, he is doing so in response to some imperative which remains a mystery to the community. The only one who approaches an understanding of that imperative is the narrator, who never explains, at least not in any ranked or ordered fashion, his understanding of it. The narrator's perception is that the father had waited all that time for the son to take over the task of staying in the canoe in the middle of the river, and that when he turned and fled he somehow failed. Yet it is also apparent that when the offer is made, the ordeal, with whatever outcome, is over, for the father is never seen again.

It is probably possible to interpret this story in a psychological fashion, or as a problem of family communication, or even as a religious tale, but that would reduce it to allegory or treatise, in which the force of the tale is at least partly derived from the evanescent nature of the imperative. The characters in other stories in the volume are eccentrics, madmen, murderers, and children, who share with the father of "The Third Bank of the River" a distance from received community perceptions that allows them to see things that normal people cannot see, and their gift of perception leads them into a state that transcends the literal and the ordinary.

Style and Technique

João Guimarães Rosa is Brazil's monster of style, in the sense that James Joyce was such a monster in English. Anyone who knows his work can identify a single line read aloud as his or not his, because the diction of all of his works is "strange"—he is fond of neologisms, back formations, foreign words, Latinisms, pleonasms, expletives, unfamiliar word order, internal rhyme, onomatopoeia—the list is long. Such diction is difficult to render into English, with the result that those few works that have been translated are all much more "flat" in English than they were in Portuguese: The story is still there, but the surprises and delights produced by language alone are largely absent.

The stories in the volume in which this story appears are probably less dizzying from the perspective of language than are many of his others, which may be one reason that this volume is one of the few translated. Yet even in English the story is too elliptical, not sufficiently informational, to satisfy readers who desire full understanding on a first reading. There is great range in the length of Guimarães Rosa's stories, from some early ones of more than one hundred pages to later ones that barely cover two printed pages. In all these stories, two elements of composition, language and perception, are at once stumbling blocks to the reader and keys to understanding the fictions. Guimarães Rosa did not write about the fantastic, but the world about which he writes is one in which the rules are not those of the rather more banal world that most people inhabit, and since the world is perceived as larger and more open to such things as three-banked rivers, the language used to narrate the tales is more elastic and less ordered than the banal language which most people speak.

Though the mystical sense of language is necessarily flattened by a rendition into English, a less elastic tongue than Portuguese, the mystical sense of the world remains intact, and sensitive readers may even discover that some of the rivers in their world have three banks as well.

Jon S. Vincent

THE THIRD PRIZE

Author: A. E. Coppard (1878-1957)
Type of plot: Realism
Time of plot: The late 1890's
Locale: A medium-sized English town
First published: 1928

> *Principal characters:*
> GEORGE ROBINS, an attractive young clerk
> NABOTH BIRD, his friend, a bicycle mechanic
> JERRY CHAMBERS, a "cockney ruffian"

The Story

George Robins and Naboth Bird are young men for whom footracing is "their pastime, their passion, their principal absorption and topic of conversation"; while neither is a champion runner, each occasionally wins "some sort of trophy."

On an August bank holiday, they go to a garrison town on the coast of England, where the holiday is being celebrated with a carnival of games. The crowd attending includes a medley of soldiers, sailors, most of the population of the town, and a number of blind beggars. The young men meet two girls who have come from London for the holiday; the "short snub" Naboth devotes his attentions to Minnie, the more demure of the girls, while the "cute good-looking" George offers "his gifts of gallantry" to Margery, who displays "some qualities not commonly associated with demureness."

After George and Margery engage in some trivial flirtation, the young men enter the mile race. George wins third prize. When the men are dressing after the race, they are pursued by Jerry Chambers, a "cockney ruffian living by his wits," who suggests that he could get the first and second place winners disqualified so that George could claim the first prize of five pounds. They reject his offer with appropriate scorn.

When the prizes are awarded by a portly countess, the only titled person the young men have ever seen, the name of W. Ballantyne is called out for the third place winner in the mile race. When no one comes forward, George quickly exchanges his tweed cap for Nab's bowler and claims the prize as W. Ballantyne. The prize is a sovereign, a gold coin worth one pound. After the awarding of the prizes is completed, George, again wearing his tweed cap, disappears, leaving his friends wondering what he is "up to." When he returns, he says that he has been to claim the third prize as George Robins. He reports that after some "palavering and running about" the persons awarding the prizes apologize for their mistake and give George a second sovereign.

Margery and Minnie rather fatuously admire George's cleverness, but Nab is perturbed by this dishonesty: All may be fair, as Margery says, in love and war, but sport is something else. To Nab, George's trick is "a bit like what Jerry Chambers might have done himself." Margery maintains that George was "jolly smart" and that Nab was actually his confederate because he lent George his hat. George offers Nab half of the questionable sovereign, but Nab resolutely refuses it. In spite of their disagreement over the ethics of George's claiming the same prize under two different names, the foursome remains amicable and continues to wander through the festive crowd.

In the midst of the stream of people a blind beggar is trying, without much success, to get contributions from the crowd by playing a hymn tune on a tin pipe. In spite of his ragged appearance, the beggar stands erect and maintains a sort of dignity; his feeble wife holds his arm with one hand and reaches out with the other for the few pennies that are given to them. George, Nab, and the girls are astonished to see Jerry Chambers standing in front of the pathetic couple, brazenly drawing attention to them with "excruciating gestures and noises." Maintaining that looking at the old couple "just breaks my heart," Jerry says that he is going to sing a comical song, dance a jig, and perform some other antics "to collect bullion for this suffering fambly." Jerry abandons his plan of dancing a jig when he discovers that the only tune the beggar knows is the hymn "Marching to Zion," but he aggressively passes his hat to collect money for the couple, whom he openly refers to as "those two old bits of mutton."

While Margery is searching for a coin, George takes the "glittering questionable sovereign" and, before Margery can prevent him, drops the coin into Jerry's hat. Then, "curiously shamefaced," he hurries away. The girls are dazzled by the generosity of George's contribution, and even Nab is "mute before its sublimity."

After they leave, Jerry counts the money and loudly thanks the crowd for the "very handsome collection" of eight shillings and fourpence. Then he hurries away, murmuring "Beau-tiful beautiful Zi-on." He keeps the golden sovereign for himself.

Themes and Meanings

The theme of this story turns on the comparison which the author invites among the varying degrees of honor exhibited by the principal male characters. Naboth, the mechanic, is clearly the most honorable: He objects to his friend's trickery in getting the second sovereign and resolutely refuses George's offer of half of the questionable prize. He cannot imagine what George is up to when he goes to get the second sovereign and is astonished when George describes his trick. The other extreme is represented by the totally unprincipled Jerry Chambers. He has lost money by betting on George, and he wants to make good his losses by inventing reasons to have the first and second place winners disqualified. His antics in calling attention to the pathetic old beggar and his wife are pure exploitation, as he is simply using them as an occasion to collect money, and, as he keeps the largest contribution, George's sovereign, for himself, giving the beggar a sum amounting to less than half the value of the sovereign.

George, the clerk, wavers between these two extremes. He is as quick-witted as Jerry in conceiving his plan to get an extra sovereign, but Nab's disapproval—significantly Nab condemns the trick as "a bit like what Jerry Chambers might have done himself"—arouses qualms of conscience that prompt him to give the sovereign to the old couple. There is a vast difference between George's extorting an extra sovereign from the sports committee and Jerry's brazen and vulgar exploitation of the impoverished old couple for the same coin.

While Nab's steadfast integrity and George's conscientious sacrifice of the sovereign that he got by deception win the praise of the girls—and, presumably, the approval of the reader—it is significant that Jerry escapes unscathed with the sovereign to which he had no legitimate claim. Honor deserves—and wins—respect in the kind of world the story depicts, but a grossly vulgar charlatan escapes with the cash.

Style and Technique

Among the most notable aspects of Coppard's technique in this story are his skillful drawing of character and his deft presentation of significant details of description. The holiday crowd gathered for the games is festive, but also a little vulgar; it is made up of "soldiers, sailors, and quite ordinary people." George and Nab are from the lower ranges of the stratified English society of the 1890's; Margery and Minnie seem typical of the "jolly girls" who "hunt in couples." Margery opens her conversation with George by complaining that the train on which they came from London was filled with "boozy men" with "half of 'em trying to cuddle you." This conversational gambit naturally invites similar flirtation from George, and the triteness of their flirtation helps define the characters. Similarly, the blatant vulgarity of the conversation of Jerry Chambers identifies him as a "cockney ruffian."

While one hesitates to insist dogmatically on the precise significance of small details, they can often provide important clues to the author's values and attitudes. What is the importance, for example, of the fact that the blind beggar, who has a "strange dignity inseparable from blindness in his erect figure," wears a clerical hat? The town where the games take place has a garrison and a dockyard and would have been considered a city except for the fact that the "only available cathedral" was "just inside an annoying little snob of a borough" that keeps itself outside the "real and proper" town. The cathedral further isolates itself from the public by charging sixpence admission. The only titled person the young men have ever seen is the countess who helps award the prizes, but Coppard says that she has "a stomach like a publican's wife." Traditionally, the institutions of the church and the aristocracy were supposed to give England its moral fibre, but such representatives of these institutions as appear in this story seem conspicuously deficient. In a world where the church is either impoverished or snobbishly withdrawn and where a countess is indistinguishable from a publican's wife, it is hardly surprising that the vulgarity of Jerry Chambers prevails.

Erwin Hester

THIS WAY FOR THE GAS, LADIES AND GENTLEMAN

Author: Tadeusz Borowski (1922-1951)
Type of plot: Social realism
Time of plot: World War II
Locale: Auschwitz
First published: "Proszę państwa do gazu," 1948 (English translation, 1967)

> *Principal characters:*
> THE NARRATOR, the protagonist, a Polish inmate at Auschwitz
> HENRI, a French inmate at the camp and the narrator's friend

The Story

Through the first-person narrator, the author describes in harsh detail the daily routines and horrors of the concentration camp. The opening scene is a surreal picture of thousands of men and women, naked, waiting through the heat and boredom until another transport, carrying thousands of Jews to the gas chambers, arrives. Like the narrator's friend Henri, many of the inmates are members of the Canada Kommando, the labor gangs who work at unloading the transports. Henri and the narrator are introduced as they discuss the transports while lying in their barracks, eating a simple snack of bread, onions, and tomatoes. The transports mean survival. As the guards look the other way, the laborers can "organize" food and clothing from the piles of personal possessions collected from the Jews on the way to their death. As Henri states, "all of us live on what they bring."

The monotony is finally broken by the approach of a transport. For the first time, the narrator joins Henri as part of the labor gang heading to the station. The station is "like any other provincial railway stop" except that the regular freight here are those sentenced to the gas chambers. While the laborers wait, Henri barters with a guard for a bottle of water, on credit, to be paid for "by the people who have not yet arrived." As the freight cars pull into the station, the desperate cries for water and air from the prisoners crammed into the cars are quickly silenced by the gunfire ordered by an officer annoyed by the disturbance. Once the doors are opened, the prisoners surge toward the light like a "multicolored wave." The Canada Kommando members work feverishly, taking bundles from the crowd, separating those destined for the labor gangs from those for the chambers, loading trucks marked as Red Cross with the dazed prisoners. In sharp contrast to the mayhem on the ramps, an SS officer, with calm precision, marks off the new serial numbers, "thousands, of course."

A more odious task yet remains for the laborers as they are ordered to clean out the dead and dying from the cars. The narrator describes the trampled bodies of infants he carries out "like chickens." He begins to be affected by the terrors. At first intensely tired, he slips into a confused and dreamlike state as he sees the scenes repeated over and over. His own feelings of helplessness and terror turn to disgust and hatred for the Jews themselves—for, as he tells Henri, he is there, acting so brutally, only because they are.

Just as the last cars leave, the tired laborers hear a whistle and "terribly slowly" a new transport pulls in. The cycle of atrocities begins anew. Now the Kommandos are impatient and brutally rip the bundles from the prisoners and hurl them into trucks. The scenes of horror intensify as a mother tries to abandon her children in the hope of making the labor gangs (for all mothers and their children are gassed together). A couple locked in each other's arms, "nails in flesh," are pulled apart "like cattle." In the cars are seething heaps of bloated corpses and the unconscious. The narrator can no longer overcome his mounting terror and runs blindly away from the horror. When Henri finds him, he tries to reassure him that one becomes seasoned to the work, as has Henri himself. There is another whistle and the "same all over again" begins but slowed by night. There are the same motionless mountains of bodies in the cars, the same cries of despair. The narrator can no longer bear the repulsion he feels, and he vomits. Yet with the vomiting, the narrator rids himself of all the horrors he has witnessed. He suddenly sees the camp as a "haven of peace" for its inmates and realizes that he and his fellow prisoners survive, that "one is somehow still alive, one has enough food." He is seasoned. As the labor gangs finish their ungodly work and prepare to return to the camp, the narrator remarks how the camp will be fed by this transport for at least a week, how this was "a good, rich transport."

Themes and Meanings

Borowski drew upon his own experiences as a prisoner at Auschwitz and Dachau for his stories on camp life. This, the first, published shortly after his release, graphically gives testimony that man is capable of doing anything to his fellowman. More troubling is the realization that ordinary people, good people, will do anything to survive. The inmates of the camp learn to survive by assisting in the atrocities. For the Canada Kommando, the piles of plunder—jewelry, money, gold—taken from the nameless thousands are not as precious as the pair of shoes or can of cocoa that they can "organize." By using a first-person narrator (one never given a name), the author clearly identifies himself with the responsibility and guilt to be shared by all. The narrator senses his responsibility when he lets his disgust turn to anger at the thousands who go passively to their deaths. He is forced to act inhumanly to survive as a human. As often noted, the narrator is both executioner and victim. He suffers the knowledge of his collaboration. Borowski called his stories on the concentration camps "a voyage to the limit of a particular experience." That experience is the realization of what a man can and will do to survive.

Style and Technique

The true horror of Borowski's experience is the routine of the collaboration in the atrocities. He has his narrator speak with the detached, objective voice of a reporter in most of the story. The phrases are simple and direct; the incredible brutality of the events needs no commentary. "I go back inside the train; I carry out dead infants; I unload luggage; I touch corpses." The normalcy of events is heightened by the descriptions and actions of the SS officers and guards. Against the backdrop of feverish action left to the camp inmates, the SS officers "move about, dignified, businesslike." They discuss the routines of their lives—children, family—as thousands are routinely executed. There is nothing out of the ordinary taking place there at Auschwitz.

There are several key images in the story. Food—the bare essence of survival—is a recurring motif. The narrator is first seen eating "crisp, crunchy bread," bacon, onions, and tomatoes. The Greek prisoners find rotting sardines and mildewed bread; as Borowski simply states, "They eat." The gangs rest with vodka, cocoa, and sugar "organized" from the transport. Even the bodies of the dead, trampled infants, are described as chickens. As the gangs return to camp, they are weighed down by the "load of bread, marmalade, and sugar" that they collected. Food as the image for survival occurs throughout the Auschwitz stories.

Another recurring image in Borowski's stories is that of insects. The mindless drive to eat and live surfaces in man as well as in insects. The Greek prisoners sit, "their jaws working greedily, like huge human insects." What Borowski calls the "animal hunger" of the camps drives them to eat whatever is available.

The relentless machinery of the transports and the corresponding helplessness of the prisoners are seen in the author's use of the wave simile. Borowski describes the prisoners of the first transport as a wave of "a blind, mad river." Nothing can stand in its way. Yet it is not an isolated phenomenon. The last transport also discharges its freight that is like a wave that "flows on and on, endlessly."

Joan A. Robertson

THREE DEATHS

Author: Leo Tolstoy (1828-1910)
Type of plot: Symbolic realism
Time of plot: The nineteenth century
Locale: Russia
First published: "Tri smerti," 1859 (English translation, 1902)

>   *Principal characters:*
>   MARYA DMITRIYEVNA, an upper-class woman in her mid-
>   twenties who is dying from consumption
>   VASILY DMITRICH, Marya's solicitous and sentimental husband
>   EDWARD IVANOVICH, Marya's doctor
>   MATRYOSHA, Marya's maid
>   UNCLE FYODOR, a poor old carriage driver, who is dying from
>   consumption
>   SERYOGA, a young peasant carriage driver
>   NASTASYA, a peasant cook at a post station on the route to
>   Moscow

The Story

In the story's four numbered sections are described the actions of two sets of characters, one from the upper class and one from the lower. Each set revolves around a character dying from consumption: Marya Dmitriyevna, attempting to flee the harsh Russian winter to reach the warm Italian climate in the hope of curing her illness, and Uncle Fyodor, lying in the last stages of his illness in the carriage drivers' quarters at a post station. The two sets of characters intersect in sections 1 and 2 of the story, when the two carriages of the small upper-class entourage make a brief rest stop at the post station, where most of the lower-class characters work.

At the station, all the passengers except Marya disembark to eat; Vasily and Edward also have wine and further discuss what should be done about Marya, who in the doctor's opinion will certainly not live to reach Italy. At the opening of section 2, the young driver of Marya's carriage, Seryoga, enters the drivers' quarters to ask for the dying Uncle Fyodor's new boots as replacements for his own worn-out ones, which are woefully inadequate in the inclement weather. Fyodor assents, subject to Seryoga's promise to provide a headstone for his grave.

After the carriages' departure, the remainder of section 2 shifts to focus on the comfort Nastasya attempts to provide for Fyodor, who dies that night and appears in Nastasya's dream. Section 3 focuses on the family of Marya gathered, along with a local priest, at a Moscow house, where she is bedridden, too ill to continue her futile flight. At the section's conclusion, she dies, and at her wake an inattentive deacon reads psalms in a lonely vigil. Section 4 shifts back to the peasant group, recounting Nastasya's chastisement of Seryoga for not fulfilling his promise to Fyodor and subsequently Seryoga's dawn venture into the forest to begin to make good his word. The "death" of the tree (described in very human terms by the narrator) that Seryoga chops down to provide a cross on Fyodor's as-yet-unmarked grave is the third death referred to in the story's title.

Themes and Meanings

As suggested by its title, the story's main subject is death, an interest in much of Tolstoy's fiction, most notably in "The Death of Ivan Ilyich," perhaps his most famous short work. In "Three Deaths" the questions of how the different social classes respond to death, how the dying respond to it, how the living respond to those who are dying, and finally what role God has in the cycle of life and death are explored.

The story, structured as an elaborate network of implicit comparisons and contrasts, shows underlying similarities despite surface differences between the upper and lower classes in how they are affected by this certain fact of experience. Marya is surrounded by family, is relatively young, is impatient with slight physical discomforts caused by her maid, attempts to flee from death, holds off serious thought of it to the end, and dies in the spring. In contrast, Uncle Fyodor is without any family, is old, puts up with cramped discomforts over a stove, seems resigned to what will shortly happen, and dies in the autumn. Yet what is important, Tolstoy shows, is that both characters come to the same terminus.

Those around Marya attempt to show almost every consideration and hesitate to speak to her explicitly about death (Marya finds even the word "die" frightening); in contrast, Seryoga bluntly asks for Fyodor's boots (tantamount to saying that a dead man will not need them), and the cook, Nastasya, explicitly comments on corpses not needing new boots and complains (demurring "God forgive me the sin") that Fyodor has too long been an inconvenience and should have died some time ago. Yet Tolstoy shows through the exact inversion of these qualities in each class that whether rich or poor, humanity reacts with fundamental similarity to the dying. Marya's tearful husband exclaims to God and covers his eyes while unfeelingly giving directions to a servant about where to put the wine he and the doctor are to enjoy; and, as Marya notes, he comes out of the station to inquire after her while insensitively still munching on his meal. Similarly, though Nastasya is frank and unsentimental, she is sympathetic to Fyodor, apologizes for her earlier wish for his death, tries to make him comfortable, and dreams about him (the latter suggesting her spiritual sensitivity or only her concern about the old man, or both). To the two young peasant girls from the station, who are trying to peep at Marya in the carriage, the dying person is simply a curiosity; to Marya's two very young children, she is a matter of indifference, as they continue to play their games just before and after her death. Thus, no matter what their social class, those around the dying are shown to have both their altruistic and their selfish, unconcerned moments.

God is referred to several times in the story, often in the exclamation "My God!" The emphatic allusion at the end of section 3 to Psalm 104 implies, considering all thirty-five verses of the psalm, that God has created a symmetrical, cyclical universe with an orderly round of spring and fall, day and night, delights and miseries, life and death, and goodness and wickedness. Nature, including several references to trees and birds, is described at length in the psalm, applying to the death of the tree in section 4, which, though sad for the tree, will happily supply a marker for Fyodor and space for the flourishing of other surrounding trees.

Style and Technique

The story has much realistic, specific detail. Details of setting, including not only sights and sounds but also smells, are described with great vividness and emotional effect, such as the closeness of Marya's carriage, which "smelt of eau de Cologne and dust." Also, like his fellow realists Gustave Flaubert and Anton Chekhov, Tolstoy does not shun the scatological component of reality, considering it not only the basest but also the most basic level of experience, noting that with the advent of spring in Moscow comes not only beauty: "Streams of water hurried gurgling between the frozen dung-heaps in the wet streets of the town."

Yet like Fyodor Dostoevski, Tolstoy in this story—as in much of his work—endows realistic details with symbolic import. The smell of Marya's carriage, for example, is part of the network of symbolic contrasts in the story, the eau de cologne of the upper-class setting representing a foil to the smell of the confined carriers' quarters: "a smell of human beings, baking bread, and cabbage, and sheepskins." Similarly, the careful physical description of Matryosha in the story's opening paragraphs creates a symbolic antithesis between her robust vitality and Marya's moribund decay.

Besides the symbolic applicability of Psalm 104 to the story (its own cyclical symmetry corresponding to the story's) and the symbolism of Nastasya's dream (which suggests that death has been a joyful release for Fyodor), perhaps the most clearly demarcated symbolic portion of the work is the long, descriptive passage in section 4, personifying the tree. The tree "trembles in dismay" in its roots as it is about to come down, while surrounding trees display "their motionless branches more gladly than ever in the newly opened space." The tree's death thus is shown to be a parallel to the human deaths. The concluding sentence of the story recalls both the hymn of praise to God the creator in Psalm 104 and the mixed joy and mourning of the human deceased's loved ones, who are happy to be alive but not unmindful of their loss: "The sappy leaves whispered joyously and calmly on the treetops, and the branches of the living trees, slowly, majestically, swayed above the fallen dead tree."

Norman Prinsky

THE THREE HERMITS

Author: Leo Tolstoy (1828-1910)
Type of plot: Religious tale
Time of plot: The nineteenth century
Locale: The White Sea, in the Russian Arctic
First published: "Tri startsa," 1886 (English translation, 1887)

> *Principal characters:*
> AN ARCHBISHOP, a prominent figure in the Church
> THE THREE OLD MEN, rumored to be "holy men" living on a remote island
> THE SHIP'S PASSENGERS AND CREW, including a little "muzhik," or simple peasant fisherman, the captain, and the helmsman

The Story

On a ship sailing from Archangel into the White Sea is an Archbishop and several of his followers. While on deck, the Archbishop overhears a little fisherman telling the other passengers about three old men, "servants of God," who live on an island barely visible on the distant horizon.

At the Archbishop's request, the fisherman tells about his encounter with the three old men, who had once helped him when his boat struck upon the remote island. The old men, he tells the Archbishop, were most peculiar in appearance. One was very old and hunchbacked, with green hairs mingled in his gray beard. Another, who had a yellowish gray beard and wore a ragged caftan, was also very old, but taller than the first and strong enough to turn the fisherman's boat over "as if it were a pail." The third was the tallest of the three, and he had a snowy beard that reached to his knees.

The Archbishop, having heard the fisherman's story, asks the helmsman about the presence of three "holy men" on the distant island. The helmsman's response indicates that the fisherman may have been merely "spinning yarns." Nevertheless, the Archbishop goes to the captain and requests that the ship be brought close enough to the island that he can be rowed to it. This request does not please the captain, who tells the Archbishop that it would not be worth his while to see the old men. They are, he has heard, "imbeciles who understand nothing and are as dumb as the fishes of the sea."

Neither the helmsman nor the captain, however, is able to dissuade the Archbishop, who offers to pay the captain well for changing the ship's course so that he can visit the island. Thus, the captain changes the ship's course and in a short while brings it to anchor near the island. A rowboat is lowered, and several rowers are commissioned to take the Archbishop to the beach, where, by telescope, three old men can already be seen standing near a large rock.

When the Archbishop lands on the shore, he finds the three old men just as the fisherman described them, all ancient in age, with long beards of varying shades of gray, and very poorly dressed. The old men say very little but are impressed by the presence of the Archbishop, who asks them how they make their devotions and how they pray to God. The oldest of the three answers for the others that they do not know how to make any devotions but know only how to serve and support themselves. As for prayer, says the old man, they only know to say, "Three are Ye, three are we. Have Ye mercy upon us." As soon as the one old man says this simple prayer, the others look to Heaven and repeat in unison, "Three are Ye, three are we. Have Ye mercy upon us."

The Archbishop is amused by the old men's simple prayer. Citing Holy Scripture, he endeavors to teach them a prayer that he considers more pleasing to God, the Lord's Prayer. Over and over he has them repeat the words after him: "Our Father, who art in Heaven. . . ." The old men are very slow to learn this prayer, but at last they do manage to say it without the Archbishop's prompting.

At dusk, the Archbishop takes his leave of the old men and returns by rowboat to the ship. He is very satisfied with himself, giving thanks to God that he has been able to provide such simple old hermits with instruction in the proper way to pray. As the island fades into the distance and the gathering darkness, however, he suddenly spots a flicker of light coming from its direction. The light seems to be overtaking them. He asks the helmsman what it might be—"a boat, or not a boat; a bird, or not a bird; a fish, or not a fish?" The helmsman, seeing the light take the shape of the three old men "moving rapidly over the sea," drops the tiller and cries out: "Oh God of Heaven! There are three old men running upon the sea as upon dry land!"

As the ship's company gathers at the stern to witness this miraculous event, the three old men, holding hands and moving rapidly over the sea "without moving their feet at all," come up to the edge of the ship and address the Archbishop. "O servant of God," they say, "we have forgotten . . . all that you taught us. So long as we repeated it, we remembered it. But for an hour we ceased repeating it, and every word escaped us. . . . Teach it to us again."

The Archbishop is struck by this experience. He crosses himself and tells the old men, "Your prayer has also been suitable enough for God. It isn't for me to teach you. Rather you should pray for us sinners!" He then bows down to their feet, whereupon they move back over the sea toward their island, from which a faint glimmer is visible until morning.

Themes and Meanings

In Russian, there is a small rhyme, "Bog i ya, my druzya . . . zachem nuzhna religiya?" which means "God and I, we are friends . . . what do I need religion for?" This rhyme epitomizes Leo Tolstoy's attitude toward organized religion as he saw it in czarist Russia. After his own development of strong pacifist beliefs in the early 1880's, Tolstoy was critical of the dominant Russian Orthodox Church for its sanctioning of the czarist government's warring and social oppression. In his stories of this period, he tried to awaken people to the superiority of individual belief over religious dogma. In "The Three Hermits," the Archbishop's self-satisfied piety is shown to be inferior to the old men's simple and direct relationship with God. Through the story, Tolstoy attempted to teach people not to allow others, no matter what institutional support possessed or authority cited, to mitigate their moral beliefs. In support of this lesson, he cited as an epigraph to the story a verse from the New Testament: "And when ye pray, make not vain repetitions as the heathen do; for they think they shall be heard for their much asking. Be not like unto them, for your Heavenly Father knows what ye have need of before ye ask Him."

Style and Technique

Tolstoy's stories, especially his later ones, are very didactic in nature. He saw himself as a teacher, one whose task was to distill the truth as he found it so that it could be understood by people whose understanding was not as profound as his own. That is why he wrote "The Three Hermits" in a simple style, recalling the apocryphal religious legends of Russia's earlier centuries. These legends are primarily an oral genre, rife with repetitions of detail and with a straightforward moral message that is clearly stated at the end. The style relies heavily upon the device of triplication: three old men, three reported descriptions of them from three different sources, one of whom is referred to in three different ways (little muzhik, peasant, and fisherman), and so on. Even the syntax reflects this device, with many sentences having a tertiary structure: "What could it be—a boat, or not a boat; a bird, or not a bird; a fish, or not a fish?" The true function of this stylistic device is mnemonic. A triple repetition of story elements on all levels ensures that the lesson transmitted by the story will be well learned. The story's main stylistic device, then, fits well with Tolstoy's perception of himself as a teacher of spiritual truth. This triplication, common in the telling of folktales and other oral narratives, reflects as well the trinity of Father, Son, and Holy Spirit that is central to Orthodox theology.

Lee B. Croft

THE THREE-DAY BLOW

Author: Ernest Hemingway (1899-1961)
Type of plot: Psychological realism
Time of plot: c. 1920
Locale: Northern Michigan
First published: 1925

> *Principal characters:*
> NICK ADAMS, the protagonist
> BILL, Nick's close friend

The Story

"The Three-Day Blow" has little external action. The story focuses on the conversation of Nick and his friend Bill as they take refuge from an autumn storm in the cottage of Bill's father. The two close friends get drunk on whiskey belonging to Bill's father and speak of common interests: baseball, fishing, favorite books and writers, their fathers, and, as the whiskey takes effect, the recent breakup of Nick's relationship with a girl named Marge. The most important action, however, occurs inside the mind of Nick Adams.

The story begins as Nick walks through an orchard to join Bill at Bill's cottage while taking note of the way the field and woods are windblown by the autumn storm. Inside the cottage, the boys warm themselves by a roaring fire and reveal that they are eager sportsmen and avid readers. They refer to the talents and limitations of particular ballplayers and speak of unscrupulous trades, corrupt managerial strategies, and baseball monopolies that have ruined many good athletes and kept certain teams on top and others at the bottom of the baseball ladder. Suggesting a conspiracy among owners, Nick says, "There's always more to it than we know about." They agree that the "Cards" will never win a pennant—that even when the Cards did get going once, a train wreck ruined a promising season.

On their second glass of whiskey, the boys convey their admiration for certain writers over others—favoring writers they perceive as personally honest and whose works issue from firsthand knowledge. Books are as real to the boys as is fishing or whiskey, and they wish that they could share their personal passions with writers to whom they feel close. Gilbert Keith Chesterton is a "better guy" than Horace Walpole, but Walpole is "a better writer." They would like to take both of them fishing.

With the pouring of a third glass of whiskey, the boys propose to get really drunk and question whether they are not drunk already. Warmed by the whiskey, the fire, and their camaraderie, each praises the other's father, but it is clear that Nick is bothered by the fact that in contrast to Bills' father, a painter who is a bit wild, his own teetotaler father, a doctor, has missed out on too much in life. Yet Nick notes philosophically, "It all evens up." As if to prove his father wrong about drinking, Nick vows to show that he can hold his liquor and still be practical. Knocking a pan off the kitchen table, Nick shows that he is far less in control than he pretends, and his unnatural rigidity is comical.

Moving to a fourth glass of whiskey, forgetting their promise to themselves to drink only from the bottle already open, the boys are more than tipsy now. On his way back from fetching water for the whiskey, Bill winks at the "strange" face that peers back at him from the mirror. The intensity of camaraderie, fueled by the biggest drinks yet, climaxes in toasts to writers and to fishing, which the boys declare is better by far than baseball. Filling their glasses a fifth time, they congratulate themselves on their wisdom.

At this point, referring to Nick's breakup with his girl, Bill speaks of "that Marge business"—which, it seems, has been on the minds of both boys all along. Bill argues that "busting it off" was Nick's only choice, since marriage, especially to a girl who is evidently Nick's social inferior, would destroy his personal freedom. Bill tells Nick, "Once a man's married, he's absolutely bitched. He hasn't got anything more. Nothing. Not a damn thing. He's done for. You've seen the guys that get married." For a while, Nick says nothing or merely nods in quiet acquiescence to Bill's insistence that Nick "came out of it damn well." Yet one can see that Nick is far more affected by the breakup than he is willing to admit; despite a sixth glass of whiskey, the knowledge that the relationship is over forever is dramatically sobering and saddening. When Bill reminds Nick that the marriage would have infringed upon their male camaraderie, that they might not even "be going fishing tomorrow," Nick seems reconciled. "I couldn't help it," he says. . . . All of a sudden everything was over . . . I don't know why it was. . . . Just like when the three-day blows come now and rip all the leaves off the trees." They agree that the breakup was no one's fault—that, as Bill puts it, "That's the way it works out."

Rationalizing that he and Marge were not even engaged, Nick determines to get truly drunk and go swimming and simply to avoid thinking about Marge anymore, or he might get back into it again. Ironically, he is consoled by the realization that he can get back into it if he wants to—that nothing was "irrevocable." Now quite drunk, the boys load shotguns and go out into the blowing gale to hunt. Feeling that he has escaped a trap, Nick concludes, "None of it was important now. The wind blew it out of his head."

Themes and Meanings

In a story such as "The Three-Day Blow," the reader must be warned against too easily accepting what happens literally in the tale, which hardly seems to constitute a story at all. What holds this story together is not its developing action but its haunting vision of a world in which human ideals and aspirations are too often thwarted by cupidity or incompetence or by the destructive forces of nature. Love ends just as suddenly and without warning as "when the three-day blows come and rip all the leaves off the trees." When Bill says, "That's the way it works out," he refers specifically to the end of young love. Yet he also voices the growing awareness of the young men that the world is unceasingly hostile and unsympathetic, that nothing of value lasts very long, and that only the tough-skinned survive.

As with life itself, love is subject to the cruel flux and dissolution of nature. It, too, has its seasons, like baseball or hunting, youth or old age. The fire that blazes up and dies down, the "second growth timber," even the autumn storm itself, reminds one that cyclical change is the great law of life. "All of a sudden," Nick says, "everything was over. I don't know why it was. I couldn't help it." At first Nick condemns himself, but then he consoles himself with the thought that everything in life dissolves into nothingness and that no one is to blame.

Marrying and settling down represent the stifling of soul, the death of male independence that every Hemingway hero abhors. This is evidently what Bill has in mind when he tells Nick, "If you'd have married her you would have had to marry the whole family. Remember her mother and that guy she married." Domesticity is seen also as a condition in which one is more vulnerable to life's storms, more subject to self-betrayal or the kind of double-cross that has ruined many good baseball players and writers. Fishing is preferred to baseball and living alone is preferred to marriage. The solitary game allows one to guard against losing control of oneself and to guide one's own destiny.

Nick's disenchantment with love may say more about his own disturbed emotional condition than about the institution of marriage. Yet if sensitivity to life's traps and storms makes both boys a bit paranoid about marriage, that same sensitivity heightens their love of that perishable physical world whose loss they know is one day inevitable—that lovely fire, for example, that warms Nick but that may "bake" him if he is not careful. Nick is especially attuned to the sensual delights of the world about him—he is intoxicated with life. The shiny apple he puts in his coat pocket, the "swell smoky taste of the whiskey," the "dried apricots, soaking in water," the feel of the heavy wool socks, even the storm itself—all are simple, concrete experiences safely removed from the troublesome world of women.

Not only do such pleasures seem most available in the out-of-doors world of male camaraderie—the world of hunting, fishing, and baseball—but also the rules for survival in that world are clear and manageable. The boys are competent with guns just as they expect writers and baseball players to be competent and to behave with integrity. It is understandably to this world that they look for consolation against the threat of the "Marge business" at the end of the story. Nick, however, may still be more pained than consoled about this world of sudden, unpredictable storms. He has not really resolved the paradox of life as both preserver and destroyer. He knows that even the lasting power of the best of logs, one to be saved against bad weather that "will burn all night," is short-lived, yet his youthful illusions lead him to insist that nothing is "absolute," nothing is "irrevocable."

Style and Technique

"I always try to write on the principle of the iceberg," Hemingway said about his craft. "There is seven-eighths of it under water for every part that shows." In drawing attention to the often unsuspected depths in his work, Hemingway provides the ground for instruction in one of the major aesthetic principles of modern fiction: the art of indirection. What most modern writers have realized, and what is achieved so well in "The Three-Day Blow," is that it is possible to convey a great many things on paper without stating them at all. The art of implication, of making one sentence say two or more different things with a minimum of description, and the possibilities of conveying depths of emotion and the most intimate and subtle of moods through the interplay of image and symbol were grasped by Hemingway as well as by any modern writer.

The surface effects of this story are so astonishingly clear and simple at first encounter, and its language so unambiguous and lucid, that the casual reader may be deceived as to the actual movement of the iceberg beneath the water. The unadorned dialogue and lack of emotional commentary, for example, reflect the boys' fear of emotional complexity as well as their emerging stoic attitudes about life and love. The concentrated use of concrete, specific physical details and the avoidance of philosophical generalities reflect in turn the boys' reliance upon physical experience as an antidote to moral complexity. Finally, the essential worldview of Nick and Bill is portrayed through a series of subtle, interlocking contrasts: dry and warm, wet and cold; country and city; weak and dishonest men, strong men of integrity; male camaraderie, marriage and domesticity. On the one hand are the initiated, such as Bill's father and those writers and sportsmen who function honestly and courageously in the world. These men know about life's treacherous storms but also know how to cope. On the other hand are the uninitiated or the defeated, such as Nick's father or the husband of Marge's mother—those who have been unalterably "bitched" or ruined by life.

Upon encountering the stylistic subtleties of "The Three-Day Blow," the casual reader might worry that little of importance is happening. Yet Hemingway obtains a maximum emotional response from his reader more by what is not said than by what is. Understanding this should enable the reader to see that indirection in storytelling may be an integral part of the meaning of the story and a way of distinguishing fiction of genuine value.

Lawrence Broer

THROWN AWAY

Author: Rudyard Kipling (1865-1936)
Type of plot: Social realism
Time of plot: The 1880's
Locale: India
First published: 1888

> *Principal characters:*
> THE BOY, a Sandhurst graduate serving as a subaltern in India
> THE MAJOR, who has kindly feelings toward The Boy
> THE NARRATOR, a British military man

The Story

The protagonist in "Thrown Away" is never identified other than as The Boy. A young subaltern in India, The Boy led a sheltered life with his family in Great Britain and never had to deal with unpleasantness. After his years at Sandhurst preparing for military life in the colonies, The Boy is sent first to a third-rate depot battalion and then to India.

At first, he finds India attractive. The ponies, the dancing, the flirtatious women, and the gambling all appeal to him. Yet The Boy has been quite protected until now. He has developed no sense of humor. He takes life and its petty tribulations very seriously. Kipling likens The Boy to a puppy, saying that if a puppy bites the ears of an old dog, the old dog will properly chastise it, making it wiser. Yet if the puppy grows to be a dog with its full set of teeth and bites the ear of an old dog, never before having learned that there are limits to what it does, it is likely to be hurt. The Boy apparently has never been placed in the situation of having to learn his limits and is now like the grown dog with a full set of teeth who is about to bite the ear of an old dog.

The Boy falls into gambling, and his losses mount alarmingly. He takes these losses seriously and broods over them. For six months, The Boy makes one personal mistake after another, and the people closest to him know that he is making them but presume that he will learn from his mistakes and will fall into line as do most other people who come out from Great Britain.

When the cold weather ends, The Boy's colonel talks to him with some severity, but not much differently from the way colonels typically talk to subalterns: "It was only an ordinary 'Colonel's wigging'!" the reader is told. The Boy, however, takes the "wigging" very much to heart. Shortly after it, one more event contributes substantially to what is ultimately to happen: "*The* thing that kicked the beam in The Boy's mind was a remark that a woman made when he was talking to her. There is no use in repeating it, for it was only a cruel little sentence, rapped out before thinking, that made him flush to the roots of his hair." Again, he has something to brood about.

For three days after this unfortunate occurrence, The Boy keeps to himself. Then he takes a two-day leave, presumably to go shooting for big game at the Canal Engineer's Rest House, about thirty miles out from his base. People laugh at his going after big game there because the only thing worth shooting in that area is partridge, hardly the big game that The Boy seems to seek.

One of the majors has grown fond of The Boy and becomes alarmed when he hears that he has gone out shooting. He alone suspects what the big game might be that The Boy seeks. He enters The Boy's quarters and discovers that he has taken with him a revolver and a writing case, hardly the equipment for game hunting. The Major enlists the aid of the omniscient narrator, asking him if he can lie, and the two set out for the Canal Engineer's Rest House in a wagon drawn by a pony, which is pushed so hard to get there in a hurry that it is almost dead when they arrive three hours later at their destination thirty miles away.

When they get to the Rest House, the Major calls for The Boy's servant and calls out The Boy's name. There is no answer. The two men notice that a hurricane lamp is burning in the window, although it is four in the afternoon and quite light. They hear only the buzzing of hordes of flies. They enter the building and find that The Boy, having written farewell letters to his loved ones, has all but shot his head off with his revolver.

The narrator reads the letters, which are filled with self-recrimination, and he and the Major decide that they must cover up the suicide in order to spare The Boy's family grief. They decide to say that he has died of cholera, attended by them until the end. They burn his letters, then burn the bed and bedding and dispose of the ashes. They gather up The Boy's watch, locket, and rings to send to his family. The Major thinks that The Boy's mother will want a lock of his hair, but because of the mode of his death, they cannot find one fit to send her. The Major's hair is about the same color as The Boy's, so the narrator cuts a lock from the Major's head, which sets them both to laughing, supporting the argument that in India it does not pay to take anything too seriously.

The two buy hoes and dig a grave for The Boy. They wait a day before going back to their base with the news of the death. They send letters off to The Boy's loved ones telling them of his death. In due course, they receive a letter from The Boy's mother saying that she is grateful and will be under an obligation to them for as long as she lives. The story ends with the line, "All things considered, she *was* under an obligation; but not exactly as she meant."

Themes and Meanings

Much of Kipling's writing focuses on problems peculiar to and generated by British colonialism, and this story certainly fits that mold. Early in the narrative, Kipling tells his readers, "Now India is a place beyond all others where one must not take things too seriously—the mid-day sun always excepted. Too much work and too much energy kill a man just as effectively as too much assorted vice or too much drink." The Boy cannot survive in India because he takes things too seriously. He cannot accept the indolence and the inefficiency that characterize service in India.

On the other hand, the Major and the narrator will survive because even in the face of The Boy's gruesome death, they can laugh. They are not heartless, otherwise they would not think to spare The Boy's family the grief of knowing that their son committed suicide. In Kipling's presentation, the Major turns a deaf ear to those who criticize him for not bringing back The Boy's body for a regimental burial on base. Kipling shows here a man who is at peace with himself, one who knows he has done what is best and who does not care what public opinion is regarding his action. He will certainly never repeat The Boy's mistake even though he understands it and once goes so far as to say that he had gone through the same "Valley of the Shadow" as did The Boy.

The Boy is never given a name because Kipling emphasizes early in the story that in colonial India, if one man dies, he will be replaced in the eight hours between death and burial. He also points out at the end of the story that The Boy and his act will be forgotten before a fortnight has elapsed. Life here is impersonal, attachments ephemeral. Early in the story, Kipling writes that flirtations do not matter because one will not be in any one place for long.

Style and Technique

"Thrown Away" is essentially a story about anonymity. Told through an unnamed omniscient narrator, the story centers on a protagonist who remains anonymous and on a Major who is fond of The Boy but who has long since lost the sensitivity that might lead him to the same end as that of The Boy.

Kipling allows the Major emotions. When the narrator reads him the letters that The Boy has written to his loved ones, the Major "simply cried like a woman without caring to hide it." Kipling leaves little doubt, however, that the Major will recover quickly from the shock of The Boy's suicide. Before he returns to base, he is laughing and joking with the narrator. Then he has a long sleep that apparently erases what is left of this horror from his mind.

What Kipling shows here is that people are quite replaceable in India—perhaps everywhere. Kipling holds his characters in this story at arm's length; readers see them but do not know them. This is not a failing on Kipling's part but is rather a reflection of the harsh realities of colonial India.

R. Baird Shuman

TICKETS, PLEASE

Author: D. H. Lawrence (1885-1930)
Type of plot: Psychological realism
Time of plot: World War I
Locale: The English Midlands
First published: 1919

>*Principal characters:*
>ANNIE STONE, a young conductor on an English interurban railway line
>JOHN THOMAS "CODDY" RAYNOR, a handsome inspector on the same line
>NORA PURDY, one of several other women conductors

The Story

"Tickets, Please" is a story of unrequited love and the vengeance that it spawns. In its psychological depth and detail, however, it also reveals the sexual war that D. H. Lawrence believed always raged between men and women.

The setting is of crucial importance to this story, for it reflects in several significant ways Lawrence's themes. The background is World War I; since most of the healthy young men are away fighting in France, the trains are being driven by "cripples" and "hunchbacks," and the conductors on this "most dangerous tram-service in England" are all women.

The chief inspector on Annie Stone's line is John Thomas Raynor (nicknamed "Coddy" by the women), who is young and good-looking and who takes full advantage of his situation. He flirts with the conductors by day and "walks out" with them by night, and not a few have been forced to leave the service in "considerable scandal."

Annie has kept her distance from John Thomas (she has a boyfriend of her own), but one night they meet unexpectedly at a local fair and spend an exciting, romantic evening together. With their continued intimacy, Annie becomes possessive. "Annie wanted to consider him a person, a man: she wanted to take an intelligent interest in him, and to have an intelligent response." Yet here, Lawrence says, "she made a mistake." John Thomas has no intention of becoming an intelligent, serious person to her. He "walks out" with another young woman conductor on the line.

Annie is devastated by the rejection and vows revenge. She plots with Nora Purdy, another of John Thomas's former girlfriends, and together they round up half a dozen former conquests of John Thomas. One dark Sunday night, when Annie has again agreed to walk home with John Thomas, they all meet in the "rough, but cosy" waiting room in the depot at the end of the line.

When John Thomas comes into the depot, he apparently senses the situation and says that he is going home by himself. Yet the girls insist that he choose one of them to walk with: "Take one!" They force him to face the wall and guess which one touches him, and then, "like a swift cat, Annie went forward and fetched him a box on the side of the head that sent his cap flying and himself staggering." All the other girls attack him now, and a game turns into a battle between the hunters and the hunted: "Their blood was now thoroughly up. He was their sport now." They beat and subdue him until he is on the floor "as an animal lies when it is defeated and at the mercy of the captor."

Even in defeat, however, John Thomas is clever, and when the women still demand that he choose one of them, he names their ringleader: "I choose Annie." Annie, however, no longer wants him—"something was broken in her." The women release him, John Thomas leaves in tatters, but there is no sense of triumph in the waiting room; the girls leave "with mute, stupefied faces." They have wreaked their revenge and defeated their enemy, but in doing so they have also somehow destroyed the object of their desire, and there is no satisfaction in this victory.

Themes and Meanings

Like so many other Lawrence stories and novels, "Tickets, Please" concerns the sexual and spiritual war that is being waged just beneath the surface of civilized life. When that veneer is scratched, the psychological jungle is revealed.

It is appropriate that it is wartime. Aside from furthering the plot, the wartime setting is also a metaphor for the constant struggle between men and women. It is a "dangerous" but "exciting" time and, as in the stories of Ernest Hemingway at about the same time, wartime tends to show life in an exaggerated but intense reality.

This is particularly clear in the crucial battle between John Thomas and his vindictive captors. "Outside was the darkness and lawlessness of wartime," Lawrence tells his readers at the beginning of this section. Inside, there is also "war" or "lawlessness" waiting in the depot, as in the hearts of these women.

When the women corner John Thomas, something happens to them, and they are transformed into powerful sexual animals. "Strange wild creatures, they hung on him and rushed at him to bear him down." They have become the aggressors, and their new, animal, sexual power makes them feel "filled with supernatural strength." Yet this conquest of the male brings them no satisfaction; it is, Lawrence writes, a "terrifying, cold triumph." Ironically, when they bring John Thomas down they destroy not only his male sexual advantage but also his sexual attractiveness; in his tattered tunic, John Thomas is nothing to them now. They have succeeded only in making him like themselves; they have gained nothing new.

Lawrence is thus predicting failure in the sexual revolution. When women band together (as they can here, under the special conditions of wartime), they can win. Their victory, however, is hollow, for they have destroyed the object of their "lust" at the same time that they have destroyed his superiority. They leave the depot "mute" and "stupefied" because they did not know their own, irrational, animal strength—and because they have really lost, not won. There has been a sexual revolt, but once the old order has been overthrown, the slaves have no new order to install and have lost the privileges of the old. It is a sad and pessimistic message. John Thomas and the women need each other as they are, Lawrence is saying, and there is apparently no way to undo the cruel and patriarchal sexual domination.

Lawrence's story treats themes and motifs that would not be treated in such depth and detail again for half a century, until the women's sexual revolution in the second half of the twentieth century became a literary revolution as well. In his sexual psychology and symbolism, Lawrence is a father of much of that literature.

Style and Technique

As in so much of Lawrence's fiction, the style in "Tickets, Please" helps to control the raw power of his content and thus becomes an integral part of the meaning. "Tickets, Please" opens almost like a children's story, and the description of the Midlands tramway system reads like something out of "The Little Engine That Could" or—in a parallel from the story itself—the carnival rides that Annie takes with John Thomas. Yet even in these opening paragraphs, there is a crucial contrast between the playful personification of the train and the "sordid streets" and "grimy cold little market-places" of this depressed and depressing industrial England. From the beginning, there is a contradiction in tone as there is in content (between, for example, the two conditions of women in the story, before and after their overthrow of John Thomas).

The narrator of "Tickets, Please" helps to mask this gap. There is a casual, familiar "we" in the opening narration: "Since we are in wartime. . . ." This editorial "we" tends to moralize: "The girls are fearless young hussies," the voice intones. After Annie starts seeing John Thomas and some of the other conductors are "huffy" to her, this voice is consoling: "But there, you must take things as you find them, in this life." The narrator is setting the reader up for the defeat at the end of the story; it is a voice of order and stability.

The language of the story also carries these themes. In the beginning of the story, the imagery is military: The tram-car is Annie's "Thermopylae" (a famous battle site in Greece); she watches John Thomas "vanquish one girl, then another." In the battle with John Thomas, however, this language becomes animal, and the girls become wild hunting creatures and bring John Thomas "at bay." Throughout the story, the language is sexual. John Thomas' name (especially his nickname, "Coddy") refers to the male organ (as in "codpiece"), and there are several other phallic references; the sight of his "white bare arm," for example, maddens the girls. While at an intellectual level the story is about an attempted overthrow of the old patriarchal order, at the level of language and imagery the story is an example of Lawrentian "blood-lust," in which the animal in woman tries to pull down the sexual power in man.

While a novice reader of the story may be struck by the sexual symbolism and the psychological realism of the story, the humor and irony of "Tickets, Please" may not be as obvious. The playfulness of the opening sections is not only in its tone; serious as this struggle is, it is also inherently comic (and here the narrator's voice helps). Similarly, the use of language can be highly ironic. When John Thomas quips to the girls in the waiting-room, "There's no place like home," the word "home" has several levels of meaning. It is ironic because it is "home" (security) with John Thomas that the girls want, and it is "home" that John Thomas assiduously avoids. Lawrence's language, in short, can be as rich and bottomless as his meaning.

David Peck

TIME THE TIGER

Author: Wyndham Lewis (1882-1957)
Type of plot: Sociopolitical satire
Time of plot: 1949
Locale: London
First published: 1951

Principal characters:
> MARK ROBINS, a bureaucrat in the Socialist Ministry of
> Education
> CHARLES DYAT, Mark's old friend, a petty bourgeois black
> marketeer
> IDA DYAT, a widowed landowner and the sister of Charles

The Story

Mark Robins (the "red," or Marxist) and Charles Dyat (the diehard reactionary) became friends when they attended Oxford University together in the early 1920's. They were both from professional, upper-middle-class families. As students, Mark was the conservative and Charles was the radical, sporting a red tie. Twenty-five years later, in the aftermath of World War II, Great Britain has a Socialist government, and Mark has swung to the Left, while Charles has swung to the Right. Yet they have remained friends: As the story opens, Charles is visiting Mark and has just spent the night in Mark's "Rotting Hill" apartment in the suburbs of London.

Lewis' portrait of postwar Britain is comically grim: It is a satire of the same sense of cultural and material debasement, shoddiness, and deterioration conveyed more somberly by George Orwell in *Nineteen Eighty-Four* (1949). In Mark Robins' apartment, the water heater has broken down, the bread is gray and hard as brick, the buttonholes on his shirts are too skimpy to push buttons through, his shoelaces are too short to tie in bows, and his nail clipper falls apart when applied to his nails. The telephone lines are fouled up, and food shortages continue, leaving nothing but bad tea, bad butter, and bad jam. All this adds up to a bad mood for Mark, who nevertheless represses his mood, dismisses the problems, and believes that soon enough the progress of socialism will cure these ills.

Unlike Mark, Charles places no faith in the current regime. As they begin to talk over breakfast, their political differences quickly become apparent, over the topic of tipping, or "oiling palms." Charles confesses that in order to get preferential treatment he always gives tips, but Mark is scandalized by this vestige of upper-class patronization. Their conversation takes up the question of the food shortages: Mark thinks that they are actual, Charles declares that they are part of a Socialist plot to beat the population into political submission. Mark declares that Charles is an "egotist" with an "individualist itch to pick holes," and Charles retorts that Mark is a "yes-man" who has opportunistically but foolishly joined the Socialist cause.

Still, they leave the apartment in good spirits, "jabbing each other mirthfully with their forefingers," and begin a round of errands in downtown London. Mark must get a blood test, and Charles needs an eye examination, which sets up a running debate concerning the National Health Service and the question of socialized medicine. Then Mark exchanges a shirt shrunken to an unwearable size after one wash. Charles attempts to make conversation with his eye-specialist by criticizing the welfare state: The doctor ignores him and then sends him to a public glasses shop. This episode puts Charles's pretensions to gentility and his prejudices against the lower classes in general and women in particular into action: He ends up in a private shop where his ego can be appropriately massaged.

Late that evening, the two are back at Mark's apartment discussing a film they have just seen, a French existentialist film called "Time the Tiger." Mark finally lets all the day's irritations get to him, and Charles sees his chance to score some ideological points. They debate life, time, and progress, with Charles nostalgically evoking the year 1900 and Mark maintaining that popular culture is not all bad. They talk about the powers unleashed by technology, "the fantastic power conferred upon the politicos in this new era of radio, automatic weapons, atomic bombs." Charles denounces the legacies of Karl Marx and Charles Darwin, and Mark denounces the British Tories: They reach no agreement.

A reunion with Charles's widowed sister Ida, whom Mark dated many years before, has been scheduled for the next day; that night Mark dreams about her. When the three of them actually meet the following afternoon, Ida appears to "step out of a dream," seeming to Mark not to have aged a bit. Their conversation dwells on visions of their more youthful days, and all the while Mark fantasizes about marrying Ida and bringing her into his new way of life. Then "Time the Tiger" leaps: "Ida—an Ida at least twenty years older—was denouncing the Socialist Government. . . . His love transformed herself with nightmare suddenness into a Tory soap-boxer." The reunion falls apart: Mark will never see Ida again; rather, he resolves to make a date with a Socialist woman of his acquaintance. Several months later, Mark replies to a letter from Charles, "I suggest you find some other correspondent."

Themes and Meanings

"Time the Tiger" is a study of friendships tested and demolished by political pressures, the interplay among political beliefs, social class, personality, and nostalgia. As the petty bureaucratic supporter of the Socialist regime, Mark is presented as a repressive type, a self-denier and a stoic, a man who is moral (that is, conformist) out of sheer lack of imagination: "Where Mark would be apt to respect the most pernicious by-law, Charles would be quite certain to break it." Mark dutifully submits to regulation and has rationalized the social need for such submission, whereas Charles defies and defames the new order. In opposition to Mark's self-denial, Charles would be self-indulgent, if he were not so broke. Mark is law-abiding, Charles, the black marketeer and free marketeer, is an outlaw. These opposing characteristics represent the standard dramatization of the antagonism between public and private, collectivist and individualist sensibilities, Mark and Charles representing the progressive Socialist mass and the beleaguered elite, respectively.

Mark is comically naïve, but Charles is comically selfish. Mark can envision a future, and his Socialist idealism buffers him a bit from the sordid bumps and bruises of actual life, but Charles despairs of his chances in this new society and longs for the halcyon era of class privileges. Mark's naïveté sets him up for the reversal delivered at the climax of the tale by Ida's metamorphosis from timeless sweetheart to time-bound ideological foe: The transition to the new social order will not be as seamless as he dreams. At this point, Charles and Ida Dyat merge in a composite portrait of petty conservatism: They are reactionaries motivated by self-interest, by the losses of power and prestige that they must suffer under the ongoing Socialist upheavals. The future appears to be Mark's, but with a distinct sense that Mark has acquiesced, and forgotten his own acquiescence, to a life of "second best." Moreover, his new world must be purchased at the price of the collapse of his old connections.

Style and Technique

For an author whose anticommunism is proverbial, Lewis delivers "Time the Tiger" with considerable restraint. The narration is deft, hard-edged, understated, sardonic, and deployed with a confident, ironic hand. This is Lewis' mature or late prose style: There is none of the syntactic experimentalism, the "blasting and bombardiering" of his earlier stories. The world of Mark and Charles is viewed not through the lenses of Lewis' earlier Vorticism but through the trained and focused eyes of the aging visual artist finding his effects in ludicrous juxtaposition of concrete objects and persons actually presented by postwar British life.

Lewis makes Mark the central character, and although Mark is not the brightest man, he is not unsympathetic: Mark has cast his lot with the new order and patiently awaits a glorious future. One suspects that Charles is primarily the spokesman for Lewis' own attitudes, but Charles is in no way idealized: He is witty but bitter, and his anarchism is not heroic but suffering. When the true antithesis to what Mark represents materializes, it does so as Ida Dyat, a walking mirage of nostalgia who then turns into a bloodthirsty female fascist. Both as literal description and as allegory for class conflict, the politics in "Time the Tiger" are never heavy-handed. Lewis has transposed his vision of ideological conflict into a fine and enduring ironic fiction.

Bruce Clarke

TLÖN, UQBAR, ORBIS TERTIUS

Author: Jorge Luis Borges (1899-1986)
Type of plot: Fantasy
Time of plot: 1935-1947
Locale: Buenos Aires, Argentina
First published: 1940 (English translation, 1962)

> *Principal characters:*
> THE NARRATOR, presumably Jorge Luis Borges
> ADOLFO BIOY CASARES, a friend of the narrator (and of the real Borges)
> HERBERT ASHE, an English engineer involved in the encyclopedia plot
> EZRA BUCKLEY, the Tennessee millionaire who financed *A First Encyclopedia of Tlön*

The Story

In "Tlön, Uqbar, Orbis Tertius," Borges presents information about a fantastic world, which gradually, during the course of the story, acquires a tenacious and undermining hold upon reality. The story is told in the form of a memoir that mixes the narrator's personal reminiscences with essayistic account, plausible events in Buenos Aires with the fantastic inventions of an imaginary land (Tlön), and fictional characters (Herbert Ashe, Ezra Buckley) with the names of Borges' real friends (Adolfo Bioy Casares, Carlos Mastronardi, Néstor Ibarra, Ezequiel Martínez Estrada, Drieu La Rochelle, Alfonso Reyes, Princess Faucigny Lucinge, Enrique Amorim). Reality and imagination are constantly intermingled: Real books such as the *Encyclopædia Britannica* are mirrored by invented ones such as *The Anglo-American Cyclopædia* and *A First Encyclopedia of Tlön*; nonexistent books are ascribed to real authors; and preposterous theories share paragraphs with Benedict de Spinoza, Arthur Schopenhauer, and David Hume. Assumptions about how to separate what is true from what is untrue are challenged, parodied, and subverted. Amid the chaos of the world, a human desire for order and organization at any cost is seen as understandable but very dangerous.

The story is divided into three parts. In the first section, the narrator and his friend and collaborator, Adolfo Bioy Casares, discuss a hypothetical "novel in the first person, whose narrator would omit or disfigure the facts and indulge in various contradictions which would permit a few readers— very few readers—to perceive an atrocious or banal reality," a novel which is this very story. The mirror in the hallway, which reflects and monstrously distorts reality, reminds Bioy of an article in *The Anglo-American Cyclopædia* (which mirrors the 1902 *Encyclopædia Britannica*) about a country named Uqbar. An extensive search reveals that it is only Bioy's copy of the encyclopedia that contains the extra pages about Uqbar and its imaginary regions of Mlejnas and Tlön. The apparent hoax article is disquieting but more puzzling than ominous.

The second section describes the narrator's discovery and perusal two years later (in 1937) of the eleventh volume of *A First Encyclopedia of Tlön*, left behind in a bar by a shadowy Englishman, Herbert Ashe. The encyclopedia has on its first page a stamped blue oval inscribed "Orbis Tertius," and it describes a "vast methodical fragment of an unknown planet's entire history," its languages, philosophy, science, mathematics, and literature. Since, says the narrator, "the popular magazines, with pardonable excess, have spread news of the zoology and topography of Tlön," he will attempt to expound its concept of the universe.

The people of this imaginary planet are "congenitally idealist" and do not believe in the material, objective existence of their surroundings. They believe only what they themselves perceive, and hence the "world for them is not a concourse of objects in space; it is a heterogeneous series of independent acts. It is successive and temporal, not spatial." In language, this means that there are no nouns for concrete objects, only aggregates of adjectives which describe the immediate moment. Cause and effect are not thought to be related. Objects are held to disappear physically when no one is thinking about them. Innumerable sciences and philosophies abound on Tlön, as many as one can imagine. Materialism is merely the most unacceptable one of a vast number of possible ways of considering reality. The happiest hypothesis is that everything in the universe exists within one supreme mind. Thus, plagiarism in literature cannot exist if all works are the creation of one supreme author, who is timeless and anonymous and whose stories are all variations on a single plot.

The narrator describes how many centuries of idealism have changed reality. Lost objects can be duplicated through memory; anyone who remembers an object can find it. These duplications are called *hrönir*, and their quality varies as they are reproduced again and again through successive memories. Objects may also be produced through hope; anything people wish to find and can imagine appears as an *ur*. Thus archaeologists reshape and document the past according to their own imaginations.

The third section of the story, the postscript, supposedly appended to the text several years later and thus confirming the historical nature of the account, appeared (labeled 1947) in 1940, as an original part of the story. It creates at once a sense of future time having passed already and a somewhat bewildered uneasiness. When the narrator makes the observation that "ten years ago any symmetry with a semblance of order—dialectical materialism, anti-Semitism, Nazism—was sufficient to entrance the minds of men," he is describing the world of the immediate moment, not the world of ten years before. He is describing that ominous time just prior to World War I, when anti-Semitism and Nazism had invaded the reality of Germany (and Argentina) just as the reality of Earth is invaded in this story by the ideology of Tlön.

The postscript purports to clear up the mystery of Tlön. It tells how a secret society of the seventeenth century set about to invent a country and describe it. In 1824, the project was financed by Ezra Buckley, an eccentric millionaire from Tennessee. It was Buckley who suggested that a *Britannica*-like encyclopedia of the invented planet be written and in 1914 (just at the onset of World War I), the last volume of the secret *A First Encyclopedia of Tlön* was distributed. By 1942, strange objects from Tlön have begun to appear on earth: a compass inscribed in one of the alphabets of Tlön, and a mysteriously heavy cone, identified as an image of the divinity in certain regions of Tlön.

In 1944, a complete set of the forty volumes of *A First Encyclopedia of Tlön* are found in a Memphis library, and the importance of this event is (according to the narrator) recognized by everyone. The encyclopedia is phenomenally popular; a mad proliferation of summaries, editions, commentaries, and pirate editions of this "Greatest Work of Man" flood the earth. The order, symmetries, and rigor of Tlön seem infinitely superior to the confusion and doubts of ordinary human existence. Tlön appeals irresistibly to those who yearn to live in an ordered and comprehensible universe, a labyrinth of complexities perhaps, but a labyrinth which has been designed to be deciphered by men. The inventors of Tlön have triumphed; they have "changed the face of the world" and will continue, unimpeded, to change it until the human world becomes Tlön.

In the meantime, the narrator disassociates himself from this eagerly changing world around him. In its enthusiasm for an orderly universe, humanity forgets that the tidy logic of Tlön is "a rigor of chess masters, not of angels." The narrator is acutely aware of the attraction of idealism, but his nostalgia is more important to him, nostalgia for a culture that believes in the mysteries of angels and for a past that includes his own childhood and its familiar (though often illogical) languages. He retreats to the hotel where he spent happy days as a child (although it is also the hotel where Herbert Ashe left *A First Encyclopedia of Tlön*) not to act decisively but to continue a revision, to continue to take pleasure in words from the past, that past which the Tlön revisionists are now obliterating and replacing. Sir Thomas Browne's *Urn Burial* of 1658 traces the inevitable mortality of man through all of Western history. The narrator's translation of the *Urn Burial* is both a refuge from a terrible present and an indication of the futility of all intellectual effort. Within a labyrinthine, incomprehensible universe, man creates further mental labyrinths, such as totalitarian ideologies. The most absurd and unrealistic of these ideologies is, in this story, the invention of a planet, whimsically presented through the provisional encyclopedia that describes it. Yet absurd as it is (far more unrealistic than Nazi expansion), the invented world begins to impinge upon and gradually to dominate reality. The world as one knows it disintegrates. There is nothing the narrator can do but watch in horror. He retreats to another futile intellectual game: the translation of a difficult seventeenth century English Baroque writer into the no-less-difficult seventeenth century Baroque Spanish of Francisco Gómez Quevedo y Villegas.

Themes and Meanings

Borges' interest in philosophical idealism and its implications is evident in "Tlön, Uqbar, Orbis Tertius." Men imagine the world as they wish it to be and then try to impose this vision upon others; Borges describes how seductive yet how dangerous this penchant can be. The chaos of the real world cannot be understood by human beings, and yet men are endlessly tempted to define and control reality by establishing rules. Tlön offers this illusion of order and purposefulness, but it is shown in this story to be a human plot to take over the earth. Borges suggests some parallels with the expansion of the Nazi movement and with Marxism; "Tlön, Uqbar, Orbis Tertius" is one of his more political stories.

Style and Technique

"Tlön, Uqbar, Orbis Tertius" plays off an indisputably real account against a preposterous fantasy, managing to make reality seem unreal and fiction seem plausible. Readers trained to believe what they see in the *Encyclopædia Britannica* and the newspapers find themselves manipulated in this story by a worldwide mysterious plot. The story is extensively documented (like a credible encyclopedia article) with real and fictional sources so intertangled that the truth is lost. Yet amid the shambles of Western civilization, the narrator in the end holds out some hope for humanity: Aggregates of words (manifestos, revisionist histories, political propaganda) may destroy, but words may also provide comfort, refuge, and communion with the past.

Mary G. Berg

TO BUILD A FIRE

Author: Jack London (1876-1916)
Type of plot: Naturalism
Time of plot: 1900
Locale: The Yukon territory, some seventy miles south of Dawson
First published: 1902

Principal character:
> A TENDERFOOT, who is attempting to travel across the Yukon wilderness in winter

The Story

"To Build a Fire" is an adventure story of a man's futile attempts to travel across ten miles of Yukon wilderness in temperatures dropping to seventy-five degrees below zero. At ten o'clock in the morning, the unnamed protagonist plans to arrive by lunchtime at a camp where others are waiting. Unfortunately, unanticipated complications make this relatively short journey impossible. By nine o'clock that morning, there is no sun in the sky, and three feet of snow have fallen in this desolate Yukon area. Despite the gloomy, bitter, numbing cold, the man is not worried, even though he has reason to worry. At first he underestimates the cold. He knows that his face and fingers· are numb, but he fails to realize the seriousness of his circumstances until later in the story. As the story unfolds, the man gets progressively more worried about the situation. At first, he is simply aware of the cold; then be becomes slightly worried; finally, he becomes frantic.

His only companion is his wolf-dog. The animal, depressed by the cold, seems to sense that something awful might occur because of the tremendously low temperatures. The dog is frightened, and its behavior should show the man that possibly he has underestimated the danger.

At ten o'clock, the man believes that he is making good time in his journey by traveling four miles an hour. He decides to stop and eat lunch. His face is numb, and his cheeks are frostbitten. He begins to wish that he had foreseen the danger of frostbite and had got a facial strap for protection. He decides that frostbitten cheeks are never serious, merely painful, as a way to soothe himself psychologically and force himself not to worry about the cold. He knows the area and realizes the danger of springs hidden beneath the snow, covered only by a thin sheet of ice. At this point, the character is very concerned about these springs but underestimates the danger. Getting wet would only delay him, for he would then have to build a fire to dry off his feet and clothes. Every time he comes upon a suspected trap, he forces the dog to go ahead to see if it is safe. He begins to feel increasingly nervous about the cold.

By twelve o'clock, he is still far away from his camp and anticipates getting there by six o'clock, in time for dinner. He is pleased with his progress,
but, in reality, he is simply reassuring himself that there is no need to worry.
He decides to stop and eat lunch, a lunch he had planned to eat with his
friends at the camp. His fingers are so numb that he cannot hold his biscuit.
He reflects back to the time when he had laughed at an old man who had
told him how dangerous cold weather could be. He now realizes that perhaps
he had reason to worry and that he had forgotten to build a fire for warmth.
He carefully builds a fire, thaws his face, and takes "his comfortable time
over a smoke." Then he decides that he should begin walking again. The fire
has restored his confidence, but the dog wants to stay by the warmth and
safety of the fire.

The man's face soon becomes frozen again as he resumes his journey.
Lulled into a false sense of security by the fire, he becomes less and less
aware of his surroundings and steps into a hidden spring, wetting himself to
his waist. His immediate reaction is anger because he will be delayed by
building another fire. He carefully builds a fire, well aware of the importance
of drying himself. He remembers the old man's advice at Sulphur Creek that
circulation cannot be restored by running in this temperature because the
feet would simply freeze faster. His fire is a success and he is safe. He now
feels superior, because although he has had an accident and he is alone, he
has saved himself from certain death. He decides that any man can travel
alone as long as he keeps his head. Although confident because of his swift
action of building a fire to dry off, he is surprised at how fast his nose and
cheeks are freezing. He can barely control his hands: His fingers are lifeless
and frostbitten. Suddenly, his fire exists no more: He has built it under a
large tree that is weighed down with snow, and when he pulls down some
twigs to feed the flame, the snow in the tree is dislodged and falls on the man
and his fire. He thinks again about the old man at Sulphur Creek and realizes
that a partner at this time would be helpful. He begins to rebuild the fire,
aware that he will lose toes, and possibly his feet, to frostbite. Because his
fingers are nearly useless, he has difficulty collecting twigs. He is so sure that
this fire will succeed that he collects large branches for when the fire is
strong. His belief that the fire will succeed is the only thing that keeps him
alive. He finishes the foundation of his fire and needs the birch bark in his
pocket to start it, but cannot clutch the wood. He panics, drops his matches,
and is unable to pick them up. He succeeds in picking them up, finally, and
by using his teeth, he rips one match out of the pack. By holding it in his
teeth and striking it against his legs twenty times, he lights it but drops it
again when the smoke gets into his nostrils. He then strikes the entire pack
of matches against his leg and tries to light the wood but only burns his flesh.
He drops the matches, and the small pieces of rotten wood burn. He knows
that this is his last chance for life and that he cannot allow the matches to go

out. Because he cannot operate his hands, in his attempt to keep the fire burning, he spreads it out too much and it goes out. Now he can only think of killing the dog to put his hands in the carcass to stop the numbness. The dog senses danger, however, and quickly moves away. The man goes wild and catches the dog but soon realizes that he cannot kill it because he cannot use his hands. He knows that death is upon him and begins running, just as the old man had warned him not to do. The man hopes that he has a chance to run to camp but knows that he really has no chance, for he lacks the strength. He curses the dog, for it is warm and alive. The dog runs on but the man crumples after running a few yards. He decides to accept death peacefully and admits to himself that the old man at Sulpher Creek had been right. The dog stays with him, but when it smells the scent of death, it runs off in the direction of the camp, where reliable food and fire providers can be found.

Themes and Meanings

The main conflict in this story of survival is between man and nature. Another central conflict, however, is that between youth and confidence as opposed to wisdom and experience. The main character is a young man who believes that he knows the frozen wilderness but is still a tenderfoot who has not yet learned to respect the power of nature. London shows early in the story that the tenderfoot lacks imagination, an asset he sorely needs when tested to the extreme by the wilderness.

The man's egotism is in conflict with his common sense. He does not understand mankind's frailty and is too proud to admit his own. He does not comprehend the danger posed by an alien, hostile environment in which he can only survive by the full exercise of his native wit, instincts, skill, and cunning.

Before the coming of winter, the old-timer from Sulpher Creek had warned him that one should always travel in winter with a partner and that one should never attempt to travel alone in temperatures colder than fifty degrees below zero. In his ignorance, the tenderfoot had laughed at the old-timer's advice. Caught in the bitter cold, the tenderfoot is made to realize the value of the old man's warning.

The tenderfoot scorns other precautions. Once caught in the wilderness, for example, he realizes the value of having a partner. He realizes, moreover, that a facial strap would have protected him against frostbite. Still, he manages to build a fire after he has broken through the ice, and, his confidence momentarily revived, he laughs again at the old-timer. Ironically, the man is doomed by his egotism and his stupidity. When the fire goes out, he has second thoughts about his superiority.

The plot development is incremental as the tenderfoot's dilemma gets more desperate and as he unwillingly learns his lesson. His absurd belief in himself and his ability to cope with the situation is retained until the very end. Although he refuses to give up hope, it becomes increasingly clear that he has lost touch with reality. "When he got back to the States," he fantasizes, as he is freezing to death, "he could tell the folks what real cold was." Ultimately the man will die and be survived by his dog. The animal, a creature of instinct untainted by pride, is better adapted to the environment than the man.

Style and Technique

The fiction of Jack London, in tandem with the work of Frank Norris, Stephen Crane, and Hamlin Garland, helped to shape an American naturalism, a particular strain of scientific realism that was influenced by European writers of the later nineteenth century, particularly the French writer Émile Zola, who described the role of the novelist as that of "a scientist, an analyst, an anatomist" who interpreted reality through the application of scientific determinism. In "To Build a Fire," London places his protagonist in a harsh natural setting that tests to the limits his ability to survive in the wilderness.

The style of this particular brand of realistic fiction depends on the cold, objective presentation of detail that respects the force and power of nature and reduces the individual man to a position of relative insignificance. The central character of London's story is a vain creature, supremely and ironically confident of his ability to survive.

The story is carefully structured upon the building of several fires. The first two fires the tenderfoot builds are merely matters of convenience, when he stops on his journey to rest and eat. In both instances, the dog is reluctant to leave the safety of the fire. The third fire is built to stave off an emergency, since the man has got his feet wet. This fire is foolishly built, however, because the tenderfoot has no foresight or common sense.

The fourth and final fire the tenderfoot attempts to build is absolutely crucial to his survival, but he is too far gone to accomplish this task. His hands are by then too frozen to manipulate his matches, and his mind is so far gone that he cannot fully understand the seriousness of his dilemma. All he can do is believe in the possibility of his survival. The story provides an interesting study in the psychology of an unhinged mind.

London's story depends for its effect upon situational irony. An ironic strain that runs throughout the story is the tenderfoot's sense of superiority and contempt for the old trapper on Sulphur Creek. The irony is dramatic in that the reader soon realizes that the old man was right, a realization that escapes the tenderfoot until the very end of the story.

James M. Welsh

TOGETHER AND APART

Author: Virginia Woolf (1882-1941)
Type of plot: Psychological realism
Time of plot: c. 1924
Locale: London
First published: 1943

> *Principal characters:*
> MISS RUTH ANNING, the protagonist, a spinster
> MR. RODERICK SERLE, a man who fancies himself a writer but never writes and with whom Miss Anning converses at Mrs. Dalloway's party

The Story

Introduced to each other for the first time by Mrs. Dalloway at her party, Miss Ruth Anning and Mr. Roderick Serle are left by their hostess to talk together. Miss Anning had been standing at the window, looking at the evening sky; yet, while "the sky went on pouring its meaning" into her, upon Mr. Serle's sudden presence beside her she feels that the sky has changed and is not "itself, any more, but . . . shored up by [Serle's] tall body, dark eyes, grey hair, clasped hands, the stern melancholy face. . . ." Just as the sky is "shored up," so too are Miss Anning's perceptions of whatever "meaning" she may have felt able to glean from the sky, for she feels suddenly "impelled" to initiate and carry on a conversation with Mr. Serle, regardless of how "foolish" or superficial the conversation, and regardless of her own feeling that "their lives, seen by moonlight, [seemed] as long as an insect's and no more important."

"Foolish! Idiotically foolish" conversation reveals to Miss Anning, in fact, what she both lacks and possesses as an individual: She lacks the energy needed for "talking with men, who frightened her rather, and so often her talks petered out into dull commonplaces, and she had very few men friends—very few intimate friends at all, she thought, but after all, did she want them? No." Indeed, what she lacks in energy and friends seems insignificant to her when compared to what she possesses: "She had Sarah, Arthur, the cottage, the chow and, of course *that* . . . the sense she had coming home of something collected there, a cluster of miracles. . . ." Yet, for the sake of the party, for the sake of conversation, and for the sake of Mr. Serle, Miss Anning must put out of her mind those "miracles" which make her life richly and uniquely meaningful, and she must force herself to carry on a meaningless talk with Mr. Serle, a man "she could afford to leave. . . ." Miss Anning asks him a question designed to elicit a response from him on a topic, she presumes, about which he cares—Canterbury and the ancestors of his which are buried there.

After presenting Miss Anning's view of this awkward situation, the omniscient narrator then shifts to Mr. Serle's perspective, and here the reader is shown the great need this man has for such superficial conversation as that which he is having with Miss Anning: "With a stranger he felt a renewal of hope because they could not say he had not done what he had promised, and yielding to his charm would give him a fresh start—at fifty!" Despite the satisfaction he takes from the illusion of a "fresh start" with this stranger, he nevertheless feels that his "extraordinary facility and responsiveness to talk" have proven to be "his undoing" over the years, for he has been unable to refuse invitations to parties, and unable to resist "society and the company of women. . . ." Consequently, he has been unable to find the time he needs to be the writer he believes he is—even though he never writes. Rather than blaming himself for putting off his writing and the test of his talent, Mr. Serle finds it easier and less damaging to his exaggeratedly positive self-image to "blame . . . the richness of his nature, which he compared favorably with Wordsworth's. . . ." Rather than seeing such parties as Mrs. Dalloway's, as well as such conversations as his with Miss Anning, as a waste of time and energy, Mr. Serle views such activities as essential to his "deep" life.

The narrator's ironic view of Mr. Serle's existence differs greatly from the man's own view, for underpinning his need for polite society, the attention of women, and idle conversation is the fact that, at home, he has an invalid wife with whom he is "grumpy, unpleasant," and "caustic"—his remarks to her "too clever for her to meet, except by gentle expostulations and a tear or two. . . ." While Miss Anning's displeasure over the superficiality germane to conversations at parties is intensified by her reflection upon the "miracles" she possesses at home, Mr. Serle's displeasure with his home intensifies his hunger for precisely such parties as this one of the Dalloways. Significantly, it is Miss Anning's desire for a meaningful and rich existence that prompts her to tell Mr. Serle "the truth" about her own relationship to Canterbury, and thereby prevent him from going away from her with any "false assumption"; she tells him, therefore, "I loved Canterbury." As a result of her truthfulness, their eyes "collided" and each of them experiences a brief exposure of the other's inner, heretofore "secluded being," and the experience is—while momentary—"alarming" and "terrific." It is, in short, "the old ecstasy of life" made apparent, and its momentary exposure punctuates Mr. Serle's otherwise "yawning, empty, capricious" existence.

Unfortunately, just as quickly as the moment of their communion occurs (that of one "secluded being" with another), it dissipates and becomes a kind of "withdrawal," a "violation of trust," and they are left as before: "She did her part; he his." Caught in awkward silence, they both feel "freed" when Mira Cartwright approaches them and accosts Mr. Serle: To the relief of both Miss Anning and Mr. Serle, Cartwright's intrusion frees them to "separate."

Themes and Meanings

In *Jacob's Room* (1922), Virginia Woolf's third novel, the narrator asserts that "life is but a procession of shadows"; then she asks, "why are we yet surprised in the window corner by a sudden vision that the young man in the chair is of all things in the world the most real, the most solid, the best known to us . . . ? For the moment after we know nothing about him." While Woolf (through her narrator) is discussing here the difficulty a biographer has in capturing, with words upon paper, the essence of an individual, she is also pointing to what she sees as an inescapable fact of human existence: One individual can never completely know another; similarly, one can never completely know oneself, since that essentially fluid self is shaded and even, at times, changed by associations with others. This last point (regarding the effect other people have upon a personality, as well as upon that personality's view of itself and others) is important to understanding Woolf's fiction; indeed, she gave expression to this point in all of her novels, in several autobiographical essays, and in a number of her short stories—one of which is "Together and Apart."

Although both Miss Anning and Mr. Serle naturally have different perspectives and responses to their conversation, and to the party itself (she mildly resents having to abandon her solitary contemplation of the sky for the sake of "empty" conversation with a man whom, she gradually realizes, she does not like; he needs such a conversation because it helps him to forget the person he is at home), the artificial situation in which they find themselves permits them a brief, transcendent moment of communion with each other. The situation itself demands that the "shallow [and] agile" side of each of these people's personalities "keeps the show going" by "tumbling and beckoning" in talk; yet below the "agile" side of each exists a "secluded being, who sits in darkness." Only when Miss Anning decides that "this man shall not glide away from me, like everybody else, on false assumption," and then decides to express her feelings by saying, "I loved Canterbury," is the reader told that Mr. Serle "kindled instantly." In other words, by articulating her emotions Miss Anning has dived below the superficial and elicited a similar—albeit nonverbalized—response from her companion. Thus they both experience what Woolf elsewhere calls "a moment of being," when, as it is described in this story, the "secluded being" in each of them "stood erect; flung off his cloak; confronted the other."

After such a moment of wordless communication, Miss Anning realizes, as her creator had before her, how inadequate language is for truthful communication—especially in the face of "how obscure the mind [is], with its very few words for all these astonishing perceptions, these alterations of pain and pleasure."

Style and Technique

Reading any of Woolf's stories for the first time, the reader may be struck by how little physical action takes place in them, yet this author's stories always contain much action—thought-as-action—because her characters' conflicts are, with few exceptions, psychological ones. In "Together and Apart," for example, Miss Anning and Mr. Serle sit down on a sofa and—except for when he occasionally crosses or uncrosses his legs—that is all the physical movement the story provides. Yet, even though the story consists of approximately three thousand words, only a hundred and fifty of which are actually spoken by the two characters, the reader learns about both characters' lives—their feelings of inadequacy and incompleteness, their aspirations and frustrations, and their essentially inescapable feelings of aloneness. It is a testament to Woolf's mastery of prose and storytelling that, while it takes place in a superficial and boring context, the story itself is neither. Yet why would Woolf choose such a context?

In *Moments of Being* (1976), Woolf suggests that most individuals are not static personalities but are, instead, fluid and subject to constant changes in being and perception. While a seemingly constant, continuous identity is imposed upon people as they inhabit the finite world of physical and social existence, during "moments of being" this identity is transcended, and the individual consciousness becomes an undifferentiated part of a greater whole; at such a moment all limits associated with the finite world cease to exist. With this in mind, then, the reader is better able to understand why "Together and Apart" takes place in the limited confines of an artificial setting, for the setting itself heightens and intensifies the "moment of being" that Miss Anning and Mr. Serle experience. In fact, the limits imposed upon Miss Anning, by the finite setting and the identity that it forces her to project, goad her into demanding more of herself, Mr. Serle, and their situation. While in the story's first paragraph Miss Anning's perception of the infinite (the sky) is "shored up" by Mr. Serle's presence (himself representing the restrictions of the finite world), she becomes the catalyst for her companion's transcendent moment of communion with the infinite behind the "cloak."

David A. Carpenter

TOMMY

Author: John Edgar Wideman (1941-   )
Type of plot: Psychological realism
Time of plot: The mid-1970's, not long after the Vietnam War
Locale: Homewood, a decaying black neighborhood in the urban Northeast
First published: 1981

> *Principal characters:*
> TOMMY LAWSON, the streetwise protagonist, a directionless
>   black youth longing to leave his crumbling home
> RUCHELL, his hip, jive partner in crime
> INDOVINA, a fraudulent, parasitic white salesman
> CHUBBY, the businessman's Uncle Tomish sidekick
> JOHN LAWSON, Tommy's elder brother who has escaped the
>   ghetto

The Story

Tommy Lawson is strolling through the deserted streets of Homewood, a once populous black community now demarcated by boarded-up buildings and cracked sidewalks. Both he and the city streets share a legacy of tough, charismatic individuals: from Tommy's grandfather John French, who jived and jitterbugged until he "got too old and got saved," to the ice-ball vendor Mr. Strayhorn, who in his youth garnered such a reputation that no one yet will shake him down for money. Yet now neither the young man nor the blocks where he bebopped have bright futures. Homewood has become a no-man's-land since the 1960's riots, so Tommy shoots pool with the junkies and assorted drifters in the Velvet Slipper.

Today, however, Tommy stalks the Avenue, lost in reminiscence, for he has found a way to escape. He and his running buddy, Ruchell, whose full-time occupation is getting as high as possible, plan to finance their flight by swindling a crooked car-salesman. They have alerted this hustler, Indovina, to a truckload of stolen television sets which they will deposit at his business for a fee. (Actually, nothing is in their borrowed van except carpeting left there by its owner.) While Tommy closes the deal inside the white man's office, Ruchell will stand guard by the goods. Then, as Indovina's bodyguard Chubby approaches to inspect the cache, Ruchell will corner him with a gun. Tommy simultaneously will hold up Indovina. Certain that the Italian will not report the incident for fear of being charged himself, the two young men will "score and blow" to the West Coast.

Yet this scam soon sours. Ruchell shoots Chubby when he sees the hefty man reaching for a concealed weapon. Panicking at the sound of shots, Tommy pistol-whips Indovina and flees toward the van, too hysterical to grab any money first. Hunted now, the unlucky pair hides away from Homewood with Tommy's older brother John Lawson and his family.

Ironically, at last Tommy and Ruchell have severed the old neighborhood's hold. Charged with first-degree murder, they literally cannot return to it. Yet their prospects are burdensome rather than uplifting and inspiring.

Tommy especially feels the dead weight of his misbegotten dream. After assuring his brother, "I'm happy you got out. One of us got out anyway," the pursued man lies on a bed thinking about Christmases past. He dwells on not the toys and food, but the sleepless, futile night spent listening for Santa, watching for the flying reindeer. Again he finds himself with a dream he longs to confirm: being free. Even if it does not make sense given his circumstances, he still yearns for it to come true.

Themes and Meanings

John Edgar Wideman admits that "Tommy," like all the linked tales of *Damballah* (1981), arose from his desire to tell a story whose "theme was to be the urge for freedom, the resolve of the runaway to live free or die." Though Tommy and his peers are not literal slaves, like his great-great-great-grandmother who escaped North, in many ways their struggles are no easier than hers and yield few long-term successes.

As Tommy walks through Homewood at the beginning of the story, he complains to himself that he has "no ride of his own so he's still walking." Yet this statement belies the fact that he has tried to thwart the area's encroaching listlessness. He once was lead singer of the Commodores, a group so popular that it drew throngs of listeners to its Sunday jam sessions. A recording deal fell through, however, thanks to a seedy agent, and the group was dissolved.

Tommy's near success has been repeated in many ways by other men from Homewood's row houses and projects. Some have traded apparent impossibilities for the tangible, quick fruition of a junkie's nod. Others have relented unwillingly, their bodies blown asunder in the rice paddies of Vietnam. All have been suppressed by forces outside the community: In lieu of slavers seizing unsuspecting tribes, twentieth century whites use drugs, wars, and legal loopholes to entrap black men.

Tommy admires his brother, once an outstanding basketball player, for skirting a dead-end life-style and establishing a career, yet he can never account for precisely why John beat the odds in the first place. With hands "bigger than his brother's," Tommy could "palm a ball when he was eleven," but he did not even try the sport as a means of liberation. On the other hand, Deacon Barclay, a longtime friend of the family, owns a home as a result of a bittersweet victory. He has earned the money by "running around yes sirring and no mamming the white folks and cleaning their toilets," by performing in effect little more than his plantation forebears did.

A slave's paths to freedom (those other than death) were all uncertain long shots: to escape, to purchase himself, to be manumitted in a kind master's will, or to enjoy a superficial independence as the mistress's cook or the master's butler and valet. For many of Homewood's men, the American dream still carries the same measure of unattainability. Thus, as the story closes, Tommy repeats a resolve that echoes the "live free or die" motto of the fugitive slave. He vows, "I ain't going back to prison. They have to kill me before I go back in prison." Yet an ugly fact unsettles his declaration: a black man, not a white, died during his heist. In their desperate attempts to use any means necessary for obtaining money and respect, black men all too often hurt their own people: It is as if the final method of containing them is turning them against themselves. The themes of this autobiographical story—John Lawson is Wideman's alter ego—are treated at length in Wideman's acclaimed *Brothers and Keepers* (1984), a work of nonfiction.

Style and Technique

The streets and people of Homewood are moldy grays and jaundiced yellows. The Avenue is "a darker gray stripe between the gray sidewalks," and Mr. Strayhorn peers at passersby out of "yellow eyes." Interestingly, despite his animosity toward this neighborhood, Tommy also is associated with these colors. In one example, he complains about "crawling all sweaty out of the gray sheets. Mom could wash them every day, they still be gray. Like his underclothes. Like every. . . thing they had and would ever have." Similarly, when he and Ruchell plot their ill-fated robbery, the lights about them cast a "yellow pall." Thus, the color imagery stresses Tommy's unfortunate ties to the community. He is already part of its human refuse, and his hopes of climbing out of the pile are as good as dead. Yet the images link him to Homewood for another purpose, too. Regardless of his scorn for the winos, methadone users, and ruthless young gangs that have burgeoned over the years, Homewood is his ancestral seat. He walks where his gambling grandfather once strutted, and he passes "rain-soaked, sun-faded" posters paying silent tribute to other relatives' lives. So, though a fresh start and unlimited advancement may never be his, he possesses a history that he cannot lose.

In one well-crafted series of bird images, Wideman vividly underscores Tommy's ineffectual hopes. The young Lawson remembers how, missing the trolley back in high school days, he "wished he was a bird soaring through the black night, a bird with shiny chrome fenders and fishtails and a Continental kit." He describes a car in such terms because a bird, more so than any other creature, suggests freedom. Upon snapping out of his daydream, however, he discovers a real, dead, barely recognizable bird. This gory corpse, "already looking like the raggedy sole somebody had walked off their shoe," adds a sense of foreboding to the story, as if his teenage aspirations for independence will go the same shredded way as that of the pitiful skeleton fusing with the ground beneath him. Then a similar ghastly memory revives in Tommy's mind. He recalls stoning the winos' camp when he was a child, then fearing the wrath of a foul-breathed boogyman. He would picture his nemesis "behind every bush, gray and bloody-mouthed. The raggedy, gray clothes flapping like a bird and a bird's feathery, smothering funk covering you as he drags you into the bushes." Since the wino of Tommy's reverie metamorphoses into a dead bird, an indicator already of dashed dreams, Wideman again conveys a sense of doom. Tommy is not impatient that opportunities will come too soon; he worries that they will disintegrate before he reaches them.

Barbara A. McCaskill

TOMORROW AND TOMORROW AND SO FORTH

Author: John Updike (1932-   )
Type of plot: Social realism
Time of plot: The 1950's
Locale: An American high school
First published: 1955

> *Principal characters:*
> MARK PROSSER, the protagonist and the story's central
>   consciousness, an eleventh-grade English teacher
> GLORIA ANGSTROM, an attractive student
> PETER FORRESTER, an antagonistic student
> GEOFFREY LANGER, a bright student
> STRUNK, a physical education teacher

The Story

The lesson for the day in Mark Prosser's English classroom is Macbeth's soliloquy upon hearing of Lady Macbeth's death:

> Tomorrow and tomorrow and tomorrow
> Creeps in this petty pace from day to day,
> To the last syllable of recorded time,
> And all our yesterdays have lighted fools
> The way to dusty death. Out, out, brief candle!
> Life's but a walking shadow, a poor player
> That struts and frets his hour upon the stage
> And then is heard no more. It is a tale
> Told by an idiot, full of sound and fury,
> Signifying nothing.

Macbeth's criticism of life, based on his experience, reflects on the lack of experience or learning taking place in the classroom.

As his students enter the eleventh-grade English classroom, Prosser flatters himself on his ability to interpret their responses to their environment, attributing their restlessness to a change in the weather. The adolescents act out their relationships with one another as they roughhouse their way to their respective seats. Prosser is particularly aware of Gloria Angstrom, whose practically sleeveless pink sweater sets off the whiteness of her arms. His libidinous feelings toward Gloria make him a rival for her attentions with red-headed Peter Forrester, who has not prepared his homework assignment, but has succeeded in making her gasp as they enter the classroom. Prosser expresses his envy in contemplating the shortcomings of redheads in general and Peter in particular by calling on Peter first to be accountable for the homework assignment. Peter is unprepared. Prosser is unable to refrain from mocking his student's superficial, inappropriate answers.

As a teacher, Prosser is very self-conscious; indeed, his self-consciousness matches that of his adolescent students. Rather than concentrating on the subject matter, he reacts to their behavior, or what he assumes to be their reactions to him. His interpretation of William Shakespeare's lines is little better than that of the students, because it depends more on the interaction between teacher and students than on the play. When Peter eventually asks for a better explication, Prosser claims that he does not really know the meaning himself. When the students express their discomfort with this response, he tells them that he does not want to force his interpretation on them; in effect, he abandons the role of teacher to become a "human-among-humans." He is more concerned with what they think of him than with teaching them to understand Shakespeare. When he does start to provide some information about Shakespeare, he allows their disinterest to determine his actions. He is continually evaluating his relationship with them, congratulating himself on what he supposes to be his acuteness of perception.

When the students each attempt to recite the passage from memory at the front of the room, Prosser remains preoccupied with the interaction among them, especially as they relate to Gloria. As he admonishes Geoffrey, the smart boy with whom Prosser identifies himself, Prosser intercepts a note from Gloria to Peter in which she asserts that Prosser is a great teacher and that she loves him. As the period ends, he tells her to stay.

When the others leave, he patronizingly admonishes her for note-passing and suggests that she does not know the meaning of love. He thinks, however, that her emotional sincerity is about to express itself in tears.

After she has left, Strunk, the physical education teacher, comes in to tell how Gloria had played a joke that morning on another of her teachers by letting him intercept a note that said she loved that teacher. Moreover, the same thing had been done to yet another teacher the day before. Prosser feels angry. He does not tell Strunk that he, too, has been a victim of this joke. He leaves the school assuring himself that Gloria had been emotional, about to cry because she really did care about him, regardless of the notes intercepted by the other teachers.

Themes and Meanings

Like Macbeth's soliloquy, this story is concerned with the failure of the passage of time to produce significant meaning. Mark Prosser, as a teacher, is supposed to help his students by guiding them in their search for meaning. Unfortunately, he lacks the self-knowledge, which ought to come with maturity, that is necessary to do this. His actions are determined by his concern with how others, students or fellow teachers, perceive him. He identifies with Geoffrey Langer, the smart boy, but he behaves like Peter Forrester, the cutup, as he vies with Peter for the attention of Gloria. He picks on Peter through envy of the relationship between the two adolescents.

He wants to retain his authority as a teacher on the one hand; on the other, he wants to be seen as a friend, as a member of the group who happens to have read a little more than the others. Instead of attempting to bring them up to his level, he consistently lowers himself to theirs. When he does attempt to say something significant about the play, he allows himself to become distracted by Gloria, becomes self-conscious about what he is saying, and consciously attempts to sound diffident, as if what he is saying is not important to him either. Naturally he loses the attention of the class. To retrieve their attention, he resorts to reprimanding them and once again attacks Peter, who has taken the opportunity to talk to Gloria. He cannot convincingly answer any of their questions, since, regardless of his intellectual maturity, his emotional maturity is no greater than theirs.

Prosser conjectures that all the students want is "the quality of glide. To skip along, always in rhythm, always cool, the little wheels humming under you, going nowhere special." So he accounts for the "petty pace" of their lives. In defining this term, however, he has ranked the work of teachers along with that of accountants and bank clerks. He is inconsistent, unsure of himself, the fool of the soliloquy. His immature need for their fellowship leads him to fall for their joke. The joke itself is somewhat cruel, but it works only because the teachers are so dependent upon their students for emotional security. Clearly, the students have the intelligence or insight to realize that. Prosser is a "poor player" because his emotional maturity has not kept up with his age. Time has not endowed him with either maturity or the security that comes with self-knowledge.

Style and Technique

This story is something of a classic in the subgenre of stories about school because of Updike's ability to capture the sense of being in the classroom. He meticulously re-creates the classroom setting by adding detail to detail in a successful evocation of the interplay between students and teacher and among students themselves. The details of description and dialogue reflect the acuteness of Updike's eye and ear: Students act this way; teachers say these things.

This rich depiction of the setting is matched by Updike's precise manipulation of point of view. Like Henry James, Updike tells his story through a center of consciousness whose intellectual and moral quality delineates theme. The narration is third-person but confined to the consciousness of Mark Prosser. The reader experiences the classroom through the sensibility of the teacher. Thus, the reader not only knows what Prosser knows but also is in a position to evaluate the quality of Prosser's processing of experience into wisdom.

The facile overgeneralizing about students as they enter the room marks Prosser as less than profound. The derogatory generalizations about redheads and about the desire of all adolescents to "glide" through life more precisely define the moral and intellectual limitations of this character. By generalizing, Prosser relieves the anxiety brought about by his need to be liked by his students, the sign of his emotional immaturity. Against the evidence of the notes to the other teachers, he insists that Gloria was sincere in his note. Macbeth's generalizations are rooted deep in his experience; Prosser's, only in the topsoil of his emotions.

William J. McDonald

TONIO KRÖGER

Author: Thomas Mann (1875-1955)
Type of plot: Psychological realism
Time of plot: The last quarter of the nineteenth century
Locale: A northern German town resembling Lübeck; Munich, the Bavarian
capital; and Aalsgaard, Denmark
First published: 1903 (English translation, 1914)

> *Principal characters:*
> TONIO KRÖGER, the protagonist and the author's fictive
> persona
> HANS HANSEN, Tonio's boyhood friend
> INGEBORG HOLM, a beautiful, blonde local girl whom young
> Tonio admires
> MAGDALENA VERMEHREN, a serious, dark-eyed girl who
> adores Tonio
> LISABETTA IVANOVNA, an artist friend of the mature Tonio

The Story

Schoolboy Tonio Kröger discovers that he deeply admires, indeed loves, his classmate Hans Hansen. The boys are physical and intellectual opposites. Hans is handsome in a Nordic way with steel-blue eyes, straw-colored hair, broad shoulders, and narrow hips, while Tonio has the dark-brown hair, dark eyes, and chiseled features of the south. Hans's walk is strong and athletic, Tonio's idle and uneven. It hurts Tonio that Hans responds to his obvious admiration with easygoing indifference. When Hans is late for their after-school walk and finally appears with other friends, Tonio almost cries, but when Hans recalls their agreed upon walk and says that it was good of Tonio to wait for him, everything in Tonio leaps for joy.

Though he is aware of the differences between himself and Hans, Tonio never tries to imitate his friend. He knows that Hans will never read the copy of Friedrich Schiller's *Don Carlos* (1787) which he gives him, that even if he did, he would probably never recognize its dual themes of indestructible friendship and forbidden love. Tonio also realizes that he cannot develop Hans's interest in riding. Tonio would prefer to read a book on horses and admire their strength and beauty rather than to be on horseback. Though Tonio recognizes that he is different, he is hurt when Hans calls him by his surname because "Tonio" sounds too "foreign." Tonio likes the unusual combination, "Tonio Kröger."

Tonio's extraordinary sensitivity causes him to feel things more deeply than most boys. Indeed, his ability to recognize sham and ill-breeding, even in his teachers, results in school absenteeism and poor grades, which trouble and anger Consul Kröger, Tonio's fastidious, tall, blue-eyed father. Tonio's beautiful, black-haired mother, Consuelo, seems to him blithely indifferent to his grades, and Tonio is glad about this, though he considers his father's attitude somehow more respectable and dignified.

Tonio, now age sixteen, has suddenly become infatuated by blonde Ingeborg Holm. Though he has known her all of his life, she suddenly seems to have acquired a special beauty. Tonio is aware that he feels the same ecstatic love for Inge that he felt for Hans several years earlier, and that this transformation has occurred during Herr Knaak's private dancing class. The perceptive Tonio has considered Knaak's effeminate and affected demonstrations and gestures those of "an unmentionable monkey" and is embarrassed when the dancing master calls him "Fräulein Kröger" after Tonio has taken a wrong turn in the dance.

Mortified by his friends' laughter, Tonio takes refuge in the corridor, wonders why he always seems to feel so much pain and longing, and wishes that he were at home reading *Immensee* (1852), a romantically joyful story by Theodor Storm. Tonio wishes Inge would come out and console him, but he realizes that she has probably laughed at him like all the rest. Dark-eyed Magdalena Vermehren, "who was falling down in the dances," would be impressed that a magazine has recently accepted one of his poems, but this would mean nothing to Inge. Tonio resolves to be faithful to Inge, even though his love remains unrequited.

By the story's next juncture, Tonio's mother and father have died, the family firm has been dissolved, and the Kröger house has been sold. Tonio goes his own way, lives in various cities in the south, and continues to acquire respect for his intellect and the power of the Word. He comes to think of life as a labyrinth, but even in the throes of depression his artistry sharpens. His exotic name becomes associated with excellence, and his writings gain a large audience. At the same time, Tonio's appearance comes to resemble his work: fastidious, precious, *raffiné*.

It is in the southern German city of Munich that the now-established Tonio meets his attractive artist friend Lisabetta Ivanovna. Lisabetta chides Tonio for his formality and fastidious appearance. She claims that he does not look like an author, but Tonio argues that wearing a velveteen jacket or adopting Bohemian ways does not make one an artist. This interview gives Tonio a chance to expound his views on art, specifically the art of writing.

The art of writing is not a blessing but a curse that one begins to feel very early. It begins with a sense of isolation and estrangement from others, and this sense grows deeper with the years until there is no hope of reconciliation. As a result, the true artist is recognizable. The writer, Tonio continues, always speaks most directly to "the same old gathering of early Christians . . . people who are falling down in the dance."

In the last section of the story, Tonio journeys north to the town he had left thirteen years earlier. He finds his boyhood home, even expects to see his father come from its entrance, but discovers that it has now become the town's public library. For a time he is detained by the police, who confuse him with a wanted man, but he proves his identity with the proof-sheets of his latest book. He quietly enjoys this little encounter as he continues his journey north to Denmark.

Tonio enjoys Aalsgaard, the Danish seaside resort where his northward journey ends. One morning after a leisurely breakfast, Hans Hansen and Ingeborg Holm walk through the room. Inge is dressed as she used to be at Herr Knaak's dancing class; Hans wears his sailor's overcoat with its gilt buttons. They are not the Hans and Inge of Tonio's youth but are similar in type. Tonio continues to observe the couple closely in his writer's way and even notices that the nasal pronunciation of the orchestra leader resembles that of Herr Knaak.

In a conversation with Lisabetta, Tonio confides the results of his trip. He has determined that it is his ability to love the ordinary that has made him an artist. Nevertheless, he stands between two worlds, a part neither of the bourgeois world about which he writes, nor of the abstract world occupied by those who coldly adore the beautiful.

Themes and Meanings

This early work of Thomas Mann encapsulates the theory of art he would develop in his novella *Der Tod in Venedig* (1912; *Death in Venice*, 1925) and in many of his subsequent works. It reflects his readings in the works of the philosophers Friedrich Nietzsche (1844-1900) and Arthur Schopenhauer (1788-1860) and uses the device of leitmotif, the short recurring phrase that distinguishes given characters, emotions, or situations in the musical dramas of Richard Wagner (1813-1883).

Nietzsche's theory of balanced opposites as the source of art appears in the story's numerous juxtapositions. Externally, these exist in the story's northern and southern locales and represent northern intellect and southern passion. Tonio's hometown and the Danish town he visits as an adult are balanced by Bavarian Munich (Tonio's place of residence as a successful writer) and the Italian pilgrimage Tonio makes when he leaves his boyhood home. Within the story, Tonio's fastidious father is complemented by his fiery, non-German mother, Consuelo, and opposition continues in Tonio's attraction to Hans and Inge. Significantly, Magdalena and Lisabetta, who more closely resemble Tonio, become the audience for his art. The ultimate fusion of opposites, and by Nietzsche's definition art's origins, is appropriately in the name of the story's protagonist.

Schopenhauer's theory of the will and representation finds expression in Tonio's careful observations of all he sees. He records these from boyhood, and as he grows older and wishes to see pattern and continuity in his life, these impressions return in altered settings. This explains the haunted journey northward which Tonio undertakes as well as his fear that his long-dead father will suddenly emerge from his boyhood home. (A connection between Danish locale, Tonio's father obsession, and the ghost of Hamlet's father seems implied.) His artist's power of will to mold representation also accounts for Tonio's ability to see Hans, Inge, and Knaak in the people at the Danish resort.

Mann loved Wagner's *Der Ring des Nibelungen* (1876) and determined to incorporate Wagnerian-style leitmotifs in his work. The wildflower that Consul Kröger wears, as well as his fastidious appearance, reappear in the dress of the successful Tonio. Similarly, Tonio writes for those "always falling down in the dance," the epithet given originally to Magdalena.

Style and Technique

Thomas Mann's works almost plunder his family and circle of acquaintances for their plots, settings, and characterizations. Tonio is the fastidious Mann, and Mann's merchant grandfather, father, and mother appear in the descriptions of Tonio's parents. Mann left Lübeck to live in Munich after his father's death just as Tonio leaves his northern town for the Bavarian capital. Mann felt a deep attachment for a school friend named Armin Martens, Tonio's Hans Hansen.

This intensely personal autobiographical style did not endear Mann to many Lübeck residents, who recognized themselves in his works (or believed they did), and often resented how they appeared. Indeed, it was with the same anxiety that Tonio experienced that Mann revisited the town of his youth when a successful author.

Robert J. Forman

TOWN AND COUNTRY LOVERS

Author: Nadine Gordimer (1923-   )
Type of plot: Social realism
Time of plot: The recent past
Locale: Johannesburg and Middleburg, South Africa, and its environs
First published: 1980

Principal characters:

> DR. FRANZ-JOSEF VON LEINSDORF, a middle-aged Austrian-born geologist who has worked in Africa for seven years
> A SOUTH AFRICAN MULATTO GIRL, a supermarket cashier and Leinsdorf's mistress
> PAULUS EYSENDYCH, a white veterinary college student, age nineteen
> THEBEDI, a black girl living on the Eysendych farm, age eighteen
> NJABULO, a laborer on the Eysendych farm

The Story

When published first in *The New Yorker* (on October 13, 1975), this story was entitled "City Lovers"; the second part was added for publication in *A Soldier's Embrace* (1980). The two parts are quite discrete stories, connected only by the central theme.

Part 1 gives a detailed account of the professional and cultural background of Dr. Franz-Josef von Leinsdorf, who has worked in Peru, New Zealand, and the United States in a senior, though not executive capacity, for companies interested in mineral research; his special interest is underground watercourses; his cultural interests are skiing, music appreciation, and reading the poetry of Rainer Maria Rilke. Though he is thought "not unattractive" by the female employees of the mining company, none has been invited to go out with him; he lives alone in a two-room apartment.

When Leinsdorf cannot find his preferred brand of razor blades, a mulatto cashier offers to see that the stock is replenished before his next visit to the supermarket. On returning home one evening after a trip away, he is told by the cashier that the blades have arrived; because he is burdened with bags and cases, she offers to get them and take them to his apartment. Quite uncomfortably, Leinsdorf offers her a tip, which she declines. He then asks her to come in for a cup of coffee.

Soon, she brings his groceries two or three times a week; he gives her chocolates. She sews a button on his trousers, and he touches her, commenting, "You're a good girl." Leinsdorf is impressed by her small and finely made body, her smooth skin, "the subdued satiny colour of certain yellow wood," and her crepey hair. The two become lovers—first during the afternoons, then overnight; she tells the caretaker that she is Leinsdorf's servant, and her mother believes the same.

Near Christmas, three policeman arrive and announce that they have been observing Leinsdorf's apartment over a three-month period and know that he has been living with the mulatto girl. They search the apartment and find her in a bedroom closet. The couple is taken to the police station for a medical examination "for signs of his seed." Leinsdorf's lawyer bails them out, and the girl returns to her mother's house in the colored township nearby. Though she confesses that they have had intercourse, the magistrate acquits both because the authorities failed to prove that carnal intercourse had occurred in violation of the Immorality Act.

Part 2 opens with an account of the childhood association of white, black, and colored children on the farm. This association ends when the white children reach school age, and strict racial segregation is imposed. "The trouble was Paulus Eysendych did not seem to realize that Thebedi was now simply one of the crowd of farm children down at the kraal (village)." The two make love at the riverbed during the summer holidays—sometimes at twilight, sometimes at dawn. When Paulus' parents are away, he and Thebedi "stayed together whole nights—almost; she had to get away before the house servants, who knew her, came in at dawn."

When Thebedi is eighteen and Paulus nineteen and preparing to enter veterinary college, a young black man, Njabulo, a bricklayer and laborer, asks Thebedi's father for permission to marry her. Two months after her marriage, Thebedi gives birth to a daughter. "There was no disgrace in that; among her people it is customary for a young man to make sure, before marriage, that the chosen girl is not barren." The child, however, is very light skinned and has "straight, fine floss," whereas both Thebedi and Njabulo were matt black. Two weeks later, Paulus returned from college and, hearing about Thebedi's baby, visited the kraal to see it, with its "spidery pink hands."

Paulus, ascertaining that Thebedi has not taken the baby to the main farmhouse, suggests that she give it away; then, saying, "I feel like killing myself," he walks out. Two days later, the child is ill with diarrhea, and during the night it dies.

Njabulo buries the baby, but since someone had reported that the baby was almost white and healthy, the police arrive and disinter the corpse. Paulus is charged with murder; Thebedi, at the preliminary investigation, says that she saw him pour liquid into the child's mouth (though she had remained outside the hut when Paulus entered to see the baby). At the court trial, Thebedi recants and the court—finding absence of proof that the child was in fact Paulus' and noting the perjury of Thebedi at one of the trials—declares Paulus not guilty.

Themes and Meanings

Through the juxtaposition of two stories of love, the author has managed to suggest that the laws against interracial association (apartheid) are a cruel interference in what are at times genuine cases of affection, if not love. Leinsdorf comments that he does accept social distinctions between people but does not believe that they should be legally imposed; Thebedi (also in an interview in a Sunday paper) says that her affair with Paulus had been "a thing of our childhood"—a natural outcome of human relationships unaffected by legalisms. Both relationships are terminated through the interference of neighbors rather than through the direct efforts of the authorities: In Part 1, it is suggested that a neighbor or the caretaker at the apartment house was the informer; in Part 2, the other laborers or their women are suspected of informing. Yet the situations are alike: There is always someone prepared to adopt a holier-than-thou attitude and to cooperate with officialdom to the discredit of a member of the group.

In both stories one sees parallel elements and can conclude that a general pattern applies in South Africa, regardless of whether love is found in city or country, in youth or middle age, with black or mulatto, by immigrant European or native Afrikaaner, with farm girl or city cashier. In both parts one sees that the treatment of whites by courts is more favorable than that of nonwhites. Nadine Gordimer is not an advocate of miscegenation or of interracial romance. Rather, she suggests that interpersonal relationships should remain exactly that and should not become the concern of government policy. Romance or sex between members of different racial groups should be guided by concern for the involved parties rather than by legislative edict.

Style and Technique

Most of Nadine Gordimer's stories and novels evoke a sense of compassion for the characters, who are enmeshed in circumstances of their own creation. She manages to develop in her readers a genuine sympathy—even an empathy—for them; understanding, forgiveness, identification are her goals rather than condemnation, advocacy, and partisanship. Further, she manages to show the ineffable bond between individuals of different races, social status, and value systems that can be developed and sustained by respect for individuals as such: Almost all of her characters come from divergent backgrounds, yet they somehow manage to find fulfillment in each other. "Town and Country Lovers" shows the gradual growth and maturation of love between couples and suggests that when that love is fulfilled in sexual relations, it is honest and honorable—though it can be destroyed through the interposition of an artificial, arbitrary, and extrinsic morality. Ultimately, this becomes a question of whether persons should be allowed to decide their own course in life or be obliged to accept a dictated one.

At times, the author distances herself somewhat too much from her characters and their situations: This distance is achieved largely through what seems at times reportage, though since both parts of the story involve police and courtroom investigations, the journalistic quality of the written style may be defended as especially appropriate. In part 1, one can imagine that the Sunday newspaper reporter was responsible for the description of the girl when the police discover her in the closet:

> She had been naked, it was true, when they knocked. But now she was wearing a long-sleeved T-shirt with an appliqued butterfly motif on one breast, and a pair of jeans. Her feet were still bare; she had managed, by feel, in the dark, to get into some of the clothing she had snatched from the bed, but she had no shoes.

Yet this factually detailed account is at times found in close juxtaposition with rather coy, Victorian language, as in the description of Leinsdorf making love to his sleeping mate: "He made his way into her body without speaking; she made him welcome without a word." All too often, as here, there is what seems an emotional understatement in which greater feeling and perhaps even passion could be justified. Apparently silent, acquiescent sex is what the lover perceives will make her "like a wife." Yet she is notably less passionate than Thebedi, as well as older and more sophisticated. One of the author's achievements is her ability to convey through her style the carefully developed and companionable relationship of part 1 and then the more natural, unrestrained sensuality of part 2.

A. L. McLeod

THE TOWN POOR

Author: Sarah Orne Jewett (1849-1909)
Type of plot: Social realism
Time of plot: Mid- to late nineteenth century
Locale: New England
First published: 1890

Principal characters:
> MRS. WILLIAM TRIMBLE, a self-sufficient individual, an
> "active" businesswoman, and a widow
> MISS REBECCA WRIGHT, a friend of Mrs. Trimble and of the
> Bray women
> ANN BRAY and
> MANDANA BRAY, two sisters who comprise the town's poor
> inhabitants
> MRS. JANES, a part owner of the home in which the Bray
> women have been placed

The Story

Mrs. William Trimble, an independent and comfortably fixed widow, and Miss Rebecca Wright, a spinster who is dependent and of marginal means, discuss the impact of the severe weather on farmers in nearby Parsley as the two women journey home in Mrs. Trimble's horse-drawn carriage. Although the two women are friends, the author emphasizes the differences between them by having the narrator shift the focus from their conversation to their demeanor—how they respond to the ride and to the cold. Mrs. Trimble, an "active business woman" who has been obliged to handle her affairs in all types of weather, is accustomed to riding in the open air. Miss Wright readily shows that she is uncomfortable.

Mrs. Trimble is more than industrious and self-sufficient. She is a generous woman who takes some interest in the affairs of Hampden's needy; she is a Lady Bountiful of a sort. Miss Wright's dependence on Mrs. Trimble for transportation, her obvious discomfort, and her timidity establish an immediate contrast with Mrs. Trimble. Although the speech of each woman is markedly regional, the differences between Mrs. Trimble and Miss Wright's speech suggests the difference between their social class and reinforces the differences between their personalities.

As the two drive along a rural road, they discover that they are approaching the farmhouse in which two of their friends—elderly sisters on welfare—have been placed by the town. These friends are the Bray sisters, Ann and Mandana, the town poor. They are old, ailing, frail, dependent, and forgotten. After deciding to visit Ann and Mandana Bray, Mrs. Trimble and Miss

Wright have some time to reminisce about better times for the Brays, about past sermons, and about the improvident father of the Bray women. His devotion of time and money to the Church are the causes of the Bray sisters' impoverished condition.

When the two visitors arrive at the farmhouse, they are greatly concerned: The yard is barren, the chickens are "ragged," the house is drab and isolated. Mrs. Abel Janes, the landlady, is as cheerless as her kitchen. She complains bitterly about her condition and lack of money, and she begrudges her boarders, the Bray women. The cold and drafty attic in which the Bray women live is far more drab than the remainder of the house. It is also poorly furnished. These conditions and the lack of a good view make the sisters virtual prisoners. They have little food to sustain them, and they have no clothing to brave the inclement weather. They speak of getting "stout shoes and rubbers . . . to fetch home plenty o' little dry boughs o' pine. . . ." Despite their poverty, the sisters, especially Ann, are hospitable. With her hand in a sling, Ann cheerfully prepares all the food in the room for their guests: tea, crackers, marmalade. In addition to making their guests feel comfortable and welcome, Ann consoles her sister, Mandana, who weeps about their situation. Mrs. Trimble is so touched by the Brays' plight that she vows to approach the selectmen the very next day. The town is going to have to do something to help these women.

Themes and Meanings

Through the descriptions of the topography, the hardships of the farmers, and the plight of the Brays, Jewett comments on the decline of rural New England. Having her characters reflect on the past and the present enables Jewett to criticize and idealize former days. Because Mrs. Trimble is the only independent character in the story, the only one able to influence positively the town leaders, Jewett is extolling the virtues of self-sufficient women.

At the time, Jewett recognizes the importance of sisterhood and cooperation. Mrs. Trimble provides transportation for Miss Wright and has made arrangements for Miss Wright to stay in the Trimble home for the night. Both women have great sympathy for Mrs. Janes's complaints. Both demonstrate great sympathy for the Brays. In fact, the visit to the Brays forces Mrs. Trimble and Mrs. Wright to give greater material and emotional support to their disabled friends than they have previously given. The discussions about the Brays explore right and wrong behavior. Ann Bray reinforces the themes of sisterhood and cooperation when she comforts her sobbing sister, Mandana.

Style and Technique

Images of mud, frost, and snow, of stony and sodden fields, foreshadow and symbolize the condition of the Brays; the indifference of the town to its aged and disabled; and the callousness and greed of Mrs. Janes, with whom the Brays live. These images, along with those images of isolation and decay, parallel the aging, the isolation, and the dependence of the Brays. In turn, each symbolizes the decay of the New England region.

A pattern of contrasts between characters—Mrs. Trimble and Miss Wright, Ann and Mandana—between the two sets of women, is an important part of the story's style and structure. Moreover, the speech patterns are correlated with the class and condition of each character; the Brays, who are the poorest, use speech that is the most regional and most obviously different from the speech of the other characters.

Ora Williams

A TREE. A ROCK. A CLOUD.

Author: Carson McCullers (Lula Carson Smith, 1917-1967)
Type of plot: Psychological realism
Time of plot: Just before dawn
Locale: A streetcar café
First published: 1942

> *Principal characters:*
> THE BOY, a newspaper carrier
> THE MAN, a transient
> LEO, the owner of the café

The Story

It is not yet dawn on a rainy morning when the twelve-year-old paperboy decides to have a cup of coffee at Leo's café before finishing his paper route. There are few customers this morning: some soldiers, some laborers from the nearby mill, and an unusual looking man drinking beer alone. Leo, the surly owner of the streetcar café, pays little attention to the boy, and he is about to leave when the man with the beer calls to him. The boy cautiously approaches the man and is taken aback when the stranger declares that he loves him. Though the other customers laugh at this declaration, the man is deadly serious. Embarrassed and unsure of what to do next, the boy sits down when the man offers to explain what he means.

With the boy seated next to him, the man pulls out two photographs and tells the boy to examine them. Old and faded, both are of the same woman, whom the man identifies as his wife. As he begins his story, the boy, anxious to leave the café and finish his paper route, looks to Leo for help; when none is forthcoming, the boy starts to leave, but something in the man's manner compels him to stay. Nervous but resigned, the boy listens, half convinced that the man is drunk.

Yet the man seems sober and almost eerily serene as he explains that, to him, love is a "science"; by way of illustration, he tells the story of his marriage. Twelve years ago, when he was working as a railroad engineer, he had married the woman in the picture. He married for love and did everything he could to make her happy, never suspecting that she might be otherwise. Not even two years into the marriage, however, the man had come home one night to find that she had run away with another man. He was devastated: His love for her had made him feel complete, integrated, for the first time in his life. He spent two years traveling about the country looking for her, unable to find even a trace.

Despite Leo's rude and vulgar interruptions, the story holds the boy's attention, and the man goes on with it. In the two years that followed his search for his wife, he continued to be tormented by her memory. Though he could not remember her face at will, he would be reminded of her unexpectedly by the smallest details of daily life. Miserable, he started drinking. Only in the fifth year after his wife left him did he start to develop his "science" of love. After meditating about love and its failures, he decided that most men go about love incorrectly, falling in love for the first time with a woman. Instead, says the man, people should work up to such a love, falling in love first with less significant things: a tree, a rock, a cloud. He has now mastered this "science," and now he can love anything: at will.

After the man has finished his story, the boy asks him if he has ever fallen in love with a woman again. The man admits that such a love is the last stage of his process, and that he has not yet worked up to it. After reminding the boy that he loves him, the man leaves the café, leaving the boy perplexed but strangely moved by the story.

Themes and Meanings

The desolate setting, the inability of the boy to understand the man's story, Leo's unfailing cynicism—all point to the theme of this story, and that of much of McCullers' fiction: the spiritual isolation inherent in the human condition. The only attempt at communication in the story—the old man's desperate attempt to explain the "science" of love to the adolescent paperboy—is necessarily a thwarted one: Like the Wedding Guest in Samuel Taylor Coleridge's long poem *The Rime of the Ancient Mariner* (1798), the boy is a captive audience, unwilling to listen, but compelled to by the strangeness of the speaker; like the Mariner in that same poem, the man is worn out from having told his story too often. Leo has only contempt for the man, and no words at all for the boy. A sad tale told by a defeated old man to a puzzled boy is the only vestige of human sympathy and communication in the dark world of this story.

Nor is love an answer to the dilemma posed by the story. Clearly, the old man is a victim of love, at least of romantic love: The unexpected loss of his wife was a blow from which he has never quite recovered, even though nearly eleven years have elapsed between her leaving and the time of the story. Having experienced the common reactions to betrayal—the period of obsession to get the loved one back, followed by a period of recklessness and dissipation—the old man has developed a "science" by which he can love everything he observes. Though he is composed, almost unnaturally so, during the telling of his story, it is important to remember that a man who, only somewhat more than a decade before, was happily married and gainfully employed is now little more than a bum. His decline is a testament to the illusory and transient nature of romantic love and to the bitter ways in which it can affect the human spirit.

Though it brings him a certain measure of peace and contentment, the man's "science" is clearly a mechanism that enables him to cope with his lingering misery. By willing himself to love anything or anyone, he thereby avoids the kind of spontaneous, but uncontrollable, love that has nearly destroyed him. The final stage of his "science," the one toward which he is presumably working, is romantic love, the love for a woman. Yet by the end of the story, the reader, and perhaps even the boy, knows that he will never again reach that stage, having been hurt by it too badly before.

Style and Technique

"A Tree. A Rock. A Cloud." is a story-within-a-story, that is, the old man's tale is framed by the dramatic situation involving the boy, Leo, and the bleak café. Here, however, the frame does not merely serve as a technical device to justify the old man's narrative; rather, the two stories complement and reinforce each other. While the tale of betrayal and lost love serves as the centerpiece of the story, an equal amount of space is given over to the action within the café: The boy shifts in his seat, the man lowers his head, Leo prepares food with characteristic stinginess. Both stories are about the failure of human sympathy, and the fact that the old man is unable to find a wholly sympathetic listener makes the story doubly tragic.

Unlike most of Carson McCullers' work, "A Tree. A Rock. A Cloud." is not set specifically in the South; indeed, no specific locale is mentioned. The two principal characters are unnamed, nor is any indication given of the date or of the season. This deliberate indeterminacy lends a chilling universality to the story, transforming it from a story about a tired old man's ramblings to a sort of allegory about the limitations of love.

J. D. Daubs

THE TREE OF KNOWLEDGE

Author: Henry James (1843-1916)
Type of plot: Psychological realism
Time of plot: The late 1890's
Locale: London, England
First published: 1900

> *Principal characters:*
> PETER BRENCH, the protagonist, a fifty-year-old bachelor of independent means
> MORGAN MALLOW, a middle-aged sculptor of independent means
> MRS. MALLOW, his middle-aged wife of independent means
> LANCELOT MALLOW, their son

The Story

At the heart of much of Henry James's fiction is the idea of an education—a gaining of knowledge by a protagonist which changes his view of the world. In the longer form of the novel, such as *The Portrait of a Lady* (1881), a number of experiences gradually educate the protagonist, but with the shorter form, such as in this story, James relies on one incident to change a character's view of the world—and himself. The concept of "knowledge"—the key term in the title "The Tree of Knowledge"—is the central concern around which the psychological action revolves. Peter Brench, the protagonist, is a man who loses his innocence, his illusions, through an experience with his godson, Lancelot Mallow.

The action begins with the announcement by Lancelot's mother, Mrs. Mallow, that her son shall not return to college at Cambridge, but instead will go to Paris and learn to become a painter. Peter, a family friend who has been secretly in love with Mrs. Mallow for twenty years, arranges a meeting with Lance in an attempt to persuade him not to go to Paris, but to return to college.

Peter does not wish Lance to go to Paris to study painting, because he fears that Lance will learn that his father, who has proclaimed himself a great artist as a sculptor, and who has devoted his life to his sculpting, is without talent. Peter primarily wishes to protect Mrs. Mallow from this knowledge, for he fears that it would bring her great pain and destroy her love for her husband. When Lance questions Peter on why Peter does not wish him to go to Paris, Peter declares, "I've the misfortune to be omniscient." Lance misinterprets the statement to mean that Peter does not believe that Lance has the talent to become an artist. Lance wishes to reassure Peter that he is mature enough to find out the truth about himself, and he replies that his "innocence" no longer needs protecting.

While Lance is in Paris, Peter continues to have Sunday dinner with the Mallows, and he observes the "fond illusion" of the Mallows when it appears that some of the sculpting finally will be sold, and Morgan will gain a reputation as an artist. Peter knows that Morgan will never really amount to anything as a sculptor, for he is without a proper sense of proportion, a necessary aspect of the art. Yet since the Mallows are independently wealthy, there is no need for Morgan to become successful, and Peter believes that for the well-being of all concerned, including himself, the present arrangement is best left as it is.

When Lance does return the following year from Paris, he has discovered that he does not have the talent to become a painter, and he also has discovered the lack of value of his father's work—the very knowledge Peter wished to conceal from him. Peter extracts a promise from Lance not to tell his parents the truth about his father. It is Peter's greatest wish that the couple retain their illusion. Peter's goal of protecting Mrs. Mallow from the truth is called into question by Lance's next visit home from Paris. In the final scene of the story, Lance tells Peter of a heated argument with his father, who castigated Lance for not developing his painting. Lance tells Peter that his mother, in order to relieve Lance's feelings, came to him after the argument, and Lance discovered that she had known the true value of her husband's work all along.

On hearing this, Peter is dumbfounded. Lance realizes how very much Peter must have cared all these years for his mother, and at the same time, Peter realizes that Mrs. Mallow is not the woman he thought she was; she was quite capable of living all these years with such knowledge while maintaining a convincing appearance that she believed in her husband's talent: a convincing appearance even to Peter.

When Lance closes the story by declaring how futile Peter's effort was to have tried to keep Lance from Paris, to have tried to keep him "from knowledge," Peter replies that he now realizes his effort was, "without my quite at the time having known it," to keep himself from the very knowledge that he has just discovered. All these years, he has been the one living under a "fond illusion." He was not all-knowing, "omniscient," as he told Lance, but was, indeed, the innocent one in assuming exactly what Mrs. Mallow was as a person.

Themes and Meanings

The nature of a man's illusions about himself is the central theme that Henry James explores in this story. On one level, Morgan Mallow lives a life of self-deception, believing that he is a great artist when, in fact, he has no talent. Yet because of this lack of knowledge, he goes on living as a happy, self-satisfied man. His situation is in direct contrast to that of Peter. On a more significant level, Peter discovers that although he always has assumed that he was a man without illusions, it is he who has been living with the illusion, not Mrs. Mallow.

This theme achieves its meaning through the refined sensibility of Peter. He is a man of taste, one who avoids "vulgarity"; he judges himself as one who feels "an extreme and general humility to be his proper portion." For such a man to discover that, for all of his humility, he lived a life based on an illusion calls that very humility into question—in fact, calls his whole life into question.

The age of the protagonist is a central factor in this theme: Peter is not a young man, with his life before him, but rather a man in his fifties, an age when one examines one's achievements in life, when one tries to determine what one's life has meant. He has devoted his life to a woman who is not the person he thought she was, and his illusion has cost him a larger life, one in which he might well have lived more fully.

Style and Technique

Henry James viewed this story as a "novel intensely compressed" without "any air of mutilation" into a short story. The rich psychological dimensions of the protagonist are achieved through the use of language, the famous James style—the sentences are long and complex, with one phrase, one thought, qualified by another, and often yet another. The style is entirely appropriate for the protagonist, for Peter Brench is a man of complex thought, a man concerned with nuance and distinctions.

That the action should be viewed through Peter's mind in third-person-limited point of view is also entirely appropriate, for the real "action" of the story is the psychological processes of Peter's thoughts and feelings. It is this point of view, a character of central intelligence, upon whom the action registers, that enabled James to explore the complexities of thought, the nuances of sensibility, for which he is famous.

The complexity of the overall structure in this story parallels the use of language. In attempting to conceal knowledge from Mrs. Mallow, Peter discovers the very knowledge that will lead to his own self-awareness. The structure also gives ironic dimension to the concepts of omniscience, innocence, illusion, and humility. Typical of James, the irony is not stark and biting, but rather complex and satiric. The various elements of the story—its language, structure, irony—are all in proper proportion to create a harmonious whole.

There are those readers who become impatient with the fiction of Henry James on a first reading, who find his prose too dense and his characters and their situations unexciting. To appreciate his work, one often requires multiple readings with a patient sensitivity. Critics and other writers refer to him as "the Master"—one of the greatest artists in the history of prose fiction—

for his ability to dramatize complex subjects. In reference to this particular story, James said his "fun" was in dramatizing the material, in making it live on the page, in compressing what was essentially a novel into the short story form. Brevity and physical action are not his forte; instead, his strengths are in portraying the rich life of the educated mind and the complex relationships between persons of sensitivity and taste.

Ronald L. Johnson

A TRIFLING OCCURRENCE

Author: Anton Chekhov (1860-1904)
Type of plot: Psychological realism
Time of plot: Late nineteenth century
Locale: St. Petersburg
First published: "Pustoy sluchay," 1886 (English translation, 1915)

> *Principal characters:*
> NIKOLAY ILYICH BELYAEV, the landlord
> OLGA IVANOVNA IRNINA, his mistress
> ALYOSHA, her son
> IRNIN, her estranged husband

The Story

The setting for the entire story is the drawing room of Olga Ivanovna Irnina, a woman who is estranged from her husband and is currently involved with Nikolay Ilyich Belyaev. The story opens with a brief description of Belyaev: He is a "well-fed," "pink young man of about thirty-two" years of age. He has three principal activities in life: He is a "St. Petersburg landlord," he is "very fond of the race-course," and he has a "liaison" with Olga.

This opening establishes that, as a landlord, Belyaev lives from the labor of others; that, as a racing addict, he has not closed the gap between his mental and his chronological age; and that, as a paramour, he prefers a liaison with Olga to marriage.

The epithets "well-fed" and "pink" applied to Belyaev are especially unflattering inasmuch as in Chekhov's works the color pink, when referring to a man, suggests the image of a soft, pampered, and effeminate individual, while the expression "well-fed" is an unmistakable sign of pettiness and vulgarity or, more precisely, what the Russians call *poshlost'*.

The narrator observes that Belyaev looks on his liaison with Olga as "a long and tedious romance" which he has "spun out," adding parenthetically that this is Belyaev's "own phrase." Here a more serious flaw in Belyaev's character is exposed: He has been insincere about the nature of his relationship with Olga. Moreover, as the words "to use his own phrase" indicate, he has obviously made their "tedious romance" the subject of discussion with others, though not with her.

The inauthenticity of their relationship—its prosaic nature—is further underscored when Belyaev refers to it metaphorically as a romance, the first pages of which—"pages of interest and inspiration"—had been read long ago, leaving only pages containing neither novelty nor interest. Significantly, the word "love" does not appear in the description of even the initial phase of this romance; only interest and novelty are of primary importance to Belyaev.

The irony is fully intended when the narrator, after presenting such an unflattering picture of Belyaev, refers to him as "my hero."

As the story opens, Belyaev has come to visit Olga and, not having found her at home, lies down on the drawing-room couch to wait for her. He is greeted by Olga's son, Alyosha, who is lying on a divan in the same room but whom Belyaev does not even notice. This incident betrays Belyaev's treatment of the boy in the past and foreshadows the treatment that he will accord him later.

In describing Alyosha, the narrator notes that the boy is "about eight years old, well built, well looked after, dressed up like a picture in a velvet jacket and long black stockings." Every detail bespeaks Alyosha's excellent material well-being. Yet, here too, there seems to be a lack of something—an emphasis upon the boy's material well-being perhaps at the expense of his spiritual welfare. The single most disturbing detail is his being "dressed up like a picture." He may appear to be "well cared for" but, as is eventually revealed, he is treated like an object—a pawn in a game whose principal players include his separated parents and Belyaev.

A close inspection of the description of Belyaev and Alyosha reveals considerable similarity between the grown-up man and the child: Each is a pampered, spoiled individual; the epithets "well fed" and "pink," used to describe the former, echo the epithets "well looked after" and "well built," used to describe the latter. Similarly, Belyaev's playing the races with his income from tenants finds its parallel in Alyosha's fascination with the circus and acrobats, which his mother's money enables him to see. Even the minor detail that both of them are reclining in the drawing room at the opening of the story underscores their basic similarity. Alyosha strives to behave and talk like an adult but remains a child whose impressions of adults and their standards of morality and conduct are naïve and incomplete. For his part, Belyaev, who is four times Alyosha's senior, demonstrates through his selfishness, irresponsibility, and inconsiderateness of others that in many respects he, too, is still a child.

As he reclines on the divan, Alyosha imitates an acrobat, but his behavior equally conjures up the antics of an insect: "He lay on a satin pillow... lifting up first one leg, then the other. When his legs began to be tired, he moved his hands, or he jumped." Next, he "took hold of the toe of his left foot in his right hand and got into a most awkward position. He turned head over heels and jumped up." Shortly thereafter, Belyaev says to him: "Come here, kid" (he uses the word *klop*, which in Russian basically means "bug" or "bedbug" and colloquially "kid"). He adds: "Let me look at you, quite close." The image of a barely perceptible bug is appropriate for Alyosha. In fact, to Alyosha's greeting, Belyaev responds: "I didn't notice you." The irony and full implication of this statement become apparent when somewhat later Belyaev reflects: "All the time he had been acquainted with Olga Ivanovna

he had never once turned his attention to the boy and had completely ignored his existence." Now, as he examines Alyosha (the bug), he asks: "How
are you?" In Russian, however, he simply asks "Zhivyosh?" which literally
means "Are you alive?"—an ironic question as it reflects Belyaev's attitude
toward Alyosha up to now. The "awkward position" that Alyosha has got
himself into while imitating the acrobat serves as a foreshadowing of the
awkward position in which he will soon find himself vis-à-vis his mother and
father after undergoing Belyaev's close "examination."

Alyosha is distracted by Belyaev's watch chain and locket, both of which
remind him of his father's—a fact he inadvertently blurts out. Surprised by
this information, Belyaev presses Alyosha for a complete confession: He and
his sister Sonya, escorted by their nurse, have been seeing their father on a
regular basis despite their mother's forbidding them to do so.

To extract this information from Alyosha, Belyaev addresses him as a
"friend to a friend," requesting him to speak "openly," "honestly," and on his
"word of honor." Alyosha then obtains from Belyaev a promise that the latter
will not say anything of it to his mother. When Alyosha requests Belyaev to
swear an oath, the latter responds: "What do you take me for?" Belyaev's
later custody of the secret gives this question exactly the answer Alyosha—
and the reader—feared.

Alyosha informs Belyaev that he and Sonya meet their father at Apfel's
sweet-shop, where he treats them to coffee, cakes, and pies, after which, at
home, they try to conceal the affair from their mother by eating as much as
they can. The father takes advantage of these meetings to extract information about the mother's activities and to set the children against Belyaev.
Such statements as "You are unhappy, I'm unhappy, and mother's unhappy"
strike even Alyosha as being "strange." Alyosha tells Belyaev (of all people):
"I can't understand why mother doesn't invite father to live with her or why
she says we musn't meet him." Here Chekhov demonstrates not only Alyosha's naïveté but also his own profound psychological insight into one of
childhood's predicaments: the confusion and uncertainty when caught between separate parents.

When asked by Belyaev what their father says about him, Alyosha, after
obtaining Belyaev's promise not to become offended, informs him that their
father blames Belyaev for their unhappiness and their mother's ruin. Accused
of ruining the family's happiness (Olga's in particular), Belyaev explodes with
anger. When Alyosha reminds him of his promise not to become offended,
Belyaev, in another psychologically authentic response, notes: "I'm not offended," and, after a brief pause, lashes out with: "and it's none of your business!"—a reaction which reinstates the dynamics of the story's opening, in
which Belyaev considered Alyosha too insignificant to notice. Belyaev's earlier feelings of being trapped in a dull, drawn-out romance have now become
concretized in his image of himself as an animal who has fallen into a trap.

As Olga and Sonya return home, Belyaev continues to rant and rave, completely absorbed in his hurt pride. Behind his hysterics is his desire to end the unhappy romance with Olga. He has been looking for a pretext but has been either unable or too weak to find one. At last the opportunity has presented itself and he seizes it. The animal extricates himself from the trap.

As Belyaev begins to reveal Alyosha's secret, Alyosha experiences a horror which reflects itself in "his face twisted in fright"—quite a contrast to his deliberately, acrobatically "twisted body" described in the story's opening. Alyosha repeatedly reminds Belyaev of his pledged word of honor. Belyaev's brutal response is perhaps the story's best example of irony: "Ah let me alone! . . . This is something more important than any words of honor. The hypocrisy revolts me, the lie." The man who demanded the word of honor from others and easily gave his own has proven dishonorable. Like a child, he has permitted his hurt feelings to take precedence over his word of honor. Now the biggest "hypocrite" and "liar" of all, he accuses others of revolting hypocrisy and lies.

The story comes full circle as Belyaev, absorbed in his insult, "now, as before, did not notice the presence of the boy. He, a big serious man, had nothing to do with boys." The story concludes, however, with Alyosha's final impressions. It is he who appears truly revolted by this entire experience—one which may have scarred him for life. How could a pledged word be so easily broken? How could it have so little value? The narrator concludes that this was Alyosha's first encounter with the world of lies—his first awareness that in this world "there exist many things which have no name in children's language."

Themes and Meanings

In "A Trifling Occurrence," Chekhov demonstrates his profound understanding of a child's psychology. The story shows how impressionable children are. It also demonstrates that what may seem trivial to an adult can be of great significance to a child and may leave a lasting imprint. To depict this "common triviality" at work, Chekhov has chosen a collision of children's emotions with a world of insincere and false relations—a world peopled by petty and dishonorable adults.

At first glance, the story may seem to be about Belyaev's failure to keep his word with Alyosha, thereby insulting the child and putting him through an emotional trauma. Such a reading would lead one to conclude that Belyaev is the villain and Alyosha the injured innocent. On rereading the story, however, one discovers that the situation is far more complex. In fact, no one in this story is innocent, not even Alyosha. To a lesser or greater extent, everyone is guilty of contributing to the tragedy. If Belyaev appears to be all bad (which he is not), Alyosha and the others are certainly not all good. Early in the story, Belyaev looks at Alyosha and reflects: "A boy is stuck in front of your eyes, but what is he doing here, what is his role?—you don't want to give a single thought to the question." The key word here is "role." A closer examination of the story reveals that all characters portrayed are guilty of role-playing rather than leading authentic lives. All of them are caught in a vast web of deceit and betrayal, a web which they themselves have erected. The "unnatural positions" which Alyosha acrobatically assumes in the opening paragraphs of the story are symbolic of the deceptive lives they all lead. Belyaev deceives Olga about the true nature of his feelings for her and continues playing the role of her lover. Alyosha and Sonya deceive their mother when they meet secretly with their father. Their father deceives their mother by setting up these clandestine meetings; he also deceives his children by telling them "funny stories" and treating them to sweets while pumping them for information about their mother and Belyaev and by faulting Belyaev for all of their unhappiness, without a hint that he himself may have colluded in it. Nor is Olga guiltless in the situation. If she had been completely unselfish, perhaps the liaison with Belyaev would never have been established. She is less than fair by forbidding the children to see their father. The grandeur of her material comforts suggests that she is milking both her husband and Belyaev to support her life-style. Even the nurse escorts the children to their meetings with the father, thereby taking part in the deception of her employer.

All the characters, therefore, are connected in a vicious circle of deception. That circle is finally broken when Belyaev, as a result of his egocentrism, betrays Alyosha. In doing so, Belyaev helps to expose all the other deceptions. Thus, the concluding lines of the story, "This was the first time in his life that Alyosha had been set, roughly, face to face with a lie", assume a deeper meaning. Before now, Alyosha himself has been guilty of lying and deceiving; now, he experiences the unpleasantness of being lied to. Given the number of similarities between the adult-child Belyaev and Alyosha pretending to be an adult in the opening two paragraphs of the story, the reader may seriously doubt whether Alyosha will behave any differently once he reaches adulthood. Chekhov's message appears to be that there is no substitute for truly authentic and honorable relationships.

Style and Technique

From its opening to its closing line, "A Trifling Occurrence" is exemplary of Chekhov's mastery of the short story. Its construction is analogous to the best of Chekhov's one-act plays. In fact, it could easily be staged: More than two thirds of its lines consist of dialogue. Another fact common to both story and play is that all major "events" leading up to the conflict take place offstage. As in the indirect plays, so, too, in this story, there are important offstage characters, most notably the father.

The story shows symmetry in its construction: from its bipartite opening, consisting of two paragraphs of ten lines each devoted to the introduction and description of the two protagonists, to its conclusion, consisting also of ten lines. Narrative passages frame what remains, which is essentially dialogue. Chekhov masterfully moves the tempo of this dramatic piece from the leisurely pace of the introductory paragraphs, where one finds both Belyaev and Alyosha reclining on sofas, to the midpoint, where Belyaev and Alyosha become more animated as the former learns the first details of the latter's secret, to Belyaev's real state of excitement once he learns that the father accuses him of the family's ruin, to its crescendo as Belyaev pours out his anger for the insult he has suffered. At this point Olga enters, totally confused, while Alyosha is overwhelmed by terror. Even the lines of dialogue become shorter, thus accelerating the tempo and contributing to the charged atmosphere. In the closing narrative passage the tempo subsides as the narrator sums up the "moral" of the story.

Leonard Polakiewicz

TRISTAN

Author: Thomas Mann (1875-1955)
Type of plot: Parody
Time of plot: The turn of the twentieth century
Locale: Einfried, an Alpine sanatorium
First published: 1903 (English translation, 1925)

Principal characters:

ANTON KLÖTERJAHN, a successful, domineering businessman
from North Germany
GABRIELE KLÖTERJAHN, his wife, a patient in the sanatorium
DETLEV SPINELL, a writer of slight reputation who is also
taking the cure

The Story

At the beginning of January, Anton Klöterjahn and his wife arrive at Einfried, a clinic in the mountain climate once favored by tuberculosis patients. Klöterjahn, who has brought his wife here for treatment of a slight tracheal disorder, is in robust good health and richly enjoys the fruits of his material success. Gabriele Klöterjahn is younger than he; her face betrays fatigue and a delicate constitution; shadows appear at the corners of her eyes, and a pale blue vein stands out under the fair skin of her forehead. Her present complaint—weakness, slight fever, and traces of blood when she coughs—appeared directly after the difficult birth of her first child, a lusty baby who immediately asserted his place in life "with prodigious energy and ruthlessness."

Detlev Spinell, a writer of no particular renown, has been resident at Einfried for a short time already. He has about him an air of illegitimacy, seemingly more dilettante than artist and more vacationer than patient. For some, he is merely amusing, an odd sort who affects the role of the unappreciated, solitary aesthete. Several inmates refer to him privately as "the dissipated baby." Once Klöterjahn returns to his flourishing business in the north, Spinell displays growing interest in his wife, and she finds a certain diversion in his conversation, eccentric as it is. He makes no secret of his dislike for her husband, insists that the name Klöterjahn is an affront to her, and queries her about her own family and her youth in Bremen. Upon learning that Gabriele and her father are amateur musicians, Spinell laments that the young woman sacrificed her artistic sensitivities to the domination of an acquisitive, boorish husband. Gabriele is vaguely charmed by this devotion; at the same time, her physical condition grows less encouraging.

One day at the end of February, a sleighing party is arranged for the patients, but she prefers not to take part. To no one's surprise, Spinell also remains behind. Gabriele and her frequent companion, Frau Spatz, retire to the salon. Spinell joins them there and proposes that Gabriele play something on the piano. He knows that her doctors have forbidden it, and she reminds him of this fact, but he invokes the image of her as a girl in the family garden in Bremen, as if to suggest that by satisfying his request she could undo her marriage, her submission to the odious Klöterjahn, and the illness that has resulted from bearing Klöterjahn's child. Finally, she consents and plays a few of Frédéric Chopin's nocturnes which have been left lying out in the room.

Then Spinell finds another volume. Gabriele takes it and begins to play as he sits reverently listening. It is the prelude to Richard Wagner's *Tristan und Isolde* (1865). The performance is inspired and moving, and when it ends, both sit without speaking. Frau Spatz, by now bored and uncomfortable, retires to her room. As the late afternoon shadows deepen, Spinell urges her to play the second act, the one in which Tristan and Isolde consummate their burning, illicit love. The music completely absorbs the pair at the piano. Gabriele passes to the opera's finale and plays Isolde's love-death. When it is finished, neither can speak until recalled to reality by the bells of the returning sleighs. Spinell rises, crosses the room, then sinks to his knees as if in veneration, while Gabriele sits pensively at the silent piano.

Two days later, her condition shows signs of worsening. Klöterjahn is notified and arrives with his infant son, irritated by the interruption of his business affairs. Spinell, meanwhile, writes Klöterjahn a long, laboriously worded letter in which he indulges all of his ecstatic devotion to Gabriele and his hatred of her husband. He calls her the personification of vulnerable, decadent loveliness, consecrated, in his words, to "death and beauty." He denounces Klöterjahn as her mortal enemy for having violated the deathly beauty of Gabriele's life and debased her by his own vulgar existence. When Klöterjahn receives the letter, he reviles Spinell as presumptuous, cowardly, and ridiculous. Yet his tirade is interrupted by a message that his wife has taken a turn for the worse and that he is needed at her bedside.

Spinell takes refuge in the garden. He gazes wistfully at Frau Klöterjahn's window and walks on, humming to himself the melody of the yearning motif from *Tristan und Isolde*. His reverie is cut short by the approach of a nursemaid with Klöterjahn's infant son in a perambulator. The sight of the chubby, happily screaming child is more than he can bear; he turns in consternation and walks the other way.

Themes and Meanings

The story's title prepares one for its allusions to the medieval tale of Tristan and Isolde's adulterous, ill-fated love. Yet Mann has transposed a number of its traditional motifs into a new key. Most striking is his casting of the writer-aesthete Spinell as a new Tristan, for Spinell is anything but lyrical, virile, attractive, or heroic, and therein lies the story's parodistic irony. Yet it is made thoroughly convincing by the appropriation, not of the medieval courtly epic, but of Richard Wagner's music-drama *Tristan und Isolde*. In "Tristan," the fateful potion which the two "lovers" share is not a magic drink, but Wagner's intoxicating music. The erotic thrall of music and text in *Tristan und Isolde* is potent, and in their susceptibility to the power of musical art both Gabriele Klöterjahn and Detlev Spinell are thoroughly Mannian characters.

One thematic strand reveals this story's kinship with another of Mann's early works, the family chronicle *Buddenbrooks* (1900; English translation, 1924). Gabriele Klöterjahn's family had entered a decline reminiscent of that in the Buddenbrook family: a waning of practical, bourgeois vitality and the corresponding emergence and refinement of artistic sensibilities. In Spinell's view, it would have been fitting, even desirable, for the decline to run its course. He harbors such a sublime vision of Gabriele's former life that he feels justified in reproaching Klöterjahn for intervening and presuming to reverse a natural process.

Spinell himself—solitary, unproductive, and even of dubious virility—bears the marks of a twilight generation. Among Mann's portraits of the artist, this is one of the most negative. If disease and artistic creativity go hand in hand, Spinell must be seen as a charlatan. It is questionable whether he is truly ill, and his writing seems to be an agonizing labor. He is clumsy, infantile, and ludicrous in his would-be elitism. While he lays claim to the intellect and the word as his avenging weapons against a philistine enemy, he is portrayed as unworthy to wield them.

Style and Technique

Richard Wagner's music is not only a subject and a medium of expression in Mann's "Tristan," but also a source of the typically Mannian device of the leitmotif. Like the musical "signatures" that mark characters, objects, and ideas in Wagner's operas, the literary leitmotif may emphasize physical traits, characterize speakers, signal deeper psychological patterns, or suggest characters' affinities and antipathies. Mann most successfully employs it in its full, "musical" value with clusters of associations. Perhaps the most striking example here is Gabriele's reminiscence of her youth, which Spinell embellishes to the point of factual distortion, insisting that a golden crown gleamed in her hair as she sat in the family garden in Bremen. He recalls it in this fantastic version as he "seduces" her to play the piano; he invokes the same images in his overwrought letter to Klöterjahn; and finally he torments himself with it by persisting in the use of Frau Klöterjahn's maiden name at the loathsome sight of the Klöterjahn baby, "Gabriele Eckhof's fat son."

Mann assumes that his reader will recognize Wagner's opera when he introduces it, though neither the composer nor the title is ever named. The clues come through his verbal re-creation of the music itself—its figures, motifs, orchestral voices, and dynamics—and then through quotation of Wagner's text. This distilled evocation of the Tristan and Isolde legend, certainly one of Mann's virtuoso performances, takes Wagner's achievement one step further, as it were: For in the opera the consummation of forbidden love is unambiguously represented in word and music; in "Tristan" it is both sublimated and evaded (if it can be called love at all) in words alone. Spinell and Frau Klöterjahn do not even touch, yet what they partake of is as binding as if they had become lovers. In Mann's terms, Gabriele's ominously rapid physical decline in the days following confirms the fact. Her imminent end was already implicit in the love-death of the legendary Isolde, the musical motif that dominated and ended the rapturous scene at the piano.

As for Tristan-Spinell, his "seduction" does succeed in estranging Gabriele Klöterjahn from husband and child, but only at the price of her physical collapse and his own exposure to Klöterjahn's rage. In the story's last section, the mystical ecstasy has reverted to ironic parody. Life has the final word in the grotesque garden scene, where the shrieking, jubilantly robust baby appears with his nurse before the dazzling aureole of the sinking sun— almost a travesty of madonna and child to mock the defeated Spinell.

Michael Ritterson

THE TRUMPET

Author: Walter de la Mare (1873-1956)
Type of plot: Symbolic
Time of plot: Late Victorian
Locale: A village in England
First published: 1936

Principal characters:

PHILIP, a small boy, the son of the rector
DICK, another small boy, the illegitimate son of the rector's
    former parlor maid
MRS. SULLIVAN, the rector's cook

The Story

It is nearly midnight on October 31, the night before All Saints' Day. The tiny church is deserted. The beams of the full moon have not yet pierced its darkness directly, but here and there a marble head, a wing tip, a pointing finger gleams coldly.

A stealthy footfall crunches on the rain-soaked gravel, a key is heard turning in a lock, a toy lantern emerges from behind the vestry curtain. The bearer is a small, pale, tousled boy wearing a coat over a pajama top and old flannel pants. He is shivering from the cold and from qualms and forebodings. He calls low and hoarsely, "Dick, are you there?" When there is no answer, he timidly enters a pew, plumps down on the hassock at his feet, rapidly repeats a prayer and half-covertly crosses himself. While he is admiring the gilded figure of an angel above a large tomb, he hears a faint shuffle in the vestry. He drops out of sight and wails, "Oh, oh, oh, oh!" No response. He is certain that this must be the friend he is expecting but worries that it is not. He leaps up and flashes the lantern into the glittering eyes of a dwarfish and motionless shape that is wearing a battered black mask. He shudders with rage and terror while Dick roars with laughter.

Philip angrily tells his friend to be quiet and to remember that he is in a church. Dick is at once solemn and contrite. He explains that he is late because he was first waiting for his father to finish reading and then stationed himself by the gate where Philip's mother had told his mother that "they" could be seen and, besides, he hardly expected Philip to come. Philip retorts that he said he would come, that he burned his hands on the rope and fell halfway from his bedroom window sill to the lawn, and that he did not know that Dick's father could read. Asked if his father would have whacked him much if he had caught him leaving, Dick replies that his mother will not let him punish the boy. Dick then says that his mother came home yesterday with an enormous bundle of old clothes, including a green silk dressing gown, which he is now wearing under his jacket. Philip immediately recognizes it as his own but says loftily that he does not want it now. He suddenly remarks that if Dick's real father had found him skulking in the church he would whack him hot and strong. Dick stiffens and denies this, adding that his real father leaves him alone although he went rabbiting with him one night last summer until the moon came up. Besides, his father is dead.

Philip immediately contradicts this. He heard his people reading aloud from a newspaper only a few days ago and he knows what has become of the man. He says cruelly that if Dick's other father had not been Chapel, he would never have had any father to show and his mother could not have continued to live in the village. The boys make friends again. Dick asserts that he will be a sailor and a comfort to his mother.

Now there is a discussion about ghosts with Philip claiming, unconvincingly, that he does not believe in them and came only because Dick dared him to come. He promises to dare Dick in a minute.

Dick goes outside to reconnoiter for ghosts while Philip stares again at the huge figure of the angel clasping a gilded trumpet held firmly at a small distance from her lips. This angel has been for some years the habitual center of his Sunday evening reveries whenever he is escorted to church by the family cook. He has asked the cook why the angel was made so that she cannot blow the trumpet, but the real question in his mind is what would happen if she did. Mrs. Sullivan, the cook, has suggested that the angel is depicted as waiting for the Last Day. Philip still wants to know what will happen after the Last Day; he is fascinated by any reference to an angel or a trumpet. As he stares at the angel, he meditates also on his ambivalent attitude toward Dick, whom he admires, despises, envies, and sometimes hates bitterly. He knows that Dick can detect these secret feelings but seems not to resent them.

Twelve o'clock strikes; nothing happens. Philip has lost faith in the angel's power. As he sits there, cold and sick, he hears a fiendish screech and sees a lean, faceless shape coming toward his pew. Recognizing Dick, he is despite his terror passionately angry. He dares Dick to stay on in the church alone; if Dick is afraid, he will never again be allowed to enter Philip's house or yard. Philip now proposes several impractical dares and finally orders Dick to climb almost to the roof and blow the trumpet. He says that if anyone blows the trumpet it will be the Last Day. Dick asks what the Bible says about angels, and Philip recounts many instances of their mention and then describes their awesome power, insisting that the Devil has crowds of angels under his command. He then talks about various trumpets mentioned in the Bible, concluding with, "The trumpet shall sound and the dead shall be raised." Thus Philip cleverly and slyly prods Dick into climbing.

Philip starts to leave. Dick detects scorn on his face and says that he has always done anything that Philip asked. He begins to climb. Philip suddenly realizes how enormously high the angel rises. He calls to Dick to come down, but Dick cannot hear him. Philip leaves the church but flies back to tempt Dick with the news that someone, not a man and not a woman, is coming. He is sobbing with rage, apprehension, and despair.

Dick shouts down to ask if they can still be friends if he blows with all his might and the trumpet does not sound. Philip begs him to come down, but Dick declares calmly, "I believe it *is* hollow, and I *think* she knows I'm here. You won't say I was afraid now! Philip, I'd do anything in the world for you."

The tapering wooden trumpet splinters off from the angel's grasp and Dick, clutching it, falls to the flagstones below. He is dead. In anguish, Philip creeps home.

Themes and Meanings

"The Trumpet" is considered by some critics to be Walter de la Mare's finest tale, but all find it difficult to classify. Unlike many others, it is not a ghost story, yet it is permeated by a ghostly atmosphere. Strictly speaking, it is not a moral fable, and while it is about children, it is not children's literature. Perhaps it is best termed a symbolic tragedy: the failure of the individual to pierce the veil between the known and the unknown, the natural and the supernatural.

In the ghostly silence of the moonlit church, the marble angel is as real as are the little boys. The recitation of stories of angels in the Bible authenticates their existence while the trumpet due to announce the Last Day poses questions about life, death, and an afterlife for the believer and the unbeliever alike. Mysticism is graphic here. Only Mrs. Sullivan's conversation offers a criterion of normality.

The clue to one meaning of this haunting tragedy lies in its two epigraphs: "For Brutus, as you know, was Caesar's angel . . ." and "And he said . . . am I my brother's keeper?" The two boys are half brothers but do not know it. This suggests that all men are brothers but fail to realize it and to behave as brothers should. Although Philip is the pathetic embodiment of arrogance and cruelty, he is understood and worshiped by the greathearted, happy, mischievous imp, Dick. Despite social distinctions and differing levels of education, brotherly love is possible, but the price is high. Dick dies in an effort to gratify his brother's obsessive urge for knowledge of life's mysteries.

Style and Technique

The descriptions in the story are pure poetry, but there are no words for their own sake. Each detail helps to build the atmosphere, to delineate character, or to further the action. The eerie quality is established at once by the date, the midnight hour, the cemetery, the dark church with fitful moonbeams playing on marble tombs, the discussion about ghosts, and the stealthy manner of Philip. His obsession introduces the ultimate mystery.

Character is built by the boys' conversations: Philip's snobbish attitude toward the used clothing that his mother has given to Dick's mother; Philip's very unkind remarks about Dick's mother and presumed father; Dick's praise of the kindness of Philip's mother and his own determination to be a comfort to his mother.

Small details serve to foreshadow the tragedy: The law of gravitation is mentioned, as are the brittle walls of Dick's neat skull; Philip announces that he would like to see Dick's ghost; Dick's beautiful singing voice "would need no angelic tuition—even in a better world." Disaster is implicit from the start.

Although some of the conversation between the boys is completely realistic, that of Philip is less believable when he recounts at length stories from the Bible. It is true that he has been forced to sit through his father's sermons since he was a baby and has searched the Bible for information about angels and trumpets. Yet the reader finds the glib recital unnatural in the mouth of a small boy, even one with a haunting obsession. Again there is the mingling of the real and the unreal.

De la Mare's true triumph in this weird story is his use of two little boys and a church monument to create an atmosphere of refined spiritual terror that symbolizes man's urge to find answers to life's mystery.

Dorothy B. Aspinwall

TRUTH AND LIES

Author: Reynolds Price (1933-   )
Type of plot: Social realism
Time of plot: The 1960's
Locale: Kinley, a small town near the North Carolina–Virginia border
First published: 1970

> *Principal characters:*
> SARAH WILSON, a forty-two-year-old schoolteacher, the wife
>   of Nathan Wilson
> NATHAN WILSON, her husband
> ELLA SCOTT, an eighteen-year-old former student of Mrs.
>   Wilson and the mistress of Nathan
> MR. WHITLOW, a stationmaster

The Story

Sarah Wilson has spent her life in Kinley, a rural community in that area north of Raleigh, North Carolina, and south of Richmond, Virginia. She has left the area only for the four years she spent in college preparing to become a teacher. When she finished her training, she had no real reason to return to Kinley. Both her parents were dead, and she was their only child. She decided to take the best offer when she entered the job market, but instead took the first offer. It came from Nathan Wilson, who had been principal for three years of the school in Ogburn, the next small town from Kinley. She married him that June before she began her first and only teaching job.

As the story opens, Sarah is in an open field at night beside the railroad tracks. She sits in her car, and at eight o'clock, she flashes the lights. Someone comes running down the embankment, through the high grasses, to her car. It is Ella Scott, her former student, now an eighteen-year-old woman, who thinks that Nathan is in the car. Sarah has come because when Nathan came home drunk, she found an unsigned note in his pocket, arranging the meeting.

When she shows Ella the note, she comments that Ella's handwriting has improved. The meeting between them is remarkably calm. Ella is properly respectful of Sarah, and she is totally candid in telling her about the relationship between herself and Nathan. Sarah, accustomed to hurt and disappointment, is not going to allow her emotions to control this tense situation.

It is hot, and she suggests to Ella that they will be more comfortable if they drive around and talk. Ella gets into the car, and as they drive the story of her meetings with Nathan, which now have been going on for eight months, unfolds, as does the story of Sarah's childhood and eventual marriage to Nathan.

Sarah drives toward the railroad station, which at this time of night should be closed, because the last train of the day has left. Mr. Whitlow, the stationmaster, is just coming out of the station when they arrive, and he talks with them, revealing elements of Sarah's background. He has known her most of her life.

When they leave the station, Sarah drives down the Ogburn road, past Holt Ferguson's land, which runs on for a quarter mile. She reveals to Ella that this land had once belonged to her grandfather. It passed on to her father, whose marriage house, the house in which Sarah was brought up, was built on it. She tells of how, being an only child, she kept begging her parents for brothers, for company. Her mother always responded, "Sarah, I thought we were happy. Why aren't you satisfied?" When Sarah was twelve, her mother had another child. It was born dead, and four months later, never having recovered from childbirth, her mother died at her twelve-year-old daughter's feet.

Sarah and her father went on living quite happily in the house until her father had a stroke when the girl was fifteen. At that point, Holt Ferguson's wife, Aunt Alice, who was the father's half sister, got Holt to move their whole family into the house with Sarah and her father. Their children were boys, and although Sarah had always wanted a brother, she regarded these children as intruders. Aunt Alice had always had designs on this property that her stepfather had owned.

When Sarah's father died two years later, the girl assumed that the property would be hers. She had always dreamed that one day she would own it. Eventually, however, it was revealed to her that Holt had bought the whole property from Sarah's father for enough money to send Sarah to college.

Sarah goes on to say that she and Nathan, who had spent his life until he came to Ogburn running away from himself, had been unable to have children. She tells Ella that the reason they are childless is that Nathan is sterile. She then begs Ella to give up Nathan.

Ella then reveals that she has been planning to give up Nathan, but she needs to see him one more time. Sarah discourages this final meeting, telling Ella that she will tell Nathan anything she wants conveyed to him. Finally, Ella reveals that she had sent Nathan the note and had tried to see him that night to tell him that she had taken the bus to Raleigh that week and "ditched a baby in a nigger kitchen for two hundred dollars," just as she had promised Nathan she would. She said she would pay her half of the two hundred dollars as soon as she could.

Themes and Meanings

"Truth and Lies" is really the story of a life that has been sustained through compromise. Sarah Wilson never got what she wanted from life, and as the action of this story develops, the reader sees a woman desperately trying to cling to whatever she can. In this case, she is clinging to a marriage that was initially based on need rather than on love. The stationmaster tells Ella that Sarah got out of Kinley, but that her mistake was in coming back. He asks her what brought her back: "*Love*, won't it, Sarah?" and she replies, "I don't remember that far. Maybe it was," and changes the subject.

Sarah has no illusions about Nathan. The first time she ever saw him, he was drunk, and he has more or less stayed drunk ever since. He told her on the first night she met him at a Christmas party that he was running away from himself, that he had hurt women in the past. By the time Sarah married him, she had grown accustomed to not having what she wanted: She had no siblings, her mother died trying to give her one, her father died, and she learned that the property that she had always thought would be hers would not be. The reader is also told that even in her youth, Sarah's face had "never won praise."

Sarah has lied to Ella, quite unnecessarily, in the hope of making her lose interest in Nathan. When she finally realizes that Ella knows that she has lied to her, Sarah can only say to herself as she drives her car homeward alone, killing a rabbit that runs into its path, "How could I, why should I tell the truth when I thought I could save what was left of our life."

One is left with the feeling that nothing will change. Nathan will go on drinking. He will find other women. Yet he needs Sarah, just as Sarah needs him, and they will play out the charade that they began twenty years earlier because they can do little else and because they have grown accustomed to living in this fashion.

Style and Technique

Reynolds Price is a consummate storyteller whose writing has done for Warren County, North Carolina, what William Faulkner's did for the area around Oxford, Mississippi. Price, born and reared in rural Macon, North Carolina, is close to his roots, and he tells his tales in the long monologues that are characteristic of much Southern conversation. He captures the conflicts and frustrations of people living in relative isolation, people who go to school, sometimes finish, sometimes do not, and then go on to work in textile mills. The women, as he notes in this story, work in the mills until they marry, then they begin producing children in substantial numbers.

Sarah is a cut above the people in her small town. Her father owned land. He earned eighty-five dollars a month as a station agent. The family, while not rich, had been relatively refined, and its members valued one another. The reader also learns that the family never stopped talking except from fatigue, and Sarah's lengthy speeches to Ella are excellent examples of the incessant talk that characterizes Southerners of the kind Price writes about in this story.

The rhythm of Southern speech obviously resonates in Price's memory, and he records it with a fidelity found in such Southern writers as Faulkner, Guy Owen, Thad Stem, and Eudora Welty. His stories are subtle, and in them he drops only the faintest hints at times of the convolutions that are the underpinnings of their action. In the present story, for example, the reader learns that there was no smile when Ella and Sarah recognized each other, and shortly thereafter, the absence of a smile is noted again. The implication is that Sarah's life has been lived without smiles. She has always done what she must, not what she would have preferred.

R. Baird Shuman

TWENTY-SIX MEN AND A GIRL

Author: Maxim Gorky (Alexey Maksimovich Peshkov, 1868-1936)
Type of plot: Social realism
Time of plot: The late 1890's
Locale: Provincial Russian town
First published: "Dvadtsat'shest' i odna," 1899 (English translation, 1902)

> *Principal characters:*
> A GROUP OF UNNAMED PRETZEL MAKERS
> TANYA, a sixteen-year-old seamstress
> A HANDSOME BAKER, a former soldier

The Story

Gorky begins this first-person narrative with a description of a wretched working environment: a basement-level bakery where twenty-six men, "living machines," as the narrator calls them, work long hours making pretzels. The room is cramped, airless, and stuffy. The huge oven that dominates the room stares pitilessly at the workers like a horrible monster. The workers themselves move and act like automatons, for their vital feelings have been crushed by their ceaseless toil. Only when they begin to sing do they feel a sense of lightness and gain a glimpse of freedom.

In addition to their singing, the twenty-six workers have one other source of consolation. Every morning, a sixteen-year-old seamstress named Tanya stops by the workshop to ask for pretzels. To these grim, coarse men, the cheerful girl seems a precious treasure, and her regular visits gradually make her a sacred being to them. As the narrator notes, all humans need something to worship; Tanya thus has become their idol. Although the men often make rude jokes about women, they never once consider viewing Tanya with anything other than the highest respect.

This situation, however, is not destined to last. A new man, a former soldier, is hired at the bakery next door, and this fellow turns out to be a dashing, bold figure who enjoys regaling the twenty-six pretzel makers with tales of his prowess with women. The pretzel makers find him an engaging individual, but his boasting touches a sensitive nerve. The head baker rashly suggests that not all women would fall prey to the boaster's charms. This assertion pricks the dandy's vanity, and he presses the baker to name the person who could resist his attentions. Angrily, the baker mutters Tanya's name, and the dandy immediately announces that he will seduce the girl within two weeks.

The pretzel makers are highly agitated by the dandy's challenge, and they become obsessed with the question of whether Tanya will indeed be able to spurn the man. Imperceptibly, this new element of curiosity and inquisitive-

ness creeps into their relationship with Tanya, and on the final day of the
two-week period they understand for the first time how much they have put
on the line through this foolish rivalry with the dandy. When Tanya makes
her regular visit that morning, they greet her with silence, and after an awkward exchange of words, she runs out without her pretzels. Later, the dashing baker enters and instructs the workers to keep their eye on the cellar
door across the yard from their building. Horrified, the men watch as Tanya
and the baker go into the cellar. After an anxious interval, they see the baker
emerge, followed a short time later by Tanya, with eyes shining in joy and
happiness.

For the pretzel makers this is unbearable. They rush out of their building,
surround Tanya, and begin to abuse her loudly with crude obscenities and insults. As they see it, she has let them down and betrayed them, and they will
make her pay for this misdeed. Yet after bearing their jeers with astonishment for a few moments, she suddenly flares up in anger herself. Proudly she
begins to walk away, breaking through their circle as if they were not even
present. Turning toward them, she calls them scum, and then, proud, erect,
and beautiful, she leaves them behind forever. The workers must now return
to their underground prison to work as before, but they have lost the one
precious human element in their otherwise dreary world.

Themes and Meanings

Dominating the first part of the story is Gorky's sympathy for the plight of
the downtrodden workers in Russia. His initial description of the bakers
accentuates the oppressive effects that a life of relentless toil can have on the
human spirit. His pretzel makers seem barely human. Deprived of sunlight
and freedom, they have nothing to say to one another, and they do not even
have the energy to curse one another. Even their songs, which are the only
vehicle of transcendence or release that they possess, are permeated with the
sorrow and yearning of slaves.

Complementing Gorky's compassion for the oppressed is his anger toward
the oppressor. The pretzel makers' boss is never seen in the story. He seems
to exist as an invincible force who has placed numerous restrictions on the
workers but who does not deign even to visit them. Instead, the huge stove
which looms so large in the bakery stands as a silent emblem for the boss and
his rapacious, insatiable appetite. All he cares for is productivity: during the
two-week period in which the workers were preoccupied with the dandy's
pursuit of Tanya, the boss managed to increase their work by an additional
five hundred pounds of flour a day.

Gorky's story offers more than an exposé of difficult working conditions in
prerevolutionary Russia. His treatment of the complex emotional attitude
demonstrated by the workers toward Tanya reveals a sensitive understanding
of human psychology. In the workers' early reverence for Tanya one finds a

basic human desire for objects worthy of adoration, and in their willingness to subject their idol to a test one sees a characteristic human weakness: a perverse impulse to submit one's idols to outside challenges. As for the dandy, Gorky indicates that his eagerness to prove his power as a ladies' man belies a deep-rooted sense of insecurity. Many people, the narrator declares, are so needy of having something distinctive in their lives that they will even embrace an illness or a vice rather than risk seeming average or ordinary.

Finally, in the workers' outraged reaction to Tanya's conduct at the end of the story, Gorky reveals the astonishing excesses to which people will go when their cherished assumptions are undermined or overturned. Tanya never asked these men to put her on a pedestal, nor did she ever pledge not to become infatuated with an attractive man. It is they who engineered a shallow test for her, and, as the final scene of the story indicates, it is they who are acting basely, not she. Tanya herself perceives this, and thus she walks away proud and undefiled, while they are left alone, bitter and abandoned. Gorky's story is filled with pathos and irony. Weighed down by the burdens of oppressive labor and confinement, these men make a feeble attempt to demonstrate that they possess something of worth in the midst of their wretched environment. As it turns out, however, this gesture only contributes further to their inescapable misery.

Style and Technique

The emotionally charged style of "Twenty-six Men and a Girl" is characteristic of Gorky's early narrative prose. The writer reveals a predilection for dramatic, bold metaphors and imagery, such as the huge oven, which he compares to the ugly head of a fantastic monster and which stares pitilessly at the workers as if they were slaves. Gorky's descriptions often have a sustained symbolic resonance. At the outset of the story, the narrator notes that the basement windows are covered so that the sunlight cannot reach the workers. Later, he states that Tanya had in some sense taken the place of the sun for them. It is significant, then, that the day on which Tanya consummates her relationship with the dandy turns out to be wet and rainy. On that day, the workers lose their sun, both literally and figuratively.

Gorky's emotional style also manifests itself in the passage about the workers' singing. His prose in that section is extremely lyrical and rhythmic. The Russian lines pulsate with a palpable beat, and one observes a complex interweaving of recurring consonant and vowel sounds. This lyrical, dynamic dimension apparent in Gorky's early prose style had a significant impact on the prose of the subsequent generation of Russian writers.

Julian W. Connolly

THE TWO DROVERS

Author: Sir Walter Scott (1771-1832)
Type of plot: Tale
Time of plot: The 1790's
Locale: The border country between Scotland and England
First published: 1827

Principal characters:
  ROBIN OIG M'COMBICH, a highland drover
  HARRY WAKEFIELD, an English drover
  JANET OF TOMAHOURICH, Robin's aunt, a seer
  HUGH MORRISON, a lowland farmer

The Story

Since the story describes an earlier time—about thirty years before the date of its telling—and tells of a way of life unfamiliar to many readers, the narrator begins by describing the occupation of the drovers, men who herded highland cattle from the fairs in Scotland down across the border to markets in England. The two drovers of the story, Robin Oig M'Combich, a Scottish highlander, and Harry Wakefield, an English lowlander, are classic representatives of their cultures. Robin embodies the fierce spirit of the Highlands: he takes pride in his skill as a drover, his highland heritage, and his name, said to be taken from the most famous of the highland outlaws, Rob Roy, his grandfather's friend. Harry Wakefield, "the model of Old England's merry yeomen," takes a yeoman's pride in his work and in his prowess as a boxer and wrestler.

After the Doune Fair, as Robin prepares to set off to the south, his aunt, Janet of Tomahourich, delays him so that she can perform the *deasil*, a traditional ceremony to protect the herd and the drover from harm. She cuts short her performance and warns Robin of danger, urging him to delay his journey. With the second sight of the highland seer, she sees English blood on his dirk, the dagger that the highlander carries for protection. Less a believer in highland superstition than his aunt, Robin tries to ignore her plea, but she insists that he leave his dirk behind. Finally, he agrees to entrust it to another drover, Hugh Morrison, who plans to follow Robin and Harry to the English markets.

Although they have traveled together for three years, Robin and Harry understand little of each other's culture. Harry cannot master Robin's unfamiliar tongue, and beyond their cattle and their occupation they have little about which to talk. Their personal friendship is deep, if unspoken, however, for they have shared many journeys, and on several occasions they have saved each other from danger.

On the fateful journey in the story, however, their personal friendship cannot overcome the cultural differences between them. Their falling out begins after they cross the English border and separate temporarily to seek pasturage for their herds. Harry negotiates for his pasture with a bailiff, the agent for a landowner. Unaware of Harry's agreement, Robin secures permission for the same field from the landowner himself. The misunderstanding between the landlord and his bailiff becomes a quarrel between Harry and Robin. Bitterly Harry takes his herd to a poorer pasture, feeling that he has been mistreated and tricked by his Scottish friend.

That evening, Robin tries to patch up the quarrel, but Harry, urged on by his countrymen in the local inn, refuses to concede without a fight. He challenges Robin to settle their differences with his fists. When Robin declines to take on the much-larger Harry at his own game, Harry calls him a coward, taunts him, and knocks him to the ground. Robin reaches under his plaid for his dirk, the natural weapon of the highlander, before he remembers that he has given it to Morrison. Harboring the humiliation of Harry's punches and the taunts of the Englishmen in the inn, Robin sets out to find Morrison and retrieve the weapon.

Two hours later, after walking six miles each way, he returns to the inn and confronts Wakefield. By this time, Harry has forgotten his injuries, and he offers his hand to his friend, but Robin pulls the knife and fatally stabs Harry through the heart. He has recovered his honor and shown that a highlander knows how to fight. Then he turns himself over to the law.

At the trial in Carlisle, the English judge recognizes that Robin's act was not an act of cowardice but one prompted by a different code of honor. Had Robin responded to Harry's taunts by pulling his dagger and stabbing his friend on the spot, the judge could have understood his crime as a highlander's natural response to provocation. In that case, the charge would have been manslaughter. Yet the two-hour delay while Robin went off to secure his dirk changed manslaughter into premeditated murder in the judge's mind. In such a case the judge is compelled to demand the death penalty.

The judge's distinctions are beyond Robin's comprehension. He considers his death the natural conclusion to his destiny. "I give a life for the life I took," he says as the tragic story ends, "and what can I do more?"

Themes and Meanings

Sir Walter Scott's best work nearly always treats Scotland's emergence to nationhood in the eighteenth century, following its union with England in 1707. The contact and struggles between the two allied nations shaped the Scottish identity, as Scotland changed its clannish past for its part in Great Britain. In the cross-cultural contact among the migratory drovers, Scott found a metaphor for the larger assimilation of Scotland into Britain and for the tumult brought on by this process of cultural transition. The friendship of the highland Scot and the English Yeoman, like the alliance between the two nations, is a recent and fragile one.

Robin's contact with English culture on his journeys across the border has diminished his belief in some Scottish superstitions. He seems to be humoring his aunt, for example, when he responds to her prophetic vision of doom by turning his dirk over to Morrison for safekeeping. For him "second sight" has become Scottish superstition. Yet he is still profoundly Scottish in his attitudes. His belief in honor to the point of death and his final act of giving his life for the life he has taken embody the traditional code of the Highlands. Similarly, Harry Wakefield is not so chauvinistically English as his countrymen in the inn. His love of boxing and his bumptious eagerness to settle their differences with a brawl represents the traditional attitude of the English yeoman, but his willingness to settle for a face-saving charade rather than a real fight marks a departure from traditional attitudes. Their occupation has begun the process of cultural assimilation, but neither Robin nor Harry understands the other's culture well enough to prevent the misunderstanding that leads to their deaths. Their friendship falls victim to the traditional distrust between highland Scots and lowland English produced over centuries by cultural isolation and national prejudice.

Scott adds a historical perspective to this cultural theme. By placing the story about thirty years before the time of its telling, Scott implies that his audience, given the advantages of the later historical point of view, will see some differences that the actors in the story fail to see. Like the English judge, they will recognize that Robin did not act out of cowardice. Unlike the judge, however, later readers may also understand Robin's unrelenting vengeance as an expression of his culture rather than as premeditation. Human beings are always limited by the perspective of their time and place. As well as showing the power of culture to mold human actions, "The Two Drovers" also suggests that men can only see this determining force of culture with the benefit of historical distance. The thirty-year gap between the story and its telling gives the reader the benefit of this distance.

Style and Technique

Scott embodies the historical and cultural differences he describes in differences of language. Robin speaks the language of the Highlands, a dialect frequently requiring parenthetical translation even for readers of Scott's time. Harry's language is that of an uneducated farmer from the north of England, and it contrasts with the more literate and literary prose of the judge of the English court where Robin is tried.

The gaps of understanding between cultures that lead to Harry's murder, Robin's execution, and the failure of understanding on the part of the judge lie at the heart of the pattern of tragic inevitability that gives this story its force. None of the actors can be said to be acting only out of individual character or to be revealing personal flaws. Each articulates the limitations of his culture. Scott sets the tone of tragic inevitability with the prophecy of Janet of Tomahourich who, like the ghost in *Hamlet* (c. 1600-1601) or the witches in *Macbeth* (1606), prophesies her nephew's doom. As the story moves forward, her prophecy becomes increasingly probable until the final meeting of Robin and Harry brings the inevitable conclusion. In his longer novels, Scott usually found ways for comic resolution to the problem of cultural assimilation: The hero could learn how to live between two cultures, between his traditional Scottish identity and his growing British allegiance. Yet in this short story, Scott presents the confrontation in stark and tragic terms. Only the distance of history, that later view shared by Scott and his readers, can provide the larger perspective necessary to understand the destruction caused by cultural prejudice and historically determined shortsightedness.

Paul B. Davis

THE TWO ELENAS

Author: Carlos Fuentes (1928-   )
Type of plot: Domestic realism
Time of plot: The 1960's
Locale: Mexico City
First published: "Las dos Elenas," 1964 (English translation, 1973)

>*Principal characters:*
>VICTOR, the narrator-protagonist, an architect in Mexico City
>ELENA, his wife
>DONA ELENA, Elena's mother
>DON JOSÉ, Elena's father

The Story

Dona Elena's complaint regarding the conduct of her daughter, Elena, the previous Sunday (she defended the idea that a woman can live with two men) causes Victor, an architect, to recall the night that he and Elena (his wife) saw the film *Jules and Jim* (1962). That night over dinner, as he recalls, they discussed the film and Elena arrived at certain conclusions—for example, that misogyny is the condition of love, that one day Victor would want another man to share their lives, and that she wanted an outfit like the one worn by Jeanne Moreau in the film. As he pondered the likelihood of the second proposition, he watched Elena among their men friends, imagining how each of them would supplement what he himself might be incapable of offering her. Later, they walked home through cobblestone streets ("a meeting ground for their common inclinations toward assimilation") and made love to the music of Brother Lateef.

At Sunday dinner with her parents, Elena and her father begin to argue about blacks when Dona Elena saves the day by changing the subject to her own activities during the past week. While she speaks, Victor observes her gestures and appearance, especially her caressing fingers, slim wrist, full arms, and taut breasts. After dinner, Don José excuses himself to reminisce over some old boleros. In another room, Elena falls asleep on her husband's lap while he and his mother-in-law carry on a conversation about Veracruz, which is in fact a description of the fundamental difference between the two Elenas: their origins and, consequently, their attitudes.

The following morning, Victor prepares to leave for work, and Elena outlines her schedule for that day, which includes a film, a class, some appointments, readings, and other activities, and mentions some plans for later on that week. On the way to work, Victor attempts to sort out that barrage of information, wondering if perhaps a vacation might not bring their lives closer together again. Suddenly, he finds himself steering his car, not in the direction of his work, but toward Lomas, the house of Elena's parents, where his other Elena awaits him.

Themes and Meanings

The cultural schizophrenia brought about by the Spanish conquest of the New World is the theme underlying the events of "The Two Elenas." The protagonist, Victor, is simultaneously attracted to two women who are completely different types. His wife is a composite of all that is foreign: She sees French and American motion pictures, drives a British car, glorifies the American black, studies French and reads French poetry, and listens to American jazz. In another sense, her ideas and behavior are foreign, that is, strange or uncharacteristic within the context of her upbringing. Victor admires her so-called naturalness, but the trait he describes has less to do with nature than with an adolescent sort of rebellion against all established norms of conduct. She denies rules, not to replace them with others, but to open a door, suggesting a fascination with the innovative. Her motives are dubious, however, because she merely challenges, regardless of the standard in question. For example, Elena continually strives to subvert the middle-class values of her parents by shocking their bourgeois morality, while at the same time, to her liberal-minded friends she dismisses the possibility of unfaithfulness since it has become as much a rule as Communion every Friday used to be. Her refusal to conform may account for her modern, vivacious attitude, but it is also a sign of immaturity or incomplete development.

The consequent limitations on her ability to understand are like a blindness that she has in common with her father; both are asleep, but whereas her dreams belong to other places, his belong to other times. Through nostalgia he sustains the myth of a victorious postrevolutionary society of opportunity, indifferent to what lies beyond the nation's borders and ignorant of the country's reality for the majority. His static vision prevents him from engaging in conversation at any level other than that of clichés, for even the most minor variation or concession would threaten his entire ideological structure. Don José's adverse physical reaction to any such disturbing notions demonstrates a fundamental inability to adapt to change. What Victor refers to in the text as "assimilation" is the resolution of the old and the new: His father-in-law's intolerance of the new is one type of failure to assimilate, while Elena's reactionism is another.

Dona Elena lives in the present, and yet she remains mindful of her past. Her reality is rooted in Mexico City (especially the Lomas area, a wealthy suburb) of the 1960's, amid her family. She willingly and conscientiously fulfills the duties and obligations that go with her social position. Nevertheless, her origins in Veracruz, a region synonymous with nature and life, determine her real character. Certain physical features such as her black, wakeful eyes, transparent skin that exposes her veins, taut breasts, caressing fingers, and full arms are the visible evidence of strong bonds with the authentic, intrinsically Mexican existence of the Gulf region. Dona Elena is a mature woman capable of understanding and reconciliation (be it of contrary points of view, present and past, or different life-styles). She is indeed the center of her family, for she supplies the deficiencies, makes up for shortcomings, and resolves potentially volatile situations.

As it is surprising to learn that it is Victor rather than Elena who is involved in a *ménage à trois*, so also it is interesting to note that it is not Elena but Victor who is undergoing an identity crisis. To the extent that he can be defined by who he is not (his opposite or complement), Victor has two nearly antithetical identities. Since both women have a complementary function in his life (compared to the supplementary role played by the other men in Elena's circle), they would seem to be of equal significance in that definition of being. Yet, in spite of his conscious desire to find completion in his wife, when Victor "liberates" himself and "ascends" to his other Elena, he seems to find his true complement.

Style and Technique

Carlos Fuentes is a master storyteller, for he has a remarkable ability to create suspense, surprise, and interest as he leads the reader from beginning to end of his tales. Often filmlike in technique, Fuentes' stories abound in direct discourse and visual images. Particularly effective uses of the script mode, for example, are the opening monologue, which draws the reader into the story; the intercalated speech of Elena and Dona Elena among the thoughts of Victor, foreshadowing other parallels between them; the fragments of conversation and the alternating voices, which vary the pace of the text; and the use of highly character-specific comments, which reinforce, animate, and instantly re-create a given character. Moreover, the numerous visual descriptions seem to function like the lens of a camera, complementing the audio and focusing on significant details which lend to the accomplished creation of character, or perhaps contribute to advancing the plot or developing the theme.

Fuentes' well-known proclivity toward rhetorical ornamentation surfaces only briefly in "The Two Elenas." One passage illustrating this tendency is the scene which describes lovemaking in terms of saxophone music and seems to function only as a tenuous link between the night in bed and the conversation at the dinner table. Many readers will find such passages unnecessary, a distraction from the story's authentic dialogue, credible characters, and captivating plot, but others will revel in Fuentes' baroque stylization.

Krista Ratkowski Carmona

TWO GALLANTS

Author: James Joyce (1882-1941)
Type of plot: Parody
Time of plot: c. 1900-1907
Locale: Dublin
First published: 1914

> *Principal characters:*
> LENEHAN, a parasite and "leech"
> CORLEY, a bully and seducer
> A "SLAVEY," a domestic who is preyed upon by Corley

The Story

"Two Gallants" sets up a series of expectations that are violated and reversed at the end of the story. First, the title suggests a world of gallantry, romance, perhaps a doubling of lovers similar to a Shakespearean comedy. This expectation is reinforced by the narrator's description of the place and mood:

> The streets, shuttered for the repose of Sunday, swarmed with a gaily coloured crowd. Like illumined pearls the lamps shone from the summits of their tall poles upon the living texture below which, changing shape and hue unceasingly, sent up into the warm grey evening air an unchanging, unceasing murmur.

There is even a moon shining above them. Also, the conversation of the two main characters, Lenehan and Corley, suggests a romantic involvement. Lenehan calls Corley a "gay Lothario" and wonders if Corley can succeed or "bring it off" with the girl whom he has recently met. Yet there are some discordant notes that undercut the romantic mood. Corley has accepted gifts of cigarettes and cigars from the girl rather than giving gifts to her. Lenehan speaks of the romantic code of giving gifts such as flowers and chocolates as a "mug's game." Both Corley and Lenehan despise the conventional love game because they do not profit from it. The fictional rules of romantic love do not seem to apply here.

Nor do the characters seem right for a romantic tale. Corley is described as "squat and ruddy" with a "large, globular and oily" head. Furthermore, his behavior and conversation show him to be rude and a braggart. He brags about his conquests of women and at being in the know at police headquarters. He is the son of a policeman and a "conqueror," which seems inappropriate for a lover or a patriotic Irishman. In contrast, Lenehan is a hanger-on and a "leech." His main role seems to be as an audience for Corley's bragging tales. If Corley talks only about himself, then Lenehan has no self: His pleasures, and his life, are vicarious. The characters, then, seem to be in the wrong story. They should be in a satiric comedy or a realistic story about Irish life.

The most important violation of the romantic story is, perhaps, the break in the narrative structure. The reader has been led to expect a romantic quest narrative; Corley is sent off to see if he can succeed with the girl, however, and the story then concentrates on the sycophant Lenehan. Why does Joyce choose such an unusual plot pattern? One reason is that Corley's success or failure must be suspended until the end of the story. One cannot see the process, only the result. Another reason may be that in Lenehan one sees what the real life of a "gallant" is. First, his "gaiety" vanishes when he is alone and can no longer play his accustomed role. He finds "trivial all that was meant to charm him." All he can do is wander aimlessly, controlled by the rhythm of the harp, a conventional symbol for Ireland. He eats a frugal meal and worries about the price of a plate of peas. His imagination is not stirred by anything around him, including the harp, except for the thought of Corley's adventure. Yet this lack makes him even more aware of his own "poverty of purse and spirit." He then imagines alternatives, a job, a home, a wife; all these would be pleasant alternatives to his aimless life on the streets. Once more, however, the vision is undercut. "He might yet be able to settle down in some snug corner and live happily if he could only come across some good simpleminded girl with a little of the ready." This "snug" life would not be a change in his leeching but a final confirmation of it. He can aim no higher than to feed upon a simpleminded girl for the rest of his life.

The narrative reaches a climax when Lenehan spots the couple and anxiously follows to see if Corley has succeeded. "Well? . . . Did it come off? Can't you tell us? Did you try her?" The answer is provided by the small gold coin in Corley's palm. The reader knows by this point that romantic love is not Corley's aim, but the reader, perhaps, then assumes that he is looking for a sexual encounter. Yet it is finally evident that he does not want sex, let alone love. What he wants and triumphantly shows Lenehan is the money he has extracted from the girl; finding a "simpleminded girl with a bit of the ready" to live on is the goal of the Dublin "gallants."

Themes and Meanings

The most important theme in "Two Gallants," and it is the great theme of *Dubliners* (1914), is the way love is turned into, or perverted into, a commodity. The "gallants" do not want love but a girl who will give them money or even support them. Corley does not even want sex from his "slavey," but the coin that she gives to him. He is, therefore, seen as a Judas who has sold out love, instead of Christ, for a coin, and he has a most willing "disciple" in Lenehan.

Another important theme is the enslavement of the Dubliners and, by extension, the Irish. First, there is a harp in the story, which is a traditional symbol for Ireland. The harp is controlled by a "master" and subject to "strangers." This, at first, may suggest the domination of Ireland by a foreign power, such as England. Yet the point that Joyce wishes to make, above all, is that the Irish have enslaved themselves. The Irish "slavey" willingly pays the coin of tribute to the "conqueror," Corley, while his anxious collaborator, Lenehan, looks on. Corley is the "base betrayer" of his own country, and Lenehan the informer; these are familiar themes in Irish history.

Style and Technique

Joyce uses a number of styles in "Two Gallants." There is, first, the formal and evocative style of the third-person narrator which is used to set up romantic expectations. Describing the lamps of a Dublin street as "illumined pearls" is a good example of this style. In contrast, these expectations are violated by the clichés of Lenehan: "That takes the biscuit!" Almost every sentence of Lenehan's conversation contains a cliché. More important, however, is the low and crude style of Corley. His many references to women as "fine tarts" are examples of this style. His advice to Lenehan on how a gallant should behave shows the reader what they are really like: "There's nothing to touch a good slavey," he affirms, "Take my tip on it."

There are two significant symbols in "Two Gallants." The first is the reference to the harp. The harpist is weary, and "His harp too, heedless that her covering had fallen about her knees, seemed weary alike of the eyes of strangers and of her master's hand." The harp, which is given female characteristics, is unable to transcend her condition. This symbol contrasts to one of the great symbols of Ireland, Cathleen ni Houlihan, who is transformed from an old servant to a grand and beautiful lady when revolution breaks out. Yet there is no revolt in Joyce's story; the harp remains sunken in weariness and oppression.

The most important technique in the story is the use of a Joycean epiphany. An epiphany is a "showing forth," a revelation of what a character or his situation is. This epiphany can be made by the character or the reader. In "Two Gallants" the characters are totally unaware of their true situation. It is the reader who, in a negative epiphany, recognizes the "coin" in the hands of Corley as a sign of the true nature of these Dublin gallants.

James Sullivan

TWO LITTLE SOLDIERS

Author: Guy de Maupassant (1850-1893)
Type of plot: Realism
Time of plot: The mid-1800's
Locale: The French countryside near the town of Courbevoie
First published: "Petit Soldat," 1885 (English translation, 1903)

> *Principal characters:*
> LUC LE GANIDEC, a soldier
> JEAN KERDEREN, also a soldier
> A YOUNG MAID, who attracts the attention of both soldiers

The Story

Luc and Jean are two soldiers who habitually spend their free time on Sundays away from the barracks, out in the countryside. Their day off has taken on the character of a ritual. Every Sunday, they bring food for breakfast to the same spot in the woods and lie back to enjoy the food, wine, and sights of an area that reminds them of home. ⁓

Eventually, their ritual comes to include a bit of innocent ogling of a young village girl who brings her cow out to pasture every week at the same time. One Sunday, however, the girl speaks to them on her way to the pasture, and when she returns later, she shares the cow's milk with them and leaves them with a promise to meet the following Sunday.

The next weekend, Jean suggests that they bring something for her. They settle on candy as an appropriate present, but when the girl arrives, both are too shy to tell her that they have brought something. Finally, Luc tells the girl of the treat, and Jean, who always carries the provisions, give the bonbons to her.

As the weeks pass, the girl becomes the topic of conversation for these soldiers as they spend time at the barracks, and the three become fast friends. The girl begins to share their Sunday breakfast meal and appears to devote equal attention to the two recruits.

Then, in an uncharacteristic move, Luc seeks leave on a Tuesday, and again the following Thursday. He borrows money from Jean on that day but offers no explanation for his behavior. Jean lends the money.

The following Sunday, when the girl appears with the cow, she immediately rushes up to Luc and they embrace ardently. Jean is hurt, since he is left out and does not understand why the girl has suddenly turned all of her attention to Luc. Luc and the girl go off to care for the cow and disappear into the woods for a long time. Jean is stupefied. When they return, the lovers kiss again, and the girl offers Jean a kind "Good evening" before going away.

Neither soldier speaks of the incident, but as they return to their barracks they stop momentarily on the bridge over the Seine. Jean leans over toward the water, farther than he should in Luc's judgment, then suddenly tumbles into the torrent. Luc can do nothing; he watches in anguish as his good friend drowns.

Themes and Meanings

A first-time reader of this story, or of many other Maupassant stories, may be surprised by the ending, since it is difficult to imagine such catastrophic consequences in the lives of characters as simple as these soldiers. For precisely this reason, though, Maupassant is able to have significant impact on readers: The universal aspects of the tale stand out sharply beneath the surface simplicity. In "Two Little Soldiers," the tragedy of the traditional "love triangle" is brought into sharp focus, and the readers' sympathies are immediately and directly engaged by these young men whose lives are forever altered by the arrival of a woman whom they both admire.

The central issue which Maupassant treats is the conflict between friendship and love. In its simplest terms, the "moral" of this story is that a person and his best friend cannot love the same person. That notion, however, takes on poignant overtones in Maupassant's skillful handling of the story of these two soldiers.

It is clear from the outset that the two recruits share a special relationship. Thrown together in a system that traditionally offers little freedom and little dignity for individuals, the soldiers have found in each other a much-needed comrade whose shared interests and similar background make military life bearable. The opening scenes show the genuine bond that exists between them: They survive the week in order to spend their Sundays together. What these men share is a kind of male bonding that often occurs in soldiers, a special friendship that the military hierarchy relies on to ensure that men will fight bravely to save their comrades in war.

Suddenly, another emotion enters the lives of both recruits, one that challenges the strength of that bonding. Both are smitten by the young girl who befriends them. In their quiet way, they vie for her attention, although neither seems aware that the other is in love. To win the girl, however, one of them must "betray" the bond of friendship; it is impossible that one should become the girl's lover and still maintain the same relationship with his fellow soldier that existed before the girl came into their lives. Thus, Luc must resort to deception to ensure that he will win the girl's favor: He seeks leave without explaining his motives to Jean and takes advantage of his comrade (by borrowing money) to further his own suit. It is small wonder that Jean is hurt and bewildered when Luc and the girl make him aware of their special relationship.

The fact that the reader does not see any difference between Luc's and Jean's initial reactions and behavior toward the girl only heightens the tragedy. It becomes apparent that Jean feels the same about the girl as Luc does. Perhaps his friendship for Luc has kept him from pursuing the girl himself; perhaps shyness has prevented him from making public his feelings. In any case, when he sees that Luc and the girl are in love, he feels betrayed, and his decision to commit suicide is a logical consequence of his realization that he will have neither friend nor lover. Thus, the happiness that Luc and the girl experience is achieved at great cost.

Style and Technique

"Two Little Soldiers" relies heavily on setting and point of view for its effectiveness. The pastoral surroundings in which the majority of the action takes place suggest serenity and appear to promise happiness. Maupassant is careful not to reveal too much of barracks life; only its regimentation intrudes on the story, adding to the sense of release the two soldiers feel when they escape to the countryside each weekend. The idyllic setting is no escape from the harsh realities of the world, however, as the reader discovers when Jean is cast aside by the two people who mean the most to him.

Perhaps the most significant technique that allows Maupassant to make his tragedy hit home with readers is his manipulation of the point of view. Though the action of the story appears to be continuous, "Two Little Soldiers" can actually be viewed as a series of dramatic scenes, and the point of view shifts as scenes change. For much of the story, Maupassant adopts what appears to be the voice of an omniscient narrator. He tells the reader what both soldiers think and do, giving each equal attention. Because he appears to be providing simple and straightforward information, it is easy to pass over the fact that he says almost nothing about what the young girl feels or thinks in these first encounters.

Then, at key points, Maupassant adopts a more limited view: When Luc decides to go on leave, and when the two soldiers travel to the countryside for the last time, he restricts himself to the viewpoint of one character, Jean. The reader sees only the confusion that wells up in this young man as his friend and the girl go off without him. When the two soldiers begin their trek back to the barracks, the scene is viewed through Luc's eyes: The reader is denied knowledge of Jean's feelings, and hence is given no explanation of his motivation for committing suicide.

This technique may lead to charges of poor writing; certainly Maupassant does not follow the tenet of many proponents of the school of realism that point of view should be consistent throughout a story, novel, or poem. Nevertheless, the author's conscious decision to move selectively between characters is directly responsible for the aura which he wished to create in this tragedy of the common man.

Laurence W. Mazzeno

TWO LOVELY BEASTS

Author: Liam O'Flaherty (1896-1984)
Type of plot: Social realism
Time of plot: 1938
Locale: The western part of Ireland
First published: 1946

> *Principal characters:*
> COLM DERRANE, the protagonist, a modest peasant farmer
> MRS. DERRANE, his wife
> KATE HIGGINS, a widow and neighbor
> ANDY GORUM, the village elder

The Story

The rather pastoral title of this story suggests that it might deal with animals and nature, two subjects common to O'Flaherty's writing. As the reader quickly discovers, however, the "two lovely beasts" are of only minor importance, for the true concerns of this story revolve around their human masters.

The story opens with the misfortunes of Kate Higgins, a widow whose cow has calved and then died. She brings her tale of woe to the kitchen of the Derranes, a neighboring family whose own cow has just given birth to a calf. Kate, in wild hysterics, begs Colm Derrane to buy her calf, so that she might purchase another cow. "I must have a cow for the children," she tells Colm. "The doctor said they must have plenty of milk. . . . They are ailing, the poor creatures."

Because "traditional law" allows only one cow for each family, Colm refuses her at once. Grazing land is scarce—there is only enough grass on each household plot to support one cow. By the same token, the milk is shared with those in the community who have been struck by misfortune—people such as Kate Higgins. As Mrs. Derrane, Colm's wife, tells Kate, "We couldn't leave neighbours without milk in order to fill a calf's belly."

Eventually, Colm agrees to allow his cow to feed her calf until she can find a buyer. She rejoices at this news, but soon she begins to tempt him again with the idea of owning two calves. "You'll be the richest man in the village," she whispers into his ear. "You'll be talked about and envied from one end of the parish to the other." Colm refuses her again, but with far less conviction than before.

The seed of temptation has been planted, and it comes into full blossom the following morning when Kate comes to him with the news that she can find no buyer. "Unless you buy him," she tells Colm, "I'll have to give him to the butcher at Kilmacalla." He refuses her one last time but is unable to sleep at night because of the idea of owning two calves. The idea, O'Flaherty writes, "gave him both pleasure and pain. The pleasure was like that derived from the anticipation of venery. The pain came from his conscience."

Despite the objections of his wife, the following day Colm buys Kate Higgins' calf. There is an immediate uproar in the community. Andy Gorum, the village elder, remonstrates with Colm about his decision, but Colm is adamant: He will keep the two calves, no matter what laws he is breaking. In the end, Gorum says that he has little choice but to have the rest of the community ostracize the Derranes. He predicts a dark fate for Colm and his family. Even Kate Higgins, who is unable to buy a cow, turns against Colm.

Instead of giving in, however, Colm becomes harder, more determined "to rise in the world." Every drop of milk from his cow goes to the mouths of his "two lovely beasts"—even at the expense of feeding his own children. The family, living on a diet of potatoes and salt, soon begins to starve. When his wife confronts him and threatens to beat him to his senses, Colm in turn gives her a savage beating.

Suddenly and inexplicably, she no longer sees Colm as an obsessed fool, but as someone who is trying to better their family. She and the children, despite a few setbacks, stand firmly behind him. They and their cows survive the next two winters, and slowly the villagers begin to turn away from the counsel of Gorum—whom they see as a jealous old fool—and come to get the advice of Colm. In the meantime, Kate Higgins has gone completely insane and has been taken away to a lunatic asylum.

In the final scene of the story, Colm has decided to start a shop in his cottage. He knows that the start of the "Emergency," as World War II is known in Ireland, will bring about a great demand for all sorts of foodstuffs. Though this means even more prolonged hardship for his family, they accept his decision. It is a successful decision because, before long, "there was full and plenty in the house. The little girls had ribbons to their hair and dai-dais to amuse their leisure. His wife got a velvet dress and a hat with feathers. There was bacon for breakfast."

Ironically, his great wealth alienates him once again from the community. Yet this isolation does not trouble him, for he is planning to open a shop in the town. As Colm is leaving his farm—having sold his two lovely beasts—Andy Gorum and his neighbors jeer him. Colm, however, is "completely unaware of their jeers. His pale blue eyes stared fixedly straight ahead, cold and resolute and ruthless."

Themes and Meanings

There are several themes running through this story, the most important being the nature of human greed. In the first part of the narrative, there is an almost direct parallel with the biblical story of Adam and Eve, especially in the manner in which Colm is tempted from his Garden of Eden by the idea of owning that which he is not allowed to possess. Instead of an apple,

Colm's obsession revolves around the two beasts.

His banishment from Eden is far more spiritual than physical, however, because, instead of leaving behind a garden of plenty, he is forced to give up a frame of mind that allows him satisfaction with all that he possesses. After he purchases the two beasts, though, nothing is good enough for him. He wants more and more and more—the vicious upward spiral of greed.

The fact that Andy Gorum ostracizes Colm and his family to the point that they decide to leave the community is trivial, because Colm has already made his decision to leave (spiritually, at least) by owning the two calves. Though Gorum prophesies that the Derranes will have their downfall, this does not happen in the latter half of the story. Indeed, Colm thrives to an extent which the community has never before seen. He becomes a hero.

By making Colm successful, O'Flaherty departs from the tale of Adam and Eve. No God of wrath, as Gorum would like to see, has made Colm tremble in fear for his transgression of the "traditional laws." No lightning bolts have come from the heavens; no diseases have killed his calves; no deaths have taken place in his family. Nothing unfortunate has happened to Colm.

In the end, however, greed has taken its toll on Colm. Whereas once he was hardworking yet amenable, he is now cold and calculating, obsessed with the idea of "rising in the world." To O'Flaherty, this is Colm's true fall from Eden—the notion that he will never escape his own greed, but that it will imprison him forever, continuously taunting and beckoning, so that in the end, he will have nothing but a restless and ruthless mind, unable to appreciate what he has, always wanting more.

Style and Technique

Though O'Flaherty wrote this story in English, it almost reads like a translation from his native Gaelic. The style is simple and straightforward, using few metaphors or other literary devices, and the brief paragraphs serve mainly as connecting points between the long portions of dialogue.

In fact, it is the dialogue which is the true strength of this story, for it is full of Irish phrases and sayings ("God between us and all harm!" or "God spare your health, Colm") which are both true-to-life and lively. This is a technique which O'Flaherty adopts again and again in his writing: simple (almost childish) prose which is strongly counterpointed by lively Irish peasant dialogue. Without the dialogue, this story (and many of his other works) would fall flat, for its theme is so universal and its prose so anonymous that it might have taken place anywhere. With the dialogue, however, the setting could be nowhere other than the west of Ireland.

Michael Verdon

TYPHOON

Author: Joseph Conrad (Józef Teodor Konrad Korzeniowski, 1857-1924)
Type of plot: Adventure
Time of plot: The 1890's
Locale: The China Seas
First published: 1902

> *Principal characters:*
> CAPTAIN TOM MACWHIRR, the master of the steamer
>   *Nan-Shan*
> YOUNG JUKES, the chief mate
> SOLOMON ROUT, the chief engineer
> THE SECOND MATE
> THE BOATSWAIN
> THE STEWARD
> TWO HUNDRED CHINESE COOLIES, who are returning to their
>   homes after several years of working in the tropics

The Story

The protagonist of Joseph Conrad's narrative of a typhoon in the China Seas is Captain Tom MacWhirr. Recommended by the builders of the *Nan-Shan* to Sigg and Sons, who want a competent and dependable master for their vessel, MacWhirr is gruff, empirical, without imagination. Although his reputation as a mariner is impeccable, his manner does not inspire confidence; yet, when he is first shown around the *Nan-Shan* by the builders, he immediately notes that its locks are poorly made.

Young Mr. Jukes, MacWhirr's first mate, full of himself, curious about others, always rushing off to meet trouble before it comes, is satiric concerning MacWhirr's limitations, especially his literal-mindedness, his inability to communicate with others in ordinary terms, and his taciturnity. For his part, MacWhirr is amazed at Jukes's capacity for small talk and his use of metaphorical language, for MacWhirr himself notes only the facts by which he lives. Yet he is astute enough to respect in others the ability to perform their tasks ably. Having just enough imagination to carry him through each day, tranquilly certain of his competence—although it has never been fully tested—MacWhirr communicates the essential details of his voyages to his wife and children in monthly letters which they read perfunctorily. These same letters are furtively and eagerly read by the steward, who, somehow, appreciates the truths that they distill.

A minor contretemps between Jukes and the captain occurs early in the narrative when, Jukes believes, MacWhirr fails to understand the implications of the *Nan-Shan*'s transfer from its original British to a Siamese registry. MacWhirr reads Jukes's displeasure at the change as a literal comment on the size and shape of the Siamese flag. He checks its dimensions, colors, and insignia in his naval guide and then tells Jukes that it is correct in every way. Jukes, nevertheless, continues to feel resentment against MacWhirr and the flag's Siamese elephant on a blue ground, lamenting the loss of the red, white, and blue of the Union Jack, symbol of security and order. Another minor disagreement concerns MacWhirr's and Jukes's differing opinions over the boatswain: Jukes dislikes the man for his lack of initiative and for a good nature that he thinks amounts almost to imbecility; MacWhirr respects him as a first-rate seaman who performs his tasks without grumbling.

The other members of the *Nan-Shan* crew are Solomon Rout, the chief engineer, who writes colorful and entertaining accounts of his voyages to his wife and aged mother; the second mate, who finds that he cannot function during the typhoon and is later dismissed for his failure of nerve; and the steward. MacWhirr and his crew are responsible for two hundred Chinese passengers, who, with their belongings and the silver dollars they have saved during the years that they have worked in the tropics, are returning home.

As MacWhirr and Jukes remark the rapidly falling barometer that portends the typhoon ahead, they react characteristically to the "fact" of the coming storm. Jukes is amazed at, yet respectful of MacWhirr's decision to meet the weather head-on rather than to sail behind or around it. MacWhirr consults the textbooks; he then concludes that one Captain Wilson's account of a "storm strategy" cannot be credited, since Wilson could not testify to the activities of a storm he had not experienced. "Let it come, then," says MacWhirr with "dignified indignation."

The gale arrives, in ever-increasing ferocity, attacking the *Nan-Shan*, the crew, and the passengers "like a personal enemy." At one point, as the storm nears its apex, the boatswain makes his way to the bridge to tell MacWhirr of the chaos that the pounding waves have caused in the hold where the coolies are billeted. The storm has buffeted those below with the same vehemence it has hit those above the decks: to the brink of dissolution. The Chinese and their unsecured silver dollars have been hurled against the stairs and the bulkheads by the savage waves. MacWhirr tells Jukes to see to the confusion below and to return to the bridge as soon as he can, for it may be necessary for him to assume command of the ship. Afraid, Jukes makes his way belowdecks. During the lull, as the *Nan-Shan* finds the eye of the storm, he and the boatswain rig lifelines and secure the hold. It is, however, only when he hears MacWhirr's voice through the speaking tube, with which the captain communicates with Solomon Rout and the engine room, that Jukes musters sufficient initiative to obey MacWhirr's order and to secure the hold.

The turning point of the story occurs when MacWhirr, uncertain of the outcome of his decision to confront the storm, finds his matches in their accustomed place. "I shouldn't like to lose her," he says of the *Nan-Shan* as he gives in, momentarily, to the unaccustomed sensation of mental fatigue.

Jukes, once he has settled the Chinese workmen, returns to the bridge and there experiences such self-confidence as to make him equal to the challenge of the storm—once the ship sails out of its eye—and to any future challenges as well.

Once the storm is over, the ship, grayed by salt, devastated by wind, sails into port with life restored, as much as possible, to normal order. The second mate, who had frozen on deck, is put off the ship. MacWhirr, the reader learns, has solved the problem of the Chinese and their money by dividing the silver dollars equally among them. The three dollars left over he has given to the three most seriously injured men.

The tale does not dramatize the second half of the storm. It concludes instead with an epilogue of sorts, during which the principal characters detail in written form their impressions of the typhoon.

Themes and Meanings

"Typhoon" is remarkable primarily for the immediacy with which the storm, in its elemental and objective fury, is dramatized. It is experience so intensely and forcefully narrated that its reality is felt as it is read. The tale is adventure so brilliantly accommodated by language that one becomes oblivious of the very words that communicate the experience.

The story is, furthermore, a perfect combination of the literal and the symbolic. As he confronts the storm, MacWhirr sees beyond the vault of the sky, past the stars into a vast and lonely cosmos beyond. He defines man's protest against nature as he finds in himself the determination to confront and conquer the facts of creation. The several references to the loneliness of command, to the privileges and burdens of authority, suggest, in addition, a simple but provocative allegory: Man confronts the self through a task provided by the subconscious as a means of determining his capacity to be. The ship can be seen, in an equally viable reading, as a microcosm, MacWhirr as a god-figure upon whom all depends, and his shortcomings as an index of the limitations of a godhead who has lost or never had control of his creation. Solomon Rout, in the bowels of the ship, can then be read as that aspect of the psyche upon which the intelligence depends for power and drive. Jukes, who discovers his place within the human community, as Everyman, who, in doing his work under the eye and encouragement of the god figure, succeeds in discovering his courage and verifying his humanity; the boatswain as one who does not fail in matters of trust; and the second mate as one who fails in responsibility and succumbs, as a result, to fear and terror.

Style and Technique

The means by which the adventure of MacWhirr and the *Nan-Shan* is narrated is the chief challenge of Conrad's tale. The principal characters are themselves all storytellers of different sorts. MacWhirr writes his dutiful letters to a wife who fears and dreads them, as she does his return to her and their children. Only the steward has some notion of the purity of the events they describe. When he reads MacWhirr's account of the storm, he is so reluctant to tear himself away from the letter that he is almost caught. Solomon Rout, in the habit of sending his wife and aged mother long and picturesque accounts of his travels, is curiously unable to lend romance to the events he has experienced. His wife is disappointed by the letters' paucity of description. Solomon, the reader infers, has perhaps learned somewhat more from the adventure than the others, for the typhoon has brought forth in him a desire to be reunited with his family, as well as making him aware of his mortality. Jukes's account, written to his friend in the western ocean trade, somewhat more animated than is usually the case in his correspondence, concludes that MacWhirr has gotten the *Nan-Shan* out of a difficult predicament and that he reconciled the claims of the Chinese workers fairly creditably "for such a stupid man."

The overall narrator of the tale, who is privy to the correspondence of MacWhirr, Rout, and Jukes, for his part recounts the adventure in a tone of astonished and incredulous surprise. His is a tone compounded as much of a satiric and ironic awareness of MacWhirr's limitations as of a grudging acceptance of the man's determination to survive and an appreciation of his ability to provide fair play, not only for the coolies but also for the second mate. It is the tone of tolerant yet bemused irony that transforms the narrative into a remarkable comedy, a form unusual within Conrad's oeuvre.

The comedy of "Typhoon" depends chiefly on the reader's awareness that neither MacWhirr nor Jukes changes as a result of his experience. Perhaps Solomon Rout changes, but if he does, it is left ambiguous so as not to intrude on the happy ending. Young Jukes, as does MacWhirr, passes the test of self, but he remains unaware that without MacWhirr he might have failed. This awareness, that the characters remain largely unchanged, comments, furthermore, on an absurd cosmos beyond the stars which allows for surprises of all kinds, even to the promise of hope in man.

Jukes and MacWhirr can ultimately be seen as comic foils for such characters of deep introspection as Jim of *Lord Jim* (1900) and Razumov of *Under Western Eyes* (1910), characters whose failure propels them into an ethical universe and defines the form of the novels in which they appear. If Marlow's willed descent into the self transforms the setting which he observes in *Heart of Darkness* (1902) into meaningful symbolism, then MacWhirr and Jukes's inability to fathom the depths of the self explains the straightforward and objective description of the storm, as well as the narrator's incredulousness. MacWhirr, Jukes, and Rout perform their comic parts admirably and make "Typhoon" equal to the best of Conrad's novels.

A. A. DeVitis

UNCLE

Author: R. K. Narayan (1906-   )
Type of plot: Psychological realism
Time of plot: Twentieth century
Locale: South India
First published: 1970

> *Principal characters:*
> BOY, the protagonist, grown-up when he tells the story
> UNCLE, the narrator's uncle
> AUNT, the narrator's aunt
> SURESH, a boy in the narrator's class
> THE TAILOR
> JAYRAJ, a frame maker

The Story

The narrator and protagonist, occupying and owning the house in which he was reared, recalls the stages by which he comes upon some crushing knowledge, how he lives with it and finally realizes his present gain. Seated in the easy chair once occupied by his uncle, he reminisces in the silent, solitary setting, ideal and natural for a reverie, on how the man and woman he called his uncle and aunt used to dote on him as though he were their own child. Memories of simple joys such as are universal in happy homes crowd his mind—how Uncle used to push his snuffbox out of his reach when the narrator was a toddler, how delighted he was when the little fellow tumbled, and how his aunt would carry him off and set him to the entertainment of water-splashing and then attempt with loving determination to feed him. He sees their lives revolve around himself not only when he was small, but also through all of his remembered days, when even under the pressure of silent agony he maintains their sweet relationship.

When the youngster starts going to school, his uncle and aunt pay meticulous attention to every detail of his daily routine. The reader, regaled with lively descriptions of the early morning scrub, the prayers and recitations, the organization of the school satchel with a pointy pencil and all, is left in no doubt whatsoever that the boy (the narrator) is happy and content in the tender, loving care of his uncle and aunt. They take absurd parental pride in all of his childish antics; his pretense at saying holy verse, for example, is seen as a sign that he will one day be renowned as a saint.

The first shadow of a doubt about Uncle falls upon the unsuspecting little boy's mind when Suresh, a classmate in the first grade, asks him his father's name, what he does for a living, and whether they are rich. This battery of questions, which would have seemed natural and which would have posed no problem to any other boy, bewilders him. When asked about his father, all he can say is that he calls him Uncle. He does not know what work his uncle does, for Uncle is home all day, either meditating or eating. To the question of riches perhaps he responds adequately; he does not know, but "they make plenty of sweets at home." (At this the reader is imperceptibly led to wonder about the child's use of the third person, an intuitive distancing of himself even from those closest to him in the whole world.) When he asks Uncle where his office is and whether he is rich, his aunt drags him off to eat some goodies and cautions him about asking things Uncle does not like to talk about.

Some days later, the same classmate informs the boy that his uncle came from another country—which sounds like a good thing. He also says, however, that Uncle "impersonated"—which sounds ominous even though neither boy knows what the word means. Eager as he is to find out, he cannot broach the subject when he gets home, and instead entertains Uncle with an imagined account of his physical prowess.

One day when he is being measured for a shirt to be expressly made for a picture-taking at school (a matter of monumental importance on which much thought and energy are expended), the boy gathers some more information about his uncle. The tailor, very respectful toward Uncle, expresses his family's gratitude by recounting how Uncle revived him when he was left for dead, and how he helped him go over mountain passes although Uncle had a baby in his arms. Uncle, however, tells him not to bring up the past.

Whenever Aunt wants to go out, she sends the boy to get a carriage from the street corner, where he hears the men talk among themselves, making disparaging remarks about Uncle, calling him "that Rangoon man."

The day the class photograph arrives amid much excitement, the boy and Uncle go on foot to Jayraj the frame maker, who, to the boy's astonishment, addresses Uncle as "Doctor." Mystified, the boy makes a timid and predictably futile attempt at asking Uncle for a clarification. As Jayraj is full of his own importance, full of talk and jokes, and has other customers to attend to, he cannot finish their work till the evening. With Jayraj's promise to give him food from a restaurant across the street and to bring him home, the boy, with a sense of adventure, begs his uncle to let him stay on at the shop.

Following Uncle's departure, Jayraj starts talking with a bald man about Uncle, speaking in undertones and casting sidelong glances at the boy, who grows more and more uncomfortable and hungry. From half-heard whispered phrases, the boy gathers that Jayraj addressed his uncle as "doctor" only for effect, for he is no doctor, but an impersonator of one. The real doctor—the boy's father—was a rich and successful doctor in Rangoon, where he had ten doctors employed under him. Uncle was then only a syringe washer. When the Japanese bombed Rangoon, the doctor and his wife, with their fifteen-day-old baby, and the syringe washer (Uncle) trekked back to

India over the mountains. Apparently, Uncle pushed the doctor over a cliff to his death and impersonated him in India, thereby acquiring his gold, jewels, and a bank account in Madras. He kept the doctor's wife a prisoner, and then, having given her a lethal injection, wound up his crimes with her speedy cremation. The baby, he reared.

After recounting all these shocking matters, Jayraj digs out an unclaimed photograph from his storage room, and, shoving it at him, asks the boy if he wants it. The boy knows by now that the stranger in European clothes is his father, the doctor. Hungry, confused, and terrified, though, he runs home without the photograph. He runs the entire unfamiliar way of looming shadows to the comforting arms of his uncle, the murderer and swindler of his parents.

When the boy confides the whole story to his aunt, she simply asks him to forget it. He suppresses questions even when he grows up. At college, he ignores unfavorable remarks about his uncle, but once tries to strangle a classmate for gossiping about him. When Uncle dies, he leaves everything to the boy, the narrator. In going through his uncle's things, he finds that the only connection to Burma is a lacquered box.

Themes and Meanings

Many of R. K. Narayan's novels and short stories paint vivid pictures of the imaginary South Indian village of Malgudi and the small world of little boys. The descriptive realism of the setting and the psychological realism of the characters convincingly unfold human predicaments and the choices that people make. Narayan's protagonists are confronted by circumstances which they either accept and learn to live with or take on as a challenge and endeavor to change. Such situations, naturally, reveal character, and, quite often, also an attitude toward life. "Uncle" is a story that conforms to this endearing pattern of universal relevance.

In this story, the boy, a mild and passive character, lives with a painful situation for many years before life, not he himself, brings about the final resolution—his uncle's death and his own substantial inheritance from his uncle of the money that was most probably his by right anyway. As the boy is only a first-grader when the crisis occurs, and as the crisis is of a magnitude that bears comparison with Hamlet's dilemma, the boy's response seems wholly credible. A scared and hungry little boy is likely to run home to a villain, even if that villain has killed his parents, if the villain is the only father he knows, and the world to him is a hostile place.

What is intriguing is that even as a grown-up with a college education, the protagonist does not confront Uncle or take him to court. A rare outburst of passion in him, a violent attempt at vindication, is not directed at Uncle. Rather, ironically, it is meant to defend Uncle's good name. Though too big to sit comfortably in Uncle's chair, and though he sees himself as "the monarch of all he surveys," the protagonist is hardly a formidable character. His reasons for not pursuing justice and truth are deliberately left unexplored, for the springs of action and inaction lie deep and hidden in the complex human psyche. His general passivity and lack of tenacity are convincing, for even as a boy he does not persist in getting answers to things about which he is curious. For example, he wants to know how a Hindu goddess in a picture can stand on a lotus without crushing it. When his aunt tells him not to ask such questions, he lets the matter rest without any protest whatsoever. Questions about Uncle's work and evil past are similarly put to rest. His character as portrayed by Narayan is consistent and credible.

Besides writing and reading an engrossing and satisfying story, the writer, as well as the reader, needs to discover a deeper significance in terms of human values. In this story, the dilemma of the protagonist creates interest. The choice he makes reveals not only his character but also his values, even the values of his culture. Nonviolence, tolerance, acceptance, loyalty, and patience bring a sweet harmony to life, and even a substantial reward. The opposite choice might well have brought bitterness and disaster.

Style and Technique

The hallmarks of Narayan's style are lucidity and humor, both of which are readily apparent in this story. The leisurely pace of a reverie suits the quiet personality of the protagonist, whereas the liveliness of phrase and observation lifts insipid details of everyday routines into sheer delight.

He delineates characters and their relationships obliquely; he does not state them directly, but presents situations from which they can be perceived. Vivid descriptions of the child's world—how he prays with Uncle, how he eats with him, or plays while Uncle naps on his bench—delightful in themselves, move the story along, for they show the close bond that is later threatened by the revelation of villainy. The enchantingly described market, which initially stands for the outside world which the boy is eager to discover, loses its allure, coming to represent a hostile world from which he flies to the safe sanctuary of the arms of Uncle—ironically, the person responsible for his agony.

His own feelings are more real to the boy than the moral judgments of other people. Narayan shows this superbly by employing the technique of juxtaposition, using contrasts to highlight an idea. Every time the boy learns something negative about Uncle, a scene follows which shows that Uncle is his world. Uncle's crimes are not real to the boy, for he has experienced only his love. To the boy, the only thing embarrassing about Uncle is his enormous girth. All the consistent testimony against Uncle cannot, therefore, indict him in the protagonist's mind. The final, tangible evidence of Uncle's mysterious and questionable past—a Burmese casket—is in like manner dismissed as negligible. Uncle and Aunt's given names are never mentioned.

People, places, and events in the story are seen not as they might appear to an objective observer, but as they appear to the protagonist. Everything has import within the psychological realism of the narrative.

Sita Kapadia

UNCLE WIGGILY IN CONNECTICUT

Author: J. D. Salinger (1919-   )
Type of plot: Social satire
Time of plot: The 1950's
Locale: Suburban Connecticut
First published: 1948

> *Principal characters:*
> ELOISE, a suburban upper-middle-class wife
> MARY JANE, her close friend and former college roommate
> RAMONA, Eloise's child, who is about ten years old

The Story

Mary Jane, the secretary to a New York executive named Mr. Weyinburg, has most of the day off as a result of her employer's illness but has promised to drop his mail off and take some dictation every afternoon for the duration of his illness. At three o'clock (two hours late for the lunch that her hostess had prepared), she stops to see her friend Eloise at her home in suburban Connecticut. Later she plans to drive on to Larchmont, New York, with Mr. Weyinburg's mail. Eloise, in her camel-hair coat, greets her in front of the house.

Eloise is comfortably well-off, with an attractive house, a husband who commutes to New York, a young daughter named Ramona, and a black maid named Grace. Mary Jane is single but about the same age as Eloise, who has been married for about ten years.

The two women gossip as they drink highballs in Eloise's living room. Much of the talk becomes nostalgic as the two women continue to drink. Mary Jane carelessly spills her drink while Eloise's conversation becomes more outspoken and her expressions more vulgar, referring to Grace as "sitting on her big black butt" in the kitchen.

Ramona appears. In the stilted conversation that ensues between Ramona and Mary Jane, it is obvious that Ramona is not taken in by Mary Jane's feigned enthusiasm ("Oh, what a pretty dress!"). Mary Jane questions Ramona about her imaginary companion, Jimmy Jimmereeno. Significantly, Jimmy is an orphan and has "no freckles."

The two women continue drinking, and by a quarter to five Eloise is lying on the floor recalling a long-dead lover, a GI named Walt. Walt's sense of humor, his tenderness to Eloise, and his manner of speaking are all remembered fondly by Eloise. Lew, Eloise's husband, is compared unfavorably to Walt in many respects as Eloise is questioned by Mary Jane. Eloise tearfully recalls Walt's death in an accident with a Japanese camp stove. Ramona reappears and is instructed to get her supper from the maid and go to bed.

Eloise reveals several rather unpleasant aspects of her character when she refuses to allow Grace's husband to spend the night with his wife, even though the weather is bad and driving hazardous. By now it is after seven o'clock, and Eloise lies to her husband, who is waiting to be picked up at the train station, claiming that she cannot find the keys to Mary Jane's car, which is blocking the driveway.

Next, Eloise looks in on Ramona and, finding that she is sleeping on one side of her bed, wakes her for an explanation. She learns of a new imaginary playmate, Mickey Mickeranno. She drags her passively resistant daughter to the middle of the bed and orders her to shut her eyes.

Finally, both mother and daughter are in tears as Eloise presses Ramona's glasses against her cheek saying "Poor Uncle Wiggily," which repeats Walt's phrase from many years before when Eloise had twisted her ankle outside the army PX.

Eloise finally returns to the living room, where Mary Jane has passed out. She wakens her and tearfully tries to invoke her sympathy in a desperate plea, "I was a nice girl . . . wasn't I?"

Themes and Meanings

The perennial themes of J. D. Salinger's stories are present in "Uncle Wiggily in Connecticut." His satire often deals with upper-middle-class alienation amid the complacency of the Eisenhower era. "Uncle Wiggily in Connecticut" is a story in this vein. The author characterizes Eloise and Mary Jane as modern, cynical suburbanites who are not always morally scrupulous and have never been meticulously honest. Eloise has been expelled from the university for an incident with a soldier in her residence hall. Mary Jane's marriage to an aviator cadet is marred by his imprisonment for two months after stabbing a member of the Military Police. It is assumed that Mary Jane will have to lie to explain her failure to reach her employer's house in Larchmont after her drunken afternoon with Eloise. Eloise seems unashamed and undisturbed when she lies to her husband about Mary Jane's car keys. She also seems to be offhand and casual in the extreme in performing her duties as a mother. The very fact that Ramona needs an imaginary friend who has "no mommy and no daddy" relates directly to her feelings toward her parents.

It is clear from the way that Eloise refers to Lew, her husband, that she has by now lost all respect for him and prefers to escape through alcohol rather than come to terms with her situation soberly.

Eloise and Mary Jane in their reminiscences seek an earlier manifestation of their lives, before they made the mistakes which now haunt them. Candidly, they seek their lost innocence.

Like the old wise rabbit with glasses, Uncle Wiggily of the nursery stories, everyone here seems to seek some solution to the puzzles of modern society.

Lew seeks some sort of agreeable relationship with his wife, who detests him; Ramona seeks love and is constantly disappointed; even Grace, the maid, seeks faith through a popularized version of biblical history.

The concern and interest in the lives of others represented by Eloise's dead former lover, Walt, when he shows concern for her injured ankle ("poor Uncle Wiggily"), is totally lacking in the sterile relationships of the contemporary characters. "[D]on't tell your husband anything" Eloise warns Mary Jane, ". . . you can tell them stuff. But never honestly." When Ramona goes to bed, she places her glasses carefully on the bedside table "folded neatly," stems down. After Eloise picks up the glasses she places them back on the night table "lenses down." Ramona's lenses allow her to see the domestic situation only too clearly; Eloise would much rather the lenses faced down rather than up. At this point she feels guilty about her relationship with her child but cannot see any easy release from her dilemma. She seeks to avoid the pitiless gaze of Ramona, whose glasses (counter-myopic lenses) tend to enlarge the child's eyes and create an impression of intense concentration.

The two women seem unpoised and rather crude, their conversation containing no cultural allusions save those of popular film fare and an obscure American romantic novelist. As with most of the other stories in this collection, Salinger's contempt for the elders is balanced by his admiration for the perceptive "wise child" mature beyond her years. Ramona has become an Uncle Wiggily to her rather adolescent parents, both lost in dreams of their youth. Mary Jane and Eloise in name and character relate back to the youngsters of the original tale, guided and advised by the wise, bespectacled Uncle Wiggily.

Style and Technique

Salinger created his reputation in the 1950's by counterpointing the whimsical with the mystical. The author's tone is critical of his characters and could even be said, at times, to be sarcastic. Mary Jane, "with little or no wherewithal for being left alone in a room," is seen to be of limited intelligence. Eloise is, perhaps, more intelligent but insensitive in her dealing with her maid and relates tasteless gossip endlessly to Mary Jane. Mary Jane at one point comes "back into drinking position"; Eloise "lunged . . . to her feet."

Salinger's satire on the college-girl speech of Eloise and Mary Jane is evident in the initial paragraph ("everything had been absolutely *perfect* . . . that she had remembered the way *exactly*"). The author's contempt for these drunken women is conveyed almost totally by the dialogue and the manner in which he describes the characters. As in some other Salinger stories, the author assumes a certain sophistication on the part of the reader regarding suburban life and even this particular section of the New York suburbs. Salinger refers glibly to the Merritt Parkway (even Mary Jane calls it "Merrick") in southwestern Connecticut, Larchmont (another fashionable commuter town in Westchester), and stores such as Lord and Taylor, which caters to an upper-middle-class clientele. Artifacts such as the camel-hair coat, the convertible car, and the elaborate luncheon menu all indicate a certain social and economic status presumably familiar to the reader. Thus, Salinger wastes little time on the setting and concentrates his focus on the appearance and speech of the three central characters. He treats Eloise and Mary Jane with a certain deliberate malice and the child Ramona with compassion.

The unhappiness and duplicity of both Mary Jane and Eloise become more evident as the plot develops, and the author cleverly intensifies not only the vulgarity but also the open hostility in the speeches of the two women. Their speech becomes slurred and their swearing more frequent: "I don't wanna go out there. The whole damn place smells of orange juice." Eloise's attitude toward her husband and her feelings of guilt toward her child are finally revealed unmistakably in her telephone conversation with Lew (to whom she gives short shrift) and her tearful breakdown in Ramona's bedroom, followed by the final anxious question to Mary Jane that concludes the narrative.

F. A. Couch, Jr.

UNDER A GLASS BELL

Author: Anaïs Nin (1903-1977)
Type of plot: Psychological lyricism
Time of plot: The 1920's and 1930's
Locale: A mansion in France
First published: 1941

> *Principal characters:*
> JEANNE, a wealthy young woman
> JEAN, Jeanne's brother and also the narrator
> PAUL, Jeanne's other brother

The Story

In "Under a Glass Bell," Anaïs Nin describes the life-style of Jeanne and her two brothers, Jean and Paul. The narrator, presumably Jean, first describes the family residence, a well-appointed French mansion where many generations have lived. The furnishings, while beautiful, are so fragile that the butlers are careful not to touch anything. The rooms are lighted by glass chandeliers which the narrator refers to as "blue icicle bushes." Giving off an indirect light, these "icicle bushes" cast an aura which makes everything in the house appear to exist "under a glass bell"—the kind of glass bell often used to preserve bouquets of flowers.

Next, the narrator records a long monologue in which Jeanne, her face seeming to be "stemless," tells of her relationship with her brothers and her mother. Speaking for her brothers as well as for herself, Jeanne insists that their relationships to one another are more important than their relationships to their spouses or their children, that all three scorn the demands of the real world in which their bodies age, and that the three need to live heroic lives, a present-day impossibility. That seeds of this unusual relationship were clearly planted by the mother becomes evident when Jeanne calls her mother the "true" Queen of France, who retreated from daily existence by taking drugs and by having hallucinatory talks with Napoleon Bonaparte.

Then the narrator tells the story of Jeanne's aborted affair with Prince Mahreb, a Georgian Prince. Jeanne cannot respond to the prince because she believes that he is too ordinary. When the narrator sends her an exquisitely romantic Persian print, Jeanne, assuming that the print has come from the prince, renews the affair. Each day, for four days, the narrator sends Jeanne another Persian print, each one more romantic than the first. Yet by the fifth day, Jeanne discovers that the prince has no imagination, and her face hangs down once more like a "stemless plant." The remainder of the story is framed by two incidents with Paul. Jeanne, finding Paul asleep in the garden, kisses his shadow.

Returning to the house, she enters the room of mirrors. Jeanne is disturbed by the fact that the multiple images show that her silk dress is eaten away and that her brooch has lost its stones. Trying to peer into the truth of her soul, she sees instead the actress in herself, not her true self.

Frightened by her experience with the mirrors, she runs back to the garden where Paul is still sleeping. The narrator intimates that at this point Jeanne reaches a crossroads. She can smash the glass bell that separates her and her brothers from the rest of the world or she can elect to remain in her comfortable womblike existence. Predictably, Jeanne's choice is the latter, and once more she kisses Paul's shadow. When Paul awakens, Jeanne tells him fearfully that she has seen the image of her body as it lies in the tomb. At that precise moment, Jeanne's guitar string breaks and she presumably dies.

Themes and Meanings

When Anaïs Nin could not get her stories published, she printed them herself on a treadle press. Nevertheless, Nin considered the thirteen stories collected in *Under a Glass Bell and Other Stories* (1944) to represent her best work. Each piece presents characters who are isolated from normal human existence by some kind of protective enclosure. The isolation is presented as alluringly peaceful on the one hand and terrifyingly devoid of life on the other.

Although two other stories in the collection, "Hejda" and "Birth," are more frequently anthologized, "Under a Glass Bell" presents Nin's protective enclosure motif most clearly. Jeanne and her two brothers are symbolically imprisoned in their family mansion where giant chandeliers or "icicle bushes" cast a blue film over the furnishings which Nin compares to a "glass bell."

Yet the isolation is more psychological than physical. It is the three siblings' feelings of superiority that isolate them from other human beings. They see themselves as more sensitive, more creative, and more appreciative of creativity than other people. As a result, they cannot love their spouses, their children, and certainly not Jeanne's Georgian prince. Turning to one another for affection and inspiration, they develop a psychological romantic triangle, the most obvious attachment being that of Jean for Jeanne when Jean courts his sister by anonymously sending her the series of romantic prints.

Jeanne, having received some insight into the nature of her existence while she is in the room of mirrors, returns to the garden where she has the opportunity to free herself from the "glass bell" that encases her life. Choosing safety, she once more kisses Paul's shadow and dies, her death being implied by the snapping of her guitar string.

Nin suggests, then, that life cannot be lived in a vacuum, no matter how attractive the inside or sordid the outside.

Style and Technique

Nin, whose first published work was entitled *D. H. Lawrence: An Unprofessional Study* (1932), was clearly influenced by Lawrence's work. Although her characters lack Lawrence's complexity and her plots lack his excitement, she shares his interest in exploring the interior lives of men and women, especially women. Nin said that her aim was to strip through the façades that human beings present to the world in order to get to the hidden self. Having practiced psychotherapy under the supervision of Otto Rank, Nin clearly had the tools for such an investigation. The room of mirrors in which images reflect images becomes a metaphor for Jeanne's attempt to discover the secrets of her soul.

Perhaps the most distinctive characteristics of Nin's style are the visual images and verbal beauties which give a poetic quality to her prose. For example, such phrases as "minuet lightness of step," "gardens cottoned the sound," Jeanne's "stemless" face, "little silver hooks clutching emptiness," and the "glass bushes" convey the dreamlike quality of life as it is lived under the glass bell.

Sandra Hanby Harris

UNDER THE ROSE

Author: Thomas Pynchon (1937-   )
Type of plot: Parody
Time of plot: September, 1898
Locale: In and around Alexandria and Cairo, Egypt
First published: 1961

> *Principal characters:*
> PORPENTINE, a British secret agent
> ROBIN GOODFELLOW, his partner
> LEPSIUS, a foreign spy
> HUGH BONGO-SHAFTSBURY, his partner
> MOLDWOERP, their chief
> VICTORIA WREN, a young Englishwoman

The Story

"Under the Rose" centers on the activities of Porpentine, a British spy in Egypt during the Fashoda crisis of 1898, when the British forces of General Kitchener encountered a French expeditionary troop in the contested area of the Sudan. The "Situation," as it is referred to in the story, portends an international crisis which could lead to war in Europe, but the real focus of "Under the Rose" is on a small company of secret agents hoping either to promote or prevent the final catastrophe.

Porpentine and his partner, Robin Goodfellow, are committed to preventing the "balloon" from "going up," their phrase for the outbreak of an international catastrophe. They are opposed in their efforts by a group of agents, presumably German, who are equally committed to the eventual outbreak of war. The foreign agents are led by an old veteran spy named Moldwoerp and include his subordinate Lepsius and one other agent unfamiliar to the British. Porpentine soon deduces, though, that the other agent is actually one Hugh Bongo-Shaftsbury, supposedly an amateur British archaeologist.

Bongo-Shaftsbury has attached himself to the family of Sir Alastair Wren, who are on tour. In turn, Goodfellow has formed an attachment to Sir Alastair's oldest daughter, Victoria. The entire company of tourists and spies embarks on the train for Cairo, and enroute Goodfellow is nearly killed by an Arab hired by Lepsius. Bongo-Shaftsbury also manages to frighten Victoria's young sister, Margaret, when he shows her an electrical throw-switch stitched into his arm.

In Cairo, Porpentine observes Goodfellow and Victoria in bed together, although Goodfellow is apparently impotent. Despite this interlude, the British agents get to work. They believe that the foreign spies are planning to assassinate Lord Cromer, the British consul-general, hoping that the incident will precipitate the general crisis into all-out war. To try to force the diplomat to take precautions, the two stage several mock assassination attempts, but Cromer seems to take no notice of them.

Finally, Porpentine and Goodfellow follow the consul-general to an opera house where *Manon Lescaut* (1893) is being performed. There, the two find Moldwoerp and Lepsius arrayed and Bongo-Shaftsbury in the audience with a gun. Porpentine is tempted to shoot Lord Cromer and resolve the situation once and for all, but when confronted by Moldwoerp, he fires "perhaps at Bongo-Shaftsbury, perhaps at Lord Cromer. He could not see and would never be sure which one he had intended as target."

Shoving aside Moldwoerp, whom he tells to "go away and die," Porpentine rejoins Goodfellow. Despite Goodfellow's misgivings, the two pick up Victoria and pursue the foreign agents into the desert, near the Great Sphinx of Gizeh. Porpentine, though, finds himself weaponless and outnumbered and is killed by Bongo-Shaftsbury for having insulted his chief. In the final paragraph of the story, the reader finds Goodfellow years later at Sarajevo, futilely hoping to prevent the rumored assassination of the Archduke Francis Ferdinand which will finally precipitate World War I.

Themes and Meanings

In this story, Thomas Pynchon introduces modernist concerns into historical settings, as he also does in his novels *V.* (1963) and *Gravity's Rainbow* (1973). (In fact, the characters and events in this story were reworked and published as chapter 3 of *V.*) Porpentine and Goodfellow already seem quaint and out of place in a world that is readying itself for the massive holocausts of the twentieth century. The two operate by "The Rules," the unspoken code of Victorian propriety that governs even international espionage. Even as they seek to prevent an Armageddon, their efforts are comical and the results are temporary at best—the story closes on the outbreak of World War I.

Hints of the new society that plays by different rules are seen in some of the other characters. Victoria, for example, is quite unlike her regal namesake by consenting to go to bed with Goodfellow. Porpentine is especially contemptuous of Bongo-Shaftsbury for frightening Victoria's sister on the train, telling him, "One doesn't frighten a child," but Bongo-Shaftsbury, too, represents a new order. The throw-switch in his arm marks him as part human, part machine, one who does not play by the old rules of espionage or even by the old rules of human behavior.

To be machinelike is to strive for a nonhuman purity. That wish drives Moldwoerp and his agents and even begins to affect Porpentine himself. Aiming his gun at Lord Cromer, Porpentine realizes that an assassination would end not only Porpentine's immediate worries but also any reason to worry about Europe itself again. Although Porpentine does falter at this thought, he does still break The Rules by insulting Moldwoerp. For that insult, Porpentine pays the ultimate price.

Underlying the characters and actions in this story is the theme of paranoia that runs through all of Pynchon's works. Defined in *Gravity's Rainbow* as the belief that everything is ultimately connected and leading to some sinister purpose, paranoia manifests itself in "Under the Rose" both generally and individually. The foreboding of international catastrophe runs through the whole story. Characters seem to have the firm conviction that if the Fashoda crisis does not result in war, then something else will later on, a feeling that is borne out by the story's ending. For Porpentine himself, the international crisis itself seems to be only a symptom of something even larger. Riding toward his final confrontation with Moldwoerp's agents, Porpentine has the suspicion that the foreign spies are really working for something nonhuman, the statistical law of averages that reduces all numbers to zero, all human action to nothing. With Porpentine dead and Goodfellow impotently trying to prevent World War I, the story concludes with the triumph of the inhuman forces which have governed this new century.

Style and Technique

Pynchon's story is not as stylistically interesting as its later reworking as chapter 3 of *V*, in which the story is fragmented into eight different segments told from eight different points of view. "Under the Rose," though, is a polished work of fiction with a number of interesting aspects. Pynchon's story is told straightforwardly by a third-person narrator, who is limited mostly to Porpentine's point of view. As a result, the reader shares Porpentine's thoughts while also regarding his actions from a distance. This narrative technique, traditional enough in modern literature, gives the story its combination of philosophical rumination and slapstick comedy. Even while Porpentine is trying to make sense out of his assignment and the actions of his partner and his enemies, he is engaged in buffoonlike behavior. He bursts into song in public, takes pratfalls, and engages in comic-opera fake assassination attempts. This combination of metaphysical musings and low comedy is typical of Pynchon's fiction, while Porpentine's surroundings mark the author's first use of a historical and foreign setting (whose details he lifted from a copy of Karl Baedecker's 1899 tourist guide to Egypt).

Also typical of Pynchon's early fiction is his subtle use of allusion. As in most of Pynchon's short stories, there are veiled references to T. S. Eliot's *The Waste Land* (1922). For example, the story opens on a dry, dusty square in Alexandria with Porpentine wishing for rain. When rain comes, though, it is only in squalls and showers, not the steady, nourishing rain that is needed to make deserts bloom. The most obvious references in the story are Giacomo Puccini's opera *Manon Lescaut*: Porpentine tends to burst into arias from the opera and it is *Manon Lescaut* which Lord Cromer is viewing during the assassination attempt. The opera itself is a story of foolish and doomed love that reflects both Goodfellow's affair with Victoria and Porpentine's foolish and romantic nature. At one point, realizing his impending failure, Porpentine compares himself to an inept singer in the Puccini opera.

While Pynchon himself, in an introduction to his collected short stories, has denigrated "Under the Rose" as an "apprentice effort," the story has an important place among the author's works. It marks the beginning of Pynchon's mature style, which would root itself in *V.* and fully blossom in *Gravity's Rainbow*. In the story, characters are more fully realized than in his earlier fiction, while Pynchon's particular style of comedy is truer and more amusing than in those stories. Perhaps the most interesting aspect of the story is Pynchon's command of physical detail. Working only from second-hand sources such as Baedecker, Pynchon is able to sketch in a physical environment and suggest a world and worldview that go with it. If not as fully accomplished as his later novels, "Under the Rose" marks a very good beginning.

Donald F. Larsson

THE UNKNOWN MASTERPIECE

Author: Honoré de Balzac (1799-1850)
Type of plot: Psychological realism
Time of plot: 1612
Locale: Paris
First published: "Le Chef-d'œuvre inconnu," 1831 (English translation, 1885)

> *Principal characters:*
> MASTER FRENHOFER, an old painter
> FRANÇOIS PORBUS, a former painter to the king of France
> NICHOLAS POUSSIN, a young painter
> GILLETTE, Poussin's mistress

The Story

In "The Unknown Masterpiece," Balzac describes two meetings of three artists, the old painter Master Frenhofer, the prominent master François Porbus, and the young man Nicholas Poussin. As the story begins, Poussin is hesitating before Porbus' door. When Frenhofer appears and is admitted, Poussin follows him into the only painter's studio he has ever seen. Here he is struck by the first important piece of art in the story, Porbus' painting of the Virgin Mary. To Poussin's surprise, Master Frenhofer criticizes the painting for lacking life. When Poussin objects, the older artists challenge him to prove his right to be in the studio by producing a sketch. To illustrate his own emphasis on life and movement, Frenhofer then applies his own touches of color to Porbus' Virgin Mary, making the figure live as he had insisted he could.

Invited to Frenhofer's home, Poussin sees a second fine painting, the *Adam* of Frenhofer's own master, Mabuse. Yet to Frenhofer, this painting, too, lacks some spark of life. As the painters talk, Poussin observes the esteem in which Frenhofer is held, his own lofty standards for art, his wealth, his knowledge. Poussin is impressed by Frenhofer's description of the painting which he hopes will be his masterpiece, a portrait of a courtesan, Catherine Lescault. Frenhofer, who has devoted ten years to this painting without completing it to his satisfaction, muses that perhaps he simply lacks the right model. At any rate, he refuses to allow anyone to see the painting.

Returning to his garret, Poussin embraces his devoted mistress Gillette, to whom love is all-important, so important that she resents his concentrating on the canvas rather than on her when she poses for him. Hesitantly, Poussin proposes that Gillette pose for Frenhofer. Only when Poussin seems to renounce art for love does she consent, but she warns him that the experiment may result in the end of their love. Perhaps he no longer loves her, she thinks; perhaps, she thinks, he is not worthy of her love for him.

The second meeting of the three artists takes place three months later. Depressed over his inability to perfect his painting, Frenhofer again thinks of finding a model. When, however, Poussin offers Gillette in return for allowing Porbus and him to view the painting, Frenhofer refuses, as if their seeing his Catherine Lescault would profane her. Yet when Gillette, still doubtful, arrives, Frenhofer agrees. At last admitted to his studio, Poussin and Porbus look in vain for the masterpiece. The canvas that Frenhofer shows them is merely a mass of paint, with no discernible image, except for the tip of a foot, which has escaped the layering of colors. To Frenhofer, the figure is there, brought to life by the paint that conceals it. When Poussin blurts out the truth—that there is nothing on the canvas—Frenhofer falls into despair, but soon his dream recaptures him, and once again he sees his Catherine Lescault. At that moment, Poussin remembers his Gillette, discarded and crying. She rebukes him and says that she hates him. Shown to the door by Frenhofer, the painters are chilled by his farewell. That night he burns his pictures and dies.

Themes and Meanings

Balzac's concern in "The Unknown Masterpiece" is the problem of reconciling the various opposing forces in life, a problem which is particularly difficult for the artist. The problem is illustrated appropriately in the very pattern of the short story.

The story is divided into two chapters, one entitled "Gillette," the second, "Catherine Lescault." Gillette is the actual mistress of Poussin: She is a devoted young woman who considers love more important than art and feels somehow diminished whenever Poussin uses her as a model. At those times, she senses, he draws away from her and into some visionary world in which she is merely an object. Catherine Lescault, on the other hand, is the vision of Frenhofer, a vision so real that he will not show his painting of her to others, as if such an action would profane their love. When the other painters see his canvas, they realize that the true painting exists only in Frenhofer's mind. Gillette's prophecy comes true when all three painters are so obsessed with their art that they completely forget her. At the end of the story, she tells Poussin that, although she loves him, she hates him for turning her over to Frenhofer, thus proving that love is far less important than art. In a sense, Poussin loves his art as completely as Frenhofer does. A Catherine Lescault will always win any artist from the Gillettes of this world.

Yet if the artists are alike in their devotion to art, they differ in their approach. Having learned his master Mabuse's secret, Frenhofer insists that he can paint the essence, the spirit of his subject. He insists that painters such as Porbus, who cannot decide between the precision of lines and the emotional splash of color, can never truly bring their subjects to life. When the younger painters at last see Frenhofer's masterpiece-in-progress, they realize that in his ten years of seeking for essence, of applying layer upon layer of color in order to attain the abstraction, he has retreated totally into his own dream. The implication of Balzac's story, then, is that the true artist must combine life and love with art, objectivity with subjectivity, mechanical copying of life with vision of the unknown and unseen essence of life. For all of his genius, Frenhofer has dedicated his life to creating a masterpiece which will always remain unknown.

Style and Technique

In a short story that is about art, it is appropriate that Balzac pictures reality as artists would perceive it. For example, young Poussin first sees Frenhofer in the light peculiar to dawn and thinks of his figure in terms of Rembrandt. In Porbus' studio, he again notes the light, as it touches objects in the clutter. Returning to Gillette, he thinks of her love in terms of light, her smile as a sun which shines in darkness. Finally, looking at Frenhofer's "masterpiece," they think that the studio light may be hiding the form which Frenhofer insists lives on his canvas, and they peer at the chaos of color in search of some form before they perceive that all that remains of reality in Frenhofer's painting is the foot of Catherine Lescault.

A consistent metaphor in the story is that of the mistress. Gillette, the living mistress, is justifiably jealous of Poussin's art, whose claim upon him is made clear in the first sentences of the story, when he waits at Porbus' door like a lover attending a new mistress. Clearly, when Gillette models for him, he thinks about his vision, not his model, and she senses his infidelity. When he wishes her to model for Frenhofer, she sees this activity as a kind of prostitution, and Poussin admits that the idea makes him feel dirty.

To Frenhofer, all living mistresses are unfaithful eventually, but his ideal—ironically, a courtesan—will always be faithful to him. Yet he senses the existence of some imperfection in his painting, which causes him to consider using a live model and finally accepting Gillette. Like Poussin, who is ashamed of having offered Gillette, Frenhofer believes that to show his canvas to other painters would be a kind of prostitution. To him, she is a wife, yet a virgin; in the painting, she is naked and must be clothed before she can be seen. Jealously, he accuses the younger painters of wishing to steal her; even after his brief suspicion that he has created nothing, he turns them away and covers the canvas where he believes Catherine exists. Finally, the metaphor of the mistress is suggested in the last lines, for, once having destroyed his painting, his beloved, Frenhofer can no longer live. Unlike Poussin, who can survive without Gillette's love, but like the most romantic of lovers, Frenhofer must die without his love, even though she is only an artistic illusion.

Rosemary M. Canfield-Reisman

UNMAILED, UNWRITTEN LETTERS

Author: Joyce Carol Oates (1938-   )
Type of plot: Interior monologue
Time of plot: 1969
Locale: Detroit
First published: 1969

Principal characters:
> AN UNNAMED WOMAN, the narrator
> GREG, her husband, a Detroit politician
> MR. KATZ, a visiting professor from Boston University who is
>   having an affair with the narrator
> MRS. KATZ, his wife, in Boston
> MARSHA KATZ, their precocious ten-year-old daughter, in
>   Boston

The Story

Unmailed letters exist in the everyday world, in some sort of objective reality, yet unwritten letters exist only in the mind. The title of the story is strategic; it forces the reader into the uncomfortable role of voyeur. As the reader looks over the shoulder of the writer of these "letters," the reader is actually looking into her mind, reading her fears and desires. Because of this, the action of the story is not sequential but psychological.

In the first letter, addressed to her parents, the narrator discusses a change of doctors and dentists. The banality of this first paragraph ("everything is lovely here and I hope the same with you") acts as a foil to the remainder of the letter. That is, the first paragraph is recognizable as a letter, perhaps "unmailed," but the second paragraph is truly "unwritten" thoughts directed at the narrator's parents. The change is obvious both in the subject matter ("your courage, so late in life, to take on space") and in diction ("I think of you and I think of protoplasm being drawn off into space"). Such is the tension between writing and thought that the reader must continually bear in mind.

The second letter addresses Marsha Katz, who, it seems, has been sending odd gifts anonymously to the narrator. The narrator and Marsha's father are having an affair; the precocious daughter is trying to incite guilt feelings in the narrator. At times the narrator tries to "read" the little girl's meanings, to interpret her stories; one story deals with a dead white kitten, representing (the narrator thinks) the victimized daughter herself.

She "writes" to Greg, her husband, next. The letter is an attempt to remember their first meeting, but its more submerged meanings deal with her inability to carry children to term and with her infidelity—her feelings of inadequacy and guilt. She refers to Marsha's father, her lover, as "X." She cannot bear to write (think) his name before her faithful husband.

Next she addresses her "darling," Marsha's father. She recounts a dream of his death, "mashed into a highway." His face is so badly disfigured that it is unrecognizable. In the same way that she converts him into a nonentity in the previous letter, an "X," so here she psychologically removes his face. She also dreams of suicide; the two deaths become equivalent in her dreamworld.

As the story proceeds, the narrator reveals the details of her marriage and of her affair. Greg has been a sincere, but at times ineffectual, politician in Detroit during the racial turmoil of the late 1960's. Ridden with guilt, the narrator writes to Greg of her infidelity with Katz; falling in love a second time, she says, is "terrifying, bitter, violent." Yet she does nothing to become fulfilled in this new love; her letters are unmailed, unwritten. Writing to Mrs. Katz in Boston, to Mother and Father in the Southwest, to an undefined Editor, the narrator demonstrates her paralysis, her claustrophobia, her inability to confront overtly the forces which have shaped, and continue to shape, her emotional life.

In the last long letter, these frustrations culminate. It is addressed to Greg and appears to be a straightforward confession. Although it begins "I want to tell you everything," the second paragraph reflects the same tortured mind: "I seem to want to tell you something else." Marsha Katz has just attempted suicide. Katz, who must return to Boston immediately to be with Marsha and his wife, has called the narrator, asking her to accompany him to the airport. He is shaken by his daughter's desperation; she is angry that the daughter has apparently conquered the mistress. In this emotional chaos, the two lovers sneak off to a deserted stairway in the airport to make love. He leaves. She has difficulty finding her "husband's car"; feeling literally and figuratively soiled, she checks into the airport motel to bathe and to write the preceding confession. The conclusion of the story is formed by the first words of a letter addressed to "My darling." She may be writing to Greg (if the confession means something), or she may be writing to Katz (if it does not).

Themes and Meanings

Because the action of the story occurs primarily within the consciousness of one character, Oates has necessarily limited her control over meaning. One must remember to distinguish what Joyce Carol Oates means from what her character means.

This writer of unmailed, unwritten letters is trapped in a tortuous world of uncertainties. She looks to Mother, Father, husband, and lover for a sense of security; her parents are literally and figuratively distant, her husband is good but ineffectual, her lover is appealing but weak. At one point, in a letter addressed to "The Editor," she asks the startling question, ". . . why are white men so weak, so feeble?" Rephrased, it might be, "Why cannot the men in my life make me a strong woman?" The question comes from the vantage point of a deep-seated neurosis, from the neurotic position of being a well-educated, middle-class woman in the United States who regresses into an infantile dependency.

The nature and consequences of this neurosis manifest themselves in the very form of the story. Because Oates allows her subject to reveal herself through a series of unuttered utterances, the story remains open-ended, unresolved. The reader remains trapped in the claustrophobic confines of an unproductive mind. The form of the story is in itself meaningful. The narrator exists within the cycle of modern lovings and leavings. Her life is directionless, pathetic. She is forced to make love in transit—on a staircase in an airport.

Appropriately, the collection of stories in which this story is included is entitled *The Wheel of Love and Other Stories* (1970); as this story ends, the wheel is about to take another turn. Oates may be questioning whether the identity of this last "darling" makes a difference at all to her troubled letter unwriter.

Style and Technique

Stories told by means of a series of letters (called epistolary narratives) were rather common in the eighteenth century; in the twentieth century, however, such a form of storytelling is rare. For this and other reasons, Oates's story is considered experimental.

Oates takes a somewhat obsolete form of narration and radically modernizes it. Because these letters have no specified destination (and therefore no respondents), one's attention is not, as it conventionally would be, on an interchange of two or more points of view, but rather on the workings of a single psyche. One's attention is paradoxically not on communication but on an inability to communicate (hence, "unmailed" and "unwritten").

The style of the work follows from the epistolary noncommunication. That is, it becomes an interior monologue which admits a broad range of styles. Whatever such a person (a white, middle-class, well-educated woman of the 1960's) could think is, in this story, stylistically appropriate. Oates's style is therefore a not very distant cousin of the stream-of-consciousness technique.

At times the prose sounds like letter-writing ("I don't know how to begin this letter except to tell you"), at times like metaphysical speculation ("that delicate hint of death"); at times, it is reminiscent ("we met about this time years ago"); at times, the prose exists in a sexually vivid present tense ("he kisses my knees, my thighs, my stomach"). In short, the story contains an ever changing style which reflects the nuances of the panic-stricken woman who is the story's center and its circumference.

Mark Sandona

UP THE BARE STAIRS

Author: Seán O'Faoláin (John Whelan, 1900-   )
Type of plot: Social criticism
Time of plot: The early 1900's and the 1930's
Locale: County Cork and the city of Cork, Ireland
First published: 1948

Principal characters:
> SIR FRANCIS JAMES NUGENT, the protagonist, an eminent civil
> servant
> BROTHER ANGELO, a monk, Nugent's teacher
> THE NARRATOR, Nugent's traveling companion

The Story

"Up the Bare Stairs" opens on a train traveling through Ireland. The first-person, anonymous narrator describes his traveling companion as a big man, about sixty years old, "dressed so conventionally that he might be a judge, a diplomat, a shopwalker, a shipowner, or an old-time Shakespearean actor." The narrator notices the man's initials, F. J. N., on a hat case and reads in the paper that a Francis James Nugent has been made a baronet for his military service. The ensuing conversation and the fact that boy went to the same school, West Abbey, leads to Nugent's recollections.

This section, the main action in the story, is narrated by Nugent, as the narrator assumes the role of listener. At West Abbey, Frankie (Nugent) was very fond of one of his teachers, Brother Angelo. Nugent describes Angelo as handsome and full of life, a man who enjoyed solving quadratic equations as much as he liked playing games with the boys. With the perspective of a sixty-year-old man looking back on his childhood, Nugent says that they were "too fond of him.... He knew it ... and it made him put too much of himself into everything we did ... perhaps he wasn't the best kind of teacher; perhaps he was too good.... With him it wasn't a job, it was his life, it was his joy and his pleasure."

Angelo frequently divided the class into teams representing two political factions, the Molly Maguires and the All for Irelanders. Frankie and Angelo both supported John Redmond of the Molly Maguires. One afternoon, Frankie caused his team to lose. Angelo laughed it off—and kept Frankie two hours after class, knowing that Frankie would be in trouble when he got home. Frankie's politically passionate father, a poor tailor, struggling to send Frankie to school, awakens Frankie's sick mother, a seamstress, with a roar: "A nice disgrace! Kept in because you didn't know your Euclid!" His fury increases when he learns that Frankie let down the Redmond side. The scene ends with the entire family in tears and Frankie promising to work harder.

The next day, Angelo asks Frankie to do the same problem, which he completes perfectly and insolently. Frankie continues to answer questions correctly and rudely, goading Angelo into striking him. Frankie never forgives Angelo, and their personal war continues until Frankie graduates. From then on, Frankie studied every night until midnight. When he sat for the civil service exam, he placed first throughout the British Isles in three out of five subjects. This experience in school caused him to despise and pity his parents.

Here the anonymous traveler begins narrating again, and the purpose for Nugent's trip to Cork is revealed: his mother's funeral. "I meant to bury her in London. But I couldn't do it. Silly, wasn't it?" The story ends with the narrator's description of Nugent with his "poor relations" as they leave the station.

Themes and Meanings

The main theme of "Up the Bare Stairs" is the relationship between individuality and (to use a neutral term) background—perhaps a more loaded and revealing term might be culture. The relationship is dealt with problematically, as a tension, not schematically, as a matter to be resolved or explained away. Within a narrow framework, O'Faoláin provides a dynamic series of contrasts: past and present, youth and age, personal and public history, poverty and reward, home and exile, self and community or institution, appearance and reality. These opposites confirm the tension and its continuing active presence in the protagonist's life.

A sense of the protagonist's context is important for an appreciation of the significance of Nugent's rising above it. It has become commonplace to describe the political life of Ireland at the beginning of the twentieth century as stagnant and degraded. (A celebrated representation of this state of affairs is James Joyce's "Ivy Day in the Committee Room.") As "Up the Bare Stairs" makes plain, however, there was much vivid political activity at the local, as distinct from the national, level. This activity is characterized in the story by a passionate, if unthinking, adherence to a given faction. Nugent's father's slavish loyalty to Redmond is presented as an inevitable counterpart to the slavery of tailoring.

It is in reaction against such subjection that Nugent immerses himself in his schoolwork. The moment of confrontation between Nugent and his parents leads to supplanting one form of coherence (the Redmondite) with a more authentic, self-generated one ("the work"). The result of that dedication is to give him the appearance of an Englishman. The "War Services" for which Nugent receives his knighthood have nothing to do with the Irish armed struggle for independence from the British Crown, a struggle whose linguistic repercussions, at least, leave him "indifferent."

Despite Nugent's scholastic brilliance, his extraordinary (perhaps even slightly incredible) success in the public realm, and his strenuous efforts to repudiate the oppressions of the past, he still remains deeply involved with his formative influences. He may have gained autonomy of action, as his war with Angelo suggests, but it remains moot as to whether he has achieved autonomy of spirit. His comprehension of and fidelity to the traditions of his people is impressively enacted in the scene of reunion with which the story closes, as well as in the reason for that scene, the decision to bury his mother in her native soil. Rejection of the dependent relationships of his youth, both the one with his parents and the one with Angelo, is a valuable declaration of personal independence. Yet to reject the anonymous traditions which animate the powerful authority articulated by parents and teacher proves to be a more difficult task, or at least a task which Nugent has not thoroughly analyzed. Yet perhaps because his rebellion is a subjective one, a substitution of self-respect for pitiable dependence, the protagonist has not felt the need to explore the more general influence of communal traditions. Thus, the story's conclusion may denote reconciliation and acquiescence as well as constraint and enclosure. Nugent, despite appearances, has remained "unmistakably a Corkonian."

It is not merely the end of "Up the Bare Stairs" which bears witness to the continuing presence of the past in the present. There are numerous subtle instances of this relationship during the course of the story. A case in point is the marked contrast between how little Nugent divulges of his present elevated position or of the career which led to it and the seemingly total recall he possesses of his days at West Abbey. Another representation of the emotional force and unexpected vitality of Nugent's memories is the fact that once he embarks on his recollections, the anonymous narrator becomes merely an auditor, a pretext for the past.

The narrator, despite his temporary obliteration and the reader's ignorance of him, is a crucial feature of the story's coherence. In a number of ways he embodies the unmediated present. It may be inferred that he came of age in the new independent Ireland of which Sir Francis knows nothing. The narrator's encounter with the great man, and his unwitting initiation of Nugent's revelations, illustrate the availability of the present to the past and its unpredictable involvement with it. At the end of the story, the narrator does not turn his back on the scene into which his traveling companion steps.

Yet the present exists in the story passively. The two narrators' companionship and the ostensibly uneventful nature of the journey facilitate a temporary suspension of the present. The past rushes in with increasing emotional vehemence to fill the apparent vacuum. Although the story's structure of conflict has rich cultural and conceptual repercussions, because its origin is located in "the heart" (as the epigraph, the opening two lines of William Butler Yeats's poem, "The Pity of Love," has it), it can only be lived and relived, not alleviated or dispelled.

Style and Technique

Like many Irish short stories of its generation, "Up the Bare Stairs" relies on the reproduction of a voice for its principal stylistic effect. Mimicry of the voice gives the material immediacy and dramatic impetus. Its use also evokes the age-old Gaelic tradition of storytelling, redolent of hearthside yarning at close of day. "Up the Bare Stairs" is not necessarily structured in terms of an updated version of the traditional scenario. Given the story's complex sense of personal and cultural legacies, however, it is not inappropriate that hints of such complexity are to be found in the story's organization.

Use of the voice also influences the story's pace and development. From a bland, innocuous, casual-sounding opening (like everything else about him, the narrator's voice is not particularly distinctive), the story builds in intensity. The gradual development, punctuated initially by revelations concerning Nugent's real indentity, gains markedly in momentum and vividness once Nugent takes over as narrator. Indeed, the anonymous narrator's mistaken assumption that his traveling companion is an actor seems in retrospect a revealing error, since Nugent displays a decided flair for the dramatic—and for self-dramatization. His story is not merely a chronicle of unhappiness and how it was overcome; it is a reenactment of the experience of that unhappiness. Nugent's excoriation of pity—so necessary if the story is to rise above sentimentality—occurs with a sense of shock and completeness appropriate to a dramatic climax.

"Up the Bare Stairs" also cleverly uses the story-within-a-story device. This device emphasizes the story's dual character, its interaction between different times and temperaments. In addition, however, although Nugent's narrative is the heart of the story, it does not overwhelm its surrounding framework. The story's technique articulates in its own right an overall sense of continuity and compatibility as well as a sense of distance and division. Nugent embodies the latter sense, while the anonymous narrator bears witness to the former. The elaborately conceived, but fluently presented, structure of "Up the Bare Stairs" unobtrusively and efficiently underpins the story's graphic comprehension of how complex and far-reaching simple, early lessons can be.

George O'Brien

UPON THE SWEEPING FLOOD

Author: Joyce Carol Oates (1938-   )
Type of plot: Naturalistic
Time of plot: Probably the early 1960's
Locale: Eden County, in an unspecified state
First published: 1963

> *Principal characters:*
> WALTER STUART, a thirty-nine-year-old man who is on his way
> home after his father's funeral
> THE GIRL, who is about eighteen
> THE BOY, her brother, who is about thirteen

The Story

In Eden County, a sheriff's deputy stops Walter Stuart, warns him about a hurricane that is developing, and continues on down the road. Stuart is in a hurry to get home to his wife and two daughters, having spent a week at his father's farm, making arrangements for his father's funeral. Stuart is a district vice president of a gypsum mining plant, a thirty-nine-year-old man who has achieved, quite naturally, success in both finance and love.

A girl of about eighteen and a boy of about thirteen jump into the road by their farmhouse and try to stop another car going back to town. It passes them, and Stuart offers to give them a ride to safety. The car gets mired in mud, however, and the boy sees that his frightened horse has got loose. Although the girl frantically protests and slaps at her brother, Stuart tries to help the boy round up the horse, but it gets away. Unable to flee the storm, they take refuge in the kitchen of the farmhouse, pushing furniture up against the door. The girl and the boy scream at each other and at Stuart, inexplicably angry at each other. When the water seeps up through the floorboards, they climb into the attic.

When the windows downstairs explode, Stuart makes a hole in the roof with an ax, and they climb out onto the roof and hold on as the wind and the rain assail them. Then the house collapses, and they float free on the roof. They cling to it, huddled together in the dark, terrified. The boy has "gone loony."

The dawn reveals a small hill and some trees, and they wade toward it. Stuart stirs up some snakes. In a frenzy, he and the boy try to kill them. For no reason, Stuart suddenly starts hitting the boy with a stick. Then he confronts the girl, who prepares to defend herself with a board. As Stuart lunges at her, she points toward a rescue boat. Wading out to meet it, Stuart cries, "Save me! Save me!"

Themes and Meanings

Stuart thinks of himself as normal and gentle. Yet interacting with the violent, unfeeling, and crude boy and girl, he finds himself taking on their characteristics. The hurricane and the flood provoke this process, as it aggravates the worst qualities in the girl and her "loony" brother. Oates shows how something in human nature produces, needs, thrives on violence, personal and vicarious. Morality and convention, according to Oates, cannot control this urge and may contribute to it. Stuart's altruism saves them, but he wants to force them to be grateful. The violent intrusions of chance can significantly aggravate a person's innate inclinations toward violence.

During the course of the story, Stuart is put through a profoundly wrenching experience. He goes from asking the deputy, "Do you need help?" to begging the rescue boat, "Save me!" He goes from declaring, "I know what I'm doing!" to doing something totally uncontrollable. Because the deputy assumes that Stuart is better off than "these folks coming along here" and that he would not care what the hurricane does to them, Stuart believes that he must act on the social obligation to "see if anybody needs help."

Stuart is isolated from his own people in this remote region of swampland. As "the slashing of rain against" his face excites him and he feels "a strange compulsion" to "laugh madly," he breaks out of his normal life. The engine of his car and the wind "roared together." In the farmhouse, he is isolated even from the other people who live in the swampland: In the attic, on the flood-surrounded roof, and finally on the hill, his isolation intensifies, allowing the free expression of his most primitive instincts.

The horse that runs amok at the beginning of the story is an expression of the violence of the storm as a pure force and of the irrational, erratic behavior of the strange boy and girl. These insane elements contrast with Stuart early in the story. The pair represents the mindless, valueless forces in nature that work on men who try to live within some rigid, civilized context. When Stuart goes for the ax, the boy thinks that he might hit him: Stuart's sense of "helplessness, at the folly of his being here, for an instant almost made him strike the boy with the ax." The girl senses his impulse and attacks Stuart.

The Good Samaritan of the beginning of the story is so transformed by psychological and natural disruptions that he is moved to kill the boy and the girl for whom he has risked his life (and neglected his own family) to save. As the horse is an expression of the violence of wind and rain, the writhing snakes are a manifestation of the flood stage of the hurricane. Beating the snakes with a stick is the trigger that releases irrational violence in Stuart, and he strikes the boy. The raw vitality of suppressed desires, impulses, urges, and instincts suddenly explodes. The girl is so impressed by the change in him that she does not defend her brother this time; she falls back on brute survival, preparing to defend herself. Thus, Stuart's instinctive altruism is converted, by a climate of natural and human violence, into hatred and homicide. In her depiction of motiveless violence, Oates suggests that much ordinary human behavior apparently is as motiveless as that of the panicked horse and the snakes.

Stuart can no longer believe that "his mind was a clear, sane circle of quiet . . . inside the chaos of the storm. . . ." He believes that he has "blundered" into "the wrong life," and that "his former life" was incomplete. He knows that he has "lost what he was just the day before," that he has "turned now into a different person, a stranger even to himself. . . ." The wind "tolled" the death knell of his former self. The howling outside becomes internalized in "the howling inside his mind." It is from external forces that he has now internalized that he begs the rescue team to "save" him.

Style and Technique

It is difficult, and perhaps unproductive, to discuss Oates's stories as literary constructs. If "Upon the Sweeping Flood" has form, it is so submerged in "experience" as to defy analysis. If there is control, it is not aesthetic control, but the control of gathered forces in a hurricane. The lack of shape and focus makes this story linger in the reader's consciousness as if it were an actual event one wants to forget. Would greater attention to style, technique, and structure dilute the intensity of her vision and the terror conveyed by her themes?

Oates very seldom uses either the first-person or the third-person central-intelligence point of view; omniscience seems most suited to her vision of life. In this story, the elements are filtered through the perceptions of Walter Stuart, except when Oates alludes to the manner in which he will remember this incident years later, and except for the tale-telling tone in the first line: "Not long ago in Eden County, in the remote marsh and swamplands to the south, a man named Walter Stuart was stopped in the rain. . . ." With stark authorial authority, that omniscient tone is sustained throughout. The author seems to have written in a frenzied burst of energy, the heat of which one feels simultaneously with a cold objectivity, as she violently renders her own involvement in the miserable predicament of her characters. Narrative drive, character depiction, the author's vision—in this as in many of Oates's stories—seem to rush upon the reader like the wind, the rain, and the panicked horse, to startle like the snakes, animated by an omnipotent God, expressed by an inspired omniscient author in a shotgun style.

The reader's sense that Oates is not aesthetically in control of her style contributes to the nightmare quality of her depiction of characters, landscapes, wind, rain, and flood, eerie darkness and light, horses and snakes, the erratic blows of the ax and the sticks, descriptions of the house, of the characters (enhanced by their dialogue)—a bizarre atmosphere of calamity, in which the characters, too, are out of control. It is a wonder that her style distracts no more than it does. Would a more refined style dissipate the way-

ward energy of all the elements in the story? The raw materials of her story
and the seriousness of the theme are more commanding than her style. Even
so, the power of her writing can be overwhelming; the reader feels the
author's compulsion to hack a path, as Stuart hacks a hole in the roof with an
ax, through a dense thicket to reach the site of a disaster.

David Madden

THE USE OF FORCE

Author: William Carlos Williams (1883-1963)
Type of plot: Psychological realism
Time of plot: Early twentieth century
Locale: The United States
First published: 1938

> *Principal characters:*
> A DOCTOR, the unnamed narrator
> MATHILDA OLSON, a little girl who is his patient
> MRS. OLSON, her mother
> MR. OLSON, her father

The Story

The doctor who narrates "The Use of Force" knows that the Olsons, a working-class couple, must fear that their young daughter is quite ill if they are willing to pay the three-dollar fee for his visit. Mathilda Olson is an unusually attractive child who clearly has a high fever, and the doctor sets out in his best professional manner to discover the cause. The unspoken possibility on his mind and on her parents' is that she might have diphtheria, several cases having been reported at the school the child attends.

The story is based on the simple premise that the doctor must examine Mathilda's throat and get a throat culture for her own protection and for the protection of others around her. It promises to be an easy enough task. A simple throat examination, however, becomes instead a battle between doctor and child, and William Carlos Williams traces the first-person narrator's shifting attitude toward the child and the task as the doctor moves well beyond reasoned professionalism to delight in the use of force.

The doctor first tries kindness: "Awe, come on, I coaxed, just open your mouth wide and let me take a look." In a single catlike movement, the child claws at his eyes and sends his glasses flying. Next, he tries firmness: "Look here, I said to the child, we're going to look at your throat. You're old enough to understand what I'm saying. Will you open it by yourself or shall we have to open it for you?" The child refuses, and the battle is on. The doctor has fallen in love with the spirited child by this point and sees her as magnificent in her terror of him. With the father's help, he manages to get a tongue depressor into Mathilda's mouth, but she splinters it with her teeth. The doctor sees that it would be best to stop and come back later, but he is beyond reason, and in his fury he asks for a makeshift tongue depressor that she cannot destroy: a spoon. In spite of Mathilda's bleeding mouth and hysterical shrieks, he persists and finally manages to reveal the secret that she has been hiding for three days: Her tonsils are covered with the membrane that indicates diphtheria.

Themes and Meanings

As Williams' title indicates, the narrative is a study of the use of force and of its effects on the individual who uses it. As the story progresses, the doctor degenerates from the reasonable professional concerned with his patient's welfare to an irrational being who takes pleasure in the pure muscular release of forcing the child to submit. The doctor remains well aware of the reasonableness of his ultimate goal—the girl's throat must be examined—but even as he persists in pursuing that goal he knows that he is no longer concerned with what is best for the child: "The worst of it was that I too had got beyond reason. I could have torn the child apart in my own fury and enjoyed it. It was a pleasure to attack her. My face was burning with it." His sense of logic tells him that it is a social necessity to protect the child and others against her idiocy in refusing the examination. Even as he acknowledges the truth in this line of reasoning, however, he knows that it has little if anything to do with the motivation behind his ruthless determination to force the child to do as he wishes: "A blind fury, a feeling of adult shame, bred of a longing for muscular release are the operatives. One goes on to the end."

With a "final unreasoning assault," the doctor overpowers the child. Then it is the child's turn to react in a blind fury, her turn to attack. She tries unsuccessfully to escape from her father's arms and fly at the doctor, "tears of defeat" blinding her. She knows that she has lost a battle, yet her anger is quite justified, considering the assault that she has just endured, as is her earlier fear of the doctor who has come to see if she has a disease that could kill her. It is as though the sore throat did not exist as long as it was her secret and hers alone. The fact that Williams chose for the story a patient who is not only a child but also a truly ill child at that emphasizes all the more the violence of the doctor's actions. Child is pitted against adult, illness against health, ignorance against experience. Reason would dictate that undue force should not have been necessary, but reason ceases to be the controlling factor once the battle begins.

The parents stand by anxious but helpless as the struggle takes place, their spiritlessness in contrast to the child's spirit, their unwillingness to hurt their daughter in contrast to the doctor's use of force. They do not interfere even when Mathilda is cut, bleeding, and hysterical because of their trust in what the doctor represents. They do not question the doctor's aggressive methods, let alone try to stop him, because of the infallibility and ultimate good that doctors represent in their minds: health as opposed to illness, life as opposed to death.

Style and Technique

Point of view is critical in this story about force. The external facts of the story are fairly simple: The doctor does what is necessary to diagnose a potentially fatal disease. The fact that the story is told from the doctor's point of view, however, makes it possible to see the changes that take place in his mind as he progresses from cool professional to animalistic assailant. He could have justified on the basis of logic alone his persistence in forcing the examination. What he cannot justify even to himself is his motivation for doing so. Still, the doctor is calm and controlled in telling the story. He exposes for analysis his mental state just as he exposes for examination the little girl's throat.

There are clear sexual undertones to the act of violence that the doctor directs against the child. That element could have been avoided completely had the patient been a little boy. As it is, the doctor acknowledges early the physical attractiveness of the child and the fact that he loves her for her spirit. The doctor's aggression toward Mathilda takes on characteristics of a rape as his anger builds up at her resistance and finally results in violence. The examination becomes an assault on her mouth cavity with the phallic tongue depressor, which she renders useless, and then with the spoon. As her fear of the doctor increases, Mathilda's breathing becomes more rapid. The doctor's face burns with the pleasure he feels in attacking her. Mathilda resists as she would resist an actual sexual assault, and she bleeds as a result of his probes into her mouth. The story and the assault reach their climax when the doctor achieves a sense of physical release by forcing Mathilda's mouth open and revealing the hidden membrane. Ironically, her parents let the assault take place and actually aid in it because they fear their child's death more than they fear any other form of assault on her. Mathilda herself, however, is left with a sense of violation and defeat.

Donna B. Haisty

THE VELDT

Author: Ray Bradbury (1920-   )
Type of plot: Science fiction
Time of plot: Early twenty-first century
Locale: An American town
First published: 1951

> *Principal characters:*
> GEORGE HADLEY, a middle-class American male
> LYDIA, his wife
> WENDY and PETER, their children
> DAVID MCCLEAN, a psychologist and a friend of the Hadleys

The Story

George and Lydia Hadley are the proud owners of a "Happylife Home which had cost them thirty thousand dollars installed, this house which clothed and fed and rocked them to sleep and played and sang and was good to them." This is the dream home of the story's futuristic world, and its most elaborate feature is a nursery, which can reproduce any scene in complete aural, visual, or olfactory detail in response to the occupants' thought waves. The Hadleys' children, Wendy and Peter, have used the nursery to conjure up such fantasies as Oz, Wonderland, or Doctor Doolittle, but lately the children have used it to re-create an African veldt. The Hadleys, investigating the nursery, are frightened by the image of a pride of lions charging at them.

Indeed, the incident so unnerves them that Lydia suggests locking the nursery for a few days even though she knows that the children almost live for the nursery. She begs George to turn off all the labor-saving devices in the house so that they can have a vacation and do things for themselves. At dinner, George thinks of how the children have become obsessed with the African veldt, with its hot sun, vultures, and feeding lions. The nursery shows that thoughts of death have become prominent in his children's minds. Returning to the nursery, he orders it to remove the veldt and bring forth an image that he thinks is more healthy for his children, but the room does not respond. The nursery's apparatus will not alter the veldt either because of a malfunction caused by excessive use or because someone, possibly Peter, has tampered with the machinery.

When the children arrive home from a carnival, George questions them about the nursery, but the children deny all knowledge of the veldt. Going to the nursery again, the Hadleys find a different scene in it, which must have been put in by Wendy. Yet George finds an old wallet of his on the nursery floor, with tooth marks, the odor of a lion, and blood on it. Later, the Hadleys hear the sounds of human screams and lion roars coming from the nursery. They know that the children have defied orders and are once again in their playroom. When George suggests to his children that the family give up the houses' mechanical aids, including the nursery, for a time, Wendy and Peter are decidedly against it. Peter apparently sees no other purpose in life than watching and hearing sophisticated electronic entertainments. He ominously tells his parents that they should forget about closing the nursery.

Worried about the growing secrecy and disobedience of the children, George and Lydia invite their friend David McClean, a psychologist, to examine the use that the children make of the nursery. As George and David enter the nursery, they see lions eating something in the distance. This carnage and the entire veldt disturbs David. He explains that the nursery can be used as a psychological aid, with the images left on the walls serving as an index of a child's mind. According to David, the veldt image reflects the children's hostility toward their parents. They resent their parent's authority, preferring instead the ever responsive nursery. The psychologist strongly urges them to leave their Happylife Home and start a new life elsewhere. As they leave the room, David finds a scarf of Lydia's with bloodstains on it. George questions him as to whether the room could ever make any of the images real, an idea that David dismisses as paranoid.

George finally turns off the nursery and the rest of the house. The children throw an elaborate temper tantrum in which Peter implores the now disconnected machinery not to let his father kill the house. The children beg for one minute more of nursery viewing, to which Lydia adds her support until George relents. The children are allowed one minute while George and Lydia await David McClean's arrival so that they can fly to a new life in Iowa. The Hadleys are preparing for departure when they hear Wendy and Peter calling to them. They run into the nursery, but all they find is the familiar veldt scene with the lions looking at them. Suddenly the door is slammed and locked, and the Hadleys hear Peter shouting to the house. Then the lions start moving toward them "and suddenly they realized why those other screams had sounded familiar." When David McClean arrives at the house, he finds only the children in the nursery watching lions feeding on something in the distance.

Themes and Meanings

On the most obvious level, "The Veldt" is a gruesome fable about the destructive consequences of sparing the rod and spoiling the child. Yet it is also a satire on the modern consumer society from a traditional, humanistic viewpoint in the style of several other Bradbury works, such as *Fahrenheit 451* (1953) and *The Martian Chronicles* (1950). In all these stories, technology, backed up by commercialism and a utilitarian philosophy, tries to remove the inconveniences, difficulties, and challenges of being human and, in its efforts to improve man's material condition, impoverishes his spiritual condition.

Technology's offering in this story is the Happylife Home, which mechanically performs almost every human function, including that of the imagination. The nursery reproduces images of the children's thoughts, in effect becoming their imagination. This relieves the children of the necessity of developing their imagination by contact with the outside world, so that, despite their high intelligence, the children never grow up; significantly, Wendy and Peter have the same names as the hero and heroine of *Peter Pan* (1904). Without the chance to mature, the children sink to the level of beasts, demonstrated when Peter says that all he wants to do is see, hear, and smell. Thus, they identify not with characters in traditional children's literature, such as "Aladdin's Lamp" or *The Wizard of Oz*, but with the predatory lions of the veldt.

The elder Hadleys also participate in this dehumanizing process. They have allowed the nursery to usurp their role as parents while becoming the childish dependents of their house. As David McClean tells them, they have built their life around creature comforts. They, too, have refused to grow up, to accept their duties as parents. Their avoidance of responsibility reduces them to the level of prey to lions. Unlike their children, they know what a more active life is like, and their present inactivity becomes constraining. They try to escape to a simpler life in Iowa, but they give in to the children once too often and are destroyed by the house.

The house itself becomes a living presence in the story, nor is this surprising, since the house is designed to provide services that should have been left to humans. When it makes the lions real, something it was not designed to do, the Happylife Home becomes almost godlike. Peter, in fact, regards it as a god. The killing of the elder Hadleys is the house's way of survival. Ironically, the technological marvel that was to provide a safe and carefree environment for the Hadleys creates instead the violent world of the veldt.

Style and Technique

Bradbury's style is marked by lyricism and a profusion of metaphors. In "The Veldt," these create an illusion of reality that brilliantly mirrors the deceptions that the characters in the story undergo. His description of the electronically produced African veldt contains such exact sensory details that it almost seems to be real, and indeed it is by the story's end. Moreover, his description of the veldt also conveys an atmosphere of menace and hostility mirroring the psychological state of the Hadley family. In a similar fashion, Bradbury employs active verbs and personifications, describing the workings of the house's mechanical devices in a way that suggests the living, human quality that the house is acquiring. When the devices are turned off, the house is a "mechanical cemetery," reinforcing the idea that the house is a living thing.

Characteristically, Bradbury's poetic style transports the reader out of the everyday world and into a fantasy world, often reminiscent of the unchecked imagination of childhood. The world of "The Veldt" is one in which childhood fantasies are made concrete. Hence, the story has an air of unreality about it as if it were simply a child's daydream of a world in which children have the power and competence given to adults and adults have the helplessness of children.

This dreamlike quality is counterbalanced by the use of clichés and advertising language, which levels a satiric thrust against modern society. Phrases such as "nothing's too good for our children" and "every home should have one" direct attention to the permissiveness, commercialism, and worship of material comforts that dominate American life. These serve to anchor the bizarre events of the story in an objective framework and give the child's daydream an adult moral.

Anthony J. Bernardo, Jr.

VENUS, CUPID, FOLLY, AND TIME

Author: Peter Taylor (1917-   )
Type of plot: Satiric realism
Time of plot: The early 1930's
Locale: Chatham, a fictional city on the northwestern edge of the American
    South
First published: 1958

Principal characters:
MR. ALFRED DORSET, an eccentric elderly bachelor
MISS LOUISA DORSET, his equally eccentric spinster sister
NED MERIWETHER, the fourteen-year-old son of an upper-
    middle-class family
EMILY MERIWETHER, his thirteen-year-old sister
TOM BASCOMB, the paperboy and an uninvited guest

The Story

To the conventional "establishment" community of Chatham's West Vesey
Place, the Dorsets are definitely peculiar. They are seen shopping in public
places wearing bedroom slippers or with the cuffs of a nightdress hanging
down beneath daytime clothing. Mr. Dorset washes his own car, not in the
driveway or in the garage but in the street of West Vesey Place. Miss Dorset
not only appears on her front terrace at midday in her bathrobe but also has
been seen (through the tiny glass panels surrounding the front door) doing
her housecleaning in the nude. Their home was once a mansion, but to
reduce their taxes, they ripped off the third floor, tore down the south wing,
and disconnected some of the plumbing—not bothering to conceal the
resulting scars. Nevertheless, they are the last two of a Chatham "first family," and in a community that prizes family above fortune, their social standing is not to be questioned.

The Dorsets were orphaned while still in their teens; afterward, they not
only refused any opportunity to marry but also deliberately cut themselves
off from wealthy relatives who had moved away from the town. They subsist
in an odd fashion: Mr. Dorset grows figs, plentiful but juiceless, and Miss
Dorset makes paper flowers, plentiful but artless, which they sell to those
members of the community whom they count as their peers. Their single
social gesture is an annual dancing party for the pubescent children of suitable families, and the parties have become a predebutante ritual, which all
the children must undergo but which give some of them nightmares.

Arrangements for the parties are as strange as the Dorsets. Alfred goes
around the neighborhood in his old car, collecting the juvenile guests; no
adults have been inside the house for twenty years. Alfred and Louisa are

always garbed in the latest fashion of tuxedo or ball gown, none of them ever worn twice. The house is festooned with paper flowers (perhaps to be sold later), with reproductions of somewhat lubricious artworks such as Auguste Rodin's *The Kiss* and Il Bronzino's *Venus, Cupid, Folly, and Time*, with lighting designed to emphasize the artworks. The Dorsets are inclined to notice and to nudge each other when they see the children paying particular attention to the prints and statues. The high point of the parties is a tour of the house, during which the Dorsets talk about their past social triumphs and display ancestral evening wear that they keep in glass cases. The only dancing is done by Alfred and Louisa, to Victrola music, while the children watch. When not dancing, they keep up a running dialogue about being wellborn, being young together, believing that "love can make us all young forever."

There comes a year when Ned and Emily Meriwether are of a proper age to be invited, and the Dorsets arrange a party to end all parties. It starts as a small, adolescent practical joke, merely a plan to smuggle in Tom Bascomb as an extra guest. (Tom does not live in West Vesey Place and is not wellborn; he delivers the morning paper and once saw Miss Louisa doing her nude housecleaning one day when he came to collect.) Yet the joke has repercussions that last for the rest of their lives.

Tom takes Ned's place in Mr. Dorset's old car; Ned walks to the Dorset house and slips in with a group of guests. As the tour of the house progresses, Tom and Emily put on a great show of affection; he kisses her ears and the tip of her nose, they embrace and pose among the flowers in front of the Rodin replica. Mr. Dorset and Miss Louisa are delighted by the show, which proves to them that love can "make us all young forever." Yet Ned's reaction is something he has not foreseen: He cannot bear the sight of his sister cuddling with Tom. Finally, he cries out in pain: "Don't you *know*? . . . They're *brother* and *sister*!" The other children, taking this to be the punch line for the joke, laugh aloud.

Yet the Dorsets do not turn on the incestuous pair. They turn on Ned, whom they thought to be Tom, saying that they knew all along that he did not belong among the wellborn. Ned flees up the front stairs, pursued by Mr. Dorset, down the back stairs, where he confront's Miss Dorset, up the front stairs again—until he is finally cornered and locked in one of the dismantled bathrooms. Tom, claiming to be Ned, offers to call the police and calls the Meriwether parents instead. Then he slips out the back door.

The aftermath of the joke is much more sad than comic. The hapless Dorsets, unwilling to believe that they cannot tell the wellborn from the paperboy, believe that the Meriwether parents as well as all the children are being mischievous. At last persuaded of their error, they simply withdraw to their rooms and leave the bewildered parents to close the house and see the children home.

Ned and Emily are sent off to boarding schools; they never regain their childhood intimacy, and later they become indifferent or even antagonistic to each other. Chatham's children are free forever from Dorset dancing parties.

Themes and Meanings

On the landing of the stairway to the Dorset's ballroom is a small color print of Il Bronzino's *Venus, Cupid, Folly, and Time*, torn out of a book and tacked to the wall. Its presence gains significance because of the story's title. The original is a Mannerist work depicting allegorical figures listed in the title: Venus and Cupid engaged in sly flirtation with each other, a dessicated shape of Time prophesying the end of Folly. It does very well as an illustration of Alfred and Louisa, with their faintly incestuous devotion to each other and their staunch refusal to acknowledge the passing of time. It is this unhealthy and unproductive relationship that poses a threat to the children of Chatham—not the Dorsets' simpleminded snobbery. The dancing parties seem designed to encourage others to follow their pattern, and perhaps the children's joke was born of a not-wholly-realized sense of the danger. Perhaps, also, that accounts ultimately for the breach between Ned and Emily.

Some readers see the story as an allegory of the decay of Southern gentility, a Faulknerian theme, but that social significance seems too heavy for the tone of this narrative. There is obvious social criticism in the mockery of Vesey Place manners, but the mockery contains more amusement than disgust. The narrator is still in and of the society he describes; he sees past the façade, acknowledges changes in the new generation, but he has not rejected either Chatham or its old-fashioned values. He seems more concerned with individual people than with the social scene as a whole—somewhat sorry for the Dorsets though glad that the children are free of them, forever puzzled and a bit unhappy about consequences for the Meriwethers.

Style and Technique

The point of view is the most important device in this story, combining schoolboy experience with mature understanding. The unnamed narrator speaks in the first person; he is a child of West Vesey Place, somewhat older than Ned Meriwether, and has served his turn at the dancing parties but was not present at the last one. He does not tell the story in chronological order but mingles memories, his own and others', with reports of the fiasco from several sources. He speaks often of "we" and "us," so that he seems to be a composite voice of the community, at least for his generation. He also tells the story in retrospect, many years after the event.

The last pages include information and impressions gleaned from Ned's wife at some time after World War II. By this means the reader knows the unhappy aftereffect for the Meriwethers of their impractical joke. Reasons for the family breach are not clear—the children were too young to analyze their own thoughts and feelings—but Ned's wife is sure that it started that night at the Dorsets'. She comes from outside Chatham, lives in it but is not part of it, and her view helps the narrator shape his reactions.

The narrator is a born storyteller. His voice is conversational, his attention sometimes digressive, his insight keen. He understands Chatham, its pretensions and its social values—Bascomb, Meriwether, and Dorset. Peter Taylor has used similar narrators in other stories, and one hears much of the author's voice in the voice of the fictional storyteller.

Rosamond Putzel

THE VERTICAL LADDER

Author: William Sansom (1912-1976)
Type of plot: Psychological realism
Time of plot: c. World War II
Locale: An abandoned gasworks in urban England
First published: 1947

> *Principal characters:*
> FLEGG, the protagonist, a young man
> OTHER YOUNG PEOPLE, two boys and two girls

The Story

A young man named Flegg, responding to a dare by a girl he wants to impress and the taunting of a group of young acquaintances, attempts to climb a vertical ladder on an old gasometer, a storage tower in a deserted gasworks. The reader experiences the event through the consciousness of the climber, living through the various perceptions and changing emotions of the performer as he undergoes a wide gamut of feelings from foolish bravado to sheer terror and dreadful isolation.

The group of three boys and two girls are probably teenagers, since they are apparently old enough to be given considerable freedom, yet young enough to have little sense of responsibility. They have walked out the back gate of a public park into a run-down, almost deserted section of town, wandered on to the abandoned gasworks, and started throwing bricks at the rusty iron gasometer, towering above all the other structures. The protagonist is showing off, casting his bricks higher than the others, claiming that he knows something about throwing grenades. Then comes the shout from one of the girls: "Bet you can't climb as high as you can throw!"

The boys immediately take up the derisive, taunting tone. The playful psychological game quickly pushes Flegg into a position of bravado from which he cannot gracefully retreat without losing face.

There are two ways of ascent, one known as a Jacob's ladder, bolted flat against the side of the tower, the other a zigzag staircase with a safety railing. Flegg saunters toward the safer stair, but the boys call him a sissy and insist that he climb the vertical ladder.

The ladder looks solid enough except that some twenty feet of the lower rungs are missing. A wooden painter's ladder is propped up against the vertical ladder, however, making it perfectly accessible. One of the girls, no longer vicious but actually encouraging and admiring, gives him her handkerchief to plant at the top of the tower like a banner.

He starts off jauntily enough, practically running up the wooden ladder but slowing significantly when he reaches the vertical ascent. Flakes of rust drop in his face, and he finds that he cannot remove a hand long enough to brush them off. He shakes his head to dislodge them, but this action makes him feel giddy and brings on the first twinge of fear. By the time he has climbed about fifty feet, he is close to panic and still far from the top.

Not only is he in constant dread of falling, but also everything around him seems unusually large, while he, and certainly his companions on the ground, seem very small. Now there is a new horror: There is a confusion of voices from below and a scream from the one girl who said nothing when the others taunted him. She seems to be shrieking, "Put it back, put it back, put it back!" The terrorized climber glances down for a second—just long enough to realize that someone has removed the wooden ladder. He can see it lying flat on the ground. The girl's hysterics are distracting the others. They are wandering away, abandoning him on the ladder with no way to get down.

He struggles to control his panic, focusing his attention compulsively on one rung at a time and creeping upward, looking neither up nor down. Only when he reaches the last rung does he dare to look up once more. The story ends with his realization that the rungs of the ladder do indeed end, but there are five more feet of impassable space before the top of the tower.

Themes and Meanings

As might be expected in a story of suspense in which even the protagonist is undefined except in the most general terms, theme is not prominent in this tale. Particularly noteworthy is the author's control over the reader's attention and the effective expression of psychological nuances in an emotionally packed situation.

The indeterminate ending creates a real cliff-hanger, leaving to the imagination of the reader what the outcome will be. Logic and a realistic mode suggest tragedy; it seems unlikely that the protagonist is going to be rescued. Since those on the ground really know nothing of the actual plight of the climber and may assume, if they think at all, that he can return from the top by the stairway, their return is improbable.

One significant meaning that emerges from the story is that human beings are often, especially at this age, at the mercy of their impulses, with precious little attention to possible consequences. Many an uneasy parent will recognize this volatile combination of peer pressure, ego-sensitivity, and inexperience which often leads to tragedy. The unique character of this exploit, different from usual misdemeanors of urban young people, lends a certain irony to the situation. Unlike pure pleasure-seekers, this young man assumes a pseudoheroic task that derives from a more archaic notion of valor: to climb the mountain and plant his lady's banner at the peak. Even the girl who starts the mean goading of the protagonist succumbs to the ancient meaning of chivalric action when she offers her handkerchief.

The story also emphasizes the existential isolation of each person in his private perception of experience. The climber has every reason to believe that no one knows the extremity of his distress. He is cut off both literally and spiritually from communication with his peers or anyone who might help or even sympathize with his predicament. If he lives through this experience, he will have learned a sobering truth about human destiny: The most stressful experiences of life are often the most solitary, and certainly every man does his own dying utterly alone.

Style and Technique

Any story depending heavily on suspense, rather than on more leisurely sources of reader interest, requires a fast opening to engage the reader's attention and a swift closing after suspense has attained its peak. The climber's abandonment on the tower where he can neither ascend nor reach the ground again certainly provides the latter. William Sansom achieves the first requirement by jumping into the middle of the climb, then backtracking to explain the situation.

> As he felt the first watery eggs of sweat moistening the palms of his hands, as with every rung higher his body seemed to weigh more heavily, this young man Flegg regretted in sudden desperation but still in vain, the irresponsible events that had thrust him up into his present precarious climb.

This promise of excitement-to-come sustains the reader for the several paragraphs of preliminary events. These lend credibility to the situation, showing how it arises from the natural self-absorption, sexual rivalries, jealousies, and insecurities of young people everywhere. The brief reference to the protagonist's aspiring to "the glamour of a uniform" when he pretends to throw bricks with the special lobbing action of throwing hand grenades suggests a wartime milieu in which heroic action is even more a part of young male psychology.

Sansom is adept at describing how the appearance of an object changes radically from different perspectives. When Flegg first looks up from his position on the vertical ladder, the effect is quite alien to the impression it gives even a few yards away from the tower. The precision of this passage is remarkable both for its visual accuracy and its psychological effect.

> From this angle flat against the iron sheeting, the gasometer appeared higher than before. The blue sky seemed to descend and almost touch it. The redness of the rust dissolved into a deepening grey shadow, the distant curved summit loomed over black and high. Although it was immensely stable, as seen in rounded perspective from a few yards away, there against the side it appeared top heavy, so that this huge segment of sheet iron seemed to have lost the support of its invisible complement behind, the support that was now unseen and therefore unfelt, and Flegg imagined despite himself that the entire erection

had become unsteady, that quite possibly the gasometer might suddenly blow over like a gigantic top-heavy sail.

The downward view is also distorted: "His friends appeared shockingly small. Their bodies had disappeared and he saw only their upturned faces." Such surrealistic appearances contribute to his impression of utter isolation. What is close at hand seems unnaturally large: "Even now the iron sheeting that stretched to either side and above and below seemed to have grown, he was lost among such huge smooth dimensions, grown smaller himself and clinging now like a child on some monstrous desert of rust."

The psychological realism of the story, rooted both in the special effects of an unfamiliar perspective and the tricks of an active imagination, eventually approaches archetypal imagery. Flegg's view of the top, still inaccessible at the end, seems more frightful even than the abyss below him. He sees it as "something removed and unhuman—a sense of appalling isolation."

It echoes its elemental iron aloofness, a wind blew around it that had never known the warmth of flesh nor the softness of green fibres. Its blind eyes were raised above the world. It was like the eyeless iron visor of an ancient god, it touched against the sky having risen in awful perpendicular to this isolation, solitary as the grey gannet cliffs that mark the end of the northern world.

At this moment, if at no other, the frivolous escapade undertaken on a dare seems to suggest the mythic quest of the epic hero to the end of the world. Sansom does not allow this impression to remain, however, for poor Flegg is not cutting a very heroic figure: "Flegg, clutching his body close to the rust, made small weeping sounds through his mouth." At the end, when he realizes he cannot attain the top, he is staring and circling his head like a lost animal. Whatever impression one might have had about the romantic connotations of such an adventure, they dissolve in grim reality.

Katherine Snipes

VICTROLA

Author: Wright Morris (1910-   )
Type of plot: Comic realism
Time of plot: 1981
Locale: A small American town
First published: 1982

> *Principal characters:*
> BUNDY, an old man who lives alone except for his dog
> VICTROLA, his dog
> MISS TYLER, the dog's previous owner
> AVERY, a druggist

The Story

Bundy is an elderly man who lives alone with his dog. He has had the dog since the death of its previous owner, Miss Tyler, who lived above Bundy. The overweight, asthmatic dog was already old at the time of Miss Tyler's death, several years before. When he lived with Miss Tyler, the dog always snarled when he met Bundy and barked wildly when he opened his mailbox. Bundy had taken the dog in even though he has never liked large dogs with short pelts and "had once been a cat man." Bundy does admire the dog's "one redeeming feature": He sits whenever he hears the word "sit."

Bundy and the dog have got along since the time they went to the park and the dog began furiously digging a large hole, only to have Bundy give him a sharp crack with the end of the leash. The dog turned on him with a look of hatred, but Bundy had "just enough presence of mind to stand there, unmoving, until they both grew calm." After this incident, they reached what Bundy considers a permanent truce.

The focus of the story is a shopping trip taken by the two of them. They go to a drugstore for Bundy's medicine and a vitamin supplement for the dog's itching. Passing an antique warehouse, Bundy realizes "that he no longer wanted other people's junk. Better yet (or was it worse?), he no longer *wanted*—with the possible exception of an English mint, difficult to find." At the supermarket, Bundy ties the dog to a bicycle rack and goes in to do his shopping. A few minutes later, he is called to the front of the store, where the dog is lying on its side "as if sleeping." A clerk explains that some other dogs rushed it and apparently frightened it to death. When a woman asks the dog's name, Bundy says that it is Victor "since he could not bring himself to admit the dog's name was Victrola." Miss Tyler believed that the dog looked like the RCA symbol: "The resemblance was feeble, at best. How could a person give a dog such a name?"

Themes and Meanings

Wright Morris has frequently written about dogs and cats. In *One Day* (1965), a dog wears goggles while riding sitting up in a car, creating the impression that he is driving, and a cat has laryngitis in "The Cat's Meow." Usually what is most important is the animals' effects on humans, as when a cat causes three people to become more alive in "DRRDLA." What is significant in "Victrola" is that the dog and the man share the same problem: old age. Bundy is bothered when Avery, the druggist, never fails to comment on Victrola's age. Bundy notices that as Victrola grows older the younger dogs, one by one, begin to ignore him: "He might have been a stuffed animal leashed to a parking meter." Bundy worries that the owners of these dogs see him in the same way: "The human parallel was too disturbing for Bundy to dwell on it." When Dr. Biddle says that he will miss Victrola, Bundy believes that the retired dentist's eyes betray his fear that the dog's owner will "check out first."

Bundy senses that the old men he encounters at the supermarket are touchy about whether he looks "sharper" than they do, but he considers elderly women less suspicious: "Bundy found them more realistic: they knew they were mortal. To find Bundy still around, squeezing the avocados, piqued the old men who returned from their vacations." Still, when Bundy thinks about what will happen "if worst came to worst," he is not certain whether he is thinking of himself or Victrola: "Impersonally appraised, in terms of survival the two of them were pretty much at a standoff: the dog was better fleshed out, but Bundy was the heartier eater." When the dog dies and someone finds Bundy a place to sit, he remains standing as if to offer firm proof, to himself if to no one else, that he is hardly ready to follow Victrola.

Morris' fiction is full of eccentric old men who wander bemused through a world that they understand much less than they are willing to admit. Sometimes, however, this world seems beyond understanding. In the supermarket, Bundy suspiciously studies "the gray matter being sold as meat-loaf mix." He is not at all nostalgic for the past, but that does not blind him to the shortcomings of what passes for civilization, as when he enters the checkout lane "hemmed in by scandal sheets and romantic novels." For Morris' characters, the vagaries of modern life are something to be passed by rather than fruitlessly grappled with.

Style and Technique

One of the most notable aspects of Morris' approach to fiction is his objective tone. He is more amused than angered by what Bundy encounters on his shopping trips. Morris is more concerned with reporting changes in American society than in mourning the loss of anything, realizing that hindsight makes the past seem better than it was. He always avoids sentimentality as well, choosing to shift the focus at the end of the story from Bundy's response to Victrola's death to something comic: An elderly woman who always keeps the shopping cart to ferry home her purchase of two frozen dinners this time allows a policeman, arriving to investigate the dog's demise, to escort her across the street.

Much of the humor in "Victrola" is derived from Bundy's inability to control the dog as much as he wants. Victrola sits off to one side "so that the short-haired pelt on one rump was always soiled. When Bundy attempted to clean it, as he once did, the spot no longer matched the rest of the dog, like a clean spot on an old rug." Morris reveals the characters of both protagonists through humor: "Without exception, the dog did not like anything he saw advertised on television. To that extent he was smarter than Bundy, who was partial to anything served with gravy." Such blending of detail, character, and humor is what makes Morris such a distinctive artist.

Michael Adams

VIEWS OF MY FATHER WEEPING

Author: Donald Barthelme (1931-   )
Type of plot: Antistory
Time of plot: A timeless present
Locale: Unspecified
First published: 1970

> *Principal characters:*
> THE UNNAMED NARRATOR, who may or may not be telling a
>   story about the life and death of his father
> LARS BANG, the coachman, who may or may not have
>   recounted a story of the death of the narrator's father
> A LITTLE GIRL, who witnesses the death of the father

The Story

In "Views of My Father Weeping," there is no realistic plot line based in the conventions of cause and effect and set in some existing time and space. Rather, Barthelme presents the reader with a story about the supposed death of a narrator's father combined with interlineations that present alternating views of a father weeping. To complicate the matter even further, the story about the death of the father may or may not be true, since the coachman, who storifies the experience, is reported to be a "bloody liar." In addition, the juxtaposition in the story of the narrator to the coachman suggests a doubling of the two men, an identification that makes the narrator a "bloody liar," too.

Asterisks separate thirty-five paragraphs which constitute the story. Paragraphs range from twenty-five lines to one line, the shortest being the last, which consists of one abbreviated word, "Etc.," which brings the reader back to the beginning of the story in an endless circle or a series of infinite regressions. The retrograde character of the action is consistent with the interlineations where "regression" operates in psychoanalytic terms to suggest a return of the libido to earlier stages of development or to infantile objects of attachment in the case of both father and son.

The opening of the story consists of two sentences establishing a possibly factual situation: "An aristocrat was riding down the street in his carriage. He ran over my father." The presence of an "aristocrat" in a "carriage" suggests a period when noblemen were driven about in coaches by liveried coachmen. The place of the accident, in King's New Square, together with references to the nobleman, the Lensgreve Aklefeldt, a count who lives at 17 rue du Bac, suggests a European setting. On the other hand, the interlineations refer to, among other things, mailmen, insurance salesmen, armadillos, Ford Mustangs, television, and the American plains in such a way as to identify a setting in modern times in the United States. Furthermore, in the interlineations, the father is alive, if aged and continually weeping.

The tie between the storified experience concerning the death of the father and the interlineations is the narrator. In the storified experience, the narrator is searching for the "truth" about the killing of his father. In the interlineations, the narrator is searching for the "truth" about his feelings for his father, which will result in his own ego identity.

Having been notified by the police of the accidental death of his father by a hit-and-run carriage, the narrator seeks witnesses to the occurrence so that he can determine for himself the real conditions of his father's death. The first witness that the narrator finds is a little girl, eleven or twelve years old, who says that she witnessed only part of the accident, since part of the time she had her back turned. She identifies the man in the carriage as an aristocrat. Later this little girl will inexplicably turn up at the narrator's door to tell him the name of the coachman who was driving the aristocrat's carriage.

The little girl is the first of three females who give the narrator some kind of guidance in his search for his father's executioner. A woman named Miranda will tell the narrator how to get inside the aristocratic quarters where the nobleman lives and how to present himself to the inhabitants of the great house. Another woman makes final comment on the story the coachman, Lars Bang, finally tells the narrator. This woman is the one who points out that "Bang is an absolute bloody liar." The only other female in the story is the narrator's mother, who apparently is at some distance from her husband and son, since she is not present at the burial, and the son telephones her with the news of his father's death.

Stories told to the narrator by various witnesses to the accident differ. According to the witnesses, either the father was drunk and was himself the cause of the accident or the driver was at fault because he could have avoided the collision had he tried. The narrator says that he smelled no alcohol on his father at the scene of the accident. Lars Bang, in telling his version of the story, says the father was thoroughly drunk and attacked the horses in such a way as to cause them to rear in fright and to run headlong over the father, dragging him forty feet over the cobblestones. Bang says that he tried but could not stop the horses.

The interlineations present the distress of a son with a father who cannot control his weeping. The fact that the son is not sure that the weeping father is his own suggests an archetypal father figure who may be "Tom's father, Phil's father, Pat's father, Pete's father, Paul's father." This archetypal figure desires in the son's mind to be thanked for his contribution to the life of the son and worshiped by the son in the manner demanded by a god. The son alternately sees himself before his father in a ceaseless attitude of painful supplication and as his father's avenger, someone who, if only he knew what was causing his father to weep, could try to do something about it:

Father, please! . . . look at me, Father . . . who has insulted you? . . . are you, then, compromised? . . . ruined . . . a slander is going around? . . . an obloquy? . . . a traducement? . . . 'sdeath! . . . I won't permit it! . . . I won't abide it! . . . I'll . . . move every mountain . . . climb . . . every river . . . etc.

Juxtaposed to images of the father weeping are images of the father not weeping but in absurd situations, such as straddling a very large dog, writing on a white wall with crayons, shaking pepper into a sugar bowl, knocking down doll's furniture in a doll's house, and playing shoot-'em-up with his son with real guns.

Both lines of narration—the storified experience of the death of the father and the interlineal comments on and description of the behavior of the weeping father—come to the same conclusion, expressed in the final paragraph: "Etc."

Themes and Meanings

There is no way for a reader of "Views of My Father Weeping" to tell whether anything described in the story has actually taken place. Nor can any reader tell anything objective about the father. What the reader does experience is the author's subjective expression on a surrealistic plane of a son's feelings about his father which are strong, but ambiguous. The son's nightmare vision of the father's continual weeping suggests that fathers can do nothing but weep and sons can do nothing to alleviate their weeping, though sons may feel compassion for fathers who weep. On the other hand, weeping fathers can get on the nerves of youthful sons (who are not yet fathers). Sons can desire their fathers dead and project visions of accidents that kill them. The sons themselves (because the visions are theirs) murder the fathers.

In this way, the two narrative lines of the story are joined. Lars Bang is a projection of the narrator, who kills the father whom the son desires dead. Lars Bang is a liar, as is the son who covers up his desire to rid himself of his father by projecting it into a dream context. Nothing the son can do, however, will rid him of the vision of the weeping father, and nothing the son can do will stop the passage of time from transforming the murderous son into a weeping father himself.

Style and Technique

Characterized by a surreal surface which combines in varying degrees elements of the fantastic, incongruous, absurd, and clichéd, this story owes much to writers, such as the great nineteenth century Continental novelists Nikolai Gogol, Fyodor Dostoevski, and Charles Dickens, and the great modernists, such as Franz Kafka, Vladimir Nabokov, James Joyce, and Jorge Luis Borges, whose novelistic dreamscapes provide a suprarational way of knowing that is distinctly different from a "realistic" view of the everyday world as apprehended through the senses. In Barthelme's story, as in others characteristic of the postmodernist mode, the ordinary or existential gives way to the fabulous; fact and fiction, as ordinarily conceived, are blended, and the story draws attention to itself not only as artifact but also as an epistemological act, a valid way of knowing. For Barthelme, as for other postmodernists, fiction is not mimetic, not an imitation of life. Rather, fiction is an act of creation, a shaping and a forming of reality that defines self. One is, according to Barthelme, what one makes. One defines oneself in one's art. Thus, changes in aesthetic structures can lead to changes in the world around the artist.

Mary Rohrberger

VILLON'S WIFE

Author: Osamu Dazai (Tsushima Shūji', 1909-1948)
Type of plot: Social realism
Time of plot: 1946
Locale: Tokyo
First published: "Viyon no tsuma," 1947 (English translation, 1956)

> *Principal characters:*
> MRS. OTANI, the narrator and wife of the celebrated poet
> MR. OTANI, the celebrated poet
> THE RESTAURANT OWNER
> THE OWNER'S WIFE

The Story

"Villon's Wife," set in the dark years of the early postwar era, is narrated by the wife of a writer who has been much celebrated but who has given himself over to drunkenness and debauchery. The story opens late on a winter night as the woman, asleep with her retarded son, hears her husband come home, drunk as usual. With uncharacteristic tenderness the husband asks if the child still has a fever. At this point a man and woman arrive at the front door and call for the writer, Mr. Otani. An argument ensues and the wife tries to intervene, but Otani pulls a knife and rushes out of the house, "flapping the sleeves of his coat like a huge crow," and disappears into the darkness.

The wife invites the two visitors into the shabby house and learns of the difficulty between these people and her husband. The couple explain that they run a small restaurant and drinking place where Otani has been a regular customer for several years, accompanied by a succession of women friends. He has run up a huge debt, but what is worse, on this particular evening, he has stolen five thousand yen which the owner needs in order to pay his wholesalers before the end of the year. Not wanting to make a scene in public, the couple have followed Otani home, hoping that they can persuade him quietly to return the money. Instead, he threatens them with a knife and runs away.

Upon hearing this story, the wife's only response is to burst out laughing—they are so poor she cannot even afford to take her sick child to a doctor, much less pay back the five thousand yen her husband stole or pay off the debts he has accumulated. The wife, however, reassures the couple that everything will be settled the following day and asks them not to file charges against her husband quite yet.

The next morning, the woman takes her child and wanders aimlessly for a time, then goes to the restaurant where her husband stole the money. Not knowing what else to do, she once again reassures the owner and his wife that someone will come soon with the money, and says that to show her good faith, she will stay at the restaurant as a sort of hostage until the debt is paid. The wife keeps herself busy waiting on customers. She is quite popular with the customers, who are in a festive mood since it is Christmas Eve. That evening, a man and woman came in dressed and masked for a masquerade party. Although realizing that it is her husband, the wife treats him as she would any other customer. His friend speaks briefly with the owner and pays back the five thousand yen that was stolen.

When the owner thanks Mrs. Otani for helping to get his money back, she offers to stay on and continue working until her husband's drinking debt is also paid. At first, she finds her life wonderfully transformed now that she has found a way to deal actively with her problems rather than simply sit at home and worry. The enthusiasm, however, does not last long, and after working for twenty days, she concludes that all men are criminals, that as poorly as her husband treats her, he is not the worst of the scoundrels she has come to know. One evening a customer follows her home, and when she shows some sympathy for him, he rapes her.

The next morning, she goes to work and finds her husband already at the restaurant and already drinking heavily. He shows her a review in the newspaper where he is referred to as a monster. He asks if she thinks he is a monster and explains that he stole the five thousand yen in the first place to buy New Year's presents for her and the child so that they could have "the first happy New Year in a long time." The wife's only response to this excuse is that there is nothing wrong with being a monster as long as one somehow manages to survive.

Themes and Meanings

Osamu Dazai, who had always been a social rebel, found himself in a paradoxical situation when Japan surrendered in 1945. For years, he had been preaching the message that accepted social values were bankrupt. With the loss of the war, society at large came to agree with him, and, indeed, saw him as something of a prophet. While he offered no new set of social values to replace the old, with this story and some postwar novels, he became a major spokesman for the values and attitudes of Japanese society at that time.

Typically for Dazai, the two central characters, Otani and his wife, represent contrasts at every level. In this regard, they become spokesmen for two different approaches to Japan's postwar condition. The wife is industrious, nurturing, practical, and willing to deal with problems. Otani, on the other hand, is frivolous, irresponsible, dissolute, and self-indulgent. In the end, the wife has the strength to recognize her situation and to adapt, accept, and endure it, while her husband cannot. For the wife, the most important thing is survival at any cost, no matter how degrading or dehumanizing that survival turns out to be. The husband cannot accept life on those terms, and for him there is only flight and despair. While the wife understands and accepts her condition and changes her way of living to ensure survival, the husband fails to come to terms with his desperate condition. It is typical of Dazai to depict strong, enduring women who nurture weak, feckless men. In this story, the women are practical realists, while the men are idealistic dreamers.

The title of the story alludes to a work written by Otani which has the title "François Villon." There are certain parallels between events in Dazai's story and the life of the French poet. Villon was a romantic and a poet who was accused of stealing five hundred gold crowns from the College of Navarre shortly before Christmas in 1456. His ballads, like Dazai's story, depict his helpless entanglement in shameless vice and are known for their grim humor and their expression of the vanity of life. At another level, the reader can see Dazai depicting himself in the character Otani, who sees himself as the François Villon of Japan. This is particularly true in the sense that Dazai's position was similar to that of Villon, who was loved by all of Paris for his poetry even while his personal life was a disreputable shambles.

Style and Technique

Dazai's favorite techniques for depicting the human condition are paradox and black humor. One sees examples of this when the restaurant owners arrive at Otani's house and fall back on social convention, telling him what a nice house it is. In fact, the mats are rotting, the paper doors are in shreds, and the cushions are filthy and torn. Again, one sees Dazai's sardonic humor when the restaurant owner refers to Otani as a genius, an aristocrat, and a man of unlimited capability; whereas the wife, immune to flattery, knows perfectly well that her husband is a drunkard, a thief, and a lecher who is brazenly unfaithful to her.

By creating the character of the wife as being an unflinching realist and giving her the narrator's role, Dazai is able to contrast Otani's self-pity with the absence of self-pity on the part of the wife, giving the work its terrible power. This effect is created because the narrator does not pass judgment on the events she recounts; she simply states the facts and her own determination to go on surviving.

Stephen W. Kohl

A VISIT OF CHARITY

Author: Eudora Welty (1909-   )
Type of plot: Moral fable
Time of plot: The 1930's
Locale: An American nursing home
First published: 1941

> *Principal characters:*
> MARIAN, a young Campfire Girl who visits a nursing home
> ADDIE, an elderly female occupant of the nursing home
> AN UNNAMED OLD WOMAN, who is Addie's roommate

The Story

The action of "A Visit of Charity" is deceptively simple. Marian, a young Campfire Girl, reluctantly visits an "Old Ladies' Home" to gain points for her charity work. While there, she meets two old women, one who chatters on in an obsequious way and another, old Addie, who, confined to bed, resents the little girl's visit as well as her own babbling roommate. When Marian leaves the home, she retrieves an apple that she hid before entering and takes a big bite out of it. Thus the story ends in a seemingly inconclusive way, leaving the reader to wonder if it is really a story at all. When one looks beneath the slight surface action of the story, however, one sees that "A Visit of Charity" has a complex structure based on a series of metaphoric devices, all of which serve to evoke the dreamlike grotesque atmosphere within the nursing home.

As Marian enters the home, the bulging linoleum on the floor makes her feel as if she is walking on the waves, and the smell in the building is like the interior of a clock. When the mannish nurse tells Marian that there are "two" in each room, Marian asks, "Two what?" The garrulous old woman is described as a birdlike creature who plucks Marian's hat off with a hand like a claw, while old Addie has a "bunchy white forehead and red eyes like a sheep"; she even "bleats" when she says, "Who—are—you?" Marian feels as if she has been caught in a robber's cave; she cannot even remember her own name. In her dreamy state, Marian cannot think clearly. When the old woman rocks faster and faster in her chair, Marian cannot understand how anyone can rock so fast.

The climax of the story occurs when it is discovered that it is old Addie's birthday. When the babbling roommate tells Marian that when she was a child she went to school, Addie lashes out in the single long speech in the story, telling her roommate that she was never young and that she never went to school: "You never were anything—only here. You never were born! You don't know anything. . . . Who are you? You're a stranger—a perfect stranger." When Marian goes over to Addie, she looks at her very closely from all sides, "as in dreams," and she wonders about her as if "there was nothing else in the world to wonder about. It was the first time such a thing had happened to Marian." When she asks the old woman how old she is, Addie says "I won't tell" and whimpers like a sheep, like a little lamb. In the last paragraph of the story, Marian has escaped her terrifying experience; when she jumps on the bus, she takes a big bite out of the apple that she hid, seemingly unaffected by her nightmarish experience with the old women.

Themes and Meanings

The basic theme of the story is suggested by the obvious irony of the title, for Marian's visit is not one of true charity, but rather a formal, institutionalized gesture. It certainly does not represent the biblical notion of charity in 1 Corinthians, which is interpreted in the Revised Standard Version of the Bible as "love," or sympathetic identification of one person with another. From the beginning of the story, Marian does not think of the two old women as people like herself. She not only is aware of the strangeness of the old ladies, but also she has become a stranger to herself. Thrown out of her familiar world, where she belongs, she is in a grotesque dreamworld, where she intensely feels her difference from the old ladies and thus her own separation and isolation. This symbolic sense of alienation explains the strange, dreamlike effect of the nursing home on Marian.

If the story were concerned only with Marian's difficulty in identifying with the old women, it would be easier to dismiss, for one might legitimately ask how it is possible for a girl to feel empathy for these strange and grotesque old women. Thus, to show that the feeling of charity, in the New Testament sense of "love," is totally lacking in the story, Welty establishes the relationship between the two old women. Why do they not love each other? It should be easy for them to perceive their common identity and thus maintain a sense of unity instead of one of total separation. Yet they do not; they seldom speak except to contradict each other; as old Addie says, they are strangers: "Is it possible that they have actually done a thing like this to anyone—sent them in a stranger to talk, and rock, and tell away her whole long rigamarole?" Addie's tirade against her roommate becomes the thematic center of the story: In a world without love, all people are strangers, for they cannot break through their own sense of separation to perceive their commonality and thus their oneness with one another. When Addie says that the other old woman is empty, she recognizes that this is so both because she is not loved and because she has no love to give. Without love, she is a stranger, just as without love all human beings are strangers to one another and to themselves.

The crisis for Marian occurs soon after the climactic moment of old Addie's tirade, for she then asks Addie how old she is and looks at the old woman very closely from all sides "as if in dreams." As Marian looks at Addie, she "wondered about her for a moment as though there was nothing else in the world to wonder about. It was the first time such a thing had happened to Marian." Yet this opportunity for identifying with the old woman is a fleeting one, for when Addie refuses to tell her age and begins crying, Marian jumps up and escapes.

Style and Technique

"A Visit of Charity" is typical of Welty's early short fiction, both in its use of a tight metaphoric structure and in its focus on the problem of love and separateness, which Welty has made her most predominant fictional theme. Symbol, metaphor, and biblical allusion are the primary devices that Welty uses to give depth and resonance to this seemingly simple story. The story is not merely a social criticism of institutional charity; it is about the difficulty, in any context, of following the biblical injunction to "love thy neighbor as thyself." Marian's final act—retrieving the apple she hid before entering the home and taking a big bite out of it—is the final symbolic gesture that unifies all the other metaphors and allusions in the story. Her biting the apple, recalling the biblical story of Adam and Eve, suggests both the sense of separation that follows the Fall and the difficulty of healing that separation through love, as mandated by the New Testament. In the Gospel of John, Jesus three times asks Peter if he loves Him. When Peter replies that he does, Jesus says, "Feed my sheep." When one recalls that Addie, the old woman who desperately needs love, is constantly referred to as a sheep or a little lamb, the implication of Marian's bite into the apple is clear. She has refused to feed the sheep—literally by refusing to give the apple to Addie and symbolically by refusing to give her love. Thus, by means of the central metaphors and the biblical allusions, the story illustrates both the Old Testament loss of union as depicted in the Genesis story and the difficulty of following the New Testament injunction to regain that union through loving the neighbor as the self. Marian takes the bite of the apple and the story is over; the reader is left with the echo of old Addie's despairing cry, "Who are you? You're a stranger—a perfect stranger. Don't you know you're a stranger."

Charles E. May

A VISIT TO GRANDMOTHER

Author: William Melvin Kelley (1937-   )
Type of plot: Social realism
Time of plot: The 1940's
Locale: New York City and the American South
First published: 1964

> *Principal characters:*
> DR. CHARLES DUNSFORD, a black, middle-class professional
>   with festering childhood memories
> CHARLES "CHIG" DUNSFORD II, his eldest child
> GL DUNSFORD, the doctor's spontaneous, hedonistic older
>   brother
> "MAMA" EVA DUNSFORD, Dr. Dunsford's mother

The Story

While the title of this story sparks images of loving company and comforting surroundings, it actually is a presage of disaster. Dr. Charles Dunsford has left his New York home to attend his twenty-year college reunion in Nashville, Tennessee. Accompanied by his oldest son, Charles "Chig" Dunsford II, he spends a festive week in the South. Then he decides to prolong their vacation, suggesting to the teenage Chig that they visit his mother, who has not seen her grandson since he was a small boy.

Once the pair arrives at "Mama" Eva Dunsford's home, their journey becomes an unpleasant one. Plied with questions and pampered by attentive relatives, Chig settles in with ease. His father, however, becomes taciturn and withdrawn. The constant, mesmerizing stories about his fun-loving brother, GL Dunsford, open old resentments that Charles had buried under his kind, gentle exterior.

Finally, unable to listen to the tales anymore, the jealous brother blurts out his anger during the family's dinner. Complaining to his mother that she never really loved him at all, he voices the familiar lament of the over-disciplined, overachieving sibling: "If GL and I did something wrong, you'd beat me first and then be too God damn tired to beat him. At dinner, he'd always get seconds and I wouldn't. You'd do things with him . . . but if I wanted you to do something with me, you were always too busy." The astonished Mama justifies her behavior, arguing that she loved all of her children even though she may have treated them differently. Yet Charles remains distraught. After repeating that it is too late for mending wounds, he runs upstairs to his room. Sadly, who should then appear at the door, "smiling broadly [with], an engaging, open, friendly smile, the innocent smile of a five-year-old," but GL himself, eager to reunite with his brother.

Themes and Meanings

When "A Visit to Grandmother" was published, one reviewer castigated it for not being "concerned enough with the race problem." Two years earlier, William Melvin Kelley himself had asserted that dealing exclusively with racism was not his intent: "A sixteenth of an inch of skin is nothing either to crow about or to feel ashamed of. If you are a human being, and know it, you will remain a human being even if you are brainwashed, deprived of food, clothes and shelter, drugged, beaten or shot. . . ." Kelley's preface to *Dancers on the Shore* (1964) underscores this thought with his vow to "depict people, not symbols or ideas disguised as people." Yet, at least in this story, Kelley breaks his own pledge. While the Dunsfords' individual motives and personalities are shallowly developed, taken as a group they deftly reveal the universal strengths and sorrows of human families.

Foremost, Kelley illustrates that the bedrock of human families is their unity. In contrast to Charles's physical separation from his birthplace and acquired bourgeois life-style (he sends his children to exclusive schools and summer camps), his extended family members still live in the same town. (In fact, Mama's very hands "were as dark as the wood" of her chair "and seemed to become part of it.") The adult Dunsfords even mimic one another in their colors of hair and clothing, white and brown, as if to externalize their shared experiences and dreams. They further demonstrate their solidarity by welcoming Charles and Chig, who are veritable strangers, without hesitation.

This sense of kinship that defies time and distance becomes most prominent in the story's final scene. As the dinner conversation focuses upon family memories, some of the Dunsfords—Chig, his aunts, and Mama—ask, answer, or direct questions. The two remaining men, Charles and his voracious brother Hiram, listen. By accounting for every member's behavior, regardless of vigor or passivity, Kelley emphasizes the importance of each individual's participation in order to make the family vibrant. Thus, Aunt Rose keeps piling food upon Chig's plate, despite his polite refusals, as though in some way the sustenance of the very least among them is necessary for the survival of the others.

Even the conflict between Charles and GL exposes a truth about family unity. These two men are so unlike each other that it seems unfathomable for them to have shared even one parent. GL, "part con man, part practical joker and part Don Juan," is the family's black sheep who has never established a career and family, constantly brushes the wrong side of the law, and cultivates his wits for survival as much as for trend-setting eminence. On the opposite end of the social spectrum, Charles, a soft-spoken, long-married father of three, owns his own home and maintains a successful medical practice. Ironically, though, both men exist on the family's periphery. Just as Charles leads a self-imposed exile in New York, GL flits from place to place outside his home. Foreigners to their own kin, GL looms as the roguish hero of the family memoirs while Charles puzzles his mother when she tries to identify him. Such similarities suggest that these two are brothers, with something in common, no matter what comes between them. Having sprung from the same bloodline and shared the same upbringing, they have more potential for ignoring their differences than first appears.

Style and Technique

Kelley's style here is unembellished and direct, almost reportorial. His typical descriptions, presented in loose, choppy sentences, are nearly juvenile in their simplicity: "She squinted. She looked like a doll, made of black straw, the wrinkles in her face running in one direction like the head of a broom. Her hair was white and coarse and grew out straight from her head. Her eyes were brown . . . and were hidden behind thick glasses. . . ." Instead of detracting from the story, however, this language is appropriate, because the action is related through the young Chig's eyes. At seventeen, he is on the threshold of adulthood, but he is an innocent in this story with regard to his father's relationship to GL and the rest of the family down South.

Unfortunately, the author neglects an opportunity to use this naïve point of view to heighten suspense. With Chig's uninformed observations, he could have deftly alerted readers to the angry confrontation that ends the tale. Instead, Kelley undercuts the plot by revealing the outcome too soon. For example, during the dinner-table discussion of GL, Chig sees his father's "face completely blank, without even a trace of a smile or a laugh." The youth is too absorbed with the fun and food to conclude that something has gone awry. Yet the impact of his description is weak because it lacks subtlety. In the very first sentence of this story, Chig discloses that "something was wrong" between his father and grandmother. Additionally, his early comments about his father's "far too offhand" manner and reticence about his childhood forebode disaster. Thus, Chig's half-conscious glance at his father during the meal is simply another part of the climax, rather than an unsettling, masterful harbinger of it.

Barbara A. McCaskill

VIY

Author: Nikolai Gogol (1809-1852)
Type of plot: Supernatural tale
Time of plot: Eighteenth or early nineteenth century
Locale: In and near Kiev
First published: 1835 (English translation, 1887)

> *Principal characters:*
> KHOMA BRUT, a philosophy student at the seminary in Kiev
> KHALIAVA, a theology student
> TIBERIY GOROBETS, a rhetorician
> THE "VEDMA," a witch, who takes different forms
> THE "SOTNIK," the commander of the Cossacks
> YEVTUKH,
> SPIRID, and
> DOROSH, Cossacks
> VIY, the chief of the gnomes, whose eyelids droop down to
> the earth

The Story

In "Viy," a description of student life in the seminary of the Bratsk Monastery in Kiev is followed by an introduction to three students who are hiking home for the summer. They are the philosopher, Khoma Brut, the theologian, Khaliava, and the rhetorician, Tiberiy Gorobets. The three students lose their way in the dark and are unable to find the road. Being hungry and afraid of wolves, they ask for lodging at the first farmyard they come upon. An old woman at first refuses to take them in, saying that she fears "such great hulking fellows." The three students swear that they will behave themselves, however, and Khoma falsely promises to pay her "the devil's bit" in the morning. The old woman invites them in, saying "What fine young gentlemen the devil has brought us!" She gives them all separate places to sleep. Khoma is given a place in the sheep pen.

In the middle of the night, Khoma is awakened by the entry into the sheep pen of the old woman. She reaches out her arms toward him. Khoma tries to reject her advances, saying that she is too old for him and that it is a time of fasting. Yet he finds himself strangely powerless to move away from her. She leaps onto his back with the swiftness of a cat and begins to ride him, beating him on his side with a broom.

To his amazement and horror, Khoma carries the old woman out into the wide plain, which seems to him to be at the bottom of a clear sea. The sun replaces the moon, and he sees a beautiful water nymph floating pale and naked before him. He feels an exhausting sensation which is at the same time voluptuous and exhilarating.

Realizing that he is in the power of a witch, Khoma begins to recite all the prayers he knows, all the exorcisms against evil spirits. The old woman's power seems to fade, and he, as quick as lightning, stops carrying her and jumps onto her back instead. As she starts to carry him, he picks up a piece of wood from the roadside and begins to beat her with it. The moon comes back into its former place, and as they soar over the plain, the old woman's angry howls become fainter and sweeter until they sound like delicate silver bells. Khoma, still beating her severely, wonders if she is really an old woman at all. At last, he hears her murmur, "I can do no more," as she sinks exhausted onto the ground. As Khoma looks at her, she is transformed into a lovely young woman with luxuriant tresses and eyelashes as long as arrows.

Khoma, shaken by his experience with the old woman, runs all the way back to Kiev, forgetting his companions. In Kiev, he passes whistling through the market three times, finally winking at a young widow in a yellow bonnet, who takes him home to regale him with her food and her favors. That same evening, he is seen in a tavern smoking his pipe and throwing a gold coin to the keeper. He thinks no more about his extraordinary adventure.

Meanwhile, rumors are circulating everywhere that the daughter of one of the richest Cossack sotniks (commanders), who lives some distance from Kiev, has returned one day from a walk, severely injured, hardly able to crawl home to her father's house, and is lying at the point of death, expressing the wish that one of the Kiev seminarists, the philosopher Khoma Brut, should read the prayers and the psalms over her for three nights after her death.

Hearing from the rector of the seminary about the sotnik's daughter's request, Khoma has a presentiment that something evil is awaiting him. He tries to excuse himself from the task and even plans to run away. The rector turns him over, though, to a detachment of the sotnik's Cossacks, who transport him in a large chaise to the sotnik's village, stopping along the way at a tavern to get drunk.

When they arrive at the sotnik's house, Khoma is informed that the daughter has died. The sotnik, despondent and angry over his daughter's death, leads Khoma to her body. Khoma almost panics as he recognizes in the beautiful young woman the luxuriant tresses and the eyelashes as long as arrows of the witch he killed earlier. He tries to excuse himself from the task of reading prayers over her body, telling the sotnik that he is sinful and unworthy, that he even "paid the baker's wife a visit on Maunday Thursday." The sotnik, however, will not relent. He insists that Khoma is to read the prayers each night from dusk to dawn.

Before the first night's reading, Khoma talks to the Cossacks Yevtukh, Spirid, and Dorosh, who eagerly affirm that the sotnik's daughter was indeed a witch. Spirid tells a chilling tale about Mikita the dog-keeper who withered and spontaneously burst into flame after the witch rode on his back all over the countryside. Then Dorosh relates how the witch, in the form of a dog, attacked the baby of Sheptun's wife, sucking its blood and even killing its mother. From these stories, Khoma is frightened, but, fortified by vodka, he goes to read the first night's prayers.

The body of the sotnik's daughter has been taken into the village church. There, at dusk, Khoma begins to read his prayers, but soon the girl's body rises up out of the coffin and walks around the church: It is the witch, reaching out her arms for him. Khoma draws a circle around himself and fervently reads all the prayers and exorcisms he has been taught. The witch is unable to penetrate the circle and, at dawn, she returns to her coffin.

The next day, Khoma witnesses the Cossacks playing a strange game, similar to skittles, called "kragli." The winner of the game gets the right to ride on the loser's back. This reminds him of the witch, but he is confident that his prayers will protect him. It is not until he is locked up for the second night in the church with the now-putrefying corpse that fear again seizes him. Indeed, the corpse does again rise to walk around the church, muttering unintelligible words and trying to possess him. He hears the wings and claws of other demons trying to enter the church, but he survives by staying within his drawn circle and reading his exorcisms with desperate zeal. In the morning, a local Cossack coquette notices that his hair has gone completely gray.

Before the third night's reading, Khoma confronts the sotnik with the knowledge of his daughter's witchcraft, trying one more time to be excused from reading the prayers over her body. The sotnik responds by threatening to flog Khoma if he does not complete his task. Khoma tries to run away, but he winds up running in a circle, back to where Yevtukh finds him and leads him back to the church at dusk. The third night's vigil is the worst of all. The witch's corpse rises as before but is now more terrible. Other monstrous demons crash through the windows of the church and scurry about, trying to find him. The witch shouts, "Bring Viy! Go get Viy!" Viy does indeed arrive: a thick-set, bandy-legged figure covered with black earth, and with eyelids drooping to the ground. "Lift up my eyelids. I do not see!" he says. The demons all rush to lift his eyelids. Now Viy's terrible gaze is fixed upon Khoma. "There he is!" he shouts, and all the demonic company pounce upon Khoma, who falls expiring to the ground, his soul fleeing his body in terror. The cock then crows to signal the dawn, and the demons panic. They wedge themselves into the doors and windows of the church while trying to get out. The priest is subsequently forced to close the church, which in later years is so overgrown with weeds that it is forgotten.

In the final scene, Tiberiy Gorobets and Khaliava are back in Kiev. Some time has passed; Khaliava is now the bell-ringer of Kiev's highest belfry, while Tiberiy Gorobets is now a philosopher, as Khoma was. At a tavern they drink to Khoma's memory, concluding that "all the old women who sit in our market in Kiev are witches."

Themes and Meanings

Especially in his earlier stories, Gogol adapted the folktales told to him as a youth by his mother. These folktales spring from the oral tradition of the Ukraine, where Gogol was born. They involve peasant legends of the supernatural and the everyday customs of the ethnic groups which inhabit the Ukraine, most notably the Cossacks. Thus "Viy" is rich in Ukrainian folklore and the boisterous character of the Cossacks. The religious undercurrent represented by the seminary and the prayer vigil is a reflection of the influence of Gogol's father, a strictly religious man who died when Gogol was still young. The clear sexual symbolism of "Viy"—being ridden by a witch until a "voluptuous" state of exhaustion is achieved—has been interpreted as evidence of Gogol's own ambivalent sexuality, feeling sexual urges but being convinced, perhaps for religious reasons or out of a misidentification with his mother, that indulgence of them leads to damnation.

Style and Technique

In general, Gogol's style is to deluge the reader with detail which seems digressive at first, but which relates to the main plot in psychologically supportive ways. He presents stories-within-stories, creating seemingly inconsequential characters who are born and are given names, lives, and interesting deaths, all within a paragraph. "Viy" is no exception to this pattern. Other interesting narrative techniques can be seen here as well—for example, the technique of triplication, which derives from the telling of folktales. The story is written in two distinct parts, each with parallel structure, yet there are three students, three "riding" incidents, and three night vigils, among other examples. In addition, there is an inordinate focus upon eyes, the "windows of the soul," and upon visual processes. In her beautiful forms, the witch has eyelashes as long as arrows. Khoma perishes when his eyes meet the gaze of Viy, that long-eyelidded gnome whose very name is a contraction of the Russian verb *videt*, which means "to see."

Lee B. Croft

WAITING

Author: Joyce Carol Oates (1938-   )
Type of plot: Psychological sketch
Time of plot: The 1960's
Locale: The United States
First published: 1974

> *Principal characters:*
> KATHERINE ALEXANDER, an unmarried woman in her thirties
> who works in a welfare office
> HER MOTHER
> BOB MOTT, who is in his late forties, married, and on welfare

The Story

As the story begins, the reader is caught in the middle of miscommunication. Bob Mott is trying to explain to Katherine Alexander why he has lost his job. She is distracted; he is embarrassed. She is suspicious, slightly disgusted by Mr. Mott. The narrator abruptly shifts attention to Katherine's life story. She has grown up barely admiring her retired father, frightened of becoming her struggling, unattractive mother. Her older sisters have married; her older brother, returned from the navy, works in a parts factory. Katherine supports her mother, yet she has saved enough to earn a degree from the university in the School of Social Work.

In her senior year, Katherine meets a young man who is studying to become a dentist. Although at first he is "on the rebound" from a love affair, he eventually falls in love with Katherine. As they begin to plan for marriage, Katherine's mother becomes ill. The consequent gall bladder operation is "a vast and complicated affair" which interrupts the young couple's plans. Katherine begins her social work; the young man strains over his studies; the mother becomes nervous for her daughter. Impatient after months, then years, of delay, the young man ends their relationship. Katherine is devastated—mostly by his "weakness."

After this happens, at age twenty-six, it seems that Katherine grows closer to her mother—sharing a loneliness. Her energies are devoted almost exclusively to work. She becomes expert at distinguishing the truth from lies. She also distances herself emotionally from the suffering that she sees; her idealism descends into cool distrust. She feels uncomfortable "with those *certain women*." At one point she takes an unhealthy pleasure in humiliating a prostitute; her victim, enraged, lashes back, calling her an "ugly bitch." It is then that she meets Mr. Mott.

The narration returns to the moment at the beginning of the story: Mr. Mott tries to explain himself; Katherine, disturbed by the prostitute's curse, cannot understand his problem. Mr. Mott makes himself clear—he has lost his job and plans to abandon his pregnant wife.

The narrator, once again, shifts back into Katherine's private life. Her mother sickens and dies, leaving "everything" to Katherine. Out of a sense of loyalty to the memory of her proud, bigoted, mother, she refuses to sell the family house to "colored." She gives herself completely to her job. By choice, she distances herself utterly from the people she had once hoped to help. She no longer meets the "candidates," but, shut off in her own office, she judges them. Her social life is bleak—meeting "awkward, polite bachelors" who quickly disappear from her life.

In a chance meeting, Mr. Mott reenters her life. Cheerful, newly employed, he offers her a ride home in his new car. Katherine, nervous, clutching her purse, is uncertain of herself and embarrassed by him, but she accepts. As they approach her mother's house, she is ashamed, defensive, maintaining that she keeps the house out of respect for her dead mother. She invites him in to "chat." She is repulsed by his manners, his language; her glances judge his every action.

With cruel abruptness, Mr. Mott turns on Katherine. He humiliates her for earning so little, for living in a neighborhood which is mostly black, for her sentimental attachment to "mommy," for her condescending demeanor in the welfare office. He tells her that he witnessed the incident with the prostitute who had cursed her; he himself calls her an "ugly dog-faced bitch." He confesses that he has been waiting for six years to "get" her. He strikes her several times. As she begins to weep, the entire tragic emptiness of her life descends upon her—but she cannot understand it.

Themes and Meanings

Oates makes an insistent comparison between Katherine's public and private lives. Initially, she seems to be completely selfless in both—supporting her wreck of a family, giving her life to the service of others. Yet soon the public and private dimensions of her life become ironically reciprocal: The less competent she becomes in gratifying her personal desires, the more competent she becomes at managing the lives of other unfortunates.

Yet "competence" in her job entails achieving a productive distrust for humanity. The more she is hurt personally, the more readily she can detect true suffering from camouflage: "With frightened people, lies were obvious because they never looked up at Katherine; with the bold and brazen, lies were obvious because they tried to stare her down. The only people who puzzled her were those who couldn't remember the truth, who didn't know themselves if they were lying." A passage such as this, placed in the very center of Katherine's story, gradually accumulates layers of irony as the story proceeds. In her domestic and professional capacities, Katherine lies to herself without knowing it.

Katherine helps others because she feels better when she does. Her fiancé becomes like one of her welfare "people" in her mind; her mother's medical expenses "equaled so many hours of her job." When Katherine "investigates" a poor neighborhood, the narrator slyly creeps into her mind, where it becomes obvious that she uses her job to prop herself up: "Wasn't she maybe, from a well-to-do family, dedicating herself to helping people? And wasn't she pretty?" This is what Katherine hopes her "people" will think of her. The brutal truth (that she is despised for her distant distrust) is revealed to her by Mr. Mott as the story ends.

Katherine feels "nervous" and "vaguely ashamed" in the presence of the prostitutes who frequent the welfare office. Does she humiliate the prostitute because she despises her, or is it more likely that her vague shame has to do with self-recognition? After her violent confrontation with the prostitute who curses her, Katherine prays "My God, don't let me get like that." Significantly, "her mind was so jostled, she didn't know whether she was thinking of her mother or of the prostitute." These two women represent possibilities to Katherine—whore and mother, both psychological and economic hostages to an unfriendly world, to the world of Mr. Mott.

Mr. Mott is the catalyst for the story's meaning; he psychologically violates Katherine. Throughout her life, Katherine has deluded herself about family, sex, loyalty, and her "social work." She has so resented the inadequacies of her private life that her public life has become a sham, a show of power. Mr. Mott explodes the distinction between what she is and what she wants the world to believe she is. He is one of her "people," someone who has "succeeded." While his success entails abandoning his wife and children, Katherine seems to resent him not so much because of his callousness as because of his success: He no longer looks up to her.

As the insults begin, the scene resembles a dog turning on a master; this is Katherine's perception of the relationship. The truth is displayed to Katherine; she weeps after many years of repressing the tears. Yet just when it seems that the truth may render Katherine whole, may heal and renew her pathetic life, the reader realizes the Mr. Mott's hatred has instead intensified Katherine's confusion. The reader is in the middle of the same miscommunication with which the story begins.

Style and Technique

The title of the story reflects its form. Oates subverts the reader's expectations: namely, that Katherine is the only character "waiting." Everyone around Katherine has been waiting: The mother waits for her daughter's success; the fiancé waits for his lover's acceptance; the welfare "candidates" wait for the social worker's attention; Mr. Mott waits for revenge.

Oates uses this important verb twice in the final paragraphs of the story. Mr. Mott reveals: "For six years I been waiting to run into one of you—"

After Mr. Mott has beaten Katherine, the narrator states very simply that "she waited." He has been waiting to vent his rage; she has been waiting to weep. The reader has also been waiting: The title of the story works as a kind of riddle—solved in the story's conclusion.

Through shifts in the narrative focus, Mr. Mott remains a peripheral concern to the story. He seems an annoyance, a diversion from the main story line—yet in the final scene he overwhelms Katherine and the reader with a ruthless reality that has been lurking in the background for pages.

Mark Sandona

WAKEFIELD

Author: Nathaniel Hawthorne (1804-1864)
Type of plot: Fable
Time of plot: The 1800's
Locale: London
First published: 1835

> *Principal characters:*
> WAKEFIELD, an average, middle-class man
> MRS. WAKEFIELD, his wife

The Story

Wakefield is a middle-aged man living in London, in a comfortable home with his wife of ten years. He has an "inactive mind," a peculiar "vanity," a "harmless love of mystery," a certain "selfishness" and "strangeness." One October evening, he tells his wife good-bye before leaving by coach for a journey into the country. Knowing his love of mystery, she does not inquire into the details of his trip. He tells her not to be alarmed if he does not return for three or four days but to expect him on Friday evening. She later recalls the "crafty smile" on his face as he departs.

Instead of going on a journey, he takes an apartment on the next street with a vague plan of observing the effect of his absence on his wife. Alone in the apartment, he seems to realize the inanity of what he is doing. Yet as time goes by, he is overcome with curiosity about the effect of his disappearance. Vanity lies at the root of his project. He watches his house to see how life proceeds without him but is fearful of being recognized. Consequently, he buys a red wig and unusual clothes to effect a disguise. Three weeks after his disappearance, Wakefield observes a physician entering his house; he knows that his wife is ill, but he tells himself that he must not disturb her at such a time. He expects that she may die and even seems to desire subconsciously to harm her. He cannot bring himself to return. When his wife recovers, Wakefield is vaguely aware that an "almost impassable gulf" separates him from her and from his former life. In due time, Mrs. Wakefield settles her husband's estate and proceeds with her life as a widow. Hawthorne comments that Wakefield has virtually no more chance of returning to his old life than if he were actually dead.

For ten years, Wakefield watches his house and observes his wife as best he can. He loses any feeling that his actions are strange. One day, he sees Mrs. Wakefield on her way to church. Jostled by the crowd into bodily contact, they look into each other's eyes, but she fails to recognize him. Returning to his lonely room, he falls upon the bed and passionately cries out that he is mad. It is the only time that he seems to be emotionally moved. He has postponed his return from month to month, year to year, with one feeble excuse or another, until now he is in limbo, neither dead nor truly alive. He has retained "his original share of human sympathies," is "still involved in human interests," but has lost "his reciprocal influence on them." Yet he has no clear concept of how he has changed and continues to think that he could return home the same man who departed years earlier.

In the last scene, twenty years after Wakefield's departure, he takes his usual walk to his house, which he still considers his own. Again it is autumn, and he sees through a window a fire on the hearth and on the ceiling, a "grotesque shadow" of Mrs. Wakefield, a "caricature." When a chilling rain begins to fall, he suddenly considers it ridiculous to stand outside when the comforts of his home are just beyond the door. He enters with the same "crafty" smile on his face that he wore when he first left. Instead of following Wakefield inside, the author comments: "Stay, Wakefield! Would you go to the sole home that is left you? Then step into your grave!" The story then concludes with a moral such as Hawthorne promised at the beginning:

> Amid the seeming confusion of our mysterious world, individuals are so nicely adjusted to a system, and systems to one another and to a whole, that, by stepping aside for a moment, a man exposes himself to a fearful risk of losing his place forever. Like Wakefield, he may become, as it were, the Outcast of the Universe.

Themes and Meanings

Many Hawthorne characters destroy themselves, or others, by some unusual action that separates them from the mainstream of life and eventually destroys their human ties. Aylmer in "The Birthmark" seeks scientific success and an abstract ideal, but in the process he kills his wife. Wakefield, more or less on a whim, abandons his domestic tranquillity and is doomed to a solitary life. When he finally wishes to return home, he discovers that the only home prepared to welcome him is the grave. The outline of the story, which Hawthorne claims in the first paragraph to have borrowed from a newspaper, he changes in the end to convey his belief that the breaking of human ties is evil and irrevocable. The man in the news article, he says, returned after twenty years to the bosom of a loving wife and became a loving husband until death. Wakefield, however, by the end of the story is an outcast of his own making.

Wakefield's sins are his changing, for selfish reasons, the course of another person's life and his withdrawing, for no good reason, from his established relationship with his wife and with society. Of all people, his wife is the one in whose life he should actively participate. Instead, he removes himself and coldly observes. By breaking his ties with his wife, his home, and the customs of his former life, he separates himself from everything that binds him to humanity and to life itself. Hence Hawthorne's references to him as dead or as a ghost and Hawthorne's leaving him on the threshold of his house. Wakefield is physically alive, but in all other respects he is dead; though he may enter his house, he cannot reenter his old life. Although he intended to withdraw for only a short time in order to observe the effect, he remains aloof so long that he loses his position in the scheme of things.

"Wakefield" contains two concepts often found in Hawthorne's stories—the isolation of a man from the world and the cruel attempt of one person to alter another person's life. The "crafty" smile on her husband's face that Mrs. Wakefield observes as he leaves reveals the beginning of his sin—deliberate estrangement from his former life and from the world. This estrangement, which initially is little more than a whim or a joke he intends playing on Mrs. Wakefield, becomes his destruction. It becomes obsessive as he watches his house and wife for twenty years, powerless to return and confess the truth of his actions. While she makes a normal adjustment to his absence, he is, ironically, trapped by his plan into becoming an outcast. Wakefield neither realizes nor anticipates how unimportant his disappearance will be in terms of the larger world. Hawthorne comments that it is dangerous to separate oneself even from loved ones, for their lives go on and one is quickly forgotten. Hence he refuses to allow a happy reunion for Wakefield and prepares the reader for the theme stated at the end of the story.

Style and Technique

The structure of "Wakefield" is quite simple. An unusual event, a husband's self-imposed absence, is expanded into a brief moral allegory, a type of story Hawthorne often employed. By claiming in the first paragraph that he took the initial incident from an old newspaper, he lends an air of reality to the strange event. Continuing to address the reader directly, Hawthorne welcomes him to an excursion into the remarkable anecdote, for an unusual incident often produces ideas worth considering, he claims. He concludes the introduction with an idea that points to the theme at the end of the story, giving the effect of a neatly wrapped package.

Throughout the story, Hawthorne uses a technique of prompting and leading the reader's reactions concerning what is happening with the characters. When Wakefield vacillates in deciding to return home, Hawthorne comments, "Poor man!" When Mrs. Wakefield falls ill after her husband's disappearance, the author injects, "Dear woman! Will she die?" The effect is that the reader is always conscious of the author's presence and of his guiding the reader's thoughts. This effect is strengthened by the numerous moralizing passages interspersed throughout the story. The author states early that unusual incidents such as the one on which the story is based have a "moral"; he then scatters didactic passages throughout the story as well as stating the clear moral message in the conclusion.

One characteristic of most stories that is virtually lacking in "Wakefield" is dialogue. Even the parting scene, in which Wakefield leaves his wife for the supposed journey, is not dramatized. Instead, Hawthorne describes everything for the reader, sometimes preparing for the next event with a phrase such as, "Now for a new scene!" Occasionally, Wakefield's thoughts are expressed within quotation marks, but these passages are as close as Hawthorne comes to using dialogue. Thus, the loneliness of Wakefield's situation is emphasized. By breaking all of his ties with his former life for the sake of a foolish whim, Wakefield condemns himself to the life of an outcast. From the climactic scene at the church in which his wife fails to recognize him, Wakefield clearly can never return to his old life. The following events and the lack of dialogue all convey the fact that Wakefield is permanently separated from the social fabric of life.

"Wakefield" shares several characteristics of the classic fable. The results of a single incident are investigated in a relatively brief narrative of about six pages. The characters do not have complete names and are not roundly defined. Mrs. Wakefield is the stereotypical widow, and Wakefield is motivated by a single obsession. Especially reminiscent of the fable are the didactic tone, the reader's constant awareness of the author's presence, and the author's insistence that here there is "much food for thought." Everything in the story is designed to make that thought clear, and it is flatly stated in the concluding paragraph.

Louise S. Bailey

THE WALK

Author: Robert Walser (1878-1956)
Type of plot: Antistory
Time of plot: 1917
Locale: Switzerland
First published: "Der Spaziergang," 1917 (English translation, 1957)

Principal character:
THE WALKER, the narrator and protagonist, a writer

The Story

One morning, the narrator, a writer, leaves the melancholy confines of his room to take a walk. Pleased with his suddenly "romantic and adventurous frame of mind," he rejoices at the beauty, freshness, and goodness of the day.

His first encounter on the street is with Professor Meili, a famous scholar with a forbidding, yet sympathetic figure. Various other people catch his attention: a priest, a chemist on a bicycle, a junk dealer, an army doctor, children at play, two elegant women in short skirts, and two men in straw hats.

Pretending to be a fussy connoisseur of books, he visits a book shop and asks in well-chosen words what is the most widely read and popular book of the day. When the book dealer returns with the treasured book in his hands, the writer, whose books do not enjoy such success, coldly leaves the shop with barely a thank-you.

Entering the next bank that he comes upon, he is pleasantly surprised to find that several anonymous benefactresses have credited his account with one thousand francs. The bank clerk notes the smile of the poor, disregarded writer, who rejoices in the unexpected gift as he continues his walk. In an aside, he calls attention to a luncheon date he has at one o'clock with Frau Aebi. He passes a bakery and is disturbed by its flamboyant gold lettering, which he sees as a symptom of contemporary egotism, ostentation, and fraudulence, where everything is allowed to appear to be more than it really is. Gone is the modesty of the baker who merely baked an honest loaf of bread.

At the sight of a busy foundry, he is at first ashamed of the fact that he is not working but is only out for a stroll. Yet in his bright yellow English suit he feels like a lord in his park, even though the country road is dotted with factories and simple houses and there is nothing really parklike about it. Two children who are playing in the street enchant him for a moment before a loud, rushing automobile disturbs their idyllic game. He looks angrily at the car's occupants, for he loves quiet and the moderate pace of walking and abhors the unnatural haste and pollution of the automobile.

He asks his readers for their indulgence as he announces in advance two significant figures on his walk, a supposed former actress and an alleged budding singer. The first woman turns out not to have been an actress after all, but as she responds pleasantly enough to his rather forward questions, he proceeds to tell her that when he arrived in the area not long ago, he was at odds with himself and the world. Slowly he overcame his hopelessness and anxiety and underwent a rebirth, so that now he is quite happy and receptive to the good around him.

After paying his respects to her, the writer once again sets out on his way. A charming milliner's shop elicits a shout of joy from him. He finds its rural setting so attractive that he promises to himself to write a play entitled "The Walk," in which it will appear. A nearby butcher shop similarly enraptures him, but he is too easily distracted and needs to reorient himself and regroup his forces, like a field marshall trying to gain an overview of circumstances and contingencies. Parenthetically, he adds that he is writing all of his elegant sentences with an Imperial Court pen, which gives them their brevity, pregnancy, and sharpness.

Continuing his stroll past vegetable and flower gardens, orchards, wheatfields, meadows, streams, and all manner of other pleasant things, he is suddenly confronted by a particularly unpleasant and sinister being—the giant Tomzack, whose terrible appearance disperses all of the writer's happy thoughts and imaginings. The writer knows him well, this half-dead phantom superman without home, love, fortune, friends, or country. Without looking back, the writer enters a fir forest, whose quiet, fairy-tale interior gives him back his joy and sense of well-being.

When he leaves the forest, he hears the voice of the singer, a young schoolgirl with a captivatingly beautiful voice. He tells her that she has a dazzling future as a great operatic singer and advises her to practice diligently. She barely comprehends his lengthy encomium on the virtues of her voice, a speech, he admits, that was given mostly for his own pleasure. In the distance he sees the railroad crossing that will be so important to him later in his walk, but before crossing it he must attend to three other important matters: trying on a new suit at a tailor's shop, paying his taxes at the town hall, and depositing a noteworthy letter at the post office.

First of all though, as it has just struck one o'clock, he has to dine with Frau Aebi. Declining conversation, she watches him devotedly as he eats. She insists that he keep eating as much as possible, for she claims that his main reason for coming was not intellectual discussion but to prove that he has a good appetite and is a hearty eater. When she persists, he leaps up from the table, asking how she dares to expect him to stuff himself. She laughs and says it was only a joke to show him how certain housewives can be overindulgent toward their guests.

His next stop is the post office, where he mails a caustic diatribe to a gentleman who has betrayed him and whose only concern is money and prestige. He then takes up battle with the tailor, whose botched work confirms the writer's worst fears. Instead of finding a faultlessly tailored suit, he finds his suit ill-fitting, misshapen, unimaginative, and amateurish. Faced with the tailor's vehement counterprotests, the writer quickly withdraws and marches to the tax office, where he hopes to correct a gross error on his tax bill.

Rather than possessing the considerable income that the tax accountants suppose, he has only the most meager income of a writer whose books find no echo among their intended readers. Yet "one always sees you out walking," remarks the tax collector. Indeed, the writer answers, walking invigorates him and keeps him in contact with the world. Deprived of his walks, he could not write a single word, for the studies, observations, thoughts, and insights that he gathers during his walks are essential to his work and well-being. He persuades the official that attentive walking is indeed a serious occupation and is promised as a result careful examination of his application for the lowest possible tax rate.

The writer at last reaches the railroad crossing, which seems to him like the high point or center of his walk. Here he waits with a crowd of people as a train filled with soldiers passes by and each group greets the other with patriotic joy. After the crossing clears, his surroundings seem transfigured: The country road, the modest houses and shops, the gardens and meadows are surrounded by a silver veil. He imagines that "the soul of the world has opened, and all evil, sadness, and pain are about to disappear." Having lost its external shell, the earth becomes a dream, and time seems to exist only in the present.

One delightful scene follows another, but as he continues his walk, his romantic exuberance gives way again to sharper observation of the landscape and its buildings and inhabitants. He meets a black dog, a stiff, finely clothed man, and a disheveled laundrywoman, passes several historically interesting buildings, reels off a lengthy list of everyday things and occurrences, and reads a placard advertising a boardinghouse for elegant gentlemen.

It is now evening, and his walk comes to an end at a lakeside. Two figures appear in his mind: a beautiful young girl and a weary and forsaken old man. He is filled with melancholy thoughts and self-reproaches and picks flowers as it begins to rain. He lies down for a long time and then remembers the pretty face of the young girl, who long ago left him without returning his love. The flowers fall out of his hand. He rises to go home, and everything is dark.

Themes and Meanings

"The Walk" is the longest and most famous of the more than fifty sketches of walks that Robert Walser wrote after his return from Berlin to Switzerland in 1913. Walking for Walser, who is clearly visible behind the transparent persona of his narrator-protagonist, was an essential creative activity and served a far different function from a normal recreational and diversionary stroll. As Walser's walker tells the tax collector, it is his principal connection to daily life, the only real means that a solitary individual has to confront and communicate with the everyday world.

Walking is also Walser's narrative means of creating space (the German word for "take a walk"—*spazieren*—means literally "to space") for the free flow of ideas and perceptions. The walk itself is the only element that binds together the numerous observations, reflections, and soliloquies that make up the story. The external world is little more than a set of slight and fleeting encounters that provoke a wide range of emotional, perceptual, and philosophical responses. In the moment of the epiphany at the railroad crossing, the narrator comments that the inner human being is the only one that truly exists. Thus, the conversations and images in the story can be seen as outward projections of inner needs and fantasies—particularly, the need for recognition as an honest, unpretentious writer in search of enduring relationships and connections. The men in the story are almost all ostentatious, dishonest, or threatening figures, whereas the women and girls are alluring, witty, and artistic. Similarly, the moments of joy, contentment, and euphoria occur usually in conjunction with images of women and are constantly threatened by memories of a frightening past (embodied in the giant Tomzack) and fear of future loneliness (the figure of the forsaken man in the forest). The celebration of the details of everyday life in "The Walk" may thus be viewed as an attempt to ward off the threats of a crude, male-dominated society and to keep open a more benign aesthetic space for future imaginative and literary excursions.

Style and Technique

The first-person narrator takes great pains to undermine conventional modes of narration, for the story that he has to tell is not a reconstruction of external events that are reputed to have occurred, but rather the willful linking together of episodes, philosophical reflections, lengthy monologues, and playful asides to the reader within the constructed framework of a day's walk. By parodying conventional foreshadowing and chronological sequence, Walser underscores the accidental nature of his peripatetic imaginative encounters.

Despite an occasional touch of sentimentality and melancholy, a light, self-ironic tone sustains the work. Walser never loses sight of his potential readers and lets his narrator remark at one point that "probably no other author has ever thought of the reader with such gentleness and tenderness as I." Without a sustained plot structure, developed characterization, or linear time flow, however, the reader's task is not easy. Nevertheless, it is not the larger structures that count here, but rather Walser's close attention to detail, a technique that has been termed an "immersion in the minimal." What results is a very personal vision that is both poignant and compellingly unaffected.

Peter West Nutting

THE WALL

Author: William Sansom (1912-1976)
Type of plot: Psychological realism
Time of plot: During World War II
Locale: London during an air raid
First published: 1947

> *Principal characters:*
> THE NARRATOR, a fire fighter
> LEN,
> LOFTY, and
> VERNO, three other fire fighters

The Story

This very short story of less than four pages describes what goes on in the narrator's mind as he perceives that a huge wall is about to fall on him and his fellow fire fighters. After an initial impression of the scene and the nature of the work that has been going on in a typical, hellish night during which fire fighters are trying to control fires during air raids in London, the lapse of time covered by the story is a very few minutes or even a matter of moments.

It is 3:00 A.M., and this is their third major blaze—a huge, brick warehouse, five stories high. The men are cold, wet, exhausted, almost mindless in their persistent, stubborn pouring of water into one crimson window after another. The narrator holds the icy nozzle while two other men share the weight of the heavy hose behind him. The fourth man of the team is off to the side, looking at the squat trailer pump which is roaring and quivering with effort. No one is thinking.

Then comes the long, rattling crack, sounding above the throb of the pump, the roaring of the flames, the background hum of aircraft. The narrator knows instantly that the wall is falling. The ratio of thought to action is immediately reversed; the protagonist is rooted to the spot, but his mind snaps alert. His vision becomes preternaturally sharp, recording every detail of the huge, black wall of brick with evenly spaced oblong windows that are bulging with fire, as well as noting and assessing with peripheral vision the possibilities of escape on either side. They stand in a narrow alley with limited access. On one side, the fire-fighting equipment blocks the way—the other side is free. He could yell "Drop it," and they could race up the free side, though the long wall leans over that area as well. He cannot move and says nothing. He meditates about the many ways a wall can fall—swaying to one side, crumbling at the base, or remaining intact and falling flat. The three men crouch, and the wall falls flat, miraculously framing the group of three in one of those symmetrical, oblong window spaces. The fourth man is killed, but the three are dug out with very little brick on top of them.

Themes and Meanings

This is a story almost purely of sensation—what it feels like to be in such a situation, how the mind works in the face of almost certain death. Although one might extract a theme from it or an observation about human experience, the particular event itself is enough. The remarkable escape from death is too unusual to warrant any generalization, except that sometimes strange things happen. They do not occur for any moral reason, for example, because the men who were saved were better, wiser, or more skillful than he who died. They do not provide evidence of an interfering God or predestined fate. In fact, the "accidental" survival of the men is perhaps more a technical convenience to lend realism than a thematic device; after all, how could one know what the narrator was thinking if he had not survived to tell the tale?

One might suggest a somewhat existential observation: how even the most dreadful experience becomes infinitely valuable, or at least notable, when the mind recognizes that death is imminent? The color, the shape of things, the significance of the environment attain some kind of absolute distinction; the "thingness" of objects which were before only vague and peripheral to existence suddenly comes into focus, concentrating time and awareness in a few vivid moments.

Such a story has some kind of significance or meaning partly because it gives the impression of undeniable authenticity, not a gothic exercise such as Edgar Allan Poe's "The Pit and the Pendulum," in which one enjoys the goosebumps of sustained suspense without believing a word of it. William Sansom was, as a matter of fact, a fire fighter in London during the German blitzkrieg of World War II. While such firsthand experience is not always necessary to an imaginative writer, it certainly lends verisimilitude to a story that depends not so much on plot as upon the subjective experience of an event.

"The Wall" departs from a somewhat romantic, popular assumption that in the moments before death one's life passes in review. The protagonist does indeed live in a mentally expanded space between the time when the wall leans above him and when it crashes around him, but that space is filled with very practical, realistic observations and reflections—not an ounce of nostalgia or regret over lost loves. In that, too, the story gives the impression of relentless realism.

Style and Technique

In her introduction to William Sansom's collection of short stories, Elizabeth Bowen says, "A Sansom story is a *tour de force*." That statement cer-

tainly applies to "The Wall," which is technically flawless, plunging the reader
into experience immediately and holding that attention while he expands a
moment almost, but not quite, to the breaking point.

He manages to convey not only the intensity of the crisis but also the
weary tedium of the unremitting struggle to contain fires in an air raid. What
would be exciting, perhaps even exhilarating in small doses, becomes simply
exhausting to the body and stupefying to the mind under constant, night-
after-night effort. The initial description conveys this tedious acceptance of
the fire fighter's nightly chore, creating an effective contrast to the feeling
tone of what follows later in the story.

> Until this thing happened, work had been without incident. There had been
> shrapnel, a few enquiring bombs, and some huge fires; but these were
> unremarkable and have since merged without identity into the neutral maze of
> fire and noise and water and night, without date and without hour, with neither
> time nor form, that lowers mistily at the back of my mind as a picture of the air-
> raid season.

The narrator offers a series of descriptive details that would typify their
experience. Although each is sharp and clear, it is prefaced by "I suppose . . ." or "Probably . . ." or "Without doubt . . . ," suggesting that these
were everynight occurrences, so familiar as almost to be unnoticed.

> I suppose we were drenched, with the cold hose water trickling in at our collars
> and settling down at the tails of our shirts. . . . Probably the open roar of the
> pumps drowned the petulant buzz of the raiders, and certainly the ubiquitous
> fire-glow made an orange stage-set of the streets.

Such things happened so often that "they were not forgotten because they
were never even remembered."

When the telltale crack of the bursting brick and mortar herald the collapse of the wall, however, the wandering mind snaps to attention. "I was
thinking of nothing and then I was thinking of everything in the world." The
sudden expansion of the narrator's powers of observation is metaphorically
expressed: "New eyes opened at the sides of my head so that, from within, I
photographed a hemispherical panorama bounded by the huge length of the
building in front of me and the narrow lane on either side."

There follow two-and-a-half pages of dense, precise description of what he
thought and saw between the time when the building heaved over toward
them and the few moments it took for the wall to come crashing down.
There is no particular sense of panic, though the men seem rooted to the
spot. Perhaps there is simply acceptance of the inevitable, with only a touch
of hindsight irony.

We dropped the hose and crouched. Afterwards Verno said that I knelt slowly on one knee with bowed head, like a man about to be knighted. Well, I got my knighting. There was an incredible noise—a thunderclap condensed into the space of an eardrum—and then the bricks and the mortar came tearing and burning into the flesh of my face.

Elizabeth Bowen suggests in the introduction that "what rivets one to a Sansom story is a form of compulsion, rather than 'interest' in the more usual, leisurely or reflective sense." Certainly the characters here are not "interesting"—in fact, the reader knows nothing at all about them. He is so caught up in the sensations of the moment that it does not matter who they are. Nor does the event have any particular moral dimension; the reader must accept the protagonist's simple judgment that they were "lucky."

Katherine Snipes

THE WALL

Author: Jean-Paul Sartre (1905-1980)
Type of plot: Psychological realism
Time of plot: c. 1937
Locale: Spain
First published: "Le Mur," 1937 (English translation, 1948)

> *Principal characters:*
> PABLO IBBIETA, the narrator, a political prisoner during the
>   Spanish Civil War
> JUAN MIRBAL and
> TOM STEINBOCK, his fellow prisoners
> A BELGIAN PHYSICIAN

The Story

Set during the Spanish Civil War of 1936-1939, "The Wall" sets forth the predicament of three men who are taken prisoner without warning or explanation by Falangist forces operating under General Francisco Franco; the story is narrated in the first person by Pablo Ibbieta, an erstwhile political activist who considers himself the most lucid of the trio, no doubt with good reason.

After a summary interrogation, the three captives are sentenced to death by firing squad. As they begin to confront their fate, Pablo finds himself increasingly preoccupied with the reactions of his fellow prisoners, implicitly comparing their behavior to his own. Tom Steinbock, a former comrade-in-arms, betrays his nervousness by talking too much; the third man, hardly more than a boy, is one Juan Mirbal, who repeatedly protests his innocence, claiming that the Falangists have mistaken him for an anarchist brother.

Throughout the long night preceding their planned execution at sunrise, the three men continue to respond in different manners as a Belgian doctor, ostensibly sent in to comfort them, records their behavior with a clinically observant eye. Pablo, meanwhile, is watching also, observing the doctor as well. Gradually it occurs to Pablo that the physician, not affected by the death sentence that hangs over the prisoners, in fact belongs to a different order of being; unlike them, he is sensitive to cold, and to hunger, no doubt because he can look forward to "tomorrow." The captives, slowly but surely, are losing touch with their bodies, with a loss of control that goes well beyond simple fear. Pablo, in moments of total recall, revisits the small pleasures of his life and political career, only to note that such moments are not utterly devalued by the immediacy of his death: "I had understood nothing. I missed nothing: there were so many things I could have missed, the taste of *manzanilla* or the baths I took in summer in a little creek near Cadiz; but death had disenchanted everything."

Reminded by Tom of his mistress Concha, whom he had once mentioned to Tom in a rare moment of weakness, Pablo reflects with some amazement that he no longer misses Concha, either: "When she looked at me something passed from her to me. But I knew it was over: if she looked at me *now* the look would stay in her eyes, it wouldn't reach me. I was alone." In Pablo's current state, even the wild fantasy of a reprieve leaves him strangely cold; as he explains, "several hours or several years is all the same when you have lost the illusion of being eternal."

Toward dawn, Tom and Juan are led from the cell to be shot; Pablo, however, is detained for further questioning concerning the activities and whereabouts of the anarchist Ramon Gris, of which he had previously denied any knowledge. Although he no longer values Gris's life any more than he does his own, Pablo will still refuse to divulge what he knows, if only out of stubbornness. Finally, overwhelmed by the apparent absurdity of his captors' fancy uniforms and self-important airs, Pablo tells an elaborate lie about Gris's supposed whereabouts: As he spins his improbable tale of Gris hiding in a nearby cemetery, he imagines the stuffy, beribboned officers running about among the graves, lifting up tombstones, and the look on their faces when they perceive that the prisoner has tricked them.

The officers have been gone for no more than half an hour when one of them returns, ordering Pablo to be turned loose among the other prisoners, those still awaiting sentence. It is from one of the latter, a baker named Garcia who has "had nothing to do with politics," that Pablo will learn the truth: Ramon Gris, improbably, had taken refuge in the cemetery after an argument with the cousin who had been hiding him; unable to seek refuge with Pablo because of the latter's arrest, he could think of no place else to go. The Falangists, reports Garcia, found Gris hiding in the gravediggers' shack, and when he shot at them they killed him with return fire. As the news begins to sink in, Pablo collapses to the ground in a fit of helpless laughter.

Themes and Meanings

Anticipating by nearly half a decade the full development of Jean-Paul Sartre's existentialist philosophy, "The Wall" presents in imaginative form some of the major themes of that philosophy, giving concrete illustration of seemingly abstract ideas.

The "wall" of the story's title is the wall of the prison courtyard against which the prisoners are lined up to be shot; by extension, however, it comes to symbolize the boundary between life and death, between "being" and "nothingness." Pablo Ibbieta, although he will survive physically at least long enough to tell his ironic tale, is, in fact, as good as dead from the moment that he first perceives and appreciates the immediate prospect of his "nothingness." The human capacities for love, friendship, and political activism have all died in him as he has passed, as it were, through the "wall" to the other side.

Awaiting execution during the small hours of the morning, Pablo has reviewed his life and found it strangely wanting: "I wondered how I'd been able to walk, to laugh with the girls: I wouldn't have moved so much as my little finger if I had only imagined I would die like this. My life was in front of me, closed, shut, like a bag and yet everything inside of it was unfinished." Like many of Sartre's later characters, Pablo senses that most of his planned actions will die with him, unperformed, with little trace of him left to posterity. Notwithstanding, he persists in observing his stubborn code of honor, in his implied commitment to the liberal cause, and in his determination to die "cleanly" and "well," in contrast to his fellow prisoners. For Sartre, there is no afterlife, no trace of individual human passage on earth save for the sum total of accomplishments to be recorded after death.

Style and Technique

Couched in the first person, limited solely to Pablo's individual perceptions and opinions, "The Wall" serves as an object-lesson in the literary and critical theories that Sartre was then developing. There is no God-like, omniscient narrator; the style is less literary than conversational, even "earthy," with frequent recourse to rough language and profanity in description, metaphor, and dialogue. Except for Pablo's random recollections, the characters and their actions are described entirely "in situation," with little attention paid to possible background or motivation. To further underscore Sartre's attempt at "authenticity," at least insofar as is possible in art or literature, the story's setting and "atmosphere" are evoked entirely through the immediate, often graphically rendered perceptions of the narrator's five senses. The story's "trick" ending, however sensational, is nevertheless amply prepared for throughout by the nature of the tale to be told, and by Pablo's awareness of contingency and irony in life.

David B. Parsell

WALTER BRIGGS

Author: John Updike (1932-   )
Type of plot: Domestic realism
Time of plot: The late 1950's
Locale: The Boston area
First published: 1959

> *Principal characters:*
> JACK, the protagonist
> CLARE, his wife
> Jo, their two-year-old daughter
> WALTER BRIGGS, a character from their past

The Story

Driving home from Boston (a fifty-minute trip), Jack and his wife, Clare, entertain their daughter Jo with a version of a familiar nursery rhyme while their infant son sleeps. After Jo also falls asleep, they talk about the people they have met at a party, which leads into an extended memory game in which they try to remember names and details about people they had known when, newly married, they had worked together at a YMCA family camp in New Hampshire for a summer five years before. Their conversation, mostly commonplace and trivial, reveals hidden conflicts. One name out of their past that eludes both of them is the surname of a man called Walter who stayed all summer and played bridge every night.

Lying in bed after arriving home, Jack starts recalling poignant details of their early married life at the summer camp, particularly of their cabin and of his habit of reading *Don Quixote de la Mancha* every evening before dinner. Thinking of his tears at the conclusion of the novel, Jack suddenly recollects the name that had escaped them; he turns to his sleeping wife and says, "Briggs. Walter Briggs."

Themes and Meanings

The themes of "Walter Briggs" are revealed mainly through the character of the protagonist and the nature of the conflict with his wife. Beneath the surface of the memory game in the car there is a quiet but strong undercurrent of resentment and jealousy. Jack begins the marital hostilities by remarking that Clare's comments at the party about Sherman Adams (a controversial figure in President Dwight D. Eisenhower's administration) were "stupid." Then, talking about another person at the party, Jack observes that Foxy "loves you so." This comment is followed by a series of exchanges in which Jack remembers attractive physical features of females at the camp, which provoke responses from Clare. He recalls the girl "with the big ears who was lovely," and then defends her pride in her ears when Clare disparages the girl's wearing of "those bobbly gold gypsy rings." Jack also calls to mind a mentally disturbed girl who was "*aw*fully good-looking," and a woman named Peg Grace who had "huge eyes." Clare counters with the observation that Peg had a "tiny long nose with the nostrils shaped like water wings" and further remembers that Peg's boyfriend was sexy in his "tiny black bathing trunks." Jack then recalls a German kitchen boy "with curly hair he thought was so cute." Clare, in response, explains, "You didn't like him because he was always making eyes at me." Jack says that he really did not like the German kitchen boy because he had beaten him in a broad-jump competition and that he was pleased when the German was, in turn, beaten by someone else.

Jack's competitive instinct is one reason for the exchanges between Jack and his wife. Early in the story, the author explains that Jack found the memory contest deficient: "A poor game, it lacked the minimal element of competition needed to excite Jack." In this light, the comments about other women are designed to make the memory game more exciting by provoking Clare to respond. On a deeper level, however, the form that this provocation takes suggests that Jack is indeed quite receptive to the charms of other women and subconsciously, out of a sense of inadequacy, wants to let his wife know of this attraction. Jack's sense of inadequacy is also brought out by Clare's obvious superiority in the memory game. He does not have her talent for accurate and vivid recall, and he believes that he has "made an unsatisfactory showing." Although he is jealous of "her store of explicit memories," he is also pleased that she so generously shares with him reminiscences from their mutual past.

In the final scene, after they are in bed and Clare is asleep, Jack's memory begins to become more precise and intense. Spurred by her statement that the German boy had made eyes at her, he begins to recollect loving details of their early married life: "Slowly this led him to remember how she had been, the green shorts and the brown legs, holding his hand as in the morning they walked to breakfast from their cabin, along a lane that was two dirty paths for the wheels of the jeep." His memories increase in poignancy: "Her hand, her height had seemed so small, the fact of her waking him so strange." He finally recalls that he had spent the whole summer, in the half hour between work and dinner, reading *Don Quixote de la Mancha* in a chair outside their cabin and how he cried at the conclusion when Sancho Panza urges his master to go on another quest, perhaps to find "the Lady Dulcinea under some hedge, stripped of her enchanted rags and fine as any queen." It is at this point that Jack triumphantly remembers the lost last name of Walter Briggs and says it softly to the sleeping Clare.

This ending, then, represents a triumphant moment of joy for Jack. He has not only scored a small victory in the memory game by recovering the name of Walter Briggs, but also he has achieved something much more substantial. He has been able to recover his early feelings for his wife and the details of their life together in the modest cabin. Moreover, the allusion to *Don Quixote de la Mancha* suggests another new dimension to their relationship. He now sees Clare as the Lady Dulcinea, a desirable and splendid woman, just as Sancho and his master perceived Dulcinea. Jack experiences a moment of epiphany, a new and deeper awareness about his feelings for his wife. He becomes aware, through the power of memory, of precious hours in his life, which, as the story suggests, come from little things, from commonplace shared experiences.

Style and Technique

The plot of "Walter Briggs" is a straightforward sequence of events, starting in the car in the drive from Boston and ending late that same night. The bulk of the action, however, is retrospective in that it takes place in the memory of the main character. Still, the emphasis is not in the events themselves, but on what they reveal about the protagonist and the effect they have on him. The journey as a plot device is a common one, and it is appropriate here in that it serves as a metaphor for Jack's journey into a part of his past self that had been forgotten.

Jack's character is revealed primarily through the exchanges with Clare. Yet it is a very subtle dialogue in that the thrusts and parries of the conversation as well as the underlying hostility between Jack and his wife are artfully concealed beneath the banal observations of a somewhat bored couple on a tedious automóbile trip. As often occurs in real life, the major issues between Jack and his wife are not directly stated but are indirectly brought out and then passed by as the conversation quickly shifts to another person or incident. In the end, Jack is revealed as a complex and dynamic character with very human failings yet also a person to like and perhaps admire. The author shows Jack as a person capable of change who manages to extract something permanently valuable from an unpromising evening in a car.

The point of view is limited omniscience; the story is told in the third person through the eyes of Jack, the protagonist. Although characterization mostly emerges from dialogue concerning memories from camp, the final important insight into Jack's character comes from the author's direct recording of what Jack is thinking and feeling, which permits one to see the intensity of Jack's new awareness. Because the point of view is restricted to Jack's consciousness, the reader learns about Clare only by what she says and does and by what Jack thinks of her, not through any authorial revelation of her thoughts.

"Walter Briggs" demonstrates those aspects of style for which Updike is widely praised. Among these are the strong sense of time and place in modern America, created here by the references to contemporary religious and political figures, by his knowledge of everyday practices of Americans, and even by his mention of brand names and common commercial products. Updike also has a careful ear for the way people speak and for the rhythms of conversation. In the dialogue between Jack and Clare, Updike expertly captures the ebb and flow, repetitions, and interruptions of two people who know each other intimately. The opening conversation between Clare and her daughter Jo is a masterpiece of mother-child dialogue. Above all, Updike is notable for a poetic style, which in a single telling phrase or in the perfect word or image evokes the essence of a character or a scene. The following description, for example, captures the bleakness of the summer cabin, which stands in contrast to the remembered richness of the experience there: "All around the cabin had stood white pines stretched to a cruel height by long competition, and the cabin itself had no windows, but broken screens."

Finally, the title itself serves a dramatic function by creating a sense of mystery. Who is this character, Walter Briggs, one wonders, whose name Jack and Clare are so desperately trying to recollect? At the end, the name, fully shown again in the last two words of the story, is a helpful instrument for the revelation of Jack's new awareness.

Walter Herrscher

THE WANDERERS

Author: Alun Lewis (1915-1944)
Type of plot: Realism
Time of plot: The 1930's
Locale: Wales
First published: 1939

> *Principal characters:*
> MICAH, a small boy
> THE GIPSY, his father
> MAM, his mother
> JOHNNY ONIONS, a French peddler

The Story

Although this story focuses primarily on the marital relations of a Gipsy and his Welsh wife, the central character is the small child, Micah, for he is the one most affected by his parents' passions. The plot is simple. A Welsh woman has married a Gipsy, obviously because she was pregnant with the boy Micah, but also because, as she says, she does not like to live in houses. Their life, which gives the story its title, is one of wandering, peddling, haggling, and hiring themselves out whenever possible.

The central event of the story occurs when the wife sees her husband coming out of a barn with a farm girl and soon after becomes sexually attracted to a French peddler and has sex with him while her husband sleeps. The next morning, Micah tells his father that the peddler took his mother into the meadow during the night. While the Gipsy goes off with the peddler, presumably to beat him, the wife leaves to meet the peddler in another town. After walking for hours, she gives up her quest, returns to the caravan, and has a physical fight with her husband, which sends Micah running in terror into the meadow. When the Gipsy finally tires of the fight, he and his wife have sex. When Micah returns and finds them asleep, he is content, knowing that when they awake everything will be the way he likes it.

The actions and passions of the story are reminiscent of the fiction of D. H. Lawrence, whose influence is clearly apparent here. This is a story of primitive desires, involving people practicing a wandering life-style. It depends on a stereotype of Gipsies as dark, violent, sexual creatures, homeless and almost animalistic in their desires—dark strangers that more civilized folk use as bogeymen with which to frighten young children. The story also depends on other reductive stereotypes. For example, when the Gipsy goes into town to pawn his wife's earrings, he deals with a "shrivelled little Jew" with a pointed nose and an ingratiating manner. It is similarly stereotypical that the Gipsy would have a literal "roll in the hay" with a somewhat mindless farm girl and that the man who is so alluring to the wife is a Frenchman.

Even the use of the little boy Micah as a central figure, slapped by his mother, boxed by his father, and terrified that his mother will be taken away by the peddler, is a convention based on the notion that children are often the bewildered victims of adult passions which they do not understand but instinctively fear. Micah intuitively knows that the Frenchman is a threat, for as he watches his mother talk to the peddler, Micah puts his arms around her and bites into the flesh at the nape of her neck, only to be thrown off quivering like an animal. Above all, he desires stability, the reassurance of the status quo, although the life that he has known with his wandering parents has hardly been ideal.

Themes and Meanings

"The Wanderers" evokes a life-style which may appear romantic from a distance but which, close up, is seen to be merely sordid and animalistic. When the Gipsy sees the farm girl, what he responds to are her breasts, strong and round, pressing against her cotton blouse, and his composure melts into an "aching tumult of desire." His wife almost as immediately responds to the French peddler. The story suggests that she is not simply trying to avenge herself, but that she has become "infected" by her husband's own powerful passions. The language used to describe her desire for the peddler is almost identical with that used to describe her husband's desire for the farm girl. She feels that she has never burned like this before.

Alun Lewis, whose death in World War II cut short a promising career, is best known as a poet. "The Wanderers" appeared in a collection of stories, *The Last Inspection* (1942), most of the stories in which deal with life during the early years of the war in England, when air raids were a nightly horror. In "The Wanderers," he shifts away from the wartime setting, but the rootlessness depicted in this story is akin to that felt by the soldiers whom he more often takes as his central characters. At the same time, the story depicts the uncontrollable force of sexuality—a force which Lewis evidently regarded with a mixture of fascination and guilt.

The basic irony of the story is that the wife of the Gipsy, who is himself the archetypal wandering character, runs away from him with another wandering character, a reversal that somewhat domesticates him and makes him the cuckolded husband. Perhaps the more profound irony is that as Micah strives to maintain the stability of his life with his parents, the reader must reflect that Micah's life has no genuine stability at all.

Style and Technique

Although the story centers on Micah, it is not told from his point of view but rather from an omniscient third-person approach in which the narrator alternately enters the mind of the brutal and sexually aroused husband, the wildly inflamed wife, and the bewildered child. By this narrative strategy, and by other means as well, Lewis sought to give the story something of the violent authority of a ballad or a folktale—an attempt not entirely successful.

The language of the story is generally straightforward, but there are traces of Lewis the poet: At the crucial sexual moment between the Gipsy and the farm girl, Lewis describes the luminous darkness of the barn as if it were "cloudy with purple, intangible grapes." In several nearly voyeuristic scenes, the wife is naked—getting ready for bed, bathing in the stream, looking in the mirror—and here the description is simple but powerfully suggestive. Many readers, it should be noted, will object to the attitudes that inform the story, particularly the link between violence and sex.

Charles E. May

WAR

Author: Luigi Pirandello (1867-1936)
Type of plot: Social realism
Time of plot: c. 1916
Locale: Fabriano, Italy
First published: "Quando si comprende," 1919 (English translation, 1939)

> *Principal characters:*
> A MOTHER, whose son is about to go to war
> A FATHER, whose son has been killed in the war

The Story

Some travelers from Rome are obliged to spend most of the night aboard a second-class railway carriage, parked at the station in Fabriano, waiting for the departure of the local train which will take them the remainder of their trip to the small village of Sulmona. At dawn, they are joined by two additional passengers: a large woman, "almost like a shapeless bundle," and her tiny, thin husband. The woman is in deep mourning and is so distressed and maladroit that she has to be helped into the carriage by the other passengers.

Her husband, following her, thanks the people for their assistance and then tries to look after his wife's comfort, but she responds to his ministrations by pulling up the collar of her coat to her eyes, hiding her face. The husband manages a sad smile and comments that it is a nasty world. He explains this remark by saying that his wife is to be pitied because the war has separated her from their twenty-year-old son, "a boy of twenty to whom both had devoted their entire life." The son, he says, is due to go to the front. The man remarks that this imminent departure has come as a shock because, when they gave permission for their son's enlistment, they were assured that he would not go for six months. Yet they have just been informed that he will depart in three days.

The man's story does not prompt too much sympathy from the others because the war has similarly touched their lives. One of them tells the man that he and his wife should be grateful that their son is leaving only now. He says that his own son "was sent there the first day of the war. He has already come back twice wounded and been sent back again to the front." Someone else, joining the conversation, adds that he has two sons and three nephews already at the front. The thin husband retorts that his child is an only son, meaning that, should he die at the front, a father's grief would be all the more profound. The other man refuses to see that this makes any difference. "You may spoil your son with excessive attentions, but you cannot love him more than you would all your other children if you had any." Therefore, this one insists that he would really suffer twice what a father with one son would suffer.

The man with the two sons at the front continues by saying that a father gives all of his love to each of his children "without discrimination," and, even if one son is killed and the other remains, this is a son left "for whom he must survive, while in the case of the father of an only son if the son dies the father can die too and put an end to his distress." Thus, the situation of a man with two sons would still be worse than that of a man with one son.

Another man interjects that this argument is nonsense because, although parents belong to their sons, the sons never belong to their parents. Boys at twenty, "decent" boys, consider the love of their country greater than the love of their parents; when they go away to fight, they do not want to see any tears "because if they die, they die inflamed and happy." One should therefore rejoice that they have thus been spared the ugly side of life, its boredom and pettiness and its bitterness and disillusion. He says that everyone should therefore laugh as he does, "because my son, before dying, sent a message saying that he was dying satisfied at having ended his life in the best way he could have wished."

The woman whose son is being sent to the front to "a probable danger of death" is stunned by the stranger's words. She suddenly realizes that her deep sorrow lies in her inability to rise to the height of all those fathers and mothers who have the ability to resign themselves to the departure and even the death of their sons. She listens with close attention to the man's account of how his son has fallen as a hero, and she believes that she has suddenly stumbled into a world "she never dreamt of, a world so far unknown to her." Moreover, she is greatly pleased when it appears that everyone else seems to feel the same and congratulate the "brave father who could so stoically speak of his child's death." Yet, reacting as if she had just heard nothing, she asks the man, "Then . . . is your son really dead?" Everyone stares at her, including the old man who has lost his son.

He tries to answer but cannot speak. The silly, incongruous question makes him realize, at last, that his son is, in fact, really dead and gone forever. His face begins to contort, and, reaching for a handkerchief, he, to everyone's amazement, breaks down "into harrowing, heart-rendering, uncontrollable sobs."

Themes and Meanings

This is a world of crumbling values, made all the more vapid because of the intense desire to rationalize attitudes and live in a mist of illusions. The characters are overwhelmed by events that they cannot control and little understand, but they pretend otherwise. The woman, who has just arrived, is somewhat of an outsider; she apparently has not had time, or is not yet willing, to submerge her natural emotions under a mask of acceptable public sentimentality.

The passengers reflect the lack of enthusiasm of the Italian people for the

Great War, in which their country became involved because of a greedy back-room deal to acquire a few more chunks of territory that only few thought worth spilling blood to get. The lands would most likely have been theirs as the price of staying out. Italy's participation was conditioned by no great outpouring of national sentiment, nor because the national interest demanded it. Yet a pretense has to be made. One character says, "Our children do not belong to us, they belong to the Country. . . ." His words, however, lack conviction. These people, despite their boastful façade, are not preoccupied with the great forces of history. They want to make it through life causing as little damage to their dignity as possible. They want to preserve the only thing that gives their life meaning and ensures their link with immortality: the lives of their offspring. One character says, "Is there any one of us here who wouldn't gladly take his son's place at the front if he could?" Everyone nods approval, but in fact such a question is academic, since the premise upon which it is built is so farfetched. Yet the concern is genuine.

In a sense, the war is far removed from this provincial railway siding—there is no mention or description of any actual fighting—but the war's presence is nevertheless overpowering, conveyed in the characters' pathetic attempts to maintain appearances through worthless intellectualizations, hollow gestures, and futile attempts to sublimate anxiety. If none of the characters is swept away by a sense of participation in a great national crusade, none seems to turn to religion for comfort; indeed, the absence of any meaningful reference to religion is remarkable for people living in such an avowedly Roman Catholic country. Nothing is accepted as being in conformity with God's plan, or with His grand design for the Italian nation. No sacrifices are sanctified by their relation to a higher purpose. One gets the impression from these people that none of the sons sacrificed in this war will have died on the field of any honor.

Pirandello's characters are prisoners of their own subjectivity and their own lack of imagination. They are morally featureless. Yet their stale words and feeble efforts to communicate, coming from their boredom and trepidation, reveal a genuinely human need. They must convince themselves of their own intrinsic worth to alleviate their desperation.

Style and Technique

Pirandello uses a well-established literary device to tell his story: He contrives a restricted setting for his characters and lets them share their thoughts with one another. Such constraint—Pirandello even honors the three classical unities of time, place, and action—more dramatically reveals a world in which all progress and hope of progress has ceased. This atmosphere is as dull, oppressive, and intrusive as yesterday's lifeless beer. Pirandello is trying to represent human experience as realistically and banally as possible and could hardly be considered a symbolist; nevertheless, the imagery is there. His characters sit in an old-fashioned train in a small railway station in a small Italian province and wait to be taken to an even more remote and backward part of their country. They wait for something to happen with the dread that it might. They wait with the same spirit of resignation in which they struggle to accept and minimize the ultimate loss of their sons.

Pirandello lets the characters speak for themselves. He offers the barest of description, saving himself the trouble by relying on the reader's own knowledge of his locale. In thus downplaying the surroundings, Pirandello is able to intensify the characters' relationships to one another. This intensification is necessary because his characters are so essentially colorless, with features made deliberately unpleasant. Consider how Pirandello describes their eyes: One has "bloodshot eyes of the palest grey"; another has "eyes small and bright and looking shy and uneasy"; still another has "his eyes [that] were watery and motionless"; and yet another has "bulging, horrible watery light grey eyes": These are people in decay.

Pirandello's style is lean, remarkably lacking in metaphors and imagery. His descriptions are sparse and gray. He seems to be repetitive and not very original, dealing almost in clichés. He reveals no great philosophical or psychological insights, perpetually distancing himself from his characters. The story ends with a sort of double resolution: The woman, after listening to the man's description of how his son had fallen for king and country "happy and without regrets," believes that she can at last come to terms with her grief. Yet her period of reconciliation will be all too brief. The man, whose son was slain, who until now has successfully been able to suppress his loss, suddenly has all of his illusions swept away. He will bear the scars of his grief for the remainder of his days. Pirandello makes a skillful use of irony: The father's damnation is also his salvation. The realization that he no longer will be able to protect himself by self-deception brings to an end his artificiality and restores his humanity. Whether a similar catharsis will affect the others is doubtful.

Wm. Laird Kleine-Ahlbrandt

WARD NO. 6

Author: Anton Chekhov (1860-1904)
Type of plot: Psychological sketch
Time of plot: The 1890's
Locale: A provincial Russian town
First published: "Palata No. 6," 1892 (English translation, 1916)

> *Principal characters:*
> ANDREI EFIMYCH RAGIN, a doctor
> IVAN DMITRICH GROMOV, a patient in a mental ward
> MIKHAIL AVER'IANYCH, a postmaster
> EVGENII FEDORYCH KHOBOTOV, a doctor

The Story

Anton Chekhov begins his tale by taking his readers on a tour of the mental ward of a hospital in a provincial Russian town. His initial description stresses the filth and disorder prevailing in the institution, as well as the cruel barbarity that the caretaker Nikita shows toward the helpless patients in the ward. One patient in particular draws the narrator's interest. This is Ivan Dmitrich Gromov, a polite but very agitated young man who suffers from a persecution complex. The narrator recounts how Gromov came to be placed in the mental ward: As a sensitive individual acutely conscious of the backwardness and hypocrisy permeating rural Russian life, he began to fear that he could be arrested and imprisoned through someone's error or through a miscarriage of justice. Increasingly paralyzed by this irrational anxiety, he was eventually institutionalized in Ward No. 6, where he now languishes with the other patients, neglected by the medical authorities.

As the narrator continues, he states that one man has unexpectedly begun to visit Gromov. This is the doctor in charge of the institution, Andrei Efimych Ragin. Now the reader learns of Ragin's life and personality. A heavily built, powerful man, Ragin possesses a curiously passive disposition. When he was appointed to the post of medical supervisor for the hospital, he was appalled by the primitive, unsanitary conditions he found there. Yet he lacked the strength of character to push for reform, and after an initial period of zealous work he "lost heart" and ceased going to the hospital. Gradually he developed a consoling rationalization for his own failure to strive for change: Illness and death are an inevitable part of the human experience; the current state of medical knowledge is relatively limited; therefore, there is no real point in trying to improve things—he himself figures as only a minor element in an entire system of inescapable social injustice. Bored and disillusioned, Ragin discovers one day that an interesting individual is lodged in the mental ward. Thus, he begins visiting Gromov to conduct extended discussions with him about life and philosophy.

The conversations between Ragin and Gromov provide the ideological core of the story. Ragin tries to convince Gromov that the human intellect is a self-contained organ that allows one to find peace of mind in any environment, even prison. Gromov counters this notion by pointing out that humans are made up of flesh and blood, and that to reject the pains of the flesh is to reject life itself. Descrying, in Ragin's words, an empty philosophy of expediency, he accuses Ragin of laziness and of ignorance about real life. Caustically he declares that Ragin may talk about intellectual peace of mind, but that if the doctor were to squeeze his finger in a door, he would certainly scream at the top of his lungs.

Gromov's prediction is borne out when Ragin himself is forced into the mental ward after antagonizing his friend the postmaster and a fellow doctor with a streak of erratic and unsociable behavior. Now Ragin undergoes a chilling awakening. Staring through the bars of the asylum window, he sees the blank stone walls of a nearby prison and the dark flames of a distant bone mill. In a flash he realizes that this is true reality. Panicked by his discovery, he tries to leave the ward, but he receives a beating from Nikita instead. The next day he suffers a stroke and dies. Chekhov concludes his gloomy tale by commenting that only the postmaster and Ragin's maid attend the doctor's funeral.

Themes and Meanings

In Gromov and Ragin, Chekhov depicts two individuals who are ill-suited to deal with the reality of contemporary life. Gromov may be the more sympathetic of the two. His confessed zest for life—"I want to live!" he exclaims at one point—contrasts favorably with Ragin's intellectual retreat from experience. On the other hand, he too finds it easier to talk about life than actually to live it. Neither man possesses the strength or confidence to combat injustice in the world; in the end, they are both defeated by their internal weaknesses.

Yet while both Gromov and Ragin are shown to be inadequate to the task of living meaningful and productive lives, they both seem more sensitive and alert than the rest of the people in their provincial town. Indeed, Gromov remarks that there are scores of madmen walking freely outside the asylum while people such as himself are imprisoned. Ragin concurs and asserts that such a fate is merely a matter of chance. His own relationship with his supposed friend the postmaster and his colleague Dr. Khobotov adds support to this view. The postmaster is an idle chatterer with no true understanding or compassion for anyone else's woes but his own, and Dr. Khobotov is a dull lackey who secretly covets Ragin's position and finally manages to replace him. Nor does the situation seem much better beyond the borders of this rural town. Ragin journeys with the postmaster to Moscow and Warsaw, but he finds nothing of stimulation in either locale. The atmosphere of unrelieved vulgarity and banality which Chekhov creates in this story led a fellow writer to declare that Ward No. 6 is Russia itself. Chekhov's tale provides vivid evidence that Russian society was prey to the twin vices of ignorance and indolence. Mere words and philosophical theories are insufficient to combat this pernicious affliction.

Style and Technique

Chekhov's narrative is structured in such a way as to lead the reader gradually into the world of the rural mental asylum. The charged descriptions at the outset of the story communicate his indignation over the way society has traditionally dealt with the emotionally disturbed. His portraits of the patients in the ward, from the intellectual Gromov to a man who once sorted mail at the post office, convey his compassion for the plight of those who suffer from mental illness. Then, with the incarceration of Ragin in the ward at the end of the story, the reader perceives directly the true horror of the setting. Chekhov endows Ragin's view from the asylum window with symbolic dimensions: The prison walls he sees echo his own involuntary confinement, and the bone mill also in sight stands as an emblem of impending death and destruction.

This symbolic mode of description surfaces again after Ragin suffers his fatal stroke. Ragin thinks for a moment about immortality, then dismisses it. Suddenly, he sees a vision of an extraordinarily beautiful herd of deer which race past him and disappear. Although Chekhov does not explain the significance of this vision, it is possible that the deer represent those aspects of life that Ragin himself ignored or overlooked. In his arid intellectual meditations he became divorced from the real world, from nature, and from living beauty. Only at the end of his life, when it is too late to change, does he undergo a mystical epiphany. This moment of beauty swiftly passes, however, just like Ragin's life itself.

Not only do Chekhov's descriptions of the natural environment carry symbolic associations; his descriptions of people, too, add depth to the reader's understanding of character and personality. The fact that Ragin is physically imposing yet walks softly and cautiously mirrors the contradictions in his psychology, too: Although he is in charge of the hospital and possesses the power to try to make changes in the system, he is too timid to utilize his strength.

Complementing Chekhov's charged descriptive passages are the passages in which Gromov and Ragin exchange opinions on life. As in several other of the short stories he wrote in the early 1890's, Chekhov constructs a situation in which two individuals with differing approaches come together and conduct a debate with each other. Chekhov himself does not take sides in any obvious way. He prefers to let the reader evaluate the two viewpoints and decide for himself the merits and flaws of each. In this tale, though, Ragin's arguments are clearly exposed as the weaker of the two, because as he himself discovers, the sufferings one encounters in real life are not as easily dismissed as they are in an intellectual debate. Taken together, Chekhov's evocative descriptions and his passages of intellectual exploration culminate in a striking indictment of the shortcomings of rural Russian society.

Julian W. Connolly

WASH

Author: William Faulkner (1897-1962)
Type of plot: Psychological realism
Time of plot: 1872
Locale: Sutpen's Hundred, Yoknapatawpha County, Mississippi
First published: 1934

> *Principal characters:*
> WASH JONES, the protagonist, a poor white man
> THOMAS SUTPEN, an arrogant, ambitious, disillusioned owner
> of a ruined plantation
> MILLY JONES, Wash's granddaughter
> MILLY'S NEWBORN DAUGHTER
> AN OLD BLACK WOMAN, a midwife

The Story

The opening page and a half, set in 1872 at dawn on Sunday morning, presents all principal characters except Wash Jones. It begins with Thomas Sutpen standing above the pallet where Milly Jones and her child lie; Sutpen's arrogance is seen in his stance, with whip in hand, as he looks down upon the mother and child. His mare has also given birth; the contrast between his attitude toward the colt and toward his and Milly's child presents the central problem of the story: The mare has borne a male; Milly, a female. If Milly were a mare, he would provide better quarters for her. Leaving the run-down fishing shack, he walks past his rusty scythe, which Wash Jones, Milly's grandfather, borrowed three months earlier. The scythe will become important both as a symbol and as an instrument of death.

The third-person narrator now embarks on a six-page digression, recounting events from 1861, when Colonel Sutpen rode away to fight in the "War Between the States," until his return to a ruined plantation in 1865, and through the years 1865 to 1870, when Sutpen and Wash together ran a country store and drank "inferior whiskey." There is reference to Sutpen's son, "killed in action the same winter in which his wife had died," and to Wash's grandchild. Emphasis is placed on the deterioration not only of Sutpen's property but also of his person. Even though he still rides the same black stallion and presents, at least to the naïve, worshipful Wash, a proud image, he is now a storekeeper best characterized by misplaced pride, unconcern for others, and habitual drunkenness. Wash is characterized throughout this section as a poor white in both the literal and the connotative meanings of the term. For many years, he has lived in the deteriorated shack by the slough on the plantation, the object of scorn by whites and blacks alike. While Sutpen was away, Wash pretended to have the responsibility of taking care of

Sutpen's place, but he was careful never to enter Sutpen's house. After the return, he achieved entry by carrying the drunken Sutpen in and putting him to bed. Wash has closed his eyes to the fact that Sutpen has been seducing Milly, as evidenced by the pretty ribbons she has worn around her waist. When Wash confronts Sutpen with the fact of Milly's new dress, the subject changes to whether Wash is afraid of Sutpen. The conversation and the digression end with Wash saying that Sutpen will make it right.

The last nine pages return to 1872 and the main narrative, the scene at the cabin on that Sunday when the mare's colt and Milly's girl are born. As Wash watches Milly and the black midwife, he thinks of Sutpen, admiring the man, and of the new relationship that will exist between him and Sutpen. He hears the sound of Sutpen riding up; the midwife announces that the baby is a girl; and it is dawn. Wash's pride in being a great-grandfather is balanced against the problem of telling Sutpen that his daughter is a girl. The words Sutpen speaks and the attitude he shows toward Milly and the baby cause Wash to realize Sutpen's true character for the first time. As Wash approaches, Sutpen lashes him with the whip. Wash then kills Sutpen with the rusty scythe. Wash is occupied through the day with tender care for Milly and with watching at the window. After a white boy discovers the body, Wash waits for the men to come. After dark, the gentle Wash once again becomes violent, killing Milly and the baby with a butcher knife, setting fire to the cabin, and attacking the sherrif's posse silently with the rusty scythe.

Themes and Meanings

The theme has to do with the contrast between the arrogance of Thomas Sutpen and the lowliness of Wash Jones, and with the ultimate consequences of this contrast. Sutpen's arrogance is everywhere evident, especially in the two parts that make up the main narrative. He rides a stallion, he carries a whip in his hand, and the story opens with him looking down on Milly and his newborn daughter. He is callous and unfeeling toward the girl he has seduced and toward his own child. He cares more for the mare and newborn colt; in fact, Wash comes to realize that Sutpen has arisen early because of the stable birth, not because of the one in the cabin. His statement that if Milly had been a mare he would have provided a stable for her and his stalking out of the cabin without any recognition of his daughter further emphasize his arrogance.

Similarly, with Wash, Sutpen displays only arrogance. When the man who has been his companion in the store and in drinking bouts, the man who has put him to bed on occasion, confronts him with the fact of his seduction of the fifteen-year-old Milly, Sutpen's only response is to note that Wash is afraid of him. He offers no explanation of his conduct nor does he accept any responsibility for Milly or her unborn child. Wash's assurance that Sutpen "will make hit right" is never confirmed; it later proves to be misplaced confidence. One can speculate about whether Sutpen would have done better had the child been a boy, but in the story he only makes a passing remark to the midwife to do whatever is needed. When Wash approaches him about his attitude, he lashes out with the whip, thus driving Wash to the act of violence with the scythe. Nowhere in the story does Sutpen express any concern for the feelings of Wash, Milly, or anyone else. He is entirely self-centered, reacting to the lowered status of the storekeeper by closing the store when his ego can stand no more and drowning his shame in alcohol.

Wash, on the other hand, has come up in the world through his association with Sutpen. He is of the lowest caste of Southern whites, living in a shack in which the blacks would never live. When he pretends to responsibility for the property of Sutpen, the blacks as well as the whites laugh at him in scorn, at a time when the former are still slaves to a white man. The borrowed scythe is a reminder that Wash owns nothing. The fact that it is rusty and has stood unused for three months among the tall weeds indicates that he is lazy and irresponsible. His admiration for Sutpen (in the latter's deterioration) is misplaced at best. His inattention to the seduction of his grandchild and his acceptance of the fact when he hopes to achieve higher status through the birth of Sutpen's child mark him as weak and devious.

Sutpen is a static character, unchanging to the end. Wash, however, is dynamic, undergoing radical change at the moment of truth. He becomes courageous, violent, tender, and patient, no longer the passive character of the past twenty years. Given the fact of such change, one senses the inevitability of swift retribution upon Sutpen for his many real and imagined injuries to Wash and his family.

Style and Technique

In this story, as in much of his work, Faulkner attempted to telescope present and past time into the present moment. In "Wash," he employs the epic techniques of *in medias res* and digression. The basic style is third-person, past-tense, direct narrative throughout, with little attention to psychological nuances except through suggestion. There is the almost objective viewpoint of reporting only what can be seen and heard. Even though Wash is followed as protagonist throughout, his inner thoughts and motivations are often inferred from words and deeds, although there is limited direct statement of such. The viewpoint, then, would seem to be limited omniscient third-person narration from the viewpoint of Wash, but with some of the qualities of objective. Basic simplicity of structure is seen in the three parts of direct narrative, long digression, direct narrative. Intensity is achieved through contrast of the two men and through the irony of their incongruous relationship. Compactness in the story is achieved through the focus upon one day in one place, the classical unities of time and place, and through the coincidence of Wash's recognition of the true nature of things with his reversal of intention (the classical unity of plot).

"Wash" may be read on two levels. As a short story it has all the internal ingredients for enjoyment and evaluation. The mass of information about Faulkner's other writings and about his fictional county of Yoknapatawpha, as well as occasional references to Thomas Sutpen in the novels, enhances such reading. Knowledge of the doctor upon whom Sutpen is based and of the genesis of the Sutpen narratives might also be helpful. On another level, "Wash" may be read against the background of complete knowledge of the greater context within which the author later placed it, for it eventually came to be part of a chapter within the novel *Absalom, Absalom!* (1936). This longer context reveals a young Thomas Sutpen of humble origins in the coal fields of what is now West Virginia, where everyone was considered equal; his deeply traumatic experience of being treated as poor white trash at a plantation house in Tidewater, Virginia; the deep psychological scars which resulted; his obsession with building a plantation of his own, first in Haiti, later in Mississippi; and his equal obsession with building a family dynasty, thwarted first through the revelation that his first wife was part black, later through the tragic consequences of relationships between his mulatto son and his white son and daughter. The reader would know that the younger son Henry had killed his half brother and was in perpetual hiding at the Mississippi plantation. Also helpful would be the knowledge that Sutpen had once proposed marriage to his young sister-in-law Rosa Coldfield provided she would first bear him a son. In the short story, Sutpen's worst qualities are emphasized, while the best, where mentioned, are tainted as seen through the eyes of Wash. In the novel, the full motivations of this driven man are delineated.

George W. Van Devender

THE WATCHER

Author: Italo Calvino (1923-1985)
Type of plot: Neorealism
Time of plot: 1953
Locale: Turin, the Cottolengo Hospital for Incurables
First published: "La giornata d'uno scrutatore," 1963 (English translation, 1971)

> *Principal characters:*
> AMERIGO ORMEA, the protagonist, a poll-watcher
> LIA, Amerigo's friend and mistress
> THE CHAIRMAN
> THE WOMAN IN ORANGE,
> THE WOMAN IN WHITE, and
> THE THIN MAN, other poll-watchers

The Story

This story focuses on the observations and reflections of a Communist Party worker, Amerigo Ormea, on a day in which he is participating as a "poll-watcher" during the 1953 Italian election. The voting place to which he has been assigned is Turin's Cottolengo Hospital for Incurables, a shelter for the mentally and physically afflicted. The voters at Cottolengo are its staff and, primarily, its inmates, and Amerigo's responsibility, especially as a Communist, is to see that the voters are all mentally capable of voting on their own without being guided by nuns and priests of the institution (who would be supporters of the Christian Democrat Party, opposing the Communists in the election). Working with Amerigo are five other volunteers—a chairman, a clerk, and three other watchers.

This is a psychological drama, in which the conflicts and resolutions are intellectual, occurring in the mind of the protagonist; the external action provides the context in which Amerigo faces the political, moral, and religious questions that are central to the story. The complexity of the story exists in Amerigo's intensely sensitive and ethical mind, which wanders through labyrinthine paths of speculations. The actual events are straightforward.

Amerigo leaves home at five-thirty in the morning and walks in the rain to Cottolengo. Throughout the day, Amerigo vacillates in his feelings about the election—whether, for example, taking the election to an institution for the mentally infirm and disabled helps democracy or harms it. Yet he begins positively, with a simple determination. He recognizes what he regards as

> The moral question: you had to go on doing as much as you could, day by day.
> In politics, as in every other sphere of life, there are two important principles

for a man of sense: don't cherish too many illusions, and never stop believing that every little bit helps.

At the polls, the task he is assigned is that of checking the voters' identity papers. One of the watchers, a woman in orange, questions the validity of a voter's medical certificate that claims that the man is blind. She notices that the voter is able to see that he has accidentally taken two ballots. A priest accompanying the voter defends the medical certificate, and Amerigo enters the argument, stating that the certificate is valid "if it tells the truth." He suggests that they test the voter's ability to see. The chairman, the two other watchers, and the priest outnumber Amerigo and the woman in orange, and the priest has his way, accompanying the voter into the voting booth to assist him. Amerigo and the woman record their protest, and Amerigo goes out for a smoke.

Amerigo feels a personal crisis at this point, in which all action seems futile: "[M]orality impels one to act; but what if the action is futile?" Progress, liberty, and justice seem the privilege of the healthy, and not universal, since the afflicted cannot share in them. The only practical attitude for the Cottolengo unfortunate seems to be a religious one, "establishing a relation between one's own afflictions and a universal harmony and completeness." Society creates the institution to help the afflicted, but nothing can really be done, so that "Cottolengo was, at once, the proof and the denial of the futility of action." Amerigo finally returns to his work as poll-watcher, believing that the only right action is to behave well in history, "even if the world is Cottolengo." Pessimistically, however, Amerigo muses that being right is not enough.

Amerigo returns to his home during his lunch break and begins reading a passage from the early writings of Karl Marx, on the relationship between man and nature. Lia, Amerigo's mistress, telephones him, interrupting his reading. They have a pointless argument about her belief in horoscopes, which Amerigo regards as irrational. They hang up, and Amerigo calls her back to tell her that she is "prelogical," but Lia will not let him speak, asking him instead to listen to a recording that she is playing. Amerigo, frustrated at not being able to speak, argues again with her and they hang up again. Lia calls back and informs Amerigo that she thinks she is pregnant. Amerigo reacts in horror and suggests abortion, which angers Lia, and she hangs up again. Amerigo makes a last call, to soothe her, and again is not able to speak because Lia wants him to listen to another recording. He feels fatalistic about their differences, illustrated for him by this interchange. While he anguishes over their future, Lia is passive. Amerigo thinks, "[F]or her it's nothing, for her it's nature, for her the logic of the mind doesn't count, only the logic of physiology." Yet Amerigo feels reassurance in Lia's consistency: She is always irrational, always unpredictable. During this episode, Amerigo feels largely disappointed in himself for not living up to his model of behavior, which is to maintain a calm, lucid mastery of situations. Depressed about Lia's pregnancy, and how lightly she seems to take it, he thinks of Cottolengo, "all that India of people born to unhappiness, that silent question, an accusation of all those who procreate."

Returning to Cottolengo, Amerigo joins the other voting officials in visiting a ward of inmates who cannot leave their beds. Amerigo objects to allowing the vote of a paralytic man who cannot express himself. After arguing with the mother superior and a priest, Amerigo prevails, and his objection is subsequently applied by the priest in charge to the remaining bedridden inmates in the ward. Amerigo has taken action that has made a difference.

Observing a peasant farmer who is visiting his paralytic and apparently noncommunicative son, Amerigo considers the quality of love. Unlike the mother superior, who attends the afflicted for no recognition other than "the good she derived from them," the father "stared into his son's eyes to be recognized, to keep from losing him." Amerigo thinks, "Those two . . . are necessary to each other. . . . Humanity reaches as far as love reaches; it has no frontiers except those we give it." This reflection leads Amerigo to acknowledge his love for Lia, and in a moment of revelation he hurries to call her. Her line is busy, and when he finally does reach her they end up arguing over her busy line and a trip she is planning, apparently in response to something Amerigo had carelessly said the day before. Amerigo is both furious at his inability to control his interactions with Lia and relieved that Lia never changes. He feels an impulse to hang up and at the same time a fatalistic sense that he is caught.

At the end of the day, Amerigo makes his last significant observation in Cottolengo, when he meets a fifty-year-old man who grew up in the hospital and has lived his whole life there. The man is without hands but manages to overcome his handicap with skillful manipulation of his arms. Amerigo's final response is a positive one: "Man triumphs even over malign biological mutation." He sees in the Cottolengo man a fitting symbol of man as *homo faber* ("man the maker"); in Cottolengo itself, which the Cottolengo man describes as being like a small city, Amerigo sees a symbol of all cities, which are to be respected for the human will and ingenuity that creates them. Thus, at the end of the story Amerigo feels a response to a question that opened the story: "[A]re institutions, which grow old, of no matter; is what matters only the human will, the human needs . . . restoring verity to the instruments they use?" His feeling now is that

> *Homo faber's* city . . . always runs the risk of mistaking its institutions for the secret fire without which cities are not founded and machinery's wheels aren't set in motion; and in defending institutions, unawares, you can let the fire die out.

Themes and Meanings

In the protagonist's contemplations, many issues are raised: the nature of democracy; progress in history; blessedness (that is, the sensation of universal harmony in which one takes part) versus personal dissatisfaction (which can be a stimulus to action and creativity); religion as the acceptance of human smallness; man's triumph over adversity; and the importance of personal experience over abstraction. The number and variety of these issues demonstrate the fecund restlessness of Amerigo's mind, and resulting as they do from Amerigo's observations during his day as poll-watcher, they dramatize the insistence in Italian neorealism of looking at events in the context of the environment.

These issues, however, are not so much thematic in the story as illustrative of how Amerigo's mind works. It is a characteristic of his mind that he can always perceive the antithesis of an idea and is challenged by the consequent conflict. Contemplating his reasons for going to Cottolengo, Amerigo observes how "his thoughts raced in such an agile objectivity that he could see with the adversary's own eyes the very things he had felt contempt for a moment earlier." This process itself—conceiving an idea, constructing its opposite, or opposition, and working toward a resolution—is a parody of Communist dialectic, with its thesis, antithesis, and synthesis.

The central theme of the story arises out of Amerigo's struggle with the ironies and paradoxes of a voting day in Cottolengo. He begins the day feeling self-confident, within his limits, and fairly positive about democracy, despite his "slightly pessimistic" outlook on politics. Watching the setting up of the polling place and reflecting on the tendency of institutions to forget the inspirations that created them and settle into meaningless bureaucracy, he senses an absurdity. The prospect becomes even bleaker when he observes the mental deficiency of most of the Cottolengo inmates and imagines history as decline, a sort of reverse march of progress, by which brilliant generations are replaced by increasingly dull ones. Finally comes a feeling of the futility of action, for as a watcher, there is nothing Amerigo can do to "stop the avalanche" of abuse as one inept voter follows another. Even the blessedness of the nuns is depressing, inasmuch as it seems to remove them from the real world of action: "Amerigo would have liked to go on clashing with things, fighting, and yet achieve at the same time . . . a calm above it all." This ideal, however, is still inaccessible to him. Moreover, his enthusiasm for Marx's early writings, in which he seeks something positive to "channel and accompany his reflections," turns sour; Amerigo reflects that Marx's notion of man's universality is pointless unless it can promise legs to the lame and eyesight to the blind.

The turning point occurs when, in spite of his frustration with trying to communicate with Lia, Amerigo begins to admire her courage in facing the possibility of her pregnancy. His overwhelming impulse then is to express his feeling of tenderness toward her. It is from this experience that Amerigo slowly climbs out of his depression. He becomes more active in enforcing the law in the election, and finally, through his observation of the peasant father visiting his son, and the Cottolengo man, he arrives at his vision of *homo faber* and his city. The story thus dramatizes the view that man can arrive at a positive vision through direct, personal experience, which includes both an intellectual interaction with events as well as human empathy and love.

Style and Technique

"The Watcher" is told from the third-person-singular point of view, which facilitates approaching the protagonist objectively while still revealing his thoughts. The clearest impressions in the story are those of Amerigo's mind. Other impressions are less detailed, or vague. Though the voting officials play dramatic roles in the story, their names are not mentioned, and they are drawn in only the harshest of outlines. The major character of Lia is never seen, and her voice is heard only over the telephone, accompanied by undescribed music. All of this serves to intensify the focus on Amerigo's thoughts and swings of mood. The world of the story is, in fact, presented only as a perception of Amerigo's. Even the rain at the outset of the story, rather than being presented objectively, independent of Amerigo, is presented as one of his perceptions: "It looked like rain." Soon afterward is the image of Amerigo "tilting his umbrella to one side and raising his face to the rain."

Paradox and symbol in this story are basic to Calvino's theme, and are obvious rather than subtle. The significant symbols are well explained: Cottolengo represents human society as a whole, and the Cottolengo man who was reared in the hospital is *homo faber*—representative, that is, of the spark within man that accounts for his humanity.

The most outstanding stylistic trait of the story is Calvino's mirroring in his sentence structures the complexity of Amerigo's thoughts. In the story's second chapter, it is learned that:

> At times the world's complexity seemed to Amerigo a superimposition of clearly distinct strata, like the leaves of an artichoke; at other times, it seemed a clump of meanings, a gluey dough.

What follows is a tour de force, a one-sentence paragraph that is nearly two pages long. To create many layers of subordination (Amerigo's qualifying comments and retakes), Calvino utilizes thirty-eight commas, nine pairs of parentheses, four sets of colons, two sets of dashes, and a semicolon. The sentence, about Amerigo's role as a Communist, is filled with contradictions and paradoxes. Within the sentence, he describes himself, by turns, as pessimistic, optimistic, and skeptical. The paragraph is, itself, like the complexity of Amerigo's world, an artichoke, each set of leaves enfolding another inside itself.

Another example of Calvino's artistry occurs in the fourth chapter of the story. The second paragraph ("It was a hidden Italy that filed through that room . . .") is another lengthy, one-sentence paragraph. This time, the sentence is periodic rather than cumulative, in order to create tension. It describes the inmates of Cottolengo as the "secret of families and of villages," poverty's "incestuous couplings," and "the mistake risked by the material of human race each time it reproduces itself." The sentence is rhythmically interrupted with the parenthetical disclaimers, "but not only," which emphasize Amerigo's caution and fastidiousness as a thinker and build up suspense toward the climax in the image of mutants, products of poisons and radiation, and the insistence on randomness as the governing agent in human generation.

Dennis C. Chowenhill

WET SATURDAY

Author: John Collier (1901-1980)
Type of plot: Satiric horror
Time of plot: The 1930's
Locale: Abbot's Laxton, England
First published: 1938

> *Principal characters:*
>> MR. PRINCEY, a head of a family who despises his wife, son,
>> and daughter but will shield them to protect his standing in
>> the community
>> MRS. PRINCEY, his hysterical wife
>> MILLICENT PRINCEY, their daughter and a killer
>> GEORGE PRINCEY, their son and a failed medical student
>> WITHERS, the local clergyman and murder victim
>> CAPTAIN SMOLLETT, a neighbor

The Story

On a rainy July day, Mr. Princey gathers together the family that he abhors because his daughter, Millicent, has done something so stupid as to
threaten his way of life. Mr. Princey's pleasures are simple: He loves his
house, likes to walk through the village, where his prestige is acknowledged,
and enjoys reminiscing about the lost pleasures of his childhood.

As he addresses his family, he mercilessly lashes at Millicent for her as yet
unnamed error. If caught, he explains, she will be hanged or committed to an
asylum for the criminally insane. He also insults George, his son, when he
asks the young man whether his abortive career as a medical student has enabled him to tell whether Millicent's crime can be disguised as an accident.
George says that it cannot. Millicent has hit the victim several times.

Calming his wife with direct abuse and his daughter with threats of asy-
lums and hanging, Princey asks Millicent to describe the afternoon's events.
Millicent, it turns out, had been packing up the croquet set in the stable on
that wet afternoon when the young neighboring curate, Withers, on his way
for a walk to Bass Hill, cut through the property and stopped to talk, shelter-
ing himself in the stable away from the heavy rain. Millicent had long loved
this young man (George interjects that the local pub has been laughing at her
infatuation for the past several years), and so, when Withers said that he was
now in a position to be married, she assumed that he was about to propose
to her. She was wrong. Apologetically, he gave her the name of another girl
with whom he would be married and turned his back to leave, at which point
Millicent struck him several times with a croquet mallet. Then she returned
to the house, trusting her family to shelter her. In this, she was correct.

They are still discussing the death of Withers when Captain Smollett, with only a tap at the door, walks in. Clearly, he has been in a position to hear some of their conversation, but he assumes that they have been joking about Withers' death. He admits that, at the moment, he is none too fond of that young man himself because he, too, has been courting the young woman whom Withers won.

This admission gives Princey an idea, and he calls George to the stables. A few minutes later, Princey returns and asks Smollett if he would like to see something interesting. When they reach the stables, Princey aims a gun at Smollett and tells him that, while he and George came out to shoot a rat, they might well have an accident and shoot Smollett instead. Holding Smollett captive, Princey explains that Withers' accident must be smoothed over. Smollett, he says, would remember the conversation that he had walked in upon when he heard that Withers had met with a fatal accident that day. Smollett, an apparently honest man, admits that he probably would.

Princey explains that he does not want Millicent arrested because he would be forced to leave the village. Smollett offers a promise of silence, but Princey insists that he must ensure the neighbor's silence by other means. He considers killing Smollett, having no more compunction about two corpses than about one, but he finds another way out. Smollett, after all, has admitted his own jealousy of Withers and thus has a motive for killing him. Therefore, offering Smollett the choice of death or compliance, he implicates Smollett in Withers' death. He orders George to hit Smollett in the face hard enough to leave traces of a struggle, and he forces Smollett to leave his own fingerprints on the murder weapon and on the ring by which the flagstone over the sewer is raised. Withers' body is deposited in the sewer.

Princey mops his brow with relief. Since no one knew that Withers would stop on his way to Bass Hill, investigators are hardly likely to check the Princey sewer. The group returns to the drawing room, where Mrs. Princey gushingly thanks Smollett for his cooperation. She still has tears of gratitude in her eyes as Smollett goes down the drive.

Princey has one last talk with his wife and daughter and, after the rain ends, one last look around the stable. Reassured, he picks up the telephone to call the Bass Hill police station and report the murder. The story ends here, but the reader has watched the evidence being manufactured and knows that Princey has done a very thorough job. Smollett will most assuredly take the blame.

Themes and Meanings

"Wet Saturday" is one of a group of stories in which John Collier satirizes social institutions, including marriage. Marriage, like the professions of law and medicine, tends, in Collier's view, to be governed by conventions and acquisitiveness, not by integrity and concern. In "Wet Saturday," the family's last name and the father's behavior alike suggest that this is a family which carries the belief that an Englishman's home is his castle to an insane extreme.

Essentially, this tightly, if unhappily, knit family is waging war against the community in which it resides. Princey despises his family; in him, Collier has deftly sketched the lines of a man who deeply resents adult responsibility and who yearns for the privileged world of childhood which he attempts to re-create. Despite his domestic emotions, however, Princey will defend his obviously deluded daughter, even if her defense allows her the freedom to prey on the community in the future.

Every detail of the story points to the family's narrow self-interest. A young man of God eagerly on the brink of success and marriage is, to this family, no more than refuse to be crammed down a sewer; at no point in the story does any member of the family utter any word of concern or remorse at his death. In the family's treatment of Smollett, the members give ample evidence that they honor no promises and no bonds of friendship; Smollett may well hang for a crime that he did not commit and that he vowed to conceal. The family, though, has gained its end: Its standing in the community will remain untainted. The Princey family, then, provides a typical Collier microcosm of an acquisitive and power-hungry society at its very worst.

Style and Technique

Collier creates horror by emphasizing the ordinariness of the Princey family. It could be any family dominated by a tyrannical father; this is Collier's point. Collier creates his effect by an intricate flattening out of events so that no single event—such as the death of a man of God—seems more significant than any other to this family, and by the flat, cold, emotionless language with which the story is told. The language is that of journalism, and it creates the illusion of truth to life. It reminds the reader that horror can lurk anywhere, even in the tightly knit circle of a pleasantly respectable family on an ordinary rainy Saturday afternoon.

The language of Mr. Princey dominates the story and sets the tone. Whether he is giving his family a tongue-lashing or discussing the death of Withers and the possible death of Smollett, his words are totally devoid of any emotion. He can speak without pity of his daughter's hanging, and he debates killing Smollett in the same language as he mentions shooting a rat. After George hits Smollett at his instruction, Princey politely apologizes; only a little while later, he frames Smollett for the clergyman's murder.

Betty Richardson

WHAT IS THE CONNECTION BETWEEN MEN AND WOMEN?

Author: Joyce Carol Oates (1938-   )
Type of plot: Psychological realism
Time of plot: The 1960's
Locale: The United States
First published: 1970

> *Principal characters:*
> SHARON, a widow, thirty-four years old, who works in a
>   department store
> HER HUSBAND, now dead, whom she remembers
> A MAN, unnamed, who follows her home

The Story

Joyce Carol Oates's story is an experimental rendering of guilt and sexual repression. Through an alternation between a series of questions (in italics) and answers (in roman), she exposes the rawness of a very vulnerable personality: a woman unable to understand her own desires and fears. The reader's burdensome task is to understand this neurosis, even if the central character never will. The rather curt, at times clinical, questions seem to come from a male universe; the irrational, at times utterly disjointed answers seem to emanate from the female narrator's defense of another woman—a woman as broken as she is. The title of the story (also one of its questions) seems to support this reading.

Sharon, this miserably unhappy woman, spends a sleepless night vaguely waiting for something or someone to happen to her. She brings into her memory a young boy from her high school days who "had died of insanity." She thinks of her mother, miles away, whose snoring disgusts her; throughout the story her mother appears as a bittersweet but inaccessibly distant memory. In the middle of these scattered reminiscences, the reader is uncomfortably aware that Sharon is terrified by the possibility that the telephone will ring.

She then recalls an unspecified afternoon before this sleepless night. She had met an old friend of her father-in-law. He reminds her of all the dead men in her life: father-in-law, father, husband, the insane high school boy. She successfully shakes him off. A stranger confronts her; he expresses concern that the old man was harassing her. Something about this man stuns her. She begins to confuse this man with her husband—reminding herself that he could not be her husband, yet considering that perhaps the stranger is a survivor of the automobile accident in which her husband had died. It becomes clear that the psychological stability of this woman is, to say the least, tentative.

She continues on her way home, stopping at a grocer's, obsessed with the stranger. The man has followed her to the store; she is oddly terrified by the coincidence. She is frightened by, yet attracted to, the stranger.

Periodically she recalls her life with her husband, his death, her meager survival. Since her husband's death, the world has become desexualized, dehumanized: "a world of bodies, directed clumsily by thoughts, by darting minnowlike ideas." Periodically the reader returns to her sleepless night; it seems that much of this woman has died with her husband.

At four-thirty in the morning, the telephone rings—as she had feared. She is certain that the stranger followed her home that afternoon. She answers; after a breathy hesitation, the voice asks: "Hello, is this Sharon?" He identifies himself as "someone you just met." Hysterical, she slams down the telephone receiver.

She spends another restless night and early morning in anticipation. The telephone rings at five o'clock; she does not answer. There is a knock at the door; the man calls her by name. In a turmoil of emotional contradictions she opens the door, "and everything comes open, comes apart." With these words the story ends.

Themes and Meanings

The very form of "What Is the Connection Between Men and Women?" is the most important aspect of its meaning. A distance establishes itself between question and response. This distance can be translated into male/female, outside/inside, sane/insane—any number of dichotomies that reflect the basic paradigm of cage/prisoner.

Yet this paradigm does not invite the reader to share a simplistic moral judgment—that women are innocent victims of thoughtless male imprisonment. To a certain extent, Sharon has created her own prison. She has translated the death of her husband into the death of her sexual desires. She feels unfaithful to him because she is attracted to another man; the fact that her husband is dead means nothing, for she is "permanently" married to him— and he is "permanently" dead.

The questions asked about Sharon vary in intensity from *"How does it feel to lie awake all night?"* to *"What does a woman feel while a man makes love to her?"* At times the female answers are completely disjointed from the male questions. For example, in answer to the second question above, one reads, "Barefoot, she is standing at the door . . ." or "She walked quickly home, threading her way around people. . . ." All but one of the questions are asked more than once—at times with serial insistence, at other times intermittently, as if the questioner is returning to a topic with renewed hope. The very disjunction between question and answer seems to be the central theme of the story: The connection between men and women is one of repeated misunderstanding.

Oates does not make it easy for the reader to understand or to sympathize with Sharon, this widow perpetually at the edge of a breakdown. The questions asked from outside remain unanswered. The reader starts to ask his own questions: How can an incident as ordinary as a conversation in a grocery store represent such anguish for this woman? What has she become? As terrifying as the stranger is to her, the real terror is Sharon's own sexuality.

In one of the answers to the question concerning a woman's feelings during lovemaking, one reads what seems to be an authentic response: "A violent penetration to the heart: up in the chest." Yet what momentarily seemed to be sexual gratification quickly turns to violence: "A sense of suffocation. Strangulation . . . with her mind broken up into pieces of white, terrified glass." Sex is death for Sharon.

Thus, the final paragraphs represent the ultimate invasion of privacy. Until the conclusion, the questions might have come from anyone, anywhere, outside this distracted personality. As the story ends, however, Oates explicitly identifies the questioner with the stranger whom Sharon has encountered. He asks: "Are you in there?" The response is: "He said that. He said something—she did not hear it exactly." Although on the surface the question has to do with whether Sharon is behind the door, the question resounds with meaning. The stranger, embodying sex, death, and experience, knocks at the door of a self-made prisoner; he comes to confront this vulnerable woman, wondering what is "inside." His next question is simply formed by her name: "Sharon?" Her name is "like a stab deep in her belly." Once again she conflates sexuality with violent self-destruction.

The ending provides the reader with no easy resolution. As Sharon opens the door to experience the reader knows only that "everything comes open, comes apart." Is she destroyed by this invasion of experience? What could she lose? Is she saved by this potential assault? What could she gain? Oates's story is strategically open-ended.

Style and Technique

"What Is the Connection Between Men and Women?" maintains a double vision; one of its major experiments is in point of view. The questions are asked directly; the answers are indirect, third-person narration. Yet the paradox is that the questions of a skeptical exterior confront the answers of a sympathetic interior. Sharon does not speak for herself—the reader knows her through a mediating narrator who keeps her in steady focus. The implication is that she cannot speak for herself.

Repetition is forcefully used to convey meaning. For example, Sharon's neurotic obsession with a dead husband emerges from the repetitions within the following passage: "She is married permanently to that man. Married. Married permanently. She is in love with that man yet, a dead man. Married, In love. When she sleeps, she sleeps with him; his body is next to her, in sleep." Later in the story, these repetitions reemerge: "She was still married. She was married permanently."

The repetition comes from outside as well; the questioner repeats himself almost maniacally. The question asked only once is: "Are you in there?" He has only thirteen questions in his repertory, yet he speaks twenty-seven times.

Repetition on each side of the double vision is a stylistic response to the title question: The connection between men and women, between experience and fear, between the outside and the tormented interior, is tenuous.

Mark Sandona

WHEN I WAS THIRTEEN

Author: Denton Welch (1915-1948)
Type of plot: Domestic realism
Time of plot: Probably 1928
Locale: A Swiss Alpine village
First published: 1948

> *Principal characters:*
> THE NARRATOR
> ARCHER, a university student
> THE NARRATOR'S BROTHER

The Story

The narrator of "When I Was Thirteen" recalls that, when he was thirteen, he went on a skiing trip to Switzerland with an older brother, spent an enjoyable day skiing with an older youth, and, for no reason he could understand, was accused of scandalous behavior of a kind unfamiliar to him.

Staying at the same lodge as the narrator and his brother, a student at Oxford University, is Archer, also a student at Oxford. The brother does not like Archer. The narrator, however, is very impressed by Archer's physique and bearing when, for example, he sees him skiing bare-chested in a cavalier, robust fashion.

He is of the impression that Archer takes little interest in him until the two meet on a sun terrace, where the narrator has gone to read a book, drink hot chocolate, and eat "delicious rhumbabas and little tarts filled with worm-castles of chestnut puree topped with caps of whipped cream." That afternoon tea illustrates the sensibility of the narrator—although he is only thirteen, he is a devotee of the luxurious.

The book the young man is reading is one by Leo Tolstoy. He is puzzled by Tolstoy's description of one of the characters as an illegitimate child. After Archer initiates conversation, the younger youth ventures to ask what the term means, but in his profound innocence he cannot believe the explanation that Archer gives him—that an illegitimate child is one born out of wedlock. The books Archer says he likes to read indicate that he is rather more worldly than the young narrator. One, he says, was entitled *Flaming Sex*; it "was by a French woman who married an English knight and then went back to France to shoot a French doctor." He calls such a book a "real life" story, but it, like others he describes, appears worldly to the point of being slightly sordid and risqué.

Archer is, then, similar to the narrator in that both gravitate toward the hedonistic. He invites his new young friend to come skiing with him the next day. The next morning, the narrator's infatuation with Archer is very apparent; he recalls, for example, that when Archer slung their skis across his shoulders, "he looked like a very tough Jesus carrying two crosses."

During the outing, Archer provides for his less robust companion with food and physical support. He also initiates him into some common luxuries of adulthood: hot black coffee, a glass of sweetened rum, and cheap Swiss cigarettes. The younger boy takes readily to the role of the initiate; when Archer hands him pieces of a tangerine on his outstretched palm, he has to restrain himself from licking them up as a horse would do. While skiing, Archer urges the young narrator to unusual boldness; when the narrator falls, Archer "hauled me out of the snow and stood me on my feet, beating me all over to get off the snow."

That paternal but curious physical intimacy continues after the two return to Archer's rooms, which are in an annex some distance from the chalet, and take baths, scrubbing each other's backs. The younger youth massages Archer's legs, which are cramped after the day's skiing. The narrator apprehends no threat from the older youth, and it transpires that he need fear none. It is clear, however, that his infatuation with Archer makes him willing to try anything that Archer recommends. The element of physical attraction that has been developed gradually and unobtrusively by Welch has blossomed. The narrator remarks, for example, that Archer's "thigh, swelling out, amazed me."

The meal the two youths then eat in a restaurant is, like everything else they have eaten, almost decadently luxurious. By the end of it, the younger youth has drunk a mixture of lemonade, lager, and crème de menthe and is tipsy. After he and Archer have returned to Archer's room—Archer sings "Silent Night" in German along the way—he is quite drunk and falls asleep, grateful that Archer has thoughtfully taken off his shoes, undone his tie, and loosened his braces.

The next morning, the two go to the chalet for breakfast. They meet the narrator's brother, who has unexpectedly returned early from his own extended skiing expedition. Archer clearly is aware that the older brother will have cause to suspect that inappropriate activities have taken place and tries to provide an explanation for his and his friend's arrival at the chalet so early in the morning. The older brother swallows neither his nor the narrator's explanation. After the narrator returns to his room with his brother, he vomits as a result of what he has drunk the night before. His older brother beats him with a slipper and shouts at him "in a hoarse, mad, religious voice: 'Bastard, Devil, Harlot, Sod!'"

The narrator, who has been recalling the incidents several years later, remembers that the violent outburst made him think that his brother had gone mad, "for, of the words he was using, I had not heard any before, except 'Devil.'"

Themes and Meanings

The narrator describes how he became unwittingly infatuated with Archer during the brief time they spent together. He was young, impressionable, and naturally given to infatuation, though he had as yet developed neither a capacity for full-blown sexual passions nor even an understanding of the kinds of friendship that exist between members of the same sex. He had, however, developed an appetite for worldly, sensual pleasures—one unusually keen in so young a youth, and of a kind that apparently struck Archer as indicative of a proclivity for homosexual love.

The motivations of Archer, however, are not clear. Nothing he does with the boy is clearly improper, but it is clear that he is homosexual, motivated by a paternalistic sentimentality and manipulative of the young narrator.

This story, like virtually all of Welch's writing, is evidently largely autobiographical reminiscence. Interestingly, Welch, as a narrator with a clearer, more mature notion of what transpires between Archer and himself, appears to relish the experience and does not suggest that it was in any way injurious. He does not impute questionable motivations to Archer; in fact, he paints him as benevolent and caring, and he depicts his experiences with Archer as wholly enjoyable, at least up to the point at which he vomits and is beaten by his older brother.

As the reader sees the friendship between Archer and the young man gradually develop, the natural tendency may be to question its propriety. Welch handles this aspect of his story carefully. The narrator at age thirteen is not totally ingenuous. At dinner after the skiing expedition, he is aware that Archer is encouraging him to do things he ordinarily should not be doing. Archer offers him a cigar, and "I had the sense to realize that he did not mean me to take one and smoke it there before the eyes of all the hotel." Yet the young man's awareness is limited. When he massages Archer's leg, for example, he is impressed by its physicality—"His calf was like a firm sponge ball"—but he does not realize that what impresses him are its sensual qualities, its firmness and sponginess.

Here the young man is ingenuous, and his innocence, and the way Welch manipulates the action to resemble at many points a sexual encounter, makes the reader expectant of a breaching by Archer of that innocence. It could be said that Welch is almost titillating the reader. From another perspective, however, it can be said that Welch is presenting a tale of first love—one in which boy meets boy, rather than girl.

Style and Technique

The central technique of the story is the narrative stance adopted by Welch. His narrator is telling a story about himself and understands the significance of the events about which he is writing, but his description makes it clear that he did not understand their significance at the time they occurred. By treating the encounter as a pleasant day of eating fine foods and skiing, Welch also suggests that in one sense it was simply that.

It is important to note that it is Welch, or his narrator, who places the narrator's experiences in a positive and idealized light. To do this, he has to provide many details that would most probably not have occurred to the narrator at age thirteen. When, for example, he refers to Archer, who is carrying two pairs of skis, as "a very tough Jesus," it is surely the adult narrator, or Welch, recalling the incidents of several years earlier, who supplies this interpretation, not the thirteen-year-old who was too naïve to know what sort of friendship Archer fancied.

The character of the precocious thirteen-year-old boy is an unusual one. The degree to which his appetite for finery is developed is almost too great to credit. More subtly drawn is his surprising independence. For example, he never refers to the older brother by name, and he never describes him. This nameless facelessness throughout the story makes his actions at the end of the story appear all the more intrusive. This intrusive personality serves Welch's purpose well, for it places in sharper focus the narrator's ultimate innocence; it seems that Welch considers it almost a failing in the suspicious, unspontaneous brother that he is morally upright.

Peter Monaghan

WHEN THE LIGHT GETS GREEN

Author: Robert Penn Warren (1905-   )
Type of plot: Local tale
Time of plot: c. 1914
Locale: A farm in the South
First published: 1936

> *Principal characters:*
> THE UNNAMED NARRATOR, Mr. Barden's grandson
> MR. BARDEN, a veteran of the Civil War
> AUNT LUCY, Mr. Barden's daughter
> UNCLE KIRBY, Aunt Lucy's husband

The Story

The first-person narrator of this story—a young boy when its events take place—remembers his grandfather from an unspecified time after 1918 and the old man's death. The memories (his own and his grandfather's, both imperfectly understood) lend depth to the tale and at the same time determine its loose-jointedness.

The story begins appropriately with a recurrent but inaccurate memory—"My grandfather had a long white beard. . . ."—and the shock the boy used to feel when he came home from school and watched his grandfather trimming his beard before the mirror: "It is gray and pointed, I would say then, remembering what I had thought before." As memories will, the boy's memories combine to create an ideal morning home for the summer from school, but even in the familiar routine of beard-trimming, ceremonious dressing (black vest, gold watch and chain, corncob pipe), and breakfast—always the same—the boy finds himself reminded of his grandfather's mortality; significantly, this is contrasted with his having been a soldier, "like General Robert E. Lee": He recalls noticing how "shrunken" his grandfather's "hips and backsides" were and the way his own stomach tightened at the sight, "like when you walk behind a woman and see the high heel of her shoe is worn and twisted and jerks her ankle every time she takes a step."

The domestic comedy of breakfast, related as another never-changing given in the boy's life, reveals a set of tensions and obstinacies not consciously understood by the boy. The laborious explanation of why Uncle Kirby called grandfather Mr. Barden indicates a clannishness perhaps not even recognized by the boy and, ironically, suggests that the grandfather is still in charge, though he clearly is not: "It was because my Uncle Kirby was not my real uncle, having married my Aunt Lucy, who lived with my grandfather." The matter of the cob pipe becomes a test of authority between husband and wife and between father and daughter, but Uncle Kirby's grin, "like a dog panting," and Mr. Barden's "Don't it stink" leave the test unresolved.

The story proceeds with three scenes. The first introduces contingency for the first time ("If it had rained right and was a good tobacco-setting season . . ."). The tobacco-setting occasions a detailed and idyllic description of the lot, the cold stream that runs through it, the rise with its sassafras and blackberries, the fields, and the setting itself, but here, as in what went before, the idyll is undercut by the grandfather's mortality and by displays of ineffectual authority. The boy notes that his grandfather rides "pretty straight for an old man" and sees "the big straw hat he wore waggle a little above his narrow neck." Later, at the field, Uncle Kirby's "Get the lead out" only brings grins to the faces of the "little niggers," and Mr. Barden's "Why don't you start 'em, sir?" has no effect at all; the work apparently begins despite, not because of, these two men, and "about ten o'clock" Mr. Barden "would leave and go home."

As in the scene that follows, the narrator's memories of his own experience of his grandfather lead into memories of Mr. Barden's more distant past. As a young man, Mr. Barden raised and showed horses, but now (because "horses were foolishness") tobacco has become his single care. Once he tried to be a tobacco-buyer but lost his warehouses and their contents in a fire. The failure is explained as bad luck by the boy and as inevitable by Mr. Barden's daughters; Mr. Barden himself shrugs it off as just as well. Now he watches as the crop is set, suckered, plowed, or wormed, and he worries, "nervous as a cat," when a summer storm threatens.

In the second scene, the narrator describes Mr. Barden's mornings when he does not go to the fields. He sits under a cedar tree, smokes his cob pipe, and, on most days, reads a book. The narrator's account of the history his grandfather reads and the poetry he recites leads into memories of the old man's more distant past by identifying him with Napoleon Bonaparte, Mr. Barden "having been a soldier and fought in the War himself." The boy listens to the history, to the poetry, and to the stories of the Civil War, and he wants to be proud of his grandfather, but he feels shame, thinking that his grandfather never killed any Yankees—his boyish explanation for his grandfather's never having been promoted beyond the rank of captain.

During the afternoons, Mr. Barden would sleep, and that is how the narrator usually remembers him. Alternatively, he says, he remembers him "trampling up and down the porch, nervous as a cat, while a cloud blew up and the trees began to ruffle." This generalized memory quickly narrows to a particular time, in 1914, when "the leaves began to ruffle like they do when the light gets green, and my grandfather said to me, 'Son, it's gonna hail.' " It did hail, and this time Mr. Barden had a stroke. As the narrator sits by the bed in the shadowy room, his grandfather speaks again: "Son, I'm gonna die." And again: "I'm on borrowed time, it's time to die." And finally: "It's time to die. Nobody loves me." The narrator's response, "Grandpa, I love you," is a lie: "I didn't feel anything." Yet outside again in the sunny yard, watching a hen peck at a hailstone, wondering whether the tobacco has been damaged, still "not feeling anything," he says it again "out loud, 'Grandpa, I love you.'"

Mr. Barden lives four more years: "I got the letter about my grandfather, who died of flu, but I thought about four years back, and it didn't matter much."

Themes and Meanings

Unlike the narrator of Robert Penn Warren's poem "Safe in Shade," who takes from an apparently identical communion with his grandfather a memory of safety and of "Truth—oh, unambiguous," the narrator of "When the Light Gets Green" carries with him a sense of disillusionment and, perhaps unconsciously, offers the reader a powerful argument against the ability of man to control his present environment, his past, or his future.

The remainders of man's mortality and of the limits of authority in the early parts of the story suggest how powerless humanity is to control or to keep its present, but the scene under the cedar tree and what follows it focuses this theme and adds the past and future to the story's purview. Mr. Barden's obsession with history has a double significance. On the one hand, his subjects are all illustrative of battles won or lost: Flodden Field, where James IV of Scotland was slain on the field, the sack of Constantinople by the Ottoman Turks, Napoleon Bonaparte's ill-fated Russian campaign. On the other hand, Mr. Barden attempts to rewrite his own history and that of the South with hypotheses modeled on his readings, asserting, for example, that "if they had done what Forrest wanted and cleaned the country ahead of the Yankees, like the Russians beat Napoleon, they'd whipped the Yankees sure."

Unlike history, Mr. Barden "never read poetry, he just said what he already knew," and what he already knows emphasizes the ironies of man's pride and his failure to control. The narrator remembers and quotes snippets from two poems by George Gordon, Lord Byron, but he does not finish the stanzas he recalls. The first is from *Don Juan* (1819-1824), Canto III, stanza 86, and though it begins in a celebratory vein, its last lines strike a different note: "Eternal summer gilds them yet,/ But all, except their sun, is set." More disturbing still is the second bit of poetry, from *Childe Harold's Pilgrimage* (1812-1818), Canto IV, stanza 179. The narrator quotes only the stirring first line, "Roll on, thou deep and dark blue ocean, roll," but Byron's stanza continues:

> Ten thousand fleets sweep over thee in vain;
> Man marks the earth with ruin—his control
> Stops with the shore;—upon the watery plain

> The wrecks are all thy deed, nor doth remain
> A shadow of man's ravage, save his own,
> When, for a moment, like a drop of rain,
> He sinks into thy depths with bubbling groan,
> Without a grave, unknell'd, uncoffin'd, and unknown.

As Warren's story moves on from the cedar tree to 1914 and then to 1918—another war, another human failure to control—through love affirmed but nonexistent to Mr. Barden's death, the reader is reminded again of Warren's poem "Safe in Shade" and its finally grim view:

> That all-devouring, funnel-shaped, mad and high-spiraling,
> Dark suction that
> We have, as the Future, named.

Style and Technique

The cluster of images attracted to the color in the title of this story creates a peculiarly appropriate ground for the tale of memory told here. Three images are particularly important. The first is the green light of the title, though it is not met again until late in the story. It is, literally, a natural phenomenon anticipating the onset of a hailstorm, but framed as it is by the other two images, it becomes a fitting portent of Mr. Barden's death. The second image is the mirror that opens the story and is reintroduced after the hailstorm: "the wavy green mirror, which in his always shadowy room reflected things like deep water riffled by a little wind." Later, as the narrator waits in his grandfather's room after the old man's stroke, he notices again "the mirror, which was green and wavy like water." This green mirror becomes an emblem of Mr. Barden's life with its depths of unhelpful, even inaccurate, memory, and its likeness to water lends it further depth—the depth of the frightening and watery world of the unconscious.

The third image is the narrator's rather than his grandfather's, the green of the cedar boughs where he listens to poetry and stories of the Civil War: "I lay on my back on the ground . . . and looked upside down into the cedar tree where the limbs were tangled and black-green like big hairy fern fronds with the blue sky all around, while he said some poetry." Again, his grandfather had told "how the dead men looked in the river bottoms in winter, and I lay on my back on the grass, looking up in the thick cedar limbs, and thought how it was to be dead." In this third image, the grandfather's long look downward into the wastes of memory becomes his grandson's upward and not yet frightened gaze into what any human being can expect of the future: at best something tangled and at last something dead.

Jonathan A. Glenn

WHERE ARE YOU GOING, WHERE HAVE YOU BEEN?

Author: Joyce Carol Oates (1938-   )
Type of plot: Psychological realism and allegory
Time of plot: A Sunday in a summer during the 1950's
Locale: A suburban community in the United States
First published: 1966

Principal characters:

CONNIE, the fifteen-year-old protagonist
ARNOLD FRIEND, her demon-lover

The Story

"Where Are You Going, Where Have You Been?" is the story of a presumably typical young girl whose romantic vision of love is abruptly confronted by reality. In the terms of the story, reality arrives at the protagonist's doorstep personified by a devil-like rapist disguised to resemble the boy of her dreams.

Joyce Carol Oates uses the first three pages of "Where Are You Going, Where Have You Been?" to establish the nature of the world in which Connie lives. It is a world dominated by Hollywood and popular music, shopping plazas and fast-food stands. For Connie and her friends, evenings spent with a boy, eating hamburgers, drinking Cokes, and "making-out" in a dark alley seem like heaven, filled with promises of love sweet and gentle, "the way it was in the movies." Clearly, Connie's parents do not understand the significance of her adolescent daydreams and activities. Her mother constantly nags at her for spending too much time in front of a mirror and for not being as steady and reliable as her twenty-four-year-old, unmarried sister. Her father appears as uninvolved in her life as the other fathers who drop off their daughters and friends at the local hangout, never questioning their evening's activities when they pick them up.

One hot summer Sunday, Connie chooses to remain at home alone while her parents and sister go to a barbecue at an aunt's house. Suddenly "an open jalopy, painted a bright gold" comes up the driveway. Her heart pounding, Connie hangs on to the kitchen door as she banters with the two boys in the jalopy, who invite her for a ride. The driver, Arnold Friend, saw her at the drive-in the night before and had "wagged a finger and laughed," saying "Gonna get you, baby" in response to Connie's smirk. At first, Connie is tempted by his invitation; she "liked the way he was dressed, which was the way all of them dressed: tight faded jeans stuffed into black scuffed boots, a belt that pulled his waist in and showed how lean he was." His clothes, his talk, the music blaring from his radio are all familiar to her. Then she begins to notice that he seems much older than her friends and that he knows too much about her, even where her parents are and how long they will be away from home.

As the story proceeds, Arnold moves closer to the porch but promises not to come in the house after Connie. Apparently, he wants her to join him of her own free will. His tone becomes more menacing, nevertheless, even as he promises to love her: "This is how it is, honey: you come out and we'll drive away, have a nice ride. But if you don't come out we're gonna wait till your people come home and they're all going to get it." With this threat to her family, Connie begins to lose control; sick with fear, she calls for her mother and starts to pick up the phone, then puts it back on Arnold's command. "That's a good girl. Now you come outside," he continues, and she slowly pushes the door open, "moving out into the sunlight where Arnold Friend waited."

Themes and Meanings

On a literal level, "Where Are You Going, Where Have You Been?" is a spine-chilling tale of rape and murder with a plot carefully controlled to create suspense. On a figurative level, it is an allegory of lost innocence, the screen door symbolizing the fragile threshold between childhood dreams and adult experience, between romantic illusions of love and the brutal reality of adult sexuality. Connie's "friend" turns out to be a "fiend"; her vague dream-lover arrives masked in the familiar trappings of her world, only to reveal the face of lust and violence beneath the false façade.

On a still deeper symbolic level, Connie's experience itself becomes a metaphor for American naïveté and vulnerability. In this story, as in much of her fiction, Oates explores the moral poverty of American popular culture and the ways in which it leaves her characters defenseless against powerful forces of evil. For Connie, "the bright-lit, fly-infested restaurant" is a "sacred building" and the omnipresent music is like a "church service" always in the background, something upon which she can depend. As if to parody Christian symbolism, Oates describes the "grinning boy," holding a hamburger aloft, which caps the bottle-shaped restaurant. It is here that Connie finds the "haven and blessing" otherwise missing in her life. Oates shows her readers how teenagers have created a strict code of dress, behavior, and language to fill the void left by the absence of conventional religion and adult authority. The inauthenticity of such a code is revealed by Arnold's ability to ape it so easily; its impotence, by Connie's absolute inability to defend herself against his attack.

In this story, Oates pays special attention to the mother-daughter relationship and the lack of meaningful communication between them. Their bickering, as described by Oates, is itself an empty ritual: "Sometimes, over coffee, they were almost friends, but something would come up—some vexation that was like a fly buzzing suddenly around their heads—and their faces went hard with contempt." In the end, it is her mother for whom Connie cries; her last thought before she finally pushes open the door is that she will never see her mother again. As she crosses over into the "vast unknown," Connie shuts the door on childhood. Oates seems to suggest that if either one of them had made the effort to communicate, Connie might have remained safely a child until old enough to choose the future. Ironically, it is Arnold Friend who promises to teach Connie about "love," typically the mother's role, while threatening to kill the entire family if she does not permit him to do so.

Style and Technique

Joyce Carol Oates's masterful mixing of literal and figurative, psychological and allegorical levels makes "Where Are You Going, Where Have You Been?" a powerful and fascinating story. This mix is particularly evident in her depiction of both Connie's and Arnold's double identities. Connie carefully pulls her sweater down tight when she leaves home: "Everything about her had two sides to it, one for home and one for anywhere that was not home." Arnold stuffs his boots in order to appear taller and more attractive or perhaps to hide the cloven feet of his satanic self. In Connie's action, the reader recognizes the adolescent beginning to break away from her family and to test the powers of her emerging sexuality. In Arnold's, the reader sees the Devil's traditional role as arch-deceiver and seducer. On still a deeper psychological level, Arnold Friend is the subconscious nightmare version of Connie's waking desires and dreams, erotic love as her sister June might suppose it, not "sweet and gentle" as promised in Bobby King's songs. Allegorically viewed, Friend brings the vehicle which will lead Connie to the "vast sunlit reaches" of the future, a metaphor which expresses the vagueness of her dreams while also representing an unknown—attractive, perilous, and as inevitable as death.

Though the story is heavy with thematic significance and symbolism, it also reads quickly because of Oates's skill in building suspense. Each stage of Arnold Friend's unmasking and Connie's resulting terror and growing hysteria is carefully delineated. When Arnold first arrives, Connie cannot decide "if she liked him or if he was just a jerk." The reader becomes more suspicious than she does as she notices his muscular neck and arms, his "nose long and hawk-like, sniffing as if she were a treat he was going to gobble up and it was all a joke." Gradually, Connie realizes that all the characteristics she "recognizes" in him—dress, gestures, the "singsong way he talked"—do not come together the way they should. Her heart begins to pound faster when she questions his age and notices that his companion has the face of a forty-year-old baby. Worse yet, Arnold seems to possess preternatural vision to the point of describing all the guests at the family barbecue, what they are doing, how they are dressed. As he states more explicitly what he wants from her, Connie's terror and the story's suspense mount. When Arnold promises not to enter the house unless Connie picks up the phone, the reader may recall that the Devil as evil spirit cannot cross a threshold uninvited. At this point, the end seems inevitable; in her presumed murderer's words, "The place where you came from ain't there any more, and where you had in mind to go is cancelled out."

It is no wonder that "Where Are You Going, Where Have You Been?" is the most frequently anthologized and critically acclaimed of Joyce Carol Oates's short stories. Its popularity is ensured by the famous Oates blend of violence, sex, and suspense; its place in the American literary canon by its thematic importance, Oates's frightening vision of the contemporary American inability to recognize evil in its most banal forms.

Though many critics have complained about the gratuitous violence of Oates's work and seem to distrust her extraordinary fluency (she has produced more than thirty-five volumes of stories, novels, and literary criticism in her first twenty years as a published writer), this particular story demonstrates her ability to achieve tight compression and careful stylistic control. From the first line, "Her name was Connie," to the last, " 'My sweet little blue-eyed girl,' he said, in a half-sung sigh that had nothing to do with her brown eyes . . . ," this is a story in which every word counts.

Jane M. Barstow

A WHITE HERON

Author: Sarah Orne Jewett (1849-1909)
Type of plot: Sentimental realism
Time of plot: Late nineteenth century
Locale: Rural Maine
First published: 1886

> *Principal characters:*
> SYLVIA, the protagonist, a nine-year-old girl
> MRS. TILLEY, her grandmother
> A YOUNG HUNTER, who is from the city

The Story

Jewett's "A White Heron," the most popular of her short stories, is a prime example of a "local color" story in its depiction of the life of a particular region—in this case, her native Maine. Jewett explores the internal conflict that a transplanted city girl experiences between her newly acquired love for nature and her natural and awakening interest in the opposite sex. Sylvia, who knows where the rare white heron has its nest, must decide between an allegiance to the things of nature and the gratitude and friendship of the young hunter who seeks to add the white heron to his collection of stuffed birds.

In the first part of the story, Jewett establishes Sylvia as a "child of nature" who is somewhat wary of people. After having spent the first eight years of her life in a "crowded manufacturing town," where she had been harassed by a "great red-faced boy," she is now at home in the "out-of-doors." Her grandmother, who rescued Sylvia from the city, believes that Sylvia had never been "alive" until her arrival at the farm. According to her grandmother, "the wild creatur's counts her one o' themselves." In fact, when Sylvia first appears, she is driving home a cow named Mistress Moolly, which is described as Sylvia's "valued companion." Sylvia feels more at home with her "natural" society than she does with "folks."

As a result, when she hears "a boy's whistle, determined, and somewhat aggressive," she is "horror-stricken," but the young man overcomes her fear and accompanies her to her grandmother's farm. Having spent the day hunting, he seeks food and shelter for the night, and Mrs. Tilley obliges him. The young hunter discusses his collection of birds, listens to Mrs. Tilley talk about her son Dan's hunting, and learns that Sylvia "knows all about birds." He then offers ten dollars for information about the whereabouts of the white heron. The next day, Sylvia accompanies him as he hunts, and his "kind and sympathetic" behavior wins her "loving admiration," although she cannot understand why he kills the very birds he professes to like.

The second part of the story concerns Sylvia's decision to climb the "great pine-tree" in order to gain a vantage point from which she can discover the white heron's nest, which she apparently plans to reveal to her new friend. Rising before her grandmother and the hunter, Sylvia "steals" out of the house and makes her way through the forest to the tall pine tree. After climbing the nearby white oak, she negotiates the "dangerous pass" from the oak to the pine and finally reaches the top, from which she can see both the "vast and awesome world" and the white heron's nest, which holds the white heron and his mate. (Jewett thereby balances the two worlds: nature and the "outside" world beyond the farm.) When she returns to the farm, however, Sylvia will not reveal the location of the nest, despite the rebukes of her grandmother and the entreaties of the hunter, who thought he had won her over.

Themes and Meanings

In "A White Heron," Jewett presents her readers with a series of conflicting values, all of which may be included under the theme of the country versus the city. By having Sylvia choose nature over civilization, Jewett clearly indicates her own preference while she also acknowledges the cost of making that choice.

Jewett's comparison of Sylvia to the "wretched dry geranium that belonged to a town neighbor" is instructive, for Sylvia thrives, as would the geranium, on being transplanted from town to country. When she first meets the hunter, Sylvia hangs her head "as if the stem of it were broken." Clearly, Jewett means to suggest that Sylvia is indeed a flower, a part of nature. She is not only accepted by the wild animals but also feels "as if she were a part of the gray shadows and the moving leaves." Sylvia's ties to nature are also reflected in Jewett's description of her bare feet and fingers, which are like "bird's claws," a simile that identifies her with birds and helps explain her decision to save the white heron.

The hunter who pursues the white heron is from the city and is therefore tainted by civilization. In fact, like the "great red-faced boy," he represents a threat to Sylvia: He may not physically harm her, but he can corrupt her by enticing her to "sell out" nature by taking money for information. Jewett does not condemn the hunter for hunting in itself; Mrs. Tilley obviously understands that hunting produces game birds ("pa'tridges," for example) to be eaten in order to survive. On the other hand, hunting all kinds of birds (including thrushes and sparrows) simply in order to stuff them for one's own "collection" is a notion "foreign" to Mrs. Tilley and incomprehensible to Sylvia: "She could not understand why he killed the very birds he seemed to like so much." In effect, her first perception of him as the "enemy" is correct.

The "persuasive" young man's corruption is signaled by his situation when Sylvia meets him. Like many other moral wanderers in dark woods (Nathaniel Hawthorne's Young Goodman Brown comes immediately to mind), the hunter is "lost." When he is guided to a hermitage and receives Mrs. Tilley's hospitality, he repays it by attempting to exploit Sylvia's obvious fondness for him and Mrs. Tilley's equally obvious need for money. He is successful in enlisting Mrs. Tilley's support, but Sylvia has grown and learned important lessons from her climb up the pine tree.

In many ways, "A White Heron" is an initiation story with mythic overtones. A young girl who lives in cloistered innocence is exposed to temptation from the outside world. The agent of temptation uses her developing interest in the opposite sex to seduce her into betraying the natural world to which she belongs. Although her "woman's heart," which had been "asleep," is "vaguely thrilled" by the young hunter, she also gains new insights into herself and the world of nature. Her morning journey, which takes her through the dangerous bog, and her subsequent climb up the pine tree both test her and teach her. When she negotiates the "passage" from the oak to the pine, she undertakes a "great enterprise," one at once challenging and fulfilling. From the top of the pine she can see the "vast and awesome world" that lies beyond the safety of the farm. Unfortunately for the hunter, she also sees the white heron and his mate. The two worlds are in conflict, and the parallel between the herons and her own situation is readily apparent to the "sadder but wiser" Sylvia: Her happiness at helping the object of her infatuation can be achieved only at the expense of destroying another "domestic" situation, which may be more significant. In a kind of epilogue Jewett writes, "Were the birds better friends than their hunter might have been—who can tell?"

Style and Technique

In her depiction of the often-reiterated conflict, Jewett is not objective; the "scales" are heavily weighted in favor of nature. Besides using stereotypical characters in a Good-versus-Evil confrontation of mythic dimension, she uses sentimentality to invest both vegetable and animal worlds with human characteristics. Sylvia's "valued companion" is not the hunter, but Mistress Moolly, the cow, who is capable of "pranks." The birds and beasts "say good-night to each other in sleepy twitters," thereby making their deaths seem more like "murder" and helping to account for Sylvia's final decision. Even the pine tree is personified and depicted as an ally in her quest for knowledge. The tree is "asleep"; it even stands still and holds away the wind as Sylvia climbs. Sylvia's very name, with its "sylvan" suggestions, indicates that her true home is in nature (she is known as "Sylvy" rather than the more formal "Sylvia"). Similarly, Mrs. Tilley, who "tills" her farm, is also in her proper habitat. On the other hand, the unnamed hunter is seen as an interloper who does not belong.

In order to elicit sympathy for Sylvia, Jewett uses the third-person-limited point of view, so that Sylvia's perceptions become the readers' perceptions. Her choice seems inevitable, but at the end of the story Jewett gains some distance from Sylvia and editorializes about the decision: "Dear loyalty, that suffered a sharp pang as the guest went away disappointed later in the day, that would have served and followed him and loved him as a dog loves!" The slavish, servile behavior Jewett describes is "puppy love," unworthy of the white heron's death. On the other hand, the epilogue concludes with the cost of Sylvia's decision: "Bring your gifts and graces and tell your secrets to this lonely child!" Jewett's last words suggest that the child needs human companionship and that nature's "gifts and graces" may only partially compensate for "whatever treasures" ("whatever" tends to undermine the value of the "treasures") she lost through her decision.

Thomas L. Erskine

THE WHITE HORSES OF VIENNA

Author: Kay Boyle (1903-   )
Type of plot: Social realism
Time of plot: 1934
Locale: The Austrian Tirol
First published: 1936

Principal characters:
THE DOCTOR, a country physician who is nevertheless
   sophisticated and widely traveled
HIS WIFE, a trained nurse
DR. HEINE, a young Jewish intern from Vienna

The Story

The fictional account of events in the Austrian mountains (Tirol) in the summer of 1934 is directly related to the political events of the period. These include the rise of the Nazi Party in Austria and the murder of the Austrian chancellor, Engelbert Dollfuss, on July 25, 1934, by right-wing elements undoubtedly encouraged and financed by the German chancellor, Adolf Hitler, who was anxious to annex Austria to the German Reich.

A country doctor has injured his knee while climbing at night with a group of local men near his mountain chalet. As his injury may take weeks to heal, he requests a student-doctor from the hospital in Vienna to help service his patients. When the young doctor arrives, his appearance is noted with disapproval by the country physician's wife. His "alien" appearance indicates his Semitic origin, his "black smooth hair. . . the arch of his nose." Yet both the doctor and his pet red fox seem relatively unaffected by the student-doctor's racial origins and initially accept him. The country doctor is more sophisticated than his wife. He has traveled widely and lived in large cities throughout the world, and thus tends to reserve judgment even while agreeing with her that an urban, Jewish physician will not be easily integrated into the society of this isolated mountain valley. The student-doctor, Dr. Heine, tries hard to cooperate with both the doctor and his wife, who assists him as his nurse. He listens carefully to instructions, "taking it all in with interest and respect." Dr. Heine even enlists the sympathy of the doctor's wife when his clothes are accidentally burned by the sterilizing lamp during a dental operation. The student gives no cause for criticism in his manner or his conversation. He solidifies his bond with his mentor by demonstrating his interest in high culture: music, painting, and books. The older man, forced to be inactive, amuses himself by carving wooden puppets ("his dolls"). The walls of the house are lined with books and his own paintings and drawings, dating from his imprisonment in Siberia and Dalmatia in World War I. After dinner one evening, Dr. Heine relates to the doctor, his wife, and their two sons a story of the purchase of a famous Viennese Lippizaner horse by a maharaja and how a groom destroys the horse and then commits suicide rather than see the beautiful animal sent off to a foreign owner in an alien land.

Two weeks after the student-doctor's arrival, the doctor invites his family, other children, and friends to attend a performance of his marionette theater, featuring the newly created characters fashioned during his illness. The play begins at eight, and it features a "gleaming" and impressive grasshopper. The strong, "green-armored" grasshopper is engaged in conversation by a small, dwarfish clown with a human face and carrying a bunch of artificial flowers, tripping at every step on his oversized sword. The clown seems powerless and ridiculous when compared to the powerful grasshopper, self-confident "and perfectly equipped for the life he had to lead." Dr. Heine's amusement evaporates when he realizes that the grasshopper is being referred to in the text as "The Leader," and the clown as "The Chancellor." The power and conviction of the grasshopper's oratory completely overcome the diminutive clown, who maintains his belief "in the independence of the individual" before falling over his sword into a field of daisies.

A few days later, Dr. Heine takes an evening walk from the chalet to view the mountain peaks. They seem cold and forbidding to him, and he yearns for the warmth and intellectual conversation he was accustomed to in Vienna. A moment later, he notices lights moving up toward the house from the valley. He sees them as "beacons of hope" come to rescue him from this bare northern environment of rock and "everlasting snow." Mentally he bids the lighted chain to come to him "a young man alone, as my race is alone, lost. . . ."

Actually, the local constabulary troops (*Heimwehr*) have come to arrest the doctor, who is suspected of clandestine antigovernment activities. The Austrian chancellor has been assassinated. Dr. Heine offers his help to the doctor, who leaves in good humor but, because of his leg, must be carried to the town hall (*Rathaus*) on a stretcher. He jokes about fruit and chocolate which his wife would throw up to his cell window from the street. He has been imprisoned before—during the riots and unrest in February. As the doctor is carried away, Dr. Heine recalls again the proud white horses of Vienna "bending their knees" to the empty royal box "where there was no royalty any more."

Themes and Meanings

Kay Boyle, an American expatriate writer who lived in Europe from the late 1920's until the early 1940's, writes on political themes in several of her best-known stories. Boyle here focuses on the summer of 1934, a period of political unrest in Austria which followed the riots of the previous winter, when the Dollfuss government had used troops and artillery against workers in the Karl Marx Hof apartment complex in Vienna. All the events of Boyle's narrative, though completely fictional, closely relate to the actual historical accounts. The elapsed time is about one month, from the end of June until July 25 (the day of Chancellor Dollfuss' murder).

The resident doctor, who has been spending so much time climbing the mountain near his house and returning late in the evening, is one of the right-wing Nazi sympathizers who have been accused of burning fiery swastikas on the mountain heights and are being investigated by the *Heimwehr*. The mountain setting ("snow shining hard and diamond-bright on their brows") is an appropriate backdrop for the action, a Wagnerian setting for the Aryan supermen of Nazi legend. Yet the fiery symbols on the mountain are only one aspect of the doctor's personality, which combines "tenderness and knowledge," "resolve" and "compassion." Even his wife is seen in a more humanitarian light when the student-doctor's coat catches fire (the Wagnerian fire of purification?) and she helps save him from serious injury. Later, the young doctor feels "defenceless" as he watches the mountain beacons of "disaster"; the silver swastikas on the black uniforms resemble too closely the burning emblems on the black mountainsides.

As the Nazi doctor is political and draws strength from the barren, snow-capped mountain peaks which symbolize the land and its heritage, so the young Jewish intern seems closely related to his urban origins and the intellectual and cultural background from which he springs and in which he feels comfortable. Young Dr. Heine is no less a product of Austrian tradition than his older and more experienced colleague. This fact is demonstrated by his story of the white horses, symbols of a graceful but impractical past. Like the Germans who want to unite the two German-speaking peoples, the maharaja who buys the white Lippizaner wants to possess what he admires but cannot understand the aristocratic cultural background, the love of something uniquely beautiful, which leads the groom to wound the horse and, finally, to destroy himself. The powerful, affluent forces of Germany seek to possess something which to the young doctor is intangible—the spirit and heritage of Austria.

In contrast, the symbolic values of the Nazi doctor are represented explicitly in the marionette play he produces for the local children. The grasshopper, sleek and green (the color of German army fieldpieces and regular army uniforms), overpowers and seduces the humble, silly clown dancing nimbly to what appears to be native tunes (Wolfgang Amadeus Mozart, Austria's most illustrious composer). The clown is on his way to his own funeral. The sheer physical power of the grasshopper makes the clown appear as inconsequential as a local hairdresser. In the political allegory presented by the doctor, Hitler, as the armored grasshopper, must triumph over the foolish clown (Dollfuss), whose strong religious faith (Christian Socialist Party) is no match for the ruthless practical politics of the Nazis.

Dr. Heine, who recognizes both the opposition and the inherent anti-Semitism of the older doctor and his wife, also realizes that the doctor has a more compassionate and intellectual nature beneath his doctrinaire political creed. He deplores the blackness that is closing in on his country, a world in which beauty and integrity will be lost ideals. He reaches out to the doctor, now being carried off by the *Heimwehr*, and recalls the powerless but supremely graceful white horses bowing to the empty royal box. He realizes that his thoughts and inclinations are "small and senseless in the enormous night" which is descending. Yet in the world now dominated by powerful political forces, the finer feelings of intellectual men appear to be out of place.

Style and Technique

The narrative is divided into three distinct parts. The first section recounts the fact of the doctor's injury and his hiring of a student-doctor. In the second section, which deals with the two stories told by the physicians (first about the white horses, then about the grasshopper and the clown), the omniscient narration shifts temporarily to the limited view in the thoughts of the wife, then the student-doctor. The shift from limited to omniscient continues throughout the remainder of the narrative. The major part of the interior monologue, however, is concerned with the thoughts of Dr. Heine. The senior physician's thoughts are never revealed except through dialogue. The third section is the shortest and is concerned only with the events of July 24 and the final significant thoughts of Dr. Heine.

The most important symbolic aspect of the narrative is the setting, and without its specific chronological frame the events would be largely meaningless. Even seemingly minor facts significantly affect the characterization. The fact, for example, that the older doctor was a prisoner of the Russians ("in Siberia") during World War I influences his political ideas and suggests motivation for his Nazi sympathies.

Boyle skillfully uses a totally uninflected (almost documentary) style in the initial sections of the tale, only gradually exposing the thoughts of the wife and the young Jewish doctor; she finally abandons the earlier narrative mode in the third and final section as the emotional development of the author's idea reaches its climax.

It may be pertinent to Boyle's purpose that only Dr. Heine, the student-doctor, is given a specific personal identity. The other characters in the story, both major and minor, are identified only as "the doctor," "his wife," "the *Burgermeister*," "the *Apotheker*" (druggist), and so forth. This device tends to focus the reader's attention and sympathies more exclusively on the young doctor's view of events, which is clearly the intention of the author.

F. A. Couch, Jr.

WHITE NIGHTS

Author: Fyodor Dostoevski (1821-1881)
Type of plot: Romantic study
Time of plot: c. 1848
Locale: St. Petersburg
First published: "Belye nochi," 1848 (English translation, 1918)

> *Principal characters:*
> THE UNNAMED NARRATOR
> AN INSOLENT GENTLEMAN
> NASTENKA, a seventeen-year-old girl
> HER GRANDMOTHER
> FEKLA, their charwoman
> THEIR LODGER
> MATRENA, the narrator's landlady

The Story

This work takes its title from the long twilight periods that, during the warm months of the year, last nearly until midnight in northern lands, including some parts of Russia. The unnamed narrator has lived in St. Petersburg for nearly eight years and knows very few people in the capital city. During bright, clear spring nights, he has habitually walked down major streets and alongside the canals; recently, he has been troubled by vague misgivings he cannot entirely identify. Quite by chance one night, he happens upon a fetching young well-dressed girl leaning against an embankment. She is preoccupied; from time to time muffled sobs escape from her. She is set upon by an older gentleman in formal evening attire, evidently with dubious intentions. Stricken with fear, the girl takes flight instantly; the narrator quickly interposes himself between them and drives back the assailant by brandishing his thick, knotted walking stick. When the girl returns, her eyes still moist from weeping, the narrator takes her arm and awkwardly asks her indulgence for his shyness. He confides in her at some length and confesses that, although he is twenty-six years old, heretofore he has only dreamed of women; he has not known any of them apart from two or three old landladies. Before they part, he extracts from her a promise to meet again the next night. He declares openly that he is overwhelmed with happiness. Throughout their conversation, he is moved and fascinated by her small, delicate hands and her gentle laughter; occasionally she blushes with deep and genuine feeling.

On the second night, the girl receives the narrator warmly; she apologizes for being overly sentimental and asks him to tell her the whole history of his life. To encourage him, she introduces herself as Nastenka and tells him that she lives with her old, blind grandmother, who is perpetually knitting stockings and is invariably solicitous about the young girl's acquaintances and whereabouts. The narrator unabashedly confesses that he is a dreamer. He is only happy during the evening, when his work is done and familiar sights are invested with heightened, highly personal qualities. His life has passed almost entirely in idleness and solitude; the return to his workday pursuits brings numbing and morose sobriety. Nastenka, who has been listening patiently and attentively, recounts her life with her grandmother and Fekla, their deaf charwoman, at their boardinghouse. Once Nastenka had been shown particular attention by a lodger, and her suspicious grandmother insisted on a strict accounting for all of her movements. Several times all three of them went out to the theater and the opera. When their tenant concluded his business in the capital about a year before and went on to Moscow, Nastenka was left isolated again. She had understood that he would write to her, but still no communication has been received; she doubts that she will ever hear from him again.

As the third night begins, the narrator fears that there will be no meeting, and for a time he waits in agonizing anticipation. When Nastenka appears, their conversation is confused and inconclusive; she is recurrently troubled by fears that her former lodger has vanished for good. The narrator is awkwardly torn between his growing affection for Nastenka and his concern about the other man.

By the fourth night, all is ended. Nastenka, who still has heard nothing from her erstwhile companion, feels abandoned and betrayed. The narrator offers to intercede for her and suggests that she write a letter that he will take to the lodger. She is troubled that her unrequited love for the other man may have compromised her relations with the narrator; he reassures her that his love for her is undiminished. If the lodger may bring her happiness, on her behalf he will be the more pleased for it. As the narrator weeps, Nastenka bursts into tears, and she lays her hand upon his shoulder. Then, each comforted by the other's suffering, they discuss the future; they consider houses where they could live together, and the narrator lightheartedly suggests that they could go to the opera. As they talk over such fondly envisioned projects, Nastenka is suddenly transfixed: She has seen the young man from their boardinghouse. He repeats her name; without a word she takes the narrator by the neck with both hands, kisses him warmly and tenderly and then hastens to join her lover.

The next day, the narrator is awakened by Matrena, his landlady. He has received a letter from Nastenka; in it, she beseeches his forgiveness and affirms that their love, though short-lived, was sincere. She will be married to the lodger in a week, but she will remember him always. The narrator, with no regrets or recriminations, thankfully invokes his recollections of her as the one ray of happiness in his otherwise dreary and uneventful existence.

Themes and Meanings

Love, both fleeting and permanently held dear, is presented in this narrative of four nights and a day. The narrator's chance meeting with Nastenka brings about an exchange of self-revealing confessions on the part of two isolated souls; as they unburden themselves and discover that they are kindred spirits, their mutual attachment grows. As in many affairs of the heart, much takes place over a relatively short period of time, while events of much longer duration are referred to in passing. Both the narrator and Nastenka experience marked emotional vicissitudes, alternately haunted by melancholy and transported with joy. Each senses the other's mood, which then is quickly and deeply reflected in the other's outlook. Moreover, the shared feelings that have drawn them together are not dissipated by the sudden, albeit long-awaited, appearance of Nastenka's lodger.

The narrator describes his relationship with Nastenka as a single blissful moment that redeems an otherwise unhappy life. This brief and illuminating period, which has infused in him a single, transcendent vision of romantic love, foreshadows the author's later concerns with religious insight and redemption. In this instance, the narrator is enthralled by the depth of feeling summoned forth during his meetings with the girl; it is this revelation that matters to him, rather than the ultimate resolution of their romantic situation. This aspect also distinguishes this story from romantic works in which it does matter whether relationships are continued and consummated and in which parting yields grief rather than elevation of the spirit.

Style and Technique

The relationships recorded here constitute what must be one of the happier love triangles on record, and the curious charm of the ending is a result, in the main, of certain forms of characterization. For all of Nastenka's own misgivings, the narrator is only too pleased that she has found love in her friend the lodger. This peculiar working of love's alchemy, by which the narrator's attraction to the girl is transmuted into ardent hopes for her happiness with another man, can occur because of the narrator's peculiar traits: He is a professed dreamer, and much of everyday experience passes him by; he has reconciled himself, for the most part, to a drab and uneventful existence. Only a certain number of people and sights inspire his imagination, and then only during the later periods of the day. For him, therefore, even a brief and evanescent relationship with a young woman seems disproportionately precious to him. He is gentle and accepting by nature; in most senses he is not a possessive sort. Thus, he may cherish his memories of Nastenka as the most fondly felt of his nocturnal reveries.

This work itself has a fragile, dreamlike quality that imbues the narrative with a light, romantic air; in some ways it seems insubstantial. The point of view is largely that of the narrator; his story is told in the first person and is presented almost as a diary, with a series of entries for the four nights and the day he wishes particularly to recollect. It is impressionistic but also highly focused: He refers to familiar buildings almost as though they were persons. Clouds and bright stars that appear during the warm spring nights have a special meaning for the narrator, but there is much also, notably his background and the details of his daily work, that appears, if at all, only in passing.

Much of the story is given over to conversation, and indeed for the most part the narrator's relationship with Nastenka is established in long passages of dialogue in which each one's dreams and aspirations are set forth at length. Many of the facts that are known about the narrator come to light in this manner; Nastenka's past association with the lodger is evoked entirely from her exchanges with the narrator. In this fashion, basic concerns of the major characters are raised directly and immediately in the course of the work.

J. R. Broadus

THE WHITE STOCKING

Author: D. H. Lawrence (1885-1930)
Type of plot: Domestic realism
Time of plot: Early twentieth century
Locale: A small town in England, probably in the Midlands
First published: 1914

Principal characters:
TED WHISTON, a young traveling salesman
ELSIE WHISTON, his wife
SAM ADAMS, an admirer of Elsie

The Story

When the smooth married life of a rather ordinary young couple is disrupted by the intrusion of a third person, the couple find themselves swept into an explosive situation which is beyond their capacity to control.

There is certainly nothing remarkable about the protagonists, Ted and Elsie Whiston. They have been married two years, and live in a small, homey dwelling, their first house. She is a former factory worker, small and pretty, but also coquettish and superficial ("she *seemed* witty, although, when her sayings were repeated, they were entirely trivial"). He is a traveling salesman, slow but solid, totally confident of his wife's love, in whom he seems to find his whole being enriched and made whole. She has grown bored, however, and now tends to take him for granted, even mocking and jeering at him, although in spite of this she feels a deep attachment to him. It is the tension between these two contradictory attitudes that propels the story along its course.

The story begins on the morning of Valentine's Day. Elsie is excited to find in the mail a package addressed to her. She discovers that it contains a long white stocking, in which a pair of pearl earrings have been placed. She puts them on immediately, and her vain pleasure at the sight of herself in the mirror sets an ominous tone for the remainder of the story. Hiding the earrings, Elsie pretends to her husband that the white stocking is only a sample, but at breakfast she feels compelled to admit that this was a lie. Throughout the story, her naïveté, her insensitivity to the subtlety and delicacy of the feelings with which she is dealing, and her vacillation and duplicity contribute to the story's violent climax.

It transpires that the stocking was a gift from her former employer and admirer, Sam Adams, and she unconsciously goads her husband more by telling him that earlier in the year Adams sent her another stocking, but she concealed it from him. Concealment followed by later confession is her regular pattern of behavior. Worse is to follow (at least from Whiston's point of view). She has been seeing Sam Adams, but only, she says, for coffee at the Royal. As Whiston goes to work, they part in a state of unresolved tension, caught in a situation which neither of them has the maturity to grasp fully or to resolve. Cut adrift from their stable, day-to-day moorings, they are now at the mercy of powerful subconscious forces.

The middle section of the story is an extended flashback, revealing the significance of the friendship which Elsie had with Sam Adams and the uneasy triangle it formed with Whiston. The flamboyance of Adams, the factory owner, is in sharp contrast to the dour steadiness of Whiston. Adams, a forty-year-old bachelor, is a ladies' man, fashionably dressed and possessed of considerable charm. He is at home on the dance floor, in contrast to Whiston, who does not dance. This is one of the critical points of the story and is highlighted by an incident, recalled in a flashback, which leads directly to the gift of the white stocking. Whiston and Elsie attend a Christmas party given by Adams. Adams invites Elsie to dance, and she finds the experience completely exhilarating. Something about Adams, "some male warmth of attraction," ignites her; the rhythm of the dance and the close physical presence of her partner seem to transport her away from herself, into the deepest recesses of her partner's being. It is a new state of consciousness for her, and a pure physical pleasure. Adams has touched a vein of feeling, sensuality, and physical response in her which is quite beyond the reach of dull Whiston, moodily playing cribbage in another room, and Elsie becomes momentarily aware of a grudge against Whiston for failing to satisfy this aspect of her being. Yet she is also disturbed by Adams. Even as she dances with him, she cannot quiet the voice of conscience. The intoxication of the dance is not free of tension. On the contrary, it strains her, and some part of her remains closed to Adams and will not be opened. That part belongs to Whiston. What she loves about him is his permanence and his solidity, yet part of her being is closed to him also. She will not allow him to penetrate her feelings. Although the situation is temporarily resolved in a flood of tenderness and compassion as they return from the dance, she is nevertheless caught between the attraction she feels toward both men. The seeds of the story's climax have been sown.

Now, however, the couple have married and Adams appears to have been forgotten. The narrative resumes as Whiston returns home from work tired and depressed. The love Elsie undoubtedly feels for him is masked by her awareness of his inability to give her everything she needs, and her behavior becomes outrageously provocative. Putting on the stockings, she cruelly and deliberately taunts him, dancing around the room, lifting her skirt to her knees and kicking her legs up at him. They exchange bitter words and the situation becomes full of barely suppressed hatred. His anger becomes uncontrollable. She is frightened but insists that she will not return the stockings. As the language becomes abusive, Whiston threatens his wife with physical violence, which finally erupts as she tells him the truth about Adams' earlier gifts of earrings and a brooch. Striking her across the mouth, Whiston is filled with the desire to destroy her utterly. A final catastrophe is avoided, however, as he is overcome with weariness and disgust at the whole situation. Slowly and deliberately, he locates the offending jewelry, packs it up, and sends it back to Adams. Returning to the sight of his wife's tear-stained face, he is moved to remorse and compassion. As she sobs a half-completed retraction and apology, "I never meant—," a flood of tenderness envelops them both, and the story ends on a note of anguished reconciliation.

Themes and Meanings

At the time of writing "The White Stocking," Lawrence was immersed in a reading of Arthur Schopenhauer's works, particularly "The Metaphysics of Love" in *Die Welt als Wille und Vorstellung* (1819; *The World as Will and Idea*, 1883-1886). He double-underlined a passage which referred to the falsity of the harmony that lovers suppose themselves to feel, since this "frequently turns out to be violent discord shortly after marriage." This is exactly what happens in the "The White Stocking"; the story reveals how hard it is for a man and a woman to attain stability and wholeness in a close relationship, and the destructive and irrational behavior that results when the attempt fails. It suggests that sexual love carries an undercurrent of hostility, even hatred. The sexual overtones of the story are clear from the outset. The reader is made aware of Elsie's "delightful limbs" and how the sight of her bare flesh excites and disturbs Whiston. Elsie's dance with Adams is described in highly erotic terms, and unbridled sexual taunting immediately precedes the story's climax.

The basic issue is one that Lawrence was to address throughout his writing career: How was an individual to preserve his or her integrity, freedom, and separate identity when intensely involved in a union with another human being? Ted and Elsie Whiston can be seen as Lawrentian pioneers—even though they are largely unaware of it—in the attempt to attain the "star equilibrium" which Lawrence described in *Women in Love* (1920): "a pure balance of two single beings," like "two single equal stars balanced in conjunction." This ideal state of perfect union and perfect separateness is glimpsed momentarily by Elsie. In the enhanced sensuality of the dance, which anticipates the mystic sexual unions of Lawrence's later novels, Elsie finds that "the movements of his [Adams'] body and limbs were her own movements, yet not her own movements." Yet she cannot maintain this union, either with Adams or with Whiston, because she has found no stable center within herself. She oscillates wildly between two poles of her being, both of which she needs: the rich vitality and dynamism of the dance, but also the "enduring form," the sense of permanence, which Whiston gives her. Since she can find no way of synthesizing the two within herself, the couple seem doomed to a series of temporary reconciliations, each followed by another outburst of hostility and mutual incomprehension.

Style and Technique

"The White Stocking" is one of Lawrence's earliest stories. It was originally entered for a competition offered by the *Nottinghamshire Guardian* in 1907, when Lawrence was twenty-two. It did not win, and the judges commented that it was "lacking finish." Like most of Lawrence's early stories, it is marked by a down-to-earth realism, and this makes an important contribution to its effectiveness. The commonplace setting, for example, Whiston's small, "seven and sixpenny" dwelling, and the homeyness and simplicity of their daily routine, are disturbingly limited and ordinary. This is reinforced by the effect of the diction. The predominance of short sentences, containing a high proportion of monosyllabic words, has a simple, almost childlike effect, suggesting that the characters are undeveloped in their understanding of life; they lack sophistication and self-knowledge. (This changes only in the rich, flowing prose used to describe the dance, which ably conveys the new reality which Elsie has discovered.) The presence of an omniscient narrator, who sees so much more than any individual character is able to see, tends to emphasize for the reader the smallness and inadequacy of the Whistons' own perspective.

These stylistic elements effectively highlight, by contrast, the surging, primeval forces which the characters unleash in themselves and in one another, for which they are totally unprepared. It is as if they are living only on the surface of life. The bewilderment expressed in Elsie's final reconciling words, "I never meant—," is highly significant. The rational, everyday world which they inhabit is helpless before the dark and irrational psychic forces which they unwittingly arouse. They might well echo the cry of St. Paul in Romans 7:15: "I do not understand my own actions. For I do not do what I want, but I do the very thing I hate."

Bryan Aubrey

A WHOLE LOAF

Author: Shmuel Yosef Agnon (1888-1970)
Type of plot: Metarealism
Time of plot: The 1930's
Locale: Jerusalem
First published: "Pat Shelema," 1933 (English translation, 1957)

Principal characters:

THE UNNAMED NARRATOR, the protagonist

DR. YEKUTIEL NE'EMAN, a writer and sage, an acquaintance of the protagonist

MR. GRESSLER, a wealthy landowner and favorite acquaintance of the protagonist

The Story

At the beginning of "A Whole Loaf," the narrator's suggestive comment, "I had made no preparations on Sabbath eve, so I had nothing to eat on the Sabbath," explains why he leaves his home in search of a meal. Other reasons for going out are the hellish heat at home and his sense of loneliness, for his wife and children are still abroad and he has to see to his own needs.

The protagonist thus joins other strollers at the end of the Sabbath day, partaking of the cool Jerusalem air. Soon he is distracted from his search for a restaurant by the great sage Dr. Yekutiel Ne'eman, sitting by his window. Expecting a word of wisdom, he hears Dr. Ne'eman rebuking him for not doing something to reunite the family back in Jerusalem.

The narrator then tells of Dr. Ne'eman's book, which has raised heated debate concerning its authenticity but which the sage claims to be a record of the words of Lord. Some believe that the book is authentic, whereas others hold that it is merely Dr. Ne'eman's own writings, attributed by him to an unknown and never-seen Lord. One undisputed effect of the book, observes the narrator, has been that people have bettered themselves by it, whereas others devote themselves heart and soul to keeping every word in it. Praising the book, the hero is surprised and grieved when Dr. Ne'eman leaves the window. Returning soon, however, he gives the hero a packet of letters to be posted. Accepting the task, the hero promises to mail the letters as asked.

When the Sabbath is over, the hero heads for the post office to mail the letters, all the while debating whether he should not go and eat first. He finally resolves first to fulfill his obligation to Dr. Ne'eman and finds himself standing before the post office. Just as he is about to enter, he is distracted by the strange sight of a carriage driven by his acquaintance from abroad, Mr. Gressler, making its way down the sidewalk. The pedestrians, far from being upset, appear to enjoy the danger of being nearly run over by the carriage.

Recalling the close, pleasure-filled friendship he has had with Mr. Gressler abroad and in Jerusalem, the narrator remembers how his friend was instrumental in amusing him and teaching him a knowledge to counter all other kinds of wisdom. Their close relationship was halted for a while when, still abroad, Mr. Gressler persuaded the hero's downstairs neighbor to set fire to his stock of cheap goods and collect the insurance. The fire, however, spread and consumed the hero's home as well, burning up his uninsured books and belongings. The remainder of his wealth was squandered on the ensuing litigation urged upon him by Mr. Gressler. Blaming Mr. Gressler for his losses, the hero abandoned him, immersing himself in Dr. Ne'eman's book and leaving for the Land of Israel. On the boat, he noticed that Mr. Gressler was headed for the same destination, but his cabin was in the first-class section, whereas the hero was spending the journey in the lowliest class. Upon landing, Mr. Gressler helped him through customs and the journey to Jerusalem, whereupon their friendship was renewed and became even stronger after the hero's family went abroad.

Now, joining Mr. Gressler on the carriage, the hero forgets the letters and his hunger. Soon they encounter Mr. Hofni, the inventor of a better mousetrap, whom the hero dislikes. He grabs the reins to lead the horses away from Mr. Hofni, causing the carriage to overturn. Both riders roll in the dirt, and the hero, his body aching, proceeds to the nearest hotel dining room and orders a meal (after a long and hungry wait) but insists on having a whole loaf to go with it.

Now the waiting truly begins, for many meals are served to others while he does not receive his—in part because of the search for a whole loaf. Hearing the clock strike half past ten, the hero leaps to his feet to go and mail the letters and collides with the waiter, spilling his own meal. The manager comforts the hero and promises that a new meal will be soon prepared for him.

With his soul flying between the restaurant kitchen and the already closed post office, the hero awaits the meal he was promised. The last of the diners having left, the lights are shut, leaving the hero still waiting for his food. When he hears the doors being locked, he knows that no one will return until morning. Although trying to sleep, the protagonist is disturbed by a mouse gnawing at some bones left on a table. He soon becomes convinced that it is he who will eventually become a meal for the mouse. Seeing a cat, he hopes that the mouse will run, but neither pays attention to the other and the cat's eyes take on an eerie green color which frightens the hero. The sound of a passing carriage prompts the hero to call on Mr. Gressler for help, but no help comes.

When the servants arrive in the morning, they are astonished to find the hero still waiting for his meal, and they laugh when the waiter identifies him as the one who ordered a whole loaf. The hero gets up, feeling dirty, sick, hungry, and thirsty, and makes his way back home, still unable to mail the letters as the post office is closed on Sunday. He washes and goes out to get some food, for he is still alone; his wife and children are abroad and the burden of providing for his own needs is still upon him.

Themes and Meanings

"A Whole Loaf" is perhaps the most frequently cited of Shmuel Yosef Agnon's *Book of Deeds* (1932), an anthology of short stories characterized by unreal, dreamlike situations and typed as metarealistic stories—namely, tales, or episodes within larger works, whose connotational import is in a higher (timeless) sphere than the denotational plot.

The key to this story's meaning has been identified by scholars as its title, with particular emphasis on the possible connotations of the term "loaf." There are a number of possible interpretations of what the loaf and the narrator's hunger for one represents, ranging from a yearning for spiritual, religious nourishment to one for selfish, material rewards, all the way to a desire by the hero to practice idolatry.

The difficulty with explaining the meaning of the term "loaf" may be skirted by focusing on the title's adjective. Thus, one may say that the protagonist's insistence on having a loaf (whatever it may mean) which is whole constitutes the crux of the difficulty in providing him with one, thereby leaving him hungry physically but even more so existentially, for an unattainable wholeness.

The story focuses on the hero's state of loneliness and his inability to commit himself to a specific set of values. He is of two minds about issues such as Dr. Ne'eman's book, his desire to eat or carry out the promise to mail the letters, and his inability to take steps to reunite the family. These, and others, are all encapsulated in the narrator's opening statement about being unprepared for the Sabbath (or for anything else), thereby having to bear the consequences of not enjoying the rewards of prior preparation. The penalty for his inaction is also an emotional one, represented by the hellish existence in his room, where flames of fire appear to torment him (an expression of his sense of guilt) on the Sabbath day.

The character of Yekutiel Ne'eman has been said to represent Moses or some Mosaic figure on the evidence of his name, both the first and last of which have been attributed by Jewish lore to Moses, and of his influential and controversial book. The letters, then, would compose that which was handed down by Moses—the commandments or the healing, spiritual, and ethical values contained in the Five Books—ostensibly recorded by Dr. Ne'eman as spoken by Lord, namely God (who is referred to in the story with four dots which stand for the tetragrammaton YHWH, God's unique four-letter name).

In respecting Dr. Ne'eman's claims regarding the book's authorship and by agreeing to mail the letters, the hero would be identified as a man of faith, eager and willing to pass the tradition on to others and into the future. His ambivalence about his ways in life, though, makes his mission to the post office dubious. His sense of responsibility to two distinct missions—the collective, religious one represented by Dr. Ne'eman and the selfish, individualistic view indicated via the restaurant and Mr. Gressler—leaves him caught in the middle, experiencing a spiritual starvation, as of the proverbial ass dying of hunger between two bales of hay because he cannot decide of which of the two to eat. Thus torn between two impulses, the hero remains perpetually in a state of imperfection, unable to have his whole loaf.

Style and Technique

In "The Whole Loaf," Agnon characteristically transformed real events into a powerfully evocative literary gem. The story's opening recaptures Agnon's own experience when, in 1925, renting a room in Jerusalem, he had yet to arrange for the immigration of his wife and children, who were still living with her family in Germany. Agnon's separation from the family, his sense of guilt at not heeding his wife's urging to arrange for their speedy reunion in Jerusalem, and the constant dependence on the postal service for linking him with his loved ones are but the most visible biographical details from that period incorporated into this tale of the struggle between modernity and tradition for the soul of the hero. For example, in a letter to his wife dated March 18, 1925, Agnon recounted the unusually hot spring weather in Jerusalem which prevented him from remaining in his room, because its outer walls were covered with sheets of metal.

Eight years later, Agnon drew upon these memories to embellish and reflect the spiritual torments of his protagonist, whose sense of loneliness is greater than the mere pain of being apart from his family. Agnon generalized and abstracted his own loneliness, hunger, and discomfort to indicate the existential predicament of the tradition-sensitive hero, who has become skeptical about the very existence of Lord and about the origins of Dr. Ne'eman's book (details mostly omitted by Agnon in the revised and translated version of the story).

The protagonist's shaken faith may also have been suggested by Agnon's decade-long exposure to modernism as manifested by the broad array of German intellectual life, at that time a new and unprecedented experience in the author's life (whether in Galicia or the Land of Israel), leaving a deep and lasting impression on his worldview and his literary creativity. Thus, Agnon observes in this story the bipolarity of modern-day Jewry, a conflict expressed in the rift within the hero's personality between allegiance to a Mosaic way of life (as represented by the character with the Hebrew name, Yekutiel Ne'eman) and allegiance to the life of secularism (indicated by the character bearing the German name, Gressler).

Furthermore, the fire which consumed the hero's books and household belongings, the outcome of the satanic temptation of Mr. Gressler, is a transmutation of an emotionally traumatic fire in 1924, which burned Agnon's library (and never-to-be-published book) while he was living in the German city of Homburg.

In the story, the events reflect the hero's sense of guilt for associating with Mr. Gressler and living abroad; his reaction to the fire, for example, was a break with Mr. Gressler and his secular life-style, an immersion into Dr. Ne'eman's book, and immigration to the Land of Israel.

"A Whole Loaf" thus bears out the point that Agnon's approach to writing stories was an intimate fusion between his experience and his imagination, the latter working upon the former to condense and refine it and reflect the ideas and values he hoped to relay to his readers.

Stephen Katz

THE WHORE OF MENSA

Author: Woody Allen (1935-   )
Type of plot: Parody
Time of plot: The 1970's
Locale: New York
First published: 1974

> *Principal characters:*
> KAISER LUPOWITZ, a private detective
> WORD BABCOCK, his client, a blackmail victim
> FLOSSIE, the blackmailer
> SHERRY, the title character, a prostitute of the mind

The Story

Kaiser Lupowitz, a New York private detective, is hired by Word Babcock to thwart a blackmail scheme. Babcock, who builds and services joy buzzers, considers himself an intellectual but does not find his wife intellectually stimulating: "She won't discuss Pound with me. Or Eliot. I didn't know that when I married her." He hears about a call-girl service providing female college students who will discuss intellectual matters for a fee, and he becomes a regular customer. Flossie, the madam, wants ten thousand dollars, or else she will turn over to his wife tapes of his "discussing *The Waste Land* and *Styles of Radical Will*, and, well, really getting into some issues" with a girl in a motel room. Babcock needs help because his wife "would die if she knew she didn't turn me on up here."

Lupowitz calls Flossie, who sends him Sherry to discuss the works of Herman Melville in a room at the Plaza. After some pseudointellectual banter, Lupowitz threatens to have Sherry arrested unless she tells him where to find Flossie. Sherry begins to cry, saying that she has reached her current state because she needs the money to complete her master's degree: "I've been turned down for a grant. *Twice.*"

Sherry sends Lupowitz to the Hunter College Book Store, a front for Flossie's operation. The detective discovers that Flossie is really a man. Flossie explains that he wanted to take over *The New York Review of Books* and went to Mexico for an operation that was supposed to make him look like Lionel Trilling: "Something went wrong. I came out looking like Auden, with Mary McCarthy's voice. That's when I started working the other side of the law."

Lupowitz disarms Flossie before the male madam can shoot him. Taking him to the police, Lupowitz learns that the FBI is after Flossie: "A little matter involving some gamblers and an annotated copy of Dante's *Inferno*."

Themes and Meanings

Literature, philosophy, intellectual pretensions, sex, and parody are the common elements in Woody Allen's fiction, and all are on display in "The Whore of Mensa." The story is Allen's second parody of the kind of detective fiction associated with Dashiell Hammett and Raymond Chandler. In the first, "Mr. Big," Kaiser Lupowitz is hired to prove or disprove the existence of God. Allen's intellectual satire can also be seen in such diverse works as "Spring Bulletin," "The Irish Genius," "No Kaddish for Weinstein," and, especially, "The Kugelmass Episode."

Allen has frequently been criticized for filling his stories, plays, and films with in-jokes aimed at a limited audience, but that audience is simply anyone reasonably well-read. Allen's satire depends upon his reader recognizing the comic incongruity of Sherry's being arrested for reading *Commentary* in a parked car, Lupowitz's threatening to have Sherry tell her story at Alfred Kazin's office, the detective's asking, "Suppose I wanted Noam Chomsky explained to me by two girls?" and Sherry's attempting to bribe Lupowitz with photographs of Dwight Macdonald reading.

Allen's humor is aimed at intellectuals while making fun of them at the same time. Lupowitz responds to his first sight of Sherry: "They really know how to appeal to your fantasies. Long straight hair, leather bag, silver earrings, no make-up." Like Alvy Singer's first wife in Allen's film *Annie Hall* (1977), Sherry is a cultural stereotype: "Central Park West upbringing, Socialist summer camps, Brandeis. She was every dame you saw waiting in line at the Elgin or the Thalia, or penciling the words 'Yes, very true' into the margin of some book on Kant."

As with all of Allen's humor, a serious purpose lurks beneath the surface gags. Allen equates the need for intellectual stimulation with prostitution because so many people approach sex, emotional involvement, and intellectuality on the same shallow level. Thus, Lupowitz prepares for his meeting with Sherry by consulting the Monarch College Outline series so that he can fake his way through their Melville encounter. Sherry also fakes her responses just as a prostitute would: "Oh, yes, Kaiser. Yes, baby, that's deep. A platonic comprehension of Christianity—why didn't I see it before?" This superficiality is what Word Babcock wants: "I don't want an involvement—I want a quick intellectual experience, then I want the girl to leave."

Allen's point is that shallowness in one segment of life is likely to spread into others. The interrelatedness of all aspects of life is emphasized when Lupowitz goes to Flossie's and learns that for three hundred dollars he can get "the works: A thin Jewish brunette would pretend to pick you up at the Museum of Modern Art, let you read her master's, get you involved in a screaming quarrel at Elaine's over Freud's conception of women, and then fake a suicide of your choosing—the perfect evening, for some guys."

Style and Technique

"The Whore of Mensa" celebrates the clichés of hard-boiled detective fiction. Sometimes Allen presents these clichés straight: "I turned and suddenly found myself standing face to face with the business end of a .38"; "He hit the ground like a ton of bricks." Sometimes he adds a touch of silliness, as when "a quivering pat of butter named Word Babcock walked into my office and laid his cards on the table," and when Sherry arrives "packed into her slacks like two big scoops of vanilla ice cream." Occasionally, he gives the expected a small twist: "I pushed a glass across the desk top and a bottle of rye I keep handy for nonmedicinal purposes." Allen tops it all off by having Flossie arrested by a Sergeant Holmes.

Allen no doubt chose the detective form as the vehicle for his satire not only for its appropriateness for the prostitution plot and the literary allusions but also because of the importance of the vernacular in American crime fiction. Like Mark Twain, S. J. Perelman, and numerous other humorists, Allen enjoys distinctively American ways of saying things such as "I owned up" and "A five-spot cools him." It is fitting that "The Whore of Mensa" ends with a parody of the master of the laconic, staccato American style, Ernest Hemingway: "Later that night, I looked up an old account of mine named Gloria. She was blond. She had graduated *cum laude*. The difference was she majored in physical education. It felt good."

Michael Adams

WHY DON'T YOU DANCE?

Author: Raymond Carver (1938-   )
Type of plot: Antistory
Time of plot: c. 1980
Locale: Somewhere in the United States
First published: 1981

> *Principal characters:*
> A MAN
> A GIRL
> A BOY

The Story

As he pours himself a drink in the kitchen, a man looks out the window to his front yard, where the bedroom furniture has been arranged almost precisely as it was arranged in the bedroom. There is the bed, flanked by two nightstands and two reading lamps; a chiffonier; a portable heater; a rattan chair. The kitchen table stands in the driveway, and on top of it are a record player, a box of silverware, and a potted plant. The rest of the furniture is also on the lawn: a desk, a coffee table, a television set, a sofa and chair. Earlier in the day, the man has run an extension cord from the house to the lawn, and now all the electrical items can be operated as well outdoors as they were inside the house.

Later, after the man has gone to the market, a boy and a girl stop at the house, thinking that the furniture on the lawn must signal a yard sale in progress. They begin to examine the items in the yard, and soon the boy turns on the television set and sits down on the sofa to watch it. The girl tries out the bed and invites the boy to join her; though it makes him feel awkward, he gets on the bed with her, since there seems to be no one in the house. After a while, the boy decides to see if anyone is at home who can tell him the prices of the items in the yard. The girl instructs him to offer the owner ten dollars less than the asking price for each item.

Meanwhile, the man returns from the market. The boy says that they are interested in the bed, the television, and the desk, and they haggle, settling on forty dollars for the bed and fifteen for the television. The man pours drinks for all three of them. While drinking his glass of whiskey, the man drops a lighted cigarette between the sofa cushions, and the girl helps him find it. The three sit together drinking whiskey in the dark.

The man decides that the young couple should buy the record player. He refills their drinks. Finding a box filled with records, he asks the girl to pick one, which she does at random, unfamiliar with any of the titles. The boy, by now slightly drunk, is writing a check when the man suggests that the boy and the girl dance to the phonograph music. Though the boy is reluctant, the couple start dancing together in the driveway, and before long the man joins them. The girl notices that the neighbors are watching, but the man seems not to mind, telling her that the neighbors only *thought* that they had seen everything at his house. The girl and the man start to dance closer together.

Some weeks later, the girl tries to describe what happened at the man's house that night. For a time, she talks about the incident frequently, trying to get it out of her system.

Themes and Meanings

Like many of Raymond Carver's short stories, "Why Don't You Dance?" is about an ordinary man moved to desperation by reversals of fortune. Though the reader is uncertain about what recent events have caused the man's bizarre behavior, there are broad hints in the text about a marital breakup. At any rate, the home is in crisis, probably as a result, at least in part, of the man's heavy drinking—he is never without a drink in the story, and he mixes beer and whiskey with ease. Similarly withheld is what happens after the man and girl start dancing together, but certainly it is something that the girl, weeks later, would like to be able to forget. The suggestion is of exhibitionism and voyeurism, though the act itself is less important than the reader's knowledge that the man is at the breaking point. Twice during the story the girl calls the man "desperate," though his behavior throughout is less frenzied and irrational than it is eerily calm. He is a man with nothing left to lose.

Much of the effect of this story is attributable to the very ordinariness of the characters, the surroundings, and the dialogue. In its ability to exploit the potential horror of the everyday, "Why Don't You Dance?" can be called surrealist. The setting, a suburban lawn, is made unfamiliar and grotesque because it is covered with furniture obsessively arranged as it was indoors. Routine objects take on weird significance in the context of the story: A garden hose dispenses water to dilute the girl's drink; a phonograph and a set of old record albums provide the musical accompaniment to the story's climax; a used bed becomes a symbol of two marriages. The characters themselves are wholly without surface distinction. Nameless, almost generic, they speak in flat, simple sentences, the tragic weight of which is apprehended by the reader only at the end of the story. The physical and emotional landscape is like that of a painting by René Magritte (1898-1967): deceptively ordinary, but charged with submerged anxiety and despair.

The namelessness and banality of each of the story's elements serves another purpose, however, and one ultimately more chilling. Their lack of differentiating characteristics makes these characters into Everyman and Everywoman, forcing the reader to realize that this situation could befall anyone. In front of the empty house, the couple, who are "furnishing a small apartment," act out a grotesquely compressed pantomime of middle-class married life. The girl tests the bed, while the boy shyly demurs. The boy sits on the couch watching television, and the girl tries the electric blender. Finally, at the man's prompting, they begin to dance, setting the stage for the story's unspeakable climax. In this sense, they are the man's heirs and his successors, and the tragedy that has ruined him seems destined to impinge on their young lives.

Style and Technique

Much of what would be called exposition and characterization in a more conventional story is omitted from "Why Don't You Dance?" The reader knows little about the man or about the young couple, and this deliberate vagueness forces the reader to speculate, to fill in the gaps in the narrative. What has become of the man's marriage? Why has he emptied the contents of his house onto the lawn? Most important, what happens at the end of the story? By posing but refusing to answer such questions, the story leaves everything to the reader's imagination, thus producing not one, but an infinite number of possible narratives. Paradoxically, this story—which is superficially so brief and so simple—is highly complex, subject to almost limitless interpretation.

Unlike many of Carver's short stories, "Why Don't You Dance?" is less a realistic portrayal of middle-class life than a parable of human relationships and human suffering. In this most minimalist of narratives, a writer famed for his spareness of style succeeds in evoking a tragedy as universal as it is disturbing.

J. D. Daubs

WHY I LIVE AT THE P. O.

Author: Eudora Welty (1909-   )
Type of plot: Comic monologue
Time of plot: The early 1940's
Locale: China Grove, Mississippi
First published: 1941

> *Principal characters:*
> SISTER, the obsessed narrator of the story
> STELLA-RONDO, her sister, a returned prodigal
> MAMA, Sister and Stella-Rondo's mother
> PAPA-DADDY, their grandfather
> UNCLE RONDO, their uncle
> SHIRLEY-T, Stella-Rondo's young daughter

The Story

This comic story is an extended dramatic monologue told by Sister to an unnamed visitor to the post office, where she now lives after having left her home because of the return of her sister Stella-Rondo. As the title suggests, the story is an apologia in which Sister attempts to explain why she has decided to live in the post office of the small town of China Grove, where she is postmistress. The first line of the story establishes the problem quite clearly: "I was getting along fine with Mama, Papa-Daddy and Uncle Rondo until my sister Stella-Rondo just separated from her husband and came back home again." Ostensibly, Sister's decision is a result of all of her family turning against her after the return of Stella-Rondo, who earlier ran off with a traveling photographer, who, to hear Sister tell it, was her own boyfriend before Stella-Rondo stole him from her.

What makes the story both comic and complex is that the reader only hears Sister's side of the story. As she says, Stella-Rondo broke her and Mr. Whitaker up by telling him that she was one-sided. To this Sister, in her own twisted logic that dominates the story, replies, "Bigger on one side than the other, which is a deliberate falsehood: I'm the same. Stella-Rondo is exactly twelve months to the day younger than I am and for that reason she's spoiled." It is this petty and petulant point of view of Sister that makes "Why I Live at the P. O." a tour de force of Southern idiom, one of Eudora Welty's most admired stories.

Indeed, Sister is one-sided, and as she recounts the events that take place around the Fourth of July in China Grove, the reader sees through her seemingly banal defense. One's response to Sister, who is a childish woman obsessed with trivia and her persecution complex as well as a delightful fictional creation made up of lovely illogic, is the key element in this hilarious story.

The family comedy begins when Stella-Rondo claims that her two-year-old daughter, Shirley-T, is adopted; Sister denies this by saying that Shirley-T is "the spit-image of Pappa-Daddy if he'd cut off his beard." Beginning with this remark by Sister, Stella-Rondo methodically turns each member of the family against Sister until Sister, unable to bear it any longer, systematically goes through the house taking everything that belongs to her and setting up housekeeping in the post office. The list of the things that Sister gathers up—a sewing-machine motor, a calendar with first-aid remedies on it, a thermometer, a Hawaiian ukulele, and bluebird wall vases—is in itself a wonderfully comic catalog.

Thus, the plot of the story is minimal, even trivial. In fact, trivia is what seems to characterize this extended monologue, for it is difficult for the reader to take any of the events of the story which Sister tells seriously. The reader feels superior to the characters in the story, as is typical of comedy, because he or she can laugh at the foolishness of the values they embody. At the end of the story, when Sister says that she likes it at the "P. O.," with everything catercornered, and that she wants the world to know that she is happy, the reader perhaps suspects that she protests too much. At this point, one must look back on the story and try to get beneath Sister's own stated justification for her actions. Only then can the reader answer the basic question: Why does Sister live at the P. O.?

Themes and Meanings

It is often difficult to discuss the theme of a comic story such as this one, for to explicate comedy too often puts one to the thankless task of explaining a joke. What makes "Why I Live at the P. O." amusing, however, according to many readers (it is one of Welty's best-known fictions) is that Sister is a comic example of the schizophrenia of obsession, that she thus becomes almost mechanical in her reactions to her persecution complex. The reader laughs at the story because the characters seemed so obsessed with trivia; yet, as is typical of most comedy, there is something serious beneath the laughter: The reader despairs to think that people can be so obsessed with such petty matters.

Many of Welty's fictional characters seem isolated in some way; this story is one in which the reader must discover the nature of that isolation. Thus, one might say that this story is about the reader's gradual discovery of why Sister does live at the P. O., and that this reason goes beyond what Sister says, although what Sister says is all the reader really has. Indeed, the reader must analyze Sister's situation as she herself describes it and develop a dual perspective: a sympathetic identification with Sister followed by a detached judgment of her actions and speech. The problem of the story is that of Sister, who is the kind of character who cannot do things herself, but instead must have someone else act out her own desires. In this story, it can be said that Sister is the thinking side of the self, while Stella-Rondo is the acting side. Thus, it is true when Sister says throughout the story that she does nothing and everything is Stella-Rondo's fault, but at the same time the reader is right to suspect that everything that happens is Sister's doing.

For example, it is Sister who first dates Mr. Whitaker, but it is Stella-Rondo who marries him and moves away from the family; Sister wants to do both but cannot act on her desires. According to Sister, Stella-Rondo turns the other members of the family against her, but what Stella-Rondo actually does is act out Sister's feelings. Sister communicates everything in an oblique way, never expressing her feelings directly but always manipulating events and people diagonally through Stella-Rondo. Consequently, she can cause many events to occur yet disclaim responsibility for any of them. Thus, because Stella-Rondo is the objective side of Sister's subjective self, it is inevitable that the more that Sister attempts to drive out Stella-Rondo, the more she herself is driven out.

Stella-Rondo is the female version of the biblical prodigal son returned. Sister desires to remain safe at home and manipulate the family from her position as dutiful daughter. Ironically, however, Stella-Rondo becomes the favorite when she returns, while Sister becomes the exile. The irony of the story is that although Sister spends the whole tale explaining why she lives at the P. O., she really does not know why. Although she talks throughout, no one listens to what she says, not even herself. No one listens to anyone else in this story, least of all Sister. As she says in the last line, if Stella-Rondo should come to her and try to explain about her life with Mr. Whitaker, "I'd simply put my fingers in both my ears and refuse to listen." In a metaphoric sense, Sister has told the entire story with her fingers in both her ears; that is, she cannot hear her story from the dual perspective that the reader can.

Style and Technique

The method of "Why I Live at the P. O." is that of a dramatic monologue. Thus, its closest literary analogue is the dramatic monologue of Robert Browning, in which there is always a gap between the way the speaker perceives himself and the way the listener perceives him. A dramatic monologue is a work in which the speaker reveals himself unawares. In such a form, the speaker, even as he seems to damn another character, actually only succeeds in damning himself. Perhaps the literary character that Sister resembles even more than a figure from Browning's poetry is Fyodor Dostoevski's Underground Man in his short novel *Zapiski iz podpolya* (1864; *Notes from the Underground*, 1954). As it is for Dostoevski's nameless antihero, Sister's logic is not so much insane as it is the rational pushed to such an extreme that it becomes irrational and perverse. It is indeed the style of her speech—that is, the whole of the story—which reveals this problem.

"Why I Live at the P. O." is different in both tone and technique from

Welty's usual fictional method. In most of her best-known stories, reality is transformed into fantasy and fable, and the logic is not that of ordinary life; here, in contrast, things remain stubbornly real. Many readers have noted that the dreamlike nature of Welty's stories depends on her ability to squeeze meaning out of the most trivial of details. Here, however, in a story that depends on the triviality of things, there is no dreamlike effect; the trivial details are comically allowed to remain trivial. Regardless of the difference in style, however, here as elsewhere in Welty's fiction, the focus is on the isolation of the self.

Charles E. May

THE WIDE NET

Author: Eudora Welty (1909-   )
Type of plot: Psychological realism
Time of plot: Early twentieth century
Locale: Dover, Mississippi, on the Natchez Trace
First published: 1942

> *Principal characters:*
> WILLIAM WALLACE JAMIESON, a recently married farmer
> HAZEL JAMIESON, his pregnant wife
> VIRGIL THOMAS, William Wallace's bachelor friend and
>   neighbor

The Story

As the vernal equinox approaches, Hazel Jamieson, three months pregnant, refuses sexual relations with her husband, William Wallace Jamieson. Mystified and hurt by this rejection, William Wallace spends a night out, drinking with his bachelor friend Virgil Thomas. Upon returning home in the morning, he finds a note from Hazel announcing that she will not put up with him any longer and has drowned herself in the Pearl River. William Wallace and Virgil then organize a party to drag the river for her, using the wide net which belongs to the local patriarch, Old Doc. The scholarly Doc questions the pair closely to be sure that they have a good reason for using the net, because William Wallace has used it within the last month, and it is not his turn. When Doc believes it possible that Hazel may have drowned herself, he reflects that "Lady Hazel is the prettiest girl in Mississippi.... A golden-haired girl." He decides to join the search.

As the search gets under way, it takes on a mystical, ritual quality. Doc observes that this is the equinox, the time of change from fall to winter, when all of creation seems made of gold. William Wallace responds by thinking of Hazel as "like a piece of pure gold, too precious to touch," then asks, mysteriously, for the name of the river they all know so well. Like Hazel, the river, though familiar, becomes mysterious, "almost as if it were a river in some dream." William Wallace's search of the river becomes a metaphor for his attempt to fathom the mysterious depths of Hazel's character.

Other ritual elements include the two black boys who push Doc in an oarless boat, the mysterious objects dredged up from the bottom, Virgil's refusal to allow strangers to watch them, William Wallace's deep dives, the fish feast, William Wallace's phallic dance with a catfish attached to his belt buckle, and their subsequent "vision" of "The King of Snakes," a large water snake which seems to be evoked by William Wallace's dance. The search ends just in time for a violent thunderstorm, which transforms the benign golden landscape temporarily into a terrifying, agitated silver landscape.

Of these ritual elements, William Wallace's deepest dive seems especially significant: He dives below the normal muddy world of the river into the "dark clear world of deepness." The narrator asks whether he found Hazel in this deepness: "Had he suspected down there, like some secret, the real, the true trouble that Hazel had fallen into, about which words in a letter could not speak . . . how (who knew?) she had been filled to the brim with that elation that comes of great hopes and changes . . . that comes with a little course of its own like a tune to run in the head, and there was nothing she could do about it—they knew—and so it had turned to this?" Diving deep into the river, William Wallace might also dive deep into Hazel, there to confront the same mystery which lies at his own center, "the old trouble" which all people share, but which they cannot articulate. Newly married Hazel, confronting the changes of marriage, of the season, of motherhood, is shown at the beginning of the story as inarticulate but filled to the brim with golden life: "When he came in the room she would not speak to him, but would look as straight at nothing as she could, with her eyes glowing." Her mystery is like the fish of the Pearl River, infinite and familiar at the same time.

When the quest is finished, Old Doc reflects that he has never been on a better river dragging: "If it took catfish to move the Rock of Gibralter, I believe this outfit could move it." Virgil replies that they did not catch Hazel, but Doc replies in turn that girls are not caught as fish are; they are more mysterious. William Wallace returns home to find a moon-made rainbow over his house and Hazel waiting for him. He tries to assert control over her, to prevent her behaving so whimsically again, but she evades him, asserting that her self belongs to her. He feels again the elation he felt upon winning her consent to marry, feeling in her loving assertion of selfhood the mystery of self which is at the center of their love and union as well as of their separation and sorrow.

Themes and Meanings

As she does in her novel/story cycle, *The Golden Apples* (1949), Eudora Welty uses ideas and images from William Butler Yeats's "The Song of Wandering Aengus" in "The Wide Net." Aengus is a fisherman who went fishing with a hazel wand as a pole and caught a silver trout which was later transformed into a glimmering girl. The girl called his name and ran, "and faded through the brightening air." He has spent his life trying to find her again, dreaming of a union with her in some paradise where, until the end of time, he will pluck "The silver apples of the moon,/ The golden apples of the sun." The minor coincidences of images suggest a connection with the poem. The two works share the theme of a man trying to fathom and thus achieve an ideal union with a woman. This ideal union is unattainable in this world, but the fascination of the mystery of the human soul, which cannot be captured in words and which seems to separate lovers, also draws the lovers together in an endless pursuit which gives depth and richness of meaning to life.

Ruth Vande Kieft, in an essay on Welty, describes this theme as central to much of Welty's fiction: "Welty shows how the most public things in life, love and death, are also the most mysterious and private, and must be kept so. Though privacy requires the risk of isolation and loneliness, it is a risk worth taking in order to achieve the proper balance between love and separateness." William Wallace and Hazel are attempting intuitively to achieve such a proper balance. The ritual of the wide net seems central to William Wallace's success. Just as it is the ritual itself rather than its products which William Wallace and his friends value, so it is the process of interaction in tension with Hazel, rather than achieving control over her, which makes their marriage rich and golden.

Style and Technique

Perhaps the central characteristic of Welty's style in this story is its evocative quality. In outline, the story is simple and realistic, the account of a marital misunderstanding which sends the young husband off upon a compensatory masculine adventure. Yet, in the telling, Welty evokes a deeper, even more universal layer of meaning. By means of suggestive images and carefully constructed narrative commentary, Welty points to and suggests the meanings of the ritual aspects of the whole expedition. For example, as William Wallace and Virgil plan to gather the men, William Wallace catches a rabbit. He demonstrates how he can "freeze" the animal, making it stand for a moment under his hand. Welty makes it clear that in exercising a kind of hypnotic control over it, he is expressing his wish to control Hazel in this way. Virgil's reaction points at the paradox of William Wallace's desire, setting up the meanings that will emerge from the ritual elements of the quest: "Anybody can freeze a rabbit, that wants to. . . . Was you out catching cottontails, or was you out catching your wife?" To control Hazel would be to reduce her to a relatively uninteresting animal.

One of the most evocative images is William Wallace's phallic fish dance. The men have finished their search without finding Hazel's body. After eating and napping on a sandbar, William Wallace feels exuberant. Doc attributes this joy to the pleasure of the chase: "The excursion is the same when you go looking for your sorrow as when you go looking for your joy." William Wallace then hooks a catfish to his belt buckle and begins to dance, "tears of laughter streaming down his cheeks." Then, a giant water snake appears, looped out of golden light rings on the river, evoking from the usually silent Malone men the cry, "The King of Snakes!" Among other possible meanings, one seems to be the celebration of their masculinity, which they affirm in the pursuit even of the essentially mysterious and uncapturable woman.

They confront their own mystery simultaneously in a meaningful ritual, an acting out of what they cannot put into words.

Welty describes her motive for writing as a lyrical impulse "to praise, to love, to call up, to prophesy." Ruth Vande Kieft says that Welty's fiction may be seen "as a celebration of so many pieces of life with 'the mysteries rushing unsubmissively through them by the minute.'" In "The Wide Net," Welty's evocative style points to and lights up some of those rushing mysteries in the lives of rural Mississippians.

Terry Heller

THE WIDOW'S SON

Author: Mary Lavin (1912-   )
Type of plot: Fable
Time of plot: Early twentieth century
Locale: Rural Ireland
First published: 1951

>   *Principal characters:*
>   THE STORYTELLER
>   AN UNNAMED WIDOW
>   PACKY, her fourteen-year-old son
>   AN OLD MAN, her neighbor

The Story

In "The Widow's Son," the storyteller presents two versions of the same story, with different endings.

A poor, illiterate widow in an isolated village has one son who is her "pride and joy," "the meaning of her life," but when he is fourteen and about to reward her sacrifices and her hope by winning a scholarship, he dies in an accident outside their home. The boy is cycling home, faster and faster down a steep hill, and at the bottom he swerves to avoid one òf his mother's hens. The mother is dismayed at the absurdity of the event and simply asks, "Why did he put the price of a hen above the price of his own life?" Her neighbors try to comfort her with "There, now." Her question and their response may imply that the event is beyond comprehension, as if it must simply be accepted as fate; nevertheless, the mother's cry reveals her impatience and irritation with a human error, her son's poor judgment when he swerved.

Earlier in the story, the widow was sketched as a person who had not only accommodated herself to her limited circumstances but also had triumphed over them. Her poverty is compounded by nature, but she is not fatalistic, and by her own industry she has made her small patch of land as productive as a larger farm. Her fierce will to make the best of her situation seems to achieve her triumph until the absurd accident ends everything.

There is a suggestion, however, that this is a story with a form of cruel justice. Perhaps she is too self-centered in her pursuits, too arrogant in the face of a fate that has already made her a widow. She tries to conceal her obsessive love for her son with a gruff exterior, as if she fears the ridicule of her neighbors for the single-mindedness of her devotion. Nor does she discuss her hopes with her son; instead, she threatens him and tries to encourage him to fulfill her goals by making him fearful. Her neighbors, who know her character well, seem to conclude that it is the boy's fear of her which brought him to his death.

This suggestion, that she has been blinded in her dealings with her son by the harsh persona which conceals her sentimental nature, is made explicit in the second version of the story. It begins in the same way as the first and "in many respects . . . is the same as the old." In the conversation between the widow and the old man as they await the son, she denies "in disgust" the suggestion that she has doted on the boy and spoiled him, a "ewe lamb." As if to prove the truth of her denial, when Packy kills the hen rather than himself, she attacks him, beating him over the head with the bleeding hen. This display of anger, which becomes a self-conscious display in front of her neighbors, compromises her; when he reveals that he was rushing home to tell her that he has won a scholarship, she wants to hug him, but she "thought how the crowd would look at each other and nod and snigger," and she does not want to "please them" by demonstrating her joy. Trapped by her own harsh, public persona and angry at the perversity of the situation which has denied her the social respect that the scholarship should have brought her, she begins to attack Packy, to humiliate him, even as she inwardly grieves at the price she is paying for maintaining her pride. The story ends this time with the disappearance of the son, who never returns to her, although he does forward her money as repayment for her sacrifices.

The storyteller presents this second version as if it were the product of the neighbors' gossip and secret speculation, for it reflects their shrewd sense of the woman's character. The narrator now generalizes in the form of a moral, which is usual at the end of a fable or, perhaps, a folktale: that "the path that is destined for us . . . no matter how tragic . . . is better than the tragedy we bring upon ourselves."

Themes and Meanings

The story invites the reader to join in the game of speculating about a road not taken in life and to share the pleasure of the storyteller by inventing an alternative outcome. There are severe limits placed on that speculation, however, for the story seems to imply that the choices made in life are mostly determined by character and by life itself—that there is little free choice. While the first version is granted the reality of action, the second is simply a daydream of what might have been; in each case, though, the outcome is remarkably similar: The mother loses her adored son and the story challenges the reader to wonder if the widow could have avoided her tragic fate.

The simplicity of the folktale in the first version gives prominence to actions which follow as inevitably as the bicycle gains momentum coming down the steep hill. The brevity of the first narrative leaves little room for character analysis; what is added are the shrewd psychological hints which suggest that the widow's motivation is complex and deeply embedded. A comparison of the two versions reveals that the angry confrontation between the widow and her son simply uncovers a hidden well of "disappointment, fear, resentment, and above all defiance." These impulses spring up "like screeching animals" at the sight of blood. The widow, who had appeared as a simple person with a single purpose going calmly about her business, now appears to have an ungovernable character which predetermines her fate; the action, which seemed to be shaped by accident, now seems to mirror the natural anarchy of her own inner self. Most poignant and most frustrating is that she cannot stop herself once the violent energy has been released.

Can this fate be avoided? The narrator offers consolation in the concluding paragraph: "It is only by careful watching, and absolute sincerity, that we follow the path that is destined for us." This path is preferable, even if it is tragic, to the self-made tragedy which issues from one's own blindness or willfulness. In an odd twist, the reader is encouraged to stand back from the obsessive, enclosed world of the proud widow and share in the gossip of her neighbors. Storytelling itself is a form of "careful watching"; the play of invention, of speculating on motive, character, and outcome, demonstrates "the art of the gossip" as well as the art of the storyteller. Both activities, it is suggested, may free people from self-deceptive blindness. The wisdom of the folktale or intuitive psychological speculation contributes to the hope that one may discover one's natural path in life.

Style and Technique

This story seems to break all the rules of modern narrative technique, yet its combination of folktale and self-conscious philosophical speculation is disarming. The mode of country storytelling with a cast of village stereotypes, nameless widow and grass-sucking old man, is mixed with a more literary dramatization of the same situation, and the risks to the fictive illusion are increased by the intrusive comments of a writer/narrator. The effect of a comment such as this is to deflect the reader's resistance to repetition: "After all, what I am about to tell you is no more fiction than what I have already told, and I lean no heavier now upon your credulity than, with your full consent, I did in the first instance." Writer and reader are united in a conspiracy, in the cooperative process of finding meaning in a fable. The brisk tone of presentation and inquiry keeps the momentum of the narrative from flagging, especially in the second version, and the writer's deference to the reader is flattering and involving, as in the process of gossiping.

Lavin's choice of this technique reflects her thematic interest. If the widow ends by appearing to be a mean and self-destructive character, it is the result of her isolation from other people. The story implies that "careful watching, and absolute sincerity" are encouraged in the confidential and cooperative exchanges of gossip or storytelling.

Denis Sampson

WILD SWANS

Author: Alice Munro (1931-   )
Type of plot: Psychological realism
Time of plot: Possibly the late 1940's
Locale: West Hanratty, a small town outside Toronto
First published: 1978

> *Principal characters:*
> ROSE, the protagonist, a high school student
> FLO, her garrulous, motherly adviser
> A UNITED CHURCH MINISTER, her traveling companion on a
>   train

The Story

Before leaving for the first time by herself on a trip to Toronto, paid for from the prize money she won in her school essay competition, young Rose, the protagonist, is warned by Flo against various sexual dangers that could befall a young woman traveling alone. Flo, a motherly, talkative woman— Rose's stepmother in *Who Do You Think You Are?* (1978), Alice Munro's collection of linked short stories from which "Wild Swans" is taken—warns Rose particularly against white slavers who commonly disguise themselves as ministers of the Church. Rose is skeptical, refusing to believe anything the garrulous Flo says on the subject of sex. She recalls an incredible story Flo told her about a retired undertaker who traveled around the countryside seducing women with chocolates and flattery and making love to them in his hearse.

Though Rose is skeptical, Flo's cautionary anecdotes about sexual seduction are very much on her mind. As the train leaves Hanratty, the small town where she lives, she is sitting by herself, absently staring at the passing countryside and thinking of what she will buy in Toronto. The train gradually fills up, and at one of its station stops, a man in his fifties takes the seat beside her. Chatting idly about the spring weather, he casually mentions that he is a United Church minister. He is not wearing a collar, explaining its absence by observing that he is not always in "uniform." He tells her about seeing a magnificent flock of wild swans during a recent drive through the country.

Rose responds to him courteously but briefly, discouraging conversation. Since the morning is cold, she covers herself with her coat. The minister turns to his newspaper and soon falls asleep or appears to fall asleep. His newspaper lies on his lap, adjoining Rose's coat. Rose becomes aware of the tip of the newspaper touching her leg just at the edge of her coat. She wonders if it is in fact the man's hand that is touching her and muses that she often looks at men's hands, wondering what they are capable of. Hands become, in her musing, a metonym for the sensual male, and she recalls fantasizing about being used as a sexual object by a virile French teacher.

In this frame of mind, she becomes aware that it is indeed a hand, not the tip of the newspaper, that is touching her leg. The hand is gradually moving to her thigh. She wants to protest, but initially curiosity and then sexual excitement weaken, then suppress, any protestation. The hand titillates her and brings her to a climax, which is described in terms of a flock of wild swans explosively taking to the sky. Munro's account of this seduction is replete with ambiguity. The reader is never certain whether the hand is imagined or actually there. Is it possible that Rose is fantasizing? She does say at one point that her "imagination seemed to have created this reality," an observation which, however, with its use of "seemed," encourages rather than eliminates ambiguity.

As the train pulls into Toronto, the passengers begin to stir and the minister awakens or appears to awaken. He offers to help her with her coat, and when she declines, he hurries out of the train ahead of her. Rose is never to see him again in her life, the narrator states, but she is often to recall him and his "simplicity, his arrogance, his perversely appealing lack of handsomeness." She speculates as she leaves the train on whether he is actually a minister, and for the first time since meeting him, she consciously recalls Flo's warning about white slavers disguised as ministers.

Munro provides a postscript to this incident. As Rose steps off the train, she remembers Flo mentioning a woman named Mavis who works at the Toronto station. Flo told her that Mavis once went for a weekend to a Georgian Bay resort, pretending to be the actress Frances Farmer. Flo, observing that she could have been arrested for impersonation, admired her "nerve." Rose, too, in the final sentence of the story, expresses admiration for Mavis' daring act: "To dare it; to get away with it, to enter on preposterous adventures in your own, but newly named, skin." Munro evidently intends this as Rose's conscious or unconscious comment on her own preposterous adventures on the train.

Themes and Meanings

Munro believes that the individual's true emotional, psychological, moral, and cerebral motivations are complex and elusive. Consequently, human experience cannot really be portrayed in any objective, categorical way. The brief but poignant incident from Rose's life illustrates clearly Munro's artistic credo. She inclusively suggests various ways of interpreting Rose's experience, leaving readers to draw their own conclusions.

In her deliberate and skillful use of ambiguity in depicting Rose's response to the liberties taken by the United Church minister, Munro wants the reader not only to know but also to experience how difficult it is at times for the individual to separate fantasy from reality. Narrated strictly from Rose's point of view, the story allows the reader into her consciousness, making it possible to experience vicariously the overwhelming force of fantasy and imagination.

Responding to the story as a portrayal of an actual seduction leads the reader into a consideration of society's immorality and hypocrisy and, more important, of Rose's motivations in reacting the way she does. Is she an innocent experiencing awakening sensuality? The narrator suggests that her acquiescence to the minister's probing hand is not sensuality or passivity, but an overpowering appetite for experience: "Curiosity. More constant, more imperious, than any lust. A lust in itself, that will make you draw back and wait, wait too long, risk almost anything, just to see what will happen." Munro, in an interview, reiterated explicitly this interpretation of Rose's inaction. She said that the story describes how the individual reacts to "something unthinkable" and that Rose exhibits not "passivity but curiosity."

In the first published version of this story, Munro did not include the concluding episode concerning Mavis' impersonation of Frances Farmer. In appending this ending to the later version published in *Who Do You Think You Are?*, Munro added another contiguous dimension to Rose's experience. Rose, who at the beginning of the story is portrayed as acquiescent to the milk vendor whom Flo challenges, now shares Flo's admiration for Mavis' audacity in pretending to be Frances Farmer, and, by extension, she perhaps reluctantly admires the minister's boldness as well. Given Munro's deliberately ambiguous portrayal, Rose quite likely also admires her own nerve in indulging in sexual fantasizing on a crowded train. Mavis' "preposterous adventure" in her "own, but newly named, skin" parallels Rose's own just-concluded adventure experienced in actuality or perhaps in her own young, vibrant imagination.

Style and Technique

In James Joyce's short story "Araby," a work with which Munro is familiar, the young narrator moves effortlessly between his real and imagined worlds, often not distinguishing between the two. In a crucial scene relating a conversation between the narrator and the girl he loves, Joyce uses deliberate ambiguity to allow the reader to feel the intensity of the boy's imagination. The reader is never categorically sure whether the conversation actually takes place or is fabricated by the highly imaginative youth.

In the crucial scene of her story, Munro also employs the technique of ambiguity to point up, like Joyce, the thin demarcation between fantasy and actuality and to induce the reader to share vicariously in the protagonist's experience. There are several ambiguous phrases and images. Many sentences overtly suggest that initially it is Rose's imagination which perceives the tip of the newspaper to be the minister's hand: "She thought for some time that it was the paper. Then she said to herself, what if it is a hand? That was the kind of thing she could imagine." Immediately after, she wonders: "What if it really was a hand?" Perhaps the sentence which most emphatically persuades the reader to acknowledge the possibility of ambiguity in Rose's perception of the seduction is this one: "Her imagination seemed to have created this reality, a reality she was not prepared for at all."

Rose's perception of the man's reclining posture is equally ambiguous. Could he be actually sleeping? As she looks at him, she observes that he "had arranged the paper so that it overlapped Rose's coat. His hand was underneath, simply resting, as if flung out in sleep." When the train reaches Toronto, Rose notes that the minister, "refreshed," opens his eyes. Is he refreshed from actually sleeping or from the sexual encounter? Rose assesses his offer to help her with her coat as "self-satisfied, dismissive." Is this because of the unprotested liberties he took with Rose or is it simply an aspect of his personality?

Munro has sharp eyes and ears for particulars of the individual's traits and behavior. For example, she alerts the reader to Flo's pronunciation of the words "bad women," which are run together like "badminton." Some details have only tenuous thematic and narrative significance and are included essentially to create authenticity of people and places. A good example of this Chekhovian technique is the account of Flo's accosting the vendor of sour milk at the Hanratty station. Munro effectively uses details of nature to convey the protagonist's feelings: The reference to the sensual wild swans in the title and the story is appropriate, and Rose's imagined or real orgasm is poetically conveyed through a host of natural (and artificial) images that flash by the train window.

Victor J. Ramraj

THE WILL

Author: Mary Lavin (1912-   )
Type of plot: Domestic realism
Time of plot: The 1940's
Locale: Rural Ireland
First published: 1944

> *Principal characters:*
> LALLY CONROY, the disinherited daughter and protagonist
> KATE CONROY, the oldest child and the family leader
> MATTHEW CONROY, the only male child
> NONNY CONROY, the youngest child

The Story

Mary Lavin's "The Will" is set in rural Ireland; in such a rural locale, the people tend to be excessively concerned about respectability and to be afflicted with a meanness of spirit. The story begins soon after the mother's will has been read by a solicitor. The four children then discuss the consequences of the mother's cutting Lally out of the will. What follows is a series of contrasts, and some conflicts: between the children who remained in the rural Irish town—Kate, Matthew, and Nonny—and Lally, who left home at an early age for the city and marriage.

The first contrast is between the practical, and socially respectable, desire of the other children to provide Lally with some of the money taken away from her by the will and Lally's steadfast refusal to violate her mother's wishes. Kate takes the lead and prods Matthew to suggest that each of them will contribute to Lally a part of the money they received. Their concern seems, for the most part, to be for what people will say rather than for their sister. Matthew says, "We won't let it be said by anyone that we'd see you in want, Lally." Lally, however, resists their attempt to circumvent their mother's will; she believes that such a plan would be in violation of her mother's wishes and that, if her mother did not wish her to have the money, she should not have it. Lally has a sense of fairness and justice that contrasts with the others' attempt to preserve respectability.

Such a contrast can also be seen in her reaction to the next proposal by Matthew. Matthew offers to pool their resources and purchase a hotel in the city for Lally to run. In his eyes, a hotel would be more respectable than the boardinghouse that Lally now has: "It would be in the interests of the family," he tells Lally, "if you were to give up keeping lodgers." Lally rejects this proposal as well. She thinks of her departed husband rather than respectability. "I'd hate to be making a lot of money and Robert gone where he couldn't profit by it." She is interested in fulfilling people's desires and does not worry about what people think.

Another contrast is that Lally, although an exile from the house, is the only one to display any feeling for her mother's death. She cries when she remembers her mother and their relationship before she left home, "but the tears upset the others, who felt no inclination to cry." She also cries when she hears that her mother's last words were "blue feathers"—Lally had worn those blue feathers the day she left home to go to the city. It is obvious that the mother felt much affection for Lally. She could not, however, rise above her social prejudices. Kate says that the mother "might have forgiven your marriage in time, but she couldn't forgive you for lowering yourself in keeping lodgers." In contrast, Lally overcomes her mother's attitude and continues to love her.

The next contrast is that all the family members except Lally treat appearance(s) as reality; Lally consistently refuses to do so. Nonny is worried that people will think that the family has quarreled about the will, but Lally responds, "What does it matter what they say, as long as we know it isn't true." Appearances mean nothing to Lally; what matters is what people know. Both Matthew and Kate, on the other hand, take their stand for, as Kate says, "keeping up appearances." The others also have a "grudge" against Lally for her run-down appearance, which reminds them of what they, too, will someday be. Kate says, "You're disgusting to look at." Nonny joins in, "I'd be ashamed to be seen talking to you." Lally does not answer them or even acknowledge their insults; she has things to do in the city and must go. The others oppose her leaving on the same day of the burial, but this is more for appearance' sake than Lally's:

All of them, even the maid servant who was clearing away the tray, were agreed that it was bad enough for people to know she was going back the very night that her mother was lowered into the clay, without adding to the scandal by giving people a chance to say that her brother, Matthew, wouldn't drive her to the train in his car, and it pouring rain.

The story shifts its focus from the conflict between Lally and her family to Lally's own thoughts as she leaves the house to return to the city. She recalls her earlier dream of escaping from the town and finding "the mystery of life." Now she realizes that she was not changed by marriage, or her life in the city, or by keeping a boardinghouse: "You were yourself always, no matter where you went or what you did." Lally does, however, believe in one change: The change of death and what happens after death is the mystery. She begins to remember tales of souls being tortured from the catechism and suddenly becomes troubled by the state of her mother's soul. She rushes into a church and asks the priest to say some masses for her mother's soul. She tells the priest, "She was very bitter against me all the time, and she died without forgiving me. I'm afraid for her soul." The priest tells her that Mrs. Conroy has left three hundred pounds for masses, but Lally believes that "it's the masses that other people have said for you that count." What is needed is a sacrifice by one person for another, not the performance of a ritual.

She rushes to catch the train, but her thoughts are still with her mother as she sits in the train. She thinks that she may have some money left after buying food for herself and her children, and this money will be used for ten masses and to light some candles at the Convent of Perpetual Reparation. Lally is confused, even feverish, but what is important is the contrast between her feelings and concern for her mother and the coldness of the others. Even Mrs. Conroy is cold and calculating, with her three hundred pounds for masses, while her daughter lives in poverty. Only Lally cares.

Themes and Meanings

The most important theme of "The Will" emerges from the contrast between outward appearance and inner reality. All but Lally are concerned with social respectability, with appearances only. Nonny says, "I don't know why you were so anxious to marry him when it meant keeping lodgers." Only Lally knows what is real and what is primary: "It was the other way around, . . . I was willing to keep lodgers because it meant I could marry him." For her, the unchanging self within, relationships with others, the feeling and knowledge of others are real. The others can never act without an eye to what others will say or think, and therefore they can have no immediate or spontaneous feelings. They are trapped by their worship of mere appearance. In contrast, Lally remains free to do what seems right and important, whether it be helping a new lodger move in, marrying someone of whom her family does not approve, or trying to lift her mother out of Purgatory with her dearly bought masses.

Style and Technique

One important technique in the story is the shift of point of view. In the first part of the story the point of view is third-person limited. The narrator describes the characters or the place but refuses to enter the thoughts of those characters. When Lally leaves the house, however, the narrator enters the mind of Lally and records her thoughts. The narration mirrors the change from a social scene to a personal and reflective one. It is essential that the reader know Lally's thoughts in the second part of the story in order to evaluate her actions in the first part, and only a change in the type of narration can accomplish this.

One element of style needs to be mentioned: the use of imagery at the end of the story. The images of darkness and those of red ("the dark train," "through the darkness," "red sparks," and "burning sparks") fill Lally's mind and remind her of the mother's suffering in Purgatory and make her feel confused and feverish, and these feelings impel her to take some action to relieve her mother's suffering. The penultimate paragraph begins with Lally feeling some "peace," but that peace is driven out by the images.

James Sullivan

WILL YOU PLEASE BE QUIET, PLEASE?

Author: Raymond Carver (1938-)
Type of plot: Psychological realism
Time of plot: The 1970's
Locale: Eureka, a town in Northern California
First published: 1976

> *Principal characters:*
> RALPH WYMAN, the protagonist, a high school teacher
> MARIAN WYMAN, his wife

The Story

The first few pages of "Will You Please Be Quiet, Please?" run quickly through ten years in the life of Ralph Wyman, a young man whose father tells him, upon Ralph's graduation from high school, that life is a "very serious matter" and "an arduous undertaking," which, despite its difficulties, can still be rewarding. Early in his college career, Ralph finds himself discarding potential careers he had envisioned for himself—law and medicine—when he finds the work too difficult or emotionally stultifying. He turns to literature and philosophy, in which he finds some stimulation. Most of his first college years, however, he spends aboard a stool in the local pub, until one special teacher, Dr. Maxwell, changes his life. Maxwell's influence reshapes Ralph's sense of his own future, and he becomes a "serious student," joins a variety of campus organizations, finds himself a wife, Marian, and diligently prepares himself, during his last year, to become a teacher.

Before taking teaching positions in a small town in Northern California, Ralph and Marian marry. One afternoon on their honeymoon, Ralph walks up the road below their hotel and catches a glimpse of his new wife standing with her arms over the ironwork balustrade, her long black hair spun out by the breeze. The image is stunning, but the memory of her pose haunts him later because somehow he cannot see himself as part of the exotic world in which he imagined her for only that moment.

Five years pass quickly, and Ralph and Marian have two children. Marian teaches music at the local community college, but Ralph continues at the high school. One Sunday night, the only event to shock the quality of their relationship emerges from a memory that each has tried to bury, a memory which has reinforced Ralph's fearful image of his wife on their Mexican honeymoon. When Marian, quite whimsically, brings up the matter of her leaving a party one night with another man two years earlier, Ralph pursues her lead and tries hard to pin her down on what it was, exactly, that had happened between them. Two years before, she had claimed that nothing at all had occurred.

Ralph's paranoia becomes evident as he pushes his wife, almost mercilessly, to reveal the truth. Slowly and painfully, the story unravels itself, and Ralph discovers that the worst fears he has carried with him since that night are warranted. Very emotionally, Marian confesses her guilt.

The second half of the story opens later that night, as Ralph has begun a drinking binge. He has left the house to drink, and he finds himself wandering in and out of downtown bars. As he staggers down the street, he picks up pieces of conversations that haunt him with their application to Marian's confession of her infidelity. He wanders through bars jammed with people, across steamy dance floors, and into restrooms where walls are marked with lurid obscenities. In his confusion, things he sees and hears strike him as haunting moral lessons only half-understood.

For a few minutes, he takes refuge in the back room of a bar, where a card game is in progress. After playing a few hands with the men around the table, he blurts out what had happened in an almost matter-of-fact tone, but the cardplayers appear untouched by his trauma. He leaves and heads out to the pier, where, as he imagines, Dr. Maxwell, his favorite professor, would likely sit and watch the waves to try to come to some understanding of his problem. Ralph finds no solace near the water, however, as he is beaten by a man in a leather jacket.

It is almost morning when he opens his eyes and realizes that he has nowhere to go but home. When his children awaken, they find him sitting up, his face laced with dried blood. He runs to the bathroom to hide. Marian, obviously distraught from his absence and the specter of his bloody face, begs him to come out. He simply tells her to be quiet and prepares to take a bath. Once the children are gone, he leaves the bathroom and gets into bed. Still unsure of how he must react to his wife, he lies perfectly still when she comes to him and tries to get him to talk. When she moves toward him sexually, he tries to stay away as long as he can, but finally he cannot battle what he feels growing within him and he turns to her, "marveling at the impossible changes he felt moving over him."

Themes and Meanings

Raymond Carver is sometimes unjustly accused of creating only the kinds of characters who lack cunning and insight. Ralph Wyman may lack the ability to understand how to deal with what is, for him, a very traumatic moment in his life, but his inability to deal with his wife's confession cannot be blamed on stupidity. Ralph's drunken wanderings occur because he is slowly discovering the basic truth of what his father had told him years before, that life is a very serious matter.

This idea is the basic theme of Carver's story: Ralph's own initiation into the very serious matter of life itself. As the son of a grade-school principal, as a college kid with too grandiose visions of his own ability, even as a student who drops out of the mold for awhile, and as a converted "serious student" who then marries and tries, not unsuccessfully, to take a respectable position in a comfortable small town, Ralph Wyman still must learn the horrors of living in a world in which one's expectations may not always be met, in which weakness is a given, and in which deceit, like a bad memory, thrives in the silence of a guilty, human heart.

The most interesting twist which Carver administers to his very traditional initiation story is the way the story ends, Ralph's surrendering to his own physicality in turning to respond to his wife's attention. Readers often expect that initiation stories will end in what James Joyce called an "epiphany," a moment of seeing the whole truth. Carver sets the reader up for such a revelation, but then concludes not with clarity but with more complexity, the mystery of that dynamic human force, desire. Trying to stay away from his wife completely, Ralph cannot keep his body from responding to her when she wants his forgiveness. He is, in fact, powerless in the surge of desire which rises in him. As confused as he is in trying to know how to act toward Marian, he cannot stop from turning to meet her. He stands in awe as he sees how very little he understands.

Does Ralph understand more about himself and Marian at the end of the story? He probably does not. Yet the limits of his experience have been reset, and he knows much more about "this serious matter" of life.

Style and Technique

Raymond Carver is often associated with those contemporary writers who have been described as "minimalists." The term is meant to describe, among other characteristics, a style which lacks amplitude, which handles both emotional extremes in monotone, as if true joy and pain do not exist. In this story, however, Carver's protagonist feels deeply the pain of his wife's revelation, even though the pain is dulled for a few hours by his drunkenness.

Another characteristic of the minimalist technique is often thought to be an extremely short and abrupt style. Carver's word choice never reaches beyond very ordinary, contemporary language, and his sentences are often short, giving the texture of his fiction an almost machine-gunlike, staccato touch and sound. Yet there is little about this story to make it anything more or less than traditional. Time is used realistically throughout; the style, while short and abrupt, never stands in the way of the story line. Carver's descriptions are never vapid and emotionless, but instead are sharp and convincing, especially when he follows Ralph's trek to a greater sense of his own mystery in those vivid scenes which capture the reality of dizzying drunkenness prompted by self-destroying paranoia.

James C. Schaap

WILLIAM WILSON

Author: Edgar Allan Poe (1809-1849)
Type of plot: Parable or allegory
Time of plot: The 1820's and 1830's
Locale: An unnamed village, Eton College and Oxford University in England,
   and Rome, Italy
First published: 1839

> Principal characters:
>   WILLIAM WILSON, the narrator and protagonist, an infamous
>   criminal
>   WILLIAM WILSON, the rival and opponent of the narrator

The Story

"William Wilson" is a tale narrated by an infamous criminal who is on the verge of death. He is ashamed to reveal his name; William Wilson is an admitted pseudonym. As death approaches, he tries to explain the momentous event that led to his life of misery and crime. His greatest fear is that he has forfeited heavenly bliss as well as earthly honor.

The path to the single event responsible for Wilson's criminality begins in an ancient, dreamlike English village whose memories alone now afford him pleasure. The village includes the church and academy that Wilson attends from age ten to fifteen. Dr. Bransby, the pastor of the church, is also principal of the academy, and Wilson marvels at the "gigantic paradox" that allows one man to be both a benign clergyman and a stern disciplinarian. The academy is set apart from the mist-enclosed village by a ponderous wall and a spike-studded gate. Old and irregular, with endless windings and subdivisions, the school building becomes for the narrator a palace of enchantment. Even the low and dismal classroom is a source of spirit-stirring and passionate excitement.

At the academy, Wilson wins control over all of his fellows but one—a classmate with the same name as his. The two William Wilsons are identical in height and figure, move and walk in the same way, and dress alike. In fact, they were born on the same date and enter school at the same time. They seem to differ only in voice: The narrator speaks in normal tones, his namesake in a low whisper.

As time passes, their rivalry intensifies. They quarrel daily because of what the narrator calls his namesake's "intolerable spirit of contradiction." Yet the narrator admits in retrospect that his rival was his superior in moral sense, if not in worldly wisdom, and that he would be a better and happier man today had he more often taken the advice given him.

Late one night, bent upon a malicious joke, the narrator steals through narrow passages to his namesake's room. There, as he looks into the sleeper's face, he is overcome with such horror that he nearly swoons: The face he sees is identical to his own. Awestruck, the narrator flees to Eton College, where he soon dismisses what he has seen as an illusion. During an evening of prolonged debauchery, however, he encounters a shadowy figure who admonishes him with the whispered words "William Wilson" and then vanishes. This scene is reenacted at Oxford University. Just as the narrator's cheating at cards brings Lord Glendinning, an aristocrat, to the brink of financial ruin, a stranger of the narrator's height mysteriously appears. He points to evidence of the narrator's cheating and, before disappearing, leaves behind a coat that is the duplicate of the narrator's own.

The narrator leaves Oxford, but he flees in vain. In Paris and Berlin, in Vienna and Moscow, he is thwarted by the figure he now regards as his archenemy and evil genius. Yet even as the narrator acknowledges his namesake's elevated character and majestic wisdom, he vows to submit no longer. The confrontation occurs in Rome at the masquerade party of Duke Di Broglio, an aged Neapolitan nobleman. As the narrator threads his way through the crowd to seduce the young and beautiful wife of the duke, he feels a light hand on his shoulder, hears a low whisper in his ear, and sees a figure attired in a costume identical to his own. In a voice husky with rage, he orders the figure to follow him to an antechamber or be stabbed on the spot.

Inside the antechamber, they struggle briefly before Wilson repeatedly stabs his namesake through the bosom. Yet it now seems as if there is a mirror in the room where none had been before, because Wilson sees his own image—spattered with blood—directly in front of him. Wilson soon realizes that what he sees is not a reflection; it is the blood-dabbled figure of his namesake. With his dying words, no longer in a whisper, the namesake says that Wilson has murdered himself and, in doing so, has lost all hope for happiness on earth or in Heaven.

Themes and Meanings

Poe often deals with the theme of the divided self or the split in personality, and "William Wilson" is his most obvious story of the war within. Poe links the two William Wilsons—they have the same name, common physical traits, and identical histories—to show that the two are doubles or twins or parts of the same self. What part of the self does each represent? The story's epigraph suggests the identity of the second William Wilson: "What say of it? what say [of] CONSCIENCE grim,/ That spectre in my path?" The second William Wilson, who comes and goes like a specter or apparition, represents the conscience or moral sense; that is why, as the gentle but persistent voice within, he speaks only in a low whisper and why no one other than the narrator ever sees him. Since the second William Wilson stands for the spiritual or heavenly part of the self, it is appropriate that his death costs the now-soulless narrator all chance for an afterlife: The narrator represents the earthly, mundane, physical part of the self that above all seeks pleasure, power, money, and conquest. So long as the conscience or spiritual self is present to restrain its earthly counterpart, Wilson's villainy is limited to drinking, swearing, and cheating at cards. Once the spiritual self is destroyed, however, there occurs a "sudden elevation in turpitude," and the earthly self turns to serious crime. The civil war in "William Wilson" ends with the triumph of the physical self over the spiritual self, but the price of victory is the loss of eternal life.

Style and Technique

One of Poe's favorite techniques is to tell a story in such a manner that the reader is not quite sure what happens. In "William Wilson," for example, it is not easy to know what Wilson actually sees when he looks into his namesake's face or, in the final scene, when he confronts the blood-spattered figure that may or may not be his reflection. Poe refuses to make his tales transparent for two major reasons. First, he is convinced that, in the nature of things, truth is difficult to know because it is difficult to separate appearance from reality. William Wilson admits that he may have hallucinated the events of his story and that his entire existence may be a dream. Second, Poe deliberately blurs events so that the reader will question the story's literal level and look beneath its surface to discover allegorical meanings.

On a literal level, William Wilson and his namesake are distinct individuals; on an allegorical level, the two represent the warring parts—the physical and the spiritual—of the divided self. Allegorically, it makes sense that William Wilson does not become aware of his namesake's existence until age ten, the age, according to Poe, at which psychic wholeness is lost and the split in consciousness emerges. It makes equally good allegorical sense that William Wilson sees less and less of his spiritual self as the split in consciousness widens and intensifies with age.

The story's major events and characters all have allegorical significance. That Dr. Bransby is both a benevolent pastor and a rigid schoolmaster underlines the theme that all human beings are made up of contradictory impulses. That William Wilson spends his early years in a remote, circumscribed, and dreamlike setting suggests, allegorically, that the child's vision has not yet been compromised by contact with the mundane world. That the final confrontation between the earthly Wilson and his spiritual counterpart occurs during a masquerade is allegorically appropriate; indeed, Poe uses this pattern in "The Cask of Amontillado," "Hop-Frog," and "The Masque of the Red Death" as well. In Poe's writings, to cover oneself with a mask or a veil or a costume is to retreat temporarily from consciousness of the outer world to consciousness of the inner world, site of the civil war that rages in every human breast. Poe's deliberate obscurity both points to the complexity of

truth and invites the reader to look for allegorical meanings beneath the surface of the tale.

Donald A. Daiker

WILLIS CARR AT BLEAK HOUSE

Author: David Madden (1933-   )
Type of plot: Historical fiction
Time of plot: March 21, 1928, with flashbacks to 1860-1867
Locale: Knoxville and Holston Mountain, Tennessee; various sites in Virginia; and out West
First published: 1985

Principal characters:

WILLIS CARR, the protagonist, a veteran of the American Civil War and a sharpshooter during the siege of Knoxville
GENERAL JAMES LONGSTREET, Confederate general and commander of Rebel forces during the Knoxville siege
WILLIAM PRICE SANDERS, a Union general subordinate to General Ambrose Burnside, the federal commander in Knoxville

The Story

David Madden sets Willis Carr's stories about his experiences as a soldier during the American Civil War within the framework of a meeting of the Knoxville Chapter of the Daughters of the Confederacy on March 21, 1928. Indeed, the entire story takes the form of the report of the organization's secretary. Introduced by Professor Jeffrey Arnow, a member of the history department at the University of Tennessee, Carr tells the women gathered in the Music Room at Bleak House what he remembers about the siege of Knoxville (in November and December of 1863), part of which he spent as a sharpshooter in the tower at Bleak House itself.

Carr's story is rambling, slightly unfocused, and structured by the process of association. He is roughly eighty-two years old, having been born on Holton Mountain, Tennessee, in 1846, and he was fourteen when he served under Confederate General James Longstreet in what his hostesses prefer to call "the War Between the States." Carr remembers that he was suffering from a fever when he reached Knoxville in 1863, which accounts for the haziness of his recollections. He does remember Bleak House clearly and tells his audience that there was a man painting a fresco on a wall downstairs during the military action. He remembers, too, that he was one of four sharpshooters sent up in the tower of the house. When one of them was killed and the other two wounded, Carr sighted an officer on a white horse dashing back and forth between the Yankee and Rebel lines. He remembers thinking that this was a hallucination induced by fever, for no officer on either side would behave so recklessly, and he shot at the man, thinking that he could do the phantom rider no harm.

Two years after the war was over, Carr returned to Tennessee from the West. Stopping in some small town—he thinks that it was Pulaski—he met and sketched a man introduced as the killer of General Sanders during the fight at Knoxville. Having returned to Holton Mountain and swept the decomposed body of his great-grandfather into the fireplace, Carr remembered one day while hunting bear the officer on the white horse in Knoxville. It came to him that this might have been General Sanders, and he remarks to his audience that he has walked all the way to Knoxville to revisit Bleak House in an attempt to determine if he, Willis Carr, is really the sharpshooter who killed the Union general.

To this point in the story, Carr has the characteristics of the kind of heroic figure his audience might be expected to admire. He goes back to the start of the war in his speech, however, and in explaining his involvement destroys his potential for heroic status in their eyes. He explains that his East Tennessee family, with the exception of his mother, were Union sympathizers. His grandfather, father, and brothers took part in raids against railroad bridges instigated by Parson Brownlow to handicap the movement of Rebel troops. Carr himself ended up in Longstreet's army because he was picked up in Knoxville as a Union sympathizer and agreed to join the Confederate troops to keep himself from being hanged. He intended to desert to the Federals as soon as possible, he remarks, but he enjoyed being a sharpshooter so much that he remained with Longstreet and served at Gettysburg and in the Wilderness.

Carr remembers the actual Confederate attack on the fort, renamed in honor of General Sanders, in Knoxville, and describes how helpless he felt watching his comrades being slaughtered. When General Longstreet himself was shot, during the Wilderness Campaign in Virginia, by one of his own troops, Carr got discouraged and deserted in a Yankee uniform. Picked up by Confederate soldiers and taken to Andersonville Prison, he was saved from execution as a deserter only because he was recognized as a sharpshooter by one of the Federal prisoners. Carr was made a guard by the Commandant of Andersonville, Captain Wirtz. A black Yankee soldier, formerly the slave of a Cherokee plantation owner, told him about the Indian Sequoyah, who invented an alphabet for Cherokee, preserving it as a written language, and this encouraged Carr to want to learn to read and write. The prisoner taught him, but one day he stepped over the dead line and was shot by his pupil.

Carr is not sure why he killed this man, just as he is not certain if he is the sharpshooter who picked off General Sanders. He has read much about the war in the years since it ended, and he tells the members of the Knoxville Daughters of the Confederacy that he cannot believe that he was really a part of the Civil War until he can answer both questions. He notes that he remembers sketching the faces of his three fellow sharpshooters on the west wall of the tower in Bleak House, and if the sketches are still there, they would provide him with firm evidence of his participation. Still, he remarks at the end of his talk, he does not think that he has the strength at his age to climb all those steps.

Themes and Meanings

On its most fundamental level, Madden's story deals with the relationship between historical fact and individual experience. Willis Carr's difficulty in finding the connection between events in his own life and statements accepted as historical truth dramatizes the problem that concerns Madden. The death of General Sanders is an event either totally separate from Carr's life or intimately part of it. The alternatives suggest differing philosophical conclusions. If Carr can prove that he was part of the war, that he did kill Sanders, then he can conclude that his actions have meaning and that he has some control over events in his life. If he cannot obtain that assurance, he must conclude that he lives in an absurd universe in which an individual is acted upon by events and cannot shape them.

Madden does not provide a clear resolution of the dilemma that his protagonist faces. Carr is aware that there are two competing historical accounts of the death of General Sanders. In the first, the general is shot while, mounted on his white horse, he leads troops along the Kingston Pike. In the second, an English adventurer named Winthrop was mounted on that horse, and the general was shot while standing on a hill overlooking the battle. If the first account is true, the man at whom Carr shot was General Sanders, and he can claim a place in history. If the second account is true, however, Carr has no place in history, even if he was present during the skirmishing around Knoxville in 1863.

"Willis Carr at Bleak House" also has its lighter side. Madden is enjoying the idea of Carr, an irreverent East Tennessee hillman, speaking to the Daughters of the Confederacy and failing to confirm any of the conventional notions about the War Between the States. Carr does not see himself as serving a noble cause; his were Union, not Confederate, sympathies, and he stayed with General Longstreet because he enjoyed shooting people, not because he believed in the Confederacy.

Style and Technique

Madden places Willis Carr's account of the past within the framework of a meeting of the Daughters of the Confederacy, and the humor of the story arises from the juxtaposition of Carr's narrative and the impersonal framework of the secretary's report. In addition to the implied comment about the unsatisfactory role Carr fills as speaker to this organization, Madden employs a broader humor in the story. The anecdote about Carr sweeping great-grandfather into the fireplace seems material straight out of folklore, as does

Carr's account of himself outrunning the horses of his grandfather, father, and brothers on the way to Knoxville.

More significant is the fact that Madden makes Willis Carr an artist. Even while working as a sharpshooter in Longstreet's forces, he sketches the faces of his companions on the west wall of the tower in Bleak House. After the wall, he tells his audience in Knoxville, he supported himself for two years out West by sketching men he met in bars. Several times during his speech, he refers to the man painting a fresco in Bleak House during the fighting going on outside. These details give substance to Carr's statement that he has come back to Knoxville to attempt to answer questions that will enable him to feel a part of the war. Like a painter, he is attempting to see the face of truth and to fix it permanently. The story suggests that both Carr's desire for certainty and his failure to attain it are inevitable.

Robert C. Petersen

THE WILLOWS

Author: Algernon Blackwood (1869-1951)
Type of plot: Horror
Time of plot: 1905
Locale: Hungary
First published: 1907

Principal characters:
THE UNNAMED NARRATOR, the protagonist
HIS COMPANION, a Swedish man

The Story

The first-person narrator and his companion, a Swedish man, are on a canoe trip, intending to travel the entire length of the Danube River to the Black Sea. The river is in flood and has swiftly carried them into Hungary and a completely wild and uninhabited area. As far as the eye can see, there is nothing on either bank but limitless clusters of large willow bushes.

They decide to stop overnight on one of the many small islands dotting the river, and upon setting up camp are almost immediately confronted by two odd sights which serve to set the tone for their stay. A strange creature, almost like an otter, is seen floating down the river turning over and over, while shortly afterward they see a "flying apparition" traveling rapidly down the river, resembling a man in a boat who seems to be making the sign of the cross and shouting wildly at them. These odd events serve as a stimulus to the narrator's imagination, and he realizes that the beauty of the wild landscape also contains weirdness, even terror, such as the howling wind, raging water, and especially the constantly moving willow branches.

Later that night, the narrator undergoes stranger encounters. Peering out of his tent, he sees in the moonlight a column of odd shapes or beings rising out of a clump of willows and disappearing into the sky, the figures appearing to melt in and out of one another. The sight is so strange and majestic that the narrator almost gets down on his knees to worship. Later that night in his tent, he hears a pattering sound, as of innumerable tiny steps, coming from outside his tent, and also feels as if a great weight is pressing down on him. He goes out and looks around and realizes that the willows seem to have moved closer to the tent during the night.

The next morning, the narrator hopes to have his staid and unimaginative traveling companion convince him that he has been dreaming, but instead he hears the astonishing revelation that a canoe paddle is missing and there is a tear in the bottom of the canoe. Adding to this ominous note, the companion divulges his feeling that mysterious forces in the area sense their presence and will try to make them victims. Increasing their tension is the discovery of small conical holes in the sand all over the island.

The damage to the canoe means that they will have to spend another day and night on the island for repairs, which is disquieting news. That night at supper, they find that the bread is missing from their provision sack. It is just at this time that a sound like a ringing gong is heard coming from the sky, although it also seems to come from the willow bushes and even from inside their bodies. They are now fully convinced that these sounds and the other manifestations can only be nonhuman in origin and are almost certainly threatening.

The narrator's companion, believing that they have trespassed on the grounds of another world, explains that they must keep quiet and especially not think about the alien forces; otherwise the two will be found and sacrificed. As if in corroboration, when one of them shouts, a strange cry is heard in the sky directly overhead and the gonging comes nearer.

Late that night, they go out hunting for firewood and see a sight so frightening that it makes one of them faint. Looking back at the camp which they have just left, they see a large, dark, rolling shape almost like the willow bushes in appearance, apparently looking for them and starting to come in their direction. They are saved only because one of them has fainted while the other is distracted by a sudden pain, thus preventing their minds from dwelling on the approaching entity, causing it to lose their location. When they get back to their camp, they see that the sand around it is completely riddled with the same conical holes.

The final confrontation comes later that night, when the narrator awakens and discovers that his companion is missing, while the gonging and pattering noises are louder than they have ever been. He finds his friend in a trance, about to jump into the river, and drags him back into the tent. At this point, all sounds cease and his friend suddenly grows calm, says that "they" have found a victim, and falls asleep peacefully.

The next morning, much relaxed, the companion repeats that a victim evidently was found and they will see evidence of this if they search. They indeed discover the corpse of a man in the water, caught in the willows. When they touch the body, the same gonging sound rises up into the air from it and fades away. To their horror, they see the same conical holes in the body that are in the sand and realize that these are the marks of the beings or entities into whose territory they have accidentally ventured.

Themes and Meanings

Algernon Blackwood was the foremost exponent of the outdoor supernatural story, although he also wrote the more claustrophobic indoor (haunted house) variety. Set in a free and untrammeled wilderness, "The Willows" luxuriates in a near-pantheistic treatment of nature; the river, the wind, and the willows are described in personifying terms and can frighten as well as charm. There is an accompanying idea, openly expressed by the narrator, that this world of nature is pure and human presence only spoils it.

Yet there appears in this story a related but more radical theme: that there is an unseen world pressing close to common reality. The story turns not on nature spirits or deities so much as on another world or dimension which intersects that of the reader and is completely unrelated to the human scheme of things. In this, "The Willows" differs from most of Blackwood's nature stories, in which the preternatural phenomena are nature spirits or demons (as in "The Wendigo" and "Glamour of the Snow"). "The Willows" is typical of Blackwood's other stories, however, in its setting in the middle of a virgin wilderness, given Blackwood's underlying idea that nature is separate from the human sphere and contact with civilization can only spoil it.

An interesting feature is that the beings or forces inhabiting this other reality are dangerous but not actually threatening to the human world if left alone, an idea differing from Arthur Machen (1863-1947), another English outdoor specialist, and especially the American H. P. Lovecraft (1890-1937), whose beings are ready to destroy the earth. Again, this idea is a reflection of Blackwood's near-worship of nature and his dim view of human presence in it. Interestingly, the narrator feels almost like worshiping the entities he sees ascending to the sky.

Style and Technique

Blackwood's stories have been most famous for their style, and it is the use of suggestion rather than literal depiction or explanation that has contributed most to his style. This use of suggestion and ambiguity adds greatly to atmosphere and tension. Lovecraft labeled Blackwood as the supreme master of weird atmosphere, and this story is regarded as Blackwood's best.

The nature of the forces that assault the travelers is never clarified, and the conception of these forces grows and changes as the story progresses. The relationship of the various things seen (the beings ascending to the sky, the dark, rolling shape) to one another is not explained, nor is it clear which of these entities is the controlling force from the other world. Even the view the author gives of these various visions is filled with ambiguity. The narrator sees an otter where the companion sees a manlike creature; the ascending beings are seen very hazily; the dark shape is seen by the narrator as "several animals grouped together, like horses, two or three, moving slowly," and by the companion as "shaped and sized like a clump of willow bushes, rounded at the top, and moving all over upon its surface."

A favorite technique of the author is to make his protagonist a visionary who is open to, and even invites, experience with another world or reality, while a second character is a man of science or at least of down-to-earth nature whose function it is to rescue the hero from the charms or dangers of the vision. Blackwood gives an interesting twist to this idea in "The Willows" when the down-to-earth character, the Swedish companion, is the first to acknowledge the presence of the supernatural and even reverses the situation when he admits to having long had a theory about another world. Aside from this, Blackwood utilizes the different viewpoints of his two characters to give alternate descriptions of the various phenomena they see, contributing to suggestion rather than literal depiction.

James V. Muhleman

THE WIND AND THE SNOW OF WINTER

Author: Walter Van Tilburg Clark (1909-1971)
Type of plot: Psychological realism
Time of plot: Early twentieth century
Locale: The desert mountains of Central Nevada
First published: 1944

> *Principal characters:*
> MIKE BRANEEN, an elderly prospector
> AN UNIDENTIFIED YOUNGER MAN

The Story

Mike Braneen has been looking for gold in the rugged desert mountains of Central Nevada for fifty-two years, roughly the last quarter of the nineteenth century and the first quarter of the twentieth century. He apparently has found enough gold to support his meager life-style, but he has long since ceased expecting to strike it rich.

Mike's life has become routine to the point of ritual; he spends eight months of every year—from April to December—in the mountains, and when the first snow falls he takes refuge in the little mining town of Gold Rock. For eight months, Mike is alone, with only his burro for company. Yet in his loneliness he perpetually relives the social phase of his life. Though comfortable with his solitary life, Mike's self-identity is clearly defined by his human relationships.

As the story begins, Mike is descending from the mountains on the rugged old wagon road, into the sunset, and toward Gold Rock. It is late December, and snow flurries are in the air. Mike is keenly attuned to nature's cycles, and he knows that this will be the first storm of winter. He picks his way down the old Comstock road, avoiding the new highway, the cars and trucks, and all other manifestations of the new era which has passed him by. Alone with his burro Annie, there is nothing to interrupt the flow of Mike's memories.

Mike thinks about the burros he has had—eighteen or twenty in all. He can remember the names of only a few, those with some unique characteristic, and for the past twenty years he has gradually felt less personal about them. He has begun to call all the jennies "Annie" and the burros "Jack."

Mike remembers women he has known, usually fleetingly, like the "little brown-haired whore" with whom he spent one night in Eureka. He cannot remember anything about her in bed, but he remembers standing with her by the open window of the hotel, listening to piano music from below. He also remembers her heart-shaped locket with the two hands gently touching. Her name was Armandy, and Mike remembers with pleasure this brief moment of human contact.

The sun sinks lower, and Mike and Annie climb the last rise before the final descent to Gold Rock. He remembers the town: John Hammersmith's livery stable, where he will take Annie; his room in Mrs. Wright's house on fourth street; the International House, where he will go for their best dinner; and most of all the Lucky Boy Saloon, where he will find the proprietor, Tom Connover, and the rest of his old friends. He relives the ritual of his arrival, how he will trim his beard, put on his suit, and go down to the Lucky Boy, how Tom will look up and greet him warmly. From somewhere in the recesses of Mike's memory, however, comes an alternate picture of a nearly empty town, of strangers who work for the highway department or talk of mining in terms that Mike does not understand.

Mike and Annie reach the summit, stop, and look down. Instead of a bright string of orange windows, Mike sees only scattered lights across the darkness, producing no "communal glow." Mike realizes that this is how Gold Rock is now, a town grown old like himself, a town which, like him, is going to die. As Mike and Annie descend into Gold Rock, a highway truck swerves to miss them. Mike stops in front of the Lucky Boy; the saloon is boarded up and dark.

A younger man approaches, and the bewildered Mike stops him. Mike learns that the Lucky Boy has been closed since Tom Connover died in June. Confused, Mike asks directions to Mrs. Wright's place. The stranger tells Mike kindly that Mrs. Wright has been dead for some time and reminds him that it was at Mrs. Branley's house where he stayed last winter. Mike is afraid to ask about John Hammersmith, afraid that he, too, is dead. Mike recognizes that he has outlived his time, that his death is also approaching. As the man and the burro turn up the street, their "lenghtening shadows" are obscured by the snowflakes.

Themes and Meanings

It is clear from the beginning of the story that Mike Braneen is nearing death. He is an old man with physical debilities, approaching senility. His memories run together, though the reader might attribute this to fifty-two years of routine rather than to senility. Mike himself, however, is well aware that he has outlived his era. The transitoriness of life is thus a central theme. Mike, the town of Gold Rock, and the era of the solitary prospector are all dying.

Yet neither Mike nor Walter Van Tilburg Clark is overly sentimental. Mike's life has been good. His chosen life-style has given him both freedom and social contact, both of which his personality requires. Though a loner, Mike defines himself by human relationships; his self-concept as rugged individualist requires the admiration of his friends, and during his eight months of solitude he relives the memories of human contact in Gold Rock, Eureka, and other Nevada towns.

Mike is comfortable with solitude, too. He is close to nature, reads her signs, and lives in harmony with her cycles. Just as Mike brings his social memories with him to the mountains, he also brings his habit of retrospection with him back to town. Suddenly Mike's friends are gone, the Lucky Boy is closed, and memories are all that Mike has left—and memories alone are not enough. The wind and snow of winter are about to claim Mike, too.

Style and Technique

"The Wind and the Snow of Winter" is a highly symbolic story. The title introduces the season of death, and the story begins "near sunset." Myriad images convey the sense of impending death, of the transience of life, of the end of Mike's era.

Mike is descending into a dying town, a town where his friends are already buried, where the social institutions which enriched his life have faded, where the prospector and his mule have been replaced by highways and trucks. Mike walks into the setting sun, it is the time of winter solstice, and the snow which covers all for the season of death is beginning to fall.

That Mike has little future left is poignantly conveyed by his living in the past. Though he does not remember that Mrs. Wright is dead, it is obvious that he has been hardened by loss and death. That he has learned from the pain of broken attachments is apparent in his increasing detachment from his burros.

Mike's introspection is prompted by what he calls "high-blue" weather. In spring high-blue, he used to think about women, to anticipate the future. Now he is more responsive to fall high-blue; he thinks of the past, of old friends—and he watches the weather carefully because he has begun to fear getting caught in a storm.

As Mike approaches the last pass, it is "getting darker rapidly." Mike looks at the sunset and remembers God. He anticipates the view from the summit of his "lighted city," the Gold Rock of his memories as well as the "lighted city" which he anticipates beyond death.

Thus the imminence of Mike Braneen's death is clearly established by Clark's symbolism. The reader is not especially surprised to look down with Mike on the dim, scattered lights of Gold Rock. One is prepared for the death of Mike's friends, for the closing of the Lucky Boy, for the approaching death of Mike himself, and one sees one's own shadows lengthen, one's own life obscured.

Mike is at peace with himself, with nature, and with his society, but he is also mortal. Clark's story not only exploits the universal symbols of human mortality and transience but also explores the human need to hold off the blast of winter—and to accept winter when it comes.

Jerry W. Wilson

WINTER DREAMS

Author: F. Scott Fitzgerald (1896-1940)
Type of plot: Domestic realism
Time of plot: Several years before and after World War I
Locale: Black Bear Lake, Minnesota, and New York City
First published: 1926

> *Principal characters:*
> DEXTER GREEN, the protagonist, seen first as a fourteen-year-old youth and later as a successful businessman
> JUDY JONES, the woman Dexter loves
> DEVLIN, a business acquaintance of Dexter

The Story

F. Scott Fitzgerald divides "Winter Dreams" into six episodes. In the first, fourteen-year-old Dexter Green, whose father owns the "second best" grocery store in Black Bear Lake, Minnesota, has been earning thirty dollars a month pocket money caddying at the Sherry Island Golf Club. He is responsible and honest, touted by at least one wealthy patron as the "best caddy in the club." His decision to quit his job comes suddenly—proclaimed, to incredulous protests, to be the result of his having got "too old." Such public excuse masks the real and private reason: Dexter has just been smitten head-over-heels by the willful, artificial, and radiant eleven-year-old Judy Jones, who, with her nurse, shows up at the club carrying five new golf-clubs in a white canvas bag and demanding a caddy. Dexter watches her engage in a sudden and passionate altercation with the nurse, which piques his interest and works to align him with Judy. He not only sympathizes with her but also senses that an equally sudden and violent act on his part (his resignation) can be the only possible response to the "strong emotional shock" of his infatuation.

In the second episode, which takes place nine years later, Dexter has become a successful entrepreneur in the business world. His laundries cater to moneyed patrons by specializing in fine woolen golfstockings and women's lingerie. Playing golf one afternoon with men for whom he once caddied, Dexter contemplates his humble past by studying the caddies serving his party, but the reverie is broken when a golfball hits one of the men in his party in the stomach. It was driven by Judy Jones, now an "arrestingly beautiful" woman of twenty, who, with her partner, nonchalantly plays through Dexter's foursome.

After an early-evening swim, Dexter is resting on the raft farthest from the club and enjoying strains of piano music from across the lake. Judy approaches by motorboat, introducing herself and requesting that Dexter drive the boat so that she can ride behind on a surfboard, making clear that she is dallying to delay returning home, where a young man is waiting for her. The encounter ends with her offhand invitation to Dexter to join her for dinner the following night.

In the third episode, visions of Judy's past beaux flit through Dexter's mind as he waits downstairs for Judy, dressed in his most elegant suit. When she does appear, though, Dexter is disappointed that she is not dressed more elaborately. In addition, her depression disturbs him, and when, after dinner, she confides that the cause of it lies in her discovery that a man she cared for had no money, Dexter is able to reveal matter-of-factly that he is perhaps the richest man of his age in the Northwest. Judy responds to this information with excited kisses.

The fourth episode forms the culmination of Judy's tantalizing and irresistible charm. It shows a dozen men, Dexter among them, circulating around her at any given moment, always entranced, alternately in and out of her favor.

After experiencing three ecstatic days of heady mutual attraction following their first dinner, Dexter is devastated to realize that Judy's attentions and affections are being turned toward a man from New York, of whom she tires after a month. Thereafter, she alternately encourages and discourages Dexter, and when, eighteen months later, he realizes the futility of thinking that he could ever completely possess Judy, he becomes engaged to a girl named Irene Scheerer, who never appears as an actual character in the story. In contrast to the passion and brilliance that Judy inspires in him, Dexter feels solid and content with the "sturdily popular" and "intensely great" Irene.

One night when Irene has a headache, which precludes her going out with him, Dexter passes the time by watching the dancers at the University Club and is startled by the sound of Judy's voice behind him. Back from Florida, Hot Springs, and a broken engagement, she seems eager to tantalize Dexter again and asks if he has a car. As they drive around the city, Judy teases him with "Oh, Dexter, have you forgotten last year?" and "I wish you'd marry me." Dexter is confused about whether the remarks are sincere or artificial, but when, for the first time, she begins to cry in his presence, lamenting that she is beautiful but not happy, Dexter is passionately drawn to her once again, despite his better judgment. When Judy invites him to come inside her house, Dexter accepts.

The fifth episode takes place ten years later. Dexter reminisces about how the passion rekindled from that one night lasted only a month, yet he feels that the deep happiness was worth the deep pain. He knows now that he will never really own Judy, but that he will always love her. At the outbreak of the war, having broken off his engagement with Irene and intending to settle in New York, Dexter instead turns over the management of his laundries to his partner and enlists in an officer's training program.

The final episode occurs seven years after the war. Dexter is now a very successful businessman in New York City. Devlin, a business acquaintance from Detroit, makes small talk by remarking that one of his best friends in Detroit, at whose wedding Devlin ushered, was married to a woman from Dexter's hometown. At the mention of Judy's name, Dexter pumps Devlin for more information and learns that Judy's life has become an unfortunate one indeed—her husband drinks and runs around with other women while she stays at home with the children. Worst of all, though, is the fact that she has lost her beauty. When Devlin leaves, Dexter weeps, not so much for the fact that Judy's physical beauty has faded, but that something spiritual within him has been lost: his illusion, his youth, his winter dream.

Themes and Meanings

In being heralded as the "laureate of the Jazz Age," Fitzgerald struck in his very American writing a balance between romance and disaster, glitter and delusion. His characters include the petted and popular and rich, who both dream and live recklessly and who have as their biggest enemy time, the time that ages and changes. The aging process is signified by the word "winter" in the title, but "winter" also signifies a transition that is more tragic than physical deterioration; by the end of the story, Dexter's emotions have become frozen. He has lost the ability to care or to feel. His "dream" of Judy had kept him energetic, passionate, and alive, and now the dream has been taken from him.

The reader cares about Dexter at the beginning of the story and wants him to succeed in career and in love. One myth associated with the American Dream is that even the poor, by spunk and luck, have a chance of making it big, and Dexter, whose mother "talked broken English to the end of her days," has worked hard to raise himself out of the poor immigrant class to which he was born. Yet the dream of material success finally proves unsatisfying to Dexter, who comes to know that money cannot buy his real dream. In contrast, Judy was born into wealth and takes it as much for granted as she does her good looks. Judy, the spoiled little rich girl, gets what she deserves. She has been a merciless flirt, using her attraction to break hearts for sport. When the story reveals that she has become careworn and commonplace, married to a bully who deceives her, it is obvious that the tragedy is not hers but Dexter's, who most wanted not riches, but a woman he could never have. What is the most tragic of all, the woman was not worth having.

Style and Technique

Fitzgerald's direct narrative style is as clear and straightforward as Dexter's romantic purpose. The flashbacks and gaps in the story mirror Dexter's on-again, off-again affair with Judy, though his unswerving obsession with her and the chronicle of it is emphasized here. Fitzgerald's tale uses poetic language and diction, yet it does not imply more than it states, and, in the story's episodic structure of fits and starts, it is loose enough to accommodate some things that are almost irrelevant. Dexter's business success, for example, is fortuitous; the real attraction and attention of the protagonist and the reader is his private life.

The third-person limited omniscient point of view allows the reader to know Dexter's story exclusively through Dexter's thoughts and reactions to what is happening. It is necessary to remember that Dexter is a romantic idealist and that his temperament is responsible for both his idealization of Judy and his subsequent disillusionment.

Dexter's enchantment with Judy and the vitality he draws from her are symbolized by the color and sparkle Fitzgerald uses to present her and to create a context in which Dexter can contemplate her. When he first sees her as a young woman, Dexter notices the blue gingham edged with white that shows off Judy's tan; then, later in the afternoon, the sun is sinking "with a riotous swirl of gold and varying blues and scarlets" and Dexter swims among waters of "silver molasses." The author establishes the painting motif when Dexter stretches out on the "wet canvas" of the springboard, which suggests that Judy's seeming art of beauty and charm is all really superficial artifice. With Judy's blue silk dress at their first dinner and her golden gown and slippers at their last dance, Dexter swoons "under the magic of her physical splendor."

During his engagement to Irene, Dexter wonders why the fire and loveliness and ecstasy have disappeared. The very direction of his life, which he let Judy dictate by her casual whim, is gone as well, until she appears to play his heartstrings once more. Irene quickly fades from Dexter's romantic imagination because there is nothing "sufficiently pictorial" about her or her grief to endure after he breaks up with her. Judy is the picture of passion and beauty, energy and loveliness, the true love and true dream that are with him until, learning of Judy's decline, he recognizes it as a signal of the demise of his own dreams.

Jill B. Gidmark

WINTER NIGHT

Author: Kay Boyle (1903-   )
Type of plot: Social realism
Time of plot: The 1940's
Locale: New York City
First published: 1946

> *Principal characters:*
> FELICIA, a seven-year-old girl
> A WOMAN, the baby-sitter for the evening
> A MAID
> FELICIA'S MOTHER

The Story

As the evening darkens one winter night, the maid tells Felicia that once again her mother will not be coming home to their apartment until after Felicia is asleep. Felicia's father is away in the war. As usual, a baby-sitter will come when it is time for the maid to leave. The maid defends the mother's absence on the grounds that, after working hard all day, she deserves her freedom at night. The maids and the baby-sitters change frequently, allowing no time for Felicia to become attached to any of them. They do their jobs, providing no emotional nourishment for the little girl.

This night, the baby-sitter is early. She is a dark-haired, sad-eyed woman who immediately shows an interest in Felicia. Unlike the other sitters, this one offers to clean up after the girl's dinner so she can be alone with her sooner. Whereas other sitters perfunctorily take care of Felicia, moving through a routine that gets her to bed as soon as possible, as if she were merely something that has to be disposed of, this sitter breaks the routine. She tells Felicia that she reminds her of another little girl whose birthday this happens to be. Always attentive to Felicia, the sitter talks to her about the other little girl. Felicia, in her innocence, is never aware, but the reader quickly realizes that the woman is talking about her experiences in a German concentration camp. Felicia interprets everything she hears according to her own experience, reflecting her own anxieties, brought on by the extended absence of the father, whom she hardly remembers, and the nightly absences of her mother.

The little girl in the concentration camp could not understand what was happening to her, why her mother was taken away, why she could not go to her ballet lessons. The baby-sitter took care of her after she was separated from her mother, until they, too, were separated; the baby-sitter assumes that the little girl died in the camp. Felicia falls asleep in the woman's arms, and that is how Felicia's mother finds them when she returns after midnight. The sight of the two of them in each other's arms shocks her.

Themes and Meanings

The first sentence of the story states the theme: "There is a time of apprehension which begins with the beginning of darkness, and to which only the speech of love can lend security." Children live with this concern continuously; adults have repressed it. In a world at war, the darkness is pervasive. Children and adults alike in this story suffer from the dearth of words of love. Both Felicia in New York and the little girl in the concentration camp are innocent victims of a world in which the adults are themselves too insecure to provide security for others. The kind baby-sitter can provide affection to both girls, but she cannot save either of them from the darkness of the adult world in which men kill children in the name of ideology and mothers spend their evenings in search of pleasure. Felicia's mother could stay at home; the frequency of her absences, however, indicates that she is herself the victim of needs beyond her control. The maid says that the mother is buying her freedom and that nobody gets hurt by this. Regardless of the success of the mother in achieving this nebulous goal, Felicia is clearly being hurt by her neglect. Whatever freedom the mother gains is at a cost to her daughter. The kind baby-sitter knows that there is no escape and offers herself as a temporary stay to the darkness for Felicia, as she did for the little girl in Germany. Through her own suffering she reaches out to Felicia for what solace, fellowship, and compassion she can provide.

Whether the mother leaves her child out of her own need or out of callous disregard, the result to Felicia is the same: No one is there to comfort her. Only the woman with the experience of the concentration camp knows the reality of the darkness, the validity of the girl's fear, the anxiety that defines life in such a world.

Style and Technique

The constant danger to authors of stories about suffering children is that they will overstep the boundary between pathos and sentimentality, as most of them do, turning pathos into bathos. The effectiveness of "Winter Night" derives in part from Boyle's skill at counterpointing Felicia's plight with that of the other little girl without losing any of the specificity that makes them worthy of compassion.

Such details as the "golden fur" on their limbs, the lilac of their eyes, and the interest they have in ballet not only unite them in the mind of the sitter, but also make them real for the reader. Felicia's plight is individualized by the details of her apartment and of her nighttime routine, by the dialogue of the maid, and by the questions she asks the sitter. When the sitter speaks of the crying of the girls in the camp, Felicia asks whether they cried because their mother had to go out to supper. Such questions ring true because they are derived from Felicia's experience. In the same fashion, the story of the girl in the camp escapes sentimentalization by the understated manner in which the woman sticks to the factual details of that experience.

The story of the other little girl, more dramatically sensational, has the potential to make Felicia's story mundane or trivial, yet in Boyle's hands it has rather the opposite effect. The failure of Felicia's mother to try to comfort her daughter in a world in which such things happen to little girls deepens the pathos of her situation. Felicia and all the other children have reason to be apprehensive.

William J. McDonald

WINTER: 1978

Author: Ann Beattie (1947-   )
Type of plot: Social realism
Time of plot: 1978
Locale: Los Angeles and Connecticut
First published: 1981

> *Principal characters:*
> NICK, the protagonist, age twenty-nine
> BENTON, a painter and Nick's friend, also age twenty-nine
> OLIVIA, Benton's girlfriend
> ELIZABETH, Benton's ex-wife
> JASON, Benton's and Elizabeth's young son
> ENA, Benton's mother
> UNCLE CAL, Benton's uncle

The Story

The story begins in Los Angeles, where the protagonist, Nick, who grew up with Benton in New England, now works in the recording industry. When Benton, with his girlfriend Olivia, flies to Los Angeles to sell his latest batch of paintings to a wealthy, eccentric patron, he calls on his old friend Nick for moral support. Nick has had trouble adjusting to the deals, drugs, and flamboyance of Southern California, but Olivia, who is constantly experimenting with drugs, seems at home with the decadent Hollywood scene. At the news that Benton's younger brother Wesley has drowned in a boating accident, the three fly home, too late for the funeral but fortunate to find a flight at all so close to Thanksgiving.

They join what remains of Benton's family (his mother Ena, his ex-wife Elizabeth, his son Jason, and his Uncle Cal), who are assembled at the dead Wesley's house in the Connecticut countryside where Wesley has recently moved, it has been speculated, either to return to simplicity or to assuage some sort of guilt Ena has caused. Nick, too, finds rural New England serene and natural, a return to simplicity and tradition, with pumpkins, apple orchards, and picturesque graveyards, a place where "snow" means not cocaine but the real thing; he wishes he could live there again. The family reunion promises to be anything but peaceful, for when the three arrive from the West Coast, the other family members have already begun taking Wesley's belongings, and they rush to confess, exposing their own self-interests. Between the traditional Elizabeth and Olivia, who is often under the influence of drugs, the atmosphere is understandably charged, a situation not helped by Olivia's tendency to monopolize the bathtub. Benton's mother entertains an impossible fantasy, that her family will gather harmoniously in front of the fireplace, but she cannot manage to get everyone together at the same time. Perhaps to compensate, she insists that they wait for Hanley Paulson to deliver a load of firewood; although he charges too much, he has always delivered her wood in the past and she finds that she "can always count on Hanley." Her brother-in-law and secret admirer, Cal, bickers with her whenever he is not worrying about his health or the vegetarian foibles of his interior decorator. The child Jason seems determined to have his divorced parents reconciled.

Wandering among these miniature dramas, taking everything in but not really involved emotionally in anything (not even in the brief sexual interlude with Elizabeth), Nick is free to observe the family as a whole and to recall Wesley's influence. Wesley, a photographer, had once taken a picture of Nick's hands which transformed them into something strange, soft, and priestlike; Nick contemplates Wesley's death as a strange still life.

When the firewood finally arrives, not Hanley but his surly son delivers it; he demands extra compensation to stack it, then carries off most of Wesley's pumpkins. Toward the end of their time together, the family joins around the table to eat Ena's large dinner, which is supposed to replace the Thanksgiving dinner she never prepared, but she cannot make pumpkin pie because, she claims, all the pumpkins are gone. During the meal, the tension which has been smoldering finally flares up, sending young Jason from the table in tears. Benton puts Jason to bed with a story about evolution, in which dinosaurs turn into deer but remember their change with sadness.

Themes and Meanings

It would be difficult to find a more traditional symbol of America than the New England family gathered together at Thanksgiving to celebrate physical survival and spiritual renewal. In this case, however, what is in addition intended to be a reaffirmation of the family in the face of the loss of one of its members becomes instead such an occasion for internal competition that it drives young Jason symbolically from the family table.

On one level, then, the story follows the disintegration of a family as a result of the internal conflicts of its members: competition of egos and lifestyles. On another, broader, level, the theme becomes one of evolution, competition, and survival. Particularly in the light of Ena's rigid insistence on ritual (no matter how empty) and her subsequent disillusionment (in Hanley, her family, and civilized behavior in general), the American family can be seen as a rather cumbersome cultural institution which must try to compete successfully with the newer and self-indulgent, amorphous, anesthetic culture represented, in the story, by Southern California. Certainly this family seems already stretched to its limits, barely able to accommodate two divorces, a wife and girlfriend under the same roof, erratic electrocardiograms, Yoga, alcohol and drugs, casual sex, and the needless death of a young man.

Even if the family does manage to adapt and survive, its individual members have already begun paying a personal price for change: guilt and a sense of loss. As times and lives continue to evolve from one form into another, the family becomes like the creatures in Benton's bedtime story, whose eyes grow "sad . . . because they were once something else." Each of the characters, yearning for a return to simplicity and security, searches for some ritual, formality, or father-confessor, as if some symbolic act might absolve guilt and restore what was lost. Wesley's death is only the catalyst for his family's private fears. Divorced Ena wants a world where fate ordains "what's in the cards," where people behave in benevolent and predictable ways—all guaranteed to relieve her of the responsibility of real choice: "I would have made pumpkin pie, but the pumpkins disappeared." Uncle Cal is so afraid of dying that he resorts to an almost superstitious regime of diets, exercises, fads, and devices in an attempt to forestall the inevitable. Olivia retreats from pain and responsibility into her drugs. Benton attempts to return to childhood innocence through little Jason. Elizabeth seduces Nick (whom she sees in the role of a priest) in order, he suspects, to exorcise Wesley's ghost. Even Nick, as he contemplates the changing relationship between Benton and himself, imagines a phone booth to be a confessional; back in New England, he wishes that he could return to a time before he learned that his father had once wanted to send him away, before he realized that death could be casual and unpredictable, before he found himself using people and burdened with the ensuing guilt.

As the characters struggle helplessly between desire to regain innocence or security and their inability to do so, Beattie offers no clear-cut answer to their dilemma, though she does suggest the paradoxical metaphor of the still life: the composition which remains of what once existed. Over the whole story hangs its title, like a photographer's caption denoting still-life order and a single, graspable point in time, all the while contrasting sharply with the theme of change or evolution, and with the particular turbulence and conflict of the characters' lives. Nick expresses the story's central irony, admitting that he is fascinated by photographs given simple still-life captions when the subject matter is alarming, disturbing, absurd: "Photograph gets a shot of a dwarf running out of a burning hotel and it's labeled 'New York: 1968.'" He goes on to caption an imagined shot of the capsized boat and floating orange life vests, all that remain of Wesley's death; "Lake Champlain: 1978." This image serves both as a colorful arrangement of objects and as evidence of the absurdity and needlessness of Wesley's death—he should not have been boating in November, and he should have been wearing a life preserver. At the same time, the still-life metaphor becomes, finally, Nick's attempt to impose order, however arbitrary, on an event which cannot be comfortingly explained using reason; an expression in lieu of any explanation; an attempt to bridge the gap between present and past, between change itself and what cannot be changed. Only Nick (though perhaps Elizabeth as well) has clearly begun to understand something about his own motives in an absurd and transient world, but this growth process allows Wesley's death to be not completely in vain.

Style and Technique

Beattie's style is deceptively simple. Related as a collection of very human, often hilarious details, this story gives (as do Wesley's photographs) the effect of life spontaneously observed rather than arranged or posed, reported rather than judged. Into the zany and poignant moments of the characters' lives are woven dozens of smaller anecdotes and observations, some experienced by the characters, others merely repeated at second hand. Irony and humor work side by side. The sequence of events seems less important than their accumulation.

Yet, upon closer inspection, the seemingly random details add up to a subtly structured and solid whole. Even small anecdotes and details carefully support (and often offer substantive clues to) the main themes. For example, the cat which Nick and Elizabeth pick up at the side of the road and take to their motel room manages to adapt comfortably to whatever surroundings in which it finds itself, reinforcing the animal secret of survival. In a detail from the past, Nick recalls Benton's feeling trapped and tossing his wallet out of the car window; Nick retrieves the wallet, which falls open on the seat to Elizabeth's picture: Benton can no more easily discard his changing identity and credentials (marriage, impending fatherhood) than he can control change itself. Ena takes the dead Wesley's chain of keys, though they open nothing she can find; still, she keeps trying, hoping perhaps to unlock an answer to her son's needless death.

In image after image, the themes reappear in major and minor variations; as they do, a single picture begins to emerge. Just as Wesley's photographs transform the ordinary into something of mystery and beauty, so the story transforms disparate and ordinary elements into a single artistic vision of contemporary life whose harshness is softened by the human touch.

Sally V. Doud

WIRELESS

Author: Rudyard Kipling (1865-1936)
Type of plot: Fantasy
Time of plot: 1902
Locale: An unnamed English seaside town, possibly Teignmouth
First published: 1902

> *Principal characters:*
> THE NARRATOR, identified only as "I"
> MR. CASHELL, SR., the proprietor of a chemist's shop
> MR. CASHELL, JR., his nephew, an amateur electrical
>   experimenter
> JOHN SHAYNOR, an assistant in the shop
> FANNY BRAND, a girl with whom Shaynor is infatuated

The Story

"Wireless" is on one level the story of a failed experiment. Mr. Cashell, Jr., has invited the narrator to join him in an attempt to send radio transmissions between his uncle's shop and an operator in Poole, some distance away. At first, Poole does not come through, and by the time it does, the narrator has lost interest and has decided to go home. In the interim, all that has been heard on Cashell's radio receiver is the sound of two warships failing to communicate with each other—their transmitters working but their receivers out of tune—ending with the phrase *"Disheartening—most disheartening."* On the scientific level, then, nothing happens in "Wireless"—though one should note that everyone in the story accepts that these mishaps will be corrected soon, if not immediately, and that this scientific failure is purely temporary and insignificant.

More significant, and potentially more disheartening, is what happens while Mr. Cashell is waiting for his signal. The narrator passes the time by talking to the young shop assistant, John Shaynor. It is soon clear that Shaynor is dying of tuberculosis. He will not admit it to himself, blaming his cough on a sore throat from smoking too many cigarettes, but Cashell does not expect him to live a year, and the narrator silently agrees. Shaynor is also, equally pathetically, infatuated with a girl who comes into the shop and takes him out—into a bitingly cold east wind, the last thing one would recommend for a tuberculosis patient—but who will clearly outlive and very probably forget him. Shaynor is a doomed nobody.

Yet for a few brief hours he is also a focus, the human "receiver" (perhaps) for a message that comes through from Somewhere. This message appears to consist of the poetry of John Keats. As Shaynor slumps into a coma—caused perhaps by his illness, or possibly by the lethal alcoholic concoction the narrator has devised to warm everyone up—he starts first to declaim, and then to write, garbled versions, fragments, even whole sections, mostly of Keats's poem "The Eve of St. Agnes," but also of "Ode to a Nightingale" and the ode "To Autumn." When Shaynor comes out of his coma, the narrator establishes that he has never heard of Keats. He is not remembering, then. Where has the poetry come from? Furthermore, how does this mysterious and supernatural event relate to the equally mysterious but scientific event (or nonevent) taking place in Cashell's makeshift signal-station next door?

Themes and Meanings

The central theme of the story is clearly the inexplicable. Twice the narrator asks Cashell for an explanation of what he is doing, asking first what is "electricity," and second what is "induction." Both times, Cashell replies by telling him, not what these phenomena are, but how they work. The propagation of radio waves through empty space remains itself mysterious, and is referred to more than once as "magic."

It is worth noting how very up-to-date Kipling was, both in his science and in his sense of amazement. "Wireless" was first published in 1902, but even if this fact were not known, the story could be precisely dated on internal evidence. Its first sentence, from Shaynor, is: "It's a funny thing, this Marconi business." This comment clearly dates the story as occurring after 1896 (the year of the first arrival of Guglielmo Marconi in England) and probably after 1901—for it was in December of that year that Marconi created a sensation with the first transatlantic radio transmission. In the center of the story, however, is a clear description of a device known as a "coherer." This was the work of Edouard Branly, and was used in the early Marconi transmissions but was supplanted after 1904 by the diode. The incident of the warships signaling further recalls an event of 1899. Yet by 1910, it is safe to say, such contacts were too regular to be any longer a matter of amazement. "Wireless" accurately records the first impact of a major new technology on popular consciousness. That impact is one of awe and fear.

The central thought of Kipling's story, then, is that if an inexplicable "Power" can send impalpable messages through the dimension of space, then maybe it, or another, can send messages through time. Radio's messages can be received only after careful preparation and "tuning." Messages from the dead, perhaps, need something analogous. What the narrator records is the tuning of Shaynor—as it were, a human "coherer"—to receive the signals of Keats.

Keats and Shaynor are alike in many respects. Both are apothecaries, both are victims of tuberculosis, both are in love—one with Fanny Brawne, the other with Fanny Brand. The chemist's shop in the story is also curiously similar to the setting of Keats's "The Eve of St. Agnes." Instead of stained glass, it has the giant colored bottles of the old-fashioned apothecary. Outside it, at the game shop, hang the dead birds and hare, ruffled by the searching wind like the animals at the start of Keats's poem. When Fanny Brand takes Shaynor out, she takes him to the church of St. Agnes. The bitter cold, the sleet on the windowpanes, the red, black, and yellow cloth, the fear of death, and the frozen churchyard are common to both poem and story.

A kind of plausibility accordingly thickens around Shaynor's unconscious recording of Keats's poem (which he does like a man in the throes of composition). The radio messages give a scientific analogue. The immediate circumstances argue that this could be an unrepeatable coincidence, an ideal man and moment for "reception." Shaynor, furthermore, is dying, perhaps drunk, certainly near somnambulism, all traditionally favorable states for moments of insight. Finally, the whole house—this is told twice—has been "electrified" by Cashell's primitive antenna. The reader is given every reason for suspending disbelief. Yet the event at the heart of the story remains inexplicable, unexplained.

It is also, in several ways, sad or disheartening. This kind of communication will not be improved. It is a "one-off." Soon, Shaynor will be dead. What he has received is in any case a travesty, a garble of brilliant lines—just as Fanny Brand and the chemist's shop appear common, cheap, and vulgar compared with Madeline and the magic setting of Keats's poem. Is it poor reception? Is it a ghost unable to recapture its own greatness? A final thought is the possibility—worst of all—that Shaynor is not a receiver but a transmitter: that it is his agony and his peculiar circumstances (hare, colored bottles, colored blanket, and so on) which in some way "went out" to Keats to be transmuted into poetry. This theory would depict creativity itself as derived from a failed experiment, subordinate art and magic (as Keats feared) to the progress of science.

Style and Technique

The main point here is Kipling's famous compression. It can safely be said that no detail in "Wireless" is without significance and, furthermore, that no reader has ever read this story with full comprehension on first attempt. The early details of birds and hare make no sense until one comes on the explicit references to "The Eve of St. Agnes." Similarly, Shaynor's cough cannot be recognized as terminal until he starts to cough blood. Once the general frame of the story has been recognized, however, the reader is challenged to return and discover every trace of explanation, hinted allusion, dramatic irony—an activity which requires a reading not only of Kipling but also of Keats. Thus, the narrator's apparently casual remark that Shaynor's eyes "shone like a drugged moth's" takes on more meaning when one remembers Keats's line near the heart of "The Eve of St. Agnes" comparing stained glass to the wings of a tiger-moth—and Shaynor indeed becomes "a tiger-moth as I thought" a few pages later. The moth imagery is, however, not only one of color but also one of doom: Fanny Brand kills Shaynor with her little excursion to the church like a candle tempting a moth to burning. Shining eyes, too, are a symptom of tuberculosis. One phrase, therefore, can work on three levels.

It is also significant that Shaynor's Keatsian language starts just before his coma, as if triggering it, and further, that as he starts to come out of the coma, the lines he quotes start to go wrong. A sense of failure and degradation is in fact vital to the story, suggesting that Shaynor's visions of love and beauty—wherever they come from—are illusions. He literally adores Fanny Brand; Cashell sees her as "a great, big, fat lump of a girl"; the narrator sees both perspectives, but on the whole sides with the latter, as he is conscious of the commercial ugliness of much of his setting.

The story's final power stems, however, from Kipling's unique ability to describe. There is hardly a better description of cold and deepening solitude in English than in this story, and it is brilliantly set off by the rich evocation of color and scent within the chemist's shop. "Wireless" is a tour de force by a prose artist determined to show what his medium could do even in rivalry with poetry at its greatest.

T. A. Shippey

THE WISH HOUSE

Author: Rudyard Kipling (1865-1936)
Type of plot: Domestic realism and fantasy
Time of plot: Early twentieth century
Locale: A small village in Sussex, England
First published: 1924

> *Principal characters:*
> MRS. ASHCROFT, an old countrywoman
> MRS. FEETLEY, her friend

The Story

On a pleasant March Saturday in the Sussex countryside, Mrs. Ashcroft entertains her old friend Mrs. Feetley for afternoon tea. At the outset, talk quickly turns to memories of the past, and the story unfolds entirely through the ensuing dialogue. Mrs. Ashcroft recalls the death of her husband many years earlier. She hints that it had not been the happiest of marriages, and that both sides carried their share of the blame. Her husband had warned her on his deathbed that retribution lay in store: "I can see what's comin' to you." Yet this ominous note does not fully prepare the reader for the strange story, involving mysterious and supernatural events, that Mrs. Ashcroft now relates to her spellbound friend.

After her husband's unlamented death, Mrs. Ashcroft, who combines the practical worldliness of Chaucer's Wife of Bath with the simplicity of the countrywoman, traveled to London, finding a job as a cook in an upper-class home. It was an easy life, and she fared well. After a year, she moved back to Smalldene, a village in Sussex, where she worked on a farm. It is there that she met Harry Mockler, and their lives were destined to become entwined in a curious and baffling manner. Mrs. Ashcroft regarded Harry as her master, although, looking back, she certainly holds no illusions about romantic love. "What did ye get out of it?" Mrs. Feetley asks. "The usuals. Everythin' at first—worse than naught after," is the reply. Although she loved Harry unquestioningly, far more than she had ever loved her husband, eventually he deserted her, and she suffered greatly.

Now her story takes an unexpected turn. She relates that one day, suffering from a bad headache, she found the playful company of young Sophy Ellis, the daughter of the local charwoman, irksome. Sophy, having discovered the reason for Mrs. Ashcroft's irritability, immediately promised to relieve her headache, as if to do so was the easiest thing in the world. She promptly left the house. Within ten minutes, the headache vanished. Mrs. Ashcroft naturally assumed this to be a coincidence, but Sophy insisted on her return that it was she who was responsible for the cure, and that she was now suffering from the same headache herself. As Mrs. Ashcroft questioned the child, she heard with increasing amazement about the Wish House, a deserted house in nearby Wadloes Road, in which a spirit, known as a Token, lived. The Token had the power, if asked, to transfer an affliction from one person to another. No one, however, could wish good for himself; the spirit dealt only in bad.

Some months elapsed, during which this incident lay at the back of Mrs. Ashcroft's mind. The next summer, she traveled once more to London, and then again to Smalldene. By chance, she met Harry, whom she still loved, but found that he was tragically changed from his former self. Having sustained a bad leg injury, which had turned poisonous, he was a broken figure and was not expected to live more than a few months. Acutely distressed, she urged him to see a doctor in London, but he refused. In desperation, Mrs. Ashcroft decided that there was only one thing that she could do for him. In the evening, single-minded in her purpose, she set off for the Wish House. On her arrival, she rang the bell boldly and immediately heard the approach of shuffling footsteps. The footsteps reached the front door, where they stopped. It was an eerie moment. Mrs. Ashcroft leaned forward to the letter box and said, "Let me take everythin' bad that's in store for my man, 'Arry Mockler, for love's sake." She heard nothing from behind the door except an expulsion of breath. Then the footsteps returned downstairs to the kitchen.

For several months nothing appeared to happen, but in November, Mrs. Ashcroft learned that Harry had fully recovered and returned to his job. Her own troubles, however, were about to begin. The following spring, she developed a boil on her shin which refused to heal. At first, she made no firm connection between this event and Harry's earlier recovery. Later, however, when Harry suffered a kick from his horse, her wound got worse, and she believed that it was drawing the strength out of her. Harry got better. At that point, she knew the truth and uttered a shout of triumph which was also a prayer: "You'll take your good from me 'thout knowin' it till my life's end. O God, send me long to live for 'Arry's sake!"

As the months and years went by, Mrs. Ashcroft learned to regulate the pain and discomfort from her wound. Sometimes the wound appeared to clear up, and she learned that this was an indication that Harry would be in good health for a while, so she conserved her strength. When the wound got worse, she knew that Harry was in need. This continued for years. She gained nothing from this strange situation, since no one knew of it except herself; Harry took little notice of her, although, to her relief, he did not take up with another woman.

The final twist in the story takes place when Mrs. Ashcroft reveals that her wound has turned cancerous. She is slowly dying. In a moment of uncertainty, she seeks reassurance from her friend that the pain she endures is not wasted, that it keeps her Harry safe. Mrs. Feetley willingly concurs. Finally,

Mrs. Ashcroft asks her friend to look at the wound before she leaves. At the sight of it Mrs. Feetley shudders but kisses Mrs. Ashcroft with sympathy and understanding. The story ends on this note of compassion for the dying woman, who has selflessly taken on the troubles of a man to whom she is devoted, and who has given her nothing in return.

Themes and Meanings

"The Wish House" was originally published with two obscure poems, one of which, "Late Came the God," provides important commentary on the story. It relates how a vengeful God inflicts continual pain and distress on a woman in payment of a debt. This theme of divine retribution for past sins, real or imagined, forms a minor element in "The Wish House." Yet the last lines of the poem reveal the first of the story's main themes, the redemptive, self-sacrificial love of woman for man: "Alone, without hope of regard or reward, but uncowed,/ Resolute, selfless, divine/ These things she did in Love's honour. . . ."

This love is unrelated to merit or desert; it sees no fault in the object of love, or seeing, chooses to disregard. There is nothing romantic about it. It is a practical, even instinctive, orientation of the will and heart, in obedience to an inner impulse. The theme has profoundly Christian implications. Mrs. Ashcroft is almost Christ-like in her ability, and her willingness, to take upon herself the sins and burdens of another, motivated by the highest love. The wound in her leg will suggest, for the Christian reader, the stigmata of the Christian saint, the wounds received in imitation of Christ. The old Mrs. Ashcroft, chattering away to her friend in country dialect, is perhaps an unlikely figure to remind one of the divine, but the implication of the story is that the simplest folk become godlike, and possess godlike powers, when motivated by a pure desire for the good of another and a resolute will to endure physical hardship and pain without complaint.

The second major theme of the story is what T. S. Eliot appreciatively called its "pagan vision" of country life lived close to nature. This "vision of the people of the soil" is of a world in which magic, in the form of spirits, spells, and curses, still exerts its age-old power. The world which the two old women inhabit consists of an intuitive, prescientific sense of the interrelationship of all creatures at all levels of existence. It is a way of seeing which unquestioningly accepts the fluidity and transferability of spiritual forces, in contradistinction, as Eliot points out, to the modern, materialistic temper. Eliot's suggestion that such a vision must be regained if "the truly Christian imagination is to be recovered by Christians" is apt commentary on "The Wish House." This is because the "pagan vision" underlies the Christian implication of the story: Individual pain and death is not random or wasted but in a mysterious way nourishes the larger good; it is part of the interwoven fabric of pain and joy in which the life of the universe consists.

Style and Technique

Somewhat less cryptic and obscure than many of Kipling's stories, "The Wish House" skillfully blends realism and fantasy in a way that suggests that the supernatural order is coextensive with the natural. This lends force to the story's themes, with their implication that in spite of surface appearances to the contrary, no part of life is in fact separate from any other part.

The realism is especially noticeable in the country dialect in which both women speak, which has the effect of grounding them in a particular locality and a particular class of character. It also suggests a lack of sophistication, a lack of exposure to modern, homogenizing culture, which makes their acceptance of ancient folk beliefs immediately plausible to the reader. After all the trappings of a March Saturday in southern England—football buses, church visitors, afternoon tea—have added to the realistic flavor, the supernatural, fantastic element creeps in unobtrusively, seemingly enfolded within the natural order. The Wish House is not placed in a mysterious, unspecified setting, but at 14 Wadloes Road, on the way to the greengrocer. There are more than twenty houses in the street exactly like it. The reader's suspension of disbelief is assured. Even the spirit itself is curiously mundane, sitting on a chair in the kitchen and shuffling upstairs, Mrs. Ashcroft observes, as if it were "a heavy woman in slippers."

The effect of this subtle interpenetration of natural and supernatural becomes clear at the end of the story. The sordid reality of the exposed wound which Mrs. Ashcroft displays to her friend remains uppermost in the reader's mind, but it no longer stands alone, without wider significance. It has become the focal point for the mysterious trading of blessing and curse which has been woven into the fabric of the old woman's life.

Bryan Aubrey

WISSLER REMEMBERS

Author: Richard Stern (1928-   )
Type of plot: Psychological realism
Time of plot: The 1970's
Locale: A large university in the United States
First published: 1980

> *Principal character:*
> CHARLES WISSLER, a professor of literature

The Story

At the end of yet another academic semester, and the dissolution of yet another group of students of whom he has become extremely fond, Professor Wissler finds himself reminiscing about his thirty years in the teaching profession. His nostalgic odyssey, full of amusing anecdotes and delightful vignettes, forms the core of the story.

He recalls how at the age of twenty-one, immediately after World War II, he won a Fulbright scholarship to teach at a school in Versailles. His French was little better than the boys' English, but the students were respectful and his stay was pleasant enough. The following year had seen him working in Heidelberg, decoding cables for the army and supplementing his income by teaching English language and literature at the university. Heidelberg was full of American soldiers, and the war was a vivid presence in his mind, as he taught the sons and daughters of those who had recently been his enemies. He recalls the beautiful, exquisitely courteous Fräulein Hochhusen, with her "heart-rending popped blue eyes," and "hypnotic lips." His amorous feelings toward her are clear enough to him ("I love you") but carefully shielded from the girl herself. Wissler is always conscious of the sexual charms of his female students, but he has carefully trained himself to feel love "with the sexuality displaced." That, he thinks to himself, has been "priestly excruciation."

At the start of the Korean War, he moved to Frankfurt, to take up a higher-paying job teaching American soldiers. Most of them could hardly read or write, yet there he had the most enjoyable and rewarding experience of his teaching career. He found the willingness and sincerity of his ragged class deeply moving.

Following his return to the United States and sojourns in Iowa and Connecticut, he found himself at a "great Gothic hive of instruction and research" where he has remained ever since. He recalls the hundreds of classes and the myriad students who have passed through his hands and who are now scattered across the globe in a host of different occupations and professions. He recalls particular individuals, such as the "dull, potato-faced" Miss Rabb, who wrote a paper which was so obscure it made sense only when she explained it to him in person, but this was too late to save her from a C grade. A similar fate befell the intense Ms. Glypher, who had "never never never never never" received a C grade before, and vigorously protested that her chances of getting into law school had been ruined. Yet her spirited response was not quite enough to earn for her a change of grade.

Everywhere on his travels, from Kansas to Kyoto, New York to Nanterre, there had been wonderful, expressive faces. Even the bored and the contemptuous had their stories to tell. Underlying all of Wissler's experience was love, not only of individuals but also of the class itself, what he calls the "humanscape." The group as a whole was like a complex organism and generated a unique collective consciousness which enthralled him.

Reminiscence over, the story comes up to date. It is December, and the last class of Wissler's current course is in session. There is the sense of "amorous ether" in the room, but Wissler's lecture does not show any trace of it. He recommends a scholarly book on the history of education in antiquity. Like the good academic that he is, he speaks intelligently and interestingly; he is alert to his students' needs and tries to remain objective. The class closes, and there are polite expressions of thanks and gratitude from both professor and students.

One last, simple episode closes the story. Outside, after class, snow falls, and the paths are covered with ice. Wissler slips and falls, only to find his attractive student Miss Fennig on hand to help him up. The simplicity and pleasantness of their brief exchange reveals mutual respect and affection. Outside the formality of the classroom, and beyond the limiting roles of teacher and student, there is only the simplicity of human contact, one hand helping another.

Themes and Meanings

It would perhaps be pedantic and heavy-handed to insist on extracting too serious a theme from such a delightful and deft story as "Wissler Remembers." It is more like a series of entertaining snapshots of the pleasures and frustrations of the teaching profession: the opportunities it gives, the restrictions it imposes. Wissler's deep commitment to and quiet love of his chosen profession is clear throughout the range of his remembrance, from the fullness of a class in full swing to the sadness of conclusion and parting.

Nevertheless, throughout the story there is a recurring motif: the gap between what Wissler thinks, what he wants to say—as he allows the reader into his uncensored mind—and what he actually does say. Early in the story, this problem of communication, or noncommunication, is symbolically and amusingly represented in the episode at the French school. Wissler gives his students a French translation of an American poem and asks them to retranslate it into English. Only five of the twenty-five students even understand the assignment, but he offers a reward to anyone who gets within twelve words of the original. Needless to say, the one effort that Wissler recalls was completely unintelligible.

In the same manner, something happens to Wissler's own thoughts in the act of translating them into words, particularly with respect to the deeper feelings which he has for his students. His reminiscences are generated by his desire to tell everything to his students: how much he has grown to love them, and how difficult it will be for him to lose them. He wants to finish the class with a warm and generous tribute: "It has been a splendid class. For me. There is almost no future I think should be denied you. What world wouldn't be better led by you?" Yet somehow the words do not come. His farewell comments are polite and restrained: He will have office hours the following week; he wishes everyone good luck.

Yet this failure to communicate does not constitute a major character weakness. Wissler is a warm and compassionate man, and his students recognize him as such. The failure arises more from the inevitable restrictions that his position imposes on him. Teacher and student have vastly different roles, and for Wissler to have transgressed his own would have been to fall from the responsibility and sense of duty, which, unstuffily and unpretentiously, he respects. Wissler accepts this limitation without regret. It is in the nature of things that some channels of communication between people may be closed; that is always so in life. Other channels may be open, offering their own kind of reward. This possibility is clear from Wissler's last moments with his students. Although he does not say what he intends to say, there is yet a subtle bond between them, which both sides recognize: "the sweetness of a farewell between those who have done well by each other."

Style and Technique

Stern's diction bears the hallmark of one who began his writing career as a poet before turning to novels and short stories. It is economical, varied, and highly compressed. As one reviewer has commented, "You read a sentence twice not because it is obscure but because you want to make sure you are extracting every nuance." This richness is noticeable in the frequency of short, elliptic sentences, as Wissler's thoughts pile quickly up on one another: "And whoops, heart gripped, I'm heading down, hand cushioning, but a jar," which conveys the sudden shock of slipping on the ice.

Also noticeable in this respect is Stern's frequent use of compounds, which occur in his descriptions of the people who pass through Wissler's mental landscape. Ms. Bainbridge, for example, has a "silver-glassed, turn-of-the-century-Rebecca-West" face; Fräulein Hochhusen is "berry-cheeked"; Herr Doppelgut is "paper-white" and "dog-eyed"; Miss Rabb is "potato-faced"; and the earnest face of Ms. Glypher is "parent-treasured, parent-driven."

The juxtaposition of the formal with the informal, which underlies the story and gives it much of its effect, can be seen stylistically in the first paragraph. As Wissler reviews the names of his current students, no first names come into his mind. He knows them as Miss Fennig, Mr. Quincey, Mr. Parcannis, Miss Shimbel, Ms. Bainbridge, and Miss Vibsayana. The latter "speaks so beautifully." Yet in the parentheses which follow (a stylistic device employed frequently by Stern), such formal and correct language gives way to an undercurrent of intense feeling aroused by the thought of Miss Vibsayana and expressed in colloquial, ungrammatical language: "You cannot relinquish a sentence, the act of speech such honey in your throat, I can neither bear nor stop it." The double comma splice and the ellipsis (the omission of the verb in the second clause) convey the sudden rush of feeling and the hurried thoughts which accompany it. This dichotomy between spoken and unspoken thoughts sets the tone for the remainder of the story.

Bryan Aubrey

WITCH'S MONEY

Author: John Collier (1901-1980)
Type of plot: Satire
Time of plot: The 1930's
Locale: A small town in the Pyrenees in France
First published: 1940

> *Principal characters:*
> FOIRAL, a native of a small town who meets a stranger to the
>   village and sells a house to him
> AN UNNAMED AMERICAN PAINTER, who buys Foiral's house
>   and is murdered there by Foiral and his friends
> ARAGO,
> GUIS,
> VIGNÉ,
> QUÈS, and
> LAFAGO, natives of the village

The Story

Foiral, having taken a load of cork to his market, is returning to his unnamed village, a tiny hamlet in the Pyrénées-Orientales district of France near the Spanish border. Along the roadside, he encounters a poorly dressed stranger whose mannerisms are eccentric; Foiral assumes that the stranger is a madman. The madman is striding aggressively down the road, but he stops, awestruck, at the top of a ridge as he first looks down on Foiral's village.

On the spot, the madman decides to stay there, perceiving the village as "surrealism come to life." The cork forests, he claims, look like "petrified ogres," while the black clothes of the natives make them seem "holes in the light." Foiral, bewildered, tries to remove himself from the vicinity of this lunatic, but the madman detains him, asking for a place to stay. When Foiral claims that there is no such place, the lunatic wanders through the village until he finds Foiral's own vacant property. Forced to admit that the property is his, Foiral finds himself selling it to the stranger, who identifies himself as an American painter who has been living in Paris.

Despite the stranger's appearance, he shows Foiral a wallet containing a number of thousand-franc notes. Having paid a deposit, the stranger returns to Paris for his possessions, while Foiral prepares the house for its new tenant. On his return to the village, the stranger offers Foiral the remainder of the sales price in the form of a check, but the villagers do not understand banking. Foiral recognizes the check only as a *billet* or note resembling a lottery ticket and is reluctant to take the scrap of paper in payment. Increasingly impatient, the artist refers him to the bank in Perpignan, the nearest city, where Foiral is astonished to learn that the *billet* can be converted into real cash—and that the bank makes a charge for this transaction. Foiral is indignant at the charge and believes that he has been cheated. Returning to the village, Foiral approaches the artist, hoping that the latter will make up the sum that the bank has charged. The artist, however, says that he, like Foiral, is a poor man. He cannot give Foiral any more money. Foiral assumes this to be a lie. After all, he has seen a little book containing many other *billets*. Since the one he took to the bank was worth thirty thousand francs, then each one of the others must be worth that amount. Not understanding that these are merely blank checks, Foiral is certain that, by the standards of the village, the artist is an extremely wealthy man.

Nursing his sense of injustice, Foiral speaks with the other village men, assuring them that the stranger admits to having no relatives and describing the little book with its many *billets*. As a result, these "very honest men" (a phrase not meant ironically) leave their homes late one night to visit the stranger. When they return, they possess the stranger's little *billets*. They quickly forget the artist himself; even his "final yelp" is forgotten as they would forget "the rattle and flash of yesterday's thunderstorm." Only one man, Guis, who has befriended the stranger, is left out; his decency causes him to be ostracized by the village and berated by his wife.

The *billets*, or blank checks, which the villagers assume to represent actual cash gradually take control of the town. The community is transformed, but not for the better. Cork concessions and other properties are exchanged for the *billets*, and the property owners swell with pride and self-importance. Marriages are arranged on the basis of possession of the *billets*; aging women take young husbands, while young girls become the property of wealthy widowers. Corruption, including gambling and prostitution, flourishes.

Eventually, the villagers feel the need for ready cash. Foiral proposes to lead the village men back to Perpignan, where all expect to exchange their blank checks for money. They go to the city as if preparing for a festival, still unaware that the scraps of paper are worthless, and they mock Guis, who once again has been left behind. Still laughing at him, they enter the bank and are last seen "choking with laughter when the swing doors closed behind them."

Themes and Meanings

The self-destructive innocence of the creative artist and the corrupting power of commercialism are recurrent motifs in Collier's fiction, providing themes for such stories as "Evening Primrose," "The Steel Cat," and "The Invisible Dove Dancer of Strathpheen Island," among others. As in "Evening Primrose," the artist of "Witch's Money" is killed because he is incapable of comprehending the meaning of money to those among whom he chooses to live.

The unnamed artist of "Witch's Money" brings about his own death, much as the villagers later initiate their own catastrophe. Dazzled by the spectacle of the village, the artist forces himself upon a reluctant Foiral. Yet he speaks to Foiral with curtness and much contempt, impatient with working-class values and oblivious to the dangers presented by those long deprived of money and possessions. The artist fails to imagine Foiral's depth of ignorance concerning banking, and he is unconcerned with the latter's festering sense of injustice. Yet the artist openly reveals the contents of his wallet and his checkbook. It is this combination of innocence, impatience, discourtesy, and tunnel vision that brings about his death.

The townspeople are, indeed, "very honest men," until they are corrupted by the prospect of the artist's wealth. From that time on, however, the killers become swollen with pride; they can neither speak to others nor be addressed, not even by their wives. The taint of corruption surrounds the marriages between old and young, while a village widow, in opening her home to "certain unattached young women" and giving "select" evening parties, introduces prostitution to a town that previously could not afford that particular vice. Similarly, the cardplayers can now afford new cards. In short, the town experiences the results of capitalistic emphasis upon money and possessions at the expense of human values. Moreover, the townspeople do not know when to stop, and, like the artist, undermine themselves, in this case by the decision to take the checks to Perpignan. As the villagers disappear through the bank doors, the reader is left uncertain as to their fate, but the "swing doors" suggest the doors of prisons and the swinging rope of the hangman.

Style and Technique

Collier's style is deceptively simple, his diction crisp and extremely precise. Beneath the seemingly simple language and sentence structure, however, lies a masterful ability to manipulate point of view, to create tone through the use of metaphor, and to exploit every ironic implication of the story.

In "Witch's Money," the tone of horror is maintained by distancing both Foiral and the artist from the reader, who can only watch, fascinated, their single-minded pursuit of self-destruction. The artist—the character with whom the reader can most readily identify—is kept distant from the reader; he is unnamed, and his actions are seen primarily through Foiral's limited viewpoint. When the artist describes his surrealistic vision of the village as a place of sterility and damnation, it is the reader—not the artist or Foiral— who realizes the implications of this vision for the artist's own life.

Ironically, the artist has only an intellectual understanding of surrealism; he does not understand that the barren and decadent landscape reflects the spirit of the place itself and that, if he enters there, he will be living out, not painting, a surrealistic nightmare. Foiral, in contrast, is brought closer to the reader, who is allowed to see the abysmal depths of ignorance and experience that allow Foiral to kill a man whom he does not perceive to be a human being like himself. Not only does Foiral lack comprehension of money and banking, but also his vision of the stranger is fragmentary and incomplete; just as the artist ironically discusses surrealism and the barren landscape without fully understanding either, so Foiral's own aspirations have ironically empty results. When he leads the townspeople to murder, they gain only worthless scraps of paper, while their triumphant entrance into the Perpignan bank will not liberate them but imprison them.

Betty Richardson

WITHIN AND WITHOUT

Author: Hermann Hesse (1877-1962)
Type of plot: Psychological symbolism
Time of plot: The 1920's
Locale: Germany
First published: "Innen und Aussen," 1920 (English translation, 1935)

> *Principal characters:*
> FRIEDRICH, the protagonist, a man who loves rationality and
>   despises superstition
> ERWIN, his friend

The Story

Friedrich is described as a man who loves and respects rationality, especially logic and the sciences. In contrast, he has little respect for unscientific forms of knowledge. Though tolerant of religion, he does not take it seriously. He considers mysticism and magic to be pointless and outmoded in the scientific age. In fact, he despises superstition wherever he encounters it, especially among educated people. Those who question the supremacy of science in the wake of recent war and suffering infuriate him. He grows increasingly disturbed as he senses a rising interest in the occult as an alternative to science.

One day, Friedrich visits Erwin, a close friend whom he has not seen for a while. Friedrich thinks that Erwin's smile is indulgent and mocking. He recalls that he sensed a rift between them when they last parted—Erwin was not vehement enough in supporting Friedrich's hatred of superstition. Now they speak awkwardly of superficial matters, and all the while Friedrich is uncomfortably aware of a distance between them, as if he no longer truly knows Erwin.

Then Friedrich spots a paper pinned to the wall, which awakens memories of his old friend's habit of noting an interesting quotation. To Friedrich's horror, however, the line written on this paper is an expression of Erwin's recent mystical interests: "Nothing is outside, nothing is inside, for that which is outside is inside." Friedrich demands that his friend explain the meaning of this sentence and learns that Erwin sees it as an introduction to an ancient form of knowledge, "magic." In disappointment and anger, Friedrich tells Erwin to choose between this superstitious nonsense and Friedrich's respect and friendship. Erwin explains that he really had no choice in the matter—magic "chose him." He begs Friedrich not to part in anger but to accept their separation as inevitable, as if one of them were dying. Friedrich agrees and asks a final favor, to have those mysterious words explained. Erwin tells him that they refer in part to the religious idea of pantheism, in which God is in all things and all things are divine. Also, once one learns to pass beyond the habitual separation of the world into opposites, such as inside and outside, one can be free of such limitations, and that is the beginning of magic. To illustrate this experience, Erwin gives Friedrich a small clay figure, tells him to observe it from time to time, and asks Friedrich to return when the object "ceases to be outside you and is inside you. . . ."

Friedrich takes this object, a glazed clay figure of a two-headed god, to his home, where it gradually begins to obsess him. He moves it from place to place in his house, annoyed by its presence, yet finding his eyes continually drawn toward the ugly little idol. Its presence torments him; he grows restless and begins to travel often. After one such trip, he feels especially anxious and unsettled the moment he enters his house. Searching for the cause of his distress, he discovers that his maid broke the idol while dusting and disposed of its shattered remains. Friedrich immediately feels relief that this hateful and annoying reminder of superstition is finally gone, but he soon finds that he misses the figurine. Its absence is almost tangible, causing a growing emptiness within him. From hours of observing the two-headed god, he is able to recall the slightest details of its grins, its crude shape, and the colors and textures of its glaze. Even the word "glaze"—*Glasur*—upsets him and, spelled backward as *"Rusalg,"* reminds him of a book, Frank Wedekind's *Princess Russalka* (1897), which both horrified and fascinated him.

The loss of the idol so consumes his thoughts that Friedrich wonders if perhaps it was magical. Perhaps Erwin had placed a spell on him through this figure, and Friedrich was a victim of the war of reason against such dark powers. Yet he forces such ideas from his mind, thinking that he would rather die than admit even the possibility of magic. He cannot control his terror, however, and he finally wakes in fear one night, to find himself mumbling the words "Now you are inside me." Realizing that indeed the idol is torturing him from within himself, Friedrich hurries to Erwin's house to ask his friend how to remove the idol from inside himself. Erwin patiently explains that Friedrich must learn to love and accept what is now within him and stop tormenting the idol, which is really himself. Friedrich has unwillingly taken the first step beyond such pairs of opposites as inside and outside and now can begin to learn the secret of magic: freely controlling the exchange of inside and outside and becoming free from the slavery to what is inside him.

Themes and Meanings

Hesse often dealt with the need for humanity to overcome dualistic thinking and realize the unity of all reality. For Hesse, the attempt to constrict experience to technological control and objective rationality resulted only in a painful separation from the more sensual aspects integral to the human spirit. He believed that World War I was the result of that sort of spiritual crisis in Europe. Afterward, Hesse devoted himself to urging the German people to turn away from materialistic attitudes toward the inward search for healing and insight. Many of Hesse's postwar works, such as "Inside and Outside" or the later *Siddhartha* (1922), also show his fascination with the spiritual insights of Buddhist and Taoist mystical traditions, which teach the dynamic unity of opposites in one interconnected reality. Everything is related to everything else; each thing is involved in all other things. For Hesse, the recognition of this reality was the key to uniting the diverse aspects of human consciousness into one integrated whole. It was also the key to becoming free from the existential anxieties caused by people's mistaken views of themselves as isolated from one another or from nature.

In "Within and Without," Friedrich is engaged in a struggle, not only against what he perceives as the superstitions of others but also against reality itself. His attempt to mold the world to his conscious ideal of logical reasoning is a war against his own deepest nature and thereby destined to fail. By denying even the possibility of other forms of knowledge, Friedrich enslaves himself to a constant need to reject experiences and ideas which do not conform to his rational attitude. Before he visits Erwin, he is already tormenting himself with the mere idea that others may not share his "enlightened" view of the world.

His internal conflict becomes much more evident once Erwin gives him the two-headed figure. Its apparent power to disturb him reveals to Friedrich the unhappy state of his own mind, as well as his inability to control his anxiety through the means of reason. Once the external form of the idol is shattered, its power over him only increases as Friedrich is left alone with his fears, now revealed as part of his own shattered subconscious. Upon Friedrich's agitated return to Erwin, it becomes clear that what Friedrich's friend has given him is not simply an ugly clay object but the gift of beginning a journey toward insight and the freedom from his own mental self-torture. This insight into himself and the world is what Hesse means by "magic."

Style and Technique

The structure of "Within and Without" plays the external events and internal anxieties of Friedrich's life against each other to reveal their interconnectedness. The story moves from an external description of Friedrich's character through Friedrich's experience of the events which lead to the discovery of his internal turmoil. His inner disharmony shapes his world, giving external objects and events their power to disturb him. The outer world allows him to see within himself.

The relationship between these two men with very different attitudes about existence is also a vehicle for the overcoming of the false polarities in Friedrich's mind. As with many other friendships in Hesse's works—Siddhartha's with Govinda, Narcissus' with Goldmund, or Demian's with Emil Sinclair—these two opposed friends represent the rational and sensual poles of human nature. Their interaction allows their underlying union to emerge through the process of their reunion.

The idol plays a striking symbolic role in this piece. Its two opposed heads remind Friedrich of the Roman god Janus, the god of gates and new beginnings. The crude little figure does indeed act as a door to Friedrich's soul and an opportunity for him to overcome his internal conflicts and enter a new life of inner harmony. Even the outer glaze on the clay god is able to reveal his inner conflict and point the way toward its resolution. He becomes obsessed with the memory of the texture and colors of it, seeing its sheen reflected in other objects around him. The idol's surface appearances are thus transcended to reveal the inner depths and interconnections of all aspects of reality. This preoccupation with the glaze also causes him to think about the sound of the word *Glasur*, relating it to seemingly disconnected bits of his past experiences, such as the sound of a book title, *Princess Russalka*. Frank Wedekind's collection of stories about the unhappiness that results from sexual repression both repels and attracts Friedrich, showing the division between his rational and sensual natures.

This object given to Friedrich, then, symbolizes the polarities within his consciousness and the freedom to go beyond them. His internal conflicts and torments result from his superficial rejection of parts of his subconscious and of reality. His attempt to narrow reality into an external objectivity leads to a painful disconnectedness in his inner life. To become whole, Friedrich must come to recognize the validity of the various aspects of the human mind and the unity of mind and world. The gift of an object outside himself is the gateway through which he is able to enter into himself and begin the process of healing. The line from Johann Wolfgang von Goethe's poem "Epirrhema," which Erwin has taken as his motto, has also proven true for Friedrich: "Nothing is outside, nothing is inside, for that which is outside is inside."

Mary J. Sturm

THE WOMAN AT THE STORE

Author: Katherine Mansfield (Kathleen Mansfield Beauchamp, 1888-1923)
Type of plot: Psychological realism
Time of plot: c. 1908
Locale: The bush country in New Zealand
First published: 1912

> *Principal characters:*
> Jo, a dapper ladies' man
> THE NARRATOR, Jo's sister
> THE WOMAN, the ugly keeper of the "store"
> ELSE, her daughter, age five
> JIM, a young traveler

The Story

Three travelers have been caravanning for more than a month in the backblocks of the North Island of New Zealand, a wild Maori country: Jim (a guide who knows the environs), the female narrator, and her dapper brother Jo. The heat has been awful, and one of their horses has developed an open belly-sore from carrying the pack. All have traveled in silence throughout the day. They anticipate reaching a "store" in this wild land, a "whare," or home which houses a storehouse of goods to supply wayfarers and which includes a pasture for the horses. Jim has been teasing the two about this stopover; it is run, he promises, by a friend generous with his whiskey, and he also speaks of the man's blue-eyed, blonde wife, who is generous with her favors.

At sundown, they reach the whare, and all is not as cheerful as has been represented. The mistress of the store looks scarcely better than an ugly hag; she is skinny, with red, pulpy hands; her front teeth are missing, her yellow hair is wild and skimpy, and she is dressed in little better than rags. She carries a rifle and is accompanied by a scraggly, undersized, five-year-old daughter and a yellow, mangy dog. She claims that her husband has been gone for the past month "shearin'," veers wildly in mood, and appears to the visitors to be "a bit off 'er dot," somewhat unhinged from being too much alone in such a disreputable setting.

After some haggling, the travelers are permitted to stop over. She fetches some liniment for the horse and sends food down to the tent that Jim has set up in the paddock. While Jim is working and the narrator bathes in the stream, Jo, the boisterous singer and ladies' man, "smartens" himself for a visit to the woman at the store. She had once been a pretty barmaid on the West Coast, Jim tells them, and she bragged at having known "one hundred and twenty-five different ways of kissing." Despite her moods and her tawdry looks, Jo is determined to flirt and to venture. "Dang it! She'll look better by night light—at any rate, my buck, she's female flesh!" He returns to her whare while the others dine.

While Jo is gone, the woman's child brings some food, and, though very young, reveals that she loves to draw pictures of almost any kind of scene. Jo returns with a whiskey bottle; he has induced the woman to play hostess to the little party, and they all return to the whare. The adults become slightly inebriated, the child threatens to draw forbidden pictures, and Jo and the woman become more brazenly flirtatious. When a violent thunderstorm ensues, the woman suggests that they all sleep at the house—Jim, the narrator, and the daughter in the store, Jo in the living room, and herself in the bedroom, close by. All are drunk and laughing as they retire. From their uncomfortable place in the storehouse, surrounded by pickles, potatoes, strings of onions, and half-hams dangling from the ceiling, they can hear Jo rather noisily sneaking into the woman's bedroom. The disgruntled child finally draws for her companions in the store a picture her mother has forbidden her to draft: It reveals the woman shooting her husband with the rifle and then digging a hole in which to bury him. Jim and the narrator are struck speechless. They cannot sleep that night and hasten on their way early the next morning. The narrator laments for her "poor brother." As they are leaving, Jo appears briefly to motion them on; he will stay a bit and catch up with them later. The meager caravan, now minus its dapper gentleman, moves out of sight.

Themes and Meanings

"The Woman at the Store" was composed in 1911, when its author was barely more than twenty-one; together with two other tales ("Ole Underwood" and "Millie"), it treats New Zealand scenes and introduces offstage violence to obtain its effect. The repulsive but rather hilarious drinking party abruptly comes to an end when the news of the woman's murder of her "missing" husband is revealed by the small child. At a stroke, the story's meanings are completely turned around. At first, the reader is induced to believe that this is a unique (if somewhat sordid) tale of the wilds—remote, unusual, worthy of being carefully recorded by the narrator. Slowly it becomes clear, however, that, far from being an atypical travelogue, it retells instead "the same old story," albeit askew and in grotesque parody: the dapper and brazen male flirting with and seducing the innocent maid. Then, with a last twist and turn, the author reveals that the woman is quite capable of giving as good as she gets, and the implicit irony becomes evident: The reader is left to contemplate a savage act quite typical of civilization; after all, Greek tragedy has often portrayed family feuds and parricide; one need not travel into the bush to find barbarism, for it is not the rude Maori tribes-

men that need be feared, but a lonely, bedraggled woman and a smart, egois-
tic gentleman caller.

Moreover, beneath the glib surface lies the psychological portrayal of loneliness and entrapment. The buxom barmaid has been captured by love, transported to the wilderness, and virtually abandoned by a husband who was
always on the run. He often left her for days, even weeks, only to return,
demanding a kiss: "Sometimes I'd turn a bit nasty, and then 'e'd go off again,
and if I took it all right, 'e'd wait till 'e could twist me round 'is finger, then
'e'd say, 'Well, so long, I'm off.'" Worst of all was her complete transformation. In six years, she has been translated from civilization to isolation, from
good looks to ugliness, from sanity to near madness. She has had one child
and four miscarriages. Incessantly she reflects upon her intolerable life and
her intolerable husband: "[Y]ou've broken my spirit and spoiled my looks,
and wot for—that's wot I'm driving at." Again and again, over and over, "I
'ear them two words knockin' inside me all the time—'Wot for!'" That "wot
for" is ultimately a question directed to the universe: What is it all about?
Why are human beings driven by whim and passion into impossible situations? In murdering her husband, she has at least initiated some action
against a cruel force in the world, but she remains caught in its web. Indeed,
her fling with the passing Jo is in one sense a refreshment from the cruel
grind of her life, but in another, it is merely the reenactment of the servitude
she had endured at the hands of her husband. Ironically, the woman at the
store continues in a hopeless round, for she is at once barbarian and citizen,
rebel and victim. In a miserable little oasis in the wild, amid a plentitude of
stores, she has somehow—maddeningly, incomprehensibly—frittered her
own small storehouse away.

Style and Technique

"The Woman at the Store" is one of Katherine Mansfield's early stories
and does not reveal many of the features of her later great tales: extreme
subtlety, indirection, tenuous but magical symbolism, impersonation of characters, total mastery of detail and of voice. It is, on the contrary, a straight
piece of flatly narrated realism. The narrator herself and Jim are given virtually no personality; all is subsumed by the surface details of travel and
encounter with the woman, related with nearly journalistic precision. Indeed,
one powerful effect in the tale is achieved when the two learn that the woman
is a murderer; understatement prevails, and the characters react almost not
at all, expressing no feelings whatsoever. Yet it is to be inferred that their
response is considerable; Mansfield's employment of indirection here is quite
effective.

Best of all, stylistically, are touches of tone and color and atmosphere that
presage the coming of a master of the twentieth century short story. Often
Mansfield's choice of words is exquisitely appropriate, and her effects are

accomplished with the seemingly easy hand of the professional. Such achievement, for example, is clearly evident even in the story's opening paragraph:

> All that day the heat was terrible. The wind blew close to the ground; it rooted among the tussock grass, slithered along the road, so that the white pumice dust swirled in our faces, settled and sifted over us like a dry-skin itching for growth on our bodies. The horses stumbled along, coughing and chuffing. . . .

The story is a masterful display, a surprising performance by a very talented young beginner.

John R. Clark

THE WOMAN WHO RODE AWAY

Author: D. H. Lawrence (1885-1930)
Type of plot: Psychological realism
Time of plot: The 1920's or somewhat earlier
Locale: Northern Mexico
First published: 1925

> *Principal characters:*
> THE WOMAN, thirty-three years old, a "Californian from
> Berkeley"
> LEDERMAN, her husband, fifty-three years old, a rancher in
> Chihuahua, Northern Mexico
> YOUNG CHILCHUI INDIAN, the Woman's guide

The Story

In this story of initiation, a Woman from Berkeley—the reader never learns her first name—the mother of two children, is restive and dispirited; her marriage to Lederman, a strong-willed rancher twenty years her senior, has long since lost its physical and spiritual vitality. Devoted to work, Lederman once morally swayed her, "kept her in an invincible slavery." Now she yearns for adventure. Beyond the confines of her ranch live the Chilchui Indians, and she determines to ride out, alone, "to wander into the secret haunts of these timeless, mysterious, marvelous Indians of the mountains."

In part 1 of this story in three parts, the Woman, on horseback, comes upon three Indians who seem like figures of fate. One of them, a young man with eyes "quick and black, and inhuman," agrees to guide her to the Chilchui, so that she may "know their gods." Controlling her horse, the Indian leads her to a shelter where other Indians, wearing what appear to be loincloths, are indifferent to her. After a sleep in the "long, long night, icy and eternal," she is aware that she has died to her former self and can never again return to her civilization.

In part 2, she follows the young Indian, descending the slopes until she comes upon a green valley between walls of rock. There, an old chief (or medicine man) questions her. After assuring him that she has not come to bring the white man's god, she is led by her guide to an old Indian, who again questions whether she is willing to bring her "heart to the god of the Chilchui." Again she assents. Ordered to take off her clothes, she is ritually touched by the old man, then offered new clothing of cotton and wool. Later, while naked, she is given a liquor to drink, made with herbs and sweetened with honey. At first ill from the potion, she soon lapses into a langorous consciousness in which her senses are sharpened and purified. Although fascinated by the "darkly and powerfully male" young Indian who still guards her, she never is made to feel "self-conscious, or sex-conscious." Instead, after weeks of captivity, while she continues to drink the ritual emetic cup, she is prepared to learn the mysteries of the Chilchui people: They await a white woman who will sacrifice herself for their gods, and then the "gods will begin to make the world again, and the white man's gods will fall to pieces."

In part 3, increasingly distanced from her past life, numbed by the potion (perhaps one containing peyote), she has visions of the Chilchui cosmology. Dressed now in blue, she prepares herself for sacrifice so that the Indian "must give the moon to the sun." Drugged, weary, she is nevertheless unafraid. When the old priest, the cacique, comes to her with two flint sacrificial knives, when she is stripped even of her mantle and her tunic, fumigated, and laid upon a large flat stone, she acquiesces to her fate. She understands—she assents: "When the red sun was about to sink, he would shine full through the shaft of ice deep into the hollow of the cave, to the innermost." At that moment, the priest would "strike, and strike home, accomplish the sacrifice and achieve the power."

Themes and Meanings

Unlike most of D. H. Lawrence's fiction, "The Woman Who Rode Away" does not focus on the theme of mating—of erotic selection. Instead, the long story concerns a psychological and spiritual initiation into the mysteries of primitive religion. As a moral parable that explores religious values distinct from those common to Western cultures, the story resembles other late fiction by Lawrence, notably "Sun" and "St. Mawr" (1925). In these tales, the writer elaborates a moral argument that runs against the grain of his society's moral conventions. In general, the argument holds that spiritual enlightenment—a mystic attainment of pure vital spirit or anima—is superior to any attainment of emotional fulfillment through erotic bonding.

In "The Woman Who Rode Away," the reader is asked to approve the Woman's acquiescence to the act of her own sacrificial slaughter in order to appease primitive gods. More audaciously, the reader is asked to approve the notion that the primitive gods should be restored to their spiritual supremacy, so that the white man's moral order may be overturned.

To understand fully the extent to which Lawrence dares to impose upon his readers a different (and, for most, unsettling) consciousness of moral reality, one should compare "The Woman Who Rode Away" with "The Princess," a story begun in 1924 and first published in 1925. Both stories originate from a core idea. Mabel Dodge Luhan records that Lawrence showed her the manuscript of "The Woman Who Rode Away" on or about July 1, 1924; it was also at about that time that the writer made a trip to a cove near the Arroyo Seco in Taos country, a setting which is represented in the story.

Both narratives concern women who escape the spiritual ennui of a Western ranch to ride off, in the company of a native guide, in search of adventure. In "The Princess," the guide is Domingo Romero, a Mexican of mostly Indian racial traits, who attempts to rouse Dollie Urquhart to passion (or erotic vitality) through his embraces. His lovemaking, however, is crude, Dollie is indifferent to his sexuality, and she returns to civilization after her love-initiation no longer a physical virgin yet still a spiritual one. The experience has failed to function as a rite of passage to erotic fulfillment. As for Domingo—he is shot down by rangers.

The Woman from Berkeley, on the other hand, completes her initiation, going beyond Eros to the point of self-sacrifice, to Thanatos. Unlike Dollie, whose experience is shallow, the Woman profoundly changes her consciousness. Her Indian guide, unlike Dollie's, demonstrates spiritual strength by initiating her into the mysteries of the primitive gods, not sex; for the Woman, the end result is extinction of ego, rather than a neurotic retention of the old ego, as in Dollie's case. Whereas Dollie remains a civilized woman-child, the Woman from Berkeley "rides" away from the Western world altogether, rides away from life itself, to become moon goddess of the Chilchui cult.

Style and Technique

For readers of this story to understand fully, let alone empathize with, the extraordinary mythic journey of the Woman, they must take the same journey in imagination. Through accumulation of details, often hypnotically repeated, and through image and symbol, Lawrence attempts to break down the moral resistance of his readers to accept his thesis; his intention is that the reader acquiesce, no less than the Woman, to a frame of mind that judges her self-sacrifice as morally correct, that absolves her murderer-priest of guilt as a surrogate of the god, that accepts as just and appropriate the fall of Western ethos.

To achieve these tasks, Lawrence creates a psychological pattern of indoctrination that corresponds to the initiation ritual. Perfectly understandable are the stages of the Woman's mental conditioning, so that she alters her consciousness according to the demands of her ritual guide. She is, after all, denied sleep for long periods; stripped of her Western clothing, forced to go naked and then to wear the special garb of the initiate; drugged with mind-altering potions; allowed long periods of silence, times which are alternated with other periods of camaraderie and instruction in the religious cosmology of her captors; finally, exposed to the sun in a ritual of rebirth. Psychologically, the Woman is conditioned to accept her fate.

To support this pattern of mind control, Lawrence's images and symbols lead the Woman (and the reader) from the familiar to the strange, from the material to the spiritual, from reality to magic. The contrasting sensory and visual images of heat and cold, of sun and moon, are brilliantly concentrated in the cave of ice illuminated by a shaft of light from the sun. With great intensity, Lawrence turns attention away from the sacrificial knife lifted over the heart of the Woman and then "deep, deep to the heart of the earth, and the heart of the sun."

Leslie B. Mittleman

THE WONDERFUL TAR-BABY STORY

Author: Joel Chandler Harris (1848-1908)
Type of plot: Animal fable
Time of plot: An age when animals could talk
Locale: The South
First published: 1880

> *Principal characters:*
> UNCLE REMUS, an aged black man who narrates the story
> MISS SALLY'S SON, a seven-year-old and an appreciative audience
> BRER FOX, the villain of the story, determined to catch Brer Rabbit
> BRER RABBIT, the trickster-protagonist of the story, who always gets away

The Story

"The Wonderful Tar-Baby Story" is only one of the many tales that Uncle Remus tells Miss Sally's son, but it is perhaps the most loved and most remembered. The story begins with the boy asking whether Brer Rabbit ever gets caught. Uncle Remus proceeds to recount one of the wiley rabbit's closest calls.

His nemesis, Brer Fox, still smarting over being fooled again by Brer Rabbit, mixes tar and turpentine to make a tar-baby. He sets his creation, which indeed looks like a little black figure wearing a hat, beside the road and hides himself in the bushes not far away. Soon Brer Rabbit comes walking down the road and stops in his tracks when he sees the tar-baby. He speaks to it, asks it questions, accuses it of being hard-of-hearing and impolite, and finally yells at it. The tar-baby, of course, says nothing, and Brer Fox stays hidden in the bushes, chuckling quietly to himself. Losing his temper, Brer Rabbit hits the tar-baby, first with one fist, then the other. With both hands stuck in the tar, he kicks it with both feet, getting them stuck as well. In desperation, he butts it with his head, which also sticks firmly in the soft tar. Now Brer Fox emerges from the bushes, laughing so hard at Brer Rabbit's plight that he rolls on the ground.

At this point, Uncle Remus stops his tale to remove a large yam from the ashes. When the boy asks if the fox ate the rabbit, he tells him that the story does not say exactly, although some say that Brer B'ar came along and released the rabbit. Anxious readers will be relieved to know that this dilemma is resolved in a later story, "How Mr. Rabbit Was Too Sharp for Mr. Fox," and that Brer Rabbit does indeed escape.

This second installment with its resolution to the first is often considered an integral part of "The Wonderful Tar-Baby Story" and, thus, should be summarized here as well. Uncle Remus begins by indicting Brer Rabbit as a scoundrel, mixed up in all kinds of shady business. He rejoins the tar-baby story as Brer Fox gleefully celebrates his capture of the wiley rabbit with the help of the still silent tar-baby. He then tries to decide how to kill him. He considers the merits of barbecuing, hanging, drowning, and skinning. Brer Rabbit professes to be in favor of any of these solutions so long as the fox does not throw him into the nearby brier patch. This reverse psychology finally sinks in, and the fox, wanting to do whatever Brer Rabbit would hate the most, flings him by his hind legs into the middle of the brier patch. A few minutes later, the unscathed rabbit jeers from the hill, "Bred en bawn in a brier-patch, Brer Fox—bred en bawn in a brier-patch." He cheerfully leaves the scene. Reading these two stories together gives a sense of completion and closure both for Miss Sally's son and the reader. "The Wonderful Tar-Baby Story" and "How the Rabbit Was Too Sharp for Mr. Fox" allow Brer Rabbit to fool Brer Fox once again, an important theme in almost all the Uncle Remus tales.

Themes and Meanings

The meanings in "The Wonderful Tar-Baby Story" range from a simple bit of moral advice about not losing one's temper and not having too much pride to complex interpretations from mythology, folklore, psychology, and sociology. On one level, the clever rabbit is an obvious persona for the black slave; inventive, sly, wise, and successful, the physically inferior rabbit inevitably triumphs over the strong, slower, more stupid animals, especially Brer Fox, a worthy opponent, as seen in this story. In Brer Rabbit's world, the weak at least have a chance. The story of the tar-baby, however, offers an interesting variation on the idea of the slave's identification with Brer Rabbit, for the rabbit demands respect from the black tar-baby as the whites expected it from the blacks. This role reversal lets the reader turn against Brer Rabbit and root for the silent tar-baby. In the conclusion, however, the reader once again applauds Brer Rabbit and his clever escape. "The Wonderful Tar-Baby Story" is not only an entertaining fable for children but also an insightful glimpse into the history, psychology, and folklore of plantation slaves. The lines between black and white, good and evil, comedy and tragedy are blurred and changing. Brer Rabbit, hero and rogue, and Brer Fox, villain and benefactor, meet before the silent audience of the tar-baby (whose role is also ambiguous), shift roles, and rearrange themselves again into the traditional, unresolved conflict between the strong and the clever, the powerful and the powerless.

Style and Technique

Joel Chandler Harris combines journalistic integrity and an ear for Afro-

American dialect to reproduce authentic oral tradition in print. The tales themselves are remnants or at least reproductions of the tale-telling traditions prevalent in West Africa, yet this story reflects the social experience and historical perspective of Afro-Americans defining themselves through the trickster hero, Brer Rabbit. It is neither the content nor the interpretation of the meaning but the dialect that may cause initial difficulty in reading this story. Harris attempted to reproduce the story the way he remembered hearing it. It was a "language" he knew well, but one that is difficult to read. Read aloud by someone who knows the dialect, however, it is clear and easy to follow.

The dialectal spelling and sentence structure are only two of the stylistic techniques noticeable in this story. The framework of the story-teller, Uncle Remus, and the small boy, there to ask questions, removes the story from direct contact with the reader; thus, the racial message is rendered less threatening. At the same time, this setting provides a context which makes the story more accessible. Miss Sally, the yams cooking in the ashes, the old black man, and the little white boy sharing secrets provide a background for a story about talking animals. The participant-observer quality of the author provides an authentic writing style that is unique to Joel Chandler Harris. "The Wonderful Tar-Baby Story" is a blend of humor, pathos, and realism, far more than simply a children's story.

Linda Humphrey

THE WONDERSMITH

Author: Fitz-James O'Brien (1828-1862)
Type of plot: Gothic romance
Time of plot: Early nineteenth century
Locale: New York City
First published: 1859

Principal characters:
> HERR HIPPE, the Wondersmith, also known as Duke
> Balthazar of Lower Egypt, the protagonist
> ZONÉLA, Hippe's daughter
> SOLON, a hunchbacked bookseller and Zonéla's lover
> MADAME FILOMEL, a fortune-teller and midwife, Hippe's
> main accomplice in evil

The Story

Fitz-James O'Brien's short story "The Wondersmith" is divided into seven sections. The first, entitled "Golosh Street and Its People," establishes the location and dark tone for the tale. The first-person, anonymous narrator is a strong presence in this section, describing the dirty street. The "eccentric mercantile settlement" contains a bird-shop with rare birds, a second-hand book-stall, a shop owned by a Frenchman who makes and sells artificial eyes, Madame Filomel, a fortune-teller, and the shop of Herr Hippe, the Wondersmith.

In section 2, "A Bottleful of Souls," Hippe is described as tall and thin, with a "long, thin moustache, that curled like a dark asp around his mouth, the expression of which was so bitter and cruel that it seemed to distill the venom of the ideal serpent. . . ." At a knock on the door, Hippe raises his head, "which vibrated on his long neck like the head of a cobra when about to strike. . . ." Filomel, a fortune-teller and midwife, enters with a bottle of fiendish souls. The evil plot of the pair is revealed: The souls will animate the evil-looking wooden soldiers and maidens carved by Hippe, the dolls' swords and daggers will be dipped in poison, and these fatal toys will then be given to little Christian children. Another knock is heard at the door, and Kerplonne and Oaksmith, "true gypsies," enter. The conspirators are all gathered. They animate the manikins, dropping a gold piece among them to provoke a vicious battle. The souls are then gathered back into Filomel's bottle, the manikins are replaced in their box, and the "four gypsies" depart to turn the dolls loose in the bird-shop.

Part 3, "Solon," introduces the second plot, the love story between Solon, the hunchbacked vendor of secondhand books, and Zonéla, the child of a nobleman who was stolen by Hippe. Zonéla is an organ-grinder with a little monkey named Furbelow. In a song, Solon confesses that he is a poet and that he loves Zonéla, and as the girl and the monkey begin to dance, an enraged Hippe enters the room.

In section 4, "The Manikins and the Minos," the four Gypsies are revealed in the bird-shop as they animate the manikins, open all the cages, and turn the savage dolls loose to kill the helpless birds. Hippe expresses his pleasure with the dolls' ferocity, saying: "They spill blood like Christians. . . . They will be famous assassins."

"Tied Up," section 5, cuts back to Solon and Zonéla caught by Hippe. Hippe viciously kicks Furbelow into the corner of the room and insults Solon. Solon, at Zonéla's touch, experiences the "great sustaining power of love," and finds the courage to speak against Hippe. Hippe responds by telling of his son who was destroyed (inadvertently) through the drinking of brandy with a Hungarian noble; in retaliation, Hippe stole the Hungarian's daughter, Zonéla, and destroyed her life through poverty and misery. Now Hippe delights in the prospect of killing her lover. Hippe wraps Solon in a web and locks Zonéla in her room.

Part 6, "The Poisoning of the Swords," takes place on New Year's Eve. Children all over the city "were lying on white pillows, dreaming of the coming of the generous Santa Claus." In Hippe's house, the four conspirators are painting the manikins' little swords and daggers with poison and are planning to let the dolls kill Solon for practice. Filomel, when questioned by Hippe, slides the black bottle of souls from her pocket to show that she has it; when she lets it slide back, it does not return to its former place, and "balance[s] itself on the edge of her pocket."

The final section, "Let Loose," opens with Solon locked in his closet, having overheard the plan for the terrible death in store for him. Something leaps from the ceiling and "alight[s] softly on the floor. . . . His heart leaps with joy" when he realizes that Zonéla has sent Furbelow with a knife. Solon cuts his cords, opens the door, finds Zonéla, and peeps through the keyhole at the four drunk and sleeping conspirators. Filomel's rocking chair gives a sudden lurch, and the black bottle shatters on the floor. The manikins spring to life and begin stabbing the four Gypsies. Maddened and already dying from the poison, the four begin hurling the manikins into the fire; some of the figures escape and set the room ablaze. Solon, Zonéla, and the monkey escape, and by morning all that remains of the conspirators and Hippe's home is "a black network of stone and charred rafters."

Themes and Meanings

Doubleness in "The Wondersmith" is not simply the enabling mechanism of the plot; it also characterizes the story's overall conception. From the outset, there is an insistence on the underside of the ordinary world. The unattractive environment in which the story is set deftly emphasizes the opposite of metropolitan zest, stimulus, and enterprise. It is in this environment that the story's socially marginal characters ply their quaint but menacing trades and plot their revenge on the conventional world of Christmastime and stable family life. The commitment of Hippe and his underlings to instability evidently derives from the tradition of unsettlement and dispossession which their classification as Gypsies and bohemians connotes. Hippe's scheme seems mindless in its cruelty, and he behaves throughout the story with a demented confidence in his own powers. Nevertheless, there is method in his madness. The scheme's irrational component is its vengeful intolerance of innocence. Yet its attack on innocence is located in an exploitation of material reality: Innocence is destroyed through the subversion of toys purchased for the holiday season. The slaughter of the innocents, as conceived by Hippe, certainly out-Herods Herod, but it is to be carried out by making normally dependable and trustworthy playthings duplicitous.

Hippe's murderous anti-Christian designs are precisely counterbalanced or doubled by Solon's loving spirit and capacity for suffering. The Wondersmith's extraordinary artistic talent is negated by the simple integrity of the deformed bookseller. Fascination with Hippe's malevolence is obliged to yield to appreciation for the hunchback's morally upright stance. The author makes it perfectly clear that Solon is more significant for his moral courage, which his behavior unequivocally exemplifies, than for being a poet, a facet of his personality for which no direct evidence is supplied. Those whom Hippe seeks to punish, represented by the innocent and exploited Zonéla, are ultimately delivered from degradation by Solon's selfless intervention. As the climax of the story makes clear, deliverance is an end in itself.

The story's double plot assists in establishing its conflict and lends distinctive color and atmosphere to it. "The Wondersmith" may be essentially a retelling, or translation to a New World setting, of standard folktale motifs or dualities such as the struggle between purity and danger, between the beauty and the beast, between artifice and honesty. Yet these general, or even stereotypical, considerations are located firmly within the story's specific context and emerge freshly as a result of the author's strong sense of character.

To add depth to the darkness of Hippe's evil mind, O'Brien gives the story a racial dimension. The Wondersmith's obscure origins (he is "one whose lineage makes Pharaoh modern") and his evident chieftainship of an international cabal embody convincingly a sense of otherness and threat. In addition, his access to ancient Gypsy lore and the dukedom with which his intimates invest him make a consistent contribution to a sense of his character's essential foreignness. Drawing, perhaps, on popular superstitions which regard Gypsies as a lost tribe, the descendants of a dispossessed royal house whose ancient rites and usages they now deploy as secret weapons of revenge, O'Brien presents a comprehensive inventory of resources resistant to reason. Supporting the revenge motif is the background to Zonéla's captivity, which, interestingly, is Hippe's method of confronting a legitimate "Hungarian nobleman." Moreover, the combination of materials pertaining to foreignness and the nocturnal side of the world enables the author to make an obvious, but nevertheless deft, connection between Romany and romance. In this regard, Solon is not given specific cultural or national origins: His is the spirit of unadulterated beneficence.

While the struggle between Solon and Hippe is for possession of Zonéla, a battle between science and poetry is also enacted (and in view of the destructively martial nature of Hippe's carvings, battle does not seem too strong a term). Solon, a poet and reader of books, has learned to interpret the promptings of his heart. His use of a story to declare his interest in Zonéla demonstrates what a valuable basis for behavior texts can be. Hippe, on the other hand, uses models and inventions of a more material kind for ends which are a terrifying inversion of Solon's salvific objectives. Hippe's aim is to change the world. Solon, on the other hand, simply wants to make it adequate. The resolution of the conflict, however, does not merely depend on the admirable nature of Solon's personality. Hippe's destruction results from a natural cause, an accident, a species of event which belongs to the ordinary world—which is where Solon desires to take up his natural, rightful place.

Solon's implicit response to Hippe's planned vengeance is to elicit the support of the animal kingdom. In a world controlled, however temporarily, by subversive and malevolent human beings, animals are a last hope, as Solon's rescue by the monkey Furbelow suggests. Prior to this event, the story has already given an unnervingly vivid demonstration of Hippe's powers in the attack on the birds. This episode, as well as confirming the important relationship between the animal, the natural, and Solon, also enacts the murder of song, an occurrence which is paralleled by the captivity of Solon the poet. An attack on nature is tantamount to the elimination of a beautiful attribute which is the natural creature's singular attribute. Nature, for which innocence seems to be a synonym, is vulnerable because it is not duplicitous. Careful to dispel any suspicion of a schematic approach to animal symbolism in the story, O'Brien emphasizes that nature, too, can be cruel and devious by associating Hippe with a serpent. Not only does this association give the Wondersmith a suitably repellent appearance, but also it suggests a familiar link between temptation and destructive knowledge.

The story's invocation of that link facilitates a subtextual consideration on the uses and abuses of knowledge. Hippe's secret lore is capable of imparting poisonous, malevolent life to his artistic creations. He is not, therefore, using knowledge for its own sake, but for the sake of power. Not content to earn his bread by the socially sanctioned use of his talents as a carver, he makes his natural creative ability the vehicle of his blind, destructive urges. His carved models should be a natural source of childish joy. Imbued by the Wondersmith's malevolence, however, they become terroristic automatons.

The Wondersmith, thereby, reveals his true, or at least alternative, identity as the horror-monger and reveals O'Brien's themes.

Style and Technique

The story is written in the recognizable style of its period, rather than in a style which communicates a strong sense of the author's personality. (Perhaps one reason for O'Brien's comparative neglect by critics is that his work lacks a sense of a strong authorial presence, in contrast to that of his powerful contemporaries Edgar Allan Poe, Nathaniel Hawthorne, and Herman Melville.) The conversational first-person narrative opening is used as a conventional means of access to the plot, and when access has been gained, the narrator no longer functions as an integral presence. The text is perhaps too cautiously anchored in allusions to classical mythology and legend, as well as to works of literature, notably Jonathan Swift's *Gulliver's Travels* (1726). Such references sometimes have the effect of cluttering the pace of the narrative. On the other hand, they also are an economical means of suggesting the archetypal nature of the story's struggle, and they lend weight to that struggle.

Perhaps the most impressive of the story's purely technical achievements is its communication of atmosphere. Beginning with the description of the neighborhood in which the story's dire deeds are planned, there is a consistent air of tension and menace. Even the ostensibly lyrical interlude in which Solon visits Zonéla's room has a claustrophobic sense to it, because of the discovery that the girl is Hippe's prisoner and slave. The visit's claustrophobic air is confirmed and intensified when, in turn, the Wondersmith makes the poet his captive. Moreover, O'Brien, as a general strategy, uses deliberately small-scale settings for the action. The use of night also contributes effectively to the prevailing mood of oppression and threat. In addition, once the introductory material has been presented, the story concentrates with impressive consistency on the characters' immediate circumstances, thereby gripping the reader's attention and ensuring that even if he is familiar with the general presuppositions of the plot, he will be entertained by this reworking of them.

George O'Brien

WORK

Author: David Plante (1940-   )
Type of plot: Minimal realism
Time of plot: c. 1980
Locale: The Italian countryside
First published: 1981

> *Principal characters:*
> ROBERT, an American meeting his lover in Italy
> GIUSEPPE (BEPPO), a neighboring farm boy
> ALESSANDRO (ALEX), Robert's Italian lover, who lives with
>   him in the United States
> THE WIDOW MAZZINI, Beppo's mother, the hardworking head
>   of an Italian farm family
> LA NONNA, Beppo's grandmother, who has an infected leg

The Story

Nothing much happens in this story, which won the New York Society of Arts and Sciences O. Henry Memorial Award in 1983. Yet the surface details and what little does happen in "Work" suggest great significance. An American named Robert is at the house of his Italian lover, Alessandro, cleaning and preparing it for Alessandro's arrival. Giuseppe (nicknamed Beppo), the young son of the widow Mazzini, spends a lot of time with Robert waiting for Alessandro, or Alex, to arrive. With childlike fascination for violence and the peasant's fatalism, Beppo imagines all the worst things which could have delayed Alex. Beppo rides his horse to Robert's house to take him to the *posto publico* to receive a telephone call from Alex. Riding bareback behind Beppo, Robert clings to the boy's body. At the *posto publico*, he learns that everyone already knows the message from his lover. The plane has been delayed and Alex will take a taxi from the railway station. Robert and Beppo get back on the horse and stop at the widow Mazzini's house before going to Alex's house to wait for the taxi. When Alex arrives, Robert serves coffee and brandy to Alex and the taxi driver and biscuits to Beppo. Early the next morning, Beppo wakes Robert to ask that he come to the widow's house. Alex cautions Robert not to agree to do anything that he does not want to do; he hints that Robert allows others to take advantage of him.

At the widow's house, Robert, though he protests that he never eats so early in the morning, has breakfast. He talks briefly to La Nonna, the widow's mother, who is suffering from an infected leg and cannot work. He agrees that he and Alex will help the widow and her family pull the tobacco in order to get it to the cooperative warehouse in time to be processed. Alex agrees to help, but makes clear that he thinks Robert has let the widow take advantage of him. In the fields, talk turns to the value of work and the relative advantages of Communism and Fascism. After the work is completed, the widow says that Robert and Alex must have supper with her family, and though Robert initially declines, Alex tells him that they must go, for the widow "has to feed us for the work we have done."

After supper, which the widow eats while she serves the others, she takes them to the stable to show them her cows. Even at the end of a day's work, she takes advantage of the opportunity to sweep the stable floor. Walking home, Robert says that when he returns to Boston he must begin to work hard to repay his father for all the work he has done. Alex says that they are approaching the ditch with the plank over it, and Robert, a little drunk from the widow's wine, takes his arm. The story ends as the lovers go down the path "to the front of the house, which shone among the elder bushes." Here the story ends.

Nothing much has happened. Everything is very quiet and restrained, but David Plante's few pages of prose establish credible people and some of their relationships. The story makes a significant comment upon relative social situations and the possibilities open to some people, closed to others.

Themes and Meanings

Plante's story is not about homosexuality, although its central characters are a homosexual couple. The relationship between Robert and Alex is simply one of the facts of the story, an important one but not the chief one. The two men's emotional and physical relationship remains implicit. The evidence of the story is that the Italian country people know the nature of the relationship, but they neither express nor imply judgment. The love relationship between Robert and Alex assumes another dimension, at once more generalized than sex and more personal than questions of social conformity. The story is about its announced topic: work. The idea of work or the image of work is present even when the word does not occur.

When Alex arrives, he says that he will make coffee for the taxi driver, but Robert makes and serves the coffee and brandy—calling attention to the division of work. Alex looks over the house and touches a wet wall; he comments that he and Robert will have to get to work on it. He asks why certain things have not been done, but he praises Robert for the work he has done to get the house ready. Robert replies, "Work?" His question raises the issue of the meaning of the word. Is it work to prepare a home for one's lover?

The conversation in the tobacco field concentrates on work and reward. One of the farmhands cannot understand how anybody can work and get nothing for it. The widow and members of her family express the belief that one should get rewards for work, but Alex says that he became a Communist because Communism "gives our work, however small, meaning in the world." The peasants are amused by his belief, even while they admire it. They have not been able to afford social or political idealism.

At the story's conclusion, Robert tells his lover that he wants to work when he returns to Boston, but the reader is not convinced that Robert will actually fulfill what he seems to regard as an obligation to his aged father. Several Italians have questioned Robert about his father and why Robert no longer lives with him. Specifically, they want to know, if the old man can no longer work, who works for him. Beppo says that if Robert's father is eighty, he will soon die. La Nonna can no longer work, and will soon die. The implication is that, without work—meaningful activity done for various reasons, including material reward, satisfaction of duty, or love—there is no life.

Style and Technique

Plante's work in this short story and in some of his novels comes close to what critics have called minimalism. What he does not say is often as important as what he does say. He resists explanations and commentary and makes the story move forward from specific detail to detail. The action is low-key, and the reader must observe how Plante's selection of details and actions build toward a statement.

The specific details of the story, provided through the subdued voice of a third-person narrator, announce Plante's intentions, and the repetition of some of those details confirms those intentions. Early in the story, Robert is cutting the grass and notices the swifts flying about him: "He thought that there were layers below him of sand and water and rock, and layers above of air and thin cloud, and, above, the layers of the sky, and all the layers rose and fell." Later, the narrator says that "the different levels of earth and air appeared to separate as the daylight lengthened, and the dim upper and lower levels began to disappear." The narrator (thus, possibly Robert) identifies the fine line between the upper and lower levels as the space where "the swifts flew out and back, out and back." The metaphorical import of this central image becomes clear with the accumulation of detail as the story progresses: What fills the gap between the upper and lower levels of day-to-day existence, constituting life, is work.

Plante augments his meaning through repetition. He repeats not only the metaphysical images of the layering of space but also actions (Beppo is always dashing around on his horse; twice the reader sees the boy lead the horse to a large stone so that he can mount it), images of work, attitudes toward work—indeed, the very word "work."

Plante's story is a tone poem and does not depend upon resolution of conflict or plot. It plays on repetition of a word and concept central to human experience, but perhaps requiring redefinition or at least reexamination. Robert's brushing away of the spiderwebs in his and his lover's vacation house and the two of them helping the widow in the fields is work of a different sort from that necessary to sustain life. The levels and layers differ, Plante tells his readers, but work has its own dignity.

Leon V. Driskell

THE WORLD ACCORDING TO HSÜ

Author: Bharati Mukherjee (1940-   )
Type of plot: Social realism
Time of plot: 1978
Locale: An island-nation off the southeastern coast of Africa
First published: 1983

Principal characters:
> RATNA CLAYTON, a thirty-three-year-old journalist, an
> expatriate from Calcutta
> GRAEME, her husband, a thirty-five-year-old professor of
> psychology in Montreal
> CAMILLE LIOON, the travel agent, a refugee from Beirut
> JUSTIN, the taxi driver, a native of the island

The Story

From Montreal, the Claytons arrive in the wintry June of a recently independent island-nation—perhaps the Malagasy Republic but unnamed and thus serving as a symbol for postcolonial states where coups come with "seasonal regularity"—for what they hope will be a peaceful vacation. They are greeted by an unexpected, unreported revolution in progress; the vaguely leftist government downplays the insurgent "melancholy students and ungenerous bureaucrats" of the neocolonial movement, but the Claytons do not panic, presuming to remain aloof from the rioting, looting, and killing. Beneath their romantic illusions of an escape to an "old-fashioned" paradisiacal retreat, both of them harbor undisclosed motives in taking the trip. Graeme Clayton, while ostensibly wishing to view the Southern Cross, a constellation not visible in Canada, actually hopes to persuade his wife to move to Toronto so that he can accept the chair of the Personality Growth Department, an offer which he has already accepted. Ratna Clayton plans, instead of lolling on the beach, "to take stock" of her previously "manageably capricious" life before the six-month debate over the move.

Using the island's events as a symbol for constant change and impermanent appearances, the limited third-person narrator, who reflects Ratna's point of view, shows a chaotic world, riddled with divisions of race, religion, class, nationality, and language in seemingly perpetual conflict. Considering Graeme's tendency to lecture at every opportunity, Ratna imagines his clinical account once they return to Montreal; she anticipates that Graeme's colleague, Freddie McLaren, will relate the coup to Catholic-Protestant fighting in Belfast, to religious and political factional strife in Beirut, and to the French separatist movement in Quebec. She recalls their travel agent Camille Lioon's warning against a stop in Saudi Arabia, because of Hindu-Moslem antipathies, and Lioon's accusation that the Saudis are insensitive, even though he is "no less an Arab than they." Ratna contemplates her fear of "Toronto racists," for whom she believes she is "not Canadian, not even Indian" but, in the derogatory "imported idiom of London, a Paki." With a Czech mother, she remembers that even her father's Indian family shunned her "as a 'white rat' " when she was "a pale, scrawny blonde" as a child: The "European strain had appeared and disappeared." Her own use of English is "a secondhand interest," a compromise in her "home," "city," "country," "career," and "even in her marriage."

Bearing the anguish of expatriation, Ratna arrives at an intended "refuge" that becomes a "prison," mirroring her own inner turmoil. That turmoil is exacerbated by Graeme's need for "some definitive order." Ironically, as "an authority on a whole rainbow of dysfunctions" and anticipating his direction of studies in personality growth, Graeme maintains a distant perspective on the pain to which he is closest: Ratna's fear of living in Toronto. His marriage is clearly secondary to his career; when Ratna recounts horror stories of Toronto bigots attacking Indian immigrants, Graeme lies: "If you don't want to go to Toronto, we won't go." Further, he dismisses her fears, resenting "this habit she had of injecting bitterness into every new scene." Under Graeme's romantic inclinations for amateur astronomy and photography, there rest the seeds of fascism, a desire for scientifically ordering the chaos around him to suit his own interests: "In place of a heart he should have had a Nikon." Graeme is utterly incapable of understanding Ratna's anxiety as an expatriate; his empathy for the emotions of others is sterile.

Both the Claytons, however, deny the events of insurrection and martial law which surround them. They insist on staying at the Hotel Papillon, two blocks away from the center of rioting, against the protests of Justin, their taxi driver and tourist guide, who advises them to stay at the Hilton with other Europeans and Indians. Graeme rejects Justin's stereotyping of himself, accurate as it is, and Ratna, rejecting Justin's pleading that the wealthier Indians are safe there, announces arrogantly that she is a Canadian. The curfew and the closing of the museum, zoo, and school prevent sight-seeing and stargazing; entire sections of the city are sealed off. Paratroopers stop them on their way from the airport to the hotel, searching their luggage; nevertheless, the Claytons insist that Justin drive them through the marketplace, where soldiers fire mock salvos at them.

Furthermore, even middle-class natives deny the conflict. Justin arranges a bizarre tour to the king's palace, deserted in 1767 when the French deposed the king but still the site of daily recitals by the royal band, which awaits nostalgically the colonial holidays banned after the revolution. Madame Papillon, the proprietress who has remained within her hotel as a recluse for the last thirteen years, depends on Justin for news of the world outside. Indians, as a matter of habitual response, lock their assets in the Hilton's safe even as rioters burn and loot their shops. Ratna, in dwelling on her fears of racism in Toronto, begins to identify with African historical persecution of Indians— who are the Jews of Africa, as Madam Papillon remarks, not altogether innocently. Her uncertainties open her to events around herself, but her focus is on her dilemma in moving to Toronto.

That evening, while the Claytons dine on bad food and good wine, they learn of yet another coup on nearby islands. Their waiter announces the assassination of an ambassador's wife, but the failure of the government-controlled media to report it suggests that the violence on the island is increasing. Graeme, apparently still isolated from the implications of danger, reads a geology article, written by Kenneth Hsü, from *Scientific American*— "his light reading." When Ratna objects to his habit of reading at the table, he replies, " 'I'm not reading,' . . . meaning *you're free to interrupt me, I'm not advancing my career.*" Continuing his reading aloud to her, he says, "According to Hsü . . . the last time the world was one must have been about six million years ago" and goes on to explain that the "island is just part of the debris," a result of the continental collision between Africa and Asia. Ratna, besieged by emotions as she reflects on the day almost past and identifying unconsciously with the island as part of the debris, decides that she can be comfortable among the dining guests: "Like her, they were non-islanders, refugees." In her conscious rejection of the thought that the day's events have anything to do with her, she nearly reconciles her own desire to remain aloof with that of Graeme.

Graeme, still bent on a glimpse of the Southern Cross, persuades the waiter to break curfew, taking him out the kitchen door to see the stars. Before he leaves, he tells Ratna of his decision to accept the job and of having already written to Toronto. He adds, "Don't worry, if anything happens to you there I promise we'll leave." He orders more wine, inviting her to renew the romantic purpose of the trip by seeing the constellation with him. Ratna refuses. After Graeme has left, she translates an entry in French from the menu for an American, numb to the "passionate consequences" of his "unilingualism." Delighted with the local wine and at ease "in that collection of Indians and Europeans babbling in English and remembered dialects," Ratna concludes to herself: "No matter where she lived, she would never feel so at home again."

Themes and Meanings

In Bharati Mukherjee's introduction to her collection of short stories *Darkness* (1985), she describes her work as an exploration in "state-of-the-art expatriation." By seeking to isolate themselves from the physical violence of the island's coup, the Claytons only intensify, in Graeme's need for clarity and order and in Ratna's aloofness, their emotional inability to understand themselves and each other. Their marriage is a metaphor for misunderstanding between natives and expatriates; Graeme's self-assured presumption of superiority contrasts with Ratna's urgent need to belong to a society free of racial and nationalistic prejudices. He cannot participate in her emotional disorientation; she cannot desist from the "mordant and self-protective irony" in which she identifies most strongly with the French separatists in Quebec. Only when Ratna resigns herself to following Graeme on yet another path in her journey as an expatriate and finds solace among the mutual English of dining Europeans and Indians (the two halves of her heritage) does she enjoy a momentary sense of belonging somewhere. She does not, however, resolve the difference between immigrant and expatriate: Her fuzzy epiphany in translating for the American both compliments her aloof use of French and undermines the illusory self-protection which it offers. The American, an implicit metaphor for the immigrant, is free to belong to the multiplicity of many cultural heritages; Ratna, explicitly an expatriate, must wonder if she "would ever belong." In her muddled search for "souvenirs of an ever-retreating past," much like Hsü's geological archaeology of unity, and in her aloof detachment, one must conclude that Ratna will "never belong, anywhere."

The irony of telescoping symbols of the marriage, the island's independence, and Hsü's prehistorical world unity for divisive change and inconsequential stability is that however ordered Graeme's worldview may be and however aloof Ratna may remain, they will both be physically and emotionally affected by change and instability. Only by recognizing cultural differences without creating stereotypes and by accepting change within their own lives can the Claytons ever come to terms with the changing circumstances around them, wherever they may be. This recognition and acceptance depends on the cultivated awareness of the immigrant, not the feigned superiority of the expatriate. Ratna fails to gain the immigrant's awareness because she believes that it is an experience restricted to the island and dependent upon her own aloofness.

Style and Technique

Mukherjee's thematic transition from expatriate to immigrant attitudes is achieved not only through her use of irony and symbol but also through her use of specific details laden with metonyms. To portray the island as both a macrocosm of the marriage and a microcosm of the world, she employs a multitude of religions and nationalities. There are references to Christians—Catholic and Protestant, Hindus, and Moslems. European references include the French, English, Germans, Irish, Swedes, Czechs, Hungarians, and Bulgarians as well as Canadian and American characters. Camille is from Lebanon; Graeme's camera is a Japanese Nikon; Hsü is a Chinese name; North Koreans provide foreign assistance; the African troops are "Peruvian-looking"; the World Cup scores originate in Argentina; and there are frequent specific references to India and Indians. The many uses of proper place-names, from Jiddah to Dar es Salaam, in contrast to the anonymity of the island and the capital city (perhaps Antananarivo), establish their universality as symbols for political upheaval everywhere. The brief scene over dinner in which a German teaches "an English folksong to three Ismaili-Indian children" provides a foreshadowing parallel to Ratna's brief experience of immigrant awareness: the song's refrain "row, row, row your boat" itself ironically juxtaposed to Graeme's pseudosophisticated, derivative explanation of continental drift.

Further, Mukherjee's use of language helps sharpen her ironies in the dialogue. When Graeme promises to leave Toronto should anything happen to Ratna, he fails to realize that then it would be too late. When Camille asserts his own Arab identity after calling the Saudis insensitive, he condemns his own insensitivity in the overgeneralized slur. When Madam Papillon complains about not being able to "carry on an honest business," she ignores the colonial exploitation of the past and the neocolonial corruption of the present, both of which she seems to condone. To accentuate the underlying metaphor of geology for politics, Mukherjee shifts the usual context of diction in such phrases as the "epicenter of the looting" and "the plate tectonics of emotions." In another twist of ironic language, the narrator's use of Graeme's borrowed scientific vocabulary itself suggests a missed potential for immigrant awareness; thus, the limited viewpoint of the narrator underscores the pitfalls of the expatriate's shortcomings, suggesting that the language one uses reflects the worldview with which one experiences oneself in the world.

Michael Loudon

A WORLD ENDS

Author: Wolfgang Hildesheimer (1916-   )
Type of plot: Aesthetic fantasy
Time of plot: Sometime in the twentieth century
Locale: The artificial island of San Amerigo
First published: "Das Ende einer Welt," 1952 (English translation, 1960)

> *Principal characters:*
> HERR SEBALD, the narrator and protagonist, who attends the
> party on San Amerigo
> THE MARCHESA MONTETRISTO, the owner of the island and
> hostess of the party

The Story

The fabulistic nature of this very brief story is indicated initially by the detached tone of its narrator and by the absence of any social context in which its events take place. There is no plot as such; instead, the story very briefly recounts the narrator's experience at the Marchesa Montetristo's last evening party and the memorable nature of its "extraordinary conclusion," in which the artificial island on which the Marchesa lives breaks up and sinks into the sea. Most of the story focuses on the narrator's recounting of the various important guests he meets during the party.

Perhaps the key word in "A World Ends" is "artificial," for what characterizes the Marchesa and her guests is their allegiance to art and artifice rather than an affirmation of social reality—which is why the Marchesa's home is on an artificial island set apart from the real world. The Marchesa hates the mainland because it is hurtful to her spiritual equilibrium; thus she devotes her life to the antique and the forgotten—qualities which she believes typify the "true and eternal." In fact, the reason the narrator is invited to the party, his one real claim to fame, is that he has sold her the bathtub in which the French revolutionary Jean-Paul Marat was murdered.

All the guests are distinguished by their artistic talents: a woman famous for her rhythmic-expressionistic dance, a famous flutist, a renowned intellectual, an astrologer, a preserver of Celtic customs, a neomystic—all of whom the narrator introduces as if they should be well-known to the reader. In short, as he says, they are the most eminent figures of the age, but all the characters in the story suggest their aesthetic rather than actual existence. Even the Marchesa's domestic servant looks as if he were a character out of the opera *Tosca* (1900). Moreover, the building is described as being of the height of opulence and splendor, representing every period of decor from the gothic onward. Over and over, in describing the place and the guests, the narrator repeats how unnecessary it is to describe, how he need hardly remind the reader of the fame and greatness of those assembled.

None of the people is presented as real; rather, they seem to be artifice itself. The performers are dressed and arranged as if they were a picture by Jean Antoine Watteau. When the servant who looks like a character out of *Tosca* comes to tell the Marchesa of the danger of the island's foundation collapsing, her paleness is described by the narrator in terms of its aesthetic effect; he notes that her paleness suits her in the dim candlelight. Even with that warning, the guests want to go on listening to the music. As the puddles begin to form and the reverberation of the imminent collapse sounds, the narrator says that the guests are sitting upright as if they were long dead already.

The narrator, the only guest to admit his fear and to try to escape, seems to accept what is happening with the same kind of detachment that he has exhibited throughout the story. As he departs and water rises higher, he thinks only that the Marchesa can no longer use the pedals of the harpsichord she is playing and that the instrument will not sound in water. In addition to the narrator, only the servants flee, for they, unlike the guests, have no obligation to the true and eternal culture. The narrator says that no less than a world is sinking beneath the ocean. As he paddles away, the guests rise from their seats and applaud with their hands high over their heads, for the water has reached their necks. The Marchesa and the flutist receive the applause with dignity, although, the narrator notes, they cannot, under the circumstances, bow.

When the building collapses with a roar, the narrator turns around only to note that the sea is dead-calm, as if no island had ever stood there. His last thought in the story is about the bathtub of Marat, a loss that can never be made good—a somewhat heartless thought, he acknowledges, but which he justifies by saying that one needs a certain distance from such events in order to appreciate their full scope.

Themes and Meanings

It is not the distance of time that the reader needs to appreciate the full scope of this cryptic and unusual short story, but rather aesthetic distance, for indeed it is aesthetic reality that the story seems to be about. On the most obvious level, the story can be read as a parable of the inevitable fate of trying to live life detached from the reality of social interaction and responsibility. All the guests, after all, seem to exist solely in their devotion to realms of reality apart from the social world—that is, in the world of artifacts and the frozen world of art. The narrator is allowed to survive because, as he says, he is taken up with everyday affairs; it is indeed the everyday that the Marchesa and her guests avoid and deny.

Thus, in terms of a moral-aesthetic parable, Wolfgang Hildesheimer could be pointing out the shaky foundation of such artifice and antiquity, and thus, in a grimly amusing way, illustrating how it must inevitably come crashing down like a stack of cards. Moreover, he does not here offer anything that seems more valuable to take the place of such aesthetic values, for the world of the Marchesa seems to have no social context outside itself. The story is more likely, however, to be one in which Hildesheimer, himself an artist, an art critic, and a stage designer, seems to be creating a world of pure decor and unreality, a world of artifice, for no other reason than to play with aesthetic reality.

The problem is that in such a world of art, one cannot always distinguish between genuine art (whatever that is) and pretension and posturing. There is much name-dropping in this story, a fascination with the antique for its own sake and for its decadent quality. For example, there is the absurdity of valuing the tub in which Marat was killed, and there is the fact that the Marchesa does not seem to know, at least according to the narrator, that the sonata that she and the flutist are playing, supposedly by Antonio Giambattista Bloch, is a forgery, for no such person as Antonio Giambattista Bloch ever lived. In this sense, Hildesheimer is writing an ironic aesthetic fantasy which poses no real moral judgment, but which simply plays with the ambiguity of what is artistic and what is only posturing. Certainly the narrator himself is as guilty of such posturing as are any of the famous guests for whom the world ends at the end of this story.

Style and Technique

The story's style depends primarily on the detached and straightforward voice of the narrator, who accepts the values of the Marchesa, even as he escapes her world's final end. The story is very similar to Edgar Allan Poe's "The Masque of the Red Death," for there, too, in a much more ornate style, a world sustained by artifice is destroyed. Even the rooms in the artificial home of the Marchesa are representative of historical stages, not the stages of one's life, as in Poe's story, but rather the stages of architecture and design. As the guests listen to the sonata, the guests move from the Silver Room, which is baroque, to the Golden Room, which is early rococo.

Furthermore, the story is characterized, as other Poe stories are, by the invention of an elaborate world of seemingly real historical figures, with which, as the narrator reminds the reader, one should be very familiar, but which are pure fabrications of the writer himself. In this respect, as well as in the collapse of the foundations of the house, the story reminds one of Poe's "The Fall of the House of Usher," in which Roderick Usher, who also attempts to detach himself from external reality and live in a world of art, collapses within the house that is identified with him. The basic difference between Hildesheimer's story and Poe's stories is that Hildesheimer seems to be, even as he imitates Poe, slightly mocking the aestheticism typical of Poe. Thus, the story is a burlesque of Poe's stories and therefore the aesthetic movement which Poe helped to initiate. The style is a combination of the haughty aloofness of the aesthetes undercut by an authorial tone of gentle mocking. Thus, "A World Ends" has the style and tone of a playful story, for it is an artwork that self-consciously makes use of the ambiguous status and nature of the artwork both to make itself and to mock itself.

Charles E. May

THE WORLD OF APPLES

Author: John Cheever (1912-1982)
Type of plot: Psychological realism
Time of plot: The 1960's
Locale: Italy
First published: 1964

> *Principal character:*
> ASA BASCOMB, a poet and the protagonist

The Story

Asa Bascomb is an eighty-two-year-old American poet living in a villa near the Italian town of Monte Carbone. Except for the fact that he is an expatriate, he resembles the American poet Robert Frost in several ways: He is from Vermont, he has unruly white hair, and he has received many international honors, though not the Nobel Prize. The story opens with him swatting hornets in his study and wondering why this greatest of all literary honors has been denied him.

The only other person living in his villa is Maria, his maid. His wife Amelia has been dead for ten years. Though one of his reasons for living in Italy is to avoid the publicity that would burden him in the United States, fans of his most popular book of poetry, *The World of Apples*, seek him out. Generally, though, his routine is simple and uninterrupted. He writes poetry in the morning; in the afternoon he takes a nap and walks to town to get his mail, which he then goes over at home. Several evenings a week, he plays backgammon with one of the locals.

Bascomb's poetry is as simple and clear-cut as is his life. It has even been compared to Paul Cézanne's paintings. Based exclusively on nostalgia, though, his poetry lacks vision and the impulsiveness that characterized the work of several American poets with whom he is often linked and who committed suicide (one drank himself to death).

The idyllic tenor of Bascomb's life begins to crumble when his memory, the chief source of his poetry, begins to fail him in small ways. He cannot remember, for example, Lord Byron's first name, and he cannot rest until he looks it up. A major difficulty soon presents itself. While on a sight-seeing tour with a Scandinavian admirer, he accidentally discovers a couple copulating in the woods. His memory of this event haunts him, and he is unable to rid his mind of the obscene thoughts which subsequently crowd into it. He goes to bed with his maid, Maria, but though this relieves his urges, it does not drive sex from his mind. Critically interrupting his desire for vision and the Nobel Prize, obscenity becomes the pivot and bane of his work and life. He starts writing obscene poems with literary titles and based on classical models, but he burns them at the end of each morning session. He ends up writing dirty limericks, which he also discards. He travels to Rome to distract himself. This does not work either, for a man exposes himself to him in a public toilet, the art in a gallery Bascomb visits turns out to be pornographic, and he finds himself mentally undressing the female singer at a concert.

Back at his villa, he probes for the source of the filth that has invaded his consciousness. Important events in his memory, such as his wife standing in light, his son's birth, and his daughter's marriage, seem linked to this invasion. The "anxiety and love" which define these events for him also seem to be the origin of his lapse from idealism.

Informed by his maid of the statue of an angel in Monte Giordano which is supposed to cleanse troubled souls, Bascomb sets off on foot with a seashell that belonged to his wife, understanding that pilgrimages require these things. He brings an offering for the angel, too—a gold medal awarded him by the Soviet Union. On the way, he watches from concealment a man, his wife, and their three daughters get out of a car. While his wife and daughters line up with their hands over their ears and in a state of delighted excitement, the man fires his shotgun into the air. Then the party gets back in the car and leaves. Bascomb falls asleep in the grass and dreams that he is back in New England, where a boy plays king and an old man gives a bone to a dog. He also dreams of a bathtub full of burning leaves.

A thunderstorm awakens Bascomb. He befriends a dog frightened by the storm and takes shelter with an old man his own age. The old man seems simple, happy, and open, surrounded by his potted plants and holding a stamp album on his lap. Envious of him, Bascomb continues to the shrine. At first the priest in charge of it does not want to let him in because of the Communist medal he has brought as an offering. The priest gives in, however, when sunlight comes through a break in the clouds and reflects off the medal, for he regards this as a sign that Bascomb's quest is legitimate. Instead of asking the angel for a personal favor, Bascomb asks it to bless a series of famous writers, all American except for the rhapsodic Welsh poet, Dylan Thomas.

Staying overnight in Monte Giordano, Bascomb sleeps peacefully and awakes renewed, his old sense of clarity and goodness intact. As he walks home, he discovers a waterfall and remembers a similar one in his childhood in Vermont, in which he had once seen his old father bathe naked. He does the same now, after which the police, alerted by his worried maid, find him and bring him home. It is a triumphal return, reminiscent of Christ's entry into Jerusalem on Palm Sunday, and Bascomb sets about writing a new poem in his true style, no longer with his eye on the Nobel Prize.

Themes and Meanings

The aim of "The World of Apples" is to show that the artist must not only serve himself but also the world around him. Asa Bascomb is disconnected from the world in many ways. He lives virtually alone, having withdrawn from his own country to avoid his public image there. He selfishly broods on his desire for the Nobel Prize and relies more on his memories of human contact than on human contact itself. He keeps the admirers who visit him in Italy at a distance, choosing only a handful to spend any time with at all. The world, in fact, serves him, from his maid and the boy who carries his mail for him to the admirer who takes him on a tour and the official bodies which have given him awards for his poetry. The reason behind all this service is the one book he has written with which people can empathize, *The World of Apples*.

The onslaught of indecent thoughts that Bascomb experiences signals the beginning of his return to an intimate connection with the world around him. These thoughts and the lust they arouse in him challenge his remoteness and abstract purity. The couple copulating in the woods, the man in the public toilet in Rome, and the singer at the concert draw him toward them until he cannot see himself apart from them. Every attempt at escape only brings him closer to the vitality of the physical, including running away to Rome, sleeping with his maid, and writing obscene poetry.

Eventually Bascomb must appeal to a source greater than himself to repair the damage to his sense of self. He must humble himself to a custom not his own, but that of the people among whom he lives. In seeking divine aid, he encounters images of healthy if perplexing human contact such as the man entertaining his family with a shotgun and the old man whose peace and happiness seem to have something to do with the living world in that he grows plants and collects stamps. By now the approach of the rainstorm has awakened Bascomb's senses to his old delight in country things, and he has been moved to serve another creature, the dog he has petted in its fear and brought to shelter.

After nature has given a sign that it approves of his humble pilgrimage— illuminating his gift with sunlight—Bascomb returns to spiritual health, which his untroubled sleep signifies and which he chooses as his own when he bathes in the waterfall, thus "baptizing" himself—cleansing himself—as one who belongs not only to himself but to the human and natural world at large.

Style and Technique

The story makes use of the details of setting to dramatize its meanings. For example, in Monte Carbone where Bascomb lives, there are springs which feed the fountains in his garden. He finds the water distasteful, for it is very cold and noisy. The noise is unlike the pure, controlled music of his poetry, but the water's coldness symbolizes his own. The same image of water occurs near the end of the story when Bascomb encounters the waterfall on his way home from Monte Giordano. The waterfall is as cold and noisy as the fountains, but this time the water represents baptism. The noise is a kind of poetry to which Bascomb adds his voice, and the coldness is his own spirit purified through pain.

Other details of setting work in the same way. The signs of age in the buildings in his environment point to Bascomb's own advanced age. The crumbling churches, however, with their still intact artwork, rich and earthy, represent a tradition of human contact with nature and the divine to which Bascomb eventually commits himself. In Rome, the public toilet where the male prostitute exhibits himself echoes Bascomb's own soul at that point, the art gallery represents his mind haunted by obscene images, and the concert hall symbolizes his poetry furtively debased by his lust. Finally, as the thunderstorm dramatizes the turmoil in Bascomb, the sunlight which follows it is an image of his hope, his acceptance by the mysterious forces which govern life, and the generosity he ultimately brings to life.

Mark McCloskey

THE WORLD OF STONE

Author: Tadeusz Borowski (1922-1951)
Type of plot: Sketch
Time of plot: 1947-1948
Locale: Warsaw
First published: "Kamienny świat," 1948 (English translation, 1967)

> *Principal characters:*
> THE UNNAMED NARRATOR
> HIS WIFE, also unnamed, perceived only from a distance

The Story
 Very few events take place in "The World of Stone," yet when the conclusion is reached, after five pages, a comprehensive attitude toward the entire world has been described, as well as a resolute course of action toward that world. The story is not impressionistic, although at the outset it seems to register the narrator's stray observations. The reader is presented with two items of information, or building blocks of the story. First, the narrator possesses the "terrible knowledge" that the universe is inflating at incredible speed, like a soap bubble. Second, the narrator enjoys taking long, lonely walks in the city, through its poorest districts. At the beginning, this is all the narrator discloses.

 If the reader is tempted to think that these two themes of the story have no relation to each other—that the first is of a purely psychological nature and the second, an innocuous everyday pastime—this is quickly dispelled by the author. Indeed, part of the artfulness of the story's beginning is that the reader is lured into it by a seeming contradiction, only to find that there is none, or that it is not what he had expected.

 As the narrator takes his daily strolls, he observes the world around him acutely. There is no psychological impressionism here. It is a specific world—a city in ruins, beginning to be rebuilt. The country is unnamed, but it is in postwar Eastern Europe; the details could describe many different European cities after the war. Fresh grass is already beginning to overgrow the ruins, and people are busy—working, selling wares—and children are playing. The narrator observes this world in its entirety and he feels indifference for it, even contempt. Although some of the first details describing the city and its inhabitants are superficially attractive—peasant women selling sour cream, workmen hammering and straightening trolley-bus rails, children chasing rag balls—the narrator has an unambiguous attitude toward it. It is ugly, meaningless, a "gigantic stew" flowing like water down a gutter into a sewer.

 At an important transition midway through the story, the narrator proceeds from one of these walks in the city to the office where he works. It is not any office of a businessman: It is grandiose, with a marble stairway and red carpet "religiously shaken out every morning" by the cleaning ladies. Inside the building is another world, ordered, important, with a hierarchy unmistakably composed of Communist Party members.

At the end of the day, the narrator returns home to his apartment. It has a curious resemblance to the building for Party members where he works and which he has just left. He lives there only because of his Party position ("it is not registered with any rent commission"). His wife is far offstage working in the distant kitchen, and he goes to his workroom, his desk, where he looks once again out the window, re-creating the world he saw earlier during his walks: the peasant women selling sour cream, the workers hammering rails. He has no feeling whatsoever for any of the people in this world. "With a tremendous intellectual effort," however, he intends to grasp their significance and give them form, chiseling out of stone "a great immortal epic." Although the Western reader might by puzzled by some details, the author states at the end of the story in an unequivocal way that the work he is chiseling from the meaningless world will be great, epic, and immortal because—and only because—it will be a Communist world. The ending of the story is a declaration of intention: The narrator intends to create a work giving form to the world. He clearly states that it will have the qualities normally associated with art—epic, immortality, greatness—not because of any craft or compassion or human quality, but solely because of political allegiance.

Themes and Meanings

Much of the interpretation of the story is done by the narrator himself; it is a story about his "knowledge," which he asserts is not simply opinion but truth. The story operates on a high level of generality. There are no dynamic relations between individual characters, but instead a single point of view (the narrator uses the first-person singular pronoun) looking out at a broad variety of detail and people that make up the world. This world is referred to by the title; it is far more important than any single character or living human being, with the exception of the narrator.

The reader will quickly notice that this "world" has two somewhat contradictory qualities: It is both light—ready to dissolve like a soap bubble, insignificant and senseless—and it is heavy, intractable, difficult to grasp, a "world of stone." Other descriptions of this cosmic world fall midway between these two poles: It is an overripe pomegranate, a cosmic gale, a huge whirlpool, a weird snarl, and gigantic stew. This contradiction is one of the most intriguing features of the story. The interpretation of this world, and resolution of Borowski's contradiction, is one of the reader's thorniest tasks. Something is missing, or withheld. There is an irrational element in the story that Borowski partly confronts, and although he stops short of full clarity, this confrontation is one of the most moving concerns of the story. The dominant impression of the narrator's observations of the outside world is not really one of lightness or even "indifference," as the author suggests, but one of disgust. When Borowski claims that the narrator feels "irreverence bordering almost on contempt," he has already created an attitude of full *de facto* contempt that borders, rather, on hatred. It is not the world, "this weird snarl," that is weird, but the narrator's attitude. What, then is the "stone" of "the world of stone"—what does the author mean by his title? The author does not establish a clear equation, and the reader must interpret the question for himself. It is open-ended, part of the strange and disquieting art of the story. It is possible to follow the author and say that the world is worthy of total indifference and contempt, that it has no objective value and is only a place of stone. The stone can also be interpreted in psychological terms; it is the author's feelings that are petrified.

The single clear, and striking, reference to stone in the story is the description of the Communist Party building in which the narrator works. It is "a massive, cool building made of granite," and its staircase is made of marble. This is the one setting in the story where the world, with its babble and meaningless chaos, is kept at bay.

The title of the story is also the title of the collection of stories; hence, its reference is also outside this particular story. When the reader turns to the other stories—"The Death of Schillinger," "The Man with the Package," "The Supper," "A True Story," "Silence," and above all the stories not about concentration camps but about the postwar, civilian world—the overall feeling of numbness and nihilism is confirmed. Borowski was a survivor of Auschwitz and Buchenwald, and his subsequent fate indicates one path taken by survivors. An abundant literature has grown up about the concentration camps, as well as the plight of survivors—Elie Wiesel and Bruno Bettelheim are two of the foremost American contributors. Tadeusz Borowski, too, has made one of the most important and lasting contributions to the literature of the Holocaust. American readers often find one of his major themes unpalatable, refusing to accept it, denying it, or sentimentally distorting it: that the human survival instinct is not necessarily a positive value. To survive in the camps often required the willingness to destroy others. (Readers of Wiesel's *Night*, 1956, will recall the father and son trying to kill each other for a small piece of bread.) No one has portrayed this better than Borowski, both in his stories and in his life. The "stone" in the title of "The World of Stone" is not only numbness but also destructiveness; it carried over into civilian life after the war and was directed against society as a whole, finding an outlet in the Communist Party. It was also directed against art; after the collection *The World of Stone* was published in 1948, Borowski ceased writing literature and devoted himself to shrill, propagandistic journalism, filled with hatred and largely directed against Americans—no matter that his 1946 book *Byliśmy w Oświęcimiu* (1946; we were in Auschwitz) was dedicated to "The American Seventh Army which brought us liberation from the Dachau-Allach Concentration camp." Borowski became consumed by a one-dimensional rage that sacrificed all art to politics. Finally, this hatred was turned against himself; he committed suicide in Warsaw in 1951.

Style and Technique

"The World of Stone" is an unusual story in that it has no real characters or plot. It still has considerable art: It is objective, careful, and maintains a very delicate ambiguity throughout; yet it is transitional, marking a point at the end of Borowski's literary career and the beginning of his propagandistic journalism.

One of the best descriptions of the story's style, as well as of Borowski himself, can be found in *The Captive Mind* (1953), by the Nobel Prize–winning poet Czeslaw Milosz; "Beta" is a thinly disguised portrait of Borowski. Milosz wrote of *The World of Stone*: "The book comprised extremely short stories devoid of almost all action, no more than sketches of what he had seen. He was a master at the art of using material details to suggest a whole human situation." In the story "The World of Stone," however, Borowski goes beyond a human situation and reaches a literary cul de sac with no escape. It asserts a destructiveness and contempt that are supposed to inhere in the world, yet the links with their causes are totally severed. "The World of Stone" is almost a work of madness, and this is its eerie, irrational art. The narrator is filled with disgust at the world, and he makes a last effort to present this, to deal with it, in a calm, detached manner. Afterward, he abandoned the calm, the detachment. He found shrill, strident propaganda much more satisfying.

John R. Carpenter

A WORN PATH

Author: Eudora Welty (1909-   )
Type of plot: Realism
Time of plot: Early twentieth century
Locale: Natchez, Mississippi
First published: 1941

> *Principal character:*
> PHOENIX JACKSON, a poor and aged black woman

The Story

Phoenix Jackson makes her biannual visit to Natchez, walking for half a day in December to reach the medical clinic at which she receives, as charity, soothing medicine for her grandson. Having swallowed lye, he has suffered without healing for several years. Phoenix has made the journey enough times that her path to Natchez seems a worn path. Furthermore, part of that is the old Natchez trace, a road worn deep into the Mississippi landscape by centuries of travelers returning northeast after boating down the Ohio and Mississippi rivers.

Phoenix is the oldest person she knows, though she does not know exactly how old she is, only that she was too old to go to school at the end of the Civil War and therefore never learned to read. Mainly because of her age, the simple walk from her remote home into Natchez is a difficult enough journey to take on epic proportions. She fears delays caused by wild animals getting in her way: foxes, owls, beetles, jack rabbits, and raccoons. She comfortably reflects that snakes and alligators hibernate in December. Thorn bushes and barbed-wire fences, log bridges and hills are major barriers for her. The cornfield she must cross from her initial path to a wagon road is a maze, haunted to her nearsightedness by a ghost which turns out to be a scarecrow. She must also struggle against her tendency to slip into a dream and forget her task, as when she stops for a rest and dreams of a boy offering her a piece of cake. Her perception of these obstacles emphasizes her intense physical, mental, and moral effort to complete this journey.

Despite the difficulty of her trip, she clearly enjoys her adventure. She talks happily to the landscape, warning the small animals to stay safely out of her way and showing patience with the thorn bush, which behaves naturally in catching her dress. She speaks good-humoredly of the dangers of the barbed wire. Her encounter with the "ghost" ends in a short, merry dance with the scarecrow, a celebration that she has not yet met death. Difficult and important as her trip is, she extracts pleasure from it which further reveals the depth of goodness in her character.

On the trace, a dog knocks her off her path, leaving her unable to rise until she is rescued by a young hunter. Though he helps her, he is also somewhat threatening. He is hunting quail, birds with whom she has spoken on her walk. When the hunter accidentally drops a nickel, she spots it quickly. She artfully diverts his attention by getting him to chase off the strange dog, so she can retrieve this nickel. Her behavior contrasts ironically with the hunter's. She feels guilty about taking the nickel, thinking of a bird which flies by as a sign that God is watching her. Meanwhile the hunter blusters and boasts of his skill and power. He assumes that her long and difficult walk is frivolous in intent, that she is going to town to see Santa Claus. The contrast between their perceptions and the reader's judgments tends to magnify the difficulty and the goodness of Phoenix, emphasizing especially her true courage in contrast to his foolish bravado.

In Natchez, she must find her way by memory, since she cannot read, to the right building and the right office in the building in order to get the medicine. There she encounters the impatience of clinic personnel who are acutely conscious that she is a charity case. Having found the right place, she momentarily forgets why she has come. Her effort and concentration have been so great in making the journey that she has lost sight of its end. When she has the medicine, one worker offers her some pennies for Christmas. She quickly responds that she would like a nickel. Then it becomes clear that she has a specific need for ten cents. She announces that she will buy her grandson a pinwheel and reflects, "He going to find it hard to believe there such a thing in the world. I'll march myself back where he waiting, holding it straight up in this hand."

Themes and Meanings

In her essay "Is Phoenix Jackson's Grandson Really Dead?" Eudora Welty speaks of "the deep-grained habit of love" which is Phoenix's motive for her trip: "The habit of love cuts through confusion and stumbles or contrives its way out of difficulty, it remembers the way even when it forgets, for a dumbfounded moment, its reason for being." The central motive of Phoenix's quest is true charity, the "deep-grained habit of love" for her grandson. This motive accounts for her apparent lapses in confiscating the lost nickel and in specifying how much money she would like when offered pennies for Christmas. Love also accounts for Phoenix's courage, making it natural and unconscious, simply necessary rather than extraordinary.

Phoenix's courage and true charity are underlined by her encounters with the young hunter and the clinic employees. When the hunter belittles her and boasts of himself because he walks as far as she does when he hunts little birds, with which Phoenix compares her grandson, because he can order his dog to drive off the strange dog which has frightened her, and because he has a gun he can point at her, the reader sees the truer courage of her heart— not merely in her lack of fear of the gun but in her whole journey as well.

The hunter's courage comes from his instruments and youthful folly, Phoenix's from her love. When the clinic employees remind her twice that hers is a charity case, expecting gratitude for what they give, they contrast sharply with Phoenix who dreams of and delights in bringing her grandson comfort and joy. In approaching true charity, in which love rather than self-praise is the motive, Phoenix achieves true courage. In Phoenix, Welty presents an ideal of goodness.

Style and Technique

Winner of an O. Henry Memorial Contest short story award, "A Worn Path," though an early story, is as accomplished as any of Welty's later fiction. This story exemplifies Welty's special power of placing the reader inside convincing and interesting characters without reducing the essential mystery of human character. This power makes her characters seem complete and real. In her essay on "A Worn Path," Welty reveals that the story originated in her vision of a solitary old woman:

> I saw her, at a middle distance, in a winter country landscape, and watched her slowly make her way across my line of vision. The sight of her made me write the story. I invented an errand for her, but that only seemed a living part of the figure she was herself: what errand other than for someone else could be making her go?

Welty also emphasizes that, though it is possible that the grandson is dead, the really important feature of the story is Phoenix's belief that he is alive and that "he going to last." This incentive for Phoenix's quest is central; the possible ambiguity of the grandson's condition is peripheral. Welty's expressed purpose in this story is to focus on Phoenix's habitual goodness.

Crucial to the story's success is Welty's choice of narrative point of view. By confining the reader to Phoenix's perceptions, Welty avoids the danger of sentimentality which she would have risked in a more external presentation of a good person. Though Phoenix may be no better morally than the Uncle Tom in Harriet Beecher Stowe's *Uncle Tom's Cabin* (1852), she seems more real, more in the world—in part because judgments of her character arise from the reader's evaluation of her actions without the insistent help of an intrusive narrator.

Phoenix's thoughts and words are enough to establish her unself-conscious love, courage, and other attractive qualities, but Welty uses the tainted evaluations of the people Phoenix meets to bring out the central qualities of love and courage which illuminate the idea Welty saw in the image which became the origin of her story. That image of a solitary old woman walking across a winter landscape came to mean "the deep-grained habit of love."

Terry Heller

WRACK

Author: Donald Barthelme (1931-   )
Type of plot: Psychological realism
Time of plot: 1972
Locale: The garden of a suburban house
First published: 1972

Principal characters:
A MAN, recently divorced
THE LAWYER, representing the divorced wife

The Story

Two unnamed men are conversing; the text reports only their dialogue, so that the reader must make sense of their remarks as if overhearing them. The opening remarks place the reader in a garden on a day of sunshine and clouds. When the sun is behind a cloud, the first speaker complains of being cold but admits to being consoled lately by the flowers, the Japanese rock garden, Social Security, philosophy, and sexuality.

Then the tone changes. Each man asserts that the other is driving him crazy, and the second man complains of the cold and reports that he still has to "muck out the stable and buff up the silver." He is working for an unspecified "they," who trust him completely. Also, he and the first man have a joint interest in deciding "what color to paint the trucks."

This apparently idle conversation begins to include some odd questions asked by the second speaker: "The kid ever come to see you?" "Where's your watch?" Then he says, "The hollowed-out book . . . is not yours. We've established that. Let's go on." Other items follow, with no system or meaning: doors, a bonbon dish, a shoe, a hundred-pound sack of saccharin, a dressing gown, and "two mattresses surrounding the single slice of salami."

This line of questioning, though obviously not literal and realistic, makes the reader realize that the first man has recently been divorced, that the second man is simultaneously an acquaintance and a lawyer for the divorced wife, and that the two men are establishing the individual ownership of possessions once held in common.

Each item gives rise to a series of remarks, in the course of which the reader learns about "my former wife"—who may not be the one now divorcing the speaker—and Shirley, a former maid. Near the end of the dialogue the lawyer describes the former husband as "too old": "You're too old, that's all it is, think nothing of it," and he denies that description "wholeheartedly" (insisting on that term). The men conclude by raising again the subject of the trucks to be painted.

Themes and Meanings

The word *wrack* came into modern English from several different sources. As a result, its meanings include destruction, the item destroyed, and that which survives destruction. Barthelme's story, like its title, brings these meanings together.

One of his frequent themes is the beginning of a love affair (see "Lightning"). A complementary theme is the ending of one, as in the divorce that lies behind "Wrack." One commonly speaks of spouses or lovers as "breaking up," and the breaking up of a marriage constitutes the wrack of this story. The dialogue provides suggestive evidence about many aspects of the breakup. The reader learns about the past (some happy times and a possible earlier marriage that also ended badly), the present (there appears to be no direct contact between the man and his ex-wife, and his son no longer visits him), and the future (sexuality is a possible consolation, but perhaps he is "too old"). Primarily, however, Barthelme appears to be interested in evoking the low-level pain of breaking up rather than its factual effects.

Another typical Barthelme theme is connected with the items mentioned by the lawyer. Barthelme is perceptive about the persistence of objects in one's life, especially when—as here—they remain after the end of a relationship. At such a time, some once-valued objects appear merely pointless, while others are radioactive with recollections of happiness or sadness. The incoherent formlessness of such objects illustrates literally the breaking up of the relationship that once justified their collection.

Style and Technique

All Barthelme's stories display his interest in the techniques of storytelling, and the use of dialogue stripped to its barest elements is a technique he has often used. (He is probably indebted to Samuel Beckett's *Waiting for Godot*, 1952, for his earliest interest in the form.) He likes the form because it engages the reader's attention, it lends itself to suggestive patterns, and it permits an almost poetic intensity of language.

The reader's attention is engaged from the start in this story, since he must figure out what situation he is witnessing. Then he must continue to read attentively, because clues appear slowly and side issues recur and accumulate emotion.

The speeches are heightened beyond ordinary conversation by their patterns of topic and phrasing. The recurrent topics of divorce—loss, sadness, isolation, alteration, need for consolation—are evoked as each item on the list of possessions is named and discussed. A rough rhythm therefore shapes the conversation. Another rhythm is imposed by the recurrence of specific sentences—for example, "Cold here in the garden" and "Well, you can't have everything." The odd exchange concerning the painting of trucks, which occurs early in the conversation and ends with "Surely not your last word on the subject," recurs almost word for word as the last words of the conversation.

The poetic intensifying of the language is too complex a topic to cover here, but a glance at one passage may suggest Barthelme's technique. At the beginning of the story, when the divorced man is listing sources of consolation, he mentions philosophy. The lawyer oddly says, "I read a book." Then the divorced man adds sexuality. The lawyer says, "They have books about it." The divorced man says, "We'll to the woods no more. I assume."

The passage is complex and fruitful. "Book" and "philosophy" combine to suggest Boethius' *The Consolation of Philosophy* (written in prison about A.D. 525). The lawyer's emphasis on books anticipates his assertion toward the end that the divorced man is "too old"; here that man says relevantly, "We'll to the woods no more"—a bookish response, since the line is from a couplet by Théodore de Banville as translated by A. E. Housman. What is more, the story sets these woods against the suburban garden and its neat Japanese formality. This opposition clarifies the divorced man's later description of what he did yesterday: "Took a walk. In the wild trees." Clearly he still hopes to return to the woods of an undomesticated sexuality experienced in life rather than in books. He is "wholeheartedly" resisting age, therefore, as he will insist at the story's end.

Consider one more literary allusion, this one occurring much later, as the breaking up recalls to the divorced man the hopeful beginning. Deep in memories now, he remarks, "In the beginning, you don't know." Here Barthelme is alluding to a sentence from "The Rise of Capitalism," one of his own stories: "Self-actualization is not to be achieved in terms of another person, but you don't know that, when you begin." The divorced man's sad truth is made sadder by this echo.

J. D. O'Hara

WUNDERKIND

Author: Carson McCullers (Lula Carson Smith, 1917-1967)
Type of plot: Psychological realism
Time of plot: 1936
Locale: Cincinnati, Ohio
First published: 1936

Principal characters:
FRANCES, the protagonist, a fifteen-year-old girl who is
considered to be a *Wunderkind*
MR. BILDERBACH, Frances' piano teacher
MR. LAFKOWITZ, a violin teacher
HEIME, Lafkowitz's prize student, also considered to be a
Wunderkind

The Story
The "she" to whom the reader is introduced in the first paragraph, as she enters the living room of Mr. Bilderbach's house, in no way seems to be the *Wunderkind* of this story. Indeed, as she enters the room her music satchel is described as "plopping against her winter-stockinged legs," her attention is "scattered" by "restlessness," she fumbles with her books, her fingers quiver, and her "sight [is] sharpened [by] fear that had begun to torment her for the past few months." Perhaps, then, this is the story of the young girl as she becomes a *Wunderkind*. Yet she is described as mumbling "phrases of encouragement" to herself, telling herself over and over: "A good lesson—a good lesson—like it used to be. . . ." Her name is Frances, the reader learns, and she is fifteen, having arrived for her Tuesday afternoon piano lesson; she is early and must wait until Mr. Bilderbach and Mr. Lafkowitz finish playing a recently acquired sonatina. Thus, Carson McCullers has set the stage and situated her characters—with Frances sitting in Mr. Bilderbach's living room—so that, through a series of flashbacks (told from Frances' point of view through a third-person, limited omniscient narrative voice), which extend back to the time when Frances was twelve and began her lessons with Mr. Bilderbach, the author can nudge the reader toward understanding the cause of her protagonist's apparent angst and fear over having lost what "used to be."

This particular Tuesday had begun badly for Frances when, after she had practiced at her piano for two hours, her father made her eat breakfast with the rest of her family: He "had put a fried egg on her plate and she had known that if it burst—so that the slimy yellow oozed over the white—she would cry." This, in fact, had happened, and "the same feeling was upon her now," as she sits in her teacher's living room and looks at a magazine wherein a photograph of her friend, Heime, appears. He had studied the violin with Mr. Lafkowitz, and he had played in a concert with Frances (the critics had praised his performance but criticized hers). He, like Frances, had been called a *Wunderkind* for his early apparent and great talent. Heime had gone to Pennsylvania (where he is during the time of this story) to study with another, presumably more advanced teacher than Mr. Lafkowitz. Now he has had his photograph and a brief biography published in a magazine devoted to music and outstanding musicians. Indeed, Heime's obvious and praised success intensifies Frances' growing doubts about her own ability to realize her early promise as a *Wunderkind* at the piano and to become a professional instead of merely a talented student.

Her dreadful self-doubts began four months before this particular Tuesday afternoon, when the notes she played on the piano began to spring out with a "glib, dead intonation." Initially, she had attributed this, as well as her displeasure over it, to adolescence: "Some kids played with promise—and worked and worked until, like her, the least little thing would start them crying, and worn out with trying to get the thing across—the longing thing they felt—something queer began to happen—But not she! She was like Heime. She had to be." Unfortunately, it has become increasingly apparent to Frances, as it becomes apparent to the reader of this story, that she is not like Heime. Her technique at the piano is—and was when, three years earlier, she began to study with Mr. Bilderbach—excellent, but he had told her then that technique was not enough: "It—playing music—is more than cleverness. If a twelve-year-old girl's fingers cover so many keys to a second—that means nothing." Naturally, Frances wants to please Mr. Bilderbach, especially since he and his wife, with no children of their own, have treated her like their own daughter over the past three years. For her graduation from junior high school, for example, he had insisted upon buying her a pair of new shoes and having Mrs. Bilderbach make her a new dress from fabric he had chosen. She frequently eats dinner with them on Saturdays after her piano lessons, often sleeping at their house and then returning to her home on Sunday mornings, after eating breakfast with them. In some unexpressed way, that "longing thing" in her and the music she plays—that emotion she has been unable to communicate through her piano—is complicated by Mr. Bilderbach's own "longing" for a child.

Upon Mr. Lafkowitz's departure, Frances goes to the piano for her lesson. "Well, Bienchen," Mr. Bilderbach says to her, "this afternoon we are going to begin all over. Start from scratch. Forget the last few months." She will make a fresh start, then, a renewal. (Yet the reader is reminded here of what Mr. Bilderbach had said to Frances during her first lesson with him three years earlier: "Now we begin all over. . . .") He next considers having her play a piece by Johann Sebastian Bach, but then he says, "No, not yet," and instead decides to have her play Ludwig van Beethoven's Variation Sonata, opus 26.

The "stiff and dead-seeming" piano keys make Frances feel "hemmed . . . in," and it bothers her that Mr. Bilderbach frequently interrupts her playing with corrections. She asks him to let her play the piece through, without stopping, for then, she says, "Maybe . . . I could do better." He consents, but he is not pleased when she has finished, nor is she pleased: "There were no flaws . . . , but the phrases shaped from her fingers before she had put into them the meaning that she felt." She had played this sonata for years; she had also played the *Harmonious Blacksmith* for years, a composition he wants her to play next, "like a real blacksmith's daughter." In other words, he wants her to play what she knows too well, what she plays automatically, and not what would challenge her and force her to grow—as a pianist and an emotional being. His demands upon her, seemingly designed to force her into regression or, worse, artistic and emotional paralysis, are too much for her suddenly: "Her heart that had been springing against her chest all afternoon felt suddenly dead. She saw it gray and limp and shriveled at the edges like an oyster." She feels caged, confused. "I can't . . . can't anymore," she whispers to him, leaving the piano to rush past him, grab her books, and hurry out of his house. Once outside, she hurries down the street "that had become confused with noise and bicycles and the games of other children."

Themes and Meanings

Just as McCullers' *The Heart Is a Lonely Hunter* (1940) and *The Member of the Wedding* (1946) have a frustrated, lonely adolescent girl as a central character, so, too, does "Wunderkind." Similarly, as with numerous other characters in McCullers' fiction, Frances' suffering is largely caused by the manner in which others she cares about perceive her, and by the crippling influence these perceptions have upon her own self-image and development.

Called a *Wunderkind* by Mr. Bilderbach for three years, since their first interactions as student and teacher, then gradually identified as such by the man's older students as well, Frances' potential for greater, more mature personal and artistic growth is undercut because she is understandably hungry for such praise and adopts it as essential to her identity before she understands the great demands and costs such success requires, if it is to be more than merely titular. While McCullers suggests that Frances does possess an extraordinary natural talent as a pianist, she makes it clear that the teacher of such a gifted student must himself have extraordinary professional talent. In this regard, it becomes apparent to the reader that Mr. Bilderbach, because of a significant lack in his personal life, is not equipped to guide Frances toward the realization of mature artistic achievement; he is unable to teach her how to fuse style with content, form with substance.

McCullers points directly to Mr. Bilderbach's professional inadequacy in several cases, the most obvious of which are two scenes: one that Frances recalls as she sits in her teacher's living room and waits for her lesson, and the other occurring near the end of the story, moments before she runs out of his house. The first concerns the night when Mr. Bilderbach demanded that Frances play Bach's Fantasia and Fugue for him and Mr. Lafkowitz, which she did, and did "well," she had thought. Yet when she had finished, Mr. Lafkowitz, displeased by her performance, reminds her that Bach, the father of many children, "could not have been so cold," as her rendition of the composer's music would lead one to believe. This comment, she recalls, upset Mr. Bilderbach; during his angry reply, furthermore, she is careful to keep "her face blank and immature because that was the way... Bilderbach wanted her to look." The second and more pointed revelation of her teacher's subprofessional perception of her occurs at the end of this story, after Frances has finished playing Beethoven's music and Mr. Bilderbach wants her to play the piece about the blacksmith, "like a real blacksmith's daughter. You see, Bienchen," he confesses, "I know you so well—as if you were my own girl. . . ." After a few more words he becomes, "in confusion," silent; then he asks her to play the piece so it sounds "happy and simple." In short, the teacher wants the student to play what he needs and wants to hear, but not what she needs to play in order to grow and develop as a versatile artist independent of her teacher's shortcomings.

Style and Technique

One of the most remarkable aspects of "Wunderkind" is its narrative voice and vantage point. While it is that of the third person, with its omniscience limited to Frances' thoughts and perceptions, McCullers communicates the mental and emotional states of her young protagonist by rendering the narrative voice almost neutral where judgments of the other characters in the story are concerned. Because Frances' personality is portrayed at a critical moment of her development—a moment during which she is uncertain about who she is or will be, as she feels a past identity crumbling away from her— the fact that her identity is not fixed precludes her judging others for what they are or are not. In such a transitional state, in fact, Frances is critical of no one but herself.

An excellent example of the above-mentioned neutral narrative perception or portrayal of a character is that of Mrs. Bilderbach. As Frances thinks about her, the reader is told that the woman "was much different from her husband. She was quiet and fat and slow. When she wasn't in the kitchen, cooking the rich dishes that both of them loved, she seemed to spend all her time in their bed upstairs, reading magazines or just looking with a half-smile at nothing." Significantly, the observations with which the reader is presented about Mrs. Bilderbach are nonjudgmental; consequently, the reader is left to decide if any aspects of the woman or her habits are to be seen pejoratively. Similarly, the portraits of Mr. Bilderbach, Mr. Lafkowitz, and even Heime are all seemingly composed of objective observations, or observations stated objectively. McCullers utilizes this narrative approach for at least three reasons: first, because it gives the reader a sense of Frances' overly self-critical frame of mind, as well as her tendency to observe others (especially adults) in a nonevaluative manner; second, because it portrays a complex psychological struggle, for which there is no easy solution, in a largely impartial manner; and third, because it demands from the reader compassion for both Frances and Mr. Bilderbach as they suffer the effects of her painful growth.

David A. Carpenter

YELLOW WOMAN

Author: Leslie Marmon Silko (1948-   )
Type of plot: Realistic folktale
Time of plot: c. 1970
Locale: New Mexico
First published: 1974

> *Principal characters:*
> A YOUNG PUEBLO WOMAN, the "yellow woman" of the story
> SILVA, a mysterious Indian male, a rustler from the mountains

The Story

On one level, "Yellow Woman" is a simple but haunting story of a young, married Pueblo Indian woman's two-day affair with a maverick Navajo who lives alone in the mountains and steals cattle from white and Mexican ranchers. The story is divided into four brief sections, ranging in length from four and a half pages to less than a page: Section 1 describes the morning after their first night together, and section 4 depicts (sections 3 and 4 are brief) the woman's return to her home and family on the evening of the following day.

When the woman awakens on the first morning, the man is still sleeping soundly, "rolled in the red blanket on the white river sand." She peacefully watches "the sun rising up through the tamaracks and willows," listens to "the water... in the narrow fast channel," rises, and walks along "the river south the way... [they] had come the afternoon before." She intends to return to her pueblo, but she cannot go without saying goodbye. She goes back to the river, wakes up the man, and tells him that she is leaving. The man smiles at her, calls her "Yellow Woman," and calmly asserts that she is coming with him. The night before, she had talked of the "old stories about the ka'tsina spirit and Yellow Woman," stories of a mountain spirit who takes mortal women away to live with him. The woman apparently had suggested that she was Yellow Woman and Silva was the ka'tsina spirit; now the man's words and actions assert that he is, in fact, the ka'tsina and that she has become the Yellow Woman of the stories: "What happened yesterday has nothing to do with what you will do today, Yellow Woman."

She is drawn to the sexuality, strength, and danger of this stranger and to the potency of the Yellow Woman myths. She allows herself to be pulled down once again onto the "red blanket on the white river sand," and then she leaves with him. It seems that he forces her to come, but she acquiesces complacently: "I had stopped trying to pull away from him, because his hand felt cool and the sun was high." The woman's pueblo has been out of sight from the opening of the story, and the farther she gets from the pueblo, the less sure she is of her identity or of her understanding of reality. As they travel northward, she hopes to meet ordinary people in order to regain her clear, normal perception of reality: "Eventually I will see someone, and then I will be certain that he is only a man . . . and I will be sure that I am not Yellow Woman." They meet no one as they travel through the foothills and into the dark lava hills and finally to his house of "black lava rock and red mud . . . high above the spreading miles of arroyos and long mesas."

In section 2, she enters into his small home and into the rhythms of his life. She cooks for him, makes love to him, sleeps with him. When she awakens to find him gone the next morning, she thinks idly of returning home but waits passively, lost in the silence and beauty of the mountains. She is awed by this man who has assumed the role of a ka'tsina with complete assurance, who has the power to "destroy" her, and who defies the white man and his ways. She knows that life will go on as before in the pueblo: "My mother and grandmother will raise the baby like they raised me. Al will find someone else, and they will go on like before, except that there will be a story about the day I disappeared." She seems to lose interest in going home: "that didn't seem important any more, maybe because there were little blue flowers growing in the meadow behind the store house."

When Yellow Woman wanders back to the house from a peaceful walk in the big pine trees, the man is waiting. He has stolen and butchered a steer and is preparing to go to "sell the meat in Marquez." He expects her to come with him, and she agrees.

In the third section, they descend from the serenity and beauty of the mountains and the myth into the world of harsh and banal reality which the woman has imagined that she had left behind. They encounter an ordinary man, and suddenly this Yellow Woman–ka'tsina story appears to be exposed as a vulgar tale of adultery, theft, and murder. The man is a white rancher who accuses Silva of "rustling cattle" as soon as he sees "the blood-soaked gunny sacks" hanging from the woman's saddle. Silva tells her to go back up the mountain. She rides to the "ridge where the trail forked" and waits. When she hears "four hollow explosions" of the Indian's .30-.30 rifle as he apparently kills the rancher, she takes the trail leading down and to the southeast, rather than returning to the mountain. When she can see the "dark green patches of tamaracks that grew along the river," she releases the horse, first turning it around so that it will return to "the corral under the pines on the mountain," and begins the long walk back to her pueblo.

In the brief final section, the woman follows "the river back the way" Silva and she had come. She drinks the cool river water and thinks about Silva, feeling "sad at leaving" this "strange" man. When she sees the "green willow leaves that he had trimmed" from a branch, she wants "to go back to him— to kiss him and to touch him—but the mountains were too far away now." Moreover, she believes that "he will come back sometime and be waiting again by the river."

She walks into the village in the twilight. When she reaches the "screen door of her house," she can "smell supper cooking" and hear "my mother . . . telling my grandmother how to fix the Jell-O and . . . Al . . . playing with the baby." She decides to "tell them that some Navajo had kidnaped" her and regrets that her Grandpa is not alive to hear a Yellow Woman story.

Themes and Meanings

At first glance, "Yellow Woman" is a common version of the old story of a married woman seeking to escape from her boring and unfulfilling family life by having an affair with an exciting, unconventional male. The woman here seems to be rather aimless, listless, and irresponsible: She does not really "decide" to go with Silva or to leave him, but rather finds herself doing certain things. She does not appear to have a very strong attachment to her husband or child, nor does she believe that they will mourn her loss very much. When she does return to her pueblo, she holds on to the belief that the "strange" man will come back to get her one day.

Closer scrutiny reveals "Yellow Woman" to be a rich and melancholy story written by a Native American author who is well acquainted with tribal folklore and quite sensitive to the pathos of the American Indian's life in the modern world. The woman longs not so much for a lover as for a richness, a oneness of life which she has heard about in the stories of her grandfather. She lives in the banal poverty of a modern pueblo with paved roads, screen doors, and Jell-O. She seeks to make contact with the vital world of Coyote (a traditional Native American figure of the creator-trickster), ka'tsina spirits, blue mountains, and cactus flowers—a world in which man, animal, spirit, and nature are one, a dynamic world where reality itself is multidimensional and mystical.

"Yellow Woman" is not a simple story of an unfulfilled housewife seeking excitement, nor a tribal folktale of a woman lured out of sight of her pueblo by a spirit (who is linked to Coyote) and who is then unable to escape from his power. Rather, it is a fusion of those stories and more. The woman is not seduced by a man or a ka'tsina spirit so much as by the possibility that "what they tell in stories" may be true in the present, that the world may not have been wholly stripped of its magic and its unity. She is not deceiving herself when she thinks that she might be Yellow Woman; rather, she is trusting to her Indian heritage, which would free her from the white dogma that personal identity is both absolute and final.

She returns to the pueblo somewhat chastened, for she knows that Silva is, among other things, a rustler and a murderer; she knows, too, that he is fierce and free of white domination and that he may be a ka'tsina as well as a man. She has not lost faith in stories, in Yellow Woman or Coyote. It is clear that the poverty of life in the pueblo is spiritual as well as economic, and that the Native American (but not Yellow Woman) is in grave danger of following the white man into his sterile, rational landscape where Mother Earth is plowed up and paved over, Father Sky is polluted with "vapor trails" and acid rain, Coyote is merely a coyote, identity is a prison, and stories are only stories.

Style and Technique

Perhaps the most striking technical dimension of this skillfully written story is Leslie Silko's masterful use of a first-person narrator. In fact, the real interest in this story resides not so much in the events of plot as in the character of the speaker. The narrator is absolutely credible as a young Pueblo woman: straightforward, unassuming, and unsophisticated. She is also a natural storyteller with an acute sensitivity to the beauty of the physical world and a deep longing for communion with man, nature, and spirit, for a fullness and a resonance of life she fears is lost "back in time immemorial." The simplicity and directness of her prose and the purity of her descriptions are evident from the first line: "My thigh clung to his with dampness, and I watched the sun rising up through the tamaracks and willows." There is a calmness and a wistfulness in this woman's voice which is quite affecting. She brings both the harsh loveliness of the land and the mystery and strength of the man to life seemingly without effort; they are rendered vividly, not because of ornamention or rhetorical skill but because she responds to them in an elemental, deeply felt, manner:

> It was hot and the wildflowers were closing up their deep-yellow petals. Only the waxy cactus flowers bloomed in the bright sun . . . the white ones and the red ones were still buds, but the purple and the yellow were blossoms, open full. . . .

> I looked at Silva for an instant and there was something ancient and dark— something I could feel in my stomach—in his eyes. . . .

Two other aspects of Silko's technique merit comment: her use of color and the motif of storytelling. Colors play a subdued but important role here. The author draws on traditional meanings and on naturalistic detail to weave a subtle pattern of associations. The woman is linked most strongly to yellow: "Yellow Woman," "the moon in the water," "the deep-yellow petals" of wildflowers, and the "yellow" blossoms of cactus flowers. In the lore of many Native Americans, yellow represents the south (the pueblo is southeast of Silva's home), from which comes summer and the power to grow. During this story, the woman takes root in the alkaline soil of her life, grows, and opens her petals as "moonflowers blossom in the sand hills before dawn." Her beauty, her strength and fragility, her oneness with life, and her ability to grow are all effectively symbolized by her connection with yellow. The man, on the other hand, is associated with life-giving water: the river, willows. He is "damp" and "slippery," and holds an "ancient" and mysterious darkness: His body is "dark"; his horse is "black"; he lives in "blue mountains" in a house made of "black rock." Black is traditionally linked to the west (they go northwest to reach his house), where the thunder beings live who bring rain, as he brings nourishment to her arid life and parched imagination. The darkness is also suggestive of his violence and sexuality.

The theme of storytelling—the woman's increasingly complex understanding of the relationship between story and reality—is also handled quite skillfully. The woman evolves convincingly from someone who loves to repeat the stories of her grandfather but thinks of them as speaking of a world irrevocably lost, into someone who enters consciously into the reality of a Yellow Woman story and wonders if the first Yellow Woman also "had another name." Finally, she becomes a creator of stories who knows that old stories and new stories and reality are all parts of the same truth. Leslie Silko and the woman who returns to the pueblo would agree with Black Elk: "Whether it happened so or not I do not know; but if you think about it, you can see that it is true."

Hal Holladay

YENTL THE YESHIVA BOY

Author: Isaac Bashevis Singer (1904-   )
Type of plot: Folktale
Time of plot: Late nineteenth century
Locale: The villages of Yanev, Bechev, and Lublin, Poland
First published: 1962

Principal characters:

YENTL ("ANSHEL"), a girl who poses as a young man in order
    to pursue the study of Torah and Talmud
AVIGDOR, a fourth-year yeshiva student who becomes
    "Anshel's" study partner
ALTER VISHKOWER, the richest man in Bechev
HADASS, Vishkower's daughter, once engaged to Avigdor,
    who marries "Anshel"
PESHE, a widowed shopkeeper who marries Avigdor

The Story

In the nineteenth century in the shtetls of Eastern Europe, the villages populated almost entirely by Jews, the study of Torah and Talmud is prohibited to females. In the village of Yanev, however, Yentl has pursued such studies, the passion of her life, in secret under the tutelage of her father, who recognizes that his daughter is somehow different from all the other girls of the community. Yentl, tall and bony, has little interest in the running of a household. Rather than cooking or darning socks, studying her father's books is the very center of her life. Yentl, it seems, has the soul of a man.

Dressing herself as a young man and calling herself "Anshel," Yentl leaves Bechev after her father's death to continue her studies formally in a yeshiva, a school for religious teachings. Meeting Avigdor at a roadside inn, she accompanies him to Bechev to study at the yeshiva there. As Anshel, Yentl forges with Avigdor a strong bond, the basis of which is their shared love of Torah and Talmud. Yentl learns that Avigdor has been engaged to Hadass, the loveliest girl in the town and daughter of its wealthiest citizen, that the marriage had been broken off by his prospective in-laws on learning that Avigdor's brother was a suicide. The thought occurs to Avigdor that while he requires a wife and will himself marry the shrewish widowed shopkeeper, Peshe, Anshel should marry Hadass, ensuring that the girl he still loves will not end up the bride of a total stranger.

At first, Yentl dismisses the extraordinary idea, but finding herself drawn ever closer to Avigdor, she warms to his plan, realizing that it will strengthen the bond, now turning to love on her part, between herself and Avigdor. Once Avigdor marries Peshe and spends less and less time with Yentl/

Anshel, Yentl asks Alter Vishkower for his daughter's hand in marriage. Considering it an excellent match, Vishkower agrees, and the wedding takes place.

Being completely innocent in sexual matters, Hadass is unaware that her marriage to Anshel is unlike any other, especially since Yentl, in her own way, has even managed to deflower her bride. As time passes, however, aware that Hadass loves her as Anshel, that she loves Avigdor, that Avigdor—whose marriage to Peshe is a disaster—loves Hadass, Yentl realizes that her charade cannot continue. It had begun as a way of exacting vengeance for Avigdor and drawing him closer to herself, but the lives of three people are becoming ever more complex as their fates are further enmeshed. Because Hadass is not yet pregnant after the passage of some months, and Anshel never goes to the baths and never swims with the other men, the villagers begin to gossip about them.

At last, journeying with Avigdor to the nearby town of Lublin, Yentl reveals herself to him as a woman. Avigdor is thunderstruck; he even wonders if Yentl is some kind of demon. Eventually, more sad than angry, he suggests that they divorce their wives and marry each other. Yentl insists that that kind of relationship with him is impossible for her. They have been brought together by their shared love of Torah and Talmud. She can never be wife and housekeeper, but must instead continue her studies. Yet both of them have come to understand that Yentl must disappear from the lives of Avigdor and Hadass.

Yentl does not return to Bechev but instead sends divorce papers to a bewildered Hadass who takes to her bed, grief-stricken over the loss of her beloved Anshel. Time, however, heals her wound, and Hadass recovers to marry Avigdor, now divorced from Peshe. When Hadass bears him a son, the townspeople, who have been busily pondering the disappearance of Hadass' former husband, can hardly believe their ears on learning at the ceremony of the circumcision that the child is to be named Anshel.

Themes and Meanings

Singer's entertaining but hauntingly ambiguous little tale does not reveal its meaning easily, nor is it meant to do so. Near the end of the story, the omniscient narrator suggests that the village gossips who insist on prying into the details of Anshel's mysterious leave-taking must finally accept any falsehood as fact: "Truth itself is often concealed in such a way that the harder you look for it, the harder it is to find." This device may be Singer's way of cautioning the reader not to pry too deeply into his characters' motivations, to accept the tale at the simple level of its telling. The truth lies in the story's title, by which the author proclaims that he is recounting the extraordinary circumstances of a girl, Yentl, who is at the same time a boy through her dedication to God's teachings—an androgynous being with the body of a woman and the soul of a man. Yentl herself is confused by the urgings within her that drive her to dress as a man in direct violation of the proscriptions of the beloved Talmud, the words of which have become the very core of her being.

In Singer's stage adaptation of the story, written in collaboration with Leah Napolin and first performed in New York in 1974, Singer clarifies the meaning of a tale which has intrigued but puzzled many readers. In the story, Yentl accepts Hadass' love, but in the play Yentl clearly learns to love Hadass as deeply as she has come to love Avigdor. Singer's intention, it would appear, is to portry in Yentl/Anshel a divided self that is becoming whole through the knowledge of love. Embracing the masculine part of her nature in her love for Hadass and the feminine part of her nature in her love for Avigdor, Yentl, paradoxically, reveals the depth of her love by her sacrifice of that love. Removing herself from the scene, leaving both Avigdor and Hadass, she frees herself for the transcendent love of God, for which she has at last fully prepared herself through a newfound understanding of the joys and despair that accompany human love.

With the birth of the child Anshel, both story and play offer the unstated possibility that Yentl, pursuing her study of Talmud and Torah, becomes an immortal figure to be reborn within the soul of each newborn Jewish child as Yentl herself is transformed into the mythical wandering Jew. The ending calls to mind a reverse myth in a poem by Matthew Arnold to which Singer's story seems related, that of "The Scholar-Gipsy," who deserts books and study to embrace the simple life in his immortal wanderings in the natural world. Yentl, having embraced life itself and released her hold, is finally ready to give meaning to her learning, to live fully the life of the mind as she explores the eternal verities of her God, who accepts her as she has become.

Singer's story has been popularized by the film musical *Yentl* (1983), produced and directed by Barbra Streisand and adapted by her in collaboration with Jack Rosenthal as a vehicle for herself. The otherwise effective film version, however, reverses Singer's original concept. The protagonist of the story is a being who is throughout a figure of androgyny—both Jewish girl, Yentl, and yeshiva boy, Anshel. The Yentl of the play is a young woman who is transformed into an androgynous figure, whereas the Yentl of the film is an androgyne who becomes at last—in the guise of Barbra Streisand—a modern woman with feminist inclinations.

Style and Technique

Singer's story is a third-person narrative with almost no developed scenes and few extended passages of dialogue. It is charmingly told with utter simplicity, lending it the quality of a matter-of-fact folktale that has been accepted without question by several generations of listeners or readers. The reader never pauses to question the credibility of the tale, for its complex sexuality, even the mechanics of the sexual act between Yentl and Hadass, are never allowed to overwhelm the deceptively simple, seemingly primitive, straightforward style. As the author himself understands, androgyny can be convincing on the page, but perhaps only there. Once the characters are fleshed out, as they must be, for stage and screen, and scenes are added or expanded, an element of titillation intrudes. Singer never allows this element to intrude in the story and attempts to maintain control over this aspect of the play. It is this overt element that finally mars the film version in which he had no hand and of which he disapproves.

Albert E. Kalson

YERMOLAI AND THE MILLER'S WIFE

Author: Ivan Turgenev (1818-1883)
Type of plot: Social realism
Time of plot: The 1840's
Locale: Tula Province, 120 miles south of Moscow
First published: "Yermolai i mel'nichikha," 1847 (English translation, 1855)

Principal characters:

THE NARRATOR, a country squire and amateur huntsman
YERMOLAI PETROVICH, a serf who accompanies the narrator
    on the hunt and is an expert marksman
ARINA TIMOFEYEVNA, the miller's wife
SAVELY ALEKSEYEVICH, her husband, the miller
ALEKSANDR SILYCH ZVERKOV, Arina's previous master, a
    country squire
HIS WIFE
PETRUSHKA, a footman

The Story

The author-narrator starts with the setting. He is out hunting woodcock with his assistant, Yermolai. The most productive time for such hunting is the spring mating-season of the woodcock. The specific Russian word (*tyaga*, "attraction") that indicates this activity and the hunt conducted by human beings during this season is explained by the narrator. The atmosphere of the setting carries great weight: evening, motionless air, pervasive silence, only weak and occasional sounds, the setting sun, gradual darkness, birds falling asleep, stars, indistinguishable masses of trees.

The description of the atmosphere accompanying the expectation of the woodcock's appearance is followed by a presentation of Yermolai, the narrator's companion on his hunting expeditions. A humble man, a serf owned by a neighbor landowner, Yermolai is a sort of independent type, not yet old, but no longer young either (about forty-five), adapted to and completely familiar with his natural environment, a passionate huntsman, a good shot, and in a way an eccentric. His hunting dog Valyetka is fond of him, but few people are. He does not care much about people, not even his own wife, whom he visits once a week, rarely provides for, and who "managed to get along somehow and suffered a bitter fate." Yermolai himself lives from handouts; his eccentric behavior is tolerated by the peasants, and he enjoys respect only as an expert huntsman.

The locale of the anecdote which forms the substance of the story is near the river Ista, a side river of the Oka in the Tula Province. After minor success with the woodcock hunt on the evening in question, the narrator decides to spend the night nearby and to resume the hunt early the next morning. A lodging for the night is required. A nearby mill seems suitable, but the miller's servant, on his master's instructions, refuses hospitality. After further pleading and an offer of money, both the master and Yermolai are admitted for the night. Before they lie down to sleep, a meal is prepared in the yard on an open fire, where the miller's wife gives assistance and the reader detects a certain warmth and attraction between Yermolai and this woman. His occasional "sullen fierceness" is allayed in the company of Arina. He takes an interest in her (her complaint is a tormenting and persistent cough), and she waits on him gladly.

The woman's gentle but sullen demeanor arouses the narrator's curiosity, and he asks a few questions and then informs the reader of the circumstances of Arina Timofeyevna's previous life and the background of her present situation. The child of a village elder, she caught the eye of her master, Zverkov, and his wife, who took her in as a parlor maid, later letting her advance to lady's maid because of her special devotion to her mistress. After ten years of service, the girl asked to be allowed to marry the footman Petrushka. The request was denied. Several months later, the request was repeated, as the girl was pregnant. At this point, she was dismissed from the household and sent back to her village. Here the miller bought her from her previous owners. She brought into the marriage certain qualifications, such as an ability to read and write, which were useful in the miller's business. The boy with whom she had been in love, the footman Petrushka, was sent into the army. Her husband, the miller, seems to tyrannize her. She serves and obeys him without love. Their child has died.

Yermolai displays pity and affection for her, which are important in view of the heartless egotism and exploitative treatment of her previous masters, and the surly nature of her husband, the miller. With the knowledge of the hopelessness of the situation of Arina Timofeyevna and the cruel selfishness ruling human affairs, both Yermolai and his master fall asleep under the lean-to before resuming their woodcock hunting early the next morning.

Themes and Meanings

"Yermolai and the Miller's Wife" was the second in a series of short sketches which Turgenev published in the late 1840's, largely in the St. Petersburg literary periodical, *The Contemporary*, and which were later collected under the title *Zapiski okhotnika* (1852; *A Sportsman's Sketches*, 1932). This collection has been described by D. S. Mirsky as "belonging to the highest, most lasting and least questionable achievement of Turgenev and of Russian realism." The sketches gained great popularity with the Russian reading public and were said to have influenced the young heir to the throne, Alexander II, in his decision to abolish serfdom in 1861. In these sketches, the simple man is in the foreground and is presented from a perspective of psychological complexity, which was a novelty at the time. Yermolai is interesting as a person, having both positive and negative features. Such simple folk had not previously been considered worthy of serious literary treatment. Without training and education, they did not seem to possess what were deemed interesting character features. As serfs, they were condemned to a lowly life of drudgery and were viewed with condescension.

Turgenev saw these humble people from a different point of view, foremost as individual human beings, talented, sensitive, and as complex in their emotional life as the members of his own class. He broke with the stereotype of presenting them as a dark, anonymous mass. By showing Yermolai and Arina as gifted and sensitive individuals, the narrator invites the reader to draw his own conclusions about such masters as the Zverkovs and the system of serfdom. He makes his point implicitly, but his lack of sympathy for the self-righteousness, condescension, and egotism of the masters is quite clear. Such people of the upper class see life only in terms of their own comfort and pleasure, remaining totally indifferent to the human needs of others. The elevation of humble people and the indication of the absence of justice in social relations could not help but move Turgenev's readers. Yet Turgenev was too perceptive an observer of life, even at a young age, to attribute all ills to social conditions. Human callousness seems to be as much a general condition of life as the result of social causes, as demonstrated by Yermolai's ill treatment of his wife, whom he neglects unconscionably, and the apparent coldness of the miller toward Arina.

Style and Technique

Author and narrator appear as the same person and participant in the action. The author-narrator relates, comments, reflects, and treats his reader as interlocutor. This approach creates a feeling of directness and sense of immediacy. The author-narrator directs his voice to the ear of the reader. His voice is pleasant and does not grate. Briefly, a subnarrator appears in the person of Mr. Zverkov, who relates the circumstances of Arina's life in his household. His account and the manner of his speech are used as a negative device of characterization of this man. Modulation is attained by the occasional but sparing use of dialogue. All excess is avoided in this prose style, which aims at clarity and deliberately shuns the use of ornamentation. The descriptions of nature possess a lyrical quality, but these, too, are subdued. The sounds of nature, such as the soft chirping of birds in the enveloping darkness, are gentle and accessible only to the sensitive ear. The prevailing characteristic of nature is silence.

The story has a clear structural design with seven apparent sections, starting with the opening scene in which the narrator and Yermolai lie in wait for the woodcock to appear, up to the moment when they fall asleep. The interval of time between the opening and closing of the story is only a few hours.

Moderate use is made of telling names: Zverkov (Arina's insensitive master) is derived from *zver'* ("beast").

The soft narrative voice of the author, the subdued lyricism of its setting, the theme of a lonely existence (Yermolai), and a suggestion of long, inevitable suffering (Arina) let the narrative conclude on a minor key, likely to produce in the reader a feeling of melancholy and mild sadness while also suggesting truth and giving aesthetic pleasure.

Joachim T. Baer

YOUNG GOODMAN BROWN

Author: Nathaniel Hawthorne (1804-1864)
Type of plot: Allegory
Time of plot: The 1690's
Locale: Salem, Massachusetts
First published: 1835

> *Principal characters:*
> YOUNG GOODMAN BROWN, a Salem householder, the
>   protagonist
> FAITH, his wife
> A MAN MET IN THE WOODS, who may also be the Devil, a
>   conductor of a Black Mass in the forest

The Story

Young Goodman Brown is bidding his wife, Faith, farewell at their front door. It is evening in the village, and he is going on a guilty errand, a fact which he clearly recognizes and deplores but an errand he has chosen to undertake nevertheless. Taking a route into the forest, he meets, as by appointment, an older man who bears a fatherly resemblance to both Brown and the Devil.

Brown initially considers his decision to go on his unholy errand an exceptional one, but he soon discovers that other presumably exemplary villagers are on the same path, including, to his amazement, Goody Cloyse, a pious old woman who once taught him his catechism but who readily confesses to the practice of witchcraft. With Brown still confident that he can turn back, his older companion departs, leaving behind his curiously snakelike staff and fully expecting that Brown will soon follow.

Brown hides from another group of approaching figures, which includes the minister and deacon of his church and even—to his horror—his wife, Faith. At this point, he yields to despair and sets forth to join in what is obviously a witches' Sabbath or Black Mass. Laughing and blaspheming, Brown rushes toward the throng in the forest. Literally everyone noted for sanctity seems to be gathered together in communion with known sinners before a rock altar amid blazing pine trees. He is led to the latter with another initiate; when her veil is removed, he recognizes Faith. A dark satanic figure welcomes them to "the communion of your race."

Here, conscious that they are standing at the edge of some irredeemable wickedness, they hesitate, and Brown calls out to his wife to resist. A second later, the scene has dissolved, and he finds himself in the forest alone, shivering and confused. The following morning, he returns to the village to find all apparently normal, but he cannot help but shun contact with Goody Cloyse and the other good people—even his own wife.

In his final paragraph, Hawthorne summarizes the later, permanently blighted life of Goodman Brown. He scowls and mutters during prayers, suspects all the pious, recoils from his wife in bed at night, and finally dies without hope.

Themes and Meanings

"Young Goodman Brown" is the classic American short story of the guilty conscience. The question Brown confronts is whether his heritage of Original Sin incapacitates him for resisting personal sin. In this profoundly ambiguous story, Brown wavers between the desperate cynicism of the corrupt soul and the hopefulness of the believer. At the beginning of the story, he has already made his bargain with the Devil—hardly a token that he is among God's Elect but not necessarily a sign of damnation, either, if he can reject the consummation in the form of the perverted communion service in the woods. Whether by act of will or by divine grace, Brown appears to have resisted the power of evil at the climactic moment and given evidence of at least the possibility of salvation for his wife and himself.

Yet if he has, what can be made of his life thereafter? All family and community relationships have been poisoned, and if he can be said to retain his faith, he appears to have lost hope completely. If the ability to resist the Devil at his own table is victory, he has triumphed; if he has made the effort at the expense of his capability for human trust, he has met spiritual defeat. Hawthorne raises the question of whether Brown fell asleep in the forest and dreamed the witches' Sabbath. The reader, invited to ponder whether one dream could have such an intensive and extensive effect, may well proceed to wonder why Brown found it necessary to invade the forest at night merely to have a bad dream. If, on the other hand, any part of the forest encounter with devils and witches is "real," is Hawthorne to be regarded as a Manichaean who is demonstrating the power of evil?

"Young Goodman Brown" may also be read as a story concerned less with measuring the extent of evil in the world and assessing the moral prospects of the guilty than with studying the psychology of guilt. It may be doubted that Hawthorne would exercise his creative powers merely to affirm or quarrel with Calvinism, which had largely lost its grip on New Englanders' allegiance by 1835, but he clearly retained a strong interest in the psychological atmosphere fostered by Calvinism. Dilemmas such as the opposition between divine foreordination and free will and that between God's stern and irrevocable judgment and the possibility of His mercy and proffered grace continued to baffle conservative Christians in an era which offered a doctrinally less strenuous alternative such as Unitarianism. The old habits of mind had been challenged, but they were not dead.

Hawthorne's insight into the stages of Brown's guilt is acute. Part of

Brown's initial firmness in his resolve to go into the woods and in his confidence that his wife, by staying at home, saying her prayers, and going to bed early will remain unharmed, is his sense of the uniqueness of his own daring. Departing from the ways of the pious and arranging an interview with the Devil lends glamour to his quest. He imagines a "devilish Indian behind every tree" but cannot suppose any other Christian in these precincts. He exudes the confidence of a person who expects to retain control of the situation and pull back if he so decides. When he discovers that he is simply another sinner, simply another member of a corrupt race, he loses all dignity, all capacity for moral inquiry. Giving in to a mindless, emotional indulgence, he is later checked by the awesome finality of the Black Mass and acknowledges his insufficiency; then, for the first and only time in the story, he calls upon God for assistance.

In this story and in such other fictions as "The Minister's Black Veil," "Ethan Brand," and *The Scarlet Letter* (1850), Hawthorne depicts the inner conflict resulting from a guilt that is suppressed, felt to be unshareable and unforgivable. Regardless of whether it is justified, Brown's feeling of guilt is real, and to call his experience "only a dream" is to undervalue dreams, which, though read in vastly different ways over the centuries, have always been considered vitally significant by interpreters. Even if Brown is regarded as irrational, letting one night destroy his life, Hawthorne makes the reader feel such irrationality as a dreadful possibility.

Style and Technique

Hawthorne renders Brown's deterioration plausible by a blend of means, one of them being his surprising ability to adapt to his purposes a fictional mode seemingly much better suited to the purposes of medieval and Renaissance authors than those of nineteenth century novelists. Normally, allegory is sharp and clear as far as it goes, the limits of its applicability plain. Hawthorne's story portrays the traditional Christian conviction that when a Good Man forsakes his Faith, he is liable to Hell. When the Devil taxes Brown with being late for his appointment in the forest, his answer, "Faith kept me back a while," is as purely allegorical as it can be.

Hawthorne, however, goes on to complicate this idea. Not only are presumably pious people—guardians of the faith such as the minister and deacon—on the way to a satanic communion, but also the character who symbolizes faith. It may not be noticed at the beginning that Brown seems more protective of Faith than she of him. It may even pass unnoticed that Brown identifies Faith by her pink ribbon, a very fragile and decorative artifact for a character representing such a presumably powerful virtue. At the climax of the story, however, for the good man to counsel faith, rather than the opposite, is an incongruity that can hardly be missed. Then Hawthorne has them separated in a way that casts doubt on whether she, and indeed the whole diabolical crowd, were ever there. Brown was certainly there, but whether he has dreamed all or part of the night's events cannot be determined conclusively. Finally, he is reunited with her again for the duration of his life, but unhappily, his only alternative to full-scale evil is a life of gloom and misanthropy. Yet the story offers nothing more effective than faith to combat moral debasement.

Unlike the authors of the medieval morality plays, Edmund Spenser, John Bunyan, and other moral allegorists, Hawthorne employed allegory not to demonstrate a moral proposition or the effects of accepting or rejecting the proposition but to establish a moral context in which good and evil deeds remain identifiable while their causes, effects, and interrelationships become mysterious and problematic. To abandon faith is still evil; to rejoin faith is not so obviously good. The sins remain the traditional ones: lust, murder, worshiping false gods. No one, however, seems to remember how to live cleanly and charitably.

Hawthorne accentuates the ambiguity of his allegory by frequent use of such expressions as "perhaps," "as if," "seemed," "as it were," "some affirm that," and "he could have well-nigh sworn." Thus hedged about, the full meaning of his story is as shadowy as his forest. In addition, he poses a number of unanswered and often unanswerable questions, such as whether Brown had somehow dreamed his lurid adventure.

Such techniques suggest that while Hawthorne delighted in posing moral questions and examining the moral content of human behavior, his main interest here, and in his fiction generally, was plumbing the psychology of the moral life. Looking back on the Calvinist heritage, he wrote of the pressures it exerted on the psyches of believers. He was no amateur theologian but rather an artist. He does not say what Young Goodman Brown should have done or indeed whether he could have done other than what he did; rather, the author portrays a condition which is felt to be intolerable and yet irremediable.

Robert P. Ellis

YOUTH

Author: Joseph Conrad (Józef Teodor Konrad Korzeniowski, 1857-1924)
Type of plot: Sea adventure
Time of plot: 1880
Locale: Aboard an English freighter bound for the East
First published: 1902

> *Principal characters:*
> MARLOWE, the protagonist and second mate
> CAPTAIN JOHN BEARD, the skipper of the *Judea*
> MAHON, the first mate

The Story

At age forty-two, Marlowe sits drinking with four other Englishmen who began their lives in the merchant service. Most have other work ashore now, but they share the bond of seafaring men. He tells them the story of his first trip to the East, when he was an adventurous young man of twenty and had hired on for the first time as an officer, second mate on an old freighter bound for Bangkok.

Engraved on the stern of the ship was "Judea, London. Do or Die," a grandiloquent motto that appealed to the youthful enthusiasm of her youngest officer. Her skipper, John Beard, was also on his first voyage as captain, but at sixty years of age, he was an old hand in the merchant service. The first mate Mahon was also an old man. Much of the underlying irony that pervades this adventure is the implied contrast between what such an experience meant to a high-spirited young man and what it must have meant to the old captain. The storyteller, now midway between the ignorant youth he once was and the sorrowful but dignified old man, appreciates both perspectives.

The ill-fated *Judea* had nothing but trouble from the very beginning. She had not even reached the port where she was to be loaded with coal, when her ballast shifted dangerously in a murderous North Sea storm. Everyone began shoveling sand ballast to right the listing ship. It took them sixteen days to get from London to the Tyne, where they were delayed for two months because they had lost their turn at loading. When at last all was ready, they were rammed by a steamer, requiring further repair and three weeks' delay.

The *Judea* actually made it out into the Atlantic when another storm brought on an even more desperate struggle with multiple leaks. The crew pumped water furiously from the leaky hold for days and nights as the ship began to break in pieces about them. Only with great difficulty did they flounder back to the English coast, where the ship was unloaded and put in dry dock for repair.

The crew departed in disgust at that point, and the frustrated officers had to bring in another crew from far away, since everyone around had learned of the bad luck of the *Judea*. Even the rats deserted the ship at Falmouth, a development of ominous portent. Marlowe and Mahon joked of the obvious stupidity of rats, however, since they should have left before, when the ship was really unseaworthy. Now, it was well caulked and shipshape.

The freighter got clear to the Indian Ocean before further disaster assailed it. The coal in the hold started smoldering from spontaneous combustion. Whereas in the Atlantic they had pumped for dear life to prevent drowning, they now poured ocean water into the hold to prevent being burned alive, wishing for the old leaks, which would have flooded the coal more efficiently. At last the smoke stopped pouring from the pile, but only as a precursor to another calamity. As the men began to relax for the first time in many days, the hold exploded from trapped gases, resulting in serious damage to both the ship and its men.

The "Do or Die" *Judea* eventually fulfilled the second part of her motto, sinking in flames as the men watched from three small lifeboats. Marlowe eventually reached Java as the captain of a rowboat with two crew members.

Themes and Meanings

This is one of the most autobiographical of Conrad's sea stories, chronicling his own first voyage to the East and his first position as an officer. Conrad went to sea at the age of seventeen, but in 1881 he shipped in a freighter called the *Palestine*, for which the *Judea* is a pseudonym. The story probably reflects quite accurately the heartbreaking frustrations and failures, from the captain's standpoint, that often plagued such overaged seagoing vessels. It also expressed the rare power of the romantic young man's ability to convert an extremely painful, tedious, and dangerous experience into a glamorous test of his strength, courage, and ability. What must have been the most dismal failure to the old skipper on his first and probably only chance to be a captain was for the youthful mate a resounding success.

Even in the most dreadful and tedious circumstances, as when they are pumping frantically to stay afloat, the protagonist is enjoying even the misery of it all:

> And there was somewhere in me the thought: By Jove! this is the deuce of an adventure—something you read about; and it is my first voyage as second mate—and I am only twenty—and here I am lasting it out as well as any of these men, and keeping my chaps up to the mark. I was pleased. I would not have given up the experience for worlds. I had moments of exultation. Whenever the old dismantled craft pitched heavily with her counter high in the air, she seemed to me to throw up, like an appeal, like a defiance, like a cry to the clouds without mercy, the words written on her stern: "Judea, London. Do or Die."

If the story is a paean to the optimism and exhilaration of youth in the face of hardship, it is also a more muted tribute to the perseverance and honor of age when the daily battle with the sea is no longer a romantic game. The spry old skipper is treated with humor and respect, a considerate and valiant little man in the face of inevitable defeat. He insists on remaining on the burning ship until the last minute and conscientiously, though foolishly, tries to save as much as he can for his employers:

> The old man warned us in his gentle and inflexible way that it was part of our duty to save for the underwriters as much as we could of the ship's gear. Accordingly we went to work aft, while she blazed forward to give us plenty of light. We lugged out a lot of rubbish. What didn't we save? An old barometer fixed with an absurd quantity of screws nearly cost me my life: a sudden rush of smoke came upon me, and I just got away in time. There were various stores, bolts of canvas, coils of rope; the poop looked like a marine bazaar, and the boats were lumbered to the gunwales. One would have thought the old man wanted to take as much as he could of his first command with him. He was very, very quiet, but off his balance evidently. Would you believe it? He wanted to take a length of old stream-cable and a kedge-anchor with him in the long-boat. We said, "Ay, ay, sir," deferentially, and on the quiet let the things slip overboard.

"Youth," like other sea stories by Conrad, suggests that basic analogy between a voyage and the whole of human life. It may be perceived differently by the participants, but it induces in them, at least in times of danger, a rare comradeship emanating from a shared fate.

Style and Technique

Conrad combined a genius for realistic detail with an ability to embellish experience with human emotion. Though in some stories, such as *Heart of Darkness* (1902), he produced an almost too-melodramatic overlay of suggestive implications, he never seriously misrepresented the scenes he described, which he knew from personal experience. "Youth" is quite free of "purple passages," without obscuring either the grim reality of the voyage or the absurdly romantic glow in which the young mate experienced it.

Conrad's sentence style itself suggests the exhausting, mind-deadening experience of undergoing a relentless storm and the continual, repetitive struggle to stay alive. The experience is evoked by a series of short phrases presented in parallel structure—"It blew day after day: it blew with spite, without interval, without mercy, without rest"—or by rhythms that mirror the endless, mindless tedium of pumping water from the leaking hull:

> We pumped watch and watch, for dear life; and it seemed to last for months, for years, for all eternity, as though we had been dead and gone to a hell for

sailors. We forgot the day of the week, the name of the month, what year it was, and whether we had ever been ashore. The sail blew away, she lay broadside on under a weather-cloth, the ocean poured over her, and we did not care. We turned those handles, and had the eyes of idiots.

The framing of the story as a true sea yarn told to a group of drinking companions lends a convenient distance to the adventure, so that it carries a conscious irony inappropriate to the narrator's youthful self. In one sense, "Youth" is a kind of trial run for the framing technique, which became more important in *Heart of Darkness*, in which Marlowe sits cross-legged like a Buddha in a boat on the Thames with a similar group of former seamen. In "Youth," Marlowe has not yet attained that implication of inscrutable wisdom as the man initiated into the mysteries of evil at the heart of men. He speaks here not at all of the evils of men, but of the hardness of their lot and the courage with which ordinary men may face the threat of death. More than that, he marvels at the fact that such a life can seem like fun.

Katherine Snipes

THE ZULU AND THE ZEIDE

Author: Dan Jacobson (1929-   )
Type of plot: Domestic realism
Time of plot: 1956
Locale: A city in South Africa, probably Kimberley
First published: 1956

> *Principal characters:*
> HARRY GROSSMAN, a prosperous Jewish immigrant to South
>   Africa
> HIS FATHER, the "Zeide" (grandfather)
> JOHANNES and
> PAULUS, Zulu servants

The Story

Three characters in this story—Harry, his father, and Paulus—are described as physically large men, and this is reinforced by the name Dan Jacobson chooses for Harry and his father: Grossman (as *gross* means "large" in German). Yet, though Harry has inherited from his father a great strength, the old man is no longer strong and senility has destroyed much of his mental capacity. On the other hand, his "passion for freedom," which causes him constantly to run away from home, is his understandable desire to escape from a household in which he knows that he has no real place.

To Harry, the old man's senile flights are a nuisance, a social embarrassment, and a source of resentment and guilt. The resentment is against a father whose past failures were the reason for which Harry had to work so hard as a young man. When his father, setting off for South Africa, was somehow diverted to Argentina, his wife was forced to go into debt to help him come home. Harry had to work for years to pay off the debt, to finance their passage to South Africa, and, because the old man could not hold a job, to support them when they got there. Because he was forced at an early age to fill his father's economic role, he hates the old man, though he also cannot escape the sense that he owes his father filial affection. His guilt for his failings as a son is submerged in his bitterness about what he considers to have been his father's exploitation. To make matters worse, the old man in his senility demands, "What do you want in my house? . . . Out of my house!"

Harry's Zulu servant Johannes proposes using Paulus, a "raw boy" from the country, who, he claims, is his brother, as a caretaker for the old man. In fact, Paulus may only be his relative or someone from his own village. This close identification of the two Zulus with each other is important in the story because it contrasts with the mutual alienation which characterizes Harry's household. The Jews also were once a tribe, but Harry and his family are incapable of thinking even in family terms, let alone in the tribal terms of Johannes and Paulus. Harry is suspicious of Johannes' suggestion, but he consents because he thinks it would be a fine joke on his father and, because he considers Africans an inferior race, on Paulus as well.

Paulus solves the problem of the old man's constantly running away in the simplest way: He goes with him. The two men wander through the streets of the city together, often getting lost because neither can read street signs, but in a strange way they become friends. The old man calls Paulus Der Schwarzer and Paulus calls him Baas Zeide, using the Yiddish word for grandfather which he has heard Harry's children use. Paulus bathes and dresses the Zeide, trims his hair and beard, and even carries him to bed. Because Paulus clearly cares for the old man as Harry believes he himself should care for him, Harry feels a guilty irritation, yet he enjoys his joke: By reducing his father to the level of Paulus, he has reduced him to the lowest possible level in a racist society. When he makes his cruelty worse by saying that he plans to send Paulus away, he is frustrated by the response of the old man, who merely goes to Paulus' room to sit there with him "for security," as though realizing that Harry would never enter an African's room.

Because of the affection between the Zulu and the Zeide, Harry's rage is also directed at Paulus. Once, when he is accusing Paulus of tiring the old man needlessly by taking him too far—apparently forgetting that Paulus is the follower, not the leader, in the wanderings—he is enraged by Paulus' inability to understand English, accuses him of willfully misunderstanding him, and ridicules his lowly status in society: "You'll always be where you are, running to do what the white baas tells you to do. . . . Do you think I understood English when I came here?"

One day, Harry quarrels with his father when Paulus has the afternoon off. The old man calls for Der Schwarzer, and Harry tries to tell him that Paulus will return. Then he pleads with him to let him do for him what Paulus would do. "Please. . . . Why can't you ask it of me? You can ask me— haven't I done enough for you already?" By now the old man is weeping, as if in grief for the lost Paulus or perhaps in rage at Harry for sending him away at last. Finally Harry leaves him, and his father hysterically runs into the street and is hit and killed by a bicyclist. The argument which led to his father's death is a terrible secret with which Harry is left for the rest of his life.

At the funeral, Harry's wife and children and even Paulus weep for the old man. Harry, however, is unrepentant. He pays off Paulus and tells Johannes to tell him to leave; Johannes must remind the Baas that Paulus also wants his "savings" (wages withheld by the employer to keep a "boy" from wasting his earning on foolish things). When Harry asks contemptuously why Paulus would want to save money, Johannes says, "He is saving, baas . . . to bring his family to this town also." At this point, something cracks in Harry, and on the verge of tears he stares at the two Zulus and with "guilt and despair" cries, "What else could I have done? I did my best."

Themes and Meanings

This story reveals the preoccupations which appear in much of Jacobson's writing: the conflict between fathers and sons, the experience of Jews in South Africa, and the conflict of the races. Much of its power derives from the reader's realization that, in spite of Harry's obvious cruelty and his family's insensitivity to the grandfather, no one is really to blame for what happens. Harry feels a great guilt for his part in his father's death, but he is himself the victim of the burdensome duty which he has borne all of his life as the head of the family. The Zeide has always been incompetent and foolish, and even as a boy Harry had to fill his father's role. In a sense, the Zeide has always been his child.

At the same time, Paulus, though he is called a "boy" in the racist society of South Africa, is more of a man than Harry and more of a son to the Zeide. Indeed, the Zulu and the Zeide, in spite of their lack of a common language, communicate with each other more than Harry is able to communicate with his father. Harry's household is, in fact, a microcosm of the larger society of South Africa. Harry himself was once a "raw boy" from the country (Europe, in his case) and an outsider; he came to South Africa to make his way and, as Paulus hopes to do, to bring his family after him. Paulus and the Zeide are both victims of the bigotry of Harry's household. Both are wanderers in the streets, scorned by the white men, who look away when they see them because they cannot bear to see the "degradation" of the old man, reduced at the end of his life to the care of a "Kaffir."

It is the realization that he himself is an advanced version of Paulus, a noble and heroic figure toward whom he has always felt only contempt, that breaks him down at the end of the story. Paulus, working mightily to bring his family to town, is a painful reminder to Harry of what he himself once was and an even more painful reminder of his own inability to love.

Style and Technique

Jacobson's methods, here as elsewhere in his work, are subtle. The style is quiet, and the language does not reveal, except by inference, the feelings of the author. Jacobson chooses to let scene support characterization, as when he shows the lack of true family bonds in Harry's life by saying that the doors in his house were "curiously masculine in appearance, like the house of a widower." The manner of his writing most resembles that of Anton Chekhov, one of Jacobson's masters. The story is told simply, without comment, and the reader is left to reach his own conclusions about the material.

These methods contribute to the power of the story. The terrible pathos is enhanced by the quiet unfolding of the story, and the three-part plot seems painfully inevitable. The problem of what to do with the old man is defined; the advent of Paulus solves the problem but makes matters worse for Harry; finally, the old man dies and Harry is forced to grieve, not because of the death but because of the realization that he once was what the pathetic Paulus is now. Not that Jacobson tells the reader what Harry realizes. He merely lets Paulus speak, and Harry's response tells the rest. Nothing has happened in a sense, but everything has happened.

Robert L. Berner

BIBLIOGRAPHY

General Works: Critical, Historical, Theoretical

Allen, Walter. *The Short Story in English*. Oxford: The Clarendon Press, 1981. A historical study of the development of the form in England and America.

Beachcroft, T. O. *The Modest Art: A Survey of the Short Story in English*. London: Oxford University Press, 1968. A historical survey of major English short-story writers from Chaucer to Doris Lessing.

Boyce, Benjamin. "English Short Fiction in the Eighteenth Century: A Preliminary View," in *Studies in Short Fiction*. V (Winter, 1968), pp. 95-112. Boyce analyzes the types of short fiction found in periodicals during the period, such as the character sketch, the Oriental tale, and the story of passion. The most distinctive characteristics are didactic intent and formal style.

Canby, Henry S. *The Short Story in English*. New York: Holt, Rinehart and Winston, 1909, reprinted 1932. One of the first historical studies of the short story; argues that the Romantic movement gave birth to the form.

Current-Garcia, Eugene, and Walton Patrick, eds. *What Is the Short Story?* Rev. ed. New York: Scott, Foresman and Co., 1974. Contains a selection of mostly American criticism on the form arranged in alphabetical order.

Duncan, Edgar Hill. "Short Fiction in Medieval English: A Survey," in *Studies in Short Fiction*. IX (Winter, 1972), pp. 1-28. A survey of Old English short pieces, mostly in verse, which focus on singleness of character, action, or impression.

_____ . "Short Fiction in Medieval English: II," in *Studies in Short Fiction*. XI (Summer, 1974), pp. 227-242. A discussion of short fiction elements in such short romance forms as the exemplary narrative, the beast tale, and the fabliau.

Ferguson, Suzanne C. "Defining the Short Story: Impressionism and Form," in *Modern Fiction Studies*. XXVIII (Spring, 1982), pp. 13-24. Argues that there is no single characteristic or cluster of characteristics which distinguish the short story from the novel; suggests that what is called the modern short story is a manifestation of impressionism rather than a discrete genre.

Gerlach, John. *Toward the End: Closure and Structure in the American Short Story*. University: The University of Alabama Press, 1985. A detailed theoretical study of the American short story, particularly focusing on the notion of "closure."

Gullason, Thomas A. "Revelation and Evolution: A Neglected Dimension of the Short Story," in *Studies in Short Fiction*. X (Fall, 1973), pp. 347-356. Challenges the usual distinction that the short story is the art of moral revelation whereas the novel is the art of moral evolution.

Harris, Wendell V. "English Short Fiction in the Nineteenth Century," in *Studies in Short Fiction*. VI (Fall, 1968), pp. 1-93. A historical survey of short fiction during the period, in which Harris suggests that short fiction does not truly begin in England until around the 1880's.

Kenyon Review International Symposium on the Short Story. Part 1, XXX, issue 4, 1968, pp. 443-490; Part 2, XXXI, issue 1, 1969, pp. 58-94; Part 3, XXXI, issue 4, 1969, pp. 450-502. This special series features contributions from short-story writers from all over the world on the nature of the form, its history, and its significance.

Kostelanetz, Richard. "The Short Story in Search of Status," in *Twentieth Century*. CLXXIV (Autumn, 1965), pp. 65-69. A helpful study of the particular characteristics of the short story in the mid-twentieth century.

Lohafer, Susan. *Coming to Terms with the Short Story*. Baton Rouge: Louisiana State University Press, 1983. A highly suggestive theoretical study of the short story which focuses on the sentence unit of the form as a way of showing how the form differs from the novel.

Marler, Robert F. "From Tale to Short Story: The Emergence of a New Genre in the 1850's," in *American Literature*. XLVI (May, 1974), pp. 153-169. Surveys the critical condemnation of the tale form and the increasing emphasis on realism in America in the 1850's; notes that the shift is from Edgar Allan Poe's overt romance form to Herman Melville's mimetic portrayals.

May, Charles E. "The Nature of Knowledge in Short Fiction," in *Studies in Short Fiction*. XXI (Fall, 1984), pp. 227-238. A theoretical study of the epistemological bases of short fiction.

_____. "The Short Story's Unique Effect," in *Studies in Short Fiction*. XIII (Summer, 1976), pp. 289-297. Argues that Edgar Allan Poe's theory about singleness of effect refers to the mythic mode of short narrative.

_____, ed. *Short Story Theories*. Athens: Ohio University Press, 1976. The most complete collection of theoretical essays on the short story; also contains a thorough annotated bibliography of periodical articles on short-story theory and criticism.

Mish, Charles C. "English Short Fiction in the Seventeenth Century," in *Studies in Short Fiction*. VI (Spring, 1969), pp. 223-330. Mish suggests that short fiction declined into sterile imitation between 1600 and 1660, but was revitalized between 1660 and 1700 by the French movement toward interiorization, psychological analysis, and verisimilitude.

Newman, Frances. *The Short Story's Mutations: From Petronius to Paul Morand*. New York: B. W. Huebsch, 1924. Argues that the development of the short story is from the ironic mode to the impressionistic.

O'Brien, Edward J. *The Advance of the American Short Story*. Rev. ed. New York: Dodd, Mead and Co., 1931. A survey of the development of the

American short story from Washington Irving to Sherwood Anderson, focusing primarily on the contributions various authors have made to the form.

——————. *The Dance of the Machines: The American Short Story and the Industrial Age*. New York: The Macaulay Co., 1929. A rambling polemic against machinelike standardization in the industrial age; argues that the short story is patterned, impersonal, and cheap, much like the products of machines themselves.

O'Connor, Frank. *The Lonely Voice: A Study of the Short Story*. Cleveland, Ohio: The World Publishing Co., 1963. One of the best studies of the form by a master of short-story writing; impressionistic, but highly suggestive and helpful.

O'Faoláin, Seán. *The Short Story*. New York: The Devin-Adair Co., 1951. Although this is a book on technique, it argues that personality rather than technique is the most important element of short-story writing.

Pain, Barry. *The Short Story*. London: Martin Secker, 1916. One of the best early discussions of the form; claims that the short story differs from the novel in demanding more of the reader.

Pattee, Fred Lewis. *The Development of the American Short Story*. New York: Harper and Row, 1923. The most detailed and complete historical study of the form of its time; indicates the major contributions of Washington Irving, Nathaniel Hawthorne, Edgar Allan Poe, Bret Harte, and others; surveys the effect of the Ladies Books, the local-color movement, and writing handbooks.

Peden, William. *The American Short Story: Front Line in the National Defense of Literature*. Boston: Houghton Mifflin Co., 1964. A discussion of the major trends in the American short story from 1940 to the early 1960's; focuses primarily on typical themes of the period.

Pratt, Mary Louise. "The Short Story: The Long and the Short of It," in *Poetics*. X (1981), pp. 175-194. A theoretical argument which proposes eight ways in which the short story is better understood if seen as depending on the novel.

Reid, Ian. *The Short Story*. London: Methuen and Co., 1977. A brief study in the Critical Idiom Series; deals with problems of definition, historical development, and related generic forms.

Rohrberger, Mary. *Hawthorne and the Modern Short Story: A Study in Genre*. The Hague: Mouton and Col, 1966. An extremely helpful study of the Romantic origins of the short-story form.

Ross, Danforth. *The American Short Story*. Minneapolis: University of Minnesota Press, 1961. A brief survey which measures short stories since Poe against Aristotelian criteria.

Schlauch, Margaret. "English Short Fiction in the Fifteenth and Sixteenth Centuries," in *Studies in Short Fiction*. III (Summer, 1966), pp. 393-434. A survey of types of short fiction during the period, including the romantic lai, the exemplum, the fabliau, and the novella.

Shaw, Valerie. *The Short Story: A Critical Introduction*. London: Longman, 1983. A critical, rather than merely historical, study of the short story; attempts to account for the form's unique quality.

Summers, Hollis, ed. *Discussions of the Short Story*. Lexington, Mass.: D. C. Heath, 1963. Contains nine general essays on the short story.

Thurston, Jarvis, O. B. Emerson, Carl Hartman, and Elizabeth Wright, eds. *Short Fiction Criticism: A Checklist of Interpretations Since 1925 of Stories and Novelettes (American, British, Continental), 1800-1958*. Metuchen, N.J.: Swallow Press, 1960. This checklist of interpretations of individual stories was brought up to date by Elizabeth Wright in the Summer, 1969, issue of *Studies in Short Fiction* and has been supplemented by various bibliographies in each Summer issue of the journal since then.

Ward, Alfred C. *Aspects of the Modern Short Story: English and American*. London: University of London Press, 1924. Brief discussions of representative stories of twenty-three different writers.

West, Ray B., Jr. *The Short Story in America: 1900-1950*. Chicago: Henry Regnery Co., 1952. One of the most intelligent histories of the form, but not complete or comprehensive.

Williams, William Carlos. *A Beginning on the Short Story: Notes*. Yonkers, N.Y.: The Alicat Bookshop Press, 1950. A fragmentary and impressionistic collection of notes, some brilliant, some merely perverse.

Wright, Austin. *The American Short Story in the Twenties*. Chicago: University of Chicago Press, 1961. A detailed study of the differences between short stories of the 1920's and those of the late nineteenth century.

Works by Author
Conrad Aiken
Hoffman, Frederick J. *Conrad Aiken*. New York: Twayne, 1962.
Martin, Jay. *Conrad Aiken: A Life of His Art*. Princeton, N.J.: Princeton University Press, 1962.
Reuel, Denney. *Conrad Aiken*. Minneapolis: University of Minnesota Press, 1964.

Sherwood Anderson
Anderson, David D. *Sherwood Anderson: An Introduction and Interpretation*. New York: Holt, Rinehart and Winston, 1967.
_____, ed. *Critical Essays on Sherwood Anderson*. Boston: G. K. Hall, 1981.
_____, ed. *Sherwood Anderson: Dimensions of His Literary Art*. East Lansing: Michigan State University Press, 1976.
Burbank. Rex. *Sherwood Anderson*. New York: Twayne, 1964.

Weber, Brom. *Sherwood Anderson*. Minneapolis: University of Minnesota Press, 1964.

Isaac Babel

Carden, Patricia. *The Art of Isaac Babel*. Ithaca, N.Y.: Cornell University Press, 1972.
Falen, James. *Isaac Babel: Russian Master of the Short Story*. Knoxville: University of Tennessee Press, 1974.
Hallett, Richard W. *Isaac Babel*. New York: Frederick Ungar Publishing Co., 1973.

John Barth

Harris, Charles B. *Passionate Virtuosity: The Fiction of John Barth*. Urbana: University of Illinois Press, 1983.
Joseph, Gerhard. *John Barth*. Minneapolis: University of Minnesota Press, 1970.
Tharpe, Jac. *John Barth: The Comic Sublimity of Paradox*. Carbondale: Southern Illinois University Press, 1974.
Waldmeir, Joseph J., ed. *Critical Essays on John Barth*. Boston: G. K. Hall, 1980.

Donald Barthelme

Gordon, Lois G. *Donald Barthelme*. Boston: Twayne, 1981.
Stengel, Wayne B. *The Shape of Art in the Short Stories of Donald Barthelme*. Baton Rouge: Louisiana State University Press, 1985.

Ambrose Bierce

Davidson, Cathy N. *The Experimental Fictions of Ambrose Bierce*. Lincoln: University of Nebraska Press, 1984.
Grenander, M. E. *Ambrose Bierce*. New York: Twayne, 1971.
Wiggins, Robert. *Ambrose Bierce*. Minneapolis: University of Minnesota Press, 1964.
Woodruff, Stuart C. *The Short Stories of Ambrose Bierce: A Study in Polarity*. Pittsburgh: University of Pittsburgh Press, 1964.

Jorge Luis Borges

Christ, Ronald. *The Narrow Act: Borges' Art of Illusion*. New York: New York University Press, 1969.
Stabb, Martin S. *Jorge Luis Borges*. New York: Twayne, 1970.
Sturrock, John. *Paper Tiger: The Ideal Fictions of Jorge Luis Borges*. Oxford: The Clarendon Press, 1977.
Wheelock, Carter. *The Mythmaker: A Study of Motif and Symbol in the Short Stories of Jorge Luis Borges*. Austin: University of Texas Press, 1969.

John Cheever
Coale, Samuel. *John Cheever*. New York: Frederick Ungar Publishing Co., 1977.
Collins, R. G., ed. *Critical Essays on John Cheever*. Boston: G. K. Hall, 1982.
Hunt, George W. *John Cheever: The Hobgoblin Company of Love*. Grand Rapids, Mich.: William B. Eerdmans, 1983.
Waldeland, Lynne. *John Cheever*. Boston: Twayne, 1979.

Anton Chekhov
Clyman, Toby W., ed. *A Chekhov Companion*. Westport, Conn.: Greenwood Press, 1985.
Hahn, Beverly. *Chekhov: A Study of the Major Stories and Plays*. London: Cambridge University Press, 1977.
Kirk, Irene. *Anton Chekhov*. Boston: Twayne, 1981.
Kramer, Karl D. *The Chameleon and the Dream: The Image of Reality in Chekhov's Stories*. The Hague: Mouton, 1970.
Llewllyn Smith, Virginia. *Anton Chekhov and the Lady with the Dog*. London: Oxford University Press, 1973.
Rayfield, Donald. *Chekhov: The Evolution of His Art*. New York: Barnes and Noble, 1975.
Winner, Thomas. *Chekhov and His Prose*. New York: Holt, Rinehart and Winston, 1966.

Joseph Conrad
Daleski, H. M. *Joseph Conrad: The Way of Dispossession*. New York: Holmes and Meier, 1976.
Glassman, Peter. *Language and Being: Joseph Conrad and the Literature of Personality*. New York: Columbia University Press, 1976.
Graver, Lawrence. *Conrad's Short Fiction*. Berkeley: University of California Press, 1969.
Guerard, Albert J. *Conrad the Novelist*. Cambridge, Mass.: Harvard University Press, 1958.
Karl, Frederick. *A Reader's Guide to Joseph Conrad*. New York: Noonday Press, 1960.
Moser, Thomas. *Joseph Conrad: Achievement and Decline*. Cambridge, Mass.: Harvard University Press, 1957.
Said, Edward W. *Joseph Conrad and the Fiction of Autobiography*. Cambridge, Mass.: Harvard University Press, 1966.
Stallman, Robert W., ed. *The Art of Joseph Conrad: A Critical Symposium*. East Lansing: Michigan State University Press, 1960.

Stephen Crane
Berryman, John. *Stephen Crane*. New York: William Sloane Assoc., 1950.

Holton, Milne. *Cylinder of Vision: The Fiction and Journalistic Writing of Stephen Crane*. Baton Rouge: Louisiana State University Press, 1972.

Solomon, Eric. *Stephen Crane: From Parody to Realism*. Cambridge, Mass.: Harvard University Press, 1966.

Stallman, R. W. *Stephen Crane: A Biography*. New York: George Braziller, 1968.

Isak Dinesen

Hannah, Donald. *"Isak Dinesen" and Karen Blixen: The Mask and the Reality*. London: Putnam, 1971.

Johannesson, Eric O. *The World of Isak Dinesen*. Seattle: University of Washington Press, 1961.

Langbaum, Robert W. *The Gayety of Vision: A Study of Isak Dinesen's Art*. New York: Random House, 1964.

William Faulkner

Backman, Melvin. *Faulkner: The Major Years*. Bloomington: Indiana University Press, 1966.

Brooks, Cleanth. *Toward Yoknapatawpha and Beyond*. New Haven, Conn.: Yale University Press, 1978.

——————. *William Faulkner: The Yoknapatawpha Country*. New Haven, Conn.: Yale University Press, 1963.

Hoffman, Frederick J., and Olga W. Vickery, eds. *William Faulkner: Three Decades of Criticism*. East Lansing: Michigan State University Press, 1960.

Howe, Irving. *William Faulkner: A Critical Study*. New York: Random House, 1962.

Kinney, Arthur F. *Faulkner's Narrative Poetics: Style as Vision*. Amherst: University of Massachusetts Press, 1978.

Malin, Irving. *William Faulkner: An Interpretation*. Stanford, Calif.: Stanford University Press, 1957.

Milgate, Michael. *The Achievement of William Faulkner*. London: Constable, 1966.

Volpe, Edmond L. *A Reader's Guide to William Faulkner*. New York: Farrar, Straus and Giroux, 1964.

F. Scott Fitzgerald

Eble, Kenneth. *F. Scott Fitzgerald*. New York: Twayne, 1963.

——————. *F. Scott Fitzgerald: A Collection of Critical Essays*. New York: McGraw-Hill, 1973.

Fahey, William. *F. Scott Fitzgerald and the American Dream*. New York: Thomas Y. Crowell, 1973.

Higgins, John A. *F. Scott Fitzgerald: A Study of the Stories*. Jamaca, N.Y.: St. Johns University Press, 1971.

Hindus, Milton. *F. Scott Fitzgerald: An Introduction and Interpretation*. New
    York: Holt, Rinehart and Winston, 1969.
Lehan, Richard D. *F. Scott Fitzgerald and the Craft of Fiction*. Carbondale:
    Southern Illinois University Press, 1966.

Nikolai Gogol
Lavrin, Janko. *Nikolai Gogol: 1809-1852*. London: Sylvan Press, 1951.
Lindstrom, Thais S. *Nikolay Gogol*. New York: Twayne, 1974.
Nabokov, Vladimir. *Nikolai Gogol*. New York: New Directions Press, 1961.
Trahan, Elizabeth, ed. *Gogol's Overcoat: An Anthology of Critical Essays*.
    Ann Arbor, Mich.: Ardis, 1982.
Woodward, James B. *The Symbolic Art of Gogol: Essays on His Short Fic-
    tion*. Columbus, Ohio: Slavica, 1982.

Nathaniel Hawthorne
Arvin, Newton. *Hawthorne*. Boston: Little, Brown and Co., 1929.
Doubleday, Neal F. *Hawthorne's Early Tales: A Critical Study*. Durham,
    N.C.: Duke University Press, 1972.
Fogle, Richard Harter. *Hawthorne's Fiction: The Light and the Dark*. Nor-
    man: University of Oklahoma Press, 1952.
Male, Roy R. *Hawthorne's Tragic Vision*. New York: W. W. Norton, 1957.
Pearce, Harvey Roy, ed. *Hawthorne Centenary Essays*. Columbus: Ohio
    State University Press, 1964.
Rohrberger, Mary. *Hawthorne and the Modern Short Story*. The Hague:
    Mouton, 1966.
Turner, Arlin. *Nathaniel Hawthorne: An Introduction and Interpretation*.
    New York: Barnes and Noble, 1961.
Waggoner, Hyatt H. *Hawthorne: A Critical Study*. Cambridge, Mass.: Har-
    vard University Press, 1955, 1963.

Ernest Hemingway
Baker, Carlos. *Hemingway: The Writer and Artist*. Princeton, N.J.:
    Princeton University Press, 1952.
Baker, Sheridan. *Hemingway: An Introduction and Interpretation*. New
    York: Holt, Rinehart and Winston, 1967.
Benson, Jackson J. *The Short Stories of Ernest Hemingway: Critical Essays*.
    Durham, N.C.: Duke University Press, 1975.
Defalco, Joseph. *The Hero in Hemingway's Short Stories*. Pittsburgh:
    University of Pittsburgh Press, 1963.
Gurko, Leo. *Hemingway and the Pursuit of Heroism*. New York: Thomas Y.
    Crowell, 1968.
Killinger, John. *Hemingway and the Dead Gods: A Study in Existentialism*.
    Lexington: University of Kentucky Press, 1960.

Rovit, Earl. *Ernest Hemingway*. New York: Twayne, 1963.

Waldhorn, Arthur. *A Reader's Guide to Ernest Hemingway*. New York: Farrar, Straus and Giroux, 1972.

Young, Philip. *Ernest Hemingway: A Reconsideration*. University Park: Pennsylvania State University Press, 1966.

O. Henry

Current-Garcia, Eugene. *O. Henry*. New York: Twayne, 1965.

Ejxenbaum, B. M. *O. Henry and the Theory of the Short Story*. Translated by I. R. Titunik. Ann Arbor: University of Michigan Press, 1968.

Langford, Gerald. *Alias O. Henry: A Biography of William Sidney Porter*. New York: Macmillan, 1957.

Washington Irving

Bowden, Mary Weatherspoon. *Washington Irving*. Boston: Twayne, 1981.

Hedges, William L. *Washington Irving: An American Study, 1802-1832*. Baltimore: The Johns Hopkins University Press, 1965.

Leary, Lewis. *Washington Irving*. Minneapolis: University of Minnesota Press, 1963.

Meyers, Andrew B., ed. *A Century of Commentary on the Works of Washington Irving*. Tarrytown, N.Y.: Sleepy Hollow Restorations, 1976.

Roth, Martin. *Comedy and America: The Lost World of Washington Irving*. Port Washington, N.Y.: Kennikat Press, 1976.

Wagenknecht, Edward. *Washington Irving: Moderation Displayed*. New York: Oxford University Press, 1962.

Henry James

Dupee, F. W., ed. *The Question of Henry James: A Collection of Critical Essays*. New York: Holt, 1945.

Edel, Leon, ed. *Henry James: A Collection of Critical Essays*. Englewood Cliffs, N.J.: Prentice-Hall, 1963.

Hoffman, Charles G. *The Short Novels of Henry James*. New York: Bookman Associates, 1957.

McElderry, Bruce R., Jr. *Henry James*. New York: Twayne, 1965.

Matthiessen, F. O. *Henry James: The Major Phase*. New York: Oxford University Press, 1944.

Vaid, Krishna Baldev. *Technique in the Tales of Henry James*. Cambridge, Mass.: Harvard University Press, 1964.

Ward, J. A. *The Search for Form: Studies in the Structure of James's Fiction*. Chapel Hill: University of North Carolina Press, 1967.

Wright, Walter F. *The Madness of Art: A Study in Henry James*. Lincoln: University of Nebraska Press, 1962.

James Joyce
Beck, Warren. *Joyce's Dubliners: Substance, Vision, and Art.* Durham, N.C.: Duke University Press, 1969.
Givens, Seon, ed. *James Joyce: Two Decades of Criticism.* New York: Vanguard Press, 1948, 1963.
Hart, Clive, ed. *James Joyce's Dubliners: Critical Essays.* New York: The Viking Press, Inc., 1969.
Kenner, Hugh. *Dublin's Joyce.* Bloomington: Indiana University Press, 1956.
Levin, Harry. *James Joyce: A Critical Introduction.* New York: New Directions, 1960.
Litz, A. Walton. *James Joyce.* New York: Twayne, 1966.
Tindall, William York. *A Reader's Guide to James Joyce.* New York: Farrar, Straus and Giroux, 1959.

Franz Kafka
Flores, Angel, ed. *The Kafka Problem.* New York: Octagon, 1946, 1963.
Flores, Angel, and Homer Swander, eds. *Franz Kafka Today.* Madison: The University of Wisconsin Press, 1958.
Foulkes, A. P. *The Reluctant Pessimist: A Study of Franz Kafka.* The Hague: Mouton and Co., 1967.
Gray, Ronald, ed. *Kafka: A Collection of Critical Essays.* Englewood Cliffs, N.J.: Prentice-Hall, 1962.
Neider, Charles. *The Frozen Sea: A Study of Franz Kafka.* New York: Oxford University Press, 1948.

Rudyard Kipling
Carrington, Charles. *Rudyard Kipling: His Life and Work.* London: Macmillan, 1955.
Dobree, Bonamy. *Rudyard Kipling: Realist and Fabulist.* London: Oxford University Press, 1967.
Gilbert, Elliot L., ed. *Kipling and the Critics.* New York: New York University Press, 1965.
Rutherford, Andrew, ed. *Kipling's Mind and Art: Selected Critical Essays.* Stanford, Calif.: Stanford University Press, 1964.
Tompkins, J. M. S. *The Art of Rudyard Kipling.* London: Methuen and Co., 1959.

D. H. Lawrence
Draper, Ronald. *D. H. Lawrence.* New York: Twayne, 1964.
Hoffman, Frederick, ed. *The Achievement of D. H. Lawrence.* Norman: University of Oklahoma Press, 1953.
Hough, Graham. *The Dark Sun: A Study of D. H. Lawrence.* New York: Macmillan, 1957.

Moore, Harry T. *D. H. Lawrence: His Life and Work*. New York: Twayne, 1964.

Sagar, Keith. *The Art of D. H. Lawrence*. Cambridge: Cambridge University Press, 1966.

Spilka, Mark. *The Love Ethic of D. H. Lawrence*. Bloomington: Indiana University Press, 1955.

Bernard Malamud

Astro, Richard, and Jackson Benson, eds. *The Fiction of Bernard Malamud*. Corvallis: Oregon State University Press, 1977.

Field, Leslie, and Joyce W. Field, eds. *Bernard Malamud: A Collection of Critical Essays*. Englewood Cliffs, N.J.: Prentice-Hall, 1975.

―――――――. *Bernard Malamud and the Critics*. New York: New York University Press, 1970.

Hershinow, Sheldon J. *Bernard Malamud*. New York: Frederick Ungar Publishing Co., 1980.

Richman, Sidney. *Bernard Malamud*. New York: Twayne, 1966.

Thomas Mann

Feuerlicht, Ignace. *Thomas Mann*. New York: Twayne, 1968.

Hatfield, Henry. *Thomas Mann: An Introduction to His Fiction*. Norfolk, Conn.: New Directions, 1962.

Heller, Joseph. *The Ironic German*. Boston: Little, Brown and Co., 1958.

Kahlet, Erich. *The Orbit of Thomas Mann*. Princeton, N.J.: Princeton University Press, 1969.

Neider, Charles, ed. *The Stature of Thomas Mann*. New York: Books for Libraries Press, 1958.

Thomas, R. Hinton. *Thomas Mann: The Mediation of Art*. Oxford: The Clarendon Press, 1956.

Katherine Mansfield

Berkman, Sylvia. *Katherine Mansfield: A Critical Study*. New Haven, Conn.: Yale University Press, 1951.

Daly, Saralyn R. *Katherine Mansfield*. New York: Twayne, 1965.

Hankin. C. A. *Katherine Mansfield and Her Confessional Stories*. New York: St. Martin's Press, 1983.

Hanson, Clare, and Andrew Gurr. *Katherine Mansfield*. New York: St. Martin's Press, 1981.

Guy de Maupassant

Ignotus, Paul. *The Paradox of Maupassant*. London: University of London Press, 1967.

Steegmuller, Francis. *Maupassant: A Lion in the Path*. New York: Random House, 1949.

Sullivan, Edward D. *Maupassant: The Short Stories.* Great Neck, N.Y.: Barron's Educational Series, 1962.

Wallace, Albert. *Guy de Maupassant.* New York: Twayne, 1973.

Herman Melville

Bowen, Merlin. *The Long Encounter: Self and Experience in the Writings of Herman Melville.* Chicago: University of Chicago Press, 1960.

Chase, Richard. *Herman Melville: A Critical Study.* New York: Macmillan, 1949.

Dillingham, William B. *Melville's Short Fiction: 1853-56.* Athens: University of Georgia Press, 1977.

Fogle, Richard Harter. *Melville's Shorter Tales.* Norman: University of Oklahoma Press, 1960.

Miller, James E., Jr. *A Reader's Guide to Herman Melville.* New York: Noonday Press, 1962.

Rosenberry, Edward H. *Melville.* London: Routledge and Kegan Paul, 1979.

Stern, Milton. *The Finely Hammered Steel of Herman Melville.* Urbana: University of Illinois Press, 1957.

Thompson, Lawrance. *Melville's Quarrel with God.* Princeton, N.J.: Princeton University Press, 1952.

Joyce Carol Oates

Creighton, Joanne V. *Joyce Carol Oates.* Boston: Twayne, 1979.

Friedman, Ellen G. *Joyce Carol Oates.* New York: Frederick Ungar Publishing Co., 1980.

Grant, Mary Kathryn. *The Tragic Vision of Joyce Carol Oates.* Durham, N.C.: Duke University Press, 1978.

Wagner, Linda W., ed. *Critical Essays on Joyce Carol Oates.* Boston: G. K. Hall Publishers, 1979.

Waller, G. F. *Dreaming America: Obsession and Transcendence in the Fiction of Joyce Carol Oates.* Baton Rouge: Louisiana State University Press, 1979.

Flannery O'Connor

Asals, Frederick. *Flannery O'Connor: The Imagination of Extremity.* Athens: University of Georgia Press, 1982.

Feeley, Katherine. *Flannery O'Connor: The Voice of the Peacock.* New Brunswick, N.J.: Rutgers University Press, 1972.

Friedman, Melvin J., and Lewis A. Lawson, eds. *The Added Dimension: The Art and Mind of Flannery O'Connor.* New York: Fordham University Press, 1966, 1977.

Henden, Josephine. *The World of Flannery O'Connor.* Bloomington: Indiana University Press, 1970.

Shloss, Carol. *Flannery O'Connor's Dark Comedies: The Limits of Inference.* Baton Rouge: Louisiana State University Press, 1980.

Frank O'Connor
Matthews, James. *Frank O'Connor.* Lewisburg: Bucknell University Press, 1976.
Sheehy, Maurice, ed. *Michael/Frank: Studies on Frank O'Connor.* New York: Alfred A. Knopf, 1969.
Tomory, William M. *Frank O' Connor.* Boston: Twayne, 1980.
Wohlgelernter, Maurice. *Frank O'Connor: An Introduction.* New York: Columbia University Press, 1977.

Edgar Allan Poe
Buranelli, Vincent. *Edgar Allan Poe.* Boston: Twayne, 1977.
Carlson, Eric W., ed. *The Recognition of Edgar Allan Poe: Selected Criticism Since 1829.* Ann Arbor: University of Michigan Press, 1966.
Davidson, Edward H. *Poe: A Critical Study.* Cambridge, Mass.: Harvard University Press, 1957.
Gargano, James W. *The Masquerade Vision in Poe's Short Stories.* Baltimore: Enoch Pratt Free Library, 1977.
Hoffman, Daniel. *PoePoePoePoePoePoePoe.* Garden City, N.Y.: Doubleday and Co., 1972.
Jacobs, Robert D. *Poe: Journalist and Critic.* Baton Rouge: Louisiana State University Press, 1969.
Levine, Stuart. *Edgar Allan Poe: Seer and Craftsman.* Deland, Fla.: Everett/Edwards, 1972.
Quinn, Patrick. *The French Face of Edgar Allan Poe.* Carbondale: Southern Illinois University Press, 1957.
Thompson, G. R. *Poe's Fiction: Romantic Irony in the Gothic Tales.* Madison: University of Wisconsin Press, 1973.

Katherine Anne Porter
Demouy, Jane Krause. *Katherine Anne Porter's Women.* Austin: University of Texas Press, 1983.
Hartley, Lodwick, and George Core. *A Critical Symposium: Katherine Anne Porter.* Athens: University of Georgia Press, 1969.
Hendrick, George. *Katherine Anne Porter.* New York: Twayne, 1965.
Nance, William L. *Katherine Anne Porter and the Art of Rejection.* Chapel Hill: University of North Carolina Press, 1964.
West, Ray B., Jr. *Katherine Anne Porter.* Minneapolis: University of Minnesota Press, 1963.

J. D. Salinger
French, Warren. *J. D. Salinger.* New York: Twayne, 1963.

Grunwald, Henry A., ed. *Salinger: A Critical and Personal Portrait*. New York: Harper and Row, 1962.

Gwynn, Frederick, and Joseph Blotner. *The Fiction of J. D. Salinger*. Pittsburgh: University of Pittsburgh Press, 1958.

Hamilton, Kenneth. *J. D. Salinger: A Critical Essay*. Grand Rapids, Mich.: William B. Eerdmans, 1967.

Lundquist, James. *J. D. Salinger*. New York: Frederick Ungar Publishing Co., 1979.

Miller, James E. *J. D. Salinger*. Minneapolis: University of Minnesota Press, 1965.

Isaac Bashevis Singer

Alexander, Edward. *Isaac Bashevis Singer*. Boston: Twayne, 1980.

Buchen, Irving H. *Isaac Bashevis Singer and the Eternal Past*. New York: New York University Press, 1968.

Malin, Irving. *Isaac Bashevis Singer*. New York: Frederick Ungar Publishing Co., 1972.

_____, ed. *Critical Views of Isaac Bashevis Singer*. New York: New York University Press, 1969.

Siegel, Ben. *Isaac Bashevis Singer*. Minneapolis: University of Minnesota Press, 1969.

John Steinbeck

Fontenrose, Joseph. *John Steinbeck: An Introduction and Interpretation*. New York: Barnes and Noble, 1963.

French, Warren. *John Steinbeck*. New York: Twayne, 1961.

Lisca, Peter. *The Wide World of John Steinbeck*. New Brunswick, N.J.: Rutgers University Press, 1958.

Tedlock, E. W., Jr., and C. V. Wicker, eds. *Steinbeck and His Critics*. Albuquerque: University of New Mexico Press, 1957.

Leo Tolstoy

Christian, Reginald R. *Tolstoy: A Critical Introduction*. London: Cambridge University Press, 1969.

Maude, Aylmer. *Tolstoy and His Work*. New York: Haskell House, 1974.

Simmons, Ernest J. *Tolstoy*. London: Routledge and Kegan Paul, 1973.

Spiers, Logan. *Tolstoy and Chekhov*. London: Cambridge University Press, 1971.

Ivan Turgenev

Freeborn, Richard. *Turgenev: The Novelist's Novelist*. London: Oxford University Press, 1960.

Freeborn, Victor. *Turgenev's Russia*. Ithaca, N.Y.: Cornell University Press, 1980.

Kagan-Kans, Eve. *Hamlet and Don Quixote: Turgenev's Ambivalent Vision.* The Hague: Mouton, 1975.

Ledkovsky, Marina. *The Other Turgenev: From Romanticism to Symbolism.* Wurzburg: Jal-Verlag, 1973.

John Updike

Detweiler, Robert. *John Updike.* Boston: Twayne, 1972.

Greiner, Donald J. *The Other John Updike: Poems, Short Stories, Prose, Play.* Athens: Ohio University Press, 1981.

Hamilton, Kenneth and Alice. *The Elements of John Updike.* Grand Rapids, Mich.: William B. Eerdmans, 1970.

Hunt, George W. *John Updike and the Three Great Secret Things: Sex, Religion, and Art.* Grand Rapids, Mich.: William B. Eerdmans, 1980.

Eudora Welty

Appel, Alfred. *A Season of Dreams: The Fiction of Eudora Welty.* Baton Rouge: Louisiana State University Press, 1965.

Bryant, Joseph H. *Eudora Welty.* Minneapolis: University of Minnesota Press, 1968.

Evans, Elizabeth. *Eudora Welty.* New York: Frederick Ungar Publishing Co., 1981.

Howard, Zelma Turner. *The Rhetoric of Eudora Welty's Short Stories.* Jackson: University Press of Mississippi, 1973.

Isaacs, Neil D. *Eudora Welty.* Austin, Tex.: Steck-Vaughn, 1969.

Kreyling, Michael. *Eudora Welty's Achievement of Order.* Baton Rouge: Louisiana State University Press, 1980.

Prenshaw, Peggy Whitman, ed. *Eudora Welty: Critical Essays.* Jackson: University Press of Mississippi, 1979.

Vande Kieft, Ruth M. *Eudora Welty.* Boston: Twayne, 1962.

Charles E. May

MASTERPLOTS II

SHORT STORY
SERIES

TITLE INDEX

I

TITLE INDEX

III

TITLE INDEX

TITLE INDEX

AUTHOR INDEX

AUTHOR INDEX

GREENBERG, JOANNE
  Hunting Season, III-1085
  Supremacy of the Hunza, The, V-2285
GREENE, GRAHAM
  Basement Room, The, I-166
  Cheap in August, I-361
  Drive in the Country, A, II-636
GUIMARÁES ROSA, JOÁO
  Third Bank of the River, The, VI-2341

HALE, NANCY
  Empress's Ring, The, II-680
HALL, RADCLYFFE
  Miss Ogilvy Finds Herself, IV-1509
HAMMETT, DASHIELL
  House in Turk Street, The, III-1045
HARRIS, JOEL CHANDLER
  Sad Fate of Mr. Fox, The, V-2002
  Wonderful Tar-Baby Story, The, VI-2684
HARTE, BRET
  Luck of Roaring Camp, The, IV-1412
  Outcasts of Poker Flat, The, IV-1727
HAWTHORNE, NATHANIEL
  Ambitious Guest, The, I-78
  Artist of the Beautiful, The, I-122
  Birthmark, The, I-210
  Dr. Heidegger's Experiment, II-617
  Ethan Brand, II-720
  Minister's Black Veil, The, IV-1501
  My Kinsman, Major Molineux, IV-1556
  Rappaccini's Daughter, V-1897
  Wakefield, VI-2521
  Young Goodman Brown, VI-2737
HEAD, BESSIE
  Collector of Treasures, The, I-413
HEINLEIN, ROBERT A.
  "All You Zombies—", I-63
HELPRIN, MARK
  Schreuderspitze, The, V-2041
HEMINGWAY, ERNEST
  After the Storm, I-46
  Alpine Idyll, An, I-66
  Big Two-Hearted River, I-206
  Canary for One, A, I-323
  Clean, Well-Lighted Place, A, I-406
  Hills Like White Elephants, II-1018
  In Another Country, II-1130
  Indian Camp, II-1162
  Killers, The, III-1259
  Short Happy Life of Francis Macomber,
    The, V-2088
  Soldier's Home, V-2170
  Three-Day Blow, The, VI-2358

HENRY, O.
  Gift of the Magi, The, II-847
  Ransom of Red Chief, The, V-1894
HESSE, HERMANN
  Poet, The, IV-1828
  Within and Without, VI-2672
HILDESHEIMER, WOLFGANG
  World Ends, A, VI-2701
HILL, SUSAN
  Albatross, The, I-49
HIRAOKA, KIMITAKE. See MISHIMA,
  YUKIO
HOFFMANN, E. T. A.
  New Year's Eve Adventure, A, IV-1616
  Ritter Gluck, V-1964
  Sandman, The, V-2020
  Story of Serapion, The, V-2248
HORGAN, PAUL
  National Honeymoon, IV-1590
  Peach Stone, The, IV-1782
HUGHES, LANGSTON
  Gospel Singers, II-918
  Thank You, M'am, VI-2323
HURSTON, ZORA NEALE
  Sweat, V-2293

IRVING, WASHINGTON
  Adventure of the German Student, I-27
  Devil and Tom Walker, The, II-579
  Legend of Sleepy Hollow, The, III-1331
  Rip Van Winkle, V-1957

JACKSON, SHIRLEY
  Charles, I-359
  Lottery, The, IV-1406
  One Ordinary Day, with Peanuts, IV-1705
JACOBSON, DAN
  Beggar My Neighbor, I-181
  Zulu and the Zeide, The, VI-2745
JAMES, HENRY
  Altar of the Dead, The, I-70
  Aspern Papers, The, I-125
  Beast in the Jungle, The, I-169
  Figure in the Carpet, The, II-777
  Great Good Place, The, III-929
  In the Cage, III-1141
  Jolly Corner, The, III-1230
  Lesson of the Master, The, III-1339
  Pupil, The, V-1865
  Real Thing, The, V-1905
  Tree of Knowledge, The, VI-2407
JAMES, M. R.
  "Oh, Whistle, and I'll Come to You, My
    Lad," IV-1660

AUTHOR INDEX

AUTHOR INDEX